Praise for *Daughter of the Forest*

"Lush, poetic, and surprisingly romantic."

"Filled with action and loaded with romance, yet brimming with magical elements that seem real."
—*Midwest Book Review*

"A must-read for anyone who enjoys the power of myth."
—*The Post and Courier*

Praise for *Son of the Shadows*

"Marillier blends old legends with original storytelling to produce an epic fantasy."
—*Library Journal*

"The exquisite poetry of the story is carefully balanced with strong characterizations and more than a nod to Irish mythology."
—*RT Book Reviews*

Praise for *Child of the Prophecy*

"A wondrous world with compelling characters and passages."
—*RT Book Reviews*

BOOKS BY JULIET MARILLIER

THE SEVENWATERS SERIES
Daughter of the Forest
Son of the Shadows
Child of the Prophecy
Heir to Sevenwaters
Seer of Sevenwaters
Flame of Sevenwaters

Also set in the world of the Sevenwaters Series:

BLACKTHORN & GRIM
Dreamer's Pool
Tower of Thorns
Den of Wolves

WARRIOR BARDS
The Harp of Kings

SAGA OF THE LIGHT ISLES
Wolfskin
Foxmask

THE BRIDEI CHRONICLES
The Dark Mirror
Blade of Fortriu
The Well of Shades

Juliet Marillier

TOR

A Tom Doherty Associates Book
New York

Child of the Prophecy

❈ BOOK THREE OF THE SEVENWATERS TRILOGY ❈

CHILD OF THE PROPHECY

Copyright © 2002 by Juliet Marillier

All rights reserved.

Edited by Claire Eddy

Map by B. Marillier and K. Knappett

A Tor Book
Published by Tom Doherty Associates
120 Broadway
New York, NY 10271

www.tor.com

Tor® is a registered trademark of Macmillan Publishing Group, LLC.

The Library of Congress has cataloged the hardcover edition as follows:

Marillier, Juliet.
    Child of the prophecy / Juliet Marillier.
        p. cm.—(The sevenwaters trilogy ; bk. 3)
    "A Tom Doherty Associates book."
    ISBN 978-0-312-84881-1 (hardcover)
    ISBN 978-1-4299-1352-2 (ebook)
    I. Title.
  PR9619.3.M26755 C48 2002
  823'.92—dc21   2001057480

ISBN 978-1-250-23868-9 (trade paperback)

Our books may be purchased in bulk for promotional, educational, or business use. Please contact your local bookseller or the Macmillan Corporate and Premium Sales Department at 1-800-221-7945, extension 5442, or by email at MacmillanSpecial Markets@macmillan.com.

First Edition: May 2001
Second Trade Paperback Edition: November 2020

Printed in the United States of America

0 9 8 7 6 5 4 3 2 1

To old friends

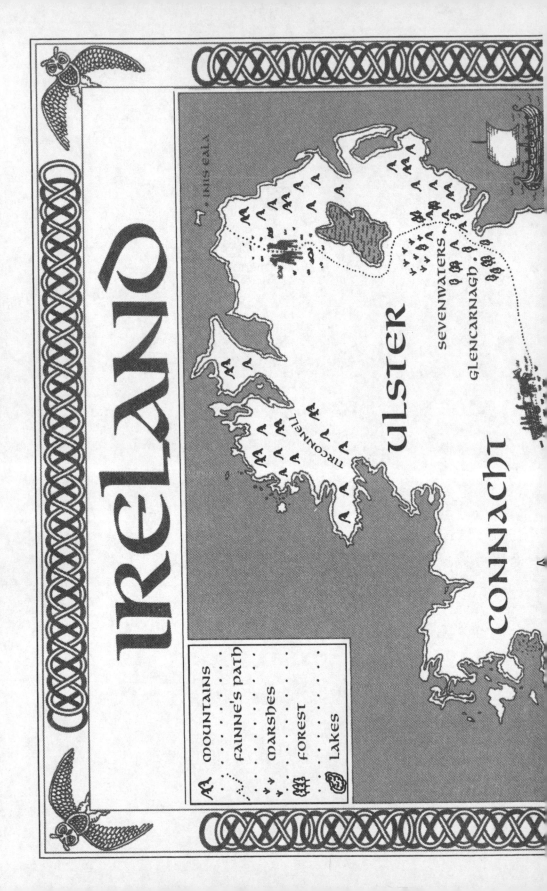

IRELAND

INIS EALA

ULSTER

SEVENWATERS

GLENCARNAGH

TIRCONNELL

CONNACHT

MOUNTAINS
FAINNE'S PATH
MARSHES
FOREST
LAKES

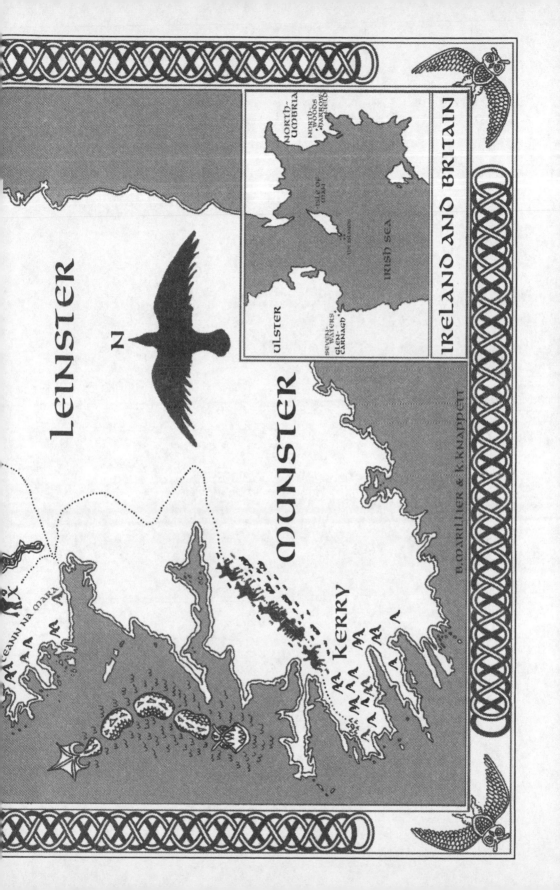

LEINSTER

N

MUNSTER

KERRY

CEANN NA MARA

ULSTER

SEVEN-
WATERS
GLEN-
CARNAGH

NORTH-
UMBRIA

WILD
WOODS
DARROW

ISLE OF
MAN

THE ISLANDS

IRISH SEA

IRELAND AND BRITAIN

B. DARILLIER & K. KNAPPETT

Child of the Prophecy

Chapter One

Every summer they came. By earth and sky, by sun and stone I counted the days. I'd climb up to the circle and sit there quiet with my back to the warmth of the rock I called Sentinel, and see the rabbits come out in the fading light to nibble at what sparse pickings might be found on the barren hillside. The sun sank in the west, a ball of orange fire diving beyond the hills into the unseen depths of the ocean. Its dying light caught the shapes of the dolmens and stretched their strange shadows out across the stony ground before me. I'd been here every summer since first I saw the travelers come, and I'd learned to read the signs. Each day the setting sun threw the dark pointed shapes a little further across the hilltop to the north. When the biggest shadow came right to my toes, here where I sat in the very center of the circle, it was time. Tomorrow I could go and watch by the track, for they'd be here.

There was a pattern to it. There were patterns to everything, if you knew how to look. My father taught me that. The real skill lay in staying outside them, in not letting yourself be caught up in them. It was a mistake to think you belonged. Such as we were could never belong. That, too, I learned from him.

I'd wait there by the track, behind a juniper bush, still as a child made of stone. There'd be a sound of hooves, and the creak of wheels turning. Then I'd see one or two of the lads on ponies, riding up ahead, keeping an eye out for any trouble. By the time they came up the hill and passed by me where I hid, they'd relaxed their guard and were joking and laughing, for they were close to camp and a summer of good fishing and relative ease, a time for mending things and making things. The season they spent here at the bay was the closest they ever came to settling down.

Then there'd be a cart or two, the old men and women sitting up on top, the smaller children perched on the load or running alongside. Danny Walker would be driving one pair of horses, his wife Peg the other. The rest of the folk would walk behind, their scarves and shawls and neckerchiefs bright splashes of color in the dun and gray of the landscape, for it was barren enough up here, even in the warmth of early summer. I'd watch and wait unseen, never stirring. And last, there was the string of ponies, and the younger lads leading them or riding alongside. That was the best moment of the summer: the first glimpse I got of Darragh, sitting small and proud on his sturdy gray. He'd be pale after the winter up north, and frowning as he watched his charges, always alert lest one of them should make a bolt for freedom. They'd a mind to go their own way, these hill ponies, until they were properly broken. This string would be trained over the warmer season, and sold when the traveling folk went north again.

Not by so much as a twitch of a finger or a blink of an eyelid would I let on I was there. But Darragh would know. His brown eyes would look sideways, twinkling, and he'd flash a grin that nobody saw, nobody but me where I hid by the track. Then the travelers would pass on and be gone down to the cove and their summer encampment, and I'd be away home, scuttling across the hill and down over the neck of land to the Honeycomb, which was where we lived, my father and I.

Father didn't much like me to go out. But he did not lay down any restrictions. It was more effective, he said, for me to set my own rules. The craft was a hard taskmaster. I would discover soon enough that it left no time for friends, no time for play, no time for swimming or fishing or jumping off the rocks as the other children did. There was much to learn. And when Father was too busy to teach me, I must spend my time practicing my skills. The only rules were the unspoken ones. Besides, I couldn't wander far, not with my foot the way it was.

I understood that for our kind the craft was all that really mattered. But Darragh made his way into my life uninvited, and once he was there he became my summer companion and my best friend; my only friend, to tell the truth. I was frightened of the other children and could hardly imagine joining in their boisterous games. They in their turn avoided me. Maybe it was fear, and maybe it was something else. I knew I was cleverer than they were. I knew I could do what I liked to them, if I chose to. And yet, when I looked at my reflection in the water, and thought of the boys and girls I'd seen running along the sand shouting to one another, and fishing from the rocks, and mending nets alongside their fathers and mothers, I wished with all my heart that I was one of them, and not myself. I wished I was one of the traveler girls, with a red scarf and a shawl with a long fringe to it, so I could perch up high on the cart and ride away in autumn time to the far distant lands of the north.

We had a place, a secret place, halfway down the hill behind big boulders and looking out to the southwest. Below us the steep, rocky promontory of the Honeycomb jutted into the sea. Inside it was a complex network of caves and chambers and concealed ways, a suitable home for a man such as my father. Behind us the slope stretched up and up to the flattened top of the hill, where the stone circle stood, and then down again to the cart track. Beyond that was the land of Kerry, and farther still were places whose names I did not know. But Darragh knew, and Darragh told me as he stacked driftwood neatly for a fire, and hunted for flint and tinder while I got out a little jar of dried herbs for tea. He told me of lakes and forests, of wild crags and gentle misty valleys. He described how the Norsemen, whose raids on our coast were so feared, had settled here and there and married Irish women, and bred children who were neither one thing nor the other. With a gleam of excitement in his brown eyes, he spoke of the great horse fair up north. He got so caught up in this, his thin hands gesturing, his voice bright with enthusiasm, that he forgot he was supposed to be lighting the little fire. So I did it myself, pointing at the sticks with my first finger, summoning the flame. The driftwood burst instantly alight, and our small pan of water began to heat. Darragh fell silent.

"Go on," I said. "Did the old man buy the pony or not?"

But Darragh was frowning at me, his dark brows drawn together in disapproval. "You shouldn't do that," he said.

"What?"

"Light the fire like that. Using sorcerer's tricks. Not when you don't need to. What's wrong with flint and tinder? I would have done it."

"Why bother? My way's quicker." I was casting a handful of the dry leaves into the pot to brew. The smell of the herbs arose freshly in the cool air of the hillside.

"You shouldn't do it. Not when there's no need." He was unable to explain any further, but his flood of words had dried up abruptly, and we brewed our tea and sat there drinking it together in silence as the seabirds wheeled and screamed overhead.

The summers were full of such days. When he wasn't needed to work with the horses or help around the camp, Darragh would come to find me, and we explored the rocky hillsides, the clifftop paths, the hidden bays and secret caves together. He taught me to fish with a single line and a steady hand. I taught him how to read what day it was from the way the shadows moved up on the hilltop. When it rained, as it had a way of doing even in summer, we'd sit together in the shelter of a little cave, down at the bottom of the land bridge that joined the Honeycomb to the shore, a place that was almost underground but not quite, for the daylight filtered through from above and washed the tiny patch of fine sand to a delicate shade of gray-blue. In this place I always felt safe. In this place sky and earth and sea met and touched and parted again, and the sound of the wavelets lapping the subterranean beach was like a sigh, at once greeting and farewell. Darragh never told me if he liked my secret cave or not. He'd simply come down with me, and sit by me, and when the rain was over, he'd slip away with never a word.

There was a wild grass that grew on the hillside there, a strong, supple plant with a silky sheen to its pale green stems. We called it rattails, though it probably had some other name. Peg and her daughters were expert basketweavers, and made use of this grass for their finer and prettier efforts, the sort that might be sold to a lady for gathering flowers maybe, rather than used for carrying vegetables or a heavy load of firewood. Darragh, too, could weave, his long fingers fast and nimble. One summer we were up by the standing stones, late in the afternoon, sitting with our backs to the Sentinel and looking out over the bay and the far promontory, and beyond to the western sea. Clouds were gathering, and the air had a touch of chill to it. Today I could not read the shadows, but I knew it was drawing close to summer's end, and another parting. I was sad, and cross with myself for being sad, and I was trying not to think about another winter of hard work and cold, lonely days. I stared at the stony ground and thought about the year, and how it turned around like a serpent biting its own tail; how it rolled on like a relentless wheel. The good times would come again, and after them the bad times.

Darragh had a fistful of rat-tails, and he was twisting them deftly and whistling under his breath. Darragh was never sad. He'd no time for it; for him, life was an adventure, with always a new door to open. Besides, he could go away if he wanted to. He didn't have lessons to learn and skills to perfect, as I did.

I glared at the pebbles on the ground. Round and round, that was my existence, endlessly repeating, a cycle from which there was no escape. Round and round. Fixed and unchangeable. I watched the pebbles as they shuddered and rolled; as they moved obediently on the ground before me.

"Fainne?" Darragh was frowning at me, and at the shifting stones on the earth in front of me.

"What?" My concentration was broken. The stones stopped moving. Now they lay in a perfect circle.

"Here," he said. "Hold out your hand."

I did as he bid me, puzzled, and he slipped a little ring of woven rat-tails on my finger, so cunningly made that it seemed without any joint or fastening.

"What's this for?" I asked him, turning the silky, springy circle of grass around and around. He was looking away over the bay again, watching the small curraghs come in from fishing.

"So you don't forget me," he said, offhand.

"Don't be silly," I said. "Why would I forget you?"

"You might," said Darragh, turning back toward me. He gestured toward the neat circle of tiny stones. "You might get caught up in other things."

I was hurt. "I wouldn't. I never would."

Darragh gave a sigh and shrugged his shoulders. "You're only little. You don't know. Winter's a long time, Fainne. And—and you need keeping an eye on."

"I do not!" I retorted instantly, jumping up from where I sat. Who did he think he was, talking as if he was my big brother? "I can look after myself quite well, thank you. And now I'm going home."

"I'll walk with you."

"You don't have to."

"I'll walk with you. Better still, I'll race you. Just as far as the junipers down there. Come on."

I stood stolid, scowling at him.

"I'll give you a head start," coaxed Darragh. "I'll count to ten."

I made no move.

"Twenty, then. Go on, off you go." He smiled, a broad, irresistible smile.

I ran, if you could call my awkward, limping gait a run. With my skirt caught up in one hand I made reasonable speed, though the steep pebbly surface required some caution. I was only halfway to the junipers when I heard his soft, quick footsteps right behind me. No race could have been less equal, and both of us knew it. He could have covered the ground in a quarter of the time it took me. But somehow, the way it worked out, the two of us reached the bushes at exactly the same moment.

"All right, sorcerer's daughter," said Darragh, grinning. "Now we walk and catch our breath. It'll be a better day tomorrow."

How old was I then? Six, maybe, and he a year or two older? I had the little ring on my finger the day the traveling folk packed up and moved out again; the day I had to wave goodbye and start waiting. It was all right for him. He had places to go and things to do, and he was eager to get on his pony and be off. Still, he made time to say farewell, up on the hillside above the camp, for he knew I would not come near where the folk gathered to load their carts and make ready for the journey. I was numb with shyness, quite unable to bear the stares of the boys and girls or to form an answer to Peg's shrewd, kindly questions. My father was down there, a tall, cloaked figure talking to Danny Walker, giving him messages to deliver, commissions to fulfill. Around them, the folk left a wide, empty circle.

"Well, then," said Darragh.

"Well, then," I echoed, trying for the same tone of nonchalance and failing miserably.

"Goodbye, Curly," he said, reaching out to tug gently at a lock of my long hair, which was the same deep russet as my father's. "I'll see you next summer. Keep out of trouble, now, until I come back." Every time he went away he said this; always just the same. As for me, I had no words at all.

The days grew shorter and the dark time of the year began. With Darragh gone there was no real reason to linger out of doors, and so I applied myself to my work and tried not to notice how cold it was inside the Honeycomb, colder, almost, than the chill of an autumn wind up on the hilltop. It was an aching feeling that lodged deep in your bones and lingered there like a burden. I never complained. Father had shown me how to deal with it and he expected me to do so. It was not that a sorcerer did not feel the heat of the fire or the bite of the north wind. A sorcerer was, after all, a man and not some Otherworld creature. What you had to do was teach your body to cope with it, so that discomfort did not make you slow or inefficient. It had to do with breathing, mostly. More I cannot say. My father was once a druid. He said he had put all that behind him when he left the brotherhood. But a man does not so easily discard all those years of training and discipline. I understood that much of what I learned was secret, to be shared only with others of our kind. One did not lay it bare before the ignorant, or those whose minds were closed. Even now there are some matters of which I cannot and will not tell.

There were many chambers in the Honeycomb. We lit lamps year round, and in my father's great workroom many candles burned, for there he stored his scrolls and books, grotesque and wondrous objects in jars, and little sacks of pungent-smelling powders. There was a dried basilisk, and a cup made from a twisted, curling horn, its base set with red stones. There was a tiny skull like a leprechaun's, with empty eyes. There was a thick grimoire whose leather cover was darkened with age and long handling. In this room my father spent days and nights in solitude, perfecting his craft, learning, always learning.

I knew how to read in more than one tongue and to write in more than one script. I could recite many, many tales and even more incantations. But I learned soon enough that the greatest magic is not set down in any book, nor mapped on any scroll for man to decipher. The most powerful spells are not created by tricks of the hand, or by mixing potions and philtres, or by chanting ancient words. I learned why it was that when my father was working hardest, all he seemed to be doing was standing very still in the center of an empty space, with his mulberry eyes fixed on nothing. For the deepest magic is that of the mind, and you will not find its lore recorded on parchment or vellum, or scratched on bark or stone. Not anywhere. Father owed his first learning to the wise ones: the druids of the forest. He had developed it through dedication and study. But our talent for the craft of sorcery was in our blood. Father was the son of a great enchantress, and from her he had acquired certain skills which he used sparingly, since they were both potent and perilous. One must take care, he said, not to venture too far and touch on dark matters best left sleeping. I could not remember my grandmother very well. I thought I recalled an elegant creature in a blue gown, who had peered into my eyes and given me a headache. I thought perhaps she had asked questions which I had answered angrily, not liking her intrusion into our ordered domain. But that had been long ago, when I was a little child. Father spoke of her seldom, save to say that our blood was tainted by the line she came from, a line of sorcerers who did not understand that some boundaries should never be crossed. And yet, said Father, she was powerful, subtle and clever, and she was my grandmother; part of her was in both of us, and we should not forget that. It ensured we would never live our lives as ordinary folk, with friends and family and honest work. It gave us exceptional talents, and it set our steps toward a destiny of darkness.

I was eight years old. It was Meán Geimhridh, and the north wind beat the stunted trees prostrate. It threw the waves crashing against the cliff face, forcing icy spray deep inside the tunnelled passages of the Honeycomb. The pebbly shore was strewn with tangles of weed and fractured shells. The fishermen hauled their curraghs up out of harm's way, and folk went hungry.

"Concentrate, Fainne," said my father, as my frozen fingers fumbled and slipped. "Use your mind, not your hands."

I set my jaw, screwed up my eyes and started again. A trick, that was all this was. It should be easy. Stretch out your arms, look at the shining ball of glass where it stood on the shelf by the far wall, with the candles' glow reflected in its deceptive surface. Bridge the gap with your mind; think the distance, think the leap. Keep still. Let the ball do the work. Will the ball into your hands. Will the ball to you. *Come. Come here. Come to me, fragile and delicate, round and lovely, come to my hands*. It was cold, my fingers ached, it was so cold. I could hear the waves smashing outside. I could hear the glass ball smashing on the stone floor. My arms fell to my sides.

"Very well," said Father calmly. "Fetch a broom, sweep it up. Then tell me why you failed." There was no judgment in his voice. As always, he wished me to judge myself. That way I would learn more quickly.

"I—I let myself think about something else," I said, stooping to gather up the knife-edged shards. "I let the link be broken. I'm sorry, Father. I can do this. I will do it next time."

"I know," he said, turning back to his own work. "Practice this twice fifty times with something unbreakable. Then come back and show me."

"Yes, Father." It was too cold to sleep anyway. I might as well spend the night doing something useful.

I was ten years old. I stood very still, right in the center of my father's workroom, with my eyes focused on nothing. Above my head the fragile ball hovered, held in its place by invisible forces. I breathed. Slow, very slow. With each outward breath, a tiny adjustment. Up, down, left, right. *Spin*, I told the ball, and it whirled, glowing in the candlelight. *Stop. Now circle around my head*. My eyes did not follow the steady movement. I need not see it to know its obedience to my will. *Stop. Now drop*. The infinitesimal pause; then the dive, a sweep before me of glittering brightness, descent to destruction. *Stop*. The diver halted a handspan above the stone floor. The ball hung in air, waiting. I blinked, and bent to scoop it up in my hand.

Father nodded gravely. "Your control is improving. These tricks are relatively easy, of course; but to perform them well requires discipline. I'm pleased with your progress, Fainne."

"Thank you." Such praise was rare indeed. It was more usual for him simply to acknowledge that I had mastered something, and go straight on to the next task.

"Don't become complacent, now."

"No, Father."

"It's time to venture into a more challenging branch of the art. For this, you'll need to find new reserves within yourself. It can be exhausting. Take a few days to rest. We'll begin at Imbolc. What apter time could there be, indeed?" His tone was bitter.

"Yes, Father." I did not ask him what he meant, though it troubled me deeply that he seemed so sad. I knew it was at Brighid's feast that he first met my mother; not that he ever spoke of her, not deliberately. That tale was well hidden within him, and he was a masterly keeper of secrets. The little I knew I had gleaned here and there, a morsel at a time over the years. There was a remark of Peg's, overheard while I waited for Darragh under the trees behind the encampment, unseen by his mother.

"She was very beautiful," Peg had said to her friend Molly. The two of them were sitting in the morning sunlight, fingers flying as they fashioned their intricate baskets. "Tall, slender, with that bright copper hair down her back. Like a faery woman. But she was always—she was always a little touched, you know what I mean? He'd watch over her like a wolf guarding its young, but he couldn't stop what happened. You could see it in her eyes, right from the first."

"Mm," Molly had replied. "Girl takes after her father, then. Strange little thing."

"She can't help what she is," said Peg.

And I remembered another time, one summer when the weather was especially warm, and Darragh finally grew impatient with my persistent refusal to go anywhere near the water.

"Why won't you let me teach you how to swim?" he'd asked me. "Is it because of her? Because of what happened to her?"

"What?" I said. "What do you mean?"

"You know. Your mother. Because she—well, because of what she did. That's what they say. That you're frightened of the water, because she jumped off the Honeycomb and drowned herself."

"Of course not," I replied, swallowing hard. "I just don't want to, that's all." How could he know that until that moment, nobody had told me how she died?

I tried to dredge up some memory of my mother, tried to picture the lovely figure Peg had described, but there was nothing. All I could remember was Father and the Honeycomb. Something had happened long since and far away, something that had damaged my mother and wounded my father, and set the path forward for all of us in a way there was no denying. Father had never told me the tale. Still, it was an unspoken lesson built into everything he taught me.

"Time to begin," said Father, regarding me rather severely. "This will be serious work, Fainne. It may be necessary to curtail your freedom this summer."

"I—yes, Father."

"Good." He gave a nod. "Stand here by me. Look into the mirror. Watch my face."

The surface was bronze, polished to a bright reflective sheen. Our images showed side by side; the same face with subtle alterations. The dark red curls; the fierce eyes, dark as ripe berries; the pale unfreckled skin. My father's countenance was handsome enough, I thought, if somewhat forbidding in expression. Mine was a child's, unformed, plain, a little pudding of a face. I scowled at my reflection, and glanced back at my father in the mirror. I sucked in my breath.

My father's face was changing. The nose grew hooked, the deep red hair frosted with white, the skin wrinkled and blotched like an ancient apple left too long in store. I stared, aghast. He raised a hand, and it was an old man's hand, gnarled and knotted, with nails like the claws of some feral creature. I could not tear my eyes away from the mirrored image.

"Now look at me," he said quietly, and the voice was his own. I forced my eyes to flicker sideways, though my heart shrank at the thought that the man standing by me might be this wizened husk of my fine, upright father. And there he was, the same as ever, dark eyes fixed on mine, hair still curling glossily auburn about his temples. I turned back to the mirror.

The face was changing again. It wavered for a moment, and stilled. This time the difference was more subtle. The hair a shade lighter, a touch straighter. The eyes a deep blue, not the unusual shade of dark purple my father and I shared. The shoulders somewhat broader, the height a handspan greater, the nose and chin with a touch of coarseness not seen there before. It was my father still; and yet, it was a different man.

"This time," he said, "when you take your eyes from the mirror, you will see what I want you to see. Don't be frightened, Fainne. I am still myself. This is the Glamour, which we use to clothe ourselves for a special purpose. It is a powerful tool if employed adeptly. It is not so much an alteration of one's appearance, as a shift in others' perception. The technique must be exercised with extreme caution."

When I looked, this time, the man at my side was the man in the mirror; my father, and not my father. I blinked, but he remained not himself. My heart was thumping in my chest, and my hands felt clammy.

"Good," said my father quietly. "Breathe slowly as I showed you. Deal with your fear and put it aside. This skill is not learned in a day, or a season, or a year. You'll have to work extremely hard."

"Then why didn't you start teaching me before?" I managed, still deeply unsettled to see him so changed. It would almost have been easier if he had transformed himself into a dog, or a horse, or a small dragon even; not this—this not quite right version of himself.

"You were too young before. This is the right age. Now come." And suddenly he was himself again, as quick as a snap of the fingers. "Step by step. Use the mirror. We'll start with the eyes. Concentrate, Fainne. Breathe from the belly. Look into the mirror. Look at the point just between the brows. Good. Will your body to utter still-ness . . . put aside the awareness of time passing . . . I will give you some words to use, at first. In time you must learn to work without the mirror, and without the incantation."

By dusk I was exhausted, my head hollow as a dry gourd, my body cold and damp with sweat. We rested, seated opposite one another on the stone floor.

"How can I know," I asked him, "how can I know what is real, and what an image? How can I know that the way I see you is the true way? You could be an ugly, wrinkled old man clothed in the Glamour of a sorcerer."

Father nodded, his pale features somber. "You cannot know."

"But—"

"It would be possible for one skilled in the art to sustain this guise for years, if it were necessary. It would be possible for such a one to deceive all. Or almost all. As I said, it is a powerful tool."

"Almost all?"

He was silent a moment, then gave a nod. "You will not blind another practitioner of our art with this magic. There are three, I think, who will always know your true self: a sorcerer, a seer and an innocent. You look weary, Fainne. Perhaps you should rest, and begin this anew in the morning."

"I'm well, Father," I said, anxious not to disappoint him. "I can go on, truly. I'm stronger than I look."

Father smiled; a rare sight. That seemed to me a change deeper than any the Glamour could effect; as if it were truly another man I saw, the man he might have been, if fate had treated him more kindly. "I forget sometimes how young you are, daughter," he said gently. "I am a hard taskmaster, am I not?"

"No, Father," I said. My eyes were curiously stinging, as if with tears. "I'm strong enough."

"Oh, yes," he said, his mouth once more severe. "I don't doubt that for a moment. Come then, let's begin again."

I was twelve years old, and for a short time I was taller than Darragh. That summer my father didn't let me out much. When he did give me a brief time for rest, I crept away from the Honeycomb and up the hill, no longer sure if this was allowed, but not prepared to ask permission in case it was refused. Darragh would be waiting for me, practicing the pipes as often as not, for Dan had taught him well, and the exercise of his skill was pleasure more than duty. We didn't explore the caves any-more, or walk along the shore looking for shells, or make little fires with twigs. Most of the time we sat in the shadow of the standing stones, or in a hollow near the cliff's edge, and we talked, and then I went home again with the sweet sound of the pipes arching through the air behind me. I say we talked, but it was usually the way of it that Darragh talked and I listened, content to sit quiet in his company. Besides, what had I to talk about? The things I did were secret, not to be spoken. And increasingly, Darragh's world was unknown to me, foreign, like some sort of thrilling dream that could never come true.

"Why doesn't he take you back to Sevenwaters?" he asked one day, somewhat incautiously. "We've been there once or twice, you know. There's an old auntie of my dad's still lives there. You've got a whole family in those parts: uncles, aunts, cousins by the cartload. They'd make you welcome, I've no doubt of it."

"Why should he?" I glared at him, finding any criticism of my father difficult, however indirectly expressed.

"Because—" Darragh seemed to struggle for words. "Because— well, because that's the way of it, with families. You grow up together, you do things together, you learn from each other and look after each other and—and—"

"I have my father. He has me. We don't need anyone else."

"It's no life," Darragh muttered. "It's not a life for a girl."

"I'm not a girl, I'm a sorcerer's daughter," I retorted, raising my brows at him. "There's no need for me to go to Sevenwaters. My home is here."

"You're doing it again," said Darragh after a moment.

"What?"

"That thing you do when you're angry. Your eyes start glowing, and little flashes of light go through your hair, like flames. Don't tell me you didn't know."

"Well, then," I said, thinking I had better exercise more control over my feelings.

"Well, what?"

"Well, that just goes to show. That I'm not just *a girl*. So you can stop planning my future for me. I can plan it myself."

"Uh-huh." He did not ask me for details. We sat silent for a while, watching the gulls wheel above the returning curraghs. The sea was dark as slate; there would be a storm before dusk. After a while he started to tell me about the white pony he'd brought down from the hills, and how his dad would be wanting him to sell her for a good price at the horse fair, but Darragh wasn't sure he could part with her, for there was a rare understanding growing between the two of them. By the time he'd finished telling me I was rapt with attention, and had quite forgotten I was cross with him.

I was fourteen years old, and summer was nearly over. Father was pleased with me, I could see it in his eyes. The Glamour was tricky. It was possible to achieve some spectacular results. My father could turn himself into a different being entirely: a bright-eyed red fox, or a strange wraith-like creature most resembling an attenuated wisp of smoke. He gave me the words for this, but he would not allow me to attempt it. There was a danger in it, if used incautiously. The risk was that one might lack the necessary controls to reverse the spell. There was always the chance that one might never come back to oneself. Besides, Father told me, such a transformation caused a major drain on a sorcerer's power. The further from one's true self the semblance was, the more severe the resultant depletion. Say one became a ferocious sea monster, or an eagle with razor-sharp talons, and then managed the return to oneself. For a while, after that, no exercise of the craft would be possible. It could be as long as a day and a night. During that time the sorcerer would be at his, or her, most vulnerable.

So I was forbidden to try the major variants of the spell, which dealt with non-human forms. But the other, the more subtle changing, that I discovered a talent for. At first it was hard work, leaving me exhausted and shaken. But I applied myself, and in time I could slip the Glamour on and off in the twinkle of an eye. I learned to conceal my weariness.

"You understand," said Father gravely, "that what you create is simply a deception of others' eyes. If your disguise is subtle, just a convenient alteration of yourself, folk will be unaware that things have changed. They will simply wonder why they did not notice, before, how utterly charming you were, or how trustworthy your expression. They will not know that they have been manipulated. And when you change back to yourself, they will not know they ever saw you differently. A complete disguise is another matter. That must be used most carefully. It can create difficulties. It is always best to keep your guise as close as possible to your own form. That way you can slip back easily and regain your strength quickly. Excuse me a moment." He turned away from me, suppressing a deep cough.

"Are you unwell?" I asked. It was unusual for him to have so much as a sniffle, even in the depths of winter.

"I'm well, Fainne," he said. "Don't fuss. Now remember what I said about the Glamour. If you use the major forms you take a great personal risk."

"But I could do it," I protested. "Change myself into a bird or a serpent. I'm sure I could. Can't I try, just once?"

Father looked at me. "Be glad," he said, "that you have no need of it. Believe that it is perilous. A spell of last resort."

It was no longer possible to take time off from my studies. I had scarcely seen the sun all summer, for Father had arranged to have our small supply of bread and fish and vegetables brought up to the Honeycomb by one of the local girls. There was a spring in one of the deep gullies, and it was Father himself who went with a bucket for water now. I stayed inside, working. I was training myself not to care. At first it hurt a lot, knowing Darragh would be out there somewhere looking for me, waiting for me. Later, when he gave up waiting, it hurt even more. I'd escape briefly to a high ledge above the water, a secret place accessible only from inside the vaulted passages of the Honeycomb. From this vantage point you could see the full sweep of the bay, from our end with its sheer cliffs and pounding breakers to the western end, where the far promontory sheltered the scattering of cottages and the bright, untidy camp of the traveling folk. You could see the boys and girls running on the shore, and hear their laughter borne on the breath of the west wind, mingled with the wild voices of seabirds. Darragh was there among them, taller now, for he had shot up this last winter away. His dark hair was thrown back from his face by the wind, and his grin was as crooked as ever. There was always a girl hanging around him now, sometimes two or three. One in particular I noticed, a little slip of a thing with skin brown from the sun, and a long plait down her back. Wherever Darragh went she wasn't far away, white teeth flashing in a smile, hand on her hip, looking. With no good reason at all, I hated her.

The lads used to dive off the rocks down below the Honeycomb, unaware of my presence on the ledge above. They were of an age when a boy believes himself invincible, when every lad is a hero who can slay whatever monsters cross his path. The ledge they chose was narrow and slippery; the sea below dark, chill and treacherous. The dive must be calculated to the instant to avoid catching the force of an incoming wave that would crush you against the jagged rocks at the Honeycomb's base. Again and again they did it, three or four of them, waiting for the moment, bare feet gripping the rock, bodies nut-brown in the sun, while the girls and the smaller children stood watching from the shore, silent in anticipation. Then, sudden and shocking no matter how often repeated, the plunge to the forbidding waters below.

Twice or three times that summer I saw them. The last time I went there, I saw Darragh leave the ledge and climb higher, nimble as a crab on the crevices of the stark cliffside, scrambling up to perch on the tiniest foothold far above the diving point. I caught my breath in shock. He could not intend—surely he did not intend—? I bit my lip and tasted salt blood; I screwed my hands into fists so tight my nails cut my palms. The fool. Why would he try such a thing? How could he possibly—?

He stood poised there a moment as his audience hushed and froze, feeling no doubt some of the same fascinated terror that gripped me. Far, far below the waves crashed and sucked, and far above the gulls screamed a warning. Darragh did not raise his arms for a dive. He simply leaned forward and plummeted down headfirst, straight as an arrow, hands by his sides, down and down until his body entered the water as neatly as a gannet diving for fish; and I watched one great wave wash over the spot where he had vanished, and another, and a third, while my heart hammered with fear, and then, much farther in toward the shore, a sleek dark head emerged from the water and he began to swim, and a cheer went up from the boys on the ledge and the girls on the sand, and when he came out of the water, dripping, laughing, she was there to greet him and to offer him the shawl from her own shoulders to dry himself off with.

I did not concentrate very well that day, and Father gave me a sharp look, but said nothing. It was my own choice not to go back and watch them after that. What Father had taught me was right. A sorcerer, or a sorcerer's daughter, could not perform the tasks required, could not practice the art to the full, if other things were allowed to get in the way.

It was close to Lugnasad and that summer's end when my father told me his own story at last. We sat before the fire after a long day's work, drinking our ale. At such times we were mostly silent, absorbed with our own thoughts. I was watching Father as he stared into the flames, and I was thinking how he was losing weight, the bones of his face showing stark beneath the skin. He was even paler than usual. Teaching me must be a trial to him sometimes. No wonder he looked weary. I would have to try harder.

"You know we are descended from a line of sorcerers, Fainne," he said suddenly, as if simply following a train of thought.

"Yes, Father."

"And you understand what that means?"

I was puzzled that he should ask me this. "That we are not the same as ordinary folk, and never can be. We are set apart, neither one thing nor the other. We can exercise the craft, for what purpose we may choose. But some elements of magic are beyond us. We may touch the Otherworld, but are not truly of it. We live in this world, but we never really belong to it."

"Good, Fainne. You understand, in theory, very well. But it is not the same to go out into the world and discover what this means. You cannot know what pain this half-existence can bring. Tell me, do you remember your grandmother? It is a long time since she came here; ten years and more. Perhaps you have forgotten her."

I frowned in concentration. "I think I can remember. She had eyes like ours, and she stared at me until my head hurt. She asked me what I'd learned, and when I told her, she laughed. I wanted her to go away."

Father nodded grimly. "My mother does not choose to go abroad in the world. Not now. She keeps to the darker places; but we cannot dismiss her, nor her arts. We bear her legacy within us, you and I, whether we will or no, and it is through her that we are both less and more than ordinary folk. I had no wish to tell you more of this, but the time has come when I must. Will you listen to my story?"

"Yes, Father," I whispered, shocked.

"Very well. Know, then, that for eighteen years of my existence I grew up in the nemetons, under the protection and nurture of the wise ones. What came before that I cannot remember, for I dwelt deep in the great forest of Sevenwaters from little more than an infant. Oak and ash were my companions; I slept on wattles of rowan, the better to hear the voice of the spirit, and I wore the plain robe of the initiate. It was a childhood of discipline and order; frugal in the provision for bodily needs, but full of rich food for the mind and spirit, devoid of the baser elements of man's existence, surrounded by the beauty of tree and stream, lake and mossy stone. I grew to love learning, Fainne. This love I have tried to impart to you, over the years of your own childhood.

"The greater part of my training in the druid way I owed to a man called Conor, who became leader of the wise ones during my time there. He took a particular interest in my education. Conor was a hard taskmaster. He would never give a straight response to a question. Always, he would set me in the right direction, but leave me to work out the answers for myself. I learned quickly, and was eager for more. I progressed; I grew older, and was a young man. Conor did not give praise easily. But he was pleased with me, and just before I had completed my training, and might at last call myself a druid, he allowed me to accompany him to the great house of Sevenwaters to assist in the ritual of Imbolc.

"It was the first time I had been outside the nemetons and the depths of the forest. It was the first time I had seen folk other than my brethren of the wise ones. Conor performed the ritual and lit the sacred fire, and I bore the torch for him. It was the culmination of the long years of training. After supper he allowed me to tell a tale to the assembled company. And he was proud of me: I could see it on his face, clever as he was at concealing his thoughts. There was a gladness in my heart that night, as if the hand of the goddess herself had touched my spirit and set my feet on a path I might follow joyfully for the rest of my days. From then on, I thought, I would be dedicated to the way of light.

"Sevenwaters is a great house and a great túath. A man called Liam was the master there, Conor's brother. And there was a sister, Sorcha, of whom wondrous things were said. She was herself a powerful storyteller and a famous healer, and her own tale was the strangest of all. Her brothers had been turned into swans by an evil enchantress, and Sorcha had won them back their human form through a deed of immense courage and sacrifice. Looking at her, it was hard to believe that it might be true, for she was such a little, fragile thing. But I knew it was true. Conor had told me; Conor who himself had taken the form of a wild creature for three long years.

They are a family of considerable power and influence, and they possess skills beyond the ordinary.

"That night everything was new to me. A great house; a feast with more food than I had ever seen before, platters of delicacies and ale flowing in abundance, lights and music and dancing. I found it— difficult. Alien. But I stood and watched. Watched a wonderful, beautiful girl dancing, whirling and laughing with her long copper-bright hair down her back, and her skin glowing gold in the flare of the torches. Later, in the great hall, it was for her I told my story. That night it was not of the goddess nor my fine ideals that I dreamed, but of Niamh, daughter of Sevenwaters, spinning and turning in her blue gown, and smiling at me as she glanced my way. This was not at all what Conor had intended in bringing me with him to the feast. But once it had begun there was no going back. I loved her; she loved me. We met in the forest, in secret. There was no doubt difficulties would be raised if we were to make our intentions known. A druid can marry if he wishes, but it is very unusual to make that choice. Besides, Conor had plans for me, and I knew he would not take the idea well. Niamh was not promised, but she said her family might take time to accept the idea of her wedded to a young man whose parentage was entirely unknown. She was, after all, the niece of Lord Liam himself. But for us there was no alternative. We could not envisage a future in which we were apart. So we met under the oaks, away from prying eyes, and while we were together the difficulties melted away. We were young. Then, it seemed as if we had all the time in the world."

He paused to cough, and took a sip of his ale. I sensed that telling this tale was very difficult for him, and kept my silence.

"In time we were discovered. How, it does not matter. Conor's nephew came galloping into the nemetons and fetched his uncle away, and I heard enough to know Niamh was in trouble. When I reached Sevenwaters I was ushered into a small room and there was Conor himself, and his brother who was ruler of the túath, and Niamh's father, the Briton. I expected to encounter some opposition. I hoped to be able to make a case for Niamh to become my wife; at least to present what credentials I had and be afforded a hearing. But this was not to be. There would be no marriage. They had no interest at all in what I had to say. That in itself seemed a fatal blow. But there was more. The reason this match was not allowed was not the one I had expected. It was not my lack of suitable breeding and resources. It was a matter of blood ties. For I was not, as I had believed, some lad of unknown parentage, adopted and nurtured by the wise ones. There had been a long lie told; a vital truth withheld. I was the offspring of a sorceress, an enemy of Sevenwaters. At the same time I was the seventh son of Lord Colum, once ruler of the túath."

I stared at him. A chieftain's son, of noble blood, and they had not told him; that was unfair. Lord Colum's son; but . . . but that meant . . .

"Yes," said my father, eyes grave as he studied my face, "I was half-brother to Conor, and to Lord Liam who now ruled there, and to Sorcha. I bore evil blood. And I was too close to Niamh. I was her mother's half-brother. Our union was forbidden by law. So, at one blow, I lost both my beloved and my future. How could the son of a sorceress aspire to the ways of light? How could the offspring of such a one ever become a druid? It was bright vision blinded, pure hope sullied. As for Niamh, they had her future all worked out. She would marry another, some chieftain of influence who would take her conveniently far away, so they would not have to think about how close she had come to besmirching the family honor."

There was a dark bitterness in his tone. He put his ale cup down on the hearth and twisted his hands together.

"That's terrible," I whispered. "Terrible and sad. Is that what happened? Did they send her away?"

"She married, and traveled far north to Tirconnell. Her husband treated her cruelly. I knew nothing for a time, for I was gone far away in search of my past. That is another story. At last Niamh escaped. Her sister saw the truth of the situation and aided her. I was sent a message and came for her. But the damage was done, Fainne. She never really recovered from it."

"Father?"

"What is it, Fainne?" He sounded terribly tired; his voice faint and rasping.

"Wasn't my mother happy here in Kerry?"

For a while I thought he was not going to answer. It seemed to me he had to reach deep within himself for the words.

"Happiness is relative. There were times of content; your birth was one. In that, Niamh believed she had at last done something right. We knew the choice we had made went against natural laws; that choice condemned us to a life in exile, here where men neither knew us nor judged us. Some would call such love an abomination. Yet it was the only fine thing, the only true thing in my life. I had not the strength to deny it. Niamh's eyes grew bright once more; I thought she was well again. I was ill prepared for what happened in the end. It seems she never recaptured what she had lost. Perhaps her final answer was the only one she had left."

"It is a very sad story," I said. "But I'm glad you told me."

"It has been necessary to tell you, Fainne," Father said very quietly. "I've been giving some consideration to your future. I think the time has come for you to move on."

"What do you mean, move on?" My heart began to thump in alarm. "Can I begin to learn some other branch of the craft? I am eager to progress, Father. I will work hard, I promise."

"No, Fainne, that is not what I mean. The time is coming when you must go away for a while, to make yourself known to the family of whom I told you, those who have by now completely forgotten that Niamh ever existed to cause them embarrassment and inconvenience. It is time for you to go to Sevenwaters."

"*What!*" I was aghast. Leave Kerry, leave the cove, travel all that way, to end up in the midst of those who had treated my parents so abominably that they had never been able to return to their home? How could he suggest such a thing?

"Now, Fainne, be calm and listen." Father looked very grave; the firelight showed me the hollows and lines of his face, a shadow of the old man to come. I bit back a flood of anxious questions. "You're getting older," he said. "You are the granddaughter of a chieftain of Ulster, the other side of your lineage does not change that. Your mother would not have wished you to grow up alone here with me, knowing no more than this narrow circle of fisherfolk and travelers, spending your whole life in practice of the craft. There is a wider world, daughter, and you must go forward and take your place in it. The folk of the forest have a debt to repay, and they will do so."

"But, Father—" His words made no sense to me; I knew nothing but the terror of being sent away, of leaving the only safe place I knew in all the world. "The craft, what are you telling me, the craft is the only important thing, I've spent so long learning and I'm good at it now, really good, you said so yourself—"

"Hush, Fainne. Breathe slowly; make your mind calm. There is no need to distress yourself. Do not fear that you will lose your skills or lack the opportunity to use them once you are gone from here. I have prepared you too well for that to occur."

"But—Sevenwaters? A great house, with so many strangers—Father, I . . ." I could not begin to explain how much that terrified me.

"There is no need for such anxiety. It is true, Sevenwaters was a place of grief and loss both for me and for your mother. But the folk of that family are not all bad. I have no quarrel with your mother's sister. Liadan did me a great favor once. If it were not for her, Niamh would never have escaped that travesty of a marriage. I have not forgotten it. Liadan followed her mother's pattern in choosing to wed a Briton. She went against Conor's will; she allied herself with an outlaw and took her child away from the forest. Both Liadan and her husband arc good people, though it may be some time before you see them, for they dwell now at Harrowfield, across the water. It is appropriate that you should meet Conor. I want him to know of you. You will be ready, Fainne. You'll go next summer; we have a full year to prepare. Those things which I cannot teach you, my mother will." His lips twisted in a mirthless smile.

"Oh," I said in a small voice. "Is she coming here? My grandmother?"

"Later," Father replied coolly. "It may not be greatly to your liking or mine, but my mother has a part to play in this, and there is no doubt she has many skills you'll find helpful. In a place like Sevenwaters you must be able to conduct yourself in every way as the daughter of a chieftain would. That you can never learn from me. I acquired deep knowledge in the nemetons, but I never discovered how to go out into the world as Lord Colum's son."

"I'm sorry, Father," I said, aware that my own distress was nothing beside his. "I had thought—I had thought one day I might become like you, a great scholar and mage. The lessons you have taught me, the long seasons of practice and study, won't all that be wasted if I am sent away to be some kind of—fine lady?"

Father's lips curved. "You will use all your skills at Sevenwaters, I think," he said. "I have taught you the craft as my mother taught me—oh, yes," he added, seeing my eyes widen in surprise, "she is an adept, unparalleled in certain branches of magic. And such as she is need not be present in body in order to teach."

I thought of the locked chamber, the long times of silence. He had indeed kept his secrets well.

"I don't invite her here lightly, Fainne. My mother is a dangerous woman. I've kept her away from you as long as I could, but we need her now. It's time. You should have no misgivings. You are my daughter, and I am proud of your skills and all you have achieved. That I send you away is a sign of the great faith I have in you, Fainne, faith in your talents, and trust in your ability to find the right purpose for them. I hope one day it will become clear to you what I mean. Now, it's late, and we've work to do in the morning. Best get some sleep, daughter."

There was a sadness in his eyes, and in the set of his shoulders, but I did not know how to comfort him. Peg and Molly and the others, they were free with hugs and kisses, with tears and laughter, as if such matters were simple. It hurt me to see my father's sorrow; it hurt more that I was powerless to mend it.

"Good night, Father," I whispered, vowing inwardly that I would work harder than ever, and do my best to please him by mastering whatever skills he chose to teach me.

I was deeply shocked by what my father had told me, and inwardly much troubled. Still, a year was a long time. Anything could happen in a year. Perhaps I would not have to go. Maybe he would change his mind. Meanwhile, there was nothing for it but to continue with the practice of the craft, for if the worst happened and my father did send me away by myself, I wanted as much skill as I could master to help me. I put aside my misgivings and applied myself to work.

The weather was quite warm, but Father still had a persistent cough and a shortness of breath. He tried to conceal it, but I heard him, late at night when I lay awake in the darkness.

I was practicing without the mirror. Gradually I had reduced the incantation to a couple of words. I made my eyes blue, or green, or clear winter-sky gray. I shaped them long and slanted, or round as a cat's, thick-lashed, bulbous, sunken and old. As the season passed I moved on to the other features: the nose, the mouth, the bones of the face. The hair. The garments. An old crone in tatters, myself in future guise, maybe. A fishergirl with her hand on her hip, and her come-hither smile, white teeth flashing. A Fainne who was like myself, almost a twin, but subtly changed. The lips sweeter, the brows more arched, the lashes longer. The figure slighter and more shapely. The skin pale and fine as translucent pearl. A dangerous Fainne.

"Good," said my father, watching me as I slipped from one guise to the next. "You've an aptitude for this, there's no doubt of it. The semblance is quite convincing. But can you sustain it, I wonder?"

"Of course I can," I responded instantly. "Try me, if you will."

"I'll do just that." Father was gathering up a bundle of scrolls and letters, and a tightly strapped goatskin bag whose contents might have been anything. "Here, carry this. The walk will be good for you."

He was already making for the passageway to the outside, his san-daled feet noiseless on the stone floor.

"Where are we going?" I was taken aback, and hastened after him, still in the guise of not-myself.

"Dan heads back north in the morning. I've business for him to conduct on my behalf, and messages to be delivered. Stay as you are. Act as you seem. Maintain this until we return. Let me see your strength."

"But—won't they notice that I am—different?"

"They've not seen you for a year. Girls grow up quickly. No cause for concern."

"But—"

Father glanced back over his shoulder as we came out of the Honeycomb onto the cliff path. His expression was neutral. "Is there a problem?" he asked.

"No, Father." There was no problem. Only Dan and Peg and the other men and women with their sharp looks and their ready com-ments. Only the girls with their giggling whispers and the boys with their jokes. Only the fact that I had not once gone right into the encampment without Darragh by my side, not in all the long years Dan Walker's folk had been spending their summers at the bay. Only that going among people still filled me with terror, even though I was a sorcerer's daughter, for my clever tricks scarcely outweighed my limping, awkward gait and crippling shyness.

But then, I thought as I followed my father's striding, dark-cloaked figure along the path and down the hillside toward the cove, today I was not that girl; not that Fainne. Instead, I was whatever I pleased. I was the other Fainne, the Glamour wrapping me in a soft raiment of gracefulness, smoothing my curls into a glossy flow of silk, making my walk straight and even, drawing the eye to my long curling lashes and my demure, pretty smile. They would see me, Dan and Peg and the others, and they would admire me, and never notice that anything had changed.

"Ready?" Father asked under his breath as we came along the path and caught sight of the cluster of folk preparing livestock and belongings for next morning's early departure. Dogs were racing around yapping, and children chased each other in and out between carts and ponies and the legs of men and women about their tasks. As we came closer and were seen, people drew back as was their habit, leaving a neat untenanted space around my father. He was unperturbed, striding on forward until he spotted Dan Walker making some fine adjustments to a piece of harness. A couple of lads were bringing their ponies up from the shore, and they glanced my way. I put a hand on one hip, casually, and looked back at them under my lashes as I had seen that girl do, the one with the teeth. One lad looked down, as if abashed, and moved on past. The other one gave an appreciative whistle.

"And drop this off at St. Ronan's," my father was telling Dan Walker. "I'm grateful to you, as always."

"It's nothing. Got to go that way regardless, this year. It's close enough to Sevenwaters. Can't pass those parts without calling in on the old auntie, I'd never be forgiven. She's getting long in the tooth, but she's a sharp one, always has been: Got any messages for the folk up there?" The question was thrown in as if quite by chance.

Father's features tightened almost imperceptibly. "Not this time."

I took a step forward, and then another, and I was aware that Peg and the other women were watching me from where they hung clothing on the bushes to dry, and I saw that now Dan's eyes, too, were fixed on me, appraising. I looked away, down toward the sea.

"Girl's turned out a credit to you, Ciarán," Dan said. He had lowered his voice, but I heard him all the same. "Who'd have thought it? Right little beauty, she's turning into; takes after her mother. You'd best be finding a husband for her before too long."

There was a pause.

"No offense," Dan added without emphasis.

"The suggestion was inappropriate," my father said. "My daughter is a child."

Dan made no comment, but I could feel his eyes following me as I walked over to the line of ponies tied up loosely in the shade under the trees, cropping at the rough grass. I could feel many eyes following me, and they were not amused or pitying or scornful, but curious, admiring, intrigued. It made me feel quite strange.

I reached up a hand to stroke the long muzzle of a placid gray beast, and the lad who had whistled before appeared at my side. He was a gangling, freckled fellow somewhat older than myself. I had seen him many times with the others, and never exchanged so much as a word. Behind him a couple more boys hovered.

"His name's Silver." This was offered with diffidence, as if the speaker were not quite sure of his possible reception. There was a pause. Some response from me was clearly expected. It was all very well to maintain the Glamour, to keep myself as this not-quite-myself that they all seemed to want to look at and talk to. My techniques were well up to that. But I must also act in keeping; find the words, the smiles, the little gestures. Find the courage. I slipped a hand into the pocket of my gown, repeated the words of an old spell silently in my head, and drew out a wrinkled apple that had not been there when we left home.

"Is it all right if I give him this?" I asked sweetly, arching my brows and trying for a shy smile.

The boy nodded, grinning. Now I had five of them around me, leaning with studied casualness on the wall, or half-hiding behind one another, peering around for a better look without being conspicuous. I put the apple on the palm of my hand, and the horse ate it. His ears were laid back. He was uneasy with me, and I knew why.

"Is it true you can make fire with your hands?" blurted out one of the lads suddenly.

"Hush your mouth, Paddy," said the first one with a scowl.

"What are you thinking of, asking the young lady something like that?"

"None of our business, I'm sure," said another, though doubtless he, like all of them, had exchanged his fair share of speculative gossip about what we got up to, those long lonely times in the Honeycomb.

"It's my father who's the sorcerer, not me," I said softly, still stroking the horse's muzzle with delicate fingers. "I'm just a girl."

"Haven't seen you out and about much this summer," commented the freckled boy. "Keeps you busy, does he?"

I gave a nod, allowing my expression to become crestfallen. "There's only my father and me, you see." I imagined myself as a dutiful daughter, cooking sustaining meals, mending and sweeping and tending to my father, and I could see the same image in their eyes.

"A shame, that," said one of the lads. "You should come down sometimes. There's dancing and games and good times here in the camp. Pity to miss it."

"Maybe—" began the other boy, but I never heard what he was about to say, for it was at that point my father called me, and the lads melted away quicker than spring snow, leaving me alone with the horse. And as I turned to follow my father obediently back home I saw Darragh, over on the far side of the horse lines, brushing down his white pony. Aoife, her name was; he'd argued long and hard with Dan to be allowed to keep her, and he'd had his way in the end. Now Darragh glanced at me and looked away, and not by so much as a twitch of the brow or a movement of the hand did he give me any recognition.

"Very good," my father said as we walked home in the chill of a rising west wind. "Very good indeed. You're getting the feeling of this. However, this is just the beginning. I'd like you to develop a degree of sophistication. You'll need that at Sevenwaters. The folk there are somewhat different from these fishermen and simple travelers. We must begin work on that."

"Yes, Father." For all his words of praise, he seemed tired and sad, as if something weighed on him. I saw a look in his eyes that I recognized well, a look that told me he was planning, calculating, seeing things so far ahead I could not hope to understand. What was it he wanted me to do at Sevenwaters? Was it so dangerous there that I must cloak myself in magic every waking moment? I wished he would explain. But that was never his way. If there was a puzzle to be solved, I was expected to do it myself.

"We might start sooner than planned, I think. As soon as Dan's folk are away we'll take the next step. You can have one day's rest. You've earned that much; we cannot afford more. Use the day wisely."

There was no choice in it; there never had been. "Yes, Father," I said, and as we made our way up the cliff path and into the dark tunnels of the Honeycomb, I let the Glamour slip away and was once more my limping, clumsy self. I had done what my father asked. Why, then, did I feel so unhappy? Hadn't I proved I could be what I pleased? Hadn't I shown I could make people admire me and bend them to my will? Yet later, lying on my bed, I stared into the darkness and felt an emptiness inside me that bore no relation whatever to spells, and enchantments, and the mastery of the craft.

It was a night of restless dreams, and I awoke before dawn, shivering under my woollen blanket, hearing the howl of the wind, and the roar of the sea as it pounded the rocks of the Honeycomb. Not a good day to be abroad. Perhaps Dan Walker and his folk would decide to stay a little longer. But it never did happen that way. They were as true to their time as birds flying away for the winter, their arrivals and departures as precise as the movement of shadows in a sacred circle. You could count your year by them. The golden times. The gray times. It seemed to me the voice of the wind had words in it. *I will sweep you bare . . . bare . . . I will take all . . . all . . .* And the sea responded in kind. *I am hungry . . . give me . . . give . . .*

I put my hands over my ears and curled up tight. It was supposed to be a day of rest, after all. Might I not sleep in peace, at least until the sun rose? But the voices would not go away, so I got up and dressed, not sure what the day might hold, but thinking I would make myself very busy indeed, and try to ignore the sick, empty feeling in my stomach. It was as I pulled on my boots that I heard, very faintly through the blast of the wind, another sound. A note or two, fragments of a tune over a steady, solid drone. The voice of the pipes. So, they were not gone yet. Not stopping to think, I grabbed my shawl and was away, out of doors and up the hill toward the standing stones, my hair whipped this way and that in the wild weather, the sea spray pursuing me as far from the cliffs as its icy fingers could stretch.

Darragh stopped playing when he saw me. He'd found a sheltered spot among the stones, and sat with his legs outstretched and his back to the great dolmen we called the Guardian, not disrespectful exactly, just blending in as if he belonged there, the same as the rabbits. I stumbled forward, pushing my hair back from my eyes, and sat down beside him. I clutched my shawl closer around me. It was still barely dawn, and the air held the first touch of a distant winter.

It took me a while to catch my breath.

"Well," said Darragh eventually, which wasn't much help.

"Well," I echoed.

"You're abroad early."

"I heard you playing."

"I've played up here often enough, this summer. Didn't bring you out before. We're leaving this morning. But I suppose you knew that."

I nodded, sudden misery near overwhelming me. "I'm sorry," I mumbled. "I've been busy. Too busy to come out. I—"

"Don't apologize. Not if you don't mean it," said Darragh lightly.

"But I did want—I hadn't any choice," I told him.

Darragh looked at me straight, his brown eyes very serious and a little frown on his face. "There's always a choice, Fainne," he said soberly.

Then we sat in silence for a while, and at length he took up the pipes and began to play again, some tune I did not recognize that was sad enough to bring the tears to your eyes. Not that I'd have cried over so foolish a thing, even if I'd been capable of it.

"There's words to that tune," Darragh ventured. "I could teach you. It sounds bonny, with the pipes and the singing."

"Me, sing?" I was jolted out of my misery. "I don't think so."

"Never tried, have you?" said Darragh. "Odd, that. I've never yet met a soul without some music in them. I bet you could sing fit to call the seals up out of the ocean, if you gave it a try." His tone was coaxing.

"Not me," I said flatly. "I've better things to do. More important things."

"Like what?"

"Things. You know I can't talk about it."

"Fainne."

"What?"

"I don't like to see you doing that—that—doing what you were doing yesterday. I don't like it."

"Doing what?" I lifted my brows as haughtily as I could manage, and stared straight at him. He looked steadily back.

"Carrying on with the lads. Flirting. Behaving like some—some silly girl. It's not right."

"I can't imagine what you mean," I retorted scornfully, though I was struck to the heart by his criticism. "Anyway, you weren't even looking at me."

Darragh gave his crooked grin, but there was no mirth in it. "I was looking, all right. You made sure everyone would be looking."

I was silent.

"My father was right, you know," he said after a while. "You should get wed, have a brood of children, settle down. You need looking after."

"Nonsense," I scoffed. "I can look after myself."

"You need keeping an eye on," persisted Darragh. "Maybe you can't see it, and maybe your father can't see it, but you're a danger to yourself."

"Rubbish," I said, bitterly offended that he should think me so inadequate. "Besides, who would I wed, here in the bay? A fisherman? A tinker's lad? Hardly."

"You're right, of course," Darragh said after a moment. "Quite unsuitable, it'd be. I see that." Then he got to his feet, lifting the pipes neatly onto his shoulder. He had grown a lot, this last year, and had begun to show a dark shadow of beard around the chin. He had acquired a small gold ring in one ear, just like his father's.

"I'd best be off, then." He looked at me unsmiling. "Slip you in my pocket and take you with me, I would, if you were a bit smaller. Keep you out of harm's way."

"I'd be too busy anyway," I said, as the desolation of parting swept over me once again. It never got any easier, year after year, and knowing I would myself be leaving next autumn made this time even worse. "I have work to do. Difficult work, Darragh."

"Mm." He didn't really seem to be listening to me, just looking. Then he reached over to tweak my hair, not too hard, and he said what he always said. "Goodbye, Curly. I'll see you next summer. Keep out of trouble, now, until I come back."

I nodded, incapable of speech. Somehow, even though I had learned so much this season, even though I had come close to a mastery of my craft, it seemed all of a sudden that the summer had been utterly wasted, that I had squandered something precious and irreplaceable. I watched my friend as he made his way through the circle of stones, the wind tugging and tearing at his old clothes and whipping his dark hair out behind him, and then he went down the other side of the hill and was gone. And it was cold, so cold I felt it in the very marrow, a chill that no warm fire nor sheepskin coat could keep at bay. I went home, and still the sun was barely creeping up the eastern sky, dark red behind storm-tossed clouds. As I walked back to the Honeycomb, and lit a lantern to see me in through the shadowy passages, I made my breathing into a pattern. One breath in, long and deep from the belly. Out in steps, like the cascades of a great waterfall. Control, that was what it was all about. You had to keep control. Lose that, and the exercise of the craft was pointless. I was a sorcerer's daughter. A sorcerer's daughter did not have friends or feelings; she could not afford them. Look at my father. He had tried to live a different sort of life, and all it had brought him was heartache and bitterness. Far wiser to concentrate on the craft, and put the rest aside.

Back in my room I made myself picture the traveling folk loading their carts, harnessing their horses, setting off up the track northward with their dogs running alongside and the lads bringing up the rear. I made myself think of Darragh on his white pony, and forced myself to hear his words again. *I don't like to see you doing that . . . you made sure everyone would be looking . . . you're a danger to yourself . . .* If that was how he saw me, it was surely far better that our paths were separating now. Ours was a childhood friendship, untenable once we were grown, for we were of different kinds, he and I, kinds that cannot be joined for long. Other girls might sit on the cart, and flash their smiles, and think of a life like Peg's and Molly's, full of laughter and music and family. Other girls might look at Darragh and think of a future. I was not like other girls. Yet I felt the loss of him like a deep wound, as if a part of me had been torn away. Year after year, season after season I had waited for him, pinning my hope and happiness on his return. It had seemed to me, sometimes, that I was not fully alive unless he was there. Now my grandmother was coming, and I was being sent away; everything was changing. Best if I put Darragh from my thoughts and just get on with things. Best if I learn to do without him. Besides, what could a traveling boy understand about sorcery, and shape-changing, and the arts of the mind? It was a different world; a world beyond his wildest imaginings. It was a world in which, finally, one must be strong enough to move forward quite alone.

Chapter Two

That day I set all my things in order. I tidied my narrow bed and folded the blanket. I swept the stone floor of my bedchamber, which was one of many caves in the Honeycomb's maze of chambers and passages. I put away my shawl and outdoor boots in the small wooden chest which housed my few possessions. Our life was very simple. Work, rest, eat when we must. We needed little. Deep in the chest, half-hidden under winter bedding, was Riona. She was the only possession I had that was not a strict essential of life. Riona was a doll. When folk spoke of my mother, they would say how beautiful she was, and how slender, like a young birch, and how much my father had loved her. They'd say how she was always a little touched in the head, though it had shocked them when she did the terrible thing she did. But you never heard them talk about her talents, the way they'd mention that Dan was a champion on the pipes, or Molly the neatest basketweaver, or how Peg's dumplings were the tastiest anywhere in Kerry. You'd have thought my mother had no qualities at all, save beauty and madness. But I knew different. You only had to look at Riona to know my mother had been expert with the needle. After all these years Riona was more than a little threadbare, her features somewhat blurred and her gown thin in patches. But she'd been made strong and neat, with such tiny, even stitches they were near invisible. She had fingers and toes, and embroidered eyelashes. She had long woollen hair colored as yellow as tansy, and a gown of rose-hued silk over a lace petticoat. The necklace Riona wore, wound three times around her small neck for safe-keeping, was the strongest thing of all. It was strangely woven of many different fibers, and so crafted that it could not be broken, not should the greatest force be exerted on it. Threaded on this cord was a little white stone with a hole in it. I did not play with Riona in Father's presence. Of course, now I was too old for play. It was a waste of time, like taking silly, dangerous dives off the rocks when there was no need for it. But over the years Riona had shared count-less adventures with Darragh and me. She had explored deep caves and precipitous gullies; had narrowly avoided falling from cliffs into the sea, and being left behind on the sand in the path of a rising tide. She had worn crowns of threaded daisies and cloaks of rabbit skin. She had sat under the standing stones watching us as if she were a queen surveying her subjects. Her dark embroidered eyes held a knowledge of me that could at times be disturbing. Riona did not judge, not exactly. She observed. She took stock.

That day I felt a strong need to be occupied, to channel my thoughts into the strictly practical. So, when my chamber was bare and clean, I went to the place where we kept our small supply of food, and took the fish the girl had brought, and a few turnips. The fish was already gutted and scaled. My father and I were not cooks. We ate because it was necessary, that was all. But I had time to fill. So I made up the fire, and let it die down, and then I roasted the turnips in the coals, and baked the fish on top. When it was ready I took a plateful down to the workroom for my father. But the door was bolted from the inside. I could not hear his voice chanting or speaking words of magic. The only sound was the harsh cawing of a bird within the vaulted chamber. That meant Fiacha was back. My heart sank, for I disliked Fiacha intensely. The raven came and went as he pleased, and when he stayed in the household he always seemed to be staring at me with his little, bright eyes, summing me up and finding me less than impressive. Then he'd be suddenly gone again, without so much as a by-your-leave. Perhaps he brought messages. Father never said. I did not like Fiacha's sharp beak or the dangerous glint in his eye. He pecked me once when I was little, and it hurt a lot. Father said it was an accident, but I was never quite so sure.

I left the food outside the door. There was a rule which need not be spoken, that when the door was locked, one did not seek admittance. Some elements of the craft must be exercised in solitude, and my father sought always to deepen and extend his knowledge. It is too easy for an outsider to judge us wrongly, to see a threat in what we do, simply because of a lack of insight. Our kind are not always made welcome, not in all parts of Erin, for folk tell tales of us which are half truth and half a jumble of their own fears and superstitions. It was not by chance that my father had come to live in this distant, remote corner of Kerry. Here, the folk were simple souls whose lives turned on sea and season, whose world had no place for the luxury of gossip and prejudice. They had accepted him and my mother as just two more dwellers in the bay, quiet, courteous folk who left well alone. And everyone knew a settlement with its own sorcerer was the safest of places to live in. My father had quickly demonstrated that, for one summer, soon after his arrival in Kerry, the Norsemen came. All along the coast there were tales of their raids, the brutal killings, the rape, the burning, the stealing of women and children, and there were tales of the places where they'd come in their longships and simply moved in, taking the cottages and farms and settling down as if they'd a right to. But there was no Viking settlement in our cove. Ciarán had seen to that. Folk still told the story of how the longships with their carven prows had come into view, rowing in hard toward the shore with so little warning there was no time to flee for cover. The sunlight had flashed on the axes and the strange helms the men wore; the many oars had dipped and splashed, dipped and splashed as the fisherfolk stood frozen in terror, watching their death come closer. Then the sorcerer had walked out onto a high ledge of the Honeycomb with his staff of yew in his hand, and raised it aloft, and an instant later, great clouds had begun to roll in from the west, and the swell had risen till white-capped breakers began to pound the shore. The longships had begun to struggle and list, and the neat rows of oars were thrown into confusion. Within moments the sky was dark with storm, and the ocean boiled, and the folk watched round-eyed as the vessels of the Norsemen cracked and split and were torn asunder each in its turn. Later, children found strange and wondrous objects cast up on the shore. An armlet wrought with snakes and dogs, curiously patterned. A necklace in the shape of a tiny, lethal axe threaded on twisted wire. A bronze bowl. The shaft of an oar, fine-fashioned. The body of a man with pale skin and long, plaited hair the color of wheat at Lugnasad. So, there was no Viking settlement in our cove. After that my father was revered and protected, a man who could do no wrong. When my mother died they grieved with him. All the same, they gave him a wide berth.

All that long day my father stayed in the workroom with the door bolted. When at last he emerged to take up the plateful of food and eat it abstractedly, not noticing it had gone cold waiting for him, he looked pale and tired. Sitting by the remnants of my small cooking fire, he picked at the congealing fish and had nothing to say. Fiacha had followed him and sat on a ledge above, staring at me. I scowled back.

"Best go to bed, daughter," my father said, and coughed harshly. "I'm not good company tonight."

"Father, you're sick." I stared with alarm as he struggled for breath. "You need help. A physic, at least."

"Nonsense." His expression was grim. "There's nothing wrong with me. Go on now, off to bed with you. This will pass. It's nothing."

He had not convinced me in the slightest.

"Father, please tell me what's wrong."

He gave a brief laugh. It was not a happy sound. "Where could one begin? Now, enough of this. I'm weary. Good night, Fainne."

So I was dismissed, and I left him there, unmoving, staring into the heart of the dying fire. As I walked away to my chamber, the sound of his coughing followed me, echoing stark through the underground caverns.

She arrived one morning late in autumn, while Father was away fetching water. I made my way out, hearing her calling from the entrance. We had few visitors. But there she was; an old lady wrapped in shawls, trudging along on foot with never a bag or basket to her name. Her face was all wrinkled and her eyes so sunken you could scarce see what color they were. She had a crown of disheveled white hair and a very loud voice.

"Well, come on, girl! Invite me in. Don't tell me I wasn't expected. What's Ciarán playing at?"

She bustled past me and on down the tunnel toward the workroom as if the place belonged to her. I trotted after, hoping my father would not be too long. Suddenly she whirled back to face me, quicker than any old lady had the right to move, and now she was gazing intently into my eyes, as if assessing me.

"Know who I am, do you?"

"Yes, Grandmother," I said, for although she seemed quite different from the elegant woman I remembered, I could feel the magic seeping from every part of her, powerful, ancient, and it was plain to me who she must be.

"Hmm. You've grown, Fainne." Clearly unimpressed, she turned her back on me and continued her confident progress through the darkened passages of the Honeycomb. Before the great door of the workroom, she halted. She put her hand out and gave a push. The door did not budge. Carven from solid oak, and set in a heavy frame which fitted tightly within its arch of stone, this entry was sealed by iron bolts and by words of power. My father guarded his knowledge closely. The old woman pushed again.

"You can't go in there," I said, alarmed. "My father doesn't let anyone go in. Just him, and sometimes me. You'll have to wait."

"Wait?" She lifted her brows and gave an arch smile. On her ancient features, it looked hideous. Her eyes bored through me, as if she wished to read my thoughts. "Has your father taught you this trick, how to come out of a room and leave it locked from the inside?"

I nodded, scowling.

"And how to unlock such a door?"

"You needn't think I'm going to open it for you," I told her, my voice growing sharp with anger at her temerity. I felt my face flush, and knew the little flames Darragh had once noticed would be starting to show on the edges of my hair. "If my father wants it locked, it stays locked. I won't do it."

"Bet you can't." She was taunting me.

"I won't open it. I told you."

She laughed, a young girl's laugh like a peal of little bells. "Then I'll have to do it myself, won't I?" she said lightly, and raised a gnarled, knobby hand toward the heavy oak panels. She clicked her fingers just once, and a bright border of flame licked at the door, all around the edges. Smoke billowed, and I began to cough. For a moment I could see nothing. There was a popping sound, and a creak. The smoke cleared. The great door now stood ajar, its surface blackened and blistered, its heavy bolts hanging useless where they had fallen away from the charred wood.

I stood in the doorway, watching, as the old woman took three steps into my father's secret room.

"He won't be happy," I said tightly.

"He won't know," she replied coolly. "Ciarán's gone. You won't see him again until we're quite finished here, child; not until next summer nears its end. It's just not possible for him to stay, not with me here. No place can hold the two of us. It's better this way. You and I have a great deal of work to do, Fainne."

I stood frozen, feeling the shock of what she had told me like a wound to the heart. How could Father do this? Where had he gone? How could he leave me alone with this dreadful old woman?

She was standing in front of the bronze mirror now, apparently admiring herself, for she took out a comb from a pocket in her voluminous attire and proceeded to drag it through her wild tangle of hair. Despite myself, I moved closer.

"Didn't Ciarán tell you about me, child? Didn't he explain anything?" She stared intently at her reflection. I came up behind, drawn to gaze over her shoulder into the polished surface.

The woman in the mirror stared back at me. She might have been sixteen years old, no more. Her hair was a glossier, prettier version of mine, curling around her shoulders with a life of its own, a rich, deep auburn. Her skin was milk-white, so pale you could see the faint blue tracery of veins on the pearly surface. Her figure was slender but shapely, with curves in all the right places. It was the figure I had tried to create for myself that day when I went down to the camp. I had thought myself skillful, but beside this, my own efforts were paltry. This woman was a master of the craft. I looked into her eyes. They were deep, dark, the color of ripe mulberries. They were my father's eyes. They were my own eyes. The old woman smiled back from the mirror, with her red, curving lips and her small, sharp white teeth.

"As you see," she said with a mirthless chuckle, "I've a lot to teach you. And we'd best start straight away. Making you into a fine lady is going to be quite a challenge."

*   *   *

For as long as I could remember, it had been the two of us, my father and I, working together or working separately, the day devoted to the practice of the craft. Our meals, our rest, our contacts with the outside world were kept to what was strictly essential: the fetching of water, the gathering of driftwood for the fire. Fish accepted from the girl at the door. Messages entrusted to Dan Walker. I had had the summers with Darragh. But Darragh was gone, and I was grown up now. Those times were over. My father and I understood each other without much need for words. Sometimes he would explain a technique or the theory behind it. Sometimes I would ask a question. Mostly, he let me find out for myself, with a little guidance here and there. He let me make my own mistakes and learn from them. That way, he said, I would become more responsible, and retain those things I most needed to know. Indeed, in time this discipline would lead not just to knowledge, but to understanding. Sometimes, when we had mastered a new skill or solved a particularly challenging puzzle, I could persuade him to come walking with me up to the stone circle, or out along the clifftop. During these brief respites I would coax him to speak of matters outside the craft, and I might glimpse a smile on his lips, a warmth in his eyes. I treasured such times as rare jewels, for I loved my father, and wished above all to dispel the sadness that seemed to shadow him even on the sunniest day. I strove to please him in every way I could, and especially by study and hard work, which he seemed to value above all. I wanted to make him happy and perhaps, once or twice, I did. It was an orderly, well-structured existence, if somewhat outside the patterns of ordinary folk.

My grandmother had quite a different method of teaching. She began by telling me Ciarán had neglected my education sorely; the least he could have taught me was to eat politely, not shovel things with my fingers like a tinker's child. When I sought to defend my father, she silenced me with a nasty little spell that made my tongue swell up and grow fuzzy as a ripe catkin. No wonder she had said she could not live in the same place as her son. One of our most basic rules was that the craft must never be used by teacher against student, or student against teacher. My father would have recoiled from the idea of using magic to inflict punishment. Grandmother employed it with no qualms whatever. I hated the way she spoke of him, of her own son.

"Well," she observed as she watched me eating my fish, her eyes following each scrap as it traveled from platter to lips, "he's taught you shape-shifting and manipulation and sleight of hand. How much good will those skills be to you when you sit at table with the fine folk of Sevenwaters? Can you dance? Can you sing? Can you smile at a man and make his blood stir and his heart race? I thought not. Don't gape, child. Your education's been quite inadequate. I blame those druids, they got hold of your father and filled his head with nonsense. It's just as well he called me when he did. Before I'm done with you, you'll be expert at the art of twisting a man around your little finger—clumsy, plain thing that you are. I'm an artist."

"I have learned much from my father," I said angrily. "He is a great sorcerer, and deeply respected. I'm not sure we need your—artistry. I have both lore and skills, and will improve both as well as I can, for my father has given me a love of learning. Why spend time and energy on table manners?"

She laughed her young woman's laugh, so incongruous as it pealed from that wizened, gap-toothed mouth.

"Oh dear, oh dear. It stamps its little foot, and the sparks fly. The first thing you need to learn is not to give yourself away like that, child. But there's more, so much more. I know your father has given you a grounding in the skills. The bare bones, so to speak. But you can achieve great things at Sevenwaters if you make the most of your opportunities. I'll help you, child. Believe me, I know these people."

From that point on she took charge. I was used to lessons and practice. I was used to working long hours, and being perpetually tired, and keeping on regardless. But these lessons were so tedious. How to eat as neatly as a wren, in tiny little morsels. How to giggle and whisper secrets. How to hold myself upright as I walked, and sway my hips from side to side. This one was not easy, with my foot the way it was. In the end she grew exasperated.

"You'll never walk straight in your own guise," she told me bluntly. "You'll never dance without making a fool of yourself. No matter. You can use the Glamour when you will. Make yourself as graceful as you want. Have the loveliest feet in the world, if there's need of them. The only problem is, it gets tiring. Keeping it up all the time, I mean. It wears you down. Why do you think I'm a wrinkled old hag? Our kind live long. Too long, I sometimes think. But I'm the way I am from being charming for Lord Colum all that time, keeping him dancing to my will." She gave a sigh. "Ah, now, *there* was a man. Shame that little upstart Sorcha thwarted me. If she hadn't done what she did, there'd have been no need for all this. It would all have been mine, and in his turn, Ciarán's. Your wretched mother would never have existed, and nor would you, pet. Think what I could have achieved. It would all have been ours, as it should have been. But she did it, she outwitted me, she and those—those creatures that call themselves fancy names. Otherworld beings. Huh! Power went to their heads a long time ago, that's their problem. Shut our kind out. We were never good enough for them, and don't they love reminding us of it? Well, we'll see what the Fair Folk make of my little gift to them. They'll be laughing on the other sides of their faces when your work is done, girl."

I hesitated to ask her what she meant. She was quick to ridicule and to punish when she thought me slow or stupid.

It was too late, Grandmother said, for me to learn to play the harp or flute. I refused to sing, even when she punished me by taking away my voice. I did well enough without it, being used to long days of silence, and in time she abandoned her efforts to extract any form of music from me. She discovered very quickly that my skills in reading and writing far surpassed her own. My sewing was another matter; she pronounced it rudimentary in the extreme. Materials were found in a flash, fine silks, gossamer fabrics, plain linen to practice on first. By lantern light I stabbed my fingers and squinted my eyes and cursed her silently. I learned to sew. She watched me a little quizzically, and once she said, "This brings back some memories. Oh, yes."

There were other lessons she taught me, lessons I would blush to relate. It was necessary, my grandmother said, for I was a girl, and to get anywhere in the world I must be able to attract a man and to hold him. It was not just a case of learning a certain way of walking, and a particular manner of glancing, or even of knowing the right things to say and when to remain silent. Nor was it simply a matter of using the Glamour to make oneself more beautiful or more enticing, though that certainly helped. Grandmother's teaching was a great deal more specific. It made me cringe to hear her sometimes. It made me hot with embarrassment to be required to demonstrate before her what I had learned. The thought of actually doing any of it made me recoil in horror. She thought me very foolish, and said so. She reminded me that I was in my fifteenth year and of marriageable age, and that I had better make the best of what little I had in the way of natural charms, and learn how to use the craft to enhance them as required, or I'd have no hope of making anything of myself. It was plain to me, as I struggled with these lessons, why my father had summoned her to guide me. If it was true that I needed to acquire these skills, to know these intimate secrets, then it was equally clear he could not have taught me them himself. There are some things a girl cannot discuss with her father, no matter how close to him she may be. But I lay awake at night, wondering at his decision, for Grandmother was a cruel teacher, and her presence in the Honeycomb cast a cold shadow on my days and filled my nights with evil dreams. Why had he gone away, so far I did not even know where he was? Was that in itself some kind of test? He had never left me before, not even for a single night. I was heartsick and lonely, and I was worried about him. He was my world, my family, my only constant. I needed him; he surely needed me, for there was no other on whom he bestowed that rare smile which lit up his somber features and showed me the man for whom my mother had left the world behind. Was he afraid of Grandmother? Was that why he had left me to her mercies? My dreams showed him gaunt and white, coughing painfully somewhere in a dark cave all by himself. I wished he would come home.

Autumn advanced into winter, and the lessons went on at a relentless pace.

"Very well, Fainne," Grandmother said one day, quite abruptly, as we sat in the workroom resting. All afternoon she had made me turn a spider into other forms: a jewel-bright lizard; a tiny bird with fluttering wings that blundered, confused, into the stone walls; a mouse that came close to making its escape through a crack until I clicked my fingers to change it into a very small fire-dragon, which puffed out a very small cloud of vapor, flapping its leathery wings in miniature defiance. I was exhausted, as limp in my chair as the spider which now hung, still as if dead, in its web high above me. "Time for a history lesson. Listen well, and don't interrupt if there's no need of it."

"Yes, Grandmother." Obedience was the easiest course to take with her. She was ingenious in her methods of punishment, and she disliked to be challenged. I far preferred Father's methods of teaching which, though strict, were not unkind.

"Answer my questions. Who were the first folk in the land of Erin?"

"The Old Ones." This type of inquisition was easy. Father had imparted the lore over long years, and he and I were fluent in question and answer. "The Fomhóire. People of the deep ocean, the wells and the lake beds. Folk of the sea and of the dark recesses of the earth."

Grandmother gave a peremptory nod. "And who came after?"

"The Fir Bolg. The bag men."

"And after them?"

"Then came the Túatha Dé Danann, out of the west, who in time sent the others into exile and spread themselves all across the land of Erin. Long years they ruled, until the coming of the sons of Mil."

"Very well. But what do you know of the origins of our own kind?" Her eyes were sharp.

"Our kind are not in the lore. I know that we are different. We are cursed, and so we are ever outside. We are not of the Túatha Dé. Neither are we mortal men and women. We are neither one thing nor the other."

"That much you've got right. We're outside because we were put there. One of us transgressed, long ago, and they never let us forget it. Know that story, do you?"

I shook my head.

"We're their descendants, whether they like it or not. Fair Folk, or whatever they choose to call themselves. Gods and goddesses every one, superior in every way, drifting around as if they owned the place, as they did, of course, after packing the others off back into their nooks and crannies. But someone dabbled in what she shouldn't, and that started it all off."

"Dabbled? In what?"

"I said, don't interrupt." She glared at me, and I felt a sharp, piercing pain in my temple. "Back in those first days we could do it all, had every branch of the craft at our fingertips. Shape-shifting, transformation. Healing. Mastery of wind and rain, wave and tide. We were gods indeed, and no wonder the Old Ones crept back to their caves with their tails between their legs. But there are some byways of the craft that should not be tampered with, not even by a master. Everyone knew that. It's perilous to touch the dark side; best leave it alone, best stay well away. Unfortunately there was one who let curiosity get the better of her. She played with a forbidden spell; called up what should have been left sleeping. From that day on there was an evil let loose that was never going to go away. So she was cast out, and part of her penalty was to be stripped of the ability to use the higher elements of magic: the powers of light, the healing, the flight. All she had left was the dross, sorcerer's tricks: she could meddle, and she could perform transformations, a frog into a man maybe, or a girl into a cockroach. She had the Glamour. Precious little, compared with what she'd lost. She attached herself to a mortal man, since none of the high-minded ones'd have her, not after what she'd done. And you know what that means."

This time an answer seemed to be expected. "That she herself would become mortal?"

"Not exactly. Our kind live long, Fainne; far beyond the human span. But it did mean she in her turn would die. She would survive to see her family perish of old age before she herself moved on. Her descendants bore the blood of the cursed one, through the ages. Every one of us has her eyes. Your eyes, girl. Every one has the craft, but narrowly, you understand. Some things will always be beyond us. That rankles. That hurts. It should be ours. The punishment was unjust; too severe."

I opened my mouth, thought better of what I was about to say, and shut it again.

"Thinking of your father, are you?" she said, unsmiling. "Thinking he seems to manifest a somewhat wider range of talents than those I described? You're right, of course. I chose his father well: no less than Colum, Lord of Sevenwaters: They're druid folk, that family. Look how they live, shut away in their precious forest, surrounded by those Others. They've got the blood of the Old Ones, mixed with the human strain. Ciarán's different. Special. He should have ruled there after Colum. Isn't he the seventh son of a seventh son? But I was foiled. Foiled by that wretched girl and her cursed brothers. They're the ones you need to watch out for. The ones with the Fomhóire streak in them."

I frowned in concentration. "Why would that be dangerous, Grandmother? The Fomhóire were not users of high magic."

"Ah. There's high magic, and there's sorcerer's magic, and there's another kind. You might call it deep magic. That's what the folk from Sevenwaters have, and we don't, child. Not all of them, mind. Most of them are simple fools like your mother, weak-willed and weak-minded. How my son ever fell for that empty little featherhead, I cannot understand. Niamh ruined his life; she weakened him terribly. But now there's you, Fainne. You're my hope."

I had learned that snapping back was pointless, though her dismissal of my mother wounded me. "Deep magic?" I queried. "What is that?"

"The magic of the earth and the ocean. That's where those folk came from, long ago. That's why they cling to the Islands. They are no sorcerers. They don't work spells. But some of them have the ability to speak to one another in the mind, without words. You don't know how hard I tried to develop that. Wore myself out. Either you have it or you don't. One or two of them can read the future. Powerful tools, both of them. And some of them have healing skills far beyond a physician's."

"Is that all?"

"All, she says!" Her laugh mocked me. "Isn't that enough? Those gifts shut me out of achieving my goal for nigh on two generations, girl. They took my son from me and turned him soft. But now it's different. I have you, Fainne, and I have a new goal, a far grander one. You've got a little bit of everything in you, thanks to your mother. That was the one good thing she did for you, pathetic wretch that she was. I've never understood it. If Ciarán had to throw himself away on one of the Sevenwaters brats, why not choose the other sister? A child of that liaison would have had rare skills indeed. Never mind, Fainne. You bear the blood of four races. That has to count for something."

This time I found it impossible not to challenge her. "I don't like you to speak of my mother that way," I said, glaring.

"No? I speak only the truth, child. Besides, what would you care? You scarcely remember her, surely. But I suppose all your attitudes come from your father. He'll hear no ill spoken of his beloved Niamh. To him she was a princess, a creature of perfection who couldn't set a foot wrong. He let losing her eat him up. Now, Fainne." Her tone had changed abruptly. "You've done quite well so far, child; we should be ready in time if you keep your mind on learning. Tomorrow I'll outline what is expected of you at Sevenwaters. All this, you understand, the airs and graces, the easy conversation, the skills of the bedchamber, all this is only a tool, part of the means to an end. Tomorrow I'll begin to explain what that end is. You've quite a task ahead of you, granddaughter. Quite a task. Now, off to bed with you, you'll need all the rest you can get."

That night, alone in my chamber with a candle for company and the ocean roaring outside, I opened the wooden chest and brought out Riona. She seemed a little crumpled from being squashed under blankets, and I thought I detected a trace of a frown on her neatly stitched features. I untangled her yellow hair and refastened the ties at the back of her gown. Tonight, suddenly I did not feel so grown-up anymore, and as I blew out the candle and lay down on my bed I kept Riona by me, something I had not done for a long time.

"Is it true?" I whispered into the darkness. "Is that all my mother was, a stupid girl who blighted my father's life? Is that why he doesn't want to talk about her? But he said he loved her. If he would talk about her, then maybe I would remember her. Maybe I would remember something. Some little thing."

Riona did not reply. Her presence by me was comforting, nonetheless. My fingers touched the strange woven necklace she wore, stroked the cool smooth surface of the white stone threaded on it.

"Perhaps it's best," I said, to her or to myself. "Perhaps it's best that I don't know. She was one of them, the human kind, the family of Sevenwaters. I am of the other kind; I am my father's daughter. Best if I never know." But my hand brushed the soft silk of Riona's skirt, and as I fell asleep I was seeing my mother's fingers, the swift flash of the needle as she sewed the little gown with tiny, even stitches. A gift for her daughter, to remember her by; a small friend to comfort me in the darkness when she was gone.

The next morning Grandmother set things out for me.

"Now, Fainne," she said, watching me very closely as I stood before her in my plain gown and serviceable shoes, my hands clasped behind my back. "Why do you think your father wants you to go to Sevenwaters? Is not that the one place he longs to obliterate from his memory, yet cannot? Why would he send you there, his only daughter, into the heart of his enemy's territory?"

"I am the granddaughter of a chieftain of Ulster," I told her. "Father said the folk of Sevenwaters have a debt to repay. He thinks I must learn to move in that circle, since there is no real future for me here in Kerry." A shiver went through me. It occurred to me for the first time that I might never return to the Honeycomb. The thought terrified me. "I trust my father," I went on as steadily as I could. "If he wishes me to travel to Ulster, then that must be the right thing."

Grandmother grimaced, awakening a network of deep wrinkles in her ancient skin. "Your confidence in Ciarán's judgment is touching, my dear, if ill founded. His decision is sound enough, it's his reasons that leave something to be desired. I put that down to his druid training. That wretch, Conor, has a lot to answer for. He and those brothers of his robbed my son of his birthright, and muddled his head with foolish ideas, so he doesn't know what's what anymore. They should never have survived what I did to them. But that's beside the point. Your father only told you half the truth, Fainne. Ciarán's sick. Very sick. He's sending you away because he sees a day, quite soon, when he'll no longer be here to provide for you."

I felt the blood drain from my face. "What?" I whispered foolishly.

"Don't believe me? You should. I'm in the very best position to know this. Ciarán won't leave his precious little apprentice here with the fisherfolk, to become another wife with a gaggle of squalling brats at heel. He can't leave you with me; I come and go as I please. So he's left with only one option. Your uncle, Lord Sean of Sevenwaters; Conor, the archdruid; the elusive Liadan; those are the only family you've got. Your father sees no alternative."

"You mean—you mean this cough, this pallor, you mean he is—dying?" I forced the word out. "But—but how can this be? Our kind are not like ordinary men and women, we live long—how can he be so sick? He said he was well. He said there was nothing wrong—"

"Of course he said that. But there are some maladies beyond mortal remedy, Fainne; some sicknesses that can strike even the most powerful mage. He didn't tell you the truth because he knew you wouldn't agree to go, if you knew."

"He was right," I said, gritting my teeth. "I won't go. I cannot leave him. How could he not tell me?" The two of us had been so close, had shared such long times of perfect understanding, of wordless cooperation. Hurt lodged deep within me like a cold stone.

Grandmother was calm. "Let me explain something to you," she said. "It's not the human folk of Sevenwaters that matter, child. It's the power behind them: those Otherworld creatures with their fancy manners, and their grip on the rest of us. You will go to Sevenwaters, if not for your father, then for me. I've a task for you to undertake, a mission for you to complete. This is big, Fainne. Far bigger than you imagine."

"But Father said—"

"Forget that. I'm his mother. I know what I'm talking about. There's one reason for you to go to Sevenwaters, and one reason alone. My reason. Why do you think I came here, Fainne? I've been watching you, these long years; waiting until you were ready for this. You will complete what I started. You will achieve the success long denied our kind. You'll show the Fair Folk that the outcast can be strong, strong enough to deny them their heart's desire. You will thwart their long scheme. They will fall together, the folk of Sevenwaters and their Otherworld shadows. That's your task."

I gaped at her. "But—but, Grandmother, the Túatha Dé Danann? Who could challenge such power? I would be crushed."

She grinned sourly. "I did it, and I'm still here. A little battered, but I have my will. And I nearly succeeded. They're much weakened since the Islands were lost to the Britons. They had a plan for that girl, Sorcha, and her muddy-boots of a lover. They have a plan for Sevenwaters. I nearly ruined the first. But the girl was too strong for me. I forgot the Fomhóire streak. Never do that, Fainne. Watch out for it. Now you'll thwart the second plan. The Fair Folk want the Islands back. They want it all played out in accordance with the prophecy. Down to the last word. And it's all set to happen when another year has run its course. So I've heard."

"Prophecy?" My head was spinning, quite unable to come to terms with the horror, the grandeur and the folly implicit in her words.

"Didn't Ciarán tell you anything? The Islands were taken by the Britons generations back. Ever since then, Sevenwaters has warred with Northwoods. Until the Islands come back to the Irish, both Fair Folk and human folk remain in disarray. They need them. The high and mighty ones want the Islands guarded. Watched over. That's the only way they can protect themselves from what's to come. The prophecy said it would take a child who was neither of Britain nor of Erin, but at the same time both. And there's some nonsense about the mark of the raven. Well, they've got him at last, the leader long hoped for, grandson of that wretched Sorcha. He's grown up, and ready to do battle with Northwoods, and he's got a formidable force lined up behind him. It won't be long now. Not next summer but the one after, that's what's being said. Your task is to stop them. Simple, really. You must make sure they don't fight, or if they do, make sure they lose. Just think of that. We, the outcast ones, at last gaining the upper hand over the Fair Folk. I'd like to see the expressions on their faces then."

I was so astonished I could barely speak. "But how could I achieve such a thing? And why has Father never spoken of this? It would be impossible, for one girl to stop an army. I would not attempt such a task. It's ridiculous."

"Who are you calling ridiculous?" The old woman fixed me with her berry-dark eyes.

I felt my backbone turn to jelly, but I tried to hold firm. "I would not attempt such a thing without Father's approval," I said. "It is impossible to believe he would support such an idea."

Grandmother's gaze sharpened. Her expression alarmed me. I felt a prickle of fear go up and down my neck.

"Ah," she said, in a very soft voice that clutched at me like a chill hand. "You'll go, Fainne. And you'll do exactly as I bid you do, from now on. I will not see my plans thwarted a second time."

"I won't," I said, trembling. "I won't leave my father. I don't care how strong your magic is. You can't make me do it."

Grandmother laughed. This time it was not the tinkling bell-like laugh, but a harsh chuckle of triumphant amusement. "Oh, Fainne. You're so young. Wait until you begin to feel the power within yourself, wait until men commit murder for you, and betray their strongest loyalties, and turn against what is dearest to their spirits. There's no pleasure like that. Wait until you recognize what you have within you. For you may be Ciarán's daughter, and carry the influence of his druid ways and his excess of conscience, but you are my granddaughter. Never forget that. You will always bear a little part of me somewhere deep within you. There's no denying it."

"You cannot make me do bad things. You cannot force me to act against my father's will. I must at least ask him."

"You'll find I can do just that, girl. Exactly that. From this moment on, you will perform whatever tasks I set you. You will pursue my quest to the bitter end, and achieve the triumph that was denied me. You think, perhaps, that if you disobey me, you will be made to suffer. A slight headache here; a bout of purging there. Warts maybe, or a nasty little boil in an awkward spot. I'm not so simple, Fainne. Act against my orders, and it is not you who will be punished. It is your father."

My heart thumped in horror. "You can't!" I whispered. "You wouldn't! Your own son? I don't believe you." But that was not true; I had seen the look in her eyes.

She grinned, revealing her little pointed teeth, a predator's teeth. "My own son, yes, and what a disappointment he turned out to be. As for my will, you've already had a demonstration of that. Your father's malady is not some ague he picked up, or the result of nerves and exhaustion. It's entirely of my doing. I have been planning for some years, and watching the two of you. He senses it, maybe; but I caught him unawares, and now he cannot shake me off. So he sends you away to what he deems a place of safety. Straight off to Conor, his archenemy. Ironic, isn't it?"

"You're lying!" I retorted, torn between horror and fury. "Father's too quick with counter-spells, he'd never let it happen. There's no sorcerer in the world stronger than he is." My voice spoke defiance while my heart shrank with dread; she had us trapped, the two of us, trapped by the love we bore each other. It was she who was strongest; she had been all along.

"Weren't you listening?" she asked me. "Ciarán could have been what you say. He could have been the most powerful of all. But he threw it away. He let hope destroy him. He may still practice the craft, but he hasn't the will now. He was easy prey for me. You'll need to be extremely careful. I'll give you some instructions before you leave. The slightest deviation from my orders, and your father goes a little further downhill. You've seen how he is. It wouldn't take many mistakes on your part to make him very sick indeed; almost beyond saving. On the other hand, do well, and he may just get better. See what power I'm giving you."

"You won't know." My voice was shaking. "I'll be at Sevenwaters, and you said yourself you cannot read minds. I could disobey and you would be none the wiser."

Her brows rose disdainfully. "You surprise me, Fainne. Have you not mastered the use of scrying bowls, the art of mirrors? I will know."

I wrapped my arms around myself, for there was a chill in me that would remain, now, on the brightest of summer days. My father sick, suffering, dying; how could I bear it? This was cruel indeed, cruel and clever. "I—I suppose I have no choice," I muttered.

Grandmother nodded. "Very wise. It won't be long before you're enjoying it, believe me. There's an inordinate amount of pleasure that can be had in watching a great work of destruction unfold. You'll have a measure of control. After all, you do need to be adaptable. I'll give you some ideas. The rest you can work out for yourself. It's amazing what power a woman can enjoy, if she learns how to make herself irresistible. I'll show you how to identify which man in a crowd of fifty is the one to target; the one with power and influence. I did that once, and I nearly had everything I wanted. I came so close. Then that girl ruined everything. I'll be as glad as Ciarán will be to see her family fail, finally and utterly. To see them disintegrate and destroy themselves."

She fumbled in a concealed pocket.

"Now. You'll need every bit of help you can get. This will be useful. It's very old. A little amulet. Bit of nonsense, really. It'll protect you from the wrong sorts of influence." She slipped a cord over my neck. The token threaded on it seemed a harmless trinket; a little triangle of finely wrought bronze whose patterns were so small I could hardly discern the shapes. Yet the moment it settled there against my heart, I seemed to see everything more clearly; my anxiety faded, and I began to understand that perhaps I could do what my grandmother wanted after all. The craft was strong in me, I knew that. Maybe all I needed to do was follow her orders and all would be well. I closed my fingers around the amulet; it had a sweet warmth that seemed to flow into me, comforting, reassuring.

"Now, Fainne," Grandmother said almost kindly, "you must keep this little token hidden under your dress. Wear it always. Never take it off, understand? It will protect you from those who seek to thwart this plan. Ciarán would say the powers of the mind are enough. Comes of the druid discipline. But what do they know? I have lived among these folk, and I can tell you, you'll need every bit of assistance you can get."

What she said sounded entirely practical. "Yes, Grandmother," I said, fingering the bronze amulet.

"It will strengthen your resolve," Grandmother said. "Keep you from running away as soon as things get too hard."

"Yes, Grandmother."

"Now tell me. Is there anyone you've taken a dislike to, in your sheltered little corner here? Got any grudges?"

I had to think about this quite hard. My circle was somewhat limited, especially of late. But one image did come into my mind: that girl with her sun-browned skin and white-toothed smile, wrapping her shawl around Darragh's shoulders.

"There's a girl," I said cautiously, thinking I had a fair idea of what was coming. "A fishergirl, down at the cove. I've no great fondness for her."

"Very well." Grandmother was looking straight into my eyes, very intently. "You know how to turn a frog into a bird, and a beetle into a crab. What would you do with this girl?"

"I—"

"Scruples, Fainne?" Her tone sharpened.

"No, Grandmother." I had no doubt she had told me the truth, and I must do as she asked. If I failed, my father would pay. Still, a transformation need not be forever. It need not be for long at all. I could obey her, and still do this my own way.

"Good. Just as well the weather's better, isn't it? You can walk down this afternoon and stretch your legs. Take that dour excuse for a raven on an outing, it still seems to be hanging about. You can do it then. You'll need to catch her alone."

"Yes, Grandmother."

"Focus, now. Remember all you're doing is making a slight adjustment. Quite harmless, in the scheme of things."

I timed it so the boats were still out and the women indoors. If I were seen at all, two and two would most certainly be put together. I lacked the skill to command invisibility, for, as my grandmother had told me, we had been stripped of the higher powers. Still, I was able to slip from rocky outcrop to wind-whipped bushes to stone wall without drawing attention to myself, crooked foot or no, and it appeared that Fiacha knew quite well what I was doing, for he behaved exactly like any other raven that just happened to be in the settlement that day. Most of the time he sat in a tree watching me.

The girl was outside her cottage, washing clothes in a tub. Her glossy brown hair was dragged back off her face, and she seemed more ordinary than I had remembered. Two very small children played on the grass nearby. I watched for a little, unseen where I stood in the shade of an outhouse. But I did not watch for long; I did not allow too much time for thought. The girl looked up and said something to the children, and one of them shrieked with laughter, and the girl grinned, showing her white teeth. I moved my hand, and made the spell in my head, and an instant later a fine fat codfish was flapping and gasping on the earthen pathway, and the brown-skinned girl was gone. The two infants appeared not to notice, absorbed in their small game. I watched as the fish twisted and jerked, desperate for life. I would leave it just long enough to show I was strong; just long enough to prove to my grandmother that I could do this. Then I would point my finger and speak the charm of undoing. Now, maybe. I began to focus my mind again, and summon the words. But before I could whisper them, a woman came bustling out of the cottage, a sharp knife in her hand and a frown on her lined features. She was a big woman, and she stopped on the path right before me, blocking my view of the thrashing fish. And while I could not see the creature I had changed, I could not work the counter-spell.

Move, I willed her. *Move now, quick.*

"Brid!" she called. "Where are you, girl?"

Move away. Oh, please.

"Where's your sister gone?" The woman seemed to be addressing the two infants, not expecting a reply. "And what's this doing here?" Before my horrified gaze she bent and scooped up something from the path. If only she would turn a little, all I needed was a glimpse of silvery tail or staring eye or gasping mouth, and I could change the girl back. I would do it, even if it meant all knew the truth. If I did not do it, I would be a murderer.

"Who's been here?" the woman asked the children. "Tinker lads playing tricks? I'll have something to say to your sister when she gets back, make no doubt of that. Leaving the two of you alone with a tub of wash water, that's asking for trouble. Still, this'll go down well with a bit of cabbage and a dumpling or two." She made a quick movement with her hand, the one that held the knife, and then, only then, she half-turned, and I saw the fish hanging limp in her grip, indeed transformed into no more than a welcome treat for a hungry family's table. I was powerless. It was too late. The greatest sorcerer in the world cannot bestow the gift of life. A freezing terror ran through me. It was not just that I had done the unforgivable. It was something far worse. Had I not just proved my grandmother right? I bore the blood of a cursed line, a line of sorcerers and outcasts. It seemed I could not fight that; it would manifest itself as it chose. Were not my steps set inevitably toward darkness? I turned and fled in silence, and the woman never saw me.

Later we heard news from the settlement of the girl's disappearance. A search was mounted; they looked for her everywhere. But nobody mentioned the dead fish, and the children were too little to tell a tale. The incident became old news. They never found the girl. The best they could hope for her was that she'd run off with some sweetheart, and made a life elsewhere. Odd, though; she'd been such a good lass.

After that, it became more difficult to get to sleep. Riona stayed in the chest. I could imagine her small eyes looking at me, looking in the darkness, telling me truths about myself with never a word spoken. I did not want to hear what she might have to say. I did not want to think about anything in particular. I knew a lot of mind games, tricks Father had shown me for focusing the concentration, strategies for shutting out what was not wanted. But now, none of them seemed to work. Instead, my mind repeated three things, over and over. My grandmother's voice saying, *Scruples, Fainne?* Darragh, watching as I made the fire with my pointing finger. Darragh frowning. *You're a danger to yourself.* And a little image of a red-haired girl, weeping and weeping, frenzied with grief, eyes squeezed shut, hands clutching her head, nose streaming, voice hoarse and ragged with sobbing. She, of them all, I wanted out of my mind. I could not bear to witness so wild a display of anguish. It made me want to scream. It made me want to cry, I could feel the tears building up in me. But our kind do not weep. *Stop it! Stop it!* I hissed, willing her away. Then she raised her blotched and tragic face to me, and the girl was myself.

After an endless winter and a chill spring, summer came and the traveling folk returned to the cove. I passed my fifteenth birthday. This year, when I might have roamed abroad free of Father's restrictions, I did not climb the hill to see the long shadows mark out the day of Darragh's arrival. But I heard the sweet, sad voice of the pipes piercing the soft stillness of dusk, and I knew he was here. Part of me still longed to escape, to make my way up to the secret place and sit by my friend, looking out over the sea, talking, or not talking as the mood took us. But it was easy, this time, to find reasons not to go. Most of them were reasons I did not want to think about, but they were there, hidden away somewhere inside me. There was that girl, and what I had done. It didn't seem to matter that my grandmother had made me do it; it didn't seem to make a difference that I had intended only to scare her, that I had been prevented from changing her back in time. It was still I who had done it, and that made me a murderer. I knew what I had done was an abuse of the craft. And yet, all that I had, all that I was, I owed to my father. To save him, I must be prepared to do the unthinkable. I had shown myself strong enough. But I did not want anyone to ask me about it. Particularly Darragh. And there was another, even more compelling reason: something my grandmother had said one day.

"There's a further step," she'd told me. "You did well. You did considerably better than I expected, in terms of the end result. But it's easy to tamper when you hate; easy enough, when you don't care. You may need to do more than that. Tell me, Fainne, is there anyone who is a special friend? Anyone you are particularly fond of?"

I thought very quickly, and blessed my grandmother's failure to master the skill of mind-reading.

"Nobody," I said calmly. "Except Father, of course."

Grandmother grimaced. "Are you sure? No friends? No sweetheart? No, I suppose not. Pity. You do need to practice that."

"Why? Why should I? What do you mean?"

She sighed. "Tell me, what things are most important to you?"

I framed my answer with care. "The task I have been set. That's all that is important."

"Mm. Seems easy, doesn't it? You go to Sevenwaters, you insinuate your way into the household, you work your magic, and the task is complete. But what if you become friends with them? What if you like them? It may not be so easy then. That's when the real test of strength begins. These folk are closely tied with the Túatha Dé, Fainne. You will not hurt one without wounding the other."

"*Like* them?" My amazement was quite genuine. "Become friends with the family that destroyed my mother, and took away my father's dreams? How could I?"

"You'd be surprised." Grandmother's tone was dryly amused. "They're not monsters, for all they did. And you've encountered few folk here, shut away with Ciarán at the end of the world. He did you no favors by bringing you to Kerry, child. You'll need to be very canny. You'll need to remember who you are, and why you're there, every moment of every day. You cannot afford to relax your guard, not for an instant. There are dangerous folk at Sevenwaters."

"How will I know who—?"

"Some will be safe. Some are harmless. Some have the power to stop you, if you give yourself away. That's what happened to me. See that it doesn't happen to you, because this is our last chance. You'll need to beware of that fellow with the swan's wing."

"What?" Surely I had not heard her properly.

"He's the danger. He's the one who can cross over and come back when it suits him. Watch out for him."

I was eager to know what she meant. But try as I might, she would tell me no more that afternoon. Indeed, she seemed suddenly in a very ill temper, and started to punish me with sharp wasp-like stings for each small error in the casting of a spell of substitution. It became necessary to concentrate extremely hard; too hard to ask awkward questions.

I learned about pain that summer. My grandmother's earlier tricks were nothing to the punishments she inflicted on me when she thought me defiant or stubborn, when she caught me dreaming instead of applying myself to the task in hand. She could induce a headache that was like the grip of an earth-dragon's jaws, an agony that turned the bowels to water and drained whatever will I might once have summoned to aid me. She could pierce the belly with a thousand long needles, and cause every corner of the skin to itch and burn and fester, so that one screamed for mercy. Almost screamed. She knew I was young, and she would stop just before the torture became unbearable. What she thought of my strength of will she never said. I endured what she did, since there was no choice. My father could not have known she would treat me thus, or he would never have left me to her mercies. I learned, and was afraid.

She showed me, one night, a vision that struck a far deeper terror in me.

"Just in case," she said, "you think to change your mind once you are gone from here. Just to erase that last little glint of defiance from your eyes, Fainne. You think I lied to you, perhaps; that this is all some kind of elaborate fantasy. Look in the coals there, where the flame glows deepest red. Slow your breathing, and shut out all else as you have been taught to do. Look hard and tell me what you see."

But there was no need to put it into words. She must have read in my face the horror I felt as I stared into the fire and saw the tiny image of my father, his strong features contorted, his body twisted with pain, his chest racked with a coughing that seemed fit to split him asunder. Blood dribbled from his gasping mouth, his hands clutched blindly at the air, his dark eyes stared like a madman's. My whole body went cold. I heard myself whispering, "Oh no, oh no." I might have begged her then, if I had had the strength to find words for it.

"Oh, yes," Grandmother said, as the vision faded and I slumped back to crouch on the rug before the hearth. "It matters nothing to me if this is my son or a stranger, Fainne. All that matters is the task in hand."

"M—my father," I stammered. "Is he—?"

"What you see is not now, it is the future. A possible future. If you want a different picture, it is up to you to ensure you obey my orders and perform what is required of you. Defy me, and he'll die, slowly. You'll do as I tell you, and you'll keep your mouth shut about it. I hope you believe me, child. You'd be a very silly girl if you didn't. Do you believe me, Fainne?"

"Yes, Grandmother," I whispered.

The warm days passed, and the voices of children floated up on the summer breeze and made their way, laughing and shrieking, into the shadowy inner chambers of the Honeycomb. The curraghs sailed out of the cove in the dawn and returned at dusk, laden with their gleaming catch. Women mended nets on the jetty, and brown-skinned lads exercised horses along the strand, high-stepping over the mounded seaweed. I lay awake, night after night, listening to the distant lament of the pipes. Though Fiacha came and went, there was no sign at all of Father, and I began to fear I might never see him again. That hurt me terribly; and yet I did not want him to see what I was becoming, to witness my ill-use of the craft, and so in a way his absence was a relief. I hoped he would never have to learn the truth, that in sending me forth he sacrificed his only child to the most foolhardy and impossible of quests, where his own life was the price of failure. As for Grandmother, to her I was no more than a finely tuned weapon, a tool many years in the fashioning, which she would now employ for a purpose of such grandeur I still struggled to come to terms with it.

The summer was nearly ended. Grandmother had made practical preparations of a sort. My small storage chest now held two gowns of a slightly better standard than my usual garb of old working dress and serviceable apron. I had a new pair of indoor shoes as well as my walking boots. A man had made them specially, muttering to himself as he took measure of my misshapen foot. This was a trial. I would have blistered the cobbler's fingers for him; but I needed the shoes.

I had not asked my grandmother how I was to travel to Sevenwaters. It was a long way, I knew that because Darragh had told me; nearly the length and breadth of Erin. But I had no idea how many moons such a journey might take. Perhaps my grandmother would work a spell of transportation, and send me north in an instant with my baggage by my side. In the end there was no need to ask, for one day Grandmother simply announced that it was time to go.

"You'll travel north on Dan Walker's cart," she said, checking the strap which fastened my storage chest. "Very practical, if not altogether stylish."

"Practical?" I echoed in dismay. "What's practical about it?"

"You'll arouse a great deal less suspicion if you turn up with the traveling folk," she said dryly, "than by manifesting yourself in your uncle's hall amidst a shower of sparks. This way nobody'll notice you. What's one more lass among that great gaggle of people? Not nervous, are you? Surely I've worked that out of you by now. Use the Glamour if you must. Be what pleases you, child. These folk are only tinkers, Fainne. They're nothing."

"Yes, Grandmother." Her words did little to settle the nervous churning in my stomach. I knew I must be strong. The task I undertook for my grandmother, her terrible work of vengeance against those who had slighted our kind, must be pursued with the utmost strength of purpose. My father's very life was in my hands. I could not fail. I would not fail. Still, I was barely fifteen years old, tortured by shyness and quite unused to the world at large. It was this, I suppose, that made me such a subtle weapon. I must have seemed as innocuous as some little hedge creature that scuttles for cover at any imagined danger.

I took my leave of Grandmother. If she still harbored any doubts, she kept them to herself.

"I almost wish I was coming with you," she sighed, and for an instant I caught a glimpse of that other manifestation she was fond of, an alluring, curvaceous young creature with auburn hair and pearly skin. "There must be fine men in those parts still, though there'll never be another Colum. And I could still cast my net, make no doubt of it." Then, abruptly, she was herself again. "But I can see it wouldn't do. They'd know me, Glamour or no. The druid would know me. So would that other one. This is your time, child. Remember what I've taught you. Remember what I've told you. Every little thing, Fainne."

"Yes, Grandmother."

We walked out of the Honeycomb to the point where the cliff path stretched ahead all the way down to the shore and along to the western end of the cove, where Dan Walker and his folk would be making ready for departure. And there, dark-cloaked, ashen-faced, stood my father, staring silent out over the sea. My heart gave a great lurch.

"I might walk down with you," Grandmother said. "See you on your way."

It's not easy to cast a spell over a fellow practitioner of the art. You need to be quick or you'll encounter a barrier or counter-spell, and your efforts will be entirely wasted. This was exceptionally quick. In an instant, without so much as a glance at each other, both Father and I threw nets of immobility over Grandmother, so that she was held there in place from both left and right, feet rooted to the rock, mouth slightly open, eyes frozen in piercing annoyance.

"She'll be angry," I remarked to Father as we set off down the path, he carrying my small wooden chest on his shoulder, I clutching a roll of bedding for the journey. Fiacha flew overhead.

"I'll deal with it," Father said calmly. I glanced at him and thought I detected a shadow of amusement in his dark eyes. But he was thin, so thin, and he seemed far older than he had last autumn, his cheeks hollow, his severe mouth bracketed by new lines of pain. "Now, Fainne, we don't have long. Are you well? This will have been a difficult time for you, a time of great change. It was hard for me to leave you thus; hard but necessary. Are you ready for this journey now, daughter?"

I picked my way with caution down the narrow, steep pathway. It had been raining, and the surface was treacherous. Questions raced through my head. *How could you let your own mother do this to you?* And, *Why didn't you tell me the truth?* And, strongest of all, *Will I ever see you again?* I could not ask any of them, for Grandmother would know, and it would be my father who was punished for it. I longed to throw my arms around him and blurt out the whole truth, and be a child again in a world where the rules made sense. I could not tell him anything.

"Yes, I'm ready," I said, feeling an odd sensation behind my eyes, as if I were about to cry.

"Sure?"

"Yes, Father."

So we walked on in silence, and it seemed to me that although we walked quite slowly, as if reluctant to reach the end, we were very soon down on the level track that skirted the strand, and Dan and Peg and the jostle of bright-clad folk were in sight along the path.

"Father," I said abruptly.

"Yes, Fainne?"

"I want to say—I want to thank you for being such a good teacher. To thank you for your wisdom and your patience—and—and for letting me find things out for myself. For trusting me."

He said nothing for a moment. When he did speak, his voice was a touch unsteady. "Fainne, it is difficult for me to say this to you."

"What, Father?"

"I—you need not go, if you do not wish to do so. If, in your heart, you feel this way is not for you, you have that choice."

"*Not go?*" My heart thumped. Now, now that it was too late, he told me I could stay, and I was forbidden to say yes. I cleared my throat. I had never lied to him before. "When we have come so far, not do this for you? Do I not owe it to my mother to go back to Sevenwaters and become what she would wish me to be? Surely I must go." And, oh, how I longed to tell him I would give anything to stay with him in Kerry, and have things be as they once were. But he was my father, and for his own sake I must find the courage to leave him.

"I wished—I simply wished you to understand that ultimately, what occurs, what develops, is for you to determine. And—and, Fainne, this may be a far greater, a far more momentous unfolding of events than either you or I have ever envisaged. So important that I would not dare put it into words for you. We are what we are by birth and by blood. Over that, we have no control. We cannot break the mold of our kind. But one always has the choice to practice the craft, to one end or another, or to stand aside. That choice you do have, daughter."

I stared at him. "Not practice the craft? But—but what else is there?"

Father made no reply, simply gave a little nod. His expression remained impassive. He had ever been a master of control. We began to walk again, our last walk together around the cove, with the plumes of spray dashing the Honeycomb behind us, and the remote cries of the gulls above us, and ahead, Dan Walker advancing toward us, a hand reached out in greeting and a grin on his dark, bearded face.

"Well, Ciarán. You've brought the lass, I see. Give that bundle to Darragh, young lady, and we'll see you settled on the cart. All ready to go?"

I nodded nervously, staring at the ground. I did not even look at Darragh as he came up and plucked the roll of bedding out of my hands. The wooden chest was loaded unceremoniously onto one cart, and I found myself hoisted up on the other one, to be seated next to Peg's friend, Molly, and several small girls with rather loud voices. Father stood alongside, and I thought he seemed even paler than before, if that were possible.

"I'll take good care of her, Ciarán," said Dan as he leapt up on the first cart and took the reins in his hand. "She'll be safe with us."

Father nodded acknowledgment. At the back of the assembled folk the lads were herding ponies into line, whistling sharply. Dogs added their excited voices. Fiacha retreated to a vantage point atop a dead tree, and the gulls scattered.

"Well," said Father quietly. "Goodbye, daughter. It may be a long time."

Now that the final parting was come, I could hardly speak. The task ahead was so daunting it could hardly be imagined. Change the course of a battle. Beat the Fair Folk at a game they had been practicing for more years than there were grains of sand on the white shore of the cove. *A momentous unfolding of events* . . . I must complete the task my grandmother had begun, I must do it at any cost, to repay him for the years of patience and the priceless gift of knowledge.

"Goodbye, Father," I whispered, and then Peg called to the horses, and gave a practiced flick of the reins, and we were off. I looked back over my shoulder, watching my father's still figure growing smaller and smaller. I remember colors. The deep red of his hair. The ashen white of his stern face. The long black cloak, a sorcerer's cloak. Behind him the sea swept in and out, in and out, and the sky built with angry clouds, slate, purple, violet, dark and mysterious as the hide of some great ocean creature. A wind began to stir the beaten branches of the low bushes that bordered the track, and the little girls huddled together under their blanket, giggling and whispering behind their hands.

"It'll pass," said Peg to nobody in particular.

"All right, lassie?" queried Molly rather awkwardly. I gave a stiff nod, and winced as the cart went over a rock. Then we rounded a bend in the road, and Father was gone.

Chapter Three

It was not a time for looking back, so I gritted my teeth and got on with things as best I could. The worst of it was the constant noise: neighing, barking, the squeak of cart wheels and folk chattering all at the same time like a gaggle of geese. I longed to cast a spell of silence. I was tempted to put my hands over my ears. With an effort, I did neither.

We made a stop by the way quite early on, so Dan Walker could see a man about a horse. The carts were drawn up in the shelter of tall elms, and the women made a little fire and boiled a kettle for tea. But the horses stayed in harness, and were watered from a bucket. All too soon we would be on the road again.

The noise went on. The smaller children ran about laughing and yelling and getting wet in the nearby stream. Peg whistled; Molly hummed to herself. The older girls were conducting a conversation about the horse fair, and which of the lads they'd met last year might be there again. The boys were joking as they went among the animals with their clanking water buckets.

I sat under the trees and imagined the dim stillness of the Honeycomb, where a whole day might pass with barely a word spoken; where the only sounds were the whisper of sandalled feet and the distant roar of the ocean.

"Come with me."

Darragh's voice interrupted my thoughts, and then Darragh's

hand was grasping mine and hauling me to my feet, before I had a chance to say yes or no.

"I've got something to show you. Come on."

He pulled me back under the trees and, faster than was comfortable, up a precipitous grassy hillside to a vantage point crowned with a little cairn of stones. We had already traveled a long way up from the coast; the track had been hard for the horses, and at times folk had climbed down and walked alongside the carts. Peg had told me to stay where I was, and I had not argued with her. Perhaps they thought I would not keep up, because of my foot. Darragh was making no such concessions.

"Now," he said. "Look out that way. That's your last sight of the Kerry coast. You'll want to remember it. There's no sea at Sevenwaters, just lots and lots of trees."

It was far away; already so far. There was no crash of waves, no roar of power, no sound of seabirds squabbling on the shore as the fisherfolk gutted the catch. Only the gleam of sunlight on distant water; only the pearly sky, and the land stretched out in folds of green and gray and brown, dotted here and there with great stones and clumps of wind-battered trees.

"Look further out. Out beyond that promontory there. Tell me what you see." Darragh put one hand on my shoulder, turning me slightly, and with the other he pointed to what seemed to be a stretch of empty ocean. "Look carefully."

There was an island: a tiny, steep triangle of rock, far out in the inhospitable waters. If I squinted, I could detect plumes of spray as waves dashed its base. Another small isle lay close by. Even by my standards, it was a desolate spot.

"You can't see them from our cove," Darragh said. "Skellig rocks, they call that place. There's folk live there."

"Live there? How could they?"

"Christian hermits. Holy men. It's supposed to be good for the soul, so they say. The Norsemen put in there once, killed most of the brothers, smashed what little they had. But the hermits went back. Strange sort of life, that'd be. Think of all you'd be missing."

"It would be quiet, at least," I said somewhat testily, still staring out at the specks in the ocean, and wondering at such a choice.

"Finding it a bit much, are you?"

I said nothing.

"You're not used to folk, that's all it is. It'll get easier as we go. You've no need to be scared of us."

"Scared?" I bristled. "Why would I be scared?"

Darragh thought for a moment. "Because it's all new?" he ventured. "Because you're used to the quiet, just you and your father shut up alone doing what you do? Because you don't like being looked at?"

Misery settled on me like a small, personal gray cloud. I stared out toward the sea in silence.

"True, isn't it?" said Darragh.

"Maybe."

"Perhaps you'd rather be a hermit living on a rock in the sea, feeding yourself on seaweed and cockles? You'd not have to think about a soul besides yourself then."

"What's that supposed to mean?" I snapped.

"No more nor less than it says."

"There's nothing wrong with a life like that," I said. "At least it's—safe."

"Funny way of looking at it. What about the cliffs? What about the Norsemen? What about starving to death in winter? Or might you point your little finger and turn one of the brothers into a nice fat codfish maybe?"

I froze, unable to look at him. There was a difficult silence.

"Fainne?" he asked eventually. "What's wrong?"

And I knew that his words had been innocent, a joke, and that it was my own mind that had put the fear into me.

"Nothing."

"I worry about you. There was someone else there this summer, wasn't there?"

"My grandmother. On a visit."

"Uh-huh. And that was why you wouldn't come out?"

"Part of the reason."

"And what was the other part?" He was frowning, his dark brows drawn together.

"I—I can't do ordinary things anymore. I can't have—friends. I can't let that get in the way. It's hard to explain. This is bad enough, going on the cart, mixing with folk, having to talk and listen and—I just can't do those things anymore. I—I can't let anyone close."

Darragh did not reply. I stared at the ground, knowing he was looking at me, but unwilling to meet the expression in those too-honest brown eyes.

"I'm sorry," I whispered.

"So am I," he said slowly. "Sounds pretty odd to me. You might think yourself too fine for the likes of us. But there's folk of your own kind, where you're going. Family. It'll be good for you, Fainne. They'll welcome you. Folk are not so bad once you get to know them. And—it's only right, to have family and friends around you. I don't understand how you could do without them."

I drew my shawl closer around my shoulders. "No, I suppose you wouldn't," I said. "But our kind don't have friends."

Then we turned and made our way back down the hill, and he took my hand on the steepest bits, and neither of us said a word until we were nearly under the elms and could hear Molly laughing at some joke of Peg's.

"You have, you know," Darragh said softly. "Sometimes you get friends without asking for them. And once you've got them, they're not so easy to lose."

"I'm going a long way away," I said.

"I'm a traveling man, remember?" said Darragh. "Always on the move, that's me."

The journey was long. I learned to shut out some of the noise by repeating in my head, over and over, the recitation of question and answer that Father and I had perfected during the long years of my childhood.

Who were the first folk in the land of Erin?

The Old Ones. The Fomhóire.

And who came next?

So it went, as the carts trundled along under gentle autumn rain and crisp westerly breeze, and sometimes, when we were running late, under a great arch of stars.

Whence did you come?

From the Cauldron of Unknowing.

For what do you strive?

For knowledge. For wisdom. For an understanding of all things.

The lore was all that I had to keep me going. The lore was control and direction, amidst the noisy children and the chattering women and the constant company, more company than I was likely to want in a lifetime.

Peg was kind enough in her rough way. She never asked me to help with skinning rabbits, or fetching water, or washing the children's clothes. She tried to find me a quiet corner to roll out my bedding, once she saw how I edged away from the other girls and pulled the blanket over my ears. When we stopped for a single night, we'd sleep in the carts, with a sort of awning over that gave half-shelter. The boys slept out under the trees, next to the horses. There was a smell, with so many folk close together, and it was never really quiet. Often I lay awake looking up at the sky, thinking of Father back home, and listening to the small cracklings and rustlings around me, the horses shuffling, the sigh of children rolling over in their sleep, the snores of older folk worn out by a long day on the road. At dawn they'd be up again and soon ready to be off, the packing a well-practiced, speedy process. It seemed to me we were covering a great distance, despite many stops to sell baskets, or collect a pony, or simply to visit old friends. I lost count of the days after a while. There was a time when we came down through a desolate sort of valley with what looked like small lakes at the bottom, and I managed to waylay Darragh for a moment as he came by the back of the cart where I was sitting.

"Are we nearly there?" I asked him, softly so that nobody else could hear.

"Nearly where?" asked Darragh.

"Nearly at Sevenwaters," I whispered.

Darragh gave his crooked grin and shook his head. "Scarce halfway yet," he said. "It's a long way north, and east as well, before we reach the forest. Quite different, it is, in those parts. Still, you'll get a rest soon, and a bit of fun."

"Fun?" I scowled at him, bitterly disappointed that we had so far still to go, and furious with myself for having asked.

"That's right. Best days of the year. Down the bottom, where the valley opens out, we'll be stopping a while. Resting the horses. Making a proper little camp. Not far from there, you come to the Cross. That's where they hold the best horse fair in the country. Games, races, music, plenty of food and drink, finest company you're likely to meet anywhere. Get to know some great folks there, you will." He was watching me closely. "Don't look so anxious, Fainne. I'll look after you."

We stopped by the lakeside, and the menfolk went a certain distance along the shore, out of sight. The day was not so cold, for all the autumn was passing. Not that it was ever any trouble getting the children into the water, it was washing them that was the problem. I watched as the women and older girls stripped and scrubbed the little ones, to the accompaniment of squeals of protest and much splashing. The bath gave way to a sort of water fight, and then Peg and Molly and the other girls took off their own clothes without so much as a word of warning, and proceeded to wash themselves with a shared sliver of soap and a volley of ribald comments. I looked away, feeling a strange mixture of embarrassment and envy. Things seemed so much easier for them. I did not like the water. At home, I had never swum in the sea. My baths had been taken in a small tub before the fire, and I had fetched and warmed the water myself. Always, I had performed my ablutions in complete privacy. Even Grandmother had respected that. Still, I knew I was dirty and did not smell as I would wish to, and I did have two clean gowns in my little chest. But this—this was too hard.

Peg scrambled out of the water, her body still lean and shapely for all her brood of children.

"Come on, lass," she said with a smile. "Last chance to get spick-and-span before the fair. The water's not so chill, once you're in."

"I—I don't know—"

"Come, child, nobody's looking. There's a little cove there, a bit more private. Not used to this, I can see. I'll keep a watch out for you."

So, my cheeks hot with embarrassment, I picked my way down to the water's edge, separated from the others by a curve of shore and a few willows, and stripped off my clothes while Peg, who had donned a fresh gown and was now combing and re-plaiting her long dark hair, sat on a fallen tree trunk nearby and warned off the children if they came too close. The water was freezing. To make things worse, the bottom was soft, oozing mud, and it was easy to lose your footing. And it grew deep so quickly. I glanced over and saw the other girls swimming, brown arms flashing, wet hair like graceful weed across naked shoulders. Farther down the lake it sounded as if the boys were swinging from a tree branch into deep water. I washed as quickly as I could, using the scrap of soap on body and hair, grateful for the chance to rid myself of the sweat and grime of the journey, terrified that I might take one step too many, and plunge in over my head by mistake. Peg was looking the other way. I could be drowned before she noticed. Nobody knew I could not swim. Nobody but Darragh. To sink beneath the water, to gasp and strain and be unable to fill the chest with air, that would be a terrible way to go. It would be like . . . it would be the same as . . . I willed that thought out of my mind, unfinished.

When I came out Peg handed me a cloth to dry myself, and then there was Molly with a gown in her hands, a gown that was not mine, for it was a bright homespun, striped in blue and green, and over her shoulder she had a neckerchief with a little border of blue ribbon.

I stood shivering with the cloth hugged around me, barely covering my nakedness.

"I have another gown in my chest," I managed. "I don't—"

"This'll be easier," said Peg in a no-nonsense sort of voice. "Good color for you, the blue. Here, put your arms up, lass. That's it."

They had everything, even a clean shift for underneath, and stockings with blue borders. When I was dressed, Peg turned me around and began to brush out my hair.

"I don't—"

"There, child. No trouble. No trouble at all. What a head of curls. I've a nice bit of the blue ribbon left, from sewing those kerchiefs— Moll, see if you can find it, will you—that'll be just right to fasten the end of this plait. Your mother had a fine head of hair. Lovely color, like dark clover honey, it was."

I said nothing as her deft fingers began to plait my hair, as fast and nimble as could be, and tie it with the bright blue ribbon Molly produced from a basket tucked in the depths of the cart.

"There," said Peg, holding me at arm's length and looking me up and down. "Not so bad, was it? Now let's wash these things, and we'll be on our way. Plenty of time to dry them out in the morning. Proper camp tonight; a good fire, chance to relax and enjoy ourselves. You'll like it, lass. See if you don't."

Soon we were back on the cart and trundling on between ever flatter fields. There was a smell of the sea in the air again. The little girls had fallen unusually silent, staring at me with their big dark eyes. Maybe, I thought, they were tired out from their bath. Then one of them spoke up.

"You look pretty," she said, and exploded in a fit of nervous giggles. The others shushed her, and they maintained silence for a few moments, and then all three burst into hilarity again. And because I could not tell if she had meant it, or was merely teasing me, I said nothing at all.

It was just as Darragh had told me. We reached level ground and a fork in the track, and all of a sudden there were people everywhere, men on horseback, boys leading ponies, farmers with carts piled high, strangely dressed folk with juggling balls or colored birds in cages. There was an enclosed cart, with a black-clad fellow seated morosely in front, driving a skinny old horse. Beside them a younger man walked, and as he went he extolled the virtues of various elixirs for sale: love philters, magic potions of strength, curses to set on an enemy. "Come one, come all," he shouted with great vigor and greater confidence. "Ills cured! Fortunes predicted! Look for the Grand Master under the old oaks north of the racing ground. Satisfaction guaranteed." I stared as they made their way past us, and I wondered what the fellow had in his mixtures. A few herbs and a dash of honey? Nothing much of value, I suspected. But there were those who ran after his cart, babbling with excitement. More fools they, I thought. They'd soon be parted from what little silver they had, and for nothing.

We did not share the road long with the ever-increasing throng, but took a side way to the west, and soon reached a sheltered stretch of sward fringed by elder trees and bordered by a swift-running stream. Here we halted and camp was set up. This time the carts were fully unpacked, serviceable shelters erected, and a solid fireplace of stones constructed in the center of the open space, with room around it for folk to sit in comfort. The horses were unharnessed, then loosely tethered in the shelter of the trees, and the boys began the task of brushing them down, each in turn, and checking for any possible damage after the journey. I gathered we were to stay here for the duration of the fair, going up the road each day to do business and returning to our camp at night. I could hear the sea, a soft, persistent washing in and out of small waves.

The women and girls had a big tent now, and in this I was given my own corner, which Peg showed me, winking. As I rolled out my bedding and checked the lock on the wooden chest, I managed a whispered thank-you, and she gave a crooked grin, the image of her son's. As soon as my things were set out neatly I made my escape, out of the tent, between the trees, and down a little track to the west. It wasn't far. A short walk on the pebbly path, between scrubby bushes, up a gentle rise, and there it was. The breakers rolled lazily in to lick at the pure, wide beach that stretched between high promontories to north and south. Farther out there were plumes of spray, and dark rocks slick with water. A great reef, it seemed, guarded this peaceful bay. The setting sun moved ever closer to the vast expanse of water, and touched the sand to pale gold. Here and there on the shore figures could be seen: two boys galloping their ponies neck and neck in a wild race along the margin of land and water; a lad on a black horse, out there swimming, breasting the power of the swell, then coming in to shore, dripping, to shake off the excess in a shower of silver. There were folk walking, a couple hand in hand, a girl bending to pick up shells.

I sat there awhile, watching. I sat there long enough to become calm, to slow my breathing, to tell myself I could manage, I would manage. Perhaps, when they gathered around the fire in the evening, they would not think it amiss if I retired early to sleep. Maybe, when they went up to join the great throng at the horse fair, I might remain behind here and walk alone on the shore, or sit and watch the slow pattern, always changing, always still the same. Perhaps that might be possible. If it were not, I would have to use the Glamour. Indeed, Grandmother would think it foolish that I had not done so by now, to cover my awkwardness, to mask my fear of strangers. I thought it foolish myself, really. But there was something held me back. I remembered Darragh's frown, and Darragh's words. *I don't like it when you do that*. I thought of the little girl's voice. *You look pretty*. I had decided, almost, that she was joking. But for a moment her words had warmed me. If I used the Glamour, everyone would think I was pretty. But it was not the same.

In the event, there was no escaping the evening's festivities. My half-framed excuse was brushed aside by Peg, who bustled me out into the circle of folk seated on rugs and old boxes and bits and pieces around the fire. She sat me down between Molly and herself, put a cup of something steaming and fragrant into my hands, then settled herself down for the fun, all, it seemed, in the twinkling of an eye. There was simply no chance to object.

Around the fire were many faces, old and new. The smaller children sat drowsing on parents' knees, or slept curled in blankets close by a watchful sister or brother. The older folk were given pride of place, the most comfortable seats, the nearest proximity to the fire's warmth. Everyone was there: Dan Walker with his little dark beard and the gold ring in his ear; the group of youths I had encountered on my visit to the camp, back home; Darragh himself, talking to a couple of brightly clad girls I had not seen before. There were other folk I did not know, though clearly they were invited guests. The two girls seemed to have brothers, or cousins, and there was an older, gray-haired man sitting by Dan and sharing the hot drink from a great kettle set by the fire. I sipped cautiously. It was good, but strong, something like a cider with spices and honey.

"What about a tale or two?" somebody asked. "Who's got a good story? Brian? Diarmuid?"

"Not me," said the gray-haired man, shaking his head. "Got a toothache. Can't talk."

"Huh!" scoffed another. "Have some more to drink, that'll soon cure it."

"Fellow at the fair, pulls teeth neat and quick," Molly suggested. "You need to visit him, he'd have it out for you before you could so much as squeal."

"That butcher?" The man paled visibly. "I'd as soon get my old woman to lay hold of it with a pair of fire tongs."

There were several suggestions as to what other remedies he might have recourse to, none of them very practical. Then Dan Walker spoke up.

"I'll tell a tale," he said. There was a chorus of approval, then silence. "It's about a man called Daithi, Daithi O'Flaherty. No relation, you understand, of the distinguished family of that name that lives in these parts." There was a roar of appreciative laughter. "A farmer, he was. Well, this Daithi got an idea he might go and see his sweetheart, just to pass the time of day, you understand. He was making his way along the road when he heard a little noise, tap tappity tap, from down under the bushes by the track. Daithi was a sharp fellow. He didn't make a sound, but crouched down quiet-like, and peered under the twigs to see what it was. And bless me if he didn't spot a tiny wee fellow, all dressed in a pointed hat and a fine small apron of leather, and by him a pitcher with a little dipper laid by it. The small one was tapping away at a boot he was making, a boot the length of one part of your finger, fit only for a clurichaun such as himself. As Daithi watched, holding his breath, the wee fellow put down his cobbler's tool, and went to the pitcher, and he dipped the ladle in and got himself a drink of the liquor; and then he went back to his work, tap tappity tap.

"Best handle this careful, said Daithi to himself. So he kept his voice soft, not to startle the little man.

" 'Good day to you, fine sir,' he spoke up, as polite as can be.

" 'And you, sir,' replied the small one, still tapping away.

" 'And what might it be that you're a-fashioning there?' asked Daithi.

" ''Tis a shoe, to be sure,' said the clurichaun, with a touch of scorn. 'And what might you be doing, wandering the track instead of doing your day's work?'

" 'I'll be back to it soon enough,' replied Daithi, thinking, Unless I catch you first. 'Now tell me, what is it you have in your fine wee pot there?'

" 'Beer,' said the little man. 'The tastiest ever brewed. Made it meself.' He licked his lips.

" 'Indeed?' said Daithi. 'And what might you use, for such a brew? Malt, would it be?'

"The clurichaun rolled his eyes in disdain. 'Malt? Malt's for babies. This drink's brewed from heather. None better.'

" 'Heather?' exclaimed Daithi. 'You can't brew beer from heather.'

" 'Ah,' said the wee fellow. ' 'Twas the Dubh-ghaill showed me. Secret recipe. 'Tis me own family makes it, and no other.'

" 'Can I taste it then?'

" 'Surely,' said the clurichaun. 'But it's shocked I am, that a fine farmer such as yourself would be thinking to pass the time of day drinking by the road, when it's his own geese are out of the yard and running riot all over his neighbor's garden.'

"Daithi was shocked, and nearly turned away to run back down to the cottage and see if the wee man was right. But at the last instant he remembered, and instead his hand shot out to grab the clurichaun by one leg. The jug went over, and all the beer spilt out on the ground.

" 'Now,' said Daithi as sternly as he could, 'show me where you keep your store of gold, or it'll be the worse for you.'

"Well, the clurichaun was rightly trapped, for as we all know, you need only hold onto such a one and keep him in your sight, and he has to show you his treasure. So on they went down to Daithi's own fields, and into a place with many rocks still to be shifted before it would be good for planting. The clurichaun pointed to one of these big stones toward the south end of the field.

" 'There,' said the little fellow. 'Under that, there's me crock of gold, and bad cess to you.'

"Well, Daithi tried and he tried to shift the rock, pushing and heaving, and all the while holding onto the clurichaun, and eventually he knew he'd not get it out without his spade. But there were so many stones there; a whole field of stones. He'd need to mark it somehow, before he went for the spade. Daithi felt in his pocket. There was a bit of red ribbon there that he'd got from a traveling man, and planned to give to his sweetheart for a surprise. He fished it out, and tied it around the rock where the gold lay buried.

" 'There,' he said. He frowned at the wee man. 'Now, before I let you free,' he said, knowing well the trickery of such folk, 'I want your word. You're not to move the treasure before I come back with the spade. And you're not to take the ribbon off this rock. Give me your promise.'

" 'I promise, sure and I do,' said the clurichaun with absolute sincerity."

There was a ripple of laughter from those in Dan's audience who knew the end of this story.

" 'All right then,' said Daithi.

" 'Will you let me go, so?' the wee man asked, polite as can be. So Daithi released him, and the clurichaun was off in a flash. Daithi went home for his spade, and rushed back to the field with his mind full of all the things he would do when he laid his hands on that crock of gold. And as he came around the corner and clapped eyes on the field, what did he see? Every single stone in that field was wearing a red ribbon, neat as could be. And try as he might, and dig as he would, Daithi O'Flaherty never did find the clurichaun's treasure."

There was a ripple of satisfied applause. Even I had enjoyed the story, though it had lacked the grandeur of those my father told. Then the gray-haired man, apparently cured of his toothache, volunteered a song. It was a fine, uplifting tune about how hard it was to make a living in the bitter cold and harsh land of Ceann na Mara, and how he loved it so well, regardless, that his heart would always call him back there. There were more tales: funny, sad, touching. At the end, Darragh was persuaded to play his pipes. This time he did not choose one of the heart-stopping laments I had heard so often ringing across the hillside above the cove. He played music for dancing, and the young folk got up and made a circle, and there was a stamping of feet and a clapping of hands, and the bright whirl of skirts and fringed shawls in the warm golden light of the campfire. I sat and watched and sipped my drink. Darragh played on. He was not looking at the joyful dancers, or at the older folk seated comfortably, renewing friendships after a year's parting. He was looking at me. *Get up and dance*, his eyes said, challenging. *Why don't you?* And deep inside me, something wanted to do just that. The music spoke to the blood; it called to feelings best left unwoken. But I had been well trained. I spoke to myself severely. *You, dance? Don't be silly. You'll never dance, not without making a fool of yourself. Besides, you are what you are. You are outside this, and always will be.*

After that it was easy enough to get up, have a quiet word with Peg, and retire to the tent.

"Enjoyed yourself, did you, lass?" Peg queried. I gave a little nod that could have meant anything, and fled to my dark corner and privacy. Outside the music played on. At some point, Darragh's pipes were joined by a whistle and a drum. In my own small patch of stillness, I unfastened the wooden chest and, rummaging through the contents, I found Riona and took her out. Her features could barely be discerned in the shadows.

Did my mother dance? I asked her. *Is that what this once was, a dress for dancing?* My fingers touched a fold of the rose-colored silk that made up Riona's small gown. Surely only a lovely, confident girl would wear such a fabric. And yet, that same girl had become the fragile creature of Peg's words, the woman who had abandoned her little child and the young man who loved her so desperately, the woman who had simply stepped off the cliff one day and gone down, down through the wild spray into the icy grip of the ocean surge as it hammered the rocks of the Honeycomb. Her own family had done this to her; her father, her uncles, her brother who still ruled as lord of Sevenwaters. Darragh's talk of family was rubbish. They had as good as killed her, and they had all but destroyed my father. In their way they were as bad as my grandmother. Now I must confront them, and somehow I must complete the task my grandmother had laid on me. How could I think of tales, and music, and fun, when I had that ahead of me? Dan Walker and his kind were simple folk. Even the stories they told were simple. I did not belong with them, and it was foolish to believe I ever would. I must keep myself to myself and make sure I drew no undue attention. In time the journey would be ended, and I could begin the work that was required of me.

But it was not so easy. It seemed to me there was a small conspiracy afoot to bring me out of myself, and make me a part of everything whether I wanted it or not. They were up early next morning, with folk already eating their porridge as I emerged, bleary-eyed, from the tent. There was a communal water trough. I splashed my face, having learned soon enough not to be too fussy.

"Eat up quick," advised one of the girls as she hurried past me, tying her hair neatly back in a kerchief. "It's quite a walk. And trading starts early."

Mutely, I accepted a bowl of porridge and retired under the trees to sit on a fallen branch and eat. I was tired. It had been a late night. I did not want to go anyway. But they all seemed so busy; there was nobody I could ask. The ponies must look their best; Dan was inspecting them as the boys moved around putting the final touches on: the intricate plaiting of a mane here, the careful brushing of a tail there. Peg was sorting out the best of the baskets, and giving the girls instructions about trading and more instructions about not getting into trouble. Maybe there was no need to ask if I could stay behind. Maybe they would just forget me. A sudden wave of homesickness swept over me, a longing to see Father and be back in safe, familiar, quiet Kerry once more. If only I could just pack up a little bag and set off by myself, retracing the way until I came up the hill where the standing stones marked the passing of time, and found myself back in the cove again.

But I could not go. The only way was forward. I felt powerless and sad. I felt truly outside, as if there were nowhere I belonged.

"Best clean that bowl and get ready to go, lass." Peg's voice broke into my thoughts. "We'll be away soon. Busy day."

I looked up at her, framing the words. Then Darragh appeared behind her, dressed in his best, green neckerchief jaunty, boots polished to a high shine.

"It's too far for Fainne to walk," he said to his mother.

"Lass'll do well enough," Peg said, looking at him sidelong with a rather odd expression. "She's not a cripple."

"I—I would—" was as much as I got out. Two pairs of eyes regarded me intently, and I knew they knew what I was trying to say.

"Tell you what," said Darragh casually. "I'll take Fainne with me. Won't hurt Aoife to carry one more. I'll drop her off near the oaks, make sure we find you before I head off for the sale lines. Be easier for all concerned."

"If that's what you want," said his mother dryly. "Don't be late, now."

"No, Mam," grinned Darragh, and advanced to where I stood scowling under the trees, empty porridge bowl in hand. "Ready?" he queried with a lift of the brows.

"I don't even want to go," I grumbled.

"Well, you can't stay here on your own, so there's no choice really, is there?" he said lightly. "You'll need a kerchief on your head, it's windy riding. Best plait up your hair, too. Want me to do it for you?"

"I certainly do not!" I snapped. "I'm not a baby. I'll do it myself."

"Don't be long," he said calmly.

One of the other girls offered to help with my hair, and because I was in a hurry, I let her. This I regretted soon enough.

"Special treatment, huh?" she queried as her fingers worked their way through the thick, intractable mass of russet curls.

I could not look at her, to quell her gossip with an expression of disdain. I was forced, therefore, to reply. "What do you mean?"

"Getting a ride with Darragh. He's never done that before, taken a girl up to the Cross with him. Too many lasses after him, that's his problem. Very careful, is Darragh. Doesn't play favorites."

I could scarcely think of what to say. I might have slapped her face, if she had not had hold of my hair.

"There's no favorites about it," I whispered angrily. "He's just being helpful, that's all, because I can't walk very fast." I moved my right foot slightly, to show the boot that was a different shape from an ordinary one.

"That?" said the girl, offhand. "That's nothing much. You'd keep up all right. Got a bit of ribbon, have you?"

I handed her the blue ribbon, over my shoulder.

"No. You're favored all right. Not like him to hang around waiting, first day of the fair. He's always the earliest one off, straight after sun-up. Horse mad, Darragh is. Wait till he turns up at the Cross with you behind him. Break a few of the lasses' hearts, that will."

"You're wrong, I'm sure," I said, feeling my cheeks grow hot with embarrassment. "It's just that—that I am not one of you. A—a stranger, a guest. He's being polite. That's all."

The girl tied the ribbon neatly and firmly. "Maybe," she said, leaning around with a little grin that marked her out as another of Peg's seemingly endless brood. She must, therefore, be Darragh's sister. I could not even remember her name. "And maybe not." And then she was off in a flurry of red skirts and a twinkle of gold earrings, before I could even think of saying thank you.

She was completely wrong, of course. Darragh and I were old friends, that was all. And Darragh thought I would be a nuisance and get into trouble if he did not play watchdog. Anything else was far too difficult to contemplate. I tied the little kerchief with its blue border over my newly braided hair, and went out to where he waited, with no sign of impatience, while Aoife cropped tranquilly at the grass. It seemed as if Dan and the men and the other lads were already gone. Peg and Molly were organizing bigger children to carry younger ones, and making use of a couple of old horses to bear baskets and babies.

Darragh was looking at me with an odd expression, almost as if he were going to laugh.

"Quite the little traveling girl," he remarked. "All you need's a finishing touch, and you'll blend right in. Here." He reached under his jacket and brought out a bundle of silk-soft cloth, neatly folded. As I took it in my hands it flowed out of itself and was revealed as a dazzling shawl of many colors, closely patterned with tiny creatures, delicate and jewel-like, leaf-green lizards, vivid blue birds, golden butterflies and exotic, rainbow fish with fronded tails. The shawl was fringed with long shining tassels, somewhere between gold and silver. It was the most beautiful garment I had ever seen.

"I can't wear this," I said, staring at it. It seemed fit only for a princess.

"No?" said Darragh, and he plucked it out of my hands and put it around my shoulders, tying the ends in front. "Come on," he said. "I promised not to be late. Not scared to ride a pony, are you?"

"Of course not!" I retorted.

"Well, then."

With him helping, it wasn't too hard to scramble up on Aoife's back. I'd thought I would have to cling on behind him, as his sister had said; but he put me up in front, sitting across like a lady, and held onto me with one arm while the other hand kept a light hold on the reins. It seemed to me, as we went, that Aoife knew what he wanted almost without being told. When there was a fork in the track, Darragh would say a quiet word, and she'd go one way or the other. He'd touch her with his knee, or put a brown hand on her glossy white neck, and she'd understand straight away what he wanted.

"All right?" he asked me once or twice, and I nodded. In fact, it was better than all right. It felt like old times; like the days of silent companionship we had shared as children. Those times were lost now. I knew that. But for as long as this ride might take, I could pretend that nothing had changed. I could feel the soft touch of the wonderful shawl with its vibrant pattern of life, enfolding me like a talisman of protection; I could almost believe I was one of the traveling folk, riding to the fair as bold as could be, and behind me, with his arm around my waist, a fine fellow who was the best piper in all of Kerry. Here I was, riding on the whitest and cleverest pony you ever saw, with the wind in my face, and the strange, stark shapes of distant hills on the one side, and the waters of a vast inlet on the other, bordered by a rocky shore, with here and there a little beach and a boat or two drawn up for safekeeping. There were not so many folk about, not now. Perhaps we really were late. Darragh didn't seem bothered, and Aoife made her way as if she were the only creature of importance on the road anyway. We had passed Peg and Molly and the children, and Darragh's sister had winked at me.

After a while I said to him, "What's your sister's name?"

"Which one?"

"The one with the red skirt, and a bold sort of way with her. The next one down from you, I think."

There was a little pause. "Why don't you ask her?" said Darragh.

I made no reply.

"They don't bite, Fainne," he said, but there was no reproach in his tone. "That'd be Roisin. Been giving you cheek, has she?"

"Not really."

"You need to watch out for her. She'll say just what she thinks, if she's a mind to."

"Mm," I said. "I've noticed."

"She's a good girl, though. They all are."

All too soon we were there. I had never seen so many people all in the one place, nor heard such a din of voices. There was a sort of order in it, if you looked close enough. The real business was over where the horses were, with little groups of farmers and traveling men and a few with the air of a local lord or a master at arms, checking teeth and inspecting hooves, and conducting intense, private conversations. Nearer at hand, folk were trading for a variety of goods, and chattering, and there was a smell of something good roasting over a little fire, and I could see the covered cart of the Grand Master and his voluble henchman. From a distance, someone called out to Darragh. We came to a halt under a stand of great trees.

"Well, then," he said, and slipped from Aoife's back, light as a feather. "Here we are." He lifted me down, and stood there with his hands around my waist. "Ah," he said. "A smile. That's a rare treat."

I reached out to pat Aoife's well-groomed flank. "Not selling her, are you?" I queried.

"Her? Not likely. Couldn't part with her, not now. She's my luck."

I nodded. "Someone's calling you," I said.

Darragh took his hands away. "Not sure I can go," he said, frowning. "Mam's not here yet, and I said I'd make certain I found them for you. And up there's no place for a girl," jerking his head toward the horse lines.

Another voice yelled out, "Darragh! You're needed here!"

"You'd better go," I said, with more courage than I felt. "I can wait here under the oaks and look out for the others."

Darragh's brown eyes regarded me very closely. "Sure?"

"I'm not a child. I think I can be relied on to wait a little and not get lost."

"Promise you'll stay out of trouble."

"Don't be ridiculous."

"Promise, or I'll be obliged to wait here with you."

"Darragh!" This time it was Dan Walker who was calling.

"This is stupid. All right, I promise."

"See you later, then." He tweaked the corner of my kerchief, turned on his heel and was gone, with Aoife walking obediently beside him, steady as a rock in the seething, noisy press of the crowd.

I did mean it, when I promised. I really did. But you can't help who you are, and what you are. Sometimes things happen, and you have to act, you simply cannot stop yourself. That was how it was, that morning at the Cross.

I melted into the shadows under the big trees, wishing I had the power to command invisibility. For now I could stand here unobserved, brilliant-colored shawl or no, since all attention was on the Grand Master's cart. It was being opened and unpacked not ten strides away from me, to much craning of necks and ooh-ing and aahing from the crowd assembled around it. The lanky assistant was doing most of the work and all the talking, while the Master himself stood there in his tattered apology for a wizard's cloak, staring down his beak of a nose and doing his best to look haughty and mysterious. There was less magic in that lugubrious fellow, I thought, than I had in my smallest finger. You could see at first glance that he was a fake, and it was astonishing that folk seemed to be taken in by it.

The assistant was a very busy man. Soon the area to each side of the cart was a gaudy array of banners and netting, with many little cages hung on poles, in each of which was a strange creature that might be obtained for a price, to amuse a sweetheart or make a neighbor jealous. I edged a little closer, but it was hard to see without being seen. In the cage nearest to me there was a forlorn-looking bird, an owl sort of thing with ragged plumage. It edged from side to side on its perch, the movements jerky, the eyes round and wild. Below it, some furry creature sat, with a clawed hand curled around the bars of its small prison, and its head leaning over as if feigning sleep. On the other side, something was uttering shrill screeches, and folk were pointing, with little exclamations.

"Now, my fine ladies, my estimable lords, my fortunate young ones!" The assistant was shouting; essential over the racket. "Come closer, come closer, and the Master will show you the amazing remedies we have for you this year, some tried and true, some wondrous new discoveries, all astonishingly effective."

He went on in this vein for some time. I glanced around. There was still no sign of Peg and Molly and the others. I moved closer. I could see the source of the noise now: a brightly colored bird tethered to a perch on the far side of the cart. Behind it were more caged creatures. Doves. Finches. A pale-furred hare, confined very close, so close it could not turn, let alone flex its strong legs and spring as was the way of its kind. There was a boy there, poking his finger in at it, and the creature had not even the room to flinch away. I looked into its eyes: blank, staring eyes where panic had overtaken reason. The bird screamed again, and it seemed to me it was crying out the rage and the fear of all of them, for being shut up and put on show and looked at, for being a thing of beauty shackled and gawked at and enjoyed, and then thrown away without further thought.

The man was going on about a potion of strength. He pretended to drink a little, and then chose a big fellow from the crowd to come up and fight him. The result was inevitable. The two of them made a pretense of sparring, and then the Master's assistant felled his much larger opponent with a careful tap to the jaw. The giant collapsed, and the crowd gasped. After a short pause, during which a child was heard to say, "Is he dead Mam?," the fellow began to groan, and was hauled to his feet, rubbing his jaw and rolling his eyes. There was a babble of excitement, and an eager jostle of buyers. I wondered how much they had paid the large man for his performance.

"And now," said the henchman, apparently buoyed by his success, "the Master himself will demonstrate the use of the new, all-effective love philter. Made with his very own hands, this potion of power will transform the most reluctant sweetheart into . . . dear friends, you cannot imagine. It must speak for itself. Good folk, here is . . . the Master."

We were supposed to cheer, I think. I still could not see properly. But if I moved any closer, I would be right in the crowd, and folk would look at me and press up against me and maybe talk to me and . . . My fingers clutched the amulet for reassurance. *Use the Glamour, child,* said my grandmother's voice, somewhere in my head. *Be what you like.*

I did it quickly, before I could change my mind. Peg and Molly weren't there. Darragh was busy. Nobody would notice a thing. I chose the form I judged least likely to draw any attention, a much older version of myself, a woman of middle years, in plain working clothes, shawled and scarved and straggle-haired. I could have been anyone. Indeed, there were many others just like me in the throng. Not a soul noticed as I moved quietly down to stand near the front, where I could see the man who called himself the Master scanning the crowd, while maintaining his pose of disdain.

"The Master's looking," said his assistant portentously. "Looking, searching for a fellow that's lonely; for some poor soul with no sweetheart. What about you, sir?"

"He's taken!" retorted a sharp female voice from the back of the crowd. Everyone laughed.

"Ah," said the assistant as the Master pointed a bony finger. "Here's a fellow. What is your name, sir?"

The man was red with embarrassment, but grinning at the same time. "His name's Ross," offered a helpful friend, spluttering with laughter. "A few sheaves short of the full stack, but a fine man for all that." It sounded as if they'd made an early start on the ale.

"You'd like a pretty sweetheart, now, wouldn't you, Ross?" asked the assistant as he hauled his victim up on the cart steps where all could view him. "Let's see if we can find one for you. Which of you ladies wants to test our new elixir, now?"

There was a shuffling of feet, and a silence. Seemingly there were no takers. I was not surprised. The man they had chosen was skinny and none too clean-looking, and he had a bulbous nose with a drip on the end.

"Come, now," coaxed the henchman. "Who'll try it? There must be a lovely lady here who'd like a bit of fun? No? Then the Master himself must beg."

The black-cloaked man had already descended from the cart, and had begun to pace along the front where folk stood close-packed. I had been watching him, while others had all their attention on the fellow who was doing the talking. The Master had in his hand a fine gold chain with a small, shining object strung on it, and he was dangling it to and fro, to and fro.

"There might be a little something in it, for the girl that's bold enough," hinted the assistant. The Master paced back and forth. The little chain swung left and right, left and right. He halted. He paused. He stretched out a finger and pointed.

"Ah!" exclaimed the assistant. "We have a willing taker. Come up, my dear, come up and sip this exquisite potion, made from carefully selected herbs and berries and just—a—*little*," he made a circle with his thumb and first finger, "of the most secretly guarded of ingredients. Just a tiny sip."

The girl they had chosen was very young, certainly younger than myself, and poorly clad, with a gown much mended. For all that, there was a delicate bloom about her that might catch a man's fancy. Nobody raised an objection when the men led her forward. It seemed she was there alone. Nobody noticed the way she stared at the little gold chain swinging to and fro, to and fro, as if that were all she could see. Nobody but me. I felt anger building in me.

The Master put the gold chain away in his pocket. The young girl stood there before him, her pure features blank of expression. On the other side, the man with the bulbous nose leered across at her, then rolled his eyes back to his friends in the crowd, who sniggered and poked each other in the ribs.

The Master bent over and whispered in the girl's ear. All that I heard was "Drink this, my dear." But there had been more. I could guess what it was.

She took the little cup in her hand and drank. There was a hush of expectation. For a moment, nothing happened. Then she turned, expressionless, and took a step over to the man, Ross. She twined her arms around his neck, and pressed her body against his, and planted a long kiss on his lips. The crowd cheered and applauded. I watched the way the man's hand groped at her skirts, and the way his tongue went, disgustingly, in her mouth. I waited for the Master to click his fingers or wave his hand before the girl's eyes, and undo what he had done. Instead, he watched the fellow lead the young girl down the steps and away through the crowd. A rush of other men clustered around the cart, eager to buy. I was outraged. It was nothing but a sham, an old trick, easy as long as you picked a susceptible subject. Simply done. Simply undone.

But this man had not undone it. He had let that little girl go, with that fellow, and—as I said, you are what you are. Sometimes you just have to act. The rainbow bird sat on its perch just by the Master's shoulder, still shrieking abuse, as well it might do. I looked it in the eye, and spoke a word in my mind.

The tether that held it broke apart. Nobody saw. The bird shrank, and swelled, and changed. For a moment, in the commotion of jostling buyers, nobody noticed. Bright feathers became shining scales. Claws and beak disappeared. I used my imagination. The creature grew long and slender and sinuous. The serpent coiled around the perch, feeling the strength in its muscular neck, feeling the venom in its forked tongue. Feeling the almost forgotten power of freedom.

A child spoke up again. "What's that, Mam?"

The Master froze in his place as a creeping, twining presence flowed across his shoulders and around his neck, above the tattered black cloak.

"Aaah . . ." he managed, a mere thread of sound. His assistant backed away. The crowd retreated. Amongst them, the man Ross halted and stared back, still clutching the girl by one arm. I took a step forward, making sure the Master could see me.

"Undo it," I said very quietly.

His eyes bulged at me. His face was purple. Maybe the coils were tight. I did not care.

"Call that girl back here and undo what you did," I said again, softly so that only he and his assistant could hear me. "Do it now or you're dead. Don't think I care what happens to you."

"Aaaah . . ." the Master gasped again, rolling his eyes toward his assistant. The serpent shifted its grip, and its tail slid off the perch to curl neatly around the Master's arm. Now he was bearing its full weight. The small, triangular head was poised just in front of his eyes.

The assistant moved, called out. "You! You there! Bring her back!"

The crowd parted for the man and the girl. Terror held folk away from the cart; fascination kept them close enough, for this fair's entertainment would be the stuff of fireside tales for many a long winter to come. The assistant grabbed the girl's other arm and wrenched her away from the leering Ross. He didn't have to pull very hard. Ross had blanched at the sight of the serpent's wicked little eyes. He faded back into the crowd.

The girl was led up close. Her expression was quite blank; the terrifying creature might just as well have been a hedgehog or a sheep.

"Undo it," I hissed. "Hurry up. Or I'll make it bite." I was not at all sure I could do this, but it sounded good. The Master raised a shaking hand, and clicked his fingers once before the girl's blank face. She blinked and rubbed her eyes. Then she saw the snake, and screamed.

"It's all right," I told her, under cover of the crowd's excited response. "Go home. Go on. Find your family, and go home."

"Dad," she said in a panicky voice, as if remembering something. "Dad'll kill me." She looked around wildly, spotted someone away toward the horse lines, and was off at a run.

"Erggh . . ." came a strangled sound. I had not forgotten the Master. Not entirely. And I must act fast, and then disappear, for I caught a glimpse of Roisin on the edge of the crowd, and knew the others must be there, and would be searching for me.

I looked the serpent in its small, bright eye. I'd been quite pleased with this creation. But a serpent could not fly, after all. I spoke the word, and it changed. The Master gave a yelp of pain as the rainbow bird clamped its claws momentarily on his shoulder, and then it spread its gaudy wings and rose somewhat unevenly into the air, circling the crowd with a scream of derision before it flew off eastward. Everyone was looking up, craning to see the phenomenon. I hadn't long, but I was good at this sort of thing. Cage doors sprang open, latches fell apart, bolts dropped from their fastenings. Not all could be safe; some I had to change. The hare became a fine, healthy little pony, which I slapped on the rump and sent in the general direction of the horse lines. He'd do well enough. The clawed, furry creature transformed into a squirrel, that streaked across the open ground and straight up into the oaks, where it proceeded to make itself quite at home. The finches, the doves, they would be all right. Perhaps they had not been captive long, for they flew off quickly to take their chances with the winter, and the trapper, and the hawk. But there was one captive left. The little owl, whose cage was open, whose path to freedom lay before it, stood quivering on its perch, lifting one foot and then the other, unable somehow to make that first move. And now folk were noticing, pointing, staring, and the Master and his henchman were advancing on me where I stood willing the creature to move its wings and fly. I fancied I heard Peg's voice somewhere beyond the oaks, calling my name.

Fly, stupid, I told the bird. I could not transform this one; it was too fragile and too terrified to survive that. A quick decision was required. I turned to the Master.

"Give me this owl. Or I'll tell all these people what a fraud you are. How all your remedies are fakes. I can do it."

He looked down his nose at me. "You?" he hissed, quiet enough for folk not to hear. "A farmer's wife? I don't think so. Now clear off, or I'll have you whipped for ruining my performance and stealing my animals. Go on, off with—" He stopped abruptly as I fixed my gaze on his neck and applied another little spell.

"Ah . . . aaagh . . ."

"You see?" I said sweetly. "The serpent is just a fancy touch. I've no need of that, to kill you gradually from strangulation. Give me the bird."

He gestured wildly with one hand and clutched his throat with the other. The assistant lifted down the small cage and its inhabitant, and I took it.

"Good," I said calmly, and released the spell. The Master staggered back, chalk-faced, as his assistant was besieged by gesticulating, confused spectators. Now that they were sure the serpent was gone, they had questions they wanted answered.

The Master was staring at me.

"Who are you?" he breathed with real fear in his eyes.

"I am a sorcerer's daughter, and more of a master than you will ever be, with your cheap tricks," I told him. "Don't try that again, fooling a little girl into behaving like some wanton for hire. Don't even think of it." I gestured toward my own neck, as if to warn him of the consequences. Then I caught sight of Molly, and beside her Roisin, and I made myself vanish into the crowd, where I was just another farmer's wife out for a day of amusement.

I retreated to a quiet corner behind an empty cart, and sat down on the grass. I spoke the words in silence, and was myself again, a little traveler girl, striped dress, blue-bordered kerchief, long red plait, limping foot. A girl wearing the most beautiful shawl at the Cross, a shawl with a proud pattern of wonderful creatures of all kinds. A girl bearing a broken cage, with a crazy owl in it. Clearly, that part would not do.

I spoke to the creature very quietly. It seemed near-stupefied with fear, its only movement the strange, mechanical lifting of its feet, left and right, left and right.

"Don't be scared," I told it, quite unsure of whether it could even hear me, let alone understand. "You can go now. Fly. Fly away free." I reached very slowly into the cage, expecting at the least some serious damage to my fingers. The bird made no move but its mindless pacing. Perhaps it really was mad. Maybe it would be kinder to wring its neck. I could hear Peg's voice again, over the noise of the crowd.

"Come on," I said. "Give me a bit of help, can't you?" I put my hand around the creature, pinning the wings so it could not hurt itself with flapping, and lifted it out carefully, head first. I could feel the frantic drumming of its heart, and the fragility of its body, all little bones and feathers. I used both hands to hold the bird more or less upright on the ground before me, facing the open.

"Trees," I said. "Oaks. That's what those are. Fly. Use those wings. Off you go." I took my hands away. The bird stood there, trembling. At least it had stopped its pacing. "Go on," I said, giving it the tiniest push away.

It turned its head and looked at me.

"By all the powers!" I whispered in exasperation. "What am I supposed to do? I can't keep you, I've got to go, and besides—"

The bird stared at me with its big, round, mad eyes.

"Haven't I got enough to worry about?" I asked it. "Oh, come on, then." The pathetic bundle of feathers could not sustain a transformation, that I knew from bitter experience. More than one rat or beetle had been sacrificed to Grandmother's quest for perfection in the art. But a lesser change might be possible. And my gown had deep pockets, since a traveler girl might need to carry a needle and thread, or a handy knife, or a spare kerchief or two. I reached out and passed my hand over the creature's ragged form. "There," I said, picking it up in my hand. Now it was around the size of a mouse: the claws like the little thorns of a wild rose, the eyes tiny, dark and solemn. It blinked at me.

"I hope you're not hungry," I said in an undertone. "I hope you understand *keep still* and *keep quiet*." And I slipped the very small bird into my pocket, and went out into the fair.

"Fainne!" yelled Roisin, before I had gone five paces across the grass. "Where were you? Mam's going frantic, said she couldn't find you anywhere! Where were you?"

"Nowhere much," I said. "She'd no need to worry."

"That's not what Darragh said."

I looked at her sharply. "And just what did Darragh say?" I asked her, shocked out of my shyness.

Roisin grinned. "Said, given half a chance, you'd find trouble."

"Nonsense," I told her. "As you see, I'm fine. Where are we going now?"

"To sell the baskets. Once they're all gone we can look around, see the sights. Not on our own, though. Mam won't allow that." She looked at me sideways, brows raised.

"Sorry," I conceded. "I didn't know."

"Uh-huh," said Roisin, sounding just like her brother.

It was all the talk of the day. I sat watching as Peg and Molly and Roisin and the other girls haggled over their wares and pocketed their profits, and the tale of what happened that morning grew ever more elaborate. We'd seen the Grand Master and his assistant pack up and leave the fair entirely, not without many delays, for there were customers dissatisfied, and explanations required. Eventually they made their escape, and this in itself was cause for surprised conjecture, for they'd been a fixture of the fair for many a season, Peg said. Folk swore by their remedies. As for herself, she'd never seen the need for any of those potions. What you couldn't do by yourself, you couldn't do. Folk should accept that, and stop trying to be what they weren't. The fellow brought the crowds, that was the only good to be said of him. Set up close to the Master's cart, and your sales would be steady enough.

I kept well out of it. Roisin asked me what I'd seen, and I told her not much, because there'd been tall people standing in front of me. Just a lot of fuss, and some birds flying off. That was all. But all morning folk were talking about it. They were saying the magic went wrong for some reason. A curse, maybe. The creatures had gone mad, and there was a snake near killed the fellow, and some large animal with claws like knives. Never seen anything like it. And there was some woman gave the Master quite a tongue-lashing. Wouldn't want to get on the wrong side of *her*. Fierce as a sorceress, she was, for all she was just some farmer's wife. And then, all of a sudden, no sign of her. But the fellow was scared, you could see it. Face the color of fresh cheese, he had, and a red mark all around his neck.

The baskets sold out early and Peg was well pleased. She'd more back at the camp, she said, and other things as well, kerchiefs and bits and pieces. We'd bring them up tomorrow. Our afternoon was free. But, Peg told us sternly, no nonsense. None of us was to go off alone, and we must be back before the sun touched the oaks, for it was a long walk to the camp, and she didn't want the children tired out. She and Molly would pack up, and enjoy a few tankards of cider and a chance to catch up with friends.

Again, I seemed to have no choice. Roisin had attached herself to me and, in the company of two other girls, was leading me out into the press of bodies, eager for some fun. Sudden panic overtook me. There were so many people, so close, and they were all strangers. Horrible, leering men like that fellow, Ross, men reaching out hands to pinch and touch, men saying things like "How about it, sweetheart?" and then guffawing as if they'd made the wittiest joke. Women screaming abuse at unruly children. Stallholders advertising their wares in voices like braying horns. I could not excuse myself, for there was nowhere to go. I had not the power to work a spell of transportation. Father had refused to teach me that, saying I was not ready. I toyed with the idea of turning the lot of them into beetles or spiders. At least, then, the little creature in my pocket would be able to have its dinner. But I'd no quarrel with Roisin or Peg or Molly. Or with Darragh. No, I'd have to do something else. *Use the Glamour, Fainne*. It had worked before, giving just enough confidence to get by for as long as I needed it. And nobody had noticed a thing. It would be quite safe.

I did it gradually, as we threaded a way through the crowd. It was not so much of a change. The hair from tight-curled russet to smoother red-gold like fine clover honey. The eyes lighter, bluer, wider, the lashes long and dark. The brows delicately arched, the lips sweet and red. The figure not so very different: just a little curve here and a little curve there, and a change in the slope of the shoulders. Lastly, the feet. Straight, beautiful, perfect feet, in neat matching boots. Feet for dancing.

We got roasted nuts to eat from a dark-skinned fellow with a little brazier. They were paid for with a kiss. Not by me; even the Glamour was not enough to make me so bold, so soon. It was Roisin pecked the man on one cheek and then the other, with a wicked little smile. Then there was cider, and that was free for all the folk who sold their wares at the fair. But we were lured by the sound of a whistle and a bodhrán and some expert on the spoons, and we were drawn into a great circling and weaving of folk that moved to the jigs and reels ringing out over the sward. The men were starting to return, their business done for the day, and Roisin and the others had an eye out for certain lads they fancied.

Nobody noticed that I was different. After all, I had not become a farmer's wife, or an old crone, or a water-dragon. All I had done was improve upon myself as subtly as I could. As Father had told me, it is not yourself you change with the Glamour. It is other folk's perception. So, that afternoon, I did not adopt a disguise. I'd no wish to disappear and have Roisin and the others out looking for me. I simply wanted to be able to fit in, to join in, to be rid of the terror that came of being myself and always out of place. Besides, I told myself, it was good practice for Sevenwaters.

Roisin had a sweetheart. He appeared on the edge of the crowd, and I saw him watching her, then making his way through to put his hands over her eyes from behind, laughing, and ask her to dance. He'd a very determined jaw on him, and strong shoulders. Not long after, a fellow asked me, and I said yes, and managed the sort of smile my grandmother had taught me.

It was a strange feeling to be graceful. The music seemed to carry me along, and I was floating from one partner to another and smiling without even trying. It was hot, and I took off my kerchief. The blue ribbon was lost, and my hair came unplaited. I felt the long red-gold flow of it over my shoulders, and the striped skirt whirling around me, and saw the silken fringe of my beautiful shawl glittering in the afternoon sun. I felt the drumming of the bodhrán deep inside me, pushing me along. I sensed the eyes of folk on me, admiring, and I didn't mind a bit. I danced with the freckled lad from our own camp, the one with a pony named Silver, and he grinned a lot and said nothing at all. On the other side of the circle, Roisin was still with the same young man; they'd eyes for no one but each other. I danced with an older man, a farmer with a fine, silver-buttoned coat and sharp eyes. He asked me my name, and I told him. He asked would he see me again tomorrow, and I said maybe. He held me closer than I liked, and I did some very fast thinking. The man went suddenly rather pale, and excused himself quickly. I hadn't done any real harm. He'd retch up the food he had in him, and be better in the morning.

The sun was near the tops of the great oaks and clouds were gathering. I was not ready to go. Here, I was the center of something. I was myself and not-myself, both at once. It was around me that it all moved, the men with their hungry eyes, the lilt and throb of the music, the bright flare and flash of scarf and shawl and flying hair, a circle of movement and laughter and light.

A tall fellow was asking me to dance, urged on by his friends. In the distance, I could see Roisin bidding her young man farewell. And beyond them on the far side of the circle was Darragh, standing very still, watching me. His expression was not angry, not exactly. It went beyond that. It was the look of a man whose worst fears have been realized before his eyes. He gave a jerk of his head as if to say, come on, time to go. Then he moved away and was lost in the crowd. He wasn't even going to wait for me.

"Excuse me," I whispered to my would-be partner, and I slipped away as quietly as I could, shedding the Glamour as I went, limping over to the place where Darragh had left me before, close by the great oaks.

Aoife was standing under the trees in the shade. Darragh was by her, grim-faced and silent. He linked his hands to give me a lift up onto the pony's back, and vaulted up behind me, and we were off at a very quick pace indeed. He didn't say anything at all until we were well on the way, passing the little curraghs drawn up by the inlet, with the clouds growing dark in the sky above us. There was nobody else in sight.

"Can't take my eye off you for a moment, can I?" he remarked.

"I don't know what you're talking about."

"I thought you promised to stay out of trouble. Now look at you."

"What do you mean, look at me?" I snapped, hating it that he was cross with me. "I went to the fair, I sold baskets, I went dancing with your sister, and now I'm going home. Just like everyone else. Isn't that what you want?"

There was a silence.

"Well, isn't it?" Even to me, my voice sounded shrill. He was making me quite uncomfortable.

"What I want doesn't seem to come into it," said Darragh quietly.

"That's nonsense," I retorted, not understanding what he meant. We rode on in silence as drops of rain began to fall. Aoife twitched her ears.

"Of course it's good to get out among folk and enjoy yourself," he said eventually. "There's nothing wrong with dancing. But not— not like that."

"Not like what?"

"Not making an exhibition of yourself. Doing it for the attention. Making the fellows look at you as if they wanted a bit more than just a dance. Doing—doing whatever it is you do."

I bit my lip and said nothing.

"Fainne?"

"I didn't cause any trouble," I said, with what dignity I could summon, wondering why it was that he had the ability to upset me so much. "All I did was enjoy myself. And besides, it's none of your business."

There was another awkward silence, punctuated by the sound of approaching hoofbeats. The freckled youth on his gray pony rode up behind us and came alongside, grinning at me. "Want company?" he asked, and then he glanced at Darragh. I saw his expression change, and then he touched his heels to the pony's flanks and was off ahead at a sharp canter.

"Anyway," said Darragh as we turned to the right and away from the inlet, "what about before that? I heard a story about a wizard, and escaping animals, and a near-riot, and birds turning into snakes."

"I heard that too."

"So?"

"So what?"

"Come on, Fainne," he said, exasperated, and he drew Aoife to a halt. "Don't tell me that was nothing to do with you. Someone said a man was half-strangled. Now tell me the truth."

I said nothing. I didn't have to, for at that moment a small, bedraggled form put its head out of my pocket, perhaps thinking the jostling and jolting was over at last. The tiny bird hopped out and settled on the back of Aoife's neck, reaching its beak down in a vain attempt to preen its tattered plumage. Aoife stood steady as ever, a jewel among ponies.

"What in the name of Brighid is *that?*"

I cleared my throat. "I think it's some kind of owl. It wouldn't fly away, and I could hardly leave it. I had to make it smaller, so people wouldn't notice."

"I see."

"The man was a fake, Darragh. He tried to make a girl do something horrible. By trickery. His potions are worthless. He cared nothing for these animals, they were cruelly caged, and—would you have me stand by, and not act when I can?"

Darragh sighed. "I don't know. I don't know anymore." Without any visible signal from her rider, Aoife began to walk again, and the tiny owl wobbled a little. I put my hand down to steady it. Grasshoppers, I thought vaguely. Worms. Small beetles.

We were nearly back at the camp before he spoke again.

"What you need is a constant guard, night and day. I don't know what your father was thinking of, sending you away on your own. It was like—like giving an infant a lighted torch and telling it to go out and play. You're not only a danger to yourself, you're a danger to everyone else as well. And the worst of it is, you don't even know it."

"What would you know?" I muttered, thinking how happy I had been when we passed this spot in the morning, and how miserable I was now. He had taken all the joy out of the day.

"I do know, Fainne," he said quietly. "I know you better than anyone. I wish you would listen to me. What you do is—is not right. You're blighting your own future. It's not the right way for you. I wish you would heed me."

Part of me longed to tell him I was sorry; sorry our day was spoiled, sorry we had quarreled, so sorry that next summer he would go back to Kerry and I would not be there. But I could not say those things, I could not afford to listen to him lest I lose the courage to go on; to do what my grandmother had said I must do. My father's life depended on it. And Darragh had wounded me deeply, for his good opinion was everything to me. Words tumbled out of me before I could stop them, hateful, hurtful words. "You don't know! How could you? How could you ever understand what I have to do, and why? It's like—it's like some stray dog trying to interpret the movement of the stars. Impossible, and ridiculous. I wish you would leave me alone! I can't listen to you. And I can't be your friend, not anymore. I don't need you, Darragh. Not now, and not ever."

Once it was said, it could not be taken back. We finished the journey in stony silence. He dismounted without a word and helped me down politely, and I took the very small owl in my hand and slipped it back in my pocket. I looked at him, and he looked at me. Then he took Aoife's bridle and led her away, and I was alone.

Chapter Four

The rain set in, and one of the children had a cough. I offered to stay behind and tend to her, and Peg accepted gratefully. But she left Roisin as well, for company, she said. Being nursemaid suited me. The little girl was no trouble. Besides, it was wet for walking, and I would not contemplate riding with Darragh again, let alone talking to him. The very thought of him made me wretched. I knew how badly I had hurt him. Funny, it seemed to be my own heart that was aching now.

While the child rested, I occupied myself with my other small charge. It had spent the night perched on a side support of the tent, tiny, still and silent. Maybe it didn't want me to know that it could fly. It did not sleep all day, as an ordinary owl should. Instead, it kept its eyes half-open watching me, and seemed happy to accept the small morsels I produced: grubs, beetles, and the like. In the quiet of the night, while the folk lay wrapped in sleep, I had seen it, twice, lift its ragged wings and swoop, deadly and noiseless, to seize some small wriggling creature from the earth, then return to the perch to eat its meal tidily with miniature beak and talons.

"You're a fraud," I whispered as I sat by the child's bedside with the owl perched on my finger, and dangled a freshly dug worm. The little bird stared intently, then opened its beak and gave a snap. The worm disappeared. "A complete fraud." The bird closed its eyes to slits, ruffled its feathers, and appeared to go to sleep. Then I heard hoofbeats outside, and returned it hastily to its dark corner.

Roisin's voice could be heard, and a man's. I glanced out of the tent, then retreated back inside. I imagined Roisin only saw her young man once a year. It was not the easiest way to conduct a courtship, if that was what it was. I sat quietly, hearing their voices, but not catching the words. My mind was far away. I was thinking of Father, and how he had lost both his sweetheart and his dreams. I was thinking it was just as well I was going to Sevenwaters now, and not later. Some things could hurt you. Some people could wound you. There was no room in my life for that. And there was no room in any other kind of life for me, or for my kind. I knew that already. I just had to keep telling myself, that was all, and the pain would go away in time.

The rain had almost stopped. From out by the fire, Roisin called me.

"Fainne?"

I emerged from the tent. The young man was building up the fire, and Roisin was making tea.

"Come and have a drink. It's getting chilly. This is Aidan. Aidan, this is Fainne. Darragh's friend."

Not anymore, I thought, forcing a smile.

"Happy to make your acquaintance, I'm sure," said the young man, and I nodded.

"Aidan's got some news, Fainne." Roisin sounded unusually hesitant. I stared at her. I could think of no news that might possibly be any concern of mine. "Sounds as if Darragh's finally made up his mind," she went on.

"About what?" I asked, accepting a cup of her steaming chamomile brew.

"Diarmuid O'Flaherty, and his horses," said Aidan, who had settled on one of the benches with his arm around Roisin.

"Didn't he tell you?" queried Roisin, as I made no response.

I shook my head.

"Just that O'Flaherty's been on at him, and on at Dad, these two years, to let Darragh stay up there at the farm and help train his horses. Ever since Darragh worked his magic on an animal none of O'Flaherty's men could touch. That was a good while back. He's got that way with them, Darragh, like nobody else. Some of the best stock comes out of O'Flaherty's. It'd be a great chance for Darragh.

But our kind doesn't settle. He always said no. Rather be on the road or back in Kerry, horses or no horses."

"Looks like he's settling now," observed Aidan. "Maybe there's a lass in it. O'Flaherty's daughters are a bonny enough pair."

Roisin glared at him. As for me, I sat there with my cup in my hands and said not a word.

"Bit of a surprise," said Roisin. "Dad's pleased, and sad too. He knows it's a great opportunity. But we'll all miss Darragh."

"Not so hard maybe," said Aidan. "You'll see him at fair time. That's the pattern of it for us here in Ceann na Mara," he explained, looking at me. "Summers in the hill country, winters on the coast. O'Flaherty's got big holdings. Wed into that family and you'd be falling on your feet, that's certain."

"Who said anything about wedding?" scoffed Roisin, digging him in the ribs.

"Folk'll be saying it."

"Folk can say what they want. That doesn't make it true. I never thought Darragh would do it. Surprised us all." She glanced at me. "Thought you'd have been the first to know."

After that things moved very quickly. O'Flaherty was to be off home the next day, and he was taking Darragh with him. Folk gathered in the evening around the fire, but the air was biting cold and nobody was in a festive mood. I said I was tired and stayed in the tent. People talked quietly and drank their ale. There were no tales, and not much laughter. Later someone asked Darragh to play his pipes; but it was Dan Walker who entertained them with a couple of tunes. I could not see, but I could tell from the sound of it. The playing was more expert than Darragh's, but it had not the same heart.

Much later, when all were asleep and a gentle rain had begun to fall again, I heard him, a long way off, down on the shore in the dark. He was playing alone; playing some kind of farewell, to his folk and his family, to the sort of life that was in his blood and in his being. *I'm a traveling man, remember?* he'd said. *Always on the move, that's me.* The lament rang forth over the empty strand and the dark surging waters, piercing the very depths of my spirit. This would have been easy once. I would simply have got up and walked down to the shore to sit by Darragh as he played. There would have been no need for words between us, for my presence would have been enough to tell him I was sorry I had hurt him. He would have understood that he was still my friend. Things were different now. I had changed them, and now my friend was leaving me forever. It was better that way; better for me, far better for him. Why, then, did it hurt so much? I curled my hand around my grandmother's amulet, feeling its warmth, feeling the reassurance it gave me that the path I had chosen was the right one, the only one. I rolled the blanket around myself, and curled up tight, and put my hands over my ears. But the voice of the pipes cried out in my heart, and would not be silenced.

A long time later I came to Sevenwaters. It was past Meán Fómhair and there was a misty stillness in the air. There had been many days on the road, too many to count. Our party had split in two, leaving one cart at a camp not far inland from the Cross with most of the folk. Without the old people and the children we moved more quickly, stopping only at night. Dan drove the cart, Peg sat by him, and Roisin kept me company. For all their kindness, my thoughts were on the task ahead of me; beyond that I could see nothing. I told myself sternly to forget Darragh. What was past was past. I tried very hard not to think about Father.

We camped a night or two at a place called Glencarnagh where there was a great house and many armed men in green tunics going about their business with grim purpose. Already, there, I saw more trees than ever before, all kinds, tall pines dark-caped in fine needles, and lesser forms, hazel and elder, already drifting into winter's sleep. But that was nothing to the forest. As we moved along a track with great heaps of tumbled stones to left and right, you could see the edge of it in the distance where it crept across the landscape, shrouding the hills, smothering the valleys. Above it the mist clung, damp and thick.

"That's it, lass," announced Dan Walker. "The forest of Sevenwaters."

"Going right in, are we?" inquired Peg. Her tone was less than enthusiastic.

"The old auntie'd kill me," Dan said, "if I passed by these parts without a visit. Besides, I promised Ciarán I'd deliver the lass safe to her uncle's door."

"If that's the way of it, that's the way of it," said Peg.

"You'll get a good meal there, if nothing else," Dan said, looking at her sideways. "Auntie'll see to that."

Going right in, as Peg had put it, proved more difficult than I could have imagined. We came across grazing fields and up a slope to a rocky outcrop. The forest was before us, encircled by hills, stretching out like a huge dark blanket. It was daunting; a place of mystery and shadows, another world, cloaked and secret. I could not comprehend how anyone could choose to live in such a place. Would it not suffocate the spirit, to be deprived of the wind and the waves and the open spaces? In my pocket the small owl stirred. And before us on the track, where there had been nobody at all, suddenly there was a troop of armed men dressed in the same dark colors as the stones and trees around us. Their leader stood out, for over his jerkin he wore a tunic of white, emblazoned with a blue symbol: two torcs interlinked.

"Dan Walker, traveling man of Kerry," said Dan calmly, getting down off the cart without being asked. "You know me. My wife, my daughter. We've come from Glencarnagh. I'm hopeful of Lord Sean's hospitality for a night or two."

The men came around both sides of the cart, poking and prodding at the contents. They had swords and knives, and two of them were armed with bows. There was a grim efficiency about the whole exercise.

"Tell your people to step down while we search," said the leader.

"We're traveling folk." Dan's tone was mild. "There's not a thing in here but pots and pans and a basket or two. And the girls are weary."

"Tell them to step down."

We did as we were told. Standing by the track, we watched as a methodical search took place, through every single item on the cart. Even my little wooden chest was not spared. I did not like to see the men at arms taking out Riona and touching her silken skirts with their big hands. Eventually they were finished. The leader ran his eye over us. Roisin winked at him, but his face remained impassive. He looked at me and his expression sharpened.

"Who's this girl?"

He was scrutinizing me closely, and I was scared. These were druid folk, weren't they? Maybe he could look into my eyes and read my grandmother's ill intent there. Maybe they would stop me before

I had even started, and then my father would be punished. Quick as a flash I used the Glamour, subtly, to give my face a sweetness and my eyes a dewy innocence. I looked up at the man-at-arms through my long lashes.

"She's Lord Sean's niece from Kerry," said Dan. "Fainne. Entrusted to me for safekeeping on the journey here. She's to stay on awhile at Sevenwaters when we travel back."

"Niece?" said the man, but his voice had softened a little. "I don't know anything about any niece."

"Send a message to Lord Sean, if you will. Tell him his sister's daughter is here. He'll let us through."

The armed men retreated to confer in private. There were glances in my direction, and more than one in Roisin's as well.

"Worse than last time," commented Peg. "Guard's increased. Must be something afoot."

"They'll let us through," said Dan.

There was quite a wait. The first night was spent camped by the guard post, while a man rode off down a near-invisible forest track bearing a message for my uncle. The next morning, very early, we were roused by the sound of muffled hoofbeats on the soft soil. While I was still putting aside my blankets and rubbing the sleep from my eyes, two men rode up and dismounted on the track and Dan Walker went forward to greet them. Two gray dogs, the size of small ponies, stood guard by the horses.

"My lord."

"Dan Walker, isn't it? No need for formality. I trust you've slept safe here."

The man who spoke must be my uncle Sean. He had an authority about him which marked him instantly as a leader. He was of middle years, not so tall, but strongly built, with dark curling hair pulled tightly back from his face. His clothes were plain and serviceable, but of fine quality, and he, too, wore the symbol of the linked torcs. The other man, standing behind him, I could not see.

"I hear," said my uncle, "that you've brought us an unexpected visitor."

Dan Walker gave a little cough. "Promised her safekeeping to your door, my lord. She dwells close by the place we make our summer camp. The girl's called Fainne."

Because I could put it off no longer, I walked across to stand by Dan's side. I looked up at my uncle Sean and gave a guarded smile.

"Good morning, Uncle," I said very politely.

His expression changed as if he'd seen a ghost. "Brighid save us," he said softly. "You're your mother's daughter, sure enough."

Then one of the very large dogs pushed past possessively to plant itself squarely in front of him, growling low in its throat as it fixed its fierce eyes on me.

"Enough, Neassa," my uncle said, and the hound fell silent, but still she watched me. "You're most welcome to our home, Fainne." He leaned forward to kiss me on one cheek and then the other. "This is quite a surprise."

"I'm sorry if it's inconvenient."

"You'll certainly find us in some upheaval at present, for we are in the midst of a major endeavor. But there's a welcome for you at Sevenwaters, nonetheless. It will be best if you ride back with us. We've brought you a suitable mount. Dan and his folk can follow at more leisure, with an escort."

"No need for that," said Dan. "Besides, I did undertake to bring the lass all the way to Sevenwaters itself. My instructions were quite particular."

Lord Sean's eyes narrowed just a touch. "An escort is required for all coming in, and for all going out, friend or no. It's as much for your own protection as anything. The days of slipping into Sevenwaters for a wedding or a wake are long gone. These are dangerous times. As for my niece, she is assured of safety with her family. You would not question that, surely?"

Dan gave a wry smile. "No, my lord," he replied.

"You may wish to take a little time to ready yourself." My uncle looked at me more closely, perhaps observing the rumpled gown, the unplaited hair. "A bite to eat, maybe. But don't be too long. It's quite a ride."

He drew Dan slightly away, as if to confer out of earshot, and now I could see the other man, his silent companion, waiting at a short distance, holding the bridles of three horses in his hand. This was a much older man, with soft, glossy hair that had once been chestnut brown but now was frosted with white; hair in which many small plaits had been woven and tied with colored thread. He had a curiously unlined face and serene, ageless gray eyes; he wore a long white robe that shifted and changed about him, although there was no wind. He bore a staff of birch; and the pale morning sun shone on the golden torc around his neck.

"You know me, I think." The voice was a druid's voice, soft, like music, a trap to the ear and to the mind.

"You are Conor, the archdruid?"

"I am. Call me Uncle, if you don't find that too confusing."

"I—yes, Uncle."

"Come closer, Fainne."

I did so reluctantly. I needed time to prepare for this; time to collect myself, to summon what strength would be required. But there was no time. I looked straight into his eyes, knowing I had his memory of my mother to help me. This man had engineered her downfall. He had sent her away from all that she loved, and in time that had been her death sentence. He looked at me with his calm gray eyes, and I felt most uncomfortable, almost as if he were seeing right inside me. But I stared back, unblinking; I had been well trained.

"Sean was wrong," said Conor. "I think you're much more like your father."

Even in autumn, with leaves spread thick and damp under our horses' feet, the forest was dark. It seemed to stretch out its hand as we rode deeper and deeper in, enveloping us in shadows. Sometimes there were voices. They called through the air above us, high and strange, but when I looked up, all I could see was a whisper of movement on the very edge of my vision, among the bare twigs of the beeches. It was like cobwebs in the air; it was like a shroud of mist moving faster than the eye could follow. I could not hear the words. The two men rode on unperturbed; if they perceived these tricks of light and shade, it seemed they accepted them as a familiar part of this impenetrable, mysterious landscape. It was secret, enclosed. It felt like a trap.

The pace made no concessions to my weariness, and I clung on grimly, grateful my horse seemed to go the right way without any prompting. Nobody had asked me if I could ride; and I was not about to tell them I had never gone on horseback without Darragh behind me doing all the work. The dogs raced ahead, seeking out scents in the undergrowth. My uncle Sean kept up a friendly conversation as we went. At first it was just polite talk. I thought he was trying to put me at my ease. He let me know there was a council taking place, with many visitors at the house; that it was a time when they needed to be particularly careful, and that he knew I would understand that. He mentioned he had a daughter around my age, who would help me settle in. His wife, my aunt Aisling, would be delighted to see me, for she, too, had once known my mother.

"You understand, we had no idea you were coming until the fellow rode in last night," he added gravely. "Your father has been sparing with his messages. We'd have welcomed the chance to see you earlier. But Ciarán was effective in limiting contact with our family. We never saw them again, after—after what happened."

"My father had his reasons," I said into the rather awkward silence.

Sean nodded. "They could not have returned to Sevenwaters together, that was certain. I remain unconvinced that what he did was right. Still, he has sent you home now. I welcome that. You will find folk rather curious when first you arrive. Muirrin, my eldest daughter, will look after you and help you deal with their questions."

"Curious?"

"It's a long time ago now. Your mother's departure and matters leading up to it have become the stuff of tales here; a little like the story of your grandmother, and the time my uncles spent under a spell, as creatures of the wild. Already folk can scarcely discern the margin between history and legend. That's the way of things. Your arrival will spark conjecture. Folk will talk for a while. They do not know the truth of what happened to your mother. The whole situation calls for careful handling."

I did not reply. I was becoming ever more aware of the silent presence of the druid on my other side; of the way he seemed to be watching me, although his eyes were fixed on the track ahead. It felt as if he were assessing me without saying a single word. It made me very uneasy.

"We might make a brief stop," said Sean, halting his horse in a small clearing. There was a stream, with ferns growing by a pool, and light filtered through from above, giving the moss-cloaked tree trunks an eerie green glow. The tall elms wore mantles of ivy. "I'll help you down, Fainne."

I could not suppress a groan of pain when my feet touched the ground, and cramps seized my body.

"Not used to riding," Sean observed, gathering up pieces of wood to make a fire. "You should have told us."

I rubbed my sore back, then lowered myself with some difficulty onto the saddle blanket provided. I was indeed weary; but I would not drop my guard, not with that man gazing at me with his bottomless gray eyes.

Sean had rapidly stacked a neat pile of fallen branches. Being lord of Sevenwaters did not seem to have stopped him from acquiring practical skills. The dogs flopped down, long tongues hanging pink from their great open mouths.

"Wood's a bit damp," Sean observed, glancing at Conor. "Want to light it for me?"

I looked at the druid, and he looked at me, his pale features impassive.

"Why don't you light it, Fainne?" he said without emphasis.

I knew at that moment that, whatever I might have to do to outwit this man, I was never going to be able to lie to him. I could not plead girlish ignorance or attempt some kind of bluff. This was a test, and there was only one way to pass it. I raised my hand and pointed a finger at the pile of small logs and twiggy kindling. The fire flared, and caught, and began to burn, steady and hot.

"Thank you," said Sean, lifting his brows. "Your father taught you a few things, then."

"One or two," I replied cautiously, warming my hands at the blaze. "Small tricks, no more."

Conor sat down on a large flat rock, on the far side of the fire. The flames showed me his face strangely shadowed, his pallor accentuated. The eyes, now, were sharply focused on me.

"You know that Ciarán followed the druid way for many years," he observed. "Followed it with rare promise and great aptitude."

I nodded, clenching my teeth in anger. It was all very well for him to say that; he had encouraged my father and lied to him, letting him believe he could become one of the wise ones, when all along he must have known his student was the son of a sorceress. It had been a cruel thing to do.

"You say your father has taught you a few tricks. What of Ciarán himself? How does he live his life? Does he still exercise those skills he possessed in such abundance?"

Why would you care? I thought savagely. But I formed my answer with caution. "We live a very simple life, a solitary life. He searches for knowledge. He practices his craft. He employs it only rarely. That is his choice."

Conor was silent for a while. Then he asked, "Why has he sent you back?"

Sean glanced at him, frowning slightly.

"A reasonable question." Conor's tone was mild. "Why now? Why would he choose to bring up a daughter on his own, and send her away after—what is it—fifteen, sixteen years?"

"Perhaps he thinks Fainne has a better chance of a good marriage, of some reasonable prospects, if she lives here with the family for a while," Sean said. "That's only practical. She has a birthright, like all the other children of Sevenwaters, for all—" he stopped himself abruptly.

"Fainne?" Conor was not going to let his question go unanswered.

"We thought it was time." This seemed to me a good answer. It was true; and it gave nothing away.

"So it appears," said Conor, and that was the end of it for now. He did not ask, Time for what?

All too soon we were back on our horses and riding forward again.

"It's a little awkward, Fainne," Sean said after a while. "I must be blunt with you, and you may not like this. To reveal your father's identity to our kinsmen and allies and to the community of Sevenwaters would create a difficulty. It would be extremely awkward for this stage of our negotiations. But I've no wish to lie about it."

"Lie?" My astonishment was quite genuine. "Why would you need to lie?"

He gave a grim smile. "Because even now, all these years later, folk still do not know the truth. Not the whole truth. That Niamh became disturbed in her mind, that she fled to the south and was later widowed, that they do know. Within our own household, a little more, maybe. But it's thought, generally, that she retired to a Christian convent and later died there. The sudden appearance of a daughter must somehow be explained, for anyone who knew my sister must recognize you instantly as her child."

I felt Conor's eyes on me, brooding and intent, though I was looking away.

"Why not tell the truth? My parents loved each other. I know they were unwed; but that is not such great cause for shame. It's not as if I were a boy, and out to claim lands or leadership."

Sean looked at Conor. Conor said nothing.

"Fainne," Sean seemed to be choosing his words with care, "did your father ever explain to you why he could not wed your mother?"

I held my anger in check. "He does not willingly speak of her. I know their union was forbidden by blood. I know that my father left the forest, and the wise ones, when he discovered the truth about his own parentage. Later, he found her again, and that was how I came to be. But it was too late for them."

There was a little silence.

"Yes," said Sean. "Dan Walker brought us news of my sister's death, though as ever he told only what Ciarán had bid him tell, no more. It's a long time ago. You must hardly remember her."

I tightened my lips and did not reply.

"I'm sorry, Fainne," Sean said, slowing his horse to a walk as we traversed a gushing stream on its way down the hillside. "Sorry you did not have the chance to know her. For all her faults, my sister was a lovely girl, full of life and beauty. She'd have been proud of you."

You think so? Then why did she leave us on our own? Why did she choose that way? "Maybe," I said.

"To the matter in question," Sean went on. "It's a little awkward. Your mother was wed to a chieftain of the Uí Néill, a very powerful clan with two warring factions. In recent years we have been called upon to assist the leader of the northern branch in his venture against the Norsemen, and this has taken a toll on our resources and our energies for a long time. Eventually Aed Finnliath triumphed. The invaders have been swept clean from the shores of Ulster, and the peace sealed by a marriage between Aed Finnliath's daughter and a noble of the Finn-ghaill. Our support of this venture was essential not only for our own security, but to rebuild our ties with the Uí Néill of Tirconnell, which were set back by the failure of your mother's marriage. This has taken patience and diplomacy of the highest order, in addition to the diversion of our forces from the venture most dear to our hearts. The northern Uí Néill are seated this day at our council table at Sevenwaters while we formulate a strategy for our own enterprise. This will be the most important campaign of our lives. Your arrival presents a difficulty. The husband we so carefully chose for Niamh proved a cruel man, and it was to escape him she fled from a place of apparent safety, all those years ago. That fact is not known outside our family. We let folk know that she was alive; it was generally believed that she had developed a sickness of the mind, and had retreated to a house of prayer. Her husband died soon after; there was no need to speak of what he had done. Only a handful of people knew she went to join your father. Myself; my sister and her husband. My uncles. That is all. Even my wife does not know the full story. That Niamh left Fionn Uí Néill for another man, that she bore a child by a partner forbidden to her, these things are best kept secret, for your own sake as well as that of our alliance."

"I see," I said tightly.

"I'm sorry if this is distressing for you." Sean's tone was kind; that only seemed to make me feel worse. "It makes no difference to your welcome here, Fainne. You bear no responsibility for the actions of your parents. You are a daughter of this household and will be treated as such."

"You just prefer me to pretend I have no father, is that it?" These words were out before I could stop them, before I could veil the anger in my voice. How dare they? How dare they ask me to deny my strong, clever, wise father, who had been everything to me?

"This hurts you," said Conor. "He was a youth of outstanding qualities. No doubt he became a man to be proud of. We understand that. Niamh and Ciarán were young. They made a mistake, and they paid for it dearly. There is no need for you to pay as well."

"This can be handled with no need for lies." It appeared that Sean had already made the decision. "We can simply provide folk with as much of the truth as suits our purpose. There is no reason why Niamh should not have wed again after her husband's death. We will let it be known that your father was a druid of good family. We will say that Niamh bore her daughter in the south, some time after Fionn's untimely passing. You are now returned to your rightful home and the protection of your family. That must be explanation enough. Few people outside the nemetons knew of Ciarán's existence, let alone his true identity. As for our guests of the alliance, we will not draw undue attention to your presence while they are in the house. Eamonn could be a problem."

"A pity Liadan is not here," observed Conor.

"We'll need to let her know," Sean said. "I'll do that. You look weary, niece. Perhaps you should ride with me the last part of the way."

"I'm fine," I said, gritting my teeth. It was asking a lot: that I go into some dank, dreary place where endless trees blocked out the west wind, deny my father, let some girl tell me what to do and be my watchdog, and take care not to draw attention to myself, all because of their precious alliance. It was becoming rapidly apparent to me that I would have to listen hard and learn quickly if I were to have any chance of achieving the task my grandmother had set me. The men of Sevenwaters were clever and confident; these two would be formidable opponents, and there might well be more like them when we got there. There were complications here I could not even guess at, alliances and strategies and power plays. I had learned nothing in Kerry to prepare me for this. Who was Eamonn? Why would he be a problem? My father had never mentioned such a person. I would find out. And for now I would play Uncle Sean's game. But inside me, I would never forget whose daughter I was. Never. These were the men who had snatched away my father's hope and quenched my mother's dreams. Maybe they had put that behind them, but I would not forget it.

We crossed a lot of streams gurgling downhill under the trees. Then we came out from under a stand of willows, and before us there opened a great, shimmering expanse of water, its surface clear and light in the sun and dotted with little islets and the forms of drifting birds: geese, ducks, perfect white swans. We halted.

"The lake of Sevenwaters," said Sean softly. "Our keep is on the far side, to the east. The track is easy from here. You're doing well, Fainne."

I took a deep breath and tried to ease my aching back. I was glad to see the water; to be free of that endless prison of trees closing in around me. The lake was very beautiful, with its pearly sheen, its wide surface open to the sky, its little quiet coves and its unseen, secret life.

"Seven streams flow into the lake," said Conor. "They are its lifeblood. There is only one way out; the river that flows north and then eastward to the great water. The lake nourishes the forest. The forest guards the folk of Sevenwaters, and it is their sacred charge to defend and protect it and all the mysteries it holds. This you will come to know in time."

"Maybe," I said. And maybe, I thought, you will come to know that all is not as it seems; that for some, the path does not always lead to light and order. You may learn that life can be cruel and unjust.

"You could let her go now," said Conor.

"What?"

"You could let her go now. The owl. See how she looks out and turns her head skywards. She's ready to go back."

I stared at him, mute, and the small owl climbed out of my pocket to perch, teetering a little, on the back of the horse's neck. The bird was somewhat steadier now, for I had tended it carefully enough. But this was no Aoife. The horse shuddered and shied, and I gripped its mane and clung on to keep from being thrown. In an instant my uncle Sean had the creature's bridle in his hand and was holding her still, with calming words.

"What is *that*?" he asked, in a tone reminiscent of Darragh's.

As for Conor, he sat there silent. Having stirred up trouble, he now left me to deal with it.

"It was captive. I—traded for it. That was all. It wouldn't fly away."

"I have never seen an owl so small, yet fully grown. There's some magic in this, surely." Sean's tone was quite matter-of-fact. I should not, I suppose, have been surprised at that, for this was Sevenwaters, a place where old mysteries were kept safe.

"She won't go until it's undone," Conor said, moving his horse closer. "Shall I?" He reached out a hand and passed it gently over the tiny creature, and immediately the bird was itself again: still small, still somewhat bedraggled, but owl-size, and strong enough to make its own way in the woods. Sean was having difficulty controlling the wild-eyed horse.

"Go safe now," said Conor, and obediently the creature spread its tattered wings and flew, with never a sound, with never a look back; up, up into the treetops, and away into the shadowy embrace of the forest. I said not a word.

"You did well, bringing her home." Conor's tone was tranquil.

"I didn't *bring* her," I said rather crossly. "She gave me no choice."

"There's always a choice," said the druid.

There were altogether too many of them. Girls everywhere: spilling down the steps of the stone keep where at last we ended our journey, bigger girls tugging at their father's hands, chattering and laughing as their mother came out to greet me, tiny girls running about and teasing the huge dogs.

"Enough, daughters," said Sean with a smile, and in an instant they disappeared, as obedient as they were exuberant. I had not been able to count, they were so quick. Five? Six?

"I'm your aunt Aisling," said the slight, rather severe-looking woman who stood on the steps. A neat veil kept her red hair in place, and her freckled face was intent and serious. "You're very welcome here, as no doubt my husband has told you. It's a busy time. We have many guests in the house. Muirrin will look after you."

"Where is Muirrin?" inquired my uncle as we made our way inside. The horses had been quickly led away. As for Conor, he had quite simply vanished. Perhaps the bevy of little girls had been too much for him.

"We'll find her," said my aunt in capable tones. "You'd best get back to the Council. They're waiting for you."

"The representative from Inis Eala should be here today," my uncle said. "Perhaps we can conclude this on time after all." He turned to me. "I'll leave you now, niece. That was a long ride for a novice. You'd best rest those aching limbs. Muirrin should have a potion or two that will help. Perhaps we'll meet again at supper."

They seemed to think Muirrin was the answer to everything. I formed an image of her in my mind that was completely at odds with the girl we tracked down some time later, at work in a very small, rather dark room at the back of the house.

The first thing I noticed was how tiny she was; little and slender, with big green eyes, and her father's dark curls tied roughly back from her face, to keep them from her work. She was chopping up what looked like toadstools, with a rather large, dangerous-looking knife. She was concentrating hard and humming under her breath. Around her were shelves crammed with jars and bottles; bunches of drying flowers and herbs hung overhead, and a plait of garlic festooned the window. Behind her a door stood open to a little garden.

"Muirrin," said her mother, with just a touch of sharpness. "Here is your cousin Fainne. Did you forget?"

The girl looked up, her large eyes unsurprised.

"No, Mother. I'm sorry I was not there. I had a message from the cottages—this is needed urgently. How are you, Fainne? I'm your cousin Muirrin. Eldest of six. You'll have met my sisters, I should think?" She gave a wry smile, and I found myself smiling back.

"I'm rather busy," Aunt Aisling said. "Perhaps—?"

"Off you go, Mother. I'll look after Fainne. Are her things here, for unpacking?"

I explained somewhat reluctantly about Dan Walker and the carts and my little chest, and by the time I had finished, my aunt was gone.

"Sit down," said Muirrin. "I need to finish this, and give it to someone to deliver. Then I'll show you around. There, by the fire. Want some tea? The water's boiling. Use the second jar on the left— that's it—it's a mixture of peppermint and thyme, quite refreshing. Cups over there. Could you make me some too?"

While she talked her hands kept up the steady, meticulous chopping of the bronze-colored fungi on the stone slab before her. I watched as she measured spices and strained oils and finally poured her dark, pungent-smelling mixture into a small earthenware jar, which she corked neatly.

"Here's your tea," I said.

"Oh, good. I'll just wash my hands and—excuse me a moment, will you?" She stuck her head out the door to the garden. "Paddy?" she called.

A roughly dressed lad appeared, and was given the jar, and a set of instructions which she had him repeat several times to ensure no errors.

"And tell them I'll be down myself later to check on the old man. Be sure you tell them."

"Yes, my lady."

I had been glad enough to sit and watch her. Now, as she seated herself and took her cup between small, capable hands, I found it hard to know what to say. She was so confident, and so self-contained.

"Well," she ventured. "A long journey. You'll be wanting to wash, and rest, and have some time to yourself. And you'll be stiff from riding, I expect. I have a salve for that. What if we talk a little, and then I'll show you your room, and get you some spare things, and leave you on your own until later? I need to go down to the cottages; tomorrow, perhaps, you might come with me. Today, the main thing will be protecting you from my sisters. They do make a lot of noise."

"I noticed."

"Not used to so many folk?"

I relaxed a little. "It was very quiet at home. There were fishermen, and in summer the traveling folk came. But we kept ourselves to ourselves."

Muirrin nodded, her green eyes serious.

"You'll find it quite the opposite here. Especially now. The house is full of people, for the Council. And they don't like each other. Suppertimes can be quite interesting. You'll need to find out who's who, learn a few names. I'll help you. But not yet. First things first."

"Thank you. Did you say six sisters?"

Muirrin grimaced. "It's indeed so; myself and five more, and never a lad among us. It's just as well my aunt had boys, or Sevenwaters would be scratching for an heir."

"Your aunt? That would be—?"

"Our aunt Liadan. My father's twin. He had daughters. She had sons. The túath will go from uncle to nephew, as it has done before. My father is not discontent with that."

"What are your sisters' names?"

"You really want to know? Deirdre, Clodagh, Maeve, Sibeal and Eilis. You'll learn those quick enough. They'll keep reminding you which is which, until you do."

I got a lightning tour of the house, which was more comfortable inside than its grim, fortified exterior suggested. Muirrin kept me clear of the council room, whose doors were closed. The kitchen was bustling with activity: birds being plucked, pastry rolled, and a huge iron pot bubbling over the fire. The heat was fierce, the smell delicious. We were about to move on when a peremptory voice from the hearth stopped us in our tracks.

"Muirrin! Bring the girl here, lass!"

There was a very old woman seated on a bench by the fire. This was no disheveled crone, but a gaunt upright creature with dark hair pulled back into a big knot at the nape of her neck, and a fringed shawl around her bony shoulders. Her skin was wrinkled, but her eyes were very shrewd. It seemed to me nobody would dare set a foot wrong in the kitchen while she was there.

"Well, it can't be Niamh," she said as we approached. "So it must be Niamh's daughter, for it's her to the last hair of her head. Now that's something I never thought I'd see."

"This is Janis," said Muirrin, as if that should mean something. "She's been at Sevenwaters longer than anyone." She turned back to the old woman. "Fainne has come all the way from Kerry, Janis. I was just taking her to rest."

The dark eyes narrowed. "Kerry, eh? Then I know whose cart you came in on. So where's Dan? Why isn't he here to see me? Where's Darragh?"

This, then, was the auntie much mentioned.

"Dan's on his way," I said, "and Peg too. But Darragh's not coming."

"What? How can the lad be not coming? Stopped to look at a likely piece of horseflesh, has he? Playing for a wake?"

"No," I said. "He's not coming at all. He's left the traveling life and settled on a farm in the west. Training horses. A great opportunity. That's what they say."

"And what do *you* say?"

"Me? It's nothing to me."

She was unconvinced. "Training horses, eh? That wouldn't keep him off the road for long. Must be a lass in it somewhere. What else would it be?"

"There's no lass," I said severely. "Just a chance to better himself. He made a wise choice."

"You think so?" said the old woman, staring at me with her piercing dark eyes. "Then you don't know my Darragh very well. He's a traveling man, and a traveling man never settles. He might try; but sooner or later the road calls him, and he'll be off again. Different for a woman. She might yearn for it, but she can manage without it for the sake of a man, or a bairn. Well, go on then, off with you. Muirrin, make sure the lass gets her mother's old room. Put the little ones up the north end. And don't forget to give the bedding a good airing."

She spoke as if she were the mistress of the house and Muirrin a servant. But Muirrin smiled, and when we had made our way upstairs to a neat chamber whose narrow window looked out to the edge of the forest, the first thing she did was make up the fire and check the straw-filled mattress and woollen quilts. I decided my ideas of what life would be like in a great house such as Sevenwaters were badly in need of revision.

I had no wish to be grateful to Muirrin. I did not want to become her friend. I could not afford to be anyone's friend, if I were to carry out my grandmother's will. But I was forced to admit my cousin showed good judgment. What I longed for most was to be alone. The need to meet so many new people, and smile, and be polite, had taken its toll on me. Muirrin simply checked that I had all I wanted, and left me with a promise to return later. The chamber was to be mine alone, two beds or no. It would not hurt Deirdre and Clodagh one little bit to move, she had told me with a smile.

Later, there was a polite tap on the door, and a man brought in my little chest. It felt very strange to unpack in the room that had once been my mother's. Perhaps she had shared it with her sister, the Aunt Liadan they all spoke of. I had few belongings. I took out one of the good gowns and laid it flat, for later. I extracted a crumpled and cross-looking Riona and sat her in the window embrasure, looking out over the forest. Here, there seemed no special reason to hide her. It was a house of girls; probably there were dolls here aplenty. In fact, she seemed more at home here than I did. I could not rest, despite my aches and pains. My mind was too busy trying to make some sense of it all. The magnitude of the task before me meant I had no time to waste. I must find out as much as I could, and then I must formulate some sort of plan. I could not be idle. Grandmother would look, and she would find me. I had been a fool to doubt that. It was a branch of the craft I had little aptitude for, one which had frustrated and eluded me. But she, with her dark mirror, her bowl of still water, she had the skill to search and the eye to see. When she sought me there would be no place to hide.

It took time. It took courage as well. There were so many people, and so much noise, and apart from Muirrin nobody seemed to understand how much I hated that. It made my stomach clench tight and my head ache and my fingers long to make some mischief of their own. But I did not use the craft. Instead I watched and listened, and soon enough, with an application which was second nature to me after years of Father's tutelage, I learned the intricacies of the family and their allies.

There were the folk of this household, the keep of Sevenwaters, which was the center of my uncle Sean's vast túath. Him I could tolerate. Sometimes he seemed a little distant, but when he spoke to me it was as to an equal, and he took the time to explain things. I never saw him being less than fair to any of his household. I was forced to remind myself that it had been he, among others, who had banished my mother from her home. It did not seem to me that Uncle Sean would be dangerous, except maybe on the field of battle, or in a debate of strategy. Then there was Aunt Aisling. Just watching her made me tired. She was perpetually busy, supervising every aspect of the household with a whirlwind energy that totally consumed her day. As a result, the place moved with a seamless efficiency. I wondered if she was ever happy. I wondered why you would have so many children when you scarcely had time to bid them good morning before you were off again to attend to some more pressing business.

This keep had once been the only major settlement in the forest of Sevenwaters. But now there were others, established by my uncle and tenanted by his free clients, whose own bands of armed men he could call upon in time of need. Thus the túath had been made less vulnerable, with strong outposts serving as a reminder, should powerful neighbors think to stretch out a hand a little further than was appropriate. These free clients were part of the Council, as were the richly clad leaders of the Uí Néill in their tunics blazoned with the scarlet symbol of the coiled snake. In the household of Sevenwaters there was a brithem and a scribe and a poet. There was a master at arms and a fletcher and several blacksmiths. But it was others, unseen others, who intrigued me more.

Aunt Liadan was my mother's sister, and Sean's twin. My father had said she lived at Harrowfield. I had not realized how far away that was. Strangely, she dwelt in Britain among the enemies of Sevenwaters, for her husband was now master of an estate in Northumbria which had once belonged to her father. When they were not living there they were at Inis Eala, some remote place far north, surely so distant it was hardly worth thinking of. But when my uncle Sean spoke of his sister it was as if she lived as close as a skip and a jump across the fields. Conor talked of her as of an old and respected friend. I tried to remember what my grandmother had told me. I thought she'd said something about wishing Ciarán had chosen the other sister, because their child would have been cleverer, or more skillful. It had not been the most tactful of remarks to make to me. But that was Grandmother for you.

Liadan and her husband had sons. I started to learn about them not long after my arrival. For all my efforts to retreat to my room for some time alone, to shrug off the Glamour for a little, or to repeat in peace the secret incantations of the craft, I had not been able to avoid a regular influx of small, curious visitors. As Muirrin had predicted, I soon learned to distinguish them, for all their matching mops of red hair and lively freckled faces. Sibeal was the odd one out; dark, like her eldest sister, and quiet. And she had very strange eyes, clear, colorless eyes that seemed to look beyond the surface of things. Eilis was very small, and very mischievous. You had to watch her. Maeve was in the middle, and had a dog that followed her everywhere like a devoted slave. And Deirdre and Clodagh were twins. When they grew a little older, it would be just like having two more of my aunt Aisling running around making sure everything in the household was perfect. I began to understand soon enough why Muirrin spent a great deal of her time in the stillroom working, or down at the cottages tending to the sick.

On this particular day I had the twins in my room, seated one on each bed, and Maeve as well, with the dog. The dog, at least, was quiet, though its huge bulk blocked the little fire's heat from reaching the rest of us.

"Is this your doll? Can I hold her?" Maeve had queried immediately on coming in, and had picked Riona up before I could answer. Her confidence took me aback, and I did not reply.

"Did your mother make it?" asked Clodagh. Deirdre glared at her. "Yes," I said.

"What's her name?" queried Maeve, inspecting Riona's rose-pink skirt, and screwing up her nose at the strangely woven necklace.

"Riona."

"Muirrin made me a doll once. But it's not as nice as this one. Can I play with her?"

"She's not for playing with," I said, and I went over and took Riona out of the child's arms. I placed her carefully back where she belonged, gazing out of the window, down to the margin of the forest.

"Baby," said Deirdre, making a face at Maeve.

"I am not a baby! Eilis is a baby. Coll's a baby. I'm ten years old. I'm grown-up."

Deirdre lifted her brows and grimaced.

Maeve burst into tears. "I am! I am! I am, aren't I, Fainne?"

These children confused me. Their life was as different from mine as a lapdog's from a wolf's. We had nothing in common, nothing at all. What kind of girl might I have become if I had grown up among them? Maeve was still crying.

"You can play with Riona, if you like," I said magnanimously.

"Don't want to now," pouted Maeve, but she took Riona down again, and sat there hiccuping with the doll in her arms.

"Here," I said, handing her my hairbrush. "She could do with a tidy-up." I turned to the older girls. "Who's Coll?" I inquired.

"Our cousin." Clodagh liked to explain things; she enjoyed sharing her grasp of affairs. "That makes him your cousin too, I suppose."

"Aunt Liadan's son?"

"One of them. She's got heaps."

"Four, actually," put in Deirdre. "Coll's the smallest one."

"There's Cormack, he's fourteen and thinks he's quite a warrior. There's Fintan, but we don't see him, he stays at Harrowfield. And there's Johnny." This name was spoken in a very special tone, as if referring to a god.

"I'm going to marry Johnny when I'm old enough," said Deirdre in tones of great assurance.

Her twin glanced at her with a wry expression. "No, you're not," said Clodagh.

"I am so!" Deirdre looked as if she were about to explode.

"No, you're not," repeated her twin firmly. "You can't marry your first cousin, or your nephew, or your uncle. Janis told me."

"Why not?" demanded Deirdre.

"Your children would be cursed, that's why not. They'd be born with three eyes, or ears like a hare, or crooked feet or something. Everyone knows that."

"What's wrong, Fainne?" asked Maeve suddenly, looking up at me. "You've gone all white."

"Nothing," I said as cheerfully as I could, though Clodagh's words had set a chill on my heart. "Tell me. These boys, these cousins. Don't they live rather a long way away? But you seem to know them quite well."

"We see them sometimes. Not Fintan; he's the heir to Harrowfield, and Aunt Liadan says he's just like his grandfather, and would rather be on the estate plowing fields or settling arguments than spending his time traveling all the way to Ulster. And Cormack stays at Inis Eala most of the time. But Aunt Liadan brings Coll when she visits. Terrible combination, Coll and Eilis. Nothing's safe when those two get together."

"What about the other one? Johnny, is that his name?"

"Johnny's different." Clodagh's voice had softened. "He's here a lot, learning about Sevenwaters, all the people's names, and how to run the farms, and all about the alliances and the defenses and the campaigns."

"Johnny's a good rider," put in Maeve.

"What would you expect?" Clodagh said with no little scorn. "Look at the way he was brought up, among the best fighters in all of Ulster. He's a real warrior, and a great leader, even if he is only young."

"So, he is a fearsome, wild sort of man?" I queried.

"Oh, no." Maeve stared at me, brows raised. "He's lovely."

"So lovely," added Clodagh, grinning, "it's amazing he isn't wed already. Some day soon he'll turn up with a beautiful, highborn wife, I expect."

"You don't know what you're talking about," grumbled Deirdre.

"I do so," retorted Clodagh.

"Do not!"

"Is it true what they say," I ventured, "that this Johnny is the child of the old prophecy? Do you know about that?"

"*Everyone* knows that story," sniffed Maeve, who was plaiting Riona's yellow hair into an elaborate coronet.

"Well, is it true?"

The twins turned their small faces toward me.

"Oh, yes," they said in chorus, and Deirdre gave a sigh. I did not think I could ask more, without seeming unduly inquisitive. I kept silent, and after a while they grew bored with me, and went off to bother someone else.

So, there was Uncle Sean and his girls, and Aunt Liadan and her boys. A much-beloved grandfather had died recently and been laid to rest under the oaks. And there was Conor. The druids dwelt deep in a secret part of the forest, as is the habit of the wise ones. But Conor was part of the Council, and therefore remained at Sevenwaters while the discussions proceeded behind closed doors. Indeed, he was the most senior member of the family, and much deferred to. And there was another uncle, Aunt Aisling's brother. Him I met on the very first day, by chance, as I walked down the stairs with Muirrin on my way to supper and passed him coming up. I'd have thought nothing of this well-built, richly dressed man of middle years, pleasant featured, brown haired, but for the way he suddenly froze when he set eyes on me, and turned white as chalk.

"Uncle Eamonn," said Muirrin as if nothing at all were amiss, "this is my cousin Fainne. Niamh's daughter. From Kerry." A well-rehearsed statement, which said just enough, and invited no awkward questions.

The man opened his mouth and shut it again. Expressions warred on his features: shock; anger; offense; and, with a visible effort, polite welcome.

"How are you, Fainne? I'm sure Muirrin is helping you settle in here. This visit was—unexpected?"

"Father went out to meet Fainne this morning," Muirrin said smoothly. "She'll be staying here awhile."

"I see." Behind the now well-controlled features, I could tell his mind was working very quickly indeed, as if putting the pieces of a puzzle together with speed and purpose. I did not much like the look of this.

"We'd best go down now. We'll see you at supper, Uncle Eamonn."

"I expect you will, Muirrin."

That was all; but there were more than a few times after that when I saw this man watching me, at the table when other folk were engaged in talk, or across the hall when people gathered in the evening, or in the gardens walking. He was influential, I could tell that from the way the men of the alliance seemed to defer to him. Muirrin told me he was master of a huge estate, two really, that curled right around the west and north of Sevenwaters. He had acquired Glencarnagh as well as Sídhe Dubh, and that meant he controlled more men and more land than Sean did. All the same, he was family and therefore no threat. But he watched me, until I grew annoyed and began watching him back. I had no doubt what my grandmother would think of this man. She would say, *Power is everything, Fainne*.

Time passed, and Dan Walker and his folk moved on. I had scarcely seen them, for I was caught up, despite myself, in the daily routine of the family, and when I was not needed I fled to my chamber or out into the garden for precious time alone. It began to be clear to me why the druids chose to remain so isolated, emerging only at the times of the great festivals, or to perform a handfasting or a harvest blessing. To keep the lore in your mind, to tap into your inner strengths and maintain your focus required silence and solitude, for them as for us. For a druid it required also the company of trees, for trees are powerful symbols in the learning of the wise ones. In a landscape almost devoid of trees, I had learned their names and forms before I was five years old. Sean had questioned my father's wisdom in choosing to live in Kerry, so remote, so far from Sevenwaters. To me, it became ever plainer that my father had known exactly what he was doing. Perhaps, at first, he went away in order to protect my mother. But I recalled those long years of study, of silent meditation, of self-imposed privation, and I knew that if we had not dwelt there in the Honeycomb, near encircled by wild sea, canopied by rain-washed sky, watched over by the cryptic forms of the standing stones, I would never have become what I was. Father had taught me well and I had learned eagerly. What he had intended for me I still did not understand, for he had spoken of it cryptically, like the druid he still was at heart. He had said he hoped I might find the right purpose for my gifts, and had given me the tools to do so. The irony of it was that he had forged a weapon like a true master; his mother's weapon. Perhaps he had never really escaped the legacy she left him, for in this had he not done exactly as she wished? She had used the love we bore one another to twist me to her will. She need only show me that image of my father coughing, choking, suffering, to ensure I turned my hand to the most fearsome of tasks.

Despite my longing for home, I grew slowly more accustomed to the pattern of life at Sevenwaters, and it became harder and harder to remember why I was here. The memory of Grandmother's threats seemed almost like a fantasy of the mind. Distractions were many. At times I looked at the bustling domestic scene around me, and thought of the magnitude of the task I had been set, and said to myself, *This cannot be true. These things cannot exist together in the same world. Maybe I am dreaming. Let me be dreaming.*

Aunt Aisling, busy as she was, had no intention of letting me disappear to do as I wished. I would help Muirrin with her healing work; I would assist Deirdre and Clodagh with their reading and writing, as it appeared I was very capable at both, and the girls' education had been somewhat neglected recently, since everyone was so occupied. I could supervise the little ones at sewing, since I was apt at that too. I should learn to ride, properly, for one never knew when one might have to depart in a hurry. And I needed new clothes. I wondered what Aunt Aisling thought I would get up to if she did not organize every single moment of my day.

Muirrin helped. Often, when I was dispatched to assist her in the stillroom or walk with her on some errand of mercy, she would look at me with her wide green eyes, and tell me I might as well sit in the garden and have some peace and quiet, while she got on with things. Then she would work at her mixing and blending, her drying and preserving, sometimes alone and sometimes assisted by small Sibeal, an earnest, silent child. And I would sit on the stone bench in the herb garden, wrapped in my everyday shawl, for I had folded Darragh's gift neatly and laid it away in the very bottom of the wooden chest, safe from prying eyes and eager little hands. I would sit there alone in the chill of late autumn, and run the litany through my mind. I could almost hear my father's voice.

Whence came you?

From the Cauldron of Unknowing.

So it unfolded, longer than the day, longer than the season, greater than the cycle of the year, as old as the pattern of all existences. And sometimes, as I let the familiar recital of lore unfold, I would play with things just a little, scarcely conscious of what I did. There might be a subtle change in the manner in which the moss grew over the ancient stones. There might be more bees clustering on the last blooms of the lavender, and somewhat fewer small birds perched on the bare branches of the lilac. Pebbles on the ground might roll into the shape of an ancient symbol. Ash; birch; oak; spindle. Nothing grand. Just enough to keep my hand in, so to speak.

My daily life remained an effort, even when it grew more familiar. It was exhausting. I knew I would never get used to the people, the company, the need to speak the obvious and listen to the tedious, the need to participate. If you are brought up to solitude and silence, you never lose the craving for it. Sometimes I was tempted to pack a little bag and walk away, forest or no forest, Grandmother or no Grandmother. But such a venture was doomed to failure. The place was bristling with armed men, and the girls were forbidden to go past a certain point without an escort. In these times, Clodagh told me very seriously, one could not be too careful.

The Council drew to a close. I had watched to see who the representative from Inis Eala might be, for I wished to learn more of Aunt Liadan and her husband, and the fabled Johnny. But I detected no new faces at supper, and saw no riders come into the yard on the day my uncle Sean spoke of it. In the end I asked Muirrin outright.

"Are not the folk of Inis Eala represented at the Council?" I tried to sound casual. "And what about Harrowfield? If Johnny is the heir to Sevenwaters, why is not he or his father present? Do they play no role in this undertaking, whatever it is?"

Muirrin glanced at me as she stirred a pot over her small fire. "Harrowfield is not part of this," she said. "That estate has always remained outside the feud; they distance themselves from North-woods, who is our true enemy, for all they share a border. That has not changed since Liadan and the Chief took control there. For that reason, the Chief never comes to Sevenwaters. He walks a delicate path, though, for he still maintains a keen interest in the affairs of Inis Eala. And Inis Eala was most certainly represented at the Council. This venture cannot go ahead without them."

"The Chief?" I queried.

"Aunt Liadan's husband. Everyone calls him that. His real name is Bran, the raven."

"Who came from Inis Eala for the Council?" I asked. "I saw nobody arriving."

Now Muirrin wore a little frown. "Why does that interest you?" she queried.

"I'm just trying to learn about the family. Johnny seems very important. And Aunt Liadan was my mother's sister."

"Yes, it's a pity she was not here to meet you," said Muirrin, tasting a little of her mixture and making a face. "Oh dear, I'll need honey, I think. Could you reach it down, Fainne? It's no wonder you didn't see the man they sent. The Chief's folk are masters of invisibility." She saw my expression, and laughed. "Oh, no magic involved, I assure you. It's their trademark and great skill to come in and out unseen and to adopt what disguises they must, so they are not remembered. That's another reason the Chief doesn't come himself. You'd always remember *him*. A man came and left. That's all."

"Why would you always remember the—the Chief?"

"You'll know if you ever meet him. But he would not come to a Council of this kind. As I said, he is at pains to appear neutral. Besides, he has too many enemies and even now is not fully trusted by all of Father's allies."

"Really? Then why are his folk from Inis Eala involved? Isn't that risky for him?"

"Because of Johnny." She did not speak this name in the awed tone her sisters used. But she was deeply serious. "Johnny's a symbol. The son of the raven. He must lead this venture, and he cannot do so without his father's support. Besides, the Chief's unique skills and Johnny's special forces are an essential part of the campaign. It can't work without them. That's what Father says."

138 ⊛ JULIET MARILLIER

"And where does your uncle Eamonn fit into all this?"

"Just that he has the largest and best-equipped force of fighting men in all of Ulster," said Muirrin airily. "Hold this, will you, while I strain it through. Thanks. He has to be part of it. They all do. It's Father's job to keep them from each other's throats long enough for the whole thing to work. A bit like being the eldest sister, I should think it is."

I was bursting with questions, but felt I could ask her no more without arousing suspicion. Instead I watched and listened, for my father had trained me to solve puzzles. The man Eamonn was a closed book; difficult, withdrawn. He would sit at the supper table next to Aunt Aisling, and he would be very quiet, almost unnaturally so. One might think his failure to contribute to the conversation was caused by overindulgence in the good ale provided, for he would sit there drinking solidly all evening, and staring into space, and eating little. But his eyes gave him away. I could tell he was listening acutely and storing up whatever might someday be of value to him. And still I caught him watching me, time after time, as if I were the final piece of his puzzle and he had not yet decided where to put me. I looked at him under my lashes. His gaze remained unwavering. He's the one, I thought. He's the one Grandmother would tell me to target. *Find yourself a man of influence, Fainne. A woman can do wonders with such a man as her tool.* The very idea terrified me. It made my stomach churn and my skin turn to goose bumps.

One by one, the partners of the alliance made their farewells and left Sevenwaters under armed escort. For their own protection, was the explanation given, as Sean's men in their forest-colored garb rode off at front and rear, with the visitors close-guarded between. How could you work side by side, planning some sort of major campaign, I asked Muirrin, if there was such a lack of trust between you? Might not your ally turn and stab you in the back?

"Oh, it's not just that," said Muirrin. "It's the forest. The forest knows its own. Others cannot go in and out in safety. Paths change. Roots grow over the track. Voices lead people astray, and mists rise." She spoke as if of everyday matters, and I felt the hairs on the back of my neck prickle.

"Voices?" I echoed.

"Not everyone hears them," she told me. "But the forest is very old. Entrusted to our family in ancient times. We are its guardians. We are by no means its only dwellers."

I nodded. "I've heard the tale," I said cautiously. "Didn't one of your—our—ancestors wed a woman of the Fomhóire?"

"That's what they say. And from her came the secret of the Islands. They are tied up together: the Islands, the forest, the trust the Fair Folk laid on us, long ago. If one part fails, all fails. You may know of this already."

"A little. I'd like to learn more."

"You'd best ask Conor. He tells the tale better than anyone."

But I was avoiding Conor. Still he remained at Sevenwaters, but he had made no effort to seek me out, instead spending much of his time in conference with Sean, or talking with Muirrin, or seated silently in the garden gazing out toward the forest. I had the impression he was waiting.

My mind was on other things. Uncle Sean had decreed I must learn to ride properly, since one never knew when one might need to do so at short notice. It was a humiliating experience. The horses didn't trust me. And everyone could ride, even Eilis who was barely five years old. All very well for *her*, I thought crossly, watching her canter around the yard on her little black pony. She'd been brought up to it. I was almost tempted to make the pony shy and throw her off. A long time ago, in another world, Darragh had offered to teach me to ride and I had refused. Now I regretted it bitterly. Aoife would not have trembled and edged away from me. Darragh would have been patient. He might have made a joke of it, but he would never have laughed at me the way Eilis did. Not that the stable lads weren't eager to help, but that had more to do with the way I smiled at them than any natural kindness. Since my arrival at Sevenwaters I had not once gone forth among folk without clothing myself in that magical garb of beauty and sweetness the Glamour allowed. No wonder folk said I looked like my mother. Without the guise of the Glamour, I would be paralyzed by my own awkwardness. But here in the stable-yard I was tempted to shrug it off and show them just what a plain, shy thing I really was. I could have used a trick or two to put them in their place. But I resisted the urge and just got on with things. By the end of the morning I was tired and frustrated, and my teachers were scratching their heads in puzzlement.

"The horses just don't take to you," remarked one of the stable hands. "Never seen anything like it." Beside him, the mare I had been riding rolled her eyes and shivered.

"Never mind," I said. "Thank you for your time."

"It's an honor, my lady," the lad said, blushing furiously. Then I fled. I was supposed to be taking Eilis and Maeve back to the house to get cleaned up and start on some needlework. But suddenly that was more than I could face, and I slipped quietly away behind the stables, desperate for a few moments alone. There was a place where you could sit in peace, a back door with three steps coming down. Just a little respite with no unwanted company, that was all I needed.

But there was company. On the steps sat Eamonn, dressed for riding, booted legs stretched out before him, arms folded, his eyes fixed on the middle distance and his expression shadowed, as if deep in thought. He wore a dark green tunic over his riding clothes.

"Oh," I said, taken aback. "Oh—I'm sorry . . ."

He rose to his feet. "Fainne, I think I have preempted your place of refuge. In any case, I should go. I'm returning home today. I have many matters to attend to."

Frozen with shyness, Glamour or no Glamour, I could not think what to say to him or how to act. Automatically, I spoke in the soft, breathless sort of voice my grandmother would have recommended for such a situation, and I moved as she had taught me, for I could not think what else to do.

"Please—stay if you wish. I did not intend to disturb you. You're right, this is a place to flee to when things—when things become difficult. But—I don't mind sharing it. You, too, desire peace and quiet? A spell away from the hubbub of affairs? You seem a very busy man." I moved forward hesitantly, and felt myself blushing delicately, with no need for the craft.

"Please," he said. "Sit down. You have been riding, have you not? You'll be tired."

"I am somewhat weary," I said with a rueful smile, and seated myself gracefully on the top step. He stood by me, his expression guarded as always.

"You've never learned to ride? That's unusual for a girl of your age," observed Eamonn.

"I know," I said with complete honesty. "And indeed I have no wish to learn, but Uncle Sean says I must. I would prefer to spend my time on other pursuits."

"Other pursuits?"

He seemed to want to talk to me. Perhaps Grandmother's advice on how to deal with men was sounder than I had thought. I was not sure what his preferred answer to this question might be. I made a guess.

"Sewing, reading, studying. I am not accustomed to so many folk."

He gave a nod of approval. It seemed I had judged him well enough.

"You have not, then, grown up in a family such as my sister's? Were you raised in your father's household?"

It was a mistake ever to underestimate such a man. I felt the blush deepen, and lowered my eyes. "I—excuse me, this distresses me. You would need to ask my uncle Sean. I find it painful to speak of this."

Eamonn squatted down beside me, clearly concerned. But I had not missed the searching expression in his dark eyes.

"I'm sorry," he said. "I've upset you. I had no intention—"

"It's all right." My voice wobbled a little. "I—I don't care to speak of these things. I have led a rather sheltered existence, until I came here. A life of quiet and contemplation."

"For a long time I believed your mother had drowned on my own land, through my own negligence," Eamonn said. "I learned eventually that she had survived and was in a house of prayer. They said she was in fragile health. But—forgive me, but to be blunt, nobody mentioned a daughter."

"I never knew my mother," I said in a whisper. This conversation was unsettling me. I could not understand what he wanted. If he wished to learn secrets that might be of strategic advantage, he could hardly expect to get them from me.

"She was very like you," said Eamonn. "Niamh was much admired as a girl. Indeed, there were never two sisters so unlike." His mouth twisted. His face was quite close to my own.

"You will no doubt be pleased to return home at last," I said.

He stared back at me, silent.

"Your own family will be missing you," I added.

"Aisling is all the family I have," he said after a moment, and now he was looking down at the ground.

I paused. "You surprise me," I said. "No wife? No children? Perhaps my lack of exposure to the world limits my understanding of such things, but are you not anxious for an heir to your estates?"

He gave the tiniest of smiles. "You are very direct, Fainne. Startlingly so."

I employed Grandmother's teaching again, making a delicate gesture of confusion, fingers up to my lips. "I'm sorry. I had no wish to offend you. I grew up in solitude, and never learned the art of conversation. Please ignore what I said."

"It is unusual, I suppose," said Eamonn, moving around to sit by me on the steps. "Once, I imagined I could have those things. After all, a man considers them no more than a basic right. But everything changed."

"How?"

He looked down at his hands, now tightly clenched together.

"Ah. Now you venture into those matters of which I cannot speak. We must each keep our secrets, I think."

"I'm sorry, Eamonn."

He glanced at me, brows raised.

"You would prefer I called you Uncle Eamonn? It doesn't seem altogether appropriate."

"Indeed not, Fainne. And after all, I am not your uncle, though I might have been. I should go. My men will be waiting. It's a long ride to Sídhe Dubh."

"That is where you live?"

"And at Glencarnagh. You would prefer that house. It's more of a place for a woman."

"And I'd better go back to the children," I said. "They must be tidied up and given some sewing to do. Aunt Aisling keeps us all busy. I don't mind. It's just that they're so *loud*."

Eamonn smiled. It improved his appearance markedly. A pity he was so old. Nine and thirty at least, I thought. Older than my father.

"You like quiet, then?"

I nodded. "I might have better stayed in the south, and dedicated myself to a life of peace and contemplation," I said softly, pleased that I had not had to lie.

"You would not then wish for a family of your own, someday?" Eamonn asked gravely.

I guessed at what Grandmother would think appropriate here. "Indeed yes," I breathed, making my face the picture of exquisite young womanhood, on the brink of discovery. "A husband, a fine son, a lovely little daughter to watch over—doesn't every girl long for that?"

There was another pause. "I hope," said Eamonn, "I hope Sean chooses wisely for you. I would not see such a—I hope he exercises sound judgment on your behalf. Now I must be off. Good luck with your riding. I'm sure you will become as accomplished at that as no doubt you are at everything else."

"You flatter me," I said.

"I doubt that very much. Goodbye, Fainne. Perhaps we can talk again, when next I visit Sevenwaters."

"I'd like that," I said, and watched him go. I had managed, at least. Grandmother would probably have approved. So why had this interchange so disturbed me that my stomach seemed to tie itself in knots whenever I thought of it? I went through all I had said, and could find no error in it. But I kept seeing Darragh's face as he watched me dancing at the fair, the face of a man who feels somehow betrayed. And all I could think of was how glad I was that Darragh could not see me now; that he would not know what I must do, and what I must become.

Chapter Five

The forest was like a cloak of darkness around the keep and its small settlement. As the year moved forward and the weather grew damp and chill, I found it hard to shake off the feeling of oppression, of being shut in a trap that would draw close around and smother me. The forest protects its own, Muirrin had said. It seemed to me the forest lived and breathed, and sensed an intruder in its midst with destruction in her heart. Grandmother had set things out for me with devastating simplicity. *Make sure they don't fight*, she had said, *or if they do, make sure they lose*. To lose the battle was to lose the Islands. To lose the Islands was to bring ill on the forest, and on all the dwellers therein, whether of human world or Otherworld. It seemed to me the forest knew this, as a living being knows a great truth. Foolish thoughts, I said to myself briskly, as I added a log to the small fire in my room. After all, it was only trees. Trees can be cut down and burnt. Trees can be cleared to make room for crops or grazing. Stupid, to give those fears too much weight. And yet, in the lore, trees could not be underestimated. To Conor and his kind they were powerful symbols. To Muirrin and her family they were a sacred trust, to be protected at all costs. In its turn, the forest guarded all who dwelt at Sevenwaters.

I stood by my window looking down, watching the rain driven sideways by the gale, seeing the leafless forms of great oak and beech shudder under the storm's onslaught, yet stand firm together. It was nearly dark, and I had lit a candle, which struggled to remain alight there in the window. Its flickering golden glow touched Riona's embroidered features to life, and turned her silken gown the shade of autumn rose. There was the strangest of feelings about this spot, close by the narrow window. I had felt it before: some power, some significance, as if a person had waited here endlessly, as if what they felt was so strong that the memory of it still lingered there in the cold air, before the flickering candle. The sense of it chilled me. I moved away to sit on the bed, and Riona's eyes watched me.

Fears, I told myself, too many fears. I must rid myself of them, so the task could unfold. If the forest was a threat, then I must confront it. I must answer the voices, and challenge the silent sentinels. Did not my task strike at the heart of the Fair Folk themselves? And yet I quailed at the prospect of walking alone under the oaks, lest I hear their voices. Without knowledge of those whom I must defeat, I could achieve nothing. Was I not a sorcerer's daughter? Where was my courage?

The weather cleared; stormy days gave way to crisp, frosty mornings and cool afternoons under a pale sun that gave no respite to the ache deep in the bones. The little girls stopped squabbling and went outside to play, not too far from the house. The last of the season's work was completed, roofs repaired, wood stacked, winter supplies carefully stored away. In the yards, men with sword and spear and dagger rehearsed, endlessly, the lethal dances of war. More horses came in, and the stable lads were too busy to bother with a lady's riding lessons. Sean seemed grim and preoccupied, striding about with the two great dogs padding silent behind him. Other men came, and consulted with him, and left. Supplies were brought in on carts and put away before anyone could get a look at their nature. Often Conor would be there with his nephew, checking things and offering grave advice. It was not so unusual for a druid to involve himself in a military campaign, especially when it touched on something so dear to his heart.

For my grandmother had been right about the great venture planned for summer. It was indeed no less than the final onslaught on the Britons of Northwoods, the clan that had laid hold of the Islands sacred to the old faith, generations since. This was the summer when the Islands would be returned at last to their rightful guardians. Not owners; that term was not appropriate. The family were custodians only, of forest, lake, and Islands. This ancient trust had been laid on our ancestor by the folk of the Túatha Dé Danann, when first he set foot in the forest of Sevenwaters. There had been a terrible neglect of that trust, and Northwoods had laid hold of the Islands. Over countless years, the feud for control of these specks of land far out in the sea had been waged, and sons of Erin and Britain alike had laid down their lives for the cause. This would be the last onslaught. Northwoods would be driven out, his forces shattered. The time was right; the child of the prophecy was among them, and a warrior fully fledged. With him to lead, and an array of allies such as had never before been mustered, the venture could not fail.

All this I learned by listening and observation. The training my father had imparted had made me skillful at both. Indeed, there were times when I overheard rather more than I wished to; times when I wondered much about the history of this great family and the secrets which seemed woven into it. There was a day when I had fled the children's chatter and taken myself off to a secluded corner of the garden to sit in silence on an old stone bench. The air was chill; I was well wrapped in my warm cloak. I held my grandmother's amulet in my hand and tried to fix my mind on the task she had set me and how I might achieve it. Sometimes when I touched the small bronze triangle I saw her face in my mind, and heard the fierce whisper of her voice, *Don't forget, Fainne. Don't forget your father*. I remembered her punishments, and did not doubt her power. At times my spirit quailed at the impossibility of the quest which lay before me. The amulet helped in these moments of doubt. Its small form in my hand was always reassuring; while I held it I could believe myself capable of almost anything.

That day I was sitting on my bench in the shadow of a tall winter-brown hedge, when I heard voices: my uncle Sean's, and Conor's. They were walking along a gravel path on the other side of the trimmed beeches, and they paused right behind me so I could not fail to hear their words. Just in case they should decide to come around the corner where they could see me, I used a little spell to blend myself more fully into the hedge-shade, to dapple my clothing to the colors of dry winter leaf and dark clutching twig. I listened.

". . . have asked myself many questions about Ciarán's reasons for this, but no answers come to me," Conor was saying.

"It's plain enough to me, Uncle," Sean replied. "Even Ciarán must understand his daughter has no future in a remote settlement somewhere on the fringes of Kerry. He can't bring her north himself; he knows he can never be received here, for all he shares our own blood. So he sends the girl to us, hopeful that we will see her settled, find her a good husband, secure for her a future befitting a daughter of Sevenwaters."

There was a little silence.

"There's something wrong here." Conor's tone was thoughtful, as if he struggled with some challenging puzzle. "Ciarán had no love for Sevenwaters nor for his family when he stormed out of the place all those years ago. He repudiated all of us, and the brotherhood as well, as soon as he learned who he was. He set the seal on that decision in taking Niamh for himself, even after he understood that was against natural laws. In doing so he effectively cut her off from all of us. Why would he choose, now, to throw his daughter on our mercy? Even as a child Ciarán was a subtle thinker. There's a plan in this somewhere, and it's not a simple wish to see his daughter wed to some likely nobleman."

"With respect, Uncle, I think you're wrong. I think Ciarán is doing exactly what Niamh would have wanted. My sister loved this place and her family; she also loved the life it offered her, the fine things, the music and dancing, the company and festivity. Niamh was no hermit. It grieves me that I will never know if my sister forgave what we did to her, if she died still bitter that we chose so ill for her. Could not Fainne's presence here be seen as a kind of forgiveness?"

"You wish it could be so," Conor said quietly. "You overlook what the girl is, I think; what legacy she bears. She is Niamh's daughter, certainly; I see that in the toss of the head, the sudden silences, the quickness to take offense. But she is Ciarán's daughter too. You know what that means. Keeping Fainne here may be a risk to us. We must tread cautiously, I think."

"Come now, Uncle, Fainne has some skill in magic, that is true, but any druid could do what she did that day in the forest. Growing up alone with her father all these years, it is not surprising she has gleaned some knowledge from him. There's more of a danger on another front; Eamonn's been asking me questions I don't know how to answer."

"What questions?" Conor's tone was suddenly sharp.

"About the girl's father, who he was, his background. The answers I gave Aisling did not satisfy her brother; he would not accept simply that the man was a druid of good parentage. He pressed me for more."

"Hmm," said Conor. "Why would this interest Eamonn, do you think?"

"Everything interests Eamonn. He makes a point of knowing all there is to know, just in case it may come in useful someday. No doubt that is how he's made himself a man of such wealth and influence."

They were moving away along the path again. Soft as a whisper of breeze, I rose and kept pace with them on my own side of the hedge. I was well practiced at walking silently, limping foot or no.

". . . secrets there," Conor was saying. "What was the full story that day when Niamh fled from Sídhe Dubh and somehow made her way to Ciarán's side? That's a matter of great shame to Eamonn; he's never forgiven himself for allowing such a breach of security in his own home."

"It's not that story I'd like to hear," said Sean. "I'd like the truth about a time my sister Liadan went to visit Eamonn, and ended up in some outpost with two wounded men and a company of outlaws. There's a tale there that concerns me deeply. It has caused me grave misgivings all these long years."

"Yes; they've kept that secret well, Liadan and her Bran. All this time. A certain doubt still lingers concerning Eamonn's involvement in those matters."

"Still, he is my wife's brother. He is family now."

"Indeed. And an impeccable ally from that day forward. It raises interesting questions."

They fell silent. I would have to stop walking soon; the end of the hedge was close, and they would see me, spell or no spell. I had not mastered the art of invisibility.

"Don't worry about the girl," said Sean. "She's a good child, I'm sure of it. A little magic, a few special abilities, where's the harm in that? Look at Liadan, after all."

Conor laughed, but there was no gladness in it. "You're wrong. This girl's as powerful as her father was, I suspect. I see it in her, I feel what she is every time I go near her. Such potency in a girl too young to harness it with proper judgment could be disastrous for us. I know one thing. I'd greatly prefer a mage of such talents as my ally than as my enemy."

They moved on and I stayed behind. Conor was a druid; not surprising, then, that he sensed my abilities and distrusted me. If only I really were as powerful as he thought; then maybe I would be stronger than my grandmother, and could somehow say no to her and still protect my father. But Conor was wrong. My own use of the craft was puny and weak beside Grandmother's. Defy her, and I had no doubt both I and my father would be destroyed. Somewhere at the back of my mind were her words, *It wouldn't take very many mistakes on your part to make him very sick indeed*. She had said that she would know if I failed to carry out her orders, and I would be a fool to disregard that. I must make some progress or my father would suffer.

I chose a cloudless day, a day when for once Aunt Aisling had set me no tasks. Now was the time. There was nothing to be afraid of, I told myself as I put on my outdoor boots and took my shawl off the peg behind the door. Nothing at all. Just take it step by step. Today's step was to face those forest shadows, and establish that they were nothing to worry about. Tricks of the Túatha Dé, no doubt, set there to keep people in fear and stop them from asking awkward questions. My grandmother had always said that the Fair Folk were too big for their boots. Arrogant. They thought themselves better than everyone else; look at the way they had cast out their own without an inkling of how it felt to have a curse on your line forever more. It was time someone stood up to them. But, as with all that I did, carefully. My purpose must be kept secret until the very last, or failure was certain.

I wrapped the woollen shawl around me. Riona was watching. *No*, she seemed to be saying. *That won't be enough, and you know it*. I frowned at her. But I went to the little chest, and took out the beautiful silken shawl with its scattering of tiny bright creatures and its fringe that danced in the light like an ever-moving waterfall, and I tied it around my shoulders.

"Satisfied?" I muttered. Riona did not answer, since she could not. But her expression seemed to be saying, *That's better. Best hold onto what you've got left, since it's not much*. I stared at her, wondering where that thought had come from, and what it was supposed to mean. Then I picked her up and put her in the little chest, and shut the lid.

It was the middle of the day, and still the frost crunched under my boots. On the lake a few ducks floated, dipping for what morsels might be found. Smoke from the small cottage fires hung in the air; turves were stacked in orderly piles by the low doorways. I passed the settlement quickly, and made my way beside the stone walls of the grazing fields toward the margin of the forest. And there by the track were two of my uncle Sean's men, leaning on their staves and watching as I approached.

I gave them my best smile. "Good day to you."

"Good day to you, my lady. Best you don't venture any further alone."

"I'm not going far. Just a little way along the lake shore. I won't be long."

"You'd need to have a man or two with you. Lord Sean's orders."

"Oh, but—"

"Sorry, my lady. Can't let you go off on your own. Not safe."

They were both tall and broad, and the expressions on their faces told me argument was pointless. The one on the left had the slight look of a duck about him, with a full mouth and his hair pulled tightly back from the brow. The other was more like a frog. I summoned up an incantation and raised my hand.

"I'll walk with the young lady. That solves the problem to everyone's satisfaction, and no harm done." And there was Conor, standing on the path behind me, where a moment ago there had been nobody.

"Yes, my lord."

The presence of an archdruid, it seemed, automatically guaranteed safety. The men-at-arms stood aside and let us pass. We walked on in silence down the path that led beneath the canopy of leafless branches. Underfoot, the fallen leaves of oak and ash, beech and birch had rotted away to a thick, dark fabric of moist fragments in which strange fungi sprouted and creeping things busied themselves. I drew the shawl closer about me.

"You have a particular purpose in this venture out." This was a statement rather than a question. "And you would prefer to go alone. But as you see, that is not possible. The days when the children of Sevenwaters could roam the forest freely, without fear, are gone. There have been many changes here."

I nodded.

"I will not intrude, Fainne. My nephew is wise to place restrictions on movement through the forest. There's a need for complete secrecy until after the summer. I imagine you understand that."

"Besides," I said, "the forest itself is not always benign, so I'm told. Strangers are not always safe here. Muirrin said it protects its own."

There was a silence as we walked along together under the trees.

"True enough," said Conor after a while. "But that should not concern you. After all, you are one of us."

I held back my bitter response. *You think I will swallow that lie, as my father did?* "Still," I said quite truthfully, "I am not accustomed to so many trees. They make me—uneasy."

"In that case, a druid may be your best companion."

I did not reply, and we went in silence until we came to a clearing among bare-branched rowans, still hung here and there with the last shriveled remnant of the season's fruit. In the center of the open space was a huge flat stone, moss-encrusted. There was a stillness about the place that set it apart. The only sounds were the occasional call of a bird high above, and the trickling of some small unseen stream as it found its way down to the lake.

"This place is suitable," said Conor. "I will meditate awhile, for I too welcome a respite from the bustle of affairs. You must do what you will. No hurry." He settled himself cross-legged on the rock, his white robe flowing around him, his back as straight as a small child's, and closed his eyes.

There seemed to be nothing for it but to sit down, as far away from him as the breadth of the stone allowed, and do the same. I knew enough of magic, and trances, and Otherworld powers, to realize one could not simply walk out in search of manifestations and expect them to be conveniently there at one's disposal. It was necessary first to calm and slow the senses; to concentrate them on a chosen symbol or familiar snatch of the litany; to allow time. Even then you might not get what you expected. It helped to be in the right place, and it was a great deal easier when there were no distractions. The high ledges of the Honeycomb were good; the roar of the ocean and the scream of the gulls would weave themselves into a timeless, solitary sort of peace. The little cave down under the rocks, where sea and earth and filtered light met and touched and shifted in delicate balance, that was best of all. I longed for its watery blue shadows and the soft hush of wavelets on pale sand. In that place was rest for the heart. But Kerry was far away, and in the forest of Sevenwaters you could not hear the song of the sea. Here, you must think of the rock; a rock so massive and old it might be part of the very body of the earth, as if one sat safe in the lap of Dana herself. I would concentrate on the rock, and forget the trees. Slow the breath; feel it deep in the belly, feel its power through every part of the body. In and out. Pause. In and out. Slow and slower. *I am here. The earth holds me. Once I sat with my back to the standing stones, and became one with the eternal patterns of sun and moon. Now I feel the strength of this rock beneath me, and its ancient purpose through all corners of my being. Pulsing in the blood; beating in the heart; anchor and stay of mind and spirit. I am of the earth, and the earth is in me.*

A long time passed, or a short time. Without moving, without opening my eyes, I knew there was something there. It fluttered down to sit, owl-sized and a little threadbare, on the mossy surface not far from me. It fixed its strange round eyes on me, then blinked. There was a sudden change; not a flash, for there was no light. Not an explosion, for there was no sound. Just a sort of ripple of the air, an adjustment in the fabric of things. Instead of an owl, there was a small human-like being of around Eilis's size. But this was no child. I could not tell if it were man or woman, for it was clad in a voluminous cloak of feathers, brown, gray, black, tawny and striped, and wore a hood of similar hue, so that only its face could be seen, round and owl-eyed with a snub nose and bushy brows, and beneath the cloak a pair of neat small feet in bright red boots. There was no need to move or open my eyes. The eye of the spirit saw clear.

Good cross-over, fire child, said the apparition. *Learn from a druid, did you?*

From my father. It seemed to me I spoke without making a sound.

That explains it. A great loss to the wise ones; he made some very poor choices. So did your mother. At least, that's how it seemed at the time. But it all worked out for the best. Matters took a twist and a turn. Happens sometimes.

Who are you? Are you one of the—are you one of those that call themselves Fair Folk?

The small being gave a rich giggle which ended in a hoot.

Flattery'll get you nowhere, it remarked rather archly. *Fair or foul, it's all the same to me. Want to ask me anything, I'll answer you. I owe you a favor. That surprised me. Why would you choose to rescue me? Not part of any plan, was it?*

Might I not have wanted to set you free, just because it seemed the right thing to do? I asked, somewhat affronted. *An act of natural kindness?*

Not renowned for that, are you? Kindness? You're a girl who'll throw away treasure, if she thinks it's in her way. Seems to us you don't give a toss what casualties you leave behind you.

What do you mean, casualties? What is this, an inquisition? I did not come here for this.

You use your craft cleverly; you have the techniques at your fingertips. But you use it unwisely. You don't count the cost.

What cost? But in the back of my mind there was the tiny, clear image of a codfish thrashing about on the earth, gasping and drowning in the cold dry air. That picture had never really gone away. I had simply got better at not seeing it. And I recalled Riona, staring at me, and that odd little voice that was not a voice, saying, *Best hold onto what you've got.* I thought I could hear, very faintly, the keen of the pipes.

You'd want to be careful, said the small personage in the feathered cape.

Is that some sort of threat? I challenged.

Another hoot of laughter. *Threaten? Me?*

Well, what is it then? What are you trying to tell me?

You've a big job ahead of you. The biggest, fire child. Don't waste the craft. Don't splash it around. Came close a couple of times, didn't you? Save your strength for later. You'll need all you've got, and more.

I thought very hard for a moment or two. *What are you telling me? I don't understand.* Surely this small creature could not know my purpose here. Probably it was all some trick to make me talk. They must think me simple indeed.

Odd, isn't it? said the creature, squatting down on the stone beside me. It was quite impossible to tell what lay beneath the extravagant feather covering. Its eyes changed; the dark pupils growing round, the yellow border shrinking. *Even in the long plans of the Fair Folk, things don't always work out. That girl Liadan, she wasn't accounted for in the scheme. They realized too late what her importance was. By then they couldn't change her mind for her; she up and went her own way, abandoned us, left the forest, never came back save for a social call or two. Took the child with her, and near confounded the whole thing. But the child will come back. They always do. The forest calls them. Look at you. You came back. Now what are you going to do?*

Why would I tell you? I don't know who you are. Why should I tell anyone?

I could help, fire child.

I don't need help. I don't want help. Why do you keep calling me that?

When you're angry, sparks fly. Doesn't that mean something to you?

It means I have been remiss in my control. It will not happen again.

Pigheaded, aren't you? Let me know if you change your mind.

I won't. I work alone, as my father does.

Hmm. Look what happened to him. Should have come back here, where there was a place for him, if you ask me. He was a fool.

I'm not asking, and I won't hear you insult him. He is a fine man, wise and honorable, and expert at what he does.

You're doing it again. Flickering. You're a loyal daughter. Make sure loyalty's not your downfall. Best ask your questions now, if you've got any. There's rain coming.

Without opening my eyes, I could see the sky above us, pale blue and completely cloudless.

Very well. I thought I might as well use the opportunity, whether or not the answers were of any value. *What lies on the Islands? What is their importance to this family, and to the Fair Folk?*

The owl-person blinked. *Ask the druid.*

I'm asking you.

Ask the druid to tell you the story. He's got a flair for it. The Islands are the Last Place. Pity you don't have the gift.

What gift?

The gift of seeing ahead. It'll all be gone, soon enough. In your granddaughter's time, or her granddaughter's. The trees. The lake. All there'll be is a handful of barren fields for sheep to pick on, and a dried-up pond with a few sickly eels in it, gasping for breath. Nowhere to go. Nowhere for my kind, or their kind, or even for your kind. Without the Islands, it'll be the end of us all.

I thought the Islands were no more than rocks in the sea. If—if, as you say, all is to be laid waste, how can they help anyone survive? Surely they can sustain no life?

The little creature gave a huge sigh that shivered through all its feathers. *I told you. It's the Last Place. The druid'll explain.*

I don't want to ask him.

He wants you to ask him. He's waiting for you to ask him. He's been waiting since the very moment your father stormed out of Sevenwaters, and the wise ones lost their future leader. But you know that, don't you?

I did not reply. The feathered being was uncomfortably close to the mark.

Any more questions? Rain's coming. Want to know what your aunt Liadan said when she heard Ciarán's daughter had turned up at Sevenwaters? Want to know how your father's doing, all alone in Kerry? Want to hear a tale about pipers and weddings?

Stop it! How can you know so much, anyway? It might be all lies, put out just to confuse and distress me.

Distress? Thought you weren't capable of such a feeling. How do I know so much? What sort of a question is that, from a sorceress half-fledged? Didn't your father ever teach you how to scry?

I hesitated.

Well?

Yes. But I'm not very good at it.

The small being gave a nod. *There's some in your family have quite a talent in that direction*, it said. *What you need's a seer.* And then it happened again, that slight changing of the way matters were, and there was a flap of wings, and silence.

Deep in trance, I could not move or open my eyes. By the time I had completed the slow sequence of shallowing the breath and coming back to the conscious mind, of reawakening the body and, finally, emerging into the time and place of *now* and *here*, there was not a bird in sight. Just the quiet clearing, and the archdruid stretching his arms above his head, and rising gracefully to his feet with the ease of a man half his age. The day was clear and the sun still shone, glittering on the lake water down the hill between the willows.

"Ready?" Conor asked me quietly. I nodded and we began the walk homeward.

It should not have taken long. We had come only far enough to be sure of solitude and quiet. I was distracted, my mind repeating that strange conversation, and trying to puzzle out how much of it was real, and how much the product of a rather effective meditation combined with my natural unease. After a while I began to notice that, although I was certain we had simply retraced our steps along the track, now we were walking through a different kind of terrain, where surely we had not been before; a steep sort of hillside tumbled with many boulders. There was the sound of a stream very close at hand. It began to rain, fat droplets spattering, then a shivering gust of wind followed by sudden, drenching sheets of water. I could have sworn the sun was still shining. I pulled my shawl up over my head in a futile attempt to keep dry.

"In here, Fainne!" yelled Conor through the downpour, and, seizing my hand, he pulled me sideways off the narrow path and down into the shelter of the rocks. It was a long way down, through a very low opening into a place where there was a real cave, with a broad shelf above the stone floor, and a small, round opening in the roof which let in the light. Somewhere close at hand water gushed noisily.

"The stream," said Conor, stating the obvious. "One of the seven. Rain swells it quickly. Are you very wet? I suppose we could make a small fire."

"With what?" I said touchily, surveying the bleak, damp interior of the chamber. Outside, it sounded as if the rain was coming down in buckets. There was a thing about druids, and rain.

"We could improvise," he said with a little smile. "Between us, we could come up with something."

"Maybe." My tone was less than accommodating. I did not like being tricked. I did not like being cold and wet and stuck in a little cave with an archdruid, family or not. "But there's no need. This must pass quickly. The day seemed fair enough."

"It did, didn't it?" remarked Conor. "Still, I'd prefer it if you didn't catch cold." He took off the cape he wore over his long robe, and put it around my shoulders. It settled there, soft and warm and not even the tiniest bit damp. "That's better."

I could not hold my tongue any longer. "If you're deliberately trying to annoy me," I snapped, "you're succeeding."

He smiled. "And if you are deliberately avoiding extricating yourself from this situation, because you don't want me to see how much you already know, then you're wasting my time and your own."

I scowled at him. "What do you mean?"

"Could you not use a spell of transportation, and be safe before your little fire in the keep? Safe behind closed doors?"

"In fact, no," I told him crossly. "Father said I wasn't ready to learn that."

Conor nodded. "Very wise of him. It's all too easy, if you know how, to rush off home every time things get too much for you. Well, you may not know that spell just yet. But there are others."

"You mean, I could turn you into a frog, since you seem to like the wet weather so much?"

"Well, yes. You could try. But I'm somewhat older than you, and while I don't make a habit of using sorcerer's tricks, that doesn't mean I'm ignorant of them. I think you might find it just a little difficult. You'd have to be exceptionally quick."

I glared down at the stone shelf on which we sat. The sound of the downpour was all around us; cascading past the around opening above us, roaring outside the narrow passage through which we had entered. Below us, on the cave floor, water was running across the rock and pooling in the center. The walls were dripping.

"I wanted him to stay," Conor said softly. Despite the din I heard him clearly. "I asked him to stay, but he would not. He was very young, and hurt. He should not have left us. There's never been another with such aptitude; with such breadth of skill and such depth of intellect. I found it hard to forgive myself. It is part of the trust, part of the guardianship, that each generation gives a son or a daughter to the wise ones."

"Surely there have been others," I said, wondering how he could tell barefaced lies and still sound so convincing. He must know the restrictions placed on our kind. He must comprehend what Ciarán was, and how that fettered him. Yet he spoke like a father who had lost a beloved son. "There are my cousins: Sean's daughters, and my aunt Liadan's sons. Surely one of them—?"

"The apt are not easily found. It is not a vocation you choose for yourself. It chooses you. I thought once that Liadan would take that path, Liadan or her son. But she broke the pattern. And as for

Johnny, he could have been anything he wanted to be. But she took him away. Johnny is a warrior and a leader of fighting men, young as he is. Liadan made her own path. Both the strange inhabitants of Inis Eala and the good folk of her husband's estate in Britain see her as the heart of their community. And she is a skilled healer. Muirrin fulfils that role at Sevenwaters. But there is no druid."

I was silent, watching the pool on the floor as it deepened and spilled over, a great bowl of water swirling dark into the corners of the cave. I did not wish to show I was frightened.

"Did you know," said Conor conversationally, "that I myself was close to twenty years old before I entered the nemetons? I had studied, of course, and made a start on the lore and the discipline. But I left it very late. By that age, Ciarán was close to completing his apprenticeship. I'd be more content if I believed it had not been wasted. The water seems to be rising."

I nodded.

"Who were the first folk in the land of Erin?" he asked softly.

"The Old Ones. The Fomhóire. People of the deep ocean, the wells and the lake beds. Folk of the sea and of the dark recesses of the earth."

"And after them?"

"The Fir Bolg. The bag men."

"Could you go on?"

"As long as you wanted. I suppose it would be one way to die: reciting the lore as you slowly drowned."

He looked at the cave floor. The water was not only dripping down the walls, now it was gushing in through the low entrance, a sort of stream of its own. There would be no getting out that way. The level was climbing ever close to our ledge. The roar outside went on unabated.

"It does seem to be getting deeper," observed Conor.

I clenched my teeth together and tried to look as if I didn't mind a bit. I racked my brains for an appropriate spell, but nothing came to mind. It was my father who was good with the weather.

"Not frightened, are you?" Conor asked, edging back a little on the ledge. The water was splashing up close to our toes. "Didn't he bring you up in Kerry, in some place where the waves are as tall as oak trees? I'm sure that's what I heard young Maeve saying."

"Yes, well, I may be used to looking at the water, and smelling the water, and hearing it, but that doesn't mean I want to be *in* it," I said tightly.

"No. I'd say fire is your element," said the druid calmly. "I seem to be getting wet feet. Shall we attempt an escape?" He rose to stand, looking up at the small round hole in the cave roof above us. It would be possible, I thought, to squeeze out. Just. If one could scramble up first. The water was around my ankles, and rising fast.

"What do you think?" inquired Conor, and at that moment a cascade burst through the opening above his head, a sudden violent waterfall that continued relentlessly, making it impossible to hear and difficult to see. The level rose with alarming rapidity to my waist; I felt my gown dragging me down. My heart was thumping, and even if I had wanted to turn into a fish or a frog and save myself, sheer terror would have made it impossible.

Conor was yelling into my ear. "Come on! I'll help you! Take a breath, and go on up!"

"*What?*" Up through there, up through that pounding, drenching downflow, with water in my nose and eyes and ears, and no idea what was on the other side? The very thought paralyzed me.

"Quick!" shouted Conor, and he grabbed my arm as my foot slipped on the ledge, under the water, and I came close to disappearing beneath the surface. "Quick, while we can still see where it is."

"I—I—"

"Are you Ciarán's daughter, or aren't you?" he said, and putting his arms around my waist, he lifted me up toward the circle of light, through which water poured down unabated. I took a breath, remembering to fill my chest slowly from bottom to top, and then I reached out and hauled myself up as hard as I could against the weight of the descending water. I clutched at the slippery rocks, scrabbled for a root or branch or anything that might give purchase, held my breath until my chest seemed close to bursting, cursed the need for a long gown, kicked out with my booted feet and found a little ledge in the rock, pushed upward . . . and at last, found air. I gripped at the exposed roots of a willow, gasping and choking, and scrambled out onto rocks over which water ran and ran, funnelling down through the narrow opening into the cave.

"Conor!" I screamed, leaning over and peering back down into the darkness beneath the torrent. "Conor!" There was no reply. I looked around wildly, thinking a rope would be handy, or a little ladder, or even a small lantern, if I could get it to light. Light. Fire. At least then he could see the way out. I clicked my fingers, muttering. There was a pop and a fizz, and a little cloud of steam. "Oh, come on," I said, and did it again. A ball of flame appeared, and hung in the air above the dark hole in the rocks. Hurry up, Fainne, I thought grimly. The man's old enough to be your grandfather, and he did save you first. I looked around again, and was just in time to grab a stout branch of ash wood as the flood swept it by. I clutched the tree roots with one hand as the water washed around me, and reached down with the stick. Surely the cave must be near full by now. How long could an old man hold his breath? I moved the stick around, my fingers gripping tight against the sucking of the water. There had never been such rain. Cursed forest. Words ran through my head. *We think you don't give a toss what casualties you leave behind*. A pox on the Fair Folk and their owlish friends. What did they know? I cast about with the stick again, searching for something, anything. Where was he? The rain ran down my face, washing it clean, washing everything away. Was this how it felt to weep?

The stick jerked in my hand. I let go the tree roots and put both hands on the ash branch, wedging my foot between the roots to keep from being swept away over the rocks and down the steep bank. Overhead, the orb of fire maintained a steady glow, lighting the way up. I pulled as hard as I could, feeling the strain arching through my back. *Come on, come on, old man. Not far. Not very far*.

A long, pale hand appeared, gripping the stick, and then another, emerging through the cascade to grasp at the muddy roots beside me. I bent and grabbed his arm, and pulled again with all my strength. There was a splash, and his head emerged from the water, small plaits plastered damply to his cheeks, mouth open and gasping like a fish. Somehow, he still managed to look dignified.

"Manannán save me," he spluttered, "that's an experience I'd gladly not repeat. Give me your hand again, Fainne. Not as agile as I once was . . . ah, that's it. By all that's holy. And my staff's gone as well."

"Come on," I said, getting to my feet with some difficulty on the treacherous surface. "Let me help you. We're best off these rocks and onto some dry land, if there's any to be found."

"Very wise, Fainne," he said, coughing explosively as he gazed at the ball of light hovering above the hole in the ground. Water still poured in. Further down the hill, there was now the sound of a gushing exit.

I mumbled a word, and the flames died. "Come on," I said again, and we made our stumbling way, arms linked for safety, over the rocks and along the remnants of a hillside track, now crumbling away in many small landslides, until we found a stand of pine trees, and a space under them, needle-carpeted, thickly canopied, and mercifully dry. We sat on the ground side by side, breathing hard.

"It'll come back," I observed eventually.

"What will?"

"The staff. You needn't worry. They always make their way back. That's what Father said."

"Did he? I've never lost it before. There are tales. Maybe they are true, and maybe not."

"Why did you do that? Why would you do such a thing? They tell me not to use the craft unwisely, and then you—you go and nearly kill yourself. And you're an archdruid. Why?"

"Why did I do what, Fainne?"

"That. The rain and—and everything. At your age you should know better."

"Why assume it was my doing?"

I looked at him sideways as I took the shawl off my shoulders and wrung it out. The dye had not run; still it bore its brave pattern of all that was fine and fair and lovely. "Father always said you were good with weather."

"Uh-huh." Now that he had his breath back, Conor seemed remarkably his old self; almost as if nothing at all had happened.

"Father's good with weather too," I said cautiously. "He commanded winds and waves once, at the cove. The folk there think him a hero."

"I'm sure that is no less than the truth," said Conor very quietly. "A hero makes errors, and becomes strong. But he'd be the last one to recognize it. Listen. The rain's stopping. Shall we go home?"

We walked. My boots squelched, and my gown felt like a lead weight. I had lost Conor's cape somewhere in the water, and had only my wet shawl to keep out the chill. The rain dwindled to droplets, then ceased altogether. The wind died down. On the shore, where the track emerged from the trees, a long, strong piece of birch wood lay washed up, its smooth pale surface carven with many tiny symbols.

"You were right," Conor said, bending to pick it up. It seemed to me the staff rose to settle in his hand, as if coming home. Interestingly, as we made our way along the last stretch of track, between the forest and the outer fields, I felt my clothing drying, and my hair no longer heavy and damp, and my boots once more watertight and comfortable. As for Conor, you'd have thought he'd been for no more than a fair weather stroll.

I was thinking hard. I was piecing together what had happened; trying to look beyond the physical and immediate, and to perceive the less obvious, as my father had taught me to do. The darkness of the cave, under the earth. The ascent through water, the emergence through a narrow opening, into light and air. The fire. That part I had made myself. The hand stretched out in friendship, in kinship. And the strange sense of peace which had settled on me now, against all that was logical. I stopped walking.

"What is it, Fainne?" asked Conor quietly, not looking at me.

I was not sure how to frame the question.

"I don't think you can do that," I said eventually, scowling at him. "Perform an—an initiation, I suppose it was—without someone's agreement. I shouldn't think it works, unless your apprentice has done the right preparation, and enters into it in a spirit of goodwill. Besides—" I stopped myself. It was not for me to remind him that the offspring of a line of sorcerers could never become a druid. That he must know already.

"Besides what, Fainne?" He was smiling; Dana only knew what he was thinking, the devious old man.

"Nothing." I scuffed the earth with my boot, feeling my anger rising. "Just—you must know how pointless this is, with me. You know whose daughter I am. I cannot be—I cannot be part of this. The forest, the family, the—the brotherhood. You must realize that."

Conor began to walk again, steady and quiet in his old leather sandals.

"I did not plan this," he said. "I don't suppose you believe me, but it is the truth nonetheless. Perhaps it was, as you say, a test; if so, you have passed it, I think. A test set by others than myself. It may take time before its meaning becomes plain to us. You might use this as the basis for meditation and consideration, Fainne. There's always something to be learned from such an experience."

"What?" I snapped. This wasn't fair; he sounded just like my father. "That an archdruid can drown as easily as the next man, maybe?"

"You know better than to ask me what. You are the only one who can discover what lesson this carries, for yourself. Perhaps it pertains to the question *who am I*, or *what am I*. One can spend a lifetime seeking answers to such questions. You are right, of course. It held all the symbols of a druid's passage into the brotherhood; even thus do we give our kind a new birth, a new emergence into light, from the body of our mother the earth. Ask yourself why such an experience was bestowed on you."

"An error, surely. Perhaps they—whoever they were—mistook me for someone else."

Conor chuckled. "I doubt that very much. You are your father's daughter. Now, I have something to ask you, Fainne. A favor. I'd like you to help me."

We had come to the path by the cottages.

"If it's anything to do with water, the answer's no."

He grinned. "I'd like you to assist me with the celebration of Samhain. You have been taught the ritual, I assume?"

"Yes, but—you must understand, my father and I, we are no druids. What has happened today changes nothing."

Conor looked at me gravely. "You doubt yourself. But this you could do with ease. This, and a great deal more, I think."

"I—I don't know," I stammered, finding it all too easy to convey confusion, for I felt a sudden longing to confess everything to this calm old man; to tell him the reason I was there, and what my grandmother had done, and my fear for my father. *You loved him too. Help me.* But I could not tell.

"Think about it, Fainne. You'll have choices to make while you're here. Choices that will be far reaching, perhaps beyond what you imagine."

If you knew what I imagine you would tremble with fear. "I'll consider it," I said.

Conor gave a nod, and we walked up to the keep in silence. When I got back to my chamber I took off the shawl, which was quite dry, and put it away in the chest. I hesitated before I took out Riona and set her back in the window. Then I built up the small fire to a rich, rosy glow of heat, and sat before it. It had been the strangest of days. In a way, I had achieved what I set out to do. I had confronted the forest and I had survived the experience. I had heard a voice from the Otherworld, perhaps not the one I had expected, but a voice nonetheless. But I had learned nothing. The message the owlish creature had given me had been no message. The words were meaningless. I had not asked Conor the questions I wanted answered. And yet I felt a warmth inside me, as if I had got something right at last. It didn't make sense. A pox on all druids. They were just too confusing. Like owls that talked, and clothing that dried itself in a flash, and dolls that followed you with their eyes and spoke to you in your head. I gave a huge yawn, and another, and I curled up there before the fire, and slept.

Quietly, unobtrusively, in the same way as a shadow moves under the winter sun, the druids came to Sevenwaters. They were not many: one old graybeard, a few much younger, men and women with plaited hair and pale, calm faces. Inscrutable, like their leader. They were housed in an annex near the stables, preferring to be outside the stone walls of the keep, and closer to the forest. They waited.

Samhain is the darkest and most secret of the great festivals. In Kerry Father and I had performed our own ritual, just the two of us, and because of what we were, the form of it was subtly changed. Not as folk might think. We may be sorcerers, but we are no devil worshippers. We are not necromancers or practitioners of the black arts. We acknowledge the old deities. We salute the elements, fire, air, water and earth. The fifth, which is the pure essence of spirit, we cannot approach. We reverence the passing of the year and its turning points. But we use our abilities for our own ends; we do not adhere to the druid way. Still, what we do is in many aspects very close. I understood the ceremony and what my own role in it would be. Conor had shown insight, I was forced to concede. He had known my father well enough to be sure I would have learned the lore, and understood the meaning behind it. He was right; if all you looked at was education, I was well skilled to become a druid. Besides, what other prospects did I have? I was unlikely to snare a man of wealth or influence as a husband, whether or not the truth was told about my parentage. Either I was the bastard child of a forbidden coupling, or, possibly worse, I was uncharted waters, a girl whose paternity was unknown. Maybe the story was put about that I was a druid's daughter, but who could be sure? I might have been fathered by a leper, or a petty thief, or some Otherworld creature, a clurichaun maybe. What chieftain with an eye on his bloodline would so much as look at me?

That night it was especially hard to remember why I was at Sevenwaters. As I have said, the celebration of Samhain is secret. The druids had come forth, this year, only because all knew it would be the last time before the final battle. The festival marked the start of a new year, the year in which the Britons would be swept from the Islands, and the balance at last restored. Perhaps, Conor remarked, our very next Samhain would be celebrated as once before, under the sacred rowans that crowned the Needle, far out in the eastern sea. If he could witness that, he said, he would depart this life gladly. His words sent a shiver up my spine, but I said nothing.

The ritual would still be observed deep in the heart of the forest, where the druids lived their solitary existence, watched over by those other inhabitants with their strange voices and half-glimpsed manifestations. Back in the nemetons there remained a number of Conor's brethren to fulfill this purpose. Those who had come to Sevenwaters would perform a ceremony to which senior members of the family would be invited, and afterward they would emerge to acknowledge and greet the household at large, and share with them the ritual feast of Samhain. In this way, all would be included. But the sacred words themselves, and the manner of their saying, only an inner circle might witness that, and I may not tell it fully here. The smaller girls were excluded. Knowing their complete inability to be still for more than a few moments, I thought that a wise decision.

Samhain is a dangerous time. For the three days that mark the turning of the year and its descent into darkness, barriers are put aside, and the margins between worlds become less clearly defined. It no longer becomes so difficult to see the manifestations of the Otherworld, for their shadows loom close in this time of chaos. Things seem other. In the light of the Samhain bonfire, you might look at your neighbor and see, suddenly, the face of a friend long dead. You might wake in the morning and find things disturbed. Stock wander, even when closely fenced. Strange lights can be seen in the darkness of the night, and snatches of an ancient music half-heard. If you wanted to practice scrying, this would be the time to try it. You'd almost certainly see something. You might then wish you'd left well alone.

There was a part in the ritual for the youngest druid, and that part I fulfilled. It was no difficulty to speak the words with meaning and heart. Conor's own voice had a solemn power that seemed to go straight to the spirit. I had agreed to help him. I reasoned that if I were to do my grandmother's will, I must earn this man's trust; I must find a place in this household. I told myself I was simply playing a part; that it meant little to me. But as the ceremony unfolded in the candlelit chamber which had been set aside for the purpose, it became impossible to ignore the presence of unseen others among us, somewhere in the shadowy corners, or in the flame of the ritual fire. Part of the ritual is the solemn repetition of names: the names of those who have departed this life and moved on; those who might, tonight, be able to hear our words, for at Samhain their spirits are no more than a breath away. Somehow this touched me more deeply than anything that had come before, and despite myself, for a time I did forget that I did not truly belong here, and never could. I forgot Grandmother. We stood together as a family, the living hand-fast in our circle, and the others threaded between and around us.

There were many; so many, even in the time of those here present. So much sorrow. They lingered close, the lost folk of Sevenwaters, binding and strengthening the fabric of this family.

"I speak to you, my brothers," Conor said quietly. "Diarmid, ever bold and headstrong. Cormack, twin and comrade, loyal and true. Liam, once master of this hall. You leave your legacy in the fine man your nephew has become, another such as yourself."

"Sorcha, daughter of the forest," said Sean. "Healer unparalleled, and great in spirit. Iubdan, man of the earth, steadfast and wise. My hand is in yours; you guide my steps."

"Eilis, my mother," Aisling said. "In my birth you gave your life. I never knew you, but I love and honor you."

And then they looked at me, and my words came unprepared.

"Niamh," I whispered. "You danced at Imbolc, and shone bright. You are my mother, and a daughter of Sevenwaters. We hold you close, as we hold all those departed."

"And also the sons of this household, my brothers who lived but a brief span in this world," added Muirrin, taking her mother's hand. "Small Liam and Seamus; precious as bright stars in the firmament; lovely as beads of dew on the hawthorn; you live as bright flames in our minds and in our hearts. Tonight we draw near and touch you, dear ones."

"Through the shadows we feel your presence beside us," Conor said, raising his hands, "for on this night there is no barrier between us. Share our feast; be welcome and walk among us."

He proceeded with the ritual. In turn the salt, the bread, the wine and honey were shared among those present, and the spirits' portion cast into the flames. I moved around the circle, playing my part as the druids did. I recognized that the terrible losses this family had sustained were my own losses, and theirs mine. I knew the dead were there still, within us. Their legacy was in the deeds and the choices of those who lived. Did my mother look through the veil between this world and the other, and smile at what she saw? What path would she have me tread?

The circle was unwound, and the ritual complete.

"Come," said Conor. "The good folk of the household await our company. Let us feast together, and prepare ourselves for the time of shadows."

We made our way to the great hall, where all the folk of household and settlement were assembled. It was a big gathering. The numbers living at Sevenwaters had been augmented by many warriors, and others with a part to play in the preparation for war. Blacksmiths, armorers, men skilled with horses, and those who dealt with supplies and the movement of large numbers of folk at speed, and quietly. The old woman was there, Dan Walker's aunt. I saw her watching me with her dark, penetrating eyes.

Benches were set out, and some were left empty for what Otherworld visitors might care to join us. The doors stood open, for tonight no entry was barred, no passage refused. The hearth fires were cold. Outside, in the clear space between keep and stables, a great bonfire burned, sending its sparks dancing high. The moon was full, and small clouds moved across its pale, glowing surface.

"Morrigan watches from behind her veil," said Conor. "Come with me, Fainne. Let us rekindle these fires, and set our feet forward into the new year."

He had set the bonfire alight much earlier, using his hands and an incantation. Others had kept it going by more earthly means, with a regular supply of well-dried ash fagots. Now Conor took up an unlighted torch, and thrust it into the flames until it flared and caught and burned golden in the night.

"This is the fire of the new year." His voice was strong and clear, his eyes full of a serene hope. "This is the year of the reckoning. We measure the days of darkness, and take stock. We prepare for the time of sunlight and joy, and for the day of victory. I pledge to the folk of the forest, on both sides of the veil, that before Samhain next the Islands will be restored. The child of the prophecy will lead us, and we will fulfill our sacred trust. This I pledge."

Then he put the torch into my hand.

"You know what to do?" he asked me softly.

I nodded. I had the strangest feeling, as if somehow I had done this before; as if a scene from the past were being repeated, but with subtle differences. My feet moved of themselves. I bore the flaming torch into the great hall and, before the assembled folk, I reached out and touched it to the logs laid ready on the massive hearth. They flared and burned bright. Then I walked through the house, taking care to stay clear of the tapestries, until I had lit every single fire, even the small one in my own chamber. Out of the corner of my eye I thought I spotted a little smile on Riona's embroidered mouth, but when I turned to look, she was gazing out the window as solemn as ever.

My duty discharged, I returned to the hall. Tonight, suddenly, I did not fear the crowd of folk there, the talk and the brightness. There was wine and oaten bread, and some cold meats, and a little of the fine soft cheese made from ewes' milk. Only a little, for there would be no fresh milk from now to springtime, and the bulk of our butter and cheese was laid away in the caves. The last of the surplus stock had been slaughtered and the late crops gathered in. Breeding animals, the best of flock and herd, were confined in the barns or in the walled fields close by the settlement. What little grain lay still in the fields would be left now, for the spirits. It was a time to exchange the light of the sun for the warmth of the hearth fire, the action of farm and forest and field of war for the smaller sphere of household and family, and to plan for what was to come.

It was not exactly a celebration. Folk talked quietly among themselves. Even the little girls were more subdued than usual. It was well past their bedtime, and Eilis sat on Aunt Aisling's knee with her thumb in her mouth like a baby. Maeve, who had followed my progress through the house step by step with round-eyed admiration, went to sit near the hearth, leaning drowsily against her big dog. Sibeal was next to the old woman, Janis, who seemed to be telling her a story. The older girls were moving about busily, making sure goblets were refilled and platters replenished.

"You did very well tonight, Fainne." It was Muirrin, coming up with a wine flask to refill my cup. "Almost as if you were called to it, I thought. It is quite an honor, to help with the ceremony itself. It is even more of an honor to light the fires. I have never seen Conor entrust it to other than a druid."

"Really?" I said, and took a sip of the wine.

"He values you, Fainne. You should not take that lightly. Of all of them, of all the swan-brothers, Conor is the only one who remains here in the forest. He keeps the memory of the old times alive. He does not let us forget who we are, and what we must do. He sees a part for you in that, I have no doubt of it."

"Maybe," I said. "Muirrin, you said to me, your parents had daughters, and Aunt Liadan had sons. But—"

She gave a half-smile. "There were twin boys. Between Maeve and Sibeal. They lived for less than a day. I was about seven when they were born. I held them for a while. They had such little hands."

"I'm sorry. I should not have spoken of it. You said your father was content that Johnny would inherit. But I did not know they had had sons and lost them."

"Their grief was terrible. Father has come to terms with it. He is very strong. He loves and respects Johnny. With Mother it is slightly different." She hesitated.

"She is not happy that a nephew should be the heir?" I asked.

"She would never say so. She is a good wife, devoted to my father and dedicated to the seamless operation of his household. She would never say it outright, but she believes she has failed, in not giving him a healthy son. And there is a—a reservation, that is all I would call it. She likes Johnny. One cannot do otherwise. He will be an ideal ruler of Sevenwaters. But she also has some doubts."

"Doubts?" I asked her as we sat down together on a bench in the corner. "Why would she have doubts, if Johnny is the perfect creature everyone makes him out to be?"

She grinned. "He is perfect. I'm sure you will agree when you meet him. Mother's feelings have more to do with his parentage. He's a cousin, of course, but—"

"Is it Johnny's father Aunt Aisling objects to?"

"Not *objects*. I would not put it so strongly. My mother abides by my father's decisions. It is just that—there is very ill feeling, between my uncle Eamonn and the Chief. Nobody ever says what it is, or was. My mother, I think, believes that her brother can never approve of Johnny as a future master of these lands. That makes her uneasy for the future. The Chief has never come here, not since he and Aunt Liadan went away. When he needs to see Father, they meet somewhere else; a different place every time. I've only met him once myself. And Uncle Eamonn does his best to stay away when Liadan is here. It's as if they can only keep the peace if they never come face-to-face."

"How odd. How long has this been going on?"

"Since Johnny was a baby. Nearly eighteen years, it would be."

"I see," I said, although I didn't, really. There were indeed secrets here; interesting secrets. "I'm sorry, Muirrin. Sorry about your little brothers." This was no more than the truth. I had seen the look of desolation on Aunt Aisling's small, freckled features as their names had been spoken.

"Thank you, Fainne. You're such a kind girl. I'm glad you have come here. Sisters are all very well, but it's wonderful to have a friend I can talk to. Mother will come to terms with my father's plans for

Sevenwaters in time. First the battle must be won. Then we work for the future." Her face was alight with hope and purpose.

"Excuse me," I said. "I feel suddenly quite weary. Do you think Uncle Sean would mind if I went to bed now?"

"Oh, Fainne, you poor thing! I'm sorry, I forgot you worked so hard, helping Conor and carrying that big torch around—go on, off with you. I'll make your excuses."

I fled to my chamber and bolted the door, and I shrugged off the Glamour, and changed my good gown for a plain, serviceable old night shift. I lifted Riona down from the window, and sat by the hearth with her beside me. My fingers touched the graven surface of the amulet strung around my neck, moving across its tiny inscriptions. Although the small fire burned bright, the room was cold: colder than the frost at dawn; colder than the touch of the sea spray at midwinter; but not as cold as the chill that seized my spirit and would not let go. It was the frozen grip of uncertainty. I took up the poker, thinking to stir the fire to greater warmth. I touched the iron to the coals, and instantly a great sheet of flame shot up, lighting the whole chamber a vivid orange-red, filling my nose and mouth with pungent, suffocating smoke. The very air seemed to spark and hiss around me, and my heart thumped with fright. The flame died down again, the fire glowed purple, dark as mulberries, and there within its depths was my grandmother's wrinkled face, crowned with licking flames, her penetrating eyes starring out at me, and in the crackle of burning wood, I heard her mocking voice.

Shame on you, Fainne. Have you forgotten your father's suffering? Have you lost your discipline so quickly, that you play at being a druid, and forget your purpose?

I did not seem to be able to speak. My heart raced, my skin was clammy with sweat. I had known that she would seek me out. I had known that she would come, sooner or later. But not now. Not like this. "I–I–" I stammered, struggling for some vestige of control. "I haven't forgotten, I swear I haven't–"

Oh, Fainne. So weak. So easily fooled. Why did you save the druid from the flood? Why not leave your father's nemesis to drown there in the dark? Oh yes, I was watching. Your will is not as strong as you thought.

"Conor plays his own game." My teeth were chattering. Let her not show me my father's image, not that. "I have his measure; I will outwit him. He's an old man."

He's a druid. You're not convincing me, Fainne. Must I come there in body as well as spirit, to apply a little spur to your will? Have you forgotten why you are there, child?

"N-no, Grandmother."

Then why are you wasting time dreaming before the fire?

"It—it's been necessary to earn these people's trust," I faltered. This was no good at all, I must get a grip on myself quickly. Her eyes were like knives, they seemed to pierce deep inside me, seeking out every little secret. "To appear their friend; to play the part of family. My mother—" I broke off. Tonight, I had almost felt Niamh watched me, through the veil of shadows.

Your mother would be ashamed of you. Grandmother's voice was cold and hard as stone. *She despised these folk for what they did to her, and to Ciarán. You're losing your will, Fainne. And you know why.*

"What do you mean?"

These folk are subtle. They give you the semblance of welcome, the outward form of acceptance. Conor lulls you, until you believe, almost, the same lie he fed your father. You start to think perhaps you can do it, after all. Perhaps you may break through to the light; follow the way of the wise ones, until you become what he is. Huh! Look at yourself, Fainne. Look at yourself without the clothing of the Glamour. You are apart; you are not one of these folk. You bear my legacy, the blood of the outcast, and Conor knows it. He plays a little game with you, that is all. Even your father seeks simply to use you to his own ends. That is the way of it for our kind. There is no love. There is no light. There is no acceptance. The path is but confusion and shadows. At least give it some purpose.

"You say, no love. But I love my father, and he loves me. That must count for something."

That's sentimental nonsense. Ciarán thought he loved your mother. That was his biggest mistake. If he loved you he would never have sent you here. Your father knows, and I know, that you will never be other than what you are. Now pay attention. Look into the fire.

"I am looking."

Look again.

I obeyed, and the flames changed, curled around and spread out and showed me, right in the glowing center of the fire, a tiny, clear image: my father bent over, coughing as if his chest would burst with it, and bright blood seeping out between the fingers he held over his mouth. I blinked, and the image was gone. My heart turned cold.

Saw that clear enough, didn't you? That was your doing. That's right now, what you see. It's hard for a man to swallow, with a cough like that. No wonder he's so thin. Hard to breathe, sometimes. And it's cold in Kerry in the wintertime. Her eyes bored into me.

"Please!" My voice cracked with anguish. I could no longer stop myself from begging her. "Please don't do this, it's not my father's fault. Please don't hurt him like this! I am doing what you want, I am, I have plans. You're punishing him for nothing."

Plans are one thing. Action is another. What have you done, since you came here? Have you used the craft? Have you found a man to be your tool? What have you done?

"I—I went into the forest and sought out the Fair Folk. I spoke to one of them."

And?

"I—I took a man's interest," I stammered, clutching at straws in my desperation. "An influential man. He is part of my plan."

If you took his interest, where is he tonight?

"Gone home, for now. But he said he looked forward to seeing me again." It wasn't enough, I know it wasn't. My father's strangled coughing echoed in my head, a death knell.

Not good enough, Fainne. Pitifully gradual. Remember that codfish? You did that easily enough. It is the next stage that is the real challenge. You have been foolish to let these folk begin to worm their way into your heart. Best act soon, before you forget how. You'll lose your will otherwise. You will simply become one of them. Maybe you enjoy seeing your father suffer.

"Stop it! Anyway, it wasn't easy. I see that fish in my mind, every night before I fall asleep. That was evil. It was a misuse of the craft."

She was expendable, Fainne. They all are. Where's your backbone, girl? Now show me. Show me you still have it in you. Show me you don't care about these folk. They are the people who sent your mother from her home, into the arms of a man so cruel she never recovered from it. They are

the folk who planted hope in your father's heart, only to tear it from him.
They care nothing for you. Nothing. All that matters to them is their pre-
cious forest, and their Islands, and the will of the Fair Folk. Your mother
died. She killed herself, because of what these people did. Have you forgot-
ten? Are you instead drawn into their strange understanding of the world,
so you value some so-called prophecy, some garbled piece of bard's imagin-
ing, more highly than a woman's very existence? Step outside that, Fainne.
Where is your rage? Show me your strength.

I felt it then, welling within me, the craft in all its power, flowing
forth into every part of my body. I could do what she wanted. I knew
I could; I need only use what Father himself had taught me. Yet he
had said . . . "Sometimes," I whispered, "it shows greater strength of
will not to act . . ."

What's that? Some druid's nonsense? Be true to yourself. Acknowledge
your heritage. Show you can still do it. How long now, since you really used
the craft? Show me, Fainne. A little fire, maybe. Just a small one. But hot.
Give them a fright. Unsettle them. Can't do it, can you? Lost the anger.
Lost the will. So much for the love you professed for your father. That means
nothing.

"I can! Even now my fingers feel the flames within me! But—but
there seems no real purpose in this—it's just trickery—"

You ask me about purpose? Tonight, of all nights? Has not your
mother waited for you to come, year after long year between worlds, so she
might see you through the veil on Samhain night? Watching as at last you
show her brother, and her uncle, and all these folk, that they cannot walk
forward blithely on a path awash with the blood of the innocent? Tonight
your mother sees you, Fainne. Do it for her. They took away her power; they
forced her into darkness and despair. Take it back for her. Show her what
her daughter can do.

The craft was fierce in me now, a flame that seemed to hurry me
forward, yet for some reason I still fought it. These were my mother's
own people, whatever they had done. "I—I can't be sure—"

If you cannot summon up the will for this, you are a poor student
indeed. You should not hesitate, not even for a moment. Ciarán lost his
treasure, Fainne; his sweetheart and his hope. He lost his very identity. And
you have denied him, in agreeing to be fatherless here at Sevenwaters. You
know that I will make him suffer if you fail to obey my command. Now do

it. Show your father that you have not forgotten him. Find the fury within you. Make the fire.

For a moment I closed my eyes, unable to meet the power of her gaze any longer, and when I opened them again the fire had died down to glowing coals, and she was gone.

"Father," I whispered. "Father, hold on, wherever you are. Be strong."

I picked up Riona and put her away in the chest, right down the bottom underneath Darragh's shawl. Right down in the darkness where she could not see. I closed the lid. Then I went over to the window. It was very late. I had been sitting alone a long time. There seemed to be nobody about, but there would be guards; there always were. The family, the druids, the folk of household and settlement would have retired to their beds by now. All was quiet. I blew out the candle and closed my eyes. I breathed slow and deep, summoning the eye of the spirit; slow and deep, building with gradual power like the swells of the great ocean itself. In my mind I watched the bonfire Conor had made, still burning down below the walls of the keep. I saw it clear and small. There were guards stationed near the fire, alert in the dark, edging closer to warm themselves. It was a still night, and cold enough to freeze a man through sheepskin coat and woollen cloak and all. I thought about that fire, seeing it as plain as if it were right before me. Great logs in the heart of it, glowing gold and orange, crumbling to dark ash. Cinders rising in the strong draft of it, dancing in the air like glowing insects. A spark or two. Smoke curling. In the morning there would be nothing much left. I could make a fire. All I had to do was point my finger. But this would be different. An accident. Nothing to do with me. Had I not been in my room asleep, on the far side of the keep? From my window I could not even see the courtyard where the fire had so unfortunately got out of control, and spread where it should not. Eyes tight shut, I held the fire in my mind. The change was quick. It had to be, before the guards could rush in with sticks and sacks and beat out the flames. A sudden flaring up, the licking along the ground, catching at whatever might be induced to burn. Men shouting, men running. The flames were a lovely color, red-gold like the autumn sun on dark clover honey. *See, Grandmother? See what I can do?* The flames caught at the wattles of the outbuildings and stretched hungrily up toward the sky. They sang. They shrieked. They roared. And there were other noises, not inside my head now, but all too real out there in the night, sounds of people yelling, and clanking buckets, and my uncle Sean's voice shouting directions. Horses neighing, a crashing as something large was toppled or dragged out of the way, a sudden terrible sound of pain, a man screaming, screaming, on and on. I did not want to hear this. I put my fingers in my ears, but it made no difference. There were more smashing noises, and the sound of hooves on the stones of the path. I opened my eyes and now I could see, below my window, men leading terrified horses out to the safety of the fields, and running back into the mayhem. The glow from the conflagration spread their shadows long and dark across the stretch of green between keep and forest. I stood very still indeed. There was no need to undo the spell. They would put the fire out. The animals were saved. I was glad about that. The household would be unsettled. Such an event, on Samhain night, might suggest the archdruid's hope for the coming year was ill-founded. It would sow the seed of uncertainty. It had worked very well indeed. Why, then, were my hands shaking like birch leaves in an autumn gale? I clutched at the little amulet around my neck, to steady them.

There was a hammering on my door.

"Fainne! Are you awake?"

It was Muirrin. I had no choice but to open the door and let her in.

"What is it? What's happening?" I tried my best to sound half-asleep and confused.

"Oh, Fainne! Haven't you heard the noise? There's been a terrible fire. One of the druids is dead, and others badly hurt. And we can't find Maeve. I was hoping—I was thinking she might have been with you. But I see she's not here. Oh, Fainne, what will we do if—" At this point the self-contained, capable healer of Sevenwaters put her hands over her face and broke into floods of tears. I felt a terrible shiver right through my body, that had nothing at all to do with the lateness of the hour or the chill of the season.

"I'll help you look for her," I said, the unsteadiness of my voice owing nothing at all to artifice. "Let me get my cloak. I'm sure she's all right, Muirrin. By the time we're back downstairs they'll have found her, believe me." Brighid help me, why didn't I stop it in time? Why didn't I make it stop as soon as the flames began to lick at the walls? Why didn't I remember where the druids were sleeping?

If there was an answer to these questions, I did not have it. Instead, as we hastened down the stairs and outside into the yard, a very small voice spoke up inside me. *It's the same again. The same as that other time, with the fish. You can't help yourself; it's in the blood* . . .

I felt, that night, almost as if there were two of me. There was the Fainne who busied herself helping Muirrin, hunting for Maeve everywhere, through all the house, out in the garden with lantern in hand, down in the settlement where old folk and babes were now awake and fearful, and young folk all gone up to pump water and pass buckets and beat out flames. Stock were huddled together in the outer fields, boys and dogs doing their best to keep some order in the chaotic herd of terrified beasts. We asked everyone, but nobody had seen Maeve. And when we had made our way back up to the smoldering remains of the burnt outbuildings, we were just in time to see Sean bringing her out; his face was like an old man's in the torchlight, and Muirrin gave a wordless cry of anguish before she ran toward her father and the limp, doll-like figure he held in his arms.

And all the time the other Fainne looked on from inside me. Nobody could see her. Nobody could hear her little voice but me; the little voice that was my grandmother's voice. *You did this. See how strong you can be. Tomorrow your father will breathe easier.*

I put my hands over my ears, and I breathed deep, once, twice, three times. Then I forced myself to move forward and opened my mouth to ask a question whose answer I dreaded to hear. But there was no need to ask.

"Right," Muirrin was saying briskly, though her face was tearstreaked and white. "Take her up to the chamber next to mine, and you'd best put the injured men in the room alongside. Carry her carefully. We'll need a great deal of clean linen, and folk to help us. Hurry, now."

So, Maeve still lived. I cleared my throat.

"Wh-where's the dog?" I ventured. "She might want her dog, when . . ."

"The dog's dead," Sean said heavily. "She's not allowed to have him sleep inside; he came down for warmth, and the druids gave him house room."

"She was looking for the dog?" I whispered as we walked in grim procession back to the keep. In the distance somewhere, a man was still crying out in pain. "In the fire?"

Sean gave a nod. "Somehow we missed her. She must have slipped in to try to fetch him out."

"What happened? Is she badly hurt?" I forced myself to ask him.

"It seems she tripped, and in seeking to break her fall, she has laid her hands on a length of iron which once bolted the door there, not knowing how it held the heat. Her hands are—they are damaged." My uncle's voice shook. "Her hair was in flames. We put them out. Face and hands will bear the marks of this, if she survives it. I cannot forgive myself. How could I let such a thing happen?"

Chalk-faced, Muirrin ordered everything with speed and efficiency. Linen, water, herbs. A clear space with pallets set out in rows. Folk to fetch and carry. There was a young druid with terrible burns on his legs and feet. For all the discipline, he could not still his screams, and the sound of it tore through me. As for the oldest, the pallet on which he lay was shrouded with white from head to foot. This wise one would not return to see midwinter under the bare oaks. Someone had placed a sprig of yew on the snowy linen that covered him. There were five men hurt; some with burns, others dizzy and gasping from the effects of the smoke. In the room where they laid them, Conor moved from one to the next, bending to murmur soft words, to hold a hand or touch a brow. They took Maeve into the adjoining chamber and I hovered in the doorway, helpless, as they laid her down. For once Aunt Aisling seemed at a complete loss. She knelt beside her daughter, staring blankly at the singed hair and the blistering face and hands, as the sound of the child's labored breathing rasped in the candlelit room.

Muirrin was lighting more lamps. I could see her hands shaking.

"Father," she said.

Sean looked at her.

"There are too many hurt for me to tend to here," she said quietly. "And this may be beyond my skill. We need Liadan."

My uncle nodded. "It is fortunate that she is at Inis Eala and not in Britain. At least she need not travel across the sea to reach us, and so will be here sooner. What can you do for Maeve?"

Muirrin hesitated. "I'll do my best, Father," she whispered. "Now you should go. I hear men calling for you. You too, Mother."

"I should stay with her." Aunt Aisling's voice was unrecognisable; thin and quavering and not at all like herself. It frightened me that things could change so quickly. "What if she wakes, and—"

"I'll call you straight away," said Muirrin with commendable firmness. "I promise. You're right, she will want you beside her. But I'm going to give her a draft for the pain; she won't wake for a while. Folk will need you downstairs, to tell them what to do, and to reassure them that all will be well. This will unsettle everyone."

"You're right, of course." Aisling rose to her feet, a small, slight figure in her neat gown. Without the veil, her hair was bright as marigolds in the light of the candles. "I must go down." I saw her square her shoulders and swallow her tears, and then somebody called her from the other room, and she was gone.

"Can I—is there anything I can do?"

Muirrin glanced at me. "Not really, Fainne. This is a job for skilled hands; and there are plenty of helpers to fetch water and cut herbs for me. But . . ." She was looking beyond me now, and through the doorway into the passage. I turned.

They stood there still and frozen as a row of little statues. Deirdre, Clodagh, Sibeal and small Eilis, in their nightgowns, barefoot on the stone floor. Eight big, fearful eyes were fixed on me for some sort of reassurance. On me. Behind me Muirrin spoke firmly.

"It's all right, girls." She had moved up close, blocking the view into the chamber. "There's been a fire, and Maeve's hurt herself. I'm looking after her. Now Fainne will take you back to bed, and tell you a story, and in the morning you'll hear about everything." She lowered her voice. "Fainne, please?" Her tone revealed the terrible fear beneath the calmly capable words.

"I want Mother," whined Eilis, rubbing her eyes.

"Can we see Maeve?" asked Deirdre, standing on tiptoes to try to get a look. "What's wrong with her?"

There was nothing for it but to do as I was told. "Come on," I said in an imitation of Muirrin's own style. "Your mother's busy, and so is Muirrin. I know a really good story about a man who caught a clurichaun, and another about a white pony. And you," glancing at the exhausted, tearful Eilis, "can have Riona in bed with you tonight. If you're good."

Behind us, the door closed gently. In the other chamber a man still sobbed in pain. I heard Conor's soft voice, measured and calm.

"Fainne," said Clodagh quietly as we moved away. "Who's that crying?"

"A man was hurt," I said, thinking there was no point at all in lies. "One of the druids. They're looking after him. He's very badly burned."

Then there was silence, which was an extremely rare thing for them. Not one of them said a word until we were all five in my own chamber, and I was sharing out blankets and finding places on beds and making up the small fire. It was good to fill the mind with practical and immediate things.

I told them the story of the clurichaun, and then the other one, and I tucked Riona in beside Eilis. Soon enough they were all asleep, all but Clodagh who still sat before the fire, holding my silken shawl between her hands, touching the small creatures with surprisingly careful fingers.

"This is so lovely," she said, softly so as not to wake the others. "Did your sweetheart give it to you?"

"I'm not the sort of girl who has a sweetheart," I said. "It was given me by a friend." And fortunate it was that he left me when he did. At least he could not see what I had done tonight.

"Fainne?"

"Mmm?"

"Is Maeve going to die?"

I shivered. It was as if I could see the child as she had sat, there in the window, plaiting Riona's yellow hair while her great dog lay snoring before the fire.

"I don't know," I said. "Muirrin is a skillful healer, they all say so. And my uncle said Liadan will come, though it could be a long time, to get a message there and bring her back to Sevenwaters."

Clodagh stared at me. "Oh no," she said. "Father talks to her. She'll be on her way already."

"Talks to her?"

"Like Deirdre and I do. Can't you do it? Talking without speaking, I mean. Father can tell Liadan things straight away, even when she's at Harrowfield, which is far away in Northumbria. She'll come here as fast as she can. Aunt Liadan can heal anyone."

"Well, then," I said grimly, "I suppose that means Maeve has a good chance of recovery. Now, we must get some sleep. You'll have to squeeze in here with me. I hope your feet are not too cold."

But while she slept at last, I lay open-eyed as the early light of dawn crept in the window, and the house began to stir again around us. I lay and stared at the stone walls, and I thought about my mother. I wondered if her unhappy spirit wandered here, somewhere, watching me, watching everything I did. What had Father said? *There were times of content . . . your birth . . . she believed she had at last done something right.* But in the end, she had not been able to believe it. *Perhaps her final answer was the only one she had left.*

That would be one way out. To slice the wrists, or leap from the roof, or cast oneself into the cold embrace of the lake. But I could not do as she had. That would destroy my father utterly. I must do my grandmother's bidding. I owed him everything, and I could not let her torture him. Yet how could I reconcile that with what I had done tonight? Twice, now, I had killed. And there was the terrible thing I had done to Maeve, and to that young druid. How high a price must be paid for my father's safety? Tonight's evil work surely had no bearing on the battle and the Fair Folk. Why had she made me do it?

She didn't make you do it, the unwanted voice within me whispered. *You did it all by yourself. It's the blood you bear. You can't help yourself. Besides, this is no more than appropriate punishment, for what they did.*

It is not appropriate that a child should be hurt, I told myself.

Wrong. It was apt. You have unsettled your uncle, and put doubt in the hearts of the people. You have weakened the druid. Three steps toward the long goal. It's as apt as can be.

I—I don't think I want to be who I am.

And what do you want to be? A tinker's wife with a child in your belly and three at your feet, and a life on the road? Think you've got a choice, do you? That's what your father thought. Look what happened to him. And you feel sympathy for these folk?

I willed this voice to stop tormenting me, but it would not. The voice was my own, and could not be silenced. The children slept quiet around me, and as the light of dawn filled the room with a golden brightness, it seemed to me shadows crept into my mind and my heart, and the sun itself was powerless to drive them away.

Chapter Six

Fire is a fearsome thing. It starts as the merest spark, the tiniest wisp of smoke. It grows and gains power and spreads, until it becomes a great conflagration consuming whatever it can find. Unchecked, it will take all. The destructive force of what I had unleashed terrified me. It was not just the work of the flames themselves, the ruined buildings, an old man snatching his last breath in a smoke-filled nightmare, young ones suffering as they clung to life. It was not just Maeve, who now hovered on the margin between this world and the next. It was the way they were all caught by it, the way the thing that had happened spread as the flames themselves do, to touch and wound every single person at Sevenwaters. If my grandmother wished me to unsettle the household and to sow the seed of doubt over their endeavor, she must have thought this a great success. I did not want to consider what my father would have thought. I tried to imagine him using the craft to do what I had just done, but I could not. There was the time they all spoke of, when he had driven the Finn-ghaill away from the cove. Men had been drowned because of what he did. But this was different.

I watched as the little flickerings of uncertainty spread, as the wretchedness began to show itself in different ways, as the household shifted from the pure hope and inspiration of the Samhain ritual to a mood of anxious introspection. Mealtimes were subdued. Talk was sparse. Small disagreements flared which were not always resolved with speed. Sean was withdrawn and silent, and Aisling nervously busy. Conor remained but one day after the fire, and then departed for the nemetons, with four of his brethren bearing the body of the ancient one between them on a board. He must break the terrible news to his folk himself, he told Sean quietly, not leave it to reach them through idle talk. Their oldest must be sent on his way with the appropriate ritual, and his body laid to rest where it belonged, under the oaks.

It was clear Conor wanted to stay, for though some had recovered quickly, there were still three men remaining in Muirrin's care, and prospects for the youngest looked grim indeed, unless he could cling on until my aunt Liadan arrived. Their faith in her healing abilities astonished me. Liadan was only a woman, after all, Fomhóire blood or not. What could she do that Muirrin and her helpers could not?

He would return as soon as he could, Conor said. He knew his injured folk would be offered the sick-maintenance due to them both by law and kinship. Meanwhile he had obligations to those left in the forest, and these he must keep. The chill formality of his words set a distance between him and his nephew that had not been there before. I had thought Conor tireless. I had seen him endure near-drowning with an equanimity most men of one-and-twenty would be hard-pressed to summon. But the fire had shaken him. He walked out of Sevenwaters leaning heavily on his birch staff, his hood drawn up to shadow his features. There was no reading his expression. The small procession made its way down the path under the winter trees and away. Conor had not spoken to me since the night of the fire. Whether he knew, whether he guessed, or whether he had simply been too distracted to notice me, there was no way of telling.

Muirrin was a strong girl, though she was such a little thing. In the sickroom she ordered all, and there was constant activity. Women sponged fevered brows, changed dressings, brewed concoctions of herbs over the fire. Men brought firewood and carried buckets. But the place was quiet, save for the sound of painful breathing, or Muirrin's voice giving soft, precise instructions. As I passed by the doorway I closed my ears to the voice of the young druid, moaning in pain. I did not visit Maeve's sickbed. But the eye of the mind showed me her face, glistening with pus-filled blisters all down the left side, and her staring, terrified eyes.

The children were very unsettled, and Aunt Aisling seemed helpless to do much about it. Instead she moved through the strict routine of her household as if adherence to this would stop her from falling apart altogether. She did not weep, not where folk could see her. It was only when she had been sitting alone with Maeve, while Muirrin snatched a bite to eat or a brief rest, that she allowed the tears to flow. It would be visible later in her pallor and her reddened eyes.

The terrible thing I had done haunted my thoughts day and night. I had broken one of the most basic rules of the craft. I had been pushed into anger, and I had let it get the better of me. I knew it was wrong. And yet, I did not know what else I could have done. As time passed, the inner voice, the one I did not like to hear, came often to torment me.

You've grown up, it murmured. You've learned it's true. Our kind can only tread the path to chaos and destruction. We are forbidden the light. Why are you surprised? You were told this. Even your father told you.

My father does not employ the craft thus, to awaken sorrow, I told myself.

Do not make him your pattern. He lost himself, when he lost her. He is pathless. Hope was his weakness, and he let it destroy him.

Every night as I lay open-eyed longing for sleep, this voice whispered to me, harder and harder to ignore. It was as if I carried my grandmother inside me, a twin self, and I thought she grew ever stronger, and drew ever closer to snuffing out the other Fainne, the girl who had once brewed tea on a little fire, and sat quiet under the standing stones, and ridden on a white pony. I was losing that girl fast. The walls of Sevenwaters and the great blanket of the forest seemed to tighten on me day by day, and I felt the last little bit of Kerry being slowly squeezed out of me. It hurt. It hurt so much I did foolish things to try to make it better. I kept Riona by my pillow, wrapped warm in a beautiful shawl with moon-bright tassels. As I lay there I could touch its silken folds and dream of a future forbidden me. As I stroked the doll's woollen hair I could picture a past unknown to me, in which a young mother sewed a treasure for her small daughter, with love in its tiny neat stitches. My fingers moved against the fine, strong cord of Riona's strange necklace, and something whispered deep within me, *Hold on. Hold onto what you've got left.* There was magic in this little token; not the skillful, clever magic I had at my own command, but a deeper, older kind which spoke of family and belonging. This cord with its curiously twined fibers of many hues and textures was full of power. I could feel it pulling me, coaxing me, tugging me gently toward a pathway I could not follow.

Not so long ago I'd have been glad folk were too preoccupied to bother about me. I'd have welcomed the chance to be alone, to recite the lore or meditate in silence or practice spells of transference or manipulation. But now I was adrift. I could not meditate. My mind refused to rid itself of unwelcome thoughts. The lore no longer seemed to help me. It reminded me of the druid lying in pain along the hall- way, and the other gone to his long sleep. I vowed I would not exercise the craft, lest I discover again that I could use it only to destroy.

Nobody had time for me, and nobody had time for the children. The result was inevitable. I would be sitting alone, pretending to be busy with one thing or another, and they'd come creeping in on some pretext. Clodagh, wanting help with her penmanship. Deirdre, look- ing for Clodagh. Eilis, tears rolling down her cheeks, and a graze on her knee that Muirrin was too busy to look at. Sibeal like a little shadow, with no excuse at all. She would simply drift in and settle by me without a sound.

I was forced to dig deep. I'd learned a few stories on the road from Kerry. Not all were suitable for small girls' ears, so I made some adjustments here and there. My tales were well received, and I was obliged to invent more. I knew no games to speak of, but the girls taught me ringstones and some tricks with fingers and cord. They tried to teach me a song, but I pleaded that I had no singing voice, so they simply performed it for me instead. Together we wrestled with our sewing. Sheets were hemmed and gowns mended. Aunt Aisling thanked me for keeping them amused and out of everyone's way. I was able to say, quite truthfully, that I was happy to help. The day was full. The children's chatter shut out the voice of the mind. Their company exhausted me, and sleep became possible.

Still, I could not be with them all the time. Muirrin said little, but I knew Maeve was not improving, and nor was the young druid. I heard Sean say it was a miracle they'd managed to keep him alive this long, and he hoped Liadan would have some sort of answers when she got here. Muirrin was very pale, her eyes shadowed and a little frown always on her brow. When the girls were not sleeping or with me, they could usually be found in the hallway outside the sickroom, standing or sitting in a row, quite silent. Once, I would have considered their solemn stillness a rare blessing. Now I was not so sure. It gave them too much time to think. They started to ask questions I did not want to answer. Why did such a bad thing happen to Maeve? When would she be able to come out and play again? Why was Mother angry all the time, and why did she and Father snap at each other?

In the end Muirrin ordered them not to wait outside the door. Maeve was too sick to be seen, and she was doing her best. They'd just have to put up with it, she told them quite sharply, and retreated back into the sickroom, shutting the door in their faces. Eilis burst into tears. Sibeal retreated into herself. Deirdre muttered. And Clodagh said, "Muirrin's *never* cross. Maeve must be going to die. And that man too."

On the fourth day after the fire it rained so hard I was reminded of my sojourn in the cave with Conor. There was no wind. The sky was gray as slate, and the water came down in a torrent, roaring on the roof, sheeting across the pathways, turning the fields to an instant quagmire. If Liadan were indeed on her way south, this was sure to delay her arrival at Sevenwaters. Spirits already low plummeted further. Eilis got it into her head that Maeve's sickness was somehow her fault, because she had once called the dog a big dirty brute that belonged in the stableyard. She began to cry, and could not be comforted by sweetmeats or stories or any sort of blandishments I could think of. After a while Sibeal's eyes began to spill sympathetic tears, and then the others started, until my chamber was awash with misery. Sorrow was a contagion that had spread to every corner of this great house. It crept into my own heart, where guilt and doubt already warred with the long purpose I was bound to follow. It sapped my strength and tore at my will. I thought I could scarcely bear to be a moment longer here in this family, here in this house, trapped by the rain, smothered by the forest, drowning in tears, incarcerated with the thing I had done. I thought I would give anything to get away, just for a little; just to breathe and grow strong again.

Rescue came from an unexpected quarter. The girls were working themselves into a state of complete misery, and I ventured out in search of something to distract them, for I was running short of ideas. I walked along the upper hallway, deep in thought, scarcely aware of where I was going. I went past the sickroom, and did not look in. But I heard sounds. One could not block them out, however hard one tried. As I reached the stairs my legs felt suddenly weak, and I sat down on the top step and put my head in my hands. If only I could stop thinking. If only I could shut out the voices that tormented me. *We thought you didn't give a toss what casualties you left behind.*

"Fainne?"

I took my hands away and looked up. Three or four steps below me stood Eamonn, dressed in riding clothes. His brown hair was dripping wet, and his face wore an expression of friendly concern.

"You don't look well," he commented with a small frown. "You must be exhausted. I heard you are helping with the little girls. I'm very sorry to hear what happened. I came as soon as Aisling's messenger brought me the news."

I found it hard to mask my surprise. "It's rather wet," I said bluntly. "I thought nobody would venture out in such weather. Aunt Liadan will be delayed. That's what they're saying."

There was a flicker of expression, gone too fast to be read. "I thought I might be needed here," said Eamonn.

"I'm sure Aunt Aisling will be glad to see you," I said politely. "She's been much upset. Maeve is very sick."

He nodded. "And are you glad to see me, Fainne?" he asked quietly.

"Yes," I said, and it was true. He was outside all this, the weeping, the stone walls, the stifling darkness of the forest. I could look at him and not be reminded of what I had done, because he had not been a part of it.

"Ah," he said, and he reached out his hand to tuck a wayward strand of my hair behind my ear, a curiously intimate gesture. "That's a remarkable thing about you, Fainne. You always say what you think, straight out."

I felt myself blushing again. "Perhaps I lack the refinement of manners a girl should possess in a household such as this. I do speak my mind. I have never learned otherwise. But I would not wish to embarrass you by saying something inappropriate."

"You don't embarrass me, my dear," he said with a half smile. "I like your honesty. Now come, you should not be sitting on this cold stone floor. Let us go in search of a fire, and some ale perhaps. And then I have a proposal for your consideration."

He put out a hand to help me to my feet, and I took it. His hand was dry and warm and his grip very strong. I had no idea what he was about to tell me, but anything was better than facing that little chamber full of weeping girls. Their sadness only compounded my shame for what I had done.

The kitchen was the only place that was really warm, so we settled there in a corner. It was hardly private; serving men and women came in and out, chickens were being plucked and puddings wrapped for boiling, and there was a steady stream of damp-looking men-at-arms passing through for a quick tankard of ale, a hunk of oaten bread, and a moment or two before the big fire. At least, with so much noise and activity, a quiet conversation might go unheard, if not unobserved. The old woman, Janis, sat exactly where I had first seen her, bolt upright on her chair, dark eyes sharp on everything and everyone. I poured ale from the jug, and put a tankard in Eamonn's hands.

"Thank you, Fainne," he said gravely. "Now tell me. I have not yet seen my sister, or your uncle. There's flooding in one of the outer settlements, and Sean is gone to see what can be done for the folk there. I'm informed Aisling is indisposed. The situation here makes me a little uneasy. You have observed this at every stage. Is the child likely to die? And the druid? How was it this fire took hold so quickly, and could not be stopped before so much harm was done? It's unlike Sean to allow such a thing to happen. I'm concerned about the state of his security here."

I stared at him. "You mean you suspect some form of mischief? The infiltration of an enemy?"

"I don't know what I suspect. The circumstances seemed— unusual, that was all. I would not like to think another such accident might occur to undermine us. At such a time we cannot afford even one slip. What if this fire had touched a store of weapons, or carefully conserved supplies? I want you to tell me exactly how it happened."

"I can't. I had retired for the night when the fire broke out. And my chamber is on the other side. By the time I came down, the damage was already done." That was no more than the truth.

"And the child?"

"She is badly hurt. Burned on her face and hands. The druid is worse. But there is still some hope. They expect my aunt Liadan any day." I did not miss that change of expression that seemed to flash across Eamonn's features whenever this name was mentioned. Whatever had been between them, so long ago, had left an impression that still lingered painfully just beneath the surface. "They say she is a wonderful healer. Muirrin believes she can make the difference."

"I see." Under firm control now, his features were impassive. "What of my sister? She, too, is unwell?"

"Aunt Aisling is very upset. That's to be expected. She's deeply concerned for Maeve."

"Not surprising."

"She is much distressed. The girls feel it. She has little time for them, and finds their presence a burden. She fears greatly to lose another child. The household relies on her strength, I think, and finds itself somehow adrift while she is so distracted by grief. She does all that must be done, but she is—not really there."

Eamonn nodded. "Perceptive of you. I felt this as well, from the way I was received here. Life goes on, but not as before. Let us hope—let us hope Sean's sister can indeed work miracles."

"They certainly seem to think so. It's said she possesses some powers beyond the ordinary."

He gave the grimmest of smiles. "Oh, yes. That much is certainly true. It's her judgment that lets her down. Now, to the immediate situation. I've a suggestion to make, one which should suit my sister well, I think. But I need to know, first, if you are in agreement."

I raised my brows in question.

"I've a fine empty house at Glencarnagh, with plenty of folk to maintain it. Too big by far for a man on his own. Gardens to walk in, horses to ride, warmth and space. These children are wearing you out, and upsetting my sister. They could come back with me, and remain there until the situation here is resolved one way or another. And you might accompany them, not as nursemaid, you understand, but to provide another familiar face. This would please me greatly, Fainne. I'd like to see the color back in your cheeks. I'd welcome the chance to show you my home. And there are women there who can tend to the children. You'd have time to rest and recover yourself. What do you think?"

"I—I don't know," I stammered, for this had taken me by surprise. "The girls would like it, I expect; Eilis is always talking about your fine stables. But—" I could not tell him what was in my mind; that his suggestion offered me the chance to do exactly what my grandmother would wish, and that the very thought of that turned me cold with misgivings. "I'll do as Aunt Aisling wishes, of course," I said rather weakly. Aunt Aisling would refuse, I thought; it did not seem at all appropriate that I should be included in such a family visit.

"That's settled, then," Eamonn said. "I'll speak to Sean as soon as he returns. I doubt if he'll object. It's a practical solution. We might leave in the morning, if this rain eases."

"Maybe," I said, managing a smile. "That way, we'd be gone before Aunt Liadan arrives."

His gaze sharpened. "What do you mean?" he demanded.

Across the kitchen, the old woman was watching us.

"I—I simply heard the two of you take steps to avoid one another," I said. "I meant no harm by it." I did not like the sudden edge to his voice.

"It is no joking matter."

"I have offended you. I'm sorry. Whatever was between you and my aunt Liadan still hurts. I see that."

"These things are past. I don't speak of them." His mouth was tight, the brown eyes full of bitterness.

I was lost for words. It seemed I had strayed into deeper waters than I knew how to navigate.

"Fainne! There you are!" It was Clodagh, running across the kitchen from the inner doorway with the others behind her. There were still red eyes and blotched complexions, but at least the weeping had stopped. "Oh, hello, Uncle Eamonn. Where were you, Fainne?"

"Nowhere," I said with a weak smile. Tiresome as the girls could be, there were moments when they had their uses. "Your uncle Eamonn's got an idea. We'll tell you all about it. But it's only if your father agrees, mind."

Sean had some reservations when finally he returned home and was asked permission. There was enough upheaval already, he said, and besides, I had barely settled in at Sevenwaters. It was a little soon for another move. And the weather was inclement. But Aunt Aisling overruled him.

"It's a practical enough suggestion," she said briskly. "It would suit me well. The girls are best out of Muirrin's way for now. You could stop at St. Ronan's for one night, and break the journey. It's not such a very long ride."

"It's long for Fainne," put in Eilis, who had been listening hard. "She can't even ride properly, and all the horses are scared of her."

"Eilis!" her mother exclaimed. "That's less than kind. You must learn to guard your tongue."

"It's true, though." Deirdre spoke up in unaccustomed defense of her small sister.

"As to that," Eamonn said casually, "I have brought a horse for Fainne. A mare of exceptional temperament, highly suitable for a young lady. We'll take it gradually. There's no cause for concern."

Sean and Aisling both glanced at him sharply. I looked at the floor, somewhat embarrassed but just a little pleased as well. Clearly, there had been more forward planning than his casual invitation had suggested.

"I see," said Sean, frowning. "I'm not at all sure about this."

"The girls should go." Aisling seemed to have made her decision. "This house is not the best place for them just now; there is too much sadness here. It's best if they go, Sean."

"We might leave in the morning, I thought, if the rain clears." Eamonn seemed keen to press what advantage he had.

"Very well," said Sean gravely, glancing at his wife. "But there's no rush. The girls must have time to say their farewells."

"Excuse me—" Aunt Aisling turned away abruptly and made for the door, almost at a run. I thought she was choking back sudden tears.

"Come, girls," I said briskly. "We'd best have a look at your things, and make sure your boots are clean and your cloaks dry." I glanced at Eamonn. "Thank you for being so thoughtful," I said quietly.

His expression was very serious. It usually was. I thought it would be quite a challenge to persuade such a man to laugh. Grandmother had no trick for that. "It's nothing, Fainne," he said.

"The garden's nice at Glencarnagh," observed Deirdre when we were back upstairs. I had opened my wooden chest and was sorting through my pitifully small store of belongings, wondering what might be judged suitable for such a visit. "There's a pond with fish in it, and a maze of hedges, and nut trees."

"And lots and lots of horses," said Eilis. "I wonder if Uncle Eamonn would let me ride that black one?"

"Your legs are too short. Wait ten years or so, then he might consider it," said Deirdre dryly.

"Fainne," said Clodagh.

"What?" I asked absently.

"I think Uncle Eamonn likes you."

"Of course he likes her," said Eilis, puzzled. "He's our uncle, he likes all of us."

"He's not Fainne's uncle," said Clodagh. "Besides, I mean *likes* her. You wouldn't understand, you're too little."

"You mean, sweethearts sort of likes?" Deirdre's eyebrows shot up. "But he's ancient. Older than Father."

"I'm right," Clodagh said. "See if I'm not."

"I think you should go off and do some packing," I said sternly. "Sort your things out. We might be leaving tomorrow, after all."

Sibeal did not speak often. Now, her voice was soft, but her words sent a chill through every corner of my body. "What if Maeve dies, and we're not here?"

The twins went very quiet, their freckled faces white. Eilis's lower lip began to tremble ominously.

"Don't say such things." I kept my voice as steady as I could. "Isn't your aunt Liadan coming, and her the best healer in all of Ulster? Of course Maeve won't die. By the time we get back she'll be as good as new, see if she isn't." It was a credible imitation of Peg Walker's briskly positive style. But how could I hope to convince them, if I did not believe it myself?

"Fainne?" Clodagh's voice lacked its usual confidence.

"What?"

"We need to see Maeve. Before we go. Muirrin said we couldn't. But we have to. Will you ask her? She'll listen to you."

Four pairs of around eyes were fixed on me with the same expression. I had no doubt Clodagh spoke for all of them, and I wondered afresh about messages of the mind, and just who had inherited which special skills.

"I—I don't think—" I stammered.

"Please, Fainne," said Sibeal in a little, polite whisper.

"Very well," I said. "I'll ask her. But you must do two things for me. First, go to your own quarters and tidy up your things. Set aside what you plan to take with you. And stay away from the sickroom until I call you. Don't wait for me outside the door. You know how Muirrin hates that."

They disappeared without a sound. I was shivering, my heart cold with dread. I had used every excuse I could find since the night of the fire to persuade myself that I need not go into the sickroom and see what I had done. Muirrin had no use for me. She had plenty of helpers far more skilled. I was not really family anyway. It would be an intrusion. I was better occupied looking after the children. Most of the excuses were true enough. But the reason I had not gone was none of these. I had stayed away because I feared that, once I saw what was in that room, I would not have the will to go on with the task set me. And if I failed in that, my father would die in agony. But today there was no choice. I had promised. I had to go. I had to go now, right away, before I lost what little courage I could summon. It was just a matter of making my feet go straight down the hallway, one after the other, and when I got to the doorway, instead of walking past quickly and trying not to hear the sounds, I would simply go in and . . .

I picked Riona up and tucked her under my arm. And there was the shawl which had been wrapped around her, the wonderful, sun-drenched shawl. How could I wear it? It would be like letting Darragh see what I had done, like pretending I was worthy of such a gift, when what I saw before me confirmed that it was true, that my kind was capable only of destruction and mischief. But something made me put it on, all the same. Over the top I wrapped my serviceable woollen shawl, so that only the silken fringe showed, just a little at the bottom. Then I walked along the hall and tapped at the door, and I went in, my heart thumping and my skin clammy with sweat.

"Fainne!" exclaimed Muirrin in surprise. She was stirring something in a little pot by the fire. Maeve lay on a raised pallet, and Aunt

Aisling sat beside her, shielding the child from my sight. There was a small, warm fire on the hearth, and a pleasant smell of herbs. Over by the window two serving women were busy folding newly washed linen. This room adjoined the other, where the injured druids lay, but I could not see through. It was quiet, save for the sound of a man's voice reading or reciting softly.

"I'm glad you came," Muirrin said to me in an undertone, nodding toward her mother. "See if you can make Mother go and rest. She's wearing herself out, and to no good purpose. There's little for her to do here. Now you've come, perhaps she'll go."

I made myself walk forward to the bed; forced myself to look down at the child who lay there in a sort of restless half-sleep. Her hands were heavily bandaged. I could only guess at the damage she had inflicted on them, clutching at hot iron in her headlong flight. But the wrapping had been taken from her head, and on one side her bright hair was all frizzled and burned away, the left eyelid grossly swollen, brow and lashes gone. A hideous, oozing patchwork of purple and red and brown spread like a canker from the eye all the way back past the small ear. On that side, her face was a monster's. I made myself keep looking. I controlled my expression. After a little, I found I could speak.

"I'll sit with her awhile, Aunt Aisling. You should go and rest. Eilis was asking for you. She'd dearly love to show you the little cloth she's hemmed. She's very proud of it."

Aisling stared at me, her blue eyes quite blank. For a moment, I think she scarcely knew who I was.

"I'll stay here with Maeve. It's all right, Aunt. You can go." I used the craft subtly, to make my voice more convincing. I conveyed the message that she could trust me. Inside, I shuddered at my own duplicity.

Aunt Aisling blinked and seemed to come to herself. "I suppose that would be quite suitable," she said reluctantly. "Thank you, Fainne. Muirrin, I'll be back later."

For a long time I simply sat there staring at the child. To look at her was to punish myself. But all the guilt in the world would not right the wrong I had done her. If these people knew, if they understood I was responsible, I would indeed be outcast. I would be hated and reviled as my grandmother had been. No matter that I must act thus to prevent my father's suffering. No matter that I must carry out a task of such magnitude that none of their lives would ever be the same. I stared at the child and knew I had stolen her future. What I had done was every bit as bad as what Conor had done to my father. If Maeve lived, she would be scarred and hideous. I thought myself plain and awkward, with my tight-curling hair and my twisted foot, my gangling height and my shyness. But my skin was smooth and pale, my hands deft and free of blemish, my body healthy, for as Roisin had said, the limp was nothing. I was not disfigured. Not like this. It was at that moment I vowed to myself I would never again use the Glamour to make myself look beautiful. I would thank the goddess I was so lucky, and go forth as myself. Gently I let the veil of loveliness go, knowing that in the nature of things, folk would see nothing odd in the change.

"She's waking up," Muirrin said quietly. "These drafts are effective, but they don't last very long. We're all short of sleep. The pain's been bad. Will you stay while I put on the fresh dressing?"

I nodded and retreated back from the bedside. Clutching Riona to my chest, I watched as the child awoke, her damaged eye slitted by the swelling of the flesh around it, the other round and fearful, watched as Muirrin bathed her burned skin with cool herbal waters, listened as her faint, thready whimpering grew to a thin, painful keening sound while a poultice of onion skins was laid against the burned skin of face and scalp and tied there with a bandage of clean linen. I held it in place while Muirrin made the knots, and I felt Maeve's cries vibrating through my own head, as if they would lodge there forever. Then the bedding was changed, as a strapping serving woman lifted the child in her arms as carefully as a basket of new eggs. By the time Maeve was safely returned to her pallet and attempting to sip from a cup Muirrin held to her lips, I was cold with horror.

"Now, Maeve," said Muirrin calmly, "you have a visitor. Fainne is here to see you. Did you notice? Drink up, all of it, mind, and then she'll sit with you awhile. She might even tell you a story."

The child swallowed obediently, laboriously. This draft might give her another short spell of rest. I wondered at Muirrin's strength of will. She did not weep with fear at her own helplessness. She did not rail at the gods for thus striking her sister down. She did not collapse with exhaustion or ask me why I had left it so long to visit the child. She simply went on quietly doing what had to be done, accepting that matters were as they were, and taking her place in the scheme of it with a purpose that left no place for doubt. And yet, it took its toll. You could see that in her shadowed eyes.

Maeve lay back on her pillows with a little wheeze of outgoing breath that might have been a sigh. Her eyes turned toward me.

"Well, Maeve," I said as steadily as I could, seating myself on the stool by her bed. "I've brought somebody to see you." I lifted Riona up so that the child could look at her butter-yellow locks, her shrewd dark eyes and delicately embroidered mouth. The pale pink skirts fanned out over the stark linen of Maeve's coverlet. The child's lips stretched in a tiny smile.

"Good," I said. "She's glad to see you, too. I've a favor to ask. I'm going to visit your uncle Eamonn, and I'll be away awhile. Riona can't go. But I don't want to leave her on her own, seeing we're so new here. I was hoping maybe you'd look after her for me while I'm away. You'd need to keep her company, see that her hair's neat, maybe give her a corner of your bed at night. Could you do that?"

The little, painful smile was there again.

"Good," I said, and I unwound the strange necklace the doll wore, knowing somewhere deep within me that while I might give up my small companion to someone who needed her more, I could not let go this last link to my mother. I slipped the necklace into the pocket of my gown and tucked Riona in beside Maeve, under the covers. She fitted snugly into the crook of the child's arm as if she belonged there. The expression on her embroidered features seemed almost benign.

"Now I'll tell you a story, and then I have to go. Would you like a story?"

A very faint response. "Mmm." That was all she could manage. On the far side of the chamber, Muirrin sat down by the fire, and one of the women put a tankard between her hands. She stared into the flames as if suddenly too weary to move.

What sort of tale do you tell to a child as she looks across the room and sees death waiting in the shadows? I knew plenty, but none of them seemed right. What trickery can amuse a little girl as her skin twists and tightens and works itself into a crippling fabric of scars? How do you keep her heart strong and her spirit clear when you must speak from the dark turmoil of your own guilt? My fingers toyed with the little edge of fringe that hung down below my everyday shawl. Silken and sunny. Memory of innocence. The delicate, lacy pattern of wavelets lapping the sand in the tiny secret cave. Notes of a melody arching through the stillness of the dawn.

"The folk I traveled with when I came here, they tell a lot of tales around the fire at night. That's to help keep out the cold, you understand? The smallest children sit in front, and the old men and women, where it's warmest. Then there's the bigger lads and girls and the grown up folk, that's another circle. And beyond that, there's the creatures. Dogs that guard the camp, and ducks and chickens in little coops, and the horses. Enough horses to make a fine big circle all of their own. If those horses could speak, they'd have a tale or two to tell. Some of the stories are noble and grand, and some of them are silly, and some of them can make you cry and laugh at the same time. I'm going to tell you a story about a boy and a white pony. It's a new one. You are the very first person to hear it. You and Riona."

Maeve gave a little sigh, and turned her head slightly toward me, as if not to miss a single word.

"Well, now," I said, "this boy was one of the traveling folk. He'd grown up on the road. That was what he was used to. No fine houses or soft beds for him; no servants to cook or wash, no clients to tend the beasts and work in the fields. Just a cart and a pair of horses, and the sky and the sea, and the way stretching on before him, full of adventures. He didn't settle long. It's in the nature of a traveling man to be always on the move, you see."

Maeve was trying to say something. I bent my head to catch the faint words.

". . . name?"

I swallowed. "His name was Darragh. He traveled with his mother and father, and his sisters and brothers, and some cousins and uncles and aunts, and his old grandfather as well. There were plenty of folk, and even more horses, because that was what they did. They'd catch the wild ponies or buy them cheap, and train them up fine for riding, and sell them at the Cross. That's where they hold the best horse fair in all of Erin."

The room was very quiet. Not only was the child absorbed in the tale, but Muirrin's gaze was now intent on me, and the serving women had put down their work and seated themselves on a bench near the window to listen.

"Now Darragh had a rare gift with the horses. It was something about him, something you could never quite put your finger on, but the creatures trusted him. It's a hard thing for a pony to go away from his herd and be among men, you know, hard and frightening. Like saying goodbye to your family. Like going somewhere so different it could be another world. They call it breaking a horse, to tame it so that it will take a saddle, and submit to a rider's will. Sometimes what they do can seem quite cruel; tying a creature, making it lie down and accept a man's mastery over it. Breaking its spirit, that's what it is. That's the only way, the traveling men say, if you want the horse to be of any value to a buyer. Nobody wants a beast that can't be trusted to obey.

"Darragh didn't like to speak of breaking. He'd a different approach entirely. If the other men thought his methods a little odd, they never said so, because it was always the horses Darragh had brought in that were the most sought after, and fetched the best prices at the Cross.

"There was one time when they were camped under a hill, and the men and lads went out to watch for wild ponies, thinking to take a few to prepare for the next autumn's fair. The ponies were grazing on the sweet grass of the hillside. They were edgy, ears twitching, tails swishing, as if they sensed something was afoot. Ready to bolt at the least excuse, they were. Their coats were the colors of the landscape, black, gray, brown, the shades of rock and lichen and bark. But there was one who stood out. She moved among them like a lovely full moon between dark clouds, her coat as white and shining as anything you'd ever see. Her mane and tail fell like the silken fringe of a lady's shawl, lustrous and gleaming.

" 'That one's mine,' said Darragh in a whisper.

" 'Her?' muttered his father, who knew more about horses than most people could learn in a lifetime. 'Not likely. Look at her eye. That creature's mad. There's a pride and an anger in her means you'd never break her. More likely she'd be the death of you. Pick one of the others.'

"But Darragh had made up his mind. The usual thing, once they'd chosen the ones worth taking, was to come back with their own horses, and the dogs, and cut the ponies out from the herd to take back to the encampment. There they'd be confined, and subject to the usual discipline, until they were docile enough to be ridden.

"Darragh knew the white pony was different. He'd seen what his father had seen: the wildness in the eye, the flare of the nostrils, the proud carriage of the beautiful head. She was like some princess of the old tales, aloof and untouchable, and very much herself. And frightened. She had sensed his presence there. This pony could not be seized and driven by sticks, with hounds yapping at her heels. That would indeed send her mad. This princess could only be tamed by love.

"It was as well the traveling folk were camped in those parts over the summer, for Darragh needed time. He told his mother he might be away a bit, and to let his Dad know, but not quite yet. Then he went up the hill very early in the morning, when the mist still slept in the hollows and crevices and only the boldest birds sang out their challenges to the first rose tint of the dawn. He went soft-footed, without company, with a little halter in one pocket and a scrap of bread and cheese in the other, and his eyes and ears open. The white pony was on her own under the rowan trees. She was dreaming; and so quiet was Darragh, coming up to her, that she never heard a whisper until he was quite close, sitting on a rock as still as he could. She looked at him. He made no move, though truth to tell it was freezing cold and he was hard put not to shake and shiver. But he kept still, and made sure his gaze was on the grass or the trees or the sky slowly lightening to a faint lilac, and after a while she seemed almost to forget him, dropping her head to crop at the grass. But she'd her eye on him, he knew it.

"It was a long process. On one hand, Darragh was wearing her down with his patience. On the other, she was trying him to the extent of his persistence. Everywhere the white pony went, there was Darragh, silent, still, not trying anything, just keeping close by her. She'd run, she'd run swift as the west wind, up the valleys and over the passes and across the fields of shimmering grass, and Darragh would run after her as fast as his human legs could carry him, and get left behind time after time. But always, eventually, he would find her. He had ever been a lean fellow, and he grew thinner. There'd be a bite to eat at a cottage here, or a handful of berries there, but it wasn't much. His boots were nearly worn through. Back at the encampment, his folk counted the days as they passed.

" 'Boy's a fool,' said his dad. 'I told him he'd never break that pony. Anyone can see she's crazy.' His mother didn't say anything. She had her own opinion, but she kept it to herself.

"Darragh was exhausted. He'd run from dawn till sundown, and his ankle was hurt, and there were blisters on all his toes. Many days had passed since he first set out from home, and now they were back on the hillside where it had all started. The pony was watching him, and he was close, very close to where she stood. He could almost hear what she was thinking: that she found his behavior very strange indeed, and could not understand what he wanted of her. That she should be over the hill to the east, with the herd, but for some reason she was here with him. She should go, the others were waiting, but . . . but . . .

" 'Well, then,' said Darragh, and he took one step forward, and laid his thin, brown hand very gently on the white pony's neck. 'I'm off home. You'd best go back to your own folk. Keep out of trouble, now.' And with that, he turned and was off down the hill to the camp."

I paused. All was still in the room; even the voice from the neighboring chamber had ceased its steady cadence. Outside, birds were calling.

"That can't be the end," said Muirrin.

I glanced down at Maeve. She was still awake, her face turned expectantly to me.

"Indeed no," I said. "Darragh went home, and soaked his feet in a bucket of warm water, and ate a big bowlful of stew, and then he rolled up in his blanket and slept from dusk until well after cockcrow. His sister, Roisin was her name, had to wake him up, so sound was he sleeping after all that running, and all that sitting quiet, and all that trying to think the way a pony would think.

" 'Get up, Darragh,' she hissed in his ear. 'Look. Look over there.'

"He rolled out of his blanket again, blinking and rubbing his eyes. And there, delicate and graceful in the morning sunlight, stood the white pony, waiting for him on the far side of the camp among the baskets and barrels and bits and pieces. She put her beautiful head a little on one side, and looked at him with the eyes his father had called crazy, and she gave a soft whinny, as if to say, I'm here now; what comes next?

"The summer after that, Darragh's father asked him if he planned to sell Aoife, for so the white pony had been named. He'd get a good price for her at the fair, for she was a creature of exceptional intelligence, though in truth, she was only at her best when Darragh himself was on her back. Still, he'd taken a girl for a ride on her once, and her manners had been perfect. But Darragh wouldn't part with her.

" 'I can't,' he told his dad. 'She's not mine to sell.'

" 'What nonsense is that?' his father queried. 'You caught the creature, you tamed her. Of course she's yours. I know five men who would pay in good silver for such a mare.'

" 'That's not the way of it,' Darragh answered, stroking Aoife's snowy coat with gentle fingers. 'I chose her, and she chose me. There's no catching about it, and no owning. She's free to go if she wants. Besides, I could never part with her, not now. She's my luck.'

"As time passed, Darragh became much sought after for his way with horses. It's not everyone has the ability and the patience to tame a wild creature with love alone. He never parted with Aoife, nor she with him. They became a sort of legend, the two of them. People would point and whisper as they saw the dark young man with his little gold earring, riding by their cottages on the beautiful white pony.

" 'That boy's half horse himself,' somebody would say.

" 'Not what I've heard,' said another. 'They say the creature's a faery pony. Turns into a beautiful girl at night, and back into itself by day. No wonder he wouldn't give her up.'

"But Darragh only grinned his crooked grin, and nudged Aoife's flank softly, and the two of them moved on into the dusk. And that's the end of the story, for now."

Maeve seemed to be asleep, her breathing quieter, and Riona still clutched tight in her arms. I tucked the coverlet over her small form.

"Is that a true story?" asked the big serving woman with some hesitation. She had sat entranced throughout my tale.

"True enough," I said, thinking it was just as well my kind could not weep, or I would be making quite an exhibition of myself by now. "Indeed, I rode on that pony myself once. She's every bit as clever and as lovely as the tale describes."

"You tell it well." Muirrin got up from her chair and stretched wearily. "It makes you sound like—like another person entirely."

I did not reply. All the fine tales in the world, all the sweet memories, could not make things right again. Not for Maeve; not for any of us. I was glad Darragh had gone away. I was glad I would never see him again. What boy in his right mind would want someone like me for a friend?

"Muirrin," I said, remembering belatedly why I was there. "You heard we are all going to Glencarnagh, the girls and I?"

"I did," said Muirrin with a wry smile. "A surprise, that was. I wonder what inspired Uncle Eamonn to this sudden gesture of family support?"

"I think he's just trying to be helpful," I said.

"That's as may be. The girls have never gone there before except on formal visits with Mother or Father. Uncle Eamonn is a stickler for everything proper. He always works by the rules."

"This isn't breaking any rules. He is their uncle, after all."

"Mmm," Muirrin regarded me quizzically. "As long as you know what you're up to."

"I—I must ask you a favor," I said. "The children want to see Maeve before they go. It seems to be important. I was sent to persuade you to let them in, just for a little."

Muirrin frowned. "It will only upset them, and that will upset Maeve. Perhaps you do not realize how sick she is, Fainne. She has been badly shocked, and is quite weak. I don't want to risk further contagion in these wounds; that could finish her. Forgive me for being blunt, but I must do everything I can to help her hold on until Aunt Liadan arrives. This is not a good idea."

"Please let them visit." I used the craft, as subtly as I could, to make my words sound convincing. "I don't wish to distress you, but—but Sibeal said, what if Maeve dies, and we're not here? They are thinking of that. I'll warn them to keep their comments to themselves, and not to upset her. Please, Muirrin."

Now Muirrin was looking at me very closely indeed, and she had a strange expression on her face, as if she were trying to puzzle out a page of words written in a language both familiar and unknown.

"Very well," she said after a moment or two. "I can hardly say no when you put it like that. I'll send for you when she wakes. The girls must leave before the bandages are changed again. They can't be here for that. Fainne—" She bit back her words.

"What?" I asked.

"You seem—different, that's all."

"What do you mean, different?" I was alarmed. Surely she had not noticed my use of the craft?

"I don't know," Muirrin said. "It's as if sometimes you were one person and sometimes another. As if there were two of you. Sounds silly, doesn't it? I must really be tired."

"Isn't one of me enough?" I said lightly, but I knew I had been careless. I had overlooked the strange powers some members of my family possessed. I had forgotten about the Fomhóire streak. From now on I would be more watchful.

As if to ease the way for our departure, the clouds dissipated and the sun rose on a clear, cold morning. Horses and ponies were readied before the main doors, and a great many men-at-arms, whose dark green tunics blazoned with a black tower marked them as of Eamonn's household, assembled themselves into an impressive escort. This time, it seemed, none of the men of Sevenwaters were to ride with us. Eamonn was family and so, I assumed, was spared the indignity of being seen across the borders by my uncle's guards. Family could be trusted. So Darragh would have me believe; the message had been implicit in his blithe talk of the joys of growing up surrounded by sisters and brothers. It just went to show, I thought bitterly, how little I was really accepted here; Eamonn might pass as he liked, but they would not even let me take a stroll into the forest without an escort of armed men. Yet I was blood kin, and Eamonn was not.

The little girls were very quiet indeed. Visiting Maeve had been difficult for them; holding back their comments and their tears of dismay, even harder. They had done bravely, the four of them, and I had made sure I told them so, later, when the door was closed on their sister's pain. There were tears enough then, but they were as much in anger as in sorrow.

"It's not right!" Clodagh had muttered, frowning furiously as she stared down at her clenched fists. "Such things should not be allowed to happen. How can the gods let it happen?"

"It's not fair," Deirdre had added, glaring at nobody in particular.

The smaller ones had nothing to say. Sibeal was a shadow of a child; Eilis sucked her thumb. In the morning they came down in their cloaks and riding boots, and were helped onto their ponies, and soon enough we were on our way deep into the forest and headed for Glencarnagh.

Chapter Seven

Anything I knew about horses I learned from Darragh. But I had not always listened to his tales as attentively as I might, and so I did not know much. The little mare that carried me safe to Eamonn's house was very old in horse years, but still as steady as a rock. I knew she was old because Eilis told me so. You could tell by the teeth, she said. The horse was silver-gray, and gentle of eye, and like Aoife, she seemed to know where she was going without being told. She did not tremble and edge away from me as the other creatures in my uncle's stable had. Of course, now that I had shed the Glamour any animal would have been more ready to trust me. But I thought it was more than that. This mare seemed in some way different, special.

"Where did you get her?" I had asked Eamonn early on, wondering whether a great lord and owner of wide lands would travel to a horse fair, or send a man to drive bargains for him, or shun such commonplace events entirely and simply breed his own fine stock.

"She was left behind, a long time ago." Eamonn rode beside me, as if to make sure I did not stray. Perhaps he doubted my ability to handle even such a well-trained creature as this. "By a lady. She's a fine beast, and remarkably sound for all her years. Under-used."

"Has there been no lady to ride her, until now?" I ventured.

He glanced at me. "That is indeed true. For many years there has been no mistress at Glencarnagh. And since Aisling wed your uncle, my other holding at Sídhe Dubh has been a place of men. It is a long time now."

"Why did you not return the horse to her forgetful owner?" I asked him.

I thought he was not going to answer. His mouth tightened, and the brown eyes turned chill. Once again I had blundered into forbidden territory.

"There was no opportunity," he said at last. "She never came back."

I did not press him further. He had the same look on his face that had appeared when I spoke the name Liadan. I wondered if the horse had been hers.

Glencarnagh was a pretty place. I had not noticed much when I had camped here before with Dan Walker's folk, save that the house was solid and fine, and extremely efficiently guarded. Then, my head had been full of thoughts of Sevenwaters and what I might find there. Now, I had time to observe and listen.

This house had been fitted well for a family. Eamonn's own mother had grown up here, until she was wed to his father and went away to Sídhe Dubh. Later, there had been a bride in the house, the young wife taken by Eamonn's grandfather, Seamus, in his old age. There had been a child; but it seemed he had not lived to see his seventh year, and the old man had never quite recovered from the sorrow of that. When Seamus died his wife had gone back to her own folk. Now both Glencarnagh and Sídhe Dubh belonged to Eamonn himself: a middle-aged man with no wife and no heirs, and seemingly no inclination to acquire either. That was strange. Even I knew enough to realize the sudden demise of such a man, always possible in the nature of things, would lead to a time of immense instability and great risk to his neighbor, Sean of Sevenwaters, whose own lands were near-encircled by Eamonn's. There would be chieftains and petty kings from all over Ulster claiming some form of kinship and vying for the túath. In the midst of preparation for their great battle for the Islands, that would be the last thing they needed. Besides, what of Eamonn himself? Did he not care that he had no son to inherit his vast holding, his two fine houses, his personal army of warriors, his grazing lands and his various other enterprises?

There was an opportunity here that might be used, a secret Grandmother would want me to uncover, I was certain of it. That secret still made Eamonn's face tighten and his eyes darken when my aunt's name was mentioned, these long years after. Common sense told me that if Grandmother wanted these folk to be defeated, it would not be achieved by superior numbers or military strategies or even by a spectacular display of magical power, even supposing I had the mastery for such a thing. Defeat would only come from within themselves, by the division of ally from ally, and brother from sister. I knew that without ever reading it in any book, or hearing it from any teacher. I knew it from the way my grandmother had played upon my love for my father, and used it to trap me. The strongest weapons were those of the heart: hate, hurt, fear. Love, too. That could be used most cruelly. Grandmother understood that. Did not she herself act out of the desire to wreak vengeance on those who had slighted our kind? Her hatred was a force more powerful than any army. It seemed to be so easy for her to command me, to make me do bad things even when I didn't want to. I would never have hurt Maeve, never; the child was innocent, she had barely begun her life. I would never have done that. But I had done it, with a click of the fingers and the summoning of a charm, as if it had no more significance than the lighting of a little campfire to boil water. And now, even as I quailed before the prospect of completing my grandmother's task, it came to me that if I failed to progress as she wished, there were others she could make me damage. Which might be next? Fey, watchful Sibeal with her deep eyes, volatile Deirdre who had as many moods as an autumn day? Practical, perceptive Clodagh or Aunt Aisling's baby, tiny Eilis? All had become dear to me despite my best efforts to remain apart; as dear as sisters. Would I not risk them all if I did not keep to Grandmother's plan?

I knew what she would have me do here at Glencarnagh. She herself would have handled it expertly. I could almost see her, in her guise of glossy auburn curls and sweetly curved figure, of innocent smile and wide merry eyes, dancing attendance on her victim, blinding him to reality with her dazzling butterfly charm, always staying just out of reach, so that he blundered off the path of safety in his desperate pursuit. I knew how to do that. She had shown me in quite some detail. But I would not, not if there were any other way. There was something tawdry about achieving a goal by such means, however important that goal might be. It was a branch of the craft I would far rather leave untouched. I would wait a little; I would seek a different way. And so, for now, I settled at Glencarnagh with the simple gratitude of a prisoner delivered unexpectedly into freedom, and I watched the girls play ball on the grass, and chase each other through the maze, and roast nuts on the fire in a chamber cozy by candlelight, and I felt the chill on my spirit ease just a little.

I had expected to continue as before: companion to the girls by day, watcher by night, perhaps included in adult conversation from time to time if it happened to suit my host. I had no talent at music; I could not entertain. One could scarcely recite the druidic lore in company after supper. Those talents I did possess were not for sharing. I hoped to have a little time to myself, to set my thoughts in order. I did not wish to think beyond that.

But Eamonn had different ideas, and he made them clear as soon as we came to Glencarnagh. The girls were worn out by the ride and went to bed early. I too had planned to retire, for I had a fine chamber all to myself and I longed for solitude and quiet. Lately, since the fire, even my nights had rarely been spent alone, for it was common for one child or another to tiptoe in, woken by a nightmare and seeking company to keep out the dark. That they came to me was ironic indeed, and did nothing to improve my opinion of myself. But here, the children had been accommodated in a well-appointed chamber for four, with their very own maidservant, and, said Eamonn as the two of us stood before the fire together that evening, I would be able to sleep undisturbed. The hall at Glencarnagh was much smaller than the great space at Sevenwaters, and the fire's warmth spread to every corner. The furniture was polished to a gloss you could see your face in, with skillful carving on the chair backs; little creatures and scrollwork. I sipped the goblet of fine wine I had been given and nodded without speaking.

"I have observed how my sister employs you at Sevenwaters," Eamonn said evenly. "Your origins may be obscure, but you are her husband's niece, nonetheless, and should be treated as such. To use you as a convenient servant is not at all appropriate. Here, you are my guest."

"I—" His words had taken me aback. I realized, to my own surprise, that I had come to accept the tasks my aunt set me quite readily.

Indeed, I almost enjoyed them. "Aunt Aisling has never been less than kind. The children are no trouble. But I thank you for your courtesy. I will look forward to some quiet time, some time on my own."

"I must confess," said Eamonn carefully, "that that is not entirely what I intended. Although you shall most certainly have solitude and peace here, if that is what you crave. My motives are not entirely selfless. I imagine you are aware of that."

I glanced quickly at him, and back down at my wine cup. Did that mean what I thought it meant? Surely not.

"I did hope," he went on, "that we might spend some time together. I have the business of the estate to attend to, of course, and the children seem to value your company. Still, there are the evenings. And if this clear weather holds, we might ride out together. There's fine land here: grazing fields, wooded valleys, a waterfall. I'd enjoy showing you that."

"Ride?" I queried. "That's hardly my strong point."

"You did well enough on the way here, Fainne. You're quick to learn, I think."

I smiled. "That has been said of me."

Now he was looking at me very directly, and there was a brightness in his eye that my grandmother would have recognized well. "I'm a good teacher," he said softly. "You'll discover that, when you know me better."

I felt a hot blush rise to my cheeks. "I've no doubt of that," I murmured. He *did* mean that. I could scarcely believe it. For I had not employed a single one of the little tricks Grandmother had showed me, not since we rode away from Sevenwaters. I had offered him no encouragement whatever. Yet his meaning seemed clear. This was both strange and worrying. As early as was within the bounds of good manners, I pleaded weariness and retired to the solitary safety of my chamber.

The weather held fair, though cold. My cousins explored the long, low house with its walls of solid stone and its cunningly thatched roof, they investigated byre and barn, they helped feed the chickens and took little treats to the inhabitants of Eamonn's well-appointed stables. Eilis was cultivating the friendship of a long-legged black horse which dwarfed her completely. I could see she had hopes of riding forth on this daunting creature as soon as she could talk her uncle into giving permission. I envied her confidence. Clodagh worked out the way through the maze, and showed the others with a certain air of superiority. Deirdre fell into the pond chasing a ball, and had to have all her clothing cleaned and dried before the fire. They kept themselves well occupied, and smiles returned to their anxious faces. Sibeal remained quiet. She had brought her small writing tablet from Sevenwaters, and while her sisters chased each other down the paths, or threw their ball, or fed carrots to the horses, she could be seen making careful letters on the waxen surface with her little stylus. I was the one to whom she brought her work for correction, a fact that did not go unnoticed.

"You have some skill in writing, then?" Eamonn asked me later as we sat in the hall after supper. There had been others present before the meal: his brithem, his factor, his master-at-arms, and several other men of the household, with one or two wives as well. But Eamonn, it seemed, did not eat in company. This was not a place like Sevenwaters, where all sat together over supper, and the talk was vigorous and punctuated with laughter; where the children joined their parents at table, and the working folk shared the fruits of their labors with chieftain and lady. Here, the small group of trusted advisers met together to discuss serious matters: territorial disputes, cattle trading, a problem in the armory, the dispatch of men to collect goods from a vessel that had landed somewhere. The women contributed little but I could see I was under keen observation. It was men's talk. I listened carefully, but could not make a great deal of sense of it. It was odd enough to have been included in this group. My presence gave rise to a few raised eyebrows at first, and even a wink from one fellow, though I noticed they made sure Eamonn saw none of that. Then, when it was time for the meal to be served, they all melted away as if on unspoken command, and I was left with Eamonn, sitting in some splendor at a table whose fine oak shone mirror-bright. I refrained from comment, although I would indeed have been far more comfortable supping with my cousins and their waiting woman in their own quarters, or snatching a bite in a corner of the kitchens or wherever the rest of the folk of Glencarnagh ate. I thought of fish roasted over a small fire, with a turnip or two thrown in for good measure. I did not belong in this man's company, and I did not understand what he expected of me. I employed the table manners Grandmother had taught me, and said little, and at length the meal was over and we went to sit by the fire, with the flask of wine on a little table. That was when he commented on my helping Sibeal with her letters.

"I can read and write, yes," I said cautiously. "I can render Latin into Irish, and Irish into Latin. I can scribe a fair half-uncial. The teaching was excellent."

"You would be well trained, I suppose, in a house of prayer; though I understand a holy sister cannot expect the level of education provided for a young man in such an establishment. They clearly intended you for a future within those walls. And yet you have not emerged a convert to the Christian faith."

"How do you know that I am not?" I asked him, wondering how far this conversation might develop before I would have to lie.

"I know Conor was impressed by your skills and knowledge, and that he put a word in Sean's ear about maybe recruiting you to join his brothers and sisters in the nemetons. Somehow you have held onto the ways of your father. I'm told he was a druid. I found that interesting."

I made no response. The wine was good; it warmed the heart, and made the head a little light. Eamonn seemed to be able to down cup after cup and show no effect whatever.

"Do you want to know what I think?" he asked.

I said nothing.

"I think it would be something of a waste."

"What would?"

"That you should become a druid. You love children, that much is plain. I think you would not be averse to—to the opportunities a fuller life might provide for you."

I looked at him as levelly as I could manage, not so easy after the wine. "One might say the fullest life is that of the spirit," I said severely. "The spirit, and the mind. I was brought up to believe that."

"But you don't believe it, do you, Fainne?" He had moved closer, and I felt wary all of a sudden, uncomfortable, as if he were sounding me, scenting me, the way a predator fixes on his quarry. It frightened me that I had allowed him to gain control so quickly.

"I don't know," I said, swallowing. "I'm only fifteen years old, and my future is uncertain. There will be choices to make. I suppose my uncle Sean will guide me."

"Still," he said smoothly, and his hand came out to pick up the wine flask from the table, and to brush against my arm in passing, as if quite by chance, "no choice should be made blindly. It would be wise to explore the possibilities, before fixing a course. Would it not?"

"Maybe," I said, willing myself to stop shaking, willing my heart to stop thumping.

"There's no need to be frightened of me," said Eamonn.

I could not attempt an answer to such a statement, and so I ignored it. My hand moved up over the amulet, hoping desperately for some inspiration. I took a deep breath. Perhaps the only defense was to attack. "May I ask you a question?" I said.

"By all means."

"It seems to me this is a house for a family. A comfortable, pleasant house; it is full of brightness. The little girls like it here; it is safe, and they feel that."

Eamonn inclined his head slightly in apparent agreement, but his eyes were wary.

"The master of such a house must be a careful steward," I went on. "It is immaculately kept, and maintained in all its prettiness and comfort. It is a house—it is a house intended to please a woman, and to shelter her children. And yet you have chosen to have neither here. That seems odd to me."

There was a silence, and I began to regret my bold words.

"I'm sorry if I have offended you," I added.

Eamonn glanced at me, and away. "You do indeed speak what is in your mind. As for Glencarnagh, it was my grandfather's home before it came to me. Seamus Redbeard, they called him. He married late in life, a second time, and improved upon the amenities here to please his young wife. It was always a fine home. I do not live here; I visit from time to time, and I have folk who maintain it for me. My other place is quite different."

"A fortress surrounded by marshlands? That's what I've heard."

"Indeed. You might think that a more appropriate setting for a solitary man of middle years."

"Still, you have chosen to keep Glencarnagh as it is. The garden must be lovely in spring. Why would you take such trouble, when you are scarcely here to see it?"

Another little silence. "There would be an easy answer to that. I could say, so that such as yourself and my nieces could enjoy it, when you visit."

"But?"

He grimaced. "Does it matter why?" he asked. "Hope dies, and still one finds oneself going through the paces. Glencarnagh is an empty shell, Fainne. A shrine to what could never be. And yet, I cannot bring myself to let it go. It would be—it would be like the final death of dreams. Dreams that should have been buried long ago."

I stared at him. "That's terrible," I blurted out, shocked out of any fear I might have felt. "How can you say that?"

"All I wanted," he said softly, staring down at the wine in his cup, "all I wanted was what any reasonable man wants. A wife, a son, my home and lands, the chance to provide for my folk and fulfill my duty. I never set a foot wrong, Fainne. I followed the rules at every turn. And then, at a snap of the fingers, it was stolen from me, not by a man of superior standing, that I might almost have understood, but by a miscreant who'd better have died in the cradle than lived to see the light of day." His fingers clutched the cup so tight the knuckles were white. "Robbed of everything that mattered. Robbed even of the opportunity for vengeance. Worse still, forced into an unholy alliance with a creature whose very name I despise. And yet, I keep this house bright and fresh, as if spring walked in its halls, when the snows of midwinter blanket the fields outside. As if, even now, there were a chance she might come back."

He had rendered me speechless. I sat quiet, waiting for my heartbeat to slow, thinking I had been wrong about more than one thing. Thinking that, after all, Grandmother's little tricks would have been no help whatever here, for this man had only ever wanted one woman, and that was the one he could not have.

"You—you speak of my aunt Liadan, do you not?" I asked eventually.

"Did Sean tell you that?" he snapped.

"No," I said as calmly as I could. "I guessed. You make it plain enough, for all your allusive speech. You can scarcely bear to hear her name spoken; and yet you seem to be telling me you still love her."

"Love?" His tone was bitter. "I once thought I understood that word. Not any longer. There is a giving and a taking between men and women. Perhaps that's all there ever is. It cannot have been love that made her act as she did. More like some sort of perverse lust, that drove her to forget who she was, and what she had promised."

"It has been a long time," I ventured. "You still seem so angry."

It was at this point that he appeared to recall where he was, and who he was talking to. I saw him draw a deep breath, and force his features to relax just a little.

"I'm sorry, Fainne. I cannot believe I spoke thus to you. I forgot myself, and can only ask for your forgiveness. You are too young to be burdened with such foolishness."

He was a stickler for the rules. That was what Muirrin had said. It must pain him, to realize that he had thus revealed himself to a mere girl, and one of relatively short acquaintance. I framed my answer carefully.

"I have not been raised as other girls have. Please don't let this trouble you."

"You speak from your innocence," he replied, frowning. "This was incorrect of me, undisciplined and inappropriate."

"I don't think so," I said quietly. "For it seems to me this is a burden that has gone unshared for a long time. Would you carry it to your grave?"

"Fainne! You shock me. I may be an old man by your standards, but I've no intention of expiring quite yet."

"Nonetheless," I said, "you go to battle this summer. An endeavor of great peril, of high risk. It seems you care little for the future of your name or your estates. Perhaps you do not fear death. Still, it is best to rid your spirit of such hatred. The goddess calls at what time she will, not at the time you choose to step across the margin."

"You're a strange girl, Fainne," said Eamonn, and he took my hand in his and raised it to his lips. "I do not know what to make of you."

"Nor I of you," I said, withdrawing my hand. "I don't know what you want of me."

"Right now," he said, unsmiling, "I think it's time you retired to bed. Take a candle from the shelf there, by the door."

"I—"

"Best if you go, Fainne. I'm poor company tonight."

So I left him standing by the fire with the wine flask beside him, and I wondered how many cups he would need to drain, before he could win himself a brief oblivion.

I stood before the mirror. It was a fine mirror; the polished bronze sent back the light of the candle flames, glowing with a golden warmth. Around the rim, the metal was finely chased with an intricate pattern, link within link, a triple chain with here and there an oval of enamel, inset. Scarlet, sun-gold, deep blue like the fathomless ocean. It was a rich man's mirror. My reflection stared back at me, her form softened by the rosy tint of the metal, an autumn girl. I looked at myself, and heard Eamonn's words. *I'm a good teacher*, he had said, and when I thought about it, there was not much doubt which arts he believed he could share with me. The girl in the mirror was not the sort of girl to fill a man with desire. Her hair curled tightly; it was the color of flame, bonfire red. Her eyes were the intense deep purple of the ripest berries. The lips were severe. It was a hermit's mouth, suited to reciting the lore, or praying in seclusion. These were not lips for kissing, or whispering sweet words, or singing songs of love. The skin was pale, the cheeks without bloom. But my body had been changing almost without my noticing. I was developing curves here and there, so that the awkward, gangling girl now went in and out in all the right places. The twisted foot was still there. There was no cure for that legacy of a forbidden coupling, I thought savagely. But despite that, I looked . . . not unpleasant. I smiled at myself in the mirror, and the little amulet that hung around my neck sparkled back at me, catching the candlelight. My smile faded. It was foolish to believe I might ever be other than what I was. Looks were nothing. Where had looks got my mother? Sold off to the highest bidder, and miserable for the rest of her short life. Nonetheless, in Eamonn's suggestive remarks and sidelong glances there lay the seed of a solution to my problem; the beginnings of a strategy for achieving my grandmother's goal. I could hear her telling me so. *This man is powerful. And he is corruptible. Get close to him, make him want you. Use him, Fainne.*

But I could not do it. The prospect sickened me. It was a misuse of the craft and I knew that I could not make myself go through with it. I slipped my nightrobe over my head and climbed into bed, conscious of the mirror still gleaming softly across the chamber, in the light from the little hearth fire. I lacked the will for it. My body shrank from it. How could I do it, when the very words the man spoke made me shudder? It was simply wrong. To manipulate a man thus, so that he panted after you like a hound after a bitch on heat, to bend him to your will so that he would do anything for you, that was to lose the last shred of self-respect. I did not think I would ever understand men, let alone wish to lie with one and do all the things Grandmother had told me men and women did together. The very thought disgusted me. There had to be another way. Coming here had been a mistake.

Aren't you forgetting something? said the small inner voice. *What about your father? Seize this chance, Fainne. Already the alliance balances on a knife edge. Choose the weakest point, for that is fragile indeed. This man talks to you. Make him talk again. And remember, it's in the bedchamber that a man speaks his most secret thoughts.* I blocked my ears with my fingers, as if that would silence the voice within me. I curled into a tight ball under the covers. But there was no Riona to help me keep the voice at bay. There was no way to silence its relentless message. I did not need to look into the mirror to see my father's image, wheezing and gasping for breath, using every vestige of control he possessed to keep from crying out in pain as the seizure laid an iron grip around his chest, robbing him of life-giving air. I felt the small, hard form of the amulet warm against my breast. *You must go on*, said the voice, over and over. *For your father. You owe him. To the end, Fainne. Right to the end.*

The rain came back, and there was no riding out. Eamonn taught me to play brandubh, a somewhat more sophisticated game than ringstones. I was happy with this. The degree of concentration required to anticipate the opponent's next strategic move meant one could not maintain one of those difficult conversations at the same time. Sitting opposite one another, with small table and game board between, meant no touching. The playing pieces were wondrously carved, the board itself decorated with intricate wooden inlay. We started with practice games, and when he could see I understood the rules we began to play in earnest. Our third proper game went on long into the night. The rest of the household was abed, and the two of us sat alone before the fire. Eamonn drank steadily, as was his habit. I sipped at my wine, but took as little as I could. A clear head was required for the game on the board before us, and also for the subtler, unspoken game that continued between us in glance and gesture. Before dawn the black pieces had vanquished the white, and I had won. Eamonn was quite taken aback.

"Well," he remarked with a little frown, "I see I will have to watch you, Fainne."

Through a wide yawn, I could not resist saying, "You did tell me you were a good teacher."

"And you said you were a quick learner. That was true. You are almost too quick."

"You would rather I allowed you to beat me?" I asked, raising my brows.

"Of course not." His response was sharp. "You surprised me, that's all. A woman's mind is not usually able to grasp the intricate patterns of such play and use them to advantage. Next time I will be on my guard. I underestimated you as an opponent."

"And you don't like losing." These words came out before I could stop them.

He narrowed his eyes at me. "One day your outspokenness will get you into trouble," he said softly. "It might be wise to curb that tongue just a little, in other company. But you speak no more than the truth. I don't accept defeat easily. I go into any venture expecting to win."

"And do you often lose?"

"In the long term, never."

"But—"

"A man who takes what is mine can expect retribution in kind. He may forget what he has done. But I do not forget."

"What if such a man became an ally?" I asked. "Would you not then face an impossible choice?"

There was a pause. His fingers gripped the wine cup as if he were squeezing the breath from his enemy's throat.

"Such a man can never be considered an ally," he said tightly. "One would better place trust in some Otherworld monster than in such as him. The normal codes of kinship and loyalty do not apply. Better that such a creature had never been born."

His bleak tone alarmed me. I regretted asking the question. I picked up my candle, and he seemed to come back to himself.

"It's very late. Almost day. You'd best lie abed in the morning, you'll be weary."

"I may do so. But I am used to long days and early rising. Thank you for the game. I enjoyed it." And I had. It was good to exercise the mind on something other than the impossible challenge Grand-mother had set me. It was good to have to concentrate so hard that the image of Maeve's burned face faded from my mind for a little. When I went home, perhaps I could teach Father . . . no, best not take that thought any further. I must indeed be tired.

"Are you feeling faint?" Eamonn queried, stepping forward to take my arm. "You look pale. I've kept you up much too late."

"It's nothing. It will pass."

"Good night, then. Or perhaps it should be good morning." Usually he would give a grave nod or clasp my hand in his on taking leave of me. This time he bent forward and gave me a little kiss on the cheek. There was nothing in it, it was light and quick. But I saw the look in his eyes.

"Good night," I said hastily, and retreated to my own chamber. I lay in bed under my soft woollen blankets and fine linen, so weary I should have fallen asleep the moment my head touched the pillow, but unable to stop my mind from working busily. It was quite obvious what Grandmother would have me do now. Indeed, it was becoming apparent that the task she had set me might not be so impossible after all, if only I could force myself to do what must be done with Eamonn. But how could I? How could I bear it? As dawn broke outside and a cock began to crow extravagantly in the yard, I fell asleep with my problems still turning and tangling in my mind.

I did not sleep long. There was a break in the wet weather, and the girls were anxious to be off out of doors, despite the bitter cold of the day. Visitors had arrived, and were already shut away with Eamonn in his council chamber. He, too, must have had little sleep. There were fine horses being tended to in the stables, and good cloaks being hung to dry before the kitchen fires. Nobody seemed willing to say who the visitors were. Maybe nobody knew.

We went out walking, the five of us, clad in heavy, hooded capes and strong, winter boots. The sun was struggling to emerge from clouds still heavy with rain, and the breeze was biting, but the girls had smiles on their faces. They were glad to be out in the open again.

"It's good here," observed Deirdre. "You can go for a walk with-out some man-at-arms forever leaping out and barring the way."

Eilis was jumping over puddles. One, two, three—jump! One,

two, three—splash! She would need a change of clothes when we returned. As we made our way down a path between neatly clipped hedges of yew, toward a small grove of bare-limbed hazel trees, I observed that there were indeed guards. There was no leaping out, as Deirdre had put it, simply a discreet presence at a suitable distance. Men in green, well armed and silent. One might be allowed to wander, but not unwatched. It was for our safety, I supposed. Still, it riled me. I thought about Kerry, and the way Darragh and I had clambered around the cliffs like little wild goats, and scampered back and forth in the path of the advancing tide, and never a thought given by our folk as to whether we might be safe, or when we might come home. They knew we would be safe because we were together. My heart ached with the longing to be that small girl again. But there was no rewriting the past; there was no stopping the turning of the wheel.

Deirdre wanted to climb trees. She tucked her skirts into her belt and hauled herself up with impressive agility and an unladylike display of leg. Immediately Eilis was clamoring for a boost up.

"Babies," scoffed Clodagh as she lifted her small sister to reach the bottom branch, but the glint in her eye meant she was not to be outdone by her twin, and soon the three of them were scrambling about like squirrels, and swinging perilously from the leafless branches.

Sibeal was seated on a flat-topped rock, near where the rain-swollen stream came down into a small, round pool. Today the water was coated with foam, the current strong even in this place of temporary repose. Sibeal sat cross-legged, her hands still in her lap, her back very straight. It was a pose of meditation, like Conor's. Her gaze was fixed on the water. I settled quietly on the rocks beside her.

Some time passed. Sounds rose and faded: the laughter and shrieks of the others, the creaking of branches, the calls of birds; the voice of the water itself as it cascaded down into the receiving cup of the pool. The sun showed its face abruptly between the clouds, and light touched the surface of the water, piercing, dazzling in its pure brilliance. The froth of bubbles turned to gold; the wet rocks gleamed.

On the other side of me, someone was squatting; someone about the same size as my cousin, but covered with feathers. Somehow, it was possible to speak without making a sound.

You again.

Disappointed? Who were you expecting?

I did not come out here searching for Otherworld beings.

Uh-huh. If the voice of the mind can express disbelief, this was what the creature conveyed. *And I did not come to your call, but to hers.*

My—my cousin's? She called you?

She opened the way, so I could cross over. What she sees is something else entirely. She looks in the water. She sees what will be, and what may be. I'm here for you.

Why would you seek me out? I was confused enough already. The last thing I needed was another cryptic dialogue that posed more questions than it gave answers.

You're mixed up. I feel it. You've lost your way, if you ever had one. And you don't know who to ask for directions.

I need no directions. I find my own way. My father taught me to solve my own problems.

And you will. We've no doubt of that. But you're wasting time. What about a little advice?

Your advice? I think not. I don't even know who you are. What you are.

The small owl-like creature ruffled its feathers, dislodging one or two of them, which floated through the air before me, delicate, tawny fragments like autumn's last skeleton leaves. On my other side, Sibeal still sat motionless, clear gaze fixed on the water.

What I am, echoed the creature. *What we are. Have a look at us, Fainne. If you can't guess, with that headful of druidic lore, your education's been wasted.*

Us? I asked, and as the voice of the mind spoke, I saw without opening my eyes a movement of the landscape, a changing and unfolding, as if the streamlet, the great boulders, the crevices of the earth wrinkled and shifted to reveal what had been there all along, if one had only known how to look. They gathered around me in a circle, silent. None was taller than a half-grown child; each was different, each in some way resembled a known creature, a frog, a squirrel, a piglet maybe, though some seemed as much like small plants or bushes as anything; each was uniquely itself. They were not animal, and they were most certainly not human. I looked closer. There was one with a single eye in the middle of its forehead, and one had but a single leg, and hopped along on a small crutch fashioned of birch wood. One had deep wrinkles over its whole body, like an old, dried-up apple; and one seemed covered from head to toe in a gray-green, fuzzy moss.

*You are—you are—*I hesitated.

Go on. The owl-like creature nodded encouragingly. *Who were the first folk in the land of Erin?*

You were? I ventured.

There was an approving chorus of chuckles, murmurs, hoots and growls.

We are the Old Ones. It was the mossy, rock-like creature that spoke. Its form was solid, without discernible limbs, and yet it had a face of sorts: a crack of a mouth, and reddish lichen patches which might have been eyes. *We are your ancestors.*

What! I almost spoke aloud, so taken aback was I. *You? How could that be?*

There was a ripple of laughter around me. Sibeal did not stir.

Your ancestors, and your cousin's. But she does not see us. What she sees is quite other. You seem shocked. The owl-creature fixed its large around eyes on me. *You never asked the druid for the story, did you? What were you afraid of? The story tells of a union, long ago, between a man of the Gaels and one of our own. The line of Sevenwaters sprang from that coupling. And you are a child of Sevenwaters.*

I don't think so. I frowned. *I was not raised to love the forest, as these folk do. My path is different.*

There was one creature here that seemed made of water; its form changed and flowed within itself as I watched, and through the shifting fluidity of its shape I could see the rocks and grasses beyond. Its form was not unlike that of a small child, with fronds of dark pond weed for hair.

They all come back. Its voice was like the babbling of a brook over smooth pebbles. *The children come back to the forest. But it's not enough. Not anymore.*

You have come back, said the owl-creature. *You may wish to deny it, but you are one of us.*

That's nonsense. They were trying to trick me. Trying to make me reveal my purpose here. *I'm a mortal girl, that's all. I am part Irish and part Briton. A mixture. I'm as far from you as—as—*

As a stray dog is from the mysterious patterns of the stars? Wasn't that it? Ah, now I've made you angry. And I've proved my point.

What point? What do you mean?

See those little flames that flicker across the surface of your hair when you lose your temper? I don't know any mortal girls who can do that trick. Now listen. We know what you are.

Oh yes? The conversation was beginning to alarm me. I repressed the urge to use the craft. I would not reveal myself thus. *And what is that?*

The mossy one spoke again. *As you said, a mixture. A very dangerous mixture. A blend of four races. Why did your father send you here? Why come now, at the very end of things?*

These words chilled me. I must try to take control of the situation, as best I could.

Tell me, I said. *The Fair Folk want a battle won, don't they? The Islands regained? Is that what you mean by the end of things? But they have great power already. Are not the Túatha Dé gods and goddesses, able to change the patterns of wind and wave, able to strike down whole armies and to rout the strongest of opposition? Why don't they simply take the Islands back themselves? What is the need for human folk to die, generation on generation, in this long feud? This family has lost many sons. And what has it to do with such as you? With—lesser folk?*

There was a humming and a whispering and a muttering all around the circle of strange small beings. Eyebrows twitched; tails swished; feathers were ruffled and noses wrinkled in derision.

Lesser folk? The mossy creature spoke in its deep, dry voice. *They thought us lesser, when they banished us to the wells and the caves, and the depths of the sea; to the wild islands and the roots of the great oaks. But we remain, despite all. We remain and are wise. Times change, daughter. The order changes. It is thus with the Túatha Dé. With the coming of the sons of Mil, their star began to wane. A measure was set on their days. Your father and the archdruid are among the last of the wise ones in this land. Well may Conor mourn the loss of his aptest pupil, for there will not be another such, not in the time of any mortal man alive on this earth today, nor in the time of his children's children, nor of their children's children.*

Man sets his hand to games of power and influence, he quests for far horizons and wealth beyond imagining. He thinks to own what cannot be possessed. He hews the ancient trees to broaden his grazing lands; he mines the deep caves and topples the standing stones. He embraces a new faith with fervor and, perhaps, with sincerity. But he grows ever further from the old things. He can no longer hear the heartbeat of the earth, his mother. He cannot smell the change in the air; he cannot see what lies beyond the veil of shadows. Even his new god is formed in his own image, for do they not call him the son of man? By his own choice he is cut adrift from the ancient cycles of sun and moon, the ordered passing of the seasons. And without him, the Fair Folk dwindle and are nothing. They retreat and hide themselves, and are reduced to the clurichaun with his little ale jug; the brownie who steals the cow's milk at Samhain; the half-heard wailing of the banshee. They become no more than a memory in the mind of a frail old man; a tale told by a crazy old woman. We have seen this, Fainne. That time comes, and soon. Axes will be set to the great forest of Sevenwaters, until there is but a remnant of what was. An old oak here and there, hung with a wisp of goldenwood. One lovely birch by the water's edge, where once a family of clear-eyed children spoke their mother's name, and great Dana's name, in the one breath. The lake itself no more than a dried-up pond. There will be no refuge for them. And when they pass, so too does our own kind. We have seen this.

The calm, measured words chilled me to the marrow.

Can't this be stopped somehow? I asked.

We have seen it. It is what will be. In such a world there is no place for us. Around me, the creatures sighed as one.

Then why is it so important to win back the Islands? Surely it does not matter whether the prophecy is fulfilled. The mark of the raven, the chosen leader, and so on. You're saying it will all be lost anyway. The years of trust, the guard kept on the forest by the people of Sevenwaters, all for nothing?

Ah. That's just the point. All will be lost in time; the lake, the forest, druid and lord and Fair Folk alike. All that you see. It is the unseen that must endure. The seed that waits within the shriveled fruit of autumn; the jewel held safe within the silent stone. The secret hidden deep in the heart. The truth carried strong in the spirit. When the Islands themselves are no more than a memory for humankind, that kernel must survive. For this reason the battle must be won, the Islands reclaimed, before it is too late. All must be played out in accordance with the prophecy. That is as the goddess herself decrees. The Islands are the Last Place. There is preserved what is most precious. There it is guarded until the wheel turns, and the time comes again when man hears the heartbeat, and tunes to the life within. In the coming of the child of the prophecy, comes the keeper of truth, the Watcher in the Needle. This must unfold, or we are all lost indeed. Believe me, the Túatha Dé would not seek the help of human folk unless they must. It hurts their pride sorely, to be forced to demean themselves thus. But it is only through humankind that the prophecy can be fulfilled, and the mysteries kept safe.

Just a moment. The Watcher in the Needle? I don't recall any mention of that before. What does it mean? You speak in riddles.

The mossy being widened its crevice-like mouth at me. Perhaps it was trying to smile. *You should be used to that, child. Isn't your father a druid?*

We cannot tell you what will come to pass, said the owl-creature. *Prophecies and visions are never as simple as they seem. There's a battle, and blood, and death. There's sacrifice and weeping. That part's obvious to all. But it's not the killing that's important. It's the keeping. The unspoken part. The keeping of truth, in times of darkness and ignorance. Without that, we're all gone, and you are right. The years of loss and pain will have been for nothing.*

Why would you tell me this? I was shivering. If these words were true, then the quest my grandmother had set me was surely an abomination. *You know who I am, and who my father is. You must know of my grandmother, and what she did. Are you not very foolish to trust me with your secrets?*

You think so? The watery one spoke, its voice soothing and calm. *Has it never occurred to you that every girl has two grandmothers?*

Then, with a flurry of movement, a folding and concealment, they were suddenly gone.

"Did you see her?"

Sibeal's voice startled me so much I almost fell into the pool.

"See—see who?" I stammered.

"The Lady. Did you see her?"

"What lady?" I stared at her, wondering at the deep calm of her expression. Clearly she had been quite unaware of my strange companions.

"The Lady of the Forest. Didn't you see her at all? She was right there, just across the pool, on the other side."

I shook my head. "I saw no lady," I said. "Does she come to you often?"

"Sometimes." Sibeal got to her feet, brushing down her skirts. "She shows me pictures."

"Pictures?"

"In the water. I saw Maeve."

Fear gripped me. I did not speak.

"She was grown up, older than Muirrin. But I knew it was her. I could tell, because of her face."

"Her face?" I echoed stupidly, not sure I wanted to know.

"Yes, the scars. And her hands were still hurt, she had gloves on, pretty ones. Shall we go back to the others now?"

"No. Tell me the rest."

"What rest?"

"Maeve. Was she—was she all right? What was she doing? Was she happy?"

Sibeal glanced at me, apparently surprised. "She had a little baby. She was singing to it. Why do you ask?"

"Why do you think?" I exclaimed, exasperated, and forgetting she was only a little girl. "Of course I want to know! You see what's to come, don't you? This way we know she will live, and recover, and have some sort of a future! Of course I want to know!"

"Don't cry, Fainne," said Sibeal solemnly, and offered me her small linen handkerchief.

"I'm not," I said crossly, annoyed to have lost control so easily. Anyway, I could not have cried even if I had wanted to. With our kind, the tears just seemed to build up and build up inside, never to be released; an ocean of tears, flooding the depths of the heart.

"The only thing is," she went on as we began to walk slowly back up to the hazel thicket, "you never can be sure if what you see is going to come true, or if it's just something that might come true. Or it could be just a—just a symbol."

"You know what that means?" I queried, amused despite myself.

"Like a skull for death," Sibeal explained gravely. "Or a ring for a promise. Like sunlight for joy, or shadows for mystery."

"Forget I asked," I said. "Are you sure you're only eight years old?"

"I think so," answered Sibeal in puzzled tones.

I dined alone that night. Eamonn had waylaid me as I returned to my chamber to exchange my muddy boots for soft indoor shoes and attempt some tidying of my disheveled hair. As if he had sensed my presence, he stepped neatly out of the council chamber as I passed, and closed the door promptly behind him. But I had been trained in observation, and I registered a momentary glimpse of two men standing by the table within. I even caught a snatch of conversation. "It's the son who is the key," said the taller man, the one with flaxen hair braided back from his face, and shoulders set uneven, as if he bore an old injury ill healed. The other was shorter, older, with stern features and an iron-gray beard. The closing door shut off the reply.

"Fainne," said Eamonn amiably, looking me up and down. "You've been out, I see. Had a pleasant morning?"

"Thank you, yes." His scrutiny made me acutely aware of my flushed cheeks, my wild hair and crumpled gown, and the fact that I was still breathing hard after playing chase all the way back from the thicket. "The girls were climbing trees."

"Did you sleep well?"

"Well enough. Yourself?"

He grimaced. "Rest eludes me these days. It matters little. I suggest an early night tonight, Fainne. I cannot dine with you, I regret. We are in council as long as these men remain here. I must confess to a certain inclination to show you off. But under the circumstances that would be unwise. My guests will be gone in the morning. We might perhaps manage that ride I mentioned, if your cousins will spare you for the day."

"Maybe," I said, not sure if I was more relieved at the prospect of a relaxed early supper with the girls, followed by a good sleep, or alarmed at the idea of a day out in Eamonn's company. "You're busy. I'll leave you to get on with it." I turned to go, and felt his hand close around my wrist. For a man of his years, he was indeed quick.

"You are not angry? Not offended that I must exclude you?"

I spoke without turning back. "Why would I be offended? This is your house; this is your business. I have no expectation of sharing either." It sounded rather harsh, once the words were out.

"No?" said Eamonn softly, and released me. I heard the door open and close again behind me, and I fled along the hallway to my own chamber, filled with confusion. What sort of place was this, that one moment you were out in the fields chatting to Otherworld creatures that seemed to tell you the end of the world was coming, and the next moment you were playing some sort of game you didn't understand with a man who was old enough to be your father? Why couldn't I be five years old again, and the biggest of my worries the need to move my legs fast enough to keep up with Darragh? Not that that had ever been a real concern; not once had he failed to wait for me. Not until the day I told him I didn't need him anymore, and sent him away.

So much for an early night and a good sleep. I was tormented by evil dreams; dreams from which I awoke with an aching head and a sweating body, dreams which I could not remember, save that they left me more wretched and confused than before. All I could recall was running, running as fast as I could, and never quite being able to reach what it was I was pursuing.

The day started well enough. If I had expected to ride out alone, just the two of us, I had not thought logically. There had to be guards, of course, men clad in green tunics who accompanied us in silence, at a distance. After all, there was a battle pending, and an alliance whose members scarcely seemed to trust one another, let alone the opposition. I had the same little horse that had brought me to Glencarnagh; with her, I found I could almost enjoy riding. We commenced a tour of the enclosed fields, the higher grazing lands, the neat small settlements each with its own well-manned fortifications. The country was mostly open: gentle hillocks, wide, grassy valleys, with here and there a waterway fringed by willow and elder. There were trees aplenty, but the place lacked the oppressive, smothering stillness of Sevenwaters, and I liked it better. I liked even more the fact that Eamonn seemed quite content to explain it all to me, with never a suggestion that the outing was intended for any other purpose than to show me what any guest might be shown. I was much relieved and began to enjoy myself, for it was a fine day, and a fine estate, and there was a great deal to catch the interest. We looked at hives and spoke with the beekeeper about the curative properties of different flowers, and how these might be preserved and concentrated in the honey. We inspected a little dam and a mill wheel. We stopped at one of the major settlements, a big rath with a sturdy outer wall of sharpened stakes, enclosing village and small fort. Here one of Eamonn's free clients, who was leader of the community, provided us with a repast of ale and fine loaves and mutton cooked with garlic, and gave us the chance to rest a little.

"You're limping," observed Eamonn as I seated myself on a bench, and eased my foot a little in its heavy boot. "Have you hurt yourself?"

"It's nothing." I could not avoid the curtness of my tone. I hated this foot, so twisted and ugly. And I hated myself for minding so much. But I would not use the Glamour to put it right. Not after that time at the fair. Not after Maeve.

"Are you sure? Perhaps we should return home straight away. I would not wish to tire you."

"I said, it's nothing. This foot is—is a little damaged, that's all. I do walk somewhat crooked. Had you not noticed?"

Eamonn just shook his head slightly, and gave a hint of a smile. Then he returned to polite exchanges of news with our hosts.

We were riding away from the settlement, and Eamonn was speaking quietly to one of his men-at-arms. Now he rode back to me.

"Would you like to see the waterfall?" he asked. "There should be a good flow after all this rain. Not too tired?"

I shook my head.

"Good. It's up the hill to the west there."

As we rode off in that direction I saw that all but two of our guards remained behind, seemingly under instructions to wait where they were until we returned. The path went up and up under the intricate network of bare birch and ash, and emerged onto an open, rocky slope. My little horse picked her way along the difficult track with delicacy. Above us the winter sky was cloudless, a huge inverted bowl of duck-egg blue, and I was aware of an immense vista to my right, fields and trees and stone walls and, far to the east, the blanket of dark trees that marked the border with Sevenwaters.

"Don't look yet," said Eamonn over his shoulder.

I was a little alarmed at the way the hillside sloped away on one side of the path, and sharply up on the other, and could only trust to the sound instincts of my mount. My anxiety drove other thoughts from my mind; and it was only when the sound of rushing water grew to a roar in the ears, and the path broadened to a wide grassy shelf edged by great rocks, that I realized the last guards had been left behind. Eamonn helped me down, and it seemed to me his hands lingered at my waist a little longer than was strictly necessary.

The noise of the water was everywhere, echoing from the rock walls, drumming in our ears, vibrating in the very ground on which we stood. There was a fine spray in the air, and a sheen of dampness on everything.

"Come and look," Eamonn said, raising his voice to be heard over the din. "Over here. But be careful. It's slippery."

Standing at a particular point on the slick stone surface, right at the edge of the level area, you could see it. The lip of the fall was just around the corner and about a man's height above us. You could watch the sudden violent descent, a whirling veil of water crashing and splashing its way down and down to some unseen pool far below. The cliff was softened by ferns and mosses and tiny plants clinging to its cracked and creviced surface. I stared at the spilling, spraying torrent, and all I could think about was the ledge in the rock above the Honeycomb, and my mother taking a single step into space, and falling, falling down through pitiless air to the rocks and the boiling surf below. I thought of the craft, and the trick I had learned with a glass ball. *Drop. Stop. Now gently down.* Nobody had halted her descent. No great hand had reached out to catch her softly in its palm, and set her sweetly back on the earth. *Here is your second chance. Now live your life anew.* Instead, she had been allowed to go. Perhaps what purpose she had was already fulfilled. To be a rich man's toy. To break my father's heart. To bear a daughter whose mind was as confused and unhappy as her own. Once that was done, what matter if she shattered her poor, beautiful, fragile self on the hard rocks of the Honeycomb?

"Fainne!"

Perhaps I had shut my eyes. Perhaps I had been swaying, or my crooked foot had slipped just a little on the treacherous surface. As Eamonn called out, I felt his arms around my waist again, grasping me firmly, pulling me backward.

"Careful," he said sharply. "Don't frighten me like that."

But I was the one who was frightened now. For he had not let go, now that we were safe back on the grass. His hands still held me fast, and he was close, so close I could feel the warmth from his body, and hear his breathing over the sound of the water.

"I would not want to lose you, so soon after I have found you," he said softly.

"I—I don't know what you mean," I whispered. I wanted to pull away, to break free of his grip. But I feared to offend him. He turned me to face him.

"I thought—for a moment I thought—no, forget I spoke."

"You thought I would jump?"

"Fall, perhaps. You are unsteady on your feet today."

"I told you, it's nothing."

"I'm concerned that I have asked too much of you. Let me see this foot. Perhaps we can improvise a little padding for the boot, or—"

"I told you. It is not an injury. My foot is malformed, it has been always. I will never walk straight."

"Show me." He took his hands from my waist and went to seat himself on the rocks, folding his arms and observing me calmly.

"I—" How could I tell him this was the most painful thing any-one could ask me to do? How could I explain how it shamed me to reveal this deformity? If Clodagh was right, this marked me as a child who should never have been born. And the man hardly knew me. He understood nothing.

"Why are you afraid, Fainne?" Eamonn asked softly.

"I'm not afraid!" I snapped, and with shaking hands I untied my boot and eased it off my foot. I unrolled my stocking, and hobbled over to sit by him. "There," I said abruptly. "I can't imagine why you would want to see." My cheeks felt hot with embarrassment.

Then he was kneeling beside me, and his hands were moving against my bare foot, seemingly heedless of its oddity, stroking the arch of it, following the inward curve, his fingers moving to encircle my ankle, warm and strong.

"This is not such a deformity that it would blind a man to your other charms. But it troubles you, I see that," he observed, still look-ing down at the foot, though his hand seemed to be moving up my leg, under my skirt, in a way that was quite unsettling. "So much that you seem different today. More remote. Like a creature poised for flight. Are you frightened, Fainne? I have told you, I am a good teacher. I would be gentle with you, and go slowly. There is no need to shy away."

Still his hand moved, stroking my calf, lifting the skirt, straying as if by chance to the knee, and higher.

"I—I—"

"You are afraid." He withdrew his hand, and came to sit by me once more, but closer. I hoped my sigh of relief was not too audible. "I will not rush you. Only—you must understand, for a man, there is an urgency in such matters, a—a need that is hard to deny. It can at times be painful to exercise self-control."

"But you will do so," I managed, my voice squeaking with nervousness.

"You might meet me halfway."

"I—I don't understand you."

"No? You cannot be unaware of my meaning, Fainne. Your words, your glances, have led me to believe you would not be averse to my attentions. Do not deny it. Since first I met you at Sevenwaters, I have seen it in your face, and in those mysterious dark eyes. In the lift of your brow and the toss of your head, in the way your body sways as you walk. A man would have to be a monk not to want you. A man would have to be mad, not to wish to touch that snow-pale skin, to feel the purity of that flesh against his own, to look down on you lying in his bed, with only the dark flame of your hair to hide your nakedness, and to know that you were his alone, a bright jewel never to be shared. I have not the strength to deny that longing, Fainne; I must make this plain to you, fear or no fear."

I was quite unable to form a reply. My heart thumped with shock. I had done this, without even trying? I had made him feel thus, without even employing the Glamour? Surely I misunderstood his words.

"I have shocked you, and for that I am sorry. But here, there are no prying eyes, no listening ears. You spoke very plainly to me. You seemed to be saying it was time to forget; time to move on. I don't know if I can do that, Fainne. But you could help me. With you, I might begin to wipe away the past."

"I—I don't think I—" I had folded my arms tightly around me, as if to stop myself doing something I would regret forever.

"Come now. I give you my word. I will do nothing you do not

enjoy. You need but tell me and I will stop. But you cannot lie to me. I know you want me. I see it in the way you blush, like a sudden flare of fire under the translucent skin of your cheek. I hear your need for me in your breathing."

He was well practiced. Before I could say a word, I was neatly trapped in his arms, my hands against his chest, my legs across his own so that I was almost on his knee, and he was giving me a kiss that seemed quite expert, not that I had any grounds for comparison. It was a kiss that began gently and became harder; a kiss that started with a soft meeting of lips, and grew into a wet, intimate probing of tongues, a hungry, suggestive kiss that left me breathless and shivering. Under my hand his heart was racing, and his own hands were moving adeptly, one on my back, holding me to him, the other on my inner thigh. There were some very odd sensations in parts of my body I did not want to think about, and the touch of his fingers made me gasp and shudder.

"Oh, Fainne," he murmured. "Come, come closer. Put your hands on me, sweetheart. Put your hand here, let me show you."

And suddenly, Grandmother's teaching was no help at all. Indeed, so shocked was I that I could scarce remember a word of it. I simply knew this was wrong. It was so wrong I simply could not allow it to happen. To scream or fight would be undisciplined, and give great offense. I made myself focus; made myself treat this as a puzzle to be solved, while his hands caressed my body and his lips strayed to my ear, and to my neck, and down toward my breasts. I could feel, under my hand, that part of his body he had urged me to touch. It was interesting how it changed under my fingers. I was not ignorant of such matters, despite my strange upbringing. Once, at the cove, I had seen a mare brought to a stallion; had observed the act with a great deal of wonderment, and decided it did not appear very enjoyable, for the mare at least. I had been aware, in Dan Walker's encampment, of secret trysts in corners, under blankets, or out in the night beneath the trees; of sounds and movements one learned to pretend to ignore. But now, with Eamonn's body hardening against me, and his breathing becoming harsh and uncontrolled, and his hand untying my bodice to bare my breasts to the winter sun, I knew I must make this stop.

Eamonn was reaching to undo his belt, he was pressing himself against my hand. Whatever the solution was, it must be quick. I could use the craft as I had once before, and cause him a lancing pain in the gut, a sudden weakness in the stomach. That seemed a little unkind; and arbitrary enough to be viewed with suspicion.

Now I was lying on the ground, and the whole length of his body was up against me, and his hands were becoming very insistent indeed. Across the grassy shelf the little horse gave a soft whinnying sound. Horses. Something about horses. If I could just think straight for a moment. A stallion could not perform, could not enter a mare, unless his equipment was altered by desire into a more useful sort of tool. An impressive sight indeed it made, when it was. Evidently it was the same for a man. And while I knew no specific spell, I could adapt one quickly; a charm used to modify the forms of things, to make soft hard, for instance, or hard soft. Not too sudden though; there must be no suspicion.

"Eamonn," I gasped. "I can't do this. It's not right. I always—I always said I would wait." Under my breath I muttered the spell, even as my hand touched that most secret part of his body. "That I would wait until I was wed." The spell seemed to be working with alarming rapidity. I saw the expression on his face change from intense excitement to astonishment to acute mortification. He lifted himself quickly away from my touch. "I'm sorry," I said. "I know how difficult this must be for a man."

"Indeed," he said after a moment or two. "Indeed."

"I—I just can't do it," I said, sitting up and beginning to refasten my gown with trembling fingers. "I was always brought up to believe such actions were sacred to the marriage bed. For a lady, I mean. I don't wish to offend you, or to—to cause you any distress. But I vowed I would never give myself to a man, save after he set his ring on my finger."

Eamonn seemed to be having a little trouble getting his breathing back under control.

"I'm sorry," I said again.

"No. It is I who should apologize. I expected too much of you, too soon. I forgot how young you are. You make it easy to forget that, Fainne."

"I had no intention—"

"Ah. Now you are not quite telling me the truth. For I think, at heart, we speak the same language, you and I. Come, it is best if we return home. You misunderstood, perhaps."

"Misunderstood what?"

"My position. My obligations. My intentions in inviting you here to Glencarnagh."

I felt humiliation, closely followed by a rising anger, and I spoke without thinking. "You had better be straight in your words, Eamonn. Why trouble to protect me by veiling the truth? You mean, you thought I would come here, and give myself to you, and be honored that such a grand man would bother to lie with me? You mean, your intention was merely to bed me and have done with it? A man enjoys an untried girl from time to time, does he not?" I could not keep my voice steady. My lack of control troubled me. I had thought myself so clever, with my little spell. Now I felt cheap and dirty, and worse still, I had really insulted him. He was not a man I would wish as an enemy.

But I had underestimated him yet again. I had read him as a great deal simpler than he was.

"You are very beautiful when you lose your temper," he said quietly, staring at me. "Your hair seems like flame in the sunlight. Your eyes glow with feeling. How can a man look at that, and not want you? You are dangerous, Fainne. Very dangerous. But I've always liked a challenge. Now let us enjoy the ride home, for it is a fair day. This is not finished between us. We are two of a kind, you and I. Let us speak further of this later. I'm sure we will find room for—negotiation."

He helped me up onto the horse, and we started back down the hill path, with me in the lead this time. The men-at-arms would be waiting. Our time away had been rather brief. I could imagine how they might interpret that. It would do nothing to improve my reputation among these folk. The thought sickened me.

"I told you." Eamonn's voice came from behind me, just audible over the fading roar of the great waterfall. "I don't take kindly to losing. But I think you will find this is a game in which both of us can be winners in the end."

Chapter Eight

That night I retired early, and Eamonn asked no questions. But sleep eluded me. My head ached, and I tossed and turned, one moment cold as ice, the next burning hot. There were creakings and rustlings in the house, and the sounds of guards changing shifts outside, a quiet exchange of words, booted feet trudging off to the kitchen, their owners perhaps hopeful that there would still be a fire on the hearth and a bite to eat. In the end I got up and slipped a cloak over my nightrobe, and went out along the hallway myself, knowing I would not sleep if I lay on my bed willing rest to come. I would seek out some chamomile tea, and I would visit the privy, and if I still could not sleep I would simply sit by candle-light and try to put my thoughts in order. It was not as if I had any real duties here. I could rest all day if I wanted to. Why else had I been brought here but to provide Eamonn with a little amusement, a piquant diversion in his well-ordered existence? That was all it amounted to. I had been stupid not to realize that. No wonder I felt cheap.

The house was asleep. Farther along the hall, faint light glowed from the kitchen fire, through the open doorway. Perhaps there were still folk about. But the passage was in shadow, lit only by a candle here and there in a small alcove, to make the way safe for such as I who felt the need to wander at night. The side chambers were dark. I walked softly in my door slippers, careful to disturb no one. I was not in a mood for company.

It was a very small sound that caught my attention, a rhythmic gasping, *ah—ah—ah*, under the breath. I paused outside the doorway to a darkened chamber.

I should have moved on straight away, when I saw them. But I found I could not. I stood fixed to the spot, staring. The faint light from the hall candles revealed them dimly. I recognized the woman. She worked in the kitchens, Mhairi was her name, a comely enough creature if a little slatternly, with a generous figure and fine dark eyes. She had her back to the wall, and her legs apart, and her skirt up around her waist, and Eamonn was doing to her what he had been unable to do to me, up by the waterfall. The effects of my spell had been short-lived. He was not embracing the woman; he had his two hands flat against the wall, on either side of her head, and he was scarce looking at her as he thrust and thrust with a grim-faced determination that I thought was not far from anger. Mhairi did not seem unwilling; it was her little cries I had heard, and in the shadows of the room I could see her eyes half-closed, her face flushed, her lips parted. I could not make my legs move to carry me away from where I had no business to linger. The pace of their movement increased, and Mhairi gave a shuddering moan, and then Eamonn cried out and pushed inside her one last time, and I backed away on silent feet, and fled to the relative safety of the kitchen, my cheeks hot with embarrassment and shame.

My dreams did nothing to dispel my feelings of unease and self-disgust, and in the morning I found I simply could not go out and about my daily business as if nothing at all had happened. Back in Kerry, if we were feeling out of sorts, there had been a simple solution. Father would either lock himself in the workroom to wrestle with his problems in his own way, or go walking out in the wind and sea spray, with only Fiacha for company. If it was summer I would find Darragh, and recite to him my tale of woe, or sit beside him in silence while the world came slowly back to rights. In winter I would meditate: I would fix my thoughts on a single phrase of the lore, or a fragment of verse, and let the rest drop away. In Kerry there was the time and space for such things. Here it was different. The girls were always about, and eager for my company. And Eamonn was here, Eamonn who had made it clear we had unfinished business. I could not face that, not yet. There were folk everywhere. There was no place for stillness.

My head was full of unwelcome thoughts. My mind was so jumbled it was no wonder I could not see my path ahead. Already winter was upon us, and I had achieved nothing, beyond a descent into confusion and self-doubt. For that I could thank the creatures who called themselves the Old Ones. I did not want to believe what they had told me, about the battle and what it might mean. I did not want to confront that. But I must. A serving woman brought warm water for washing, and I told her I was indisposed. I wished to spend the whole day alone in my chamber, I said. No, I did not require food and drink, beyond the jug of water I had already fetched. I had logs for my fire. She was to make sure everybody knew I was not to be disturbed. Everybody. I would be fine, as long as no one came to bother me.

Then I bolted the door and made up the fire, and settled cross-legged before it, with a folded blanket between me and the stone floor. It would be a long day, and my self-discipline had weakened somewhat since Kerry. Father always said cold was a state of mind. One must learn to deal with the way it made the body shiver and tremble and long for woollen blankets and mulled wine. One must learn to put that aside. I had sat from dawn to dusk under the standing stones, or on the ledges of the Honeycomb. But today I needed my blanket and my little fire. I was slipping. I was letting the ways of these folk get under my skin and change me.

Time passed. I started with the lore, because that came almost without thinking. Its flow carried me along, to a certain point. I fixed on fire; I thought of it in all its forms, and I began to go deeper into my trance, the breathing slower, the body bathed in light, the mind beginning to release itself, just on the edge . . . and there was a polite knock on the door.

"Fainne? Fainne!"

It was Deirdre. I was far distant now, and heard her voice as if through a barrier, from the bottom of a well. I ignored it, holding onto my stillness with all my will.

"Fainne!"

"Maybe she's asleep." That was Eilis.

"It's the middle of the day. She can't be asleep."

"Better leave her alone." Clodagh's voice, the voice of common sense. "They did say—"

"Yes, but—"

"Deirdre. They did say don't disturb her for anything. Not for anything."

"Yes, but—"

Their voices faded. But they had disturbed me. I found I could not return to my trance, and I felt sick, as one does when torn too abruptly from that other state of consciousness. Now that the words had intruded, they were followed by thoughts and feelings, and my mind was retelling me the events of yesterday and of last night, and failing to make any sense of it. All right, Eamonn had wanted a woman, and when I had thwarted him with my little spell, he had gone elsewhere. That was logical enough. Why should I object to the discovery that one was as good as another? Why should I care that he had only asked me here because he thought I would be easy prey, poor, innocent, adoring thing that I seemed? I could not have it both ways. I would not play Grandmother's game with him. I had already decided that, before ever we rode out together. So why did it matter that he had thought me so cheap, and had so easily satisfied himself with a substitute? What had I believed, that he genuinely thought me beautiful? That I might prove to be the cure for all his problems? Perhaps that he would consider making me his wife?

You're nothing, I said to myself. *It's Liadan he wants. To him, all other women are the same. All you were to him was another virgin for the taking. You're nothing. Beneath notice. What man would love a girl like you? Best stick to what you're good at.*

I stared across the room at the cobwebs around the doorway. The big spider in the corner was poised above the main web, dark and still, waiting. I focused on her. She shivered and trembled, and there on the stone wall was a tiny, jewel-colored creature that was partway between a bee and a bird, clinging to the ungiving surface with little, claw-like feet. It looked quite uncomfortable there, as if it would sooner have been in some rainbow grove wreathed in exotic flowers. I willed the spider back in her place, and watched her scuttle away into hiding, doubtless somewhat shaken.

I got up, the ability to be still quite gone for now, and poured myself a cup of water. As I bent over, jug in hand, something fell into the cup with a little plop. It was the bronze amulet from around my neck, the one Grandmother had given me. *Wear this always. Never take it off, you understand? It will protect you.* I fished it out of the cup and dried it on my skirt. The cord on which it had been strung was frayed through. I would have to find another. For now, I placed the small token carefully in the wooden chest I had brought with me from Sevenwaters, down at the bottom where it would be safe. One of the girls would have a bit of cord or ribbon which I could use.

Perhaps the water had settled me. I felt clearer in the head. And the sun was coming through the clouds, outside my window. The room seemed lighter. I stretched, and went back to my place before the fire. I folded my hands in my lap and closed my eyes. This time, I would use the eye of the mind to picture my most secret place, the place of my heart. A little cave, almost underground, but not quite. The light a soft blue-gray, as if light and shadow were one in this small, mysterious space. The only sound the gentle washing of wavelets on a pure sandy beach not two strides long. A place where earth and sea and sky most wondrously and sweetly met and touched. My mind was quiet. My heart was steady. A kind of peace touched my spirit. Subtly, I began to move into that realm beyond thought, which is the realm of light.

Some time later there was a tapping at the door, and voices again.

"Fainne! Are you awake?"

Clodagh, this time. She had changed her mind about disturbing me, then. But her words passed me without meaning. I remained still; I was too far away to be called back so easily.

"Fainne!" The tone was insistent. And then there was another voice, a man's.

"I thought you were told to leave your cousin alone to rest today."

"Yes, Uncle, but—"

"Didn't your mother teach you to obey instructions?"

A short silence. "Yes, Uncle Eamonn."

"She would not be pleased, then, that you have chosen to disregard them now you are away from home."

"Yes, but—"

"You heard me, Clodagh. Your cousin is tired, unwell perhaps. We should respect her wishes. I brought her here to rest, not to be constantly bothered. Now find something useful to do with yourself. All of you."

There was a mutinous sort of pause. Then three, or maybe four, small voices muttered, "Yes, Uncle Eamonn," and footsteps retreated, and there was silence. All of this I heard, yet remained still in my secret place, my safe haven. Somewhere, deep in my mind, the thought came to me, *It's time I took them home. Home to Sevenwaters. Home to the forest.*

By dusk I had completed my meditation, and come slowly back to here and now. I felt weary, but different. I felt I might sleep, and not dream evil dreams. My mind was calm. After fasting and silence, my body seemed somehow cleaner. I was a little closer to myself, the self of Kerry, the girl who had in recent times seemed almost lost to me. Perhaps, after all, she had been there all the time, that girl who could make decisions and see ahead, and know when to start and when to stop. Perhaps I had only needed silence to find her.

I would not go down to supper. I wanted to hold on to this feeling. I wanted to let it strengthen in me, so I would have the courage to face it all again. Especially, so that I could go to Eamonn, and thank him politely for his hospitality, and tell him I wanted to take the girls home, straight away. There was nothing to be negotiated between us, I would say. It was over before it ever happened. A mistake on both our parts. A misunderstanding.

I went to lie on my bed with a blanket over me, and I rehearsed this speech in my mind. It would be important to get it right. Eamonn was a powerful man for all his shortcomings, and I did not wish to offend him. But we must leave. It was clear to me now. I simply did not have it in me to do what Grandmother wanted. I was not what she thought me to be. I could not be like her. Even if she did as she threatened, and hurt my father, I still did not think I could do it. If the Old Ones were right, this was not just about the winning or losing of a battle. It went far beyond that. It was about the difference between a future, or no future at all. Surely such momentous events must unfold regardless of anything I might do. I was going to have to tell my grandmother this. I was going to have to refuse to do her will, and live with the consequences. Maybe I would ask Conor for advice. Maybe I would tell him the truth, and throw myself on his mercy.

I was feeling drowsy. The fire glowed gold, the candle was steady on its shelf. The folk of the household would be sitting down to supper, the children in their own quarters, perhaps squabbling over whether they should have woken me or not, for whatever trivial reason it had been. The men and women in the warmth of the kitchen. The lord of the túath alone at his fine table. I willed myself not to feel sorry for him. His loneliness was of his own making. It was his choice.

Warm and relaxed, I hovered on the verge of sleep. I wondered what the girls had wanted. They had not come back after Eamonn ordered them away. Probably some little drama, a cut finger or a lost kitten. There were plenty of folk to help them. I did not understand why they always came to me. Now I would sleep, and I would dream good dreams, of the sea and the sky, of old friends and times of innocence. In the morning I would start anew, as bravely as I could.

"Fainne."

At first I refused to believe it. I squeezed my eyes tight shut, as if to deny the familiar voice I heard right there beside my bed in the firelight.

"Fainne! Get up!"

She was there. Not just her image in the glowing coals, not just the subtle whisper of her voice inside my mind, but my grandmother herself, here with me, inside my darkened and bolted chamber. Cold with shock, I turned my head and let my eyes verify what my quaking heart already knew for truth. There she stood, not two paces from me, in her old woman form, wild hair, tattered garments, claw-like fingers, baleful stare. Her voice was vibrant with anger.

"Up! Out! Stand before me and account for yourself, girl!"

I did as she bid me, shivering in my nightrobe. My feelings of peace and confidence had vanished the moment I recognized her voice.

"H—how did you get here?" I whispered.

"You think I cannot command the power of transportation?" she snapped. "You underestimate me, girl. You'll never escape my observation. Don't even think of tricking me that way. Where is the amulet? What have you done with it?"

Sudden realization struck me like an icy chill. The amulet; a charm of protection, she had told me, and I, fool that I was, had believed her. The moment I had taken it off, I had become myself again. And now here she was, livid with fury, so brimful of destructive magic that her very fingertips crackled with it. I chose my words carefully. "The cord broke. I have laid the amulet away for safekeeping. In the morning I will find another cord, and wear it again. I have not forgotten what you bid me do."

"Show me."

I went to the wooden chest, unlocked it, and began methodically to lift out folded clothes, my hairbrush, other small items. My hands were shaking. Right at the bottom was the amulet, and as I put my fingers around it they encountered something else; a tiny object long forgotten, left year after year unnoticed, perhaps awaiting this very touch. It was like a blow to the heart. *You might forget*, said a voice deep in my memory.

"Well? Do you have it? Show me!"

I held out my hand for her, the bronze amulet on the palm. She sniffed.

"Very well. Tomorrow. Without fail. Remove this, and you put yourself and our great endeavor in extreme jeopardy. Remove it and you shed your last protection against these folk. And they are strong. Do you understand me, Fainne?"

"Yes, Grandmother." I understood well enough, if somewhat too late. If I did not wear her little charm, her little spell to keep me working her will, she would be quickly at my side and ready to punish both me and my father. This was no talisman of protection, but a mind-twister, a charm of control. No wonder I had felt, at times, that my thoughts were not my own. No wonder I had hated myself.

"Now, Fainne. I wonder if you have forgotten why you are here."

"No, Grandmother. But—"

"But?" The tone of menace in this single word near froze my will. I took a deep breath, and another, and I said to myself, Fire child. Find your strength, fire child.

"I am no longer sure I can do as you wish, Grandmother. I have—I have—"

At that moment I felt a spearing pain through my right temple, a pain that drove me to my knees and left me retching there on the floor with ill-tasting bile dribbling down my chin, for my stomach was empty from the day's fasting.

"I—I—"

"What was it you wanted to say, Fainne?" she inquired sweetly.

"I—at least hear me out. You can at least let me finish, before you punish me for my words."

"I can at least let you finish? Oh, dear. When will you realize I can do anything I wish? *Anything*, girl!"

"Anything, except the practice of the higher magic?" I whispered. "Anything, except the restraint my father exercises? That is not quite *anything*."

"How dare you! How dare you defy me! How dare you answer back!"

Another stab of pain, this time on the left side. I was crouched before her, my head in my hands, and the world spinning out of control before my tight-shut eyes.

"It's wrong." My voice was like a little thread; but my father had taught me well. Through the agony that pierced my skull, still I found the words. "What you want. The forest. The Islands. You've got it wrong. The battle must be won, not lost. The Islands must be saved, not thrown away. Without that, none of us can survive. I cannot do this, Grandmother. Not for you, not for my father. Not for anyone."

"Get up."

I did not think my legs would support me. The pain was fading slowly, but my whole body ran with sweat, and my stomach churned. I struggled up to stand, swaying, before her.

"Look at me, Fainne."

I forced myself to meet her gaze. Her eyes glowed darkly; she stared back as if to read the deepest secrets of my heart.

"They told you this. You talked to them. Which was it? The lady with the blue cloak and the honeyed voice? The one that hovers on the verge of sight, elusive on the margin between light and dark? Was it the maiden all rippling locks and robes of froth and bubbles, or the flame-haired lord with his imperious manner and his little mind games? Who was it? You must not heed them. They are the enemies of our kind. Our quest is to thwart their long goal, not aid it."

"I think you are wrong. And I cannot do it. Find yourself another tool. Indeed, since you have such power that you can be here by my side in an instant, why do you not complete this task yourself? Beside you, I am nothing. You are displeased with me. You make that clear. Wreak your own act of destruction, if you will. Seek your own vengeance."

She glared at me balefully, brows arched in derision.

"You're a very silly girl at times, Fainne. There's a right way for this to happen, and a wrong way. It must unfold. It must unfold according to the prophecy, to the very last. Why do you think I haven't bid you kill their leaders or sell their secrets to the enemy? Why do you think I've left you to your own devices so long? I want you to insinuate yourself, to creep into their lives and into their hearts, child. I want them to trust you. I want them to love you. Then, at the very end, you turn. You turn, smiling, and strike the mortal blow. You're made for this task, Fainne. It's yours and yours alone."

"I won't do it. Punish me all you will. I cannot continue to hurt the innocent, and abuse my craft, and blunder on heedless of the consequences. I could not do so even if the goal were one I believed in."

A charged silence. I stood breathing with all the control I could muster, wondering where the next bolt of agony would strike.

"Haven't you forgotten something?" asked my grandmother in silken tones. She pointed to the glowing embers of the fire. I turned. As I stared, the flames rose up of themselves, twisting and flickering to make an image. There was my father, alone in the workroom. Around him, instead of the neatly stacked shelves, the orderly ranks of bottles and jars, the carefully stored scrolls and manuscripts, there was a chaotic jumble, as if every scrap of paraphernalia he possessed, every talisman, every grimoire, every secret ingredient had been tossed together by some violent act of fate. He crouched on the floor in the center, straining to breathe, his chest heaving, his mouth gaping open in the fight for air. His clothing was in rags. He was like a skeleton, a fragile collection of bones that seemed held together only by the tight-stretched, pallid skin. He looked up and right at me with my grandmother's intense dark eyes.

I turned away, my heart pounding. I summoned all my will, but still my voice trembled.

"I know my father," I said. "This is terrible to see, if it is indeed a true vision. But my father seeks the path of light, even though it is barred to him. He would sooner suffer and die than see the innocent perish, and good things destroyed because I wanted to protect him. I know my father. I know him better than you do, for all he is your only son."

Then I felt the pain again, in my foot this time, twisting and burning, as if the very bones were gripped in an iron fist and squeezed tight. I let out a gasp of terror.

"You've never liked this foot much, have you?" observed Grandmother in kindly tones. "You always wished you were more of a beauty. Who'd blame you? I can't imagine why you don't employ the Glamour more. Still, you're here, in the house of a man of influence, and him still unwed. Quite a catch. Just think, Fainne. Once Sevenwaters is defeated this fellow can take all. All three holdings in one. Your son could inherit that. Ciarán's grandson. One of our kind. He'd be the strongest landholder in all Ulster. And you'd be his mother. With power like that, who needs beauty?"

There was another wrenching wave of agony through my foot, and I clenched my teeth tight, not to cry out aloud. The pain ceased.

"There," she said calmly. "Have a look at that."

I looked down, and felt the blood drain from my face. Where, before, had been my right foot, the one whose form was just a little different, a touch crooked, a trifle inward-curved, now there was a hideous paw like that of some monster in an old tale, a travesty of a foot with hairy, swollen skin, and bulbous toes tipped by twisted, yellow claws as thick as horn.

"I could do more," she said. "A great deal more. The hands. The face. The body itself. Step by step. Men'd be running away screaming. You'd never dare put your foot outside this door again. Still want to defy my bidding, do you?" She seated herself casually on the edge of the bed, smiling.

I looked down at the monstrosity I wore in place of a foot. I summoned up a spell to change it back. I muttered the words.

"Oh, no," said Grandmother quietly. "It's not as easy as that." And before I could finish the incantation, the counterspell was already in place, and my hideous, hairy paw stayed as it was.

"Very well," I said as tears pooled behind my eyes. "Perhaps you might do your worst. Perhaps I might be turned into a monster. Then I would do as my mother did, and end it. Slice my wrists. Step from the tower at Sevenwaters. Walk out into the lake, until the waters closed over my head. Then what?"

"Wretched girl. Your father has a great deal to answer for. Here." She snapped her fingers, and my foot returned to its former self. I sucked in my breath, and bit back the abject thank-you that sprang to my lips. I would not let her know how close I had come to giving in, when I saw what she could do to me.

"Sit down, child. Put this blanket around you. It's cold. Got some nice things in your chest there, I see. A few good gowns. That's a relief. Can't come courting a rich man looking like some tattered fishwife. And what a pretty little shawl, all over colors. Comes from a tinker's market, does it?"

"It's nothing." With a great effort I kept my face and voice impassive. I thought I knew where she was heading. "You can take it if you want," I added. "It's nothing to me."

"No? Still, it's somewhat cheap and tawdry for my tastes, Fainne; the sort of trifle a traveling man might give to his sweetheart. I would hardly wear such a gaudy thing."

"Foolish of me to suggest it," I said, getting up and starting to lay my belongings back in the chest.

Behind me, my grandmother spoke again. "So, you will let your father suffer and die. You will allow yourself to become a monster. You care nothing for your own future. This surprises me, I must admit it. You are not quite the girl I thought you to be. But you will not defy me, Fainne."

"I don't know what you mean. You cannot make me do what you want. You cannot force me."

"You think not? What if you were to see all you loved, all you cared about, struck down one by one? What if you watched the slow destruction of all you hold dear? Watched this, knowing it was in your power to stop it? What then? Would you fail to act, to protect them?"

"I don't know what you mean," I breathed, but a dark horror was spreading through me as I recognized the meaning of her words. "I have nobody. I care for nobody save my father. And I told you, I know what his mind would be on this."

"Oh, make no doubt of it, he will continue to suffer. As for the others, I don't believe you. I have seen you, from time to time. I've seen the look in your eye. I've watched you playing with these children, tucking them into bed, pretending you were annoyed by their pestering. I see the way your hands linger on your tinker's trifle there, as if the memories in its folds were too precious to let go. Make no doubt of it, Fainne. You will see it all, step by agonizing step. An unfortunate fall from a horse. A young girl fallen into the wrong company. A stew eaten by the roadside, with an injudicious choice of mushrooms. A nasty incident with a fishhook. Accidents all. As for you, perhaps you will be the only one unharmed. Your job will be to watch, as they suffer around you. To watch, knowing you could have stopped it. Knowing that, without your disobedience, none of it needed to happen."

"Stop! Stop it! How do I know this is true, anyway? You could be lying to me. My father might not be sick at all. I might defy you and all could still be well!"

"You think so?" She glanced down at my foot. "If you choose to put that to the test, I cannot stop you, my dear. It would be your risk. And you're right, you cannot know about your father. Not unless you go back to Kerry. And if you do that, I assure you, his bones will be bleaching on the sand before ever you reach your little cove. Of course, you could always send a tinker's lad with a message." She glanced toward the wooden chest, where the shawl now lay neatly folded away. "You might always do that. But who's to say he would get there safely, the roads being what they are? He'd as like be murdered by the way for his little pack of cheap goods, as reach his journey's end."

"Stop it! This is evil!"

"Huh. Evil, is it? You've much to learn. Good and bad, shade and sunlight, there's but a hair's breath between them. It's all one in the end. Now tell me. Tell me everything you've done since you came here. Every detail."

"Haven't you been watching me each step of the way? Don't you know already?"

She cackled. "Hardly. I see fragments. A bit here, a bit more there. Pieces of a puzzle. A puzzle that concerns me. That's why I'm here. Now tell me. Then we'll work out what comes next. You've been wasting time. There'll be no more of that, do you hear?"

"Yes, Grandmother."

I told her. Heart clenched tight with misery, head full of unshed tears, I told her everything. I had to tell her because it was my fault. I had allowed these folk to creep under my skin. I had allowed them to charm me, and I had started to become one of them. And now, I could not stand by and see Sibeal or Clodagh or the others hurt. I could not stand by as Aunt Aisling lost yet another child. In particular, I could not let my grandmother develop any further interest in Dan Walker's family, wherever the road might have taken them. She had set a very neat trap, and I had walked right into it.

At last it was all out. The tale of the fire, though I left out how I felt about my walk in the forest with Conor, and what I had experienced at the celebration of Samhain. The story of what I had said to Eamonn, and my journey here to Glencarnagh, and how things had unfolded between us. I said nothing of the Old Ones, and as little about the children as I could. In particular I made no mention of Sibeal and her strange, clear eyes, a seer's eyes.

"Mm," said Grandmother when I had quite finished. "You must use this man Eamonn, that much is plain. Must and will. I knew his father. This is another the same. A very powerful man, Fainne. And a dangerous one. A man without honor. A man who will not hesitate to stab his brother in the back, if it should suit his purpose. A man who never forgets a slight."

"You are wrong, surely." Odd as Eamonn's manner sometimes seemed, it was hard to believe this of a man so bound by convention. Had he not said to me that he had never broken the rules?

"Don't believe it. He is the answer to our problem. Use his hatred. Use his desire. Make him want you so much he will promise you anything you ask him."

"That's ridiculous. Eamonn could have any woman he pleased. His interest in me is momentary. He does not mean to offer me marriage. I'm certain of it."

"Then you must change his mind for him. Take control. Use the craft. Make him burn for you."

"I—I cannot. This shames me, and demeans him. It is—it is not fair."

"Fair? Fair, she says?" Grandmother gave another cackling laugh. I wondered how long it would be before someone heard her and came tapping on the door to ask if I were quite well. "Forget fairness. Forget honor. Meaningless concepts, the two of them. There's only one thing that matters here, Fainne. Power. Your power over this man. His power to break the alliance. Our power to defeat the Fair Folk. Power and vengeance. The rest is nothing."

"Yes, Grandmother."

"Now tell me again. Tell me what he said about your aunt Liadan. And tell me what he said about her husband."

"I need not repeat it. I know what must be done."

"Huh! You? That's a little hard to believe, from your performance so far."

"I know what must be done," I repeated grimly. "You'd best leave me alone to get on with it."

"What? Get on with what?"

So I set it out for her, step by inevitable step: a plot that fed on jealousy and obsession, that used subterfuge and treachery to achieve its end. I could scarcely believe that I must go through with it. But there seemed to be no other way. When I was finished, my grandmother smiled at me, little pointed teeth in a mouth wizened by age.

"Good," she cooed. "Very good, Fainne. Perhaps you may become something after all, for all your unprepossessing looks."

"Grandmother, you must trust me to go through with this. There will be no need for you to come again. Do that, and it could be difficult for me to keep their trust."

She quivered with mirth. "Giving me orders now, are you? I'll come if I want, girl."

"You're not listening. I give you my word. I will do as you ask, as long as—as long as you do not—"

"Hurt those you love? Oh dear, love is such a confusing thing for a young girl, isn't it? We'd all be better off without it. The sooner you realize that, the easier life will be for you. Never choose your man for love. There's no future in that."

"Do you agree? Will you trust me to carry this out for you?"

"Trust? Huh! I'll need a safeguard. And mark my words, if you can't make this plan work, you'll need to take more drastic action. I'll give you a little time, just long enough. But I want to see progress, Fainne. I want results. You're right, I don't gladly come to these parts. Wear the amulet. Then I'll know you are safe. Don't take it off. Never, you understand?"

She was staring at me intently again, as if to see deep within. Thank the great goddess she had never mastered the art of reading another's mind, of speaking without words. *And she could only see me when I wore it.* Sweet Brighid, it was true. I had been stupid. I had been blind indeed.

"Yes, Grandmother. In the morning I will find a strong cord, and put your token back around my neck. I promise."

"I hope you're not lying to me. I'll know if you do not keep this promise. And it will be others who suffer."

I bit my lip and refrained from reply.

"Well, now," she said expansively. "What a pleasant little visit. Take care to get this right, Fainne. Don't scare me like that again. Let me down, and I will show you how creative I can be, I promise you. Do the right thing, and it may be a long time before you hear from me again."

"Yes, Grandmother."

"Farewell, then."

I watched as she faded, slowly, in the dim light from glowing fire and solitary candle. I stood staring until all trace of the hideous, disheveled old crone was quite gone. Even then, I passed my hand through the air once, twice, three times before I was satisfied there was nothing there. It was dark outside now. Supper would be over, the little girls getting ready for bed. Eamonn would be seated alone before the hall fire, with the wine jug for company. Maybe I should start tonight. My heart quailed. Why had I believed I had the strength to defy her? Why had I let myself think I might choose my path, might strive toward light instead of darkness? There was no choice for me, and there never had been.

And the amulet. How foolish had I been, not to recognize that for the witch's charm it undoubtedly was? *Wear this always. It will protect you.* A mind-twister, most potent of controls; through it she could keep watch on me and bend me to her own will. I had read of such a charm long ago, in the dusty pages of an old grimoire. While I wore it, she could find me. The moment I had taken it off she had known; known and come hastening after me, enraged and—and something else as well. Almost frightened. As if a Fainne outside her control were infinitely more dangerous to her than all the Fair Folk in the world. But that could not be right. As a sorceress I was half-trained, scarce tried in the more challenging branches of the art, hindered by my youth and inexperience. By contrast, my grandmother was a master, more powerful even than my father, for had she not captured him in her own spell of deathly sickness? I must have been mistaken. I glanced toward the wooden chest. The amulet was secure. In the morning I must put it on again. I must keep my word. It was the only way. I would protect them, my father, the girls, the family and—and everyone who was close to me. I could not watch her destroy them one by one.

I heard folk moving about in the hallway. It was not so very late. Grandmother had come and gone between the sitting down to supper and the last quenching of candles. I should go and speak to Eamonn now, while I had the courage. Quickly I stripped off my nightrobe and, shivering, dressed in a fresh gown. I pulled my hair into a ribbon at the nape of my neck. I put on my indoor slippers, and told myself I would never, ever complain about my twisted foot again. I splashed my face with water from the jug, all the while feeling the thud of my heart and the cold clutch of fear inside me. That sensation would never be gone now, not until the task she had set me was complete. And after that, nothing would matter anymore.

I opened the door cautiously, hoping I might slip along the hallway unnoticed. I took one step out and halted. Sibeal sat on the floor of the passage with her cloak around her to keep out the cold. She was so still I could only just see her there in the shadows. She did not speak, but looked up at me, and my candle flame flickered small but sure in the water-clear surface of her strange eyes. She rose to her feet in total silence. As I opened the door wider, she moved across like a small ghost, and came past me into my chamber. I closed the door behind us.

For a moment she said nothing.

"What is it, Sibeal? Why were you waiting there?"

"The others said not to tell you. Not now. They said it was too late."

"What? Not to tell me what?" Could there be anything worse than what had already befallen me this day? My mind raced through the possibilities. News from Sevenwaters. Maeve. News from farther afield. My father. "What is it? Tell me!"

The child regarded me gravely. "We did try to tell you. But you wouldn't answer. And then Uncle Eamonn got cross, and made us go away."

I grabbed her by both arms and gave her a little shake. "Tell me!" I said through gritted teeth.

"You don't need to hurt me. You don't need to be angry."

I reminded myself that she was only eight years old, and that she had waited, silent in the dark, until I was ready to come out. "I'm sorry. I'm—I'm worried, that's all. Is it bad news?"

"No. It's just that that pony was here. The one in your stories. We thought you'd like to know. We thought you'd like to see. But it's too late now."

If I had felt fear before, it was nothing to the anguish that gripped my heart now.

"What pony?" I whispered, as if I did not know the answer.

"The white pony. You know, the one in all your stories. He let us pat her, and Eilis gave her a carrot."

"He?" I breathed.

"The man. The man in the stories, the one with the little gold ring in his ear. He was asking about you."

"Darragh? Darragh was here today?" My voice shook. He was here, and Grandmother was here, and she had said—she had said, *You could send a tinker's lad with a message.* She had said, *He's as like to be murdered on his way.* "Maybe it wasn't him," I said, clinging to foolish hope. "Why would he come here? He's got work in the west, long miles from Glencarnagh. Maybe it was somebody else. Where is he now, Sibeal? Quick, tell me!"

Sibeal's tone was solemn. "Gone. Him and the pony both. Uncle Eamonn sent him away. Uncle Eamonn was cross."

"How long ago? Where was he going?"

"Away. I don't know where."

"Which way? East, to Sevenwaters? West? Which way? How long, Sibeal?"

"What's the matter, Fainne?" Her eyes were wide and questioning, almost fearful.

"I'm sorry, I'm sorry. It's all right. You did well to wait for me, so you could tell me. I'm just—I'm just—"

"Upset that you missed him? We thought you would be. That's why we tried to tell you before. But you wouldn't answer the door."

"I'm sorry," I said again. Sorrier than she would ever know. That he had been here was strange enough. Who knew why he had come? That I had not seen him was cruel indeed. But it was better this way. He was gone, and I would not see him again, and that meant he was safe from Grandmother. Perhaps he had been in these parts to visit the old woman, Janis. Perhaps that was it. In any event, this was better. Much better. Why, then, did it hurt so much that I felt as if my heart were being ripped in two?

"I'm sorry, Fainne," said Sibeal in a little tiny voice. "He went west, I think. Before sunset. He said he had to get back quickly. But he wanted to wait until you were better and could come down to talk to him. Uncle Eamonn made him go away. Uncle Eamonn was really angry."

"I—was he—was Darragh well? Did he talk to you?" Let her tell me everything, every word, every gesture. Not that it would ever be enough.

"He gave me a message for you," said Sibeal solemnly. "He made me practice it."

I waited.

"He said, Say farewell to Curly for me. Tell her to keep out of trouble until I come back. He wanted me to get it exactly right."

"But he mustn't come back!" My voice shook as fear seized my vitals anew. "He can't! I can't let him come back!"

"What's wrong, Fainne?" Sibeal's colorless eyes scrutinized me, their expression anxious.

"Nothing," I muttered. "Nothing. It's all right, Sibeal. You have done well, very well. I am in your debt. Now, it must be past your bedtime, and you're cold. Off you go, back to the others. And, Sibeal?"

She turned her small, pale face up toward mine.

"Don't talk about this. Please. I don't like asking you to keep secrets. But don't speak of this to your uncle, or to the others. It's very important."

She gave a little nod, and slipped silently out the door.

I had one night. Only one night before I must slip the talisman around my neck and be my grandmother's creature again. Darragh had come, and I had missed him. Darragh had said he would come back. He must not come back. I had until dawn to find him and tell him so. After that, I could have no more secrets from my grandmother. After that, it would not be possible to have friends.

A good pony can travel a long way between sunset and bedtime. Across open land, when her rider is in a hurry, she can traverse many miles. Beyond the borders of Glencarnagh, Aoife might be, and still moving westward, westward to the barren shores of Ceann na Mara. One thing I knew for certain. I could not ask Eamonn for help. *A man who takes what is mine, pays in kind*, he had said. I heard Sibeal's serious little voice. *Uncle Eamonn was really angry*. There would be no going along the hall and asking politely for the loan of a horse and a couple of men with torches. I must make this journey alone and unobserved, and be back in my chamber before dawn. Somehow I must cover the miles, and I must find him.

A great sorcerer like my father would have used the Glamour; used it fully, to effect a total transformation. He would have run through woodland and pasture as a fleet-footed deer, or flown on strong wings as an owl or some other bird of the night. I knew, in theory at least, how this was done. But my father had forbidden me to try it. It was too dangerous. One might make the change and be unable to return. One might be trapped in the altered form forever, or, disastrously, left as neither one thing nor the other. And it depleted the craft; sapped the strength. All the same, time was passing and I was almost desperate enough to try. My heart thumping, my blood racing, I stood by my window looking out into the night, and wondered if I dared span the distance from woman to bird, from earthbound human creature to winged being of the air. What if I failed, and dropped from the sky to crash on the stones below? But how else could I be there in time?

The moon peered between clouds. A breeze rustled through the hedges, stirring the bare branches of the old elms that sheltered the garden's orderly beds and ink-dark fishpond. Out there, close by the hedge, a horse was standing. The moon caught the shadow-gray of her coat, lighting it to a delicate pearl. Perhaps the hand of the goddess was on me this one night. I moved as swiftly as I could. A dark cloak; my outdoor shoes in my hand, for quiet. Then a spell. Not to alter my form, not much anyway. A half-change: merely a shadowy effect, so I might pass unnoticed if I were lucky. I moved on silent feet along the hallway, past the chamber where Eamonn sat alone. I went out by the kitchens, ducking into a small alcove as the guards passed by laughing and joking on their way to a late supper and good ale. I slipped away before the next shift came on duty. I followed the line of the hedge until there she was, the little horse I had ridden before, now waiting in the night for me placidly, not at all startled as I appeared right under her nose. How had she escaped her stable and made her way here unnoticed? Perhaps she was an Otherworld creature, for was she not already far older than any horse had a right to be, and still so bright and eager? She had once been Liadan's, after all, and Liadan was said to possess some powers beyond the ordinary. At any rate the mare was here and seemed willing. That did not solve the problem of how I was going to get up on her back, and ride without saddle or bridle. It did not help me know which way to go.

"Come," I whispered. "Come on. Hurry."

Now she was moving away from me, down the line of the hedge, blending into the shadows.

"Wait." I hastened after. By the stone wall that kept wandering pigs from the kitchen garden, she halted.

"Good," I muttered. "Good. You know how it's done, I see that." Pulling on my shoes, I scrambled up on the wall and thence to the horse's back, where I perched precariously without saddle or blanket, without bridle or rein to help me. "All right," I said softly. "I'm going to need all the help I can get here. You'll have to travel fast. And quietly. And not let me fall off. Understand? Now find Aoife. Find Darragh for me." I put my hand against her neck, willing her to hear me, willing her to know what must be done. Foolish, really. It was not I who could whisper in a horse's ear and win her lifelong friendship. It was not I to whom a wild creature would return, for love alone. But the gray horse lifted her head and pricked her ears, and she moved off steadily westward, past the hedges, across a little bridge, by the hazel trees and out into the shadowy night. I twisted both hands into her mane and gripped on with my knees. I would not fall off. I would not. I would get there and back by dawn. I must. When I found him I would tell him he must go straight home to O'Flaherty's and never come near me again. I would tell him that, and bid him goodbye, and then I would ride back to Glencarnagh. It was simple, really.

Time passed and the horse moved onward into the night, at first steadily, as if the moonlight were enough to show her the way. It was cold. It was so cold, I could not unbend my fingers for the cramp. My feet were numb and my ears ached with the chill. I could feel spasms of shivering through my body, like waves of icy water on a bone-cold shore.

Just as well she seemed to know where she was going, I thought grimly, wondering how long I might last before my frozen body lost the will to cling on, and I slipped from her back to the hard ground. One thing was certain. If I fell off there was no way I could summon the strength to get back on.

At first the world of night had seemed a silent one. But as we traveled onward into the west, I became more and more aware of subtle sounds. Over the quiet footsteps of the gray mare came a rustling and a creaking, as if the trees bent to observe our passing. Once I thought there was a distant howling, as of hungry wolves. I told myself I was mistaken. Something hooted in the dark branches above. A croaking chorus greeted us as we passed a darkly shining stretch of marshland. Once, there was a sudden whirring of leathery wings, and a high-pitched ringing as bats flew over our heads and away to some subterranean cavern. I was so cold I could barely stay awake, for all the urgency of the journey. I was so tired I thought I might stop pretending I could hold on, and simply curl up in the bracken and sleep. A nice long sleep. After all, who'd miss me?

The horse had slowed. Her head turned one way and then the other. She took a step and halted. She took another and paused. I was abruptly awake again, my heart thumping with alarm.

"You must know the way!" I said to her sharply. "You must! Why come so far, to give up now? Can't you follow Aoife's tracks as a hound would? What's wrong with you?"

She trembled a little, standing there in the night. We were on the verge of open ground; the moonlight showed gentle hillocks studded with groves of small trees.

"Go on!" I hissed. "Quick, before we both freeze! Don't you know we must be there and back before morning? Go! Please!"

I kicked her sides with my feet and squeezed with my knees. I had so little strength left, I doubt she noticed. "Oh, please," I whispered into the darkness, but the mare stood unmoving. My mind pondered, on some distant level, what explanation I might give Eamonn when I was discovered out here in the morning, half-frozen, with a horse that did not belong to me. Maybe I would die of cold. At least that would save having to make up excuses.

There was a hooting overhead, and something dark flew by with a sudden whoosh of wings. I thought I felt a small feather drift downward past my nose. I sneezed. There was another hoot. The tone of it sent a clear enough message. *Come on then, stupid. We haven't got all night.*

The little horse moved forward. Ahead of us the owl flew from side to side, waiting on a low branch, on a stone wall, on a rocky outcrop. Impatient. *Come on. Can't you go any faster?* The horse began to trot, and then, when we emerged onto some sort of real track, to canter. I was bounced up and down like a sack of grain. I gripped her mane anew and bent forward, willing my knees to keep hold. Pain arched through my legs and back. I clenched my teeth tight.

The owl flew onward, and the mare followed. I was put in mind of Fiacha, the raven. Just so was his manner of flight: a little in front, a little behind, a pause on one side or the other, giving the distinct impression that he thought humans unbelievably, tediously gradual, but that his job was to keep an eye on them, so he had better do it. I wondered where Fiacha was now. Did he perch on a ledge above the Honeycomb and watch the sorcerer Ciarán as he coughed out his lifeblood among the shattered tools of his ancient craft? Or had he been banished by my grandmother, leaving my father quite alone? Why did they come, these creatures of the Otherworld that guarded us and guided us as no simple owl or raven had the wit or the will to do? The bird flew onward into the night, leading my horse forward up hill and down glen, through marshland and woodland and safe beyond the borders of Glencarnagh.

At last, under bare-limbed apple trees, we halted. The owl sat above us, perched on a moss-covered branch, silhouetted against the moon. I saw her reach down, fussily, to adjust her plumage. I felt as if I had been picked up, and shaken like a churn of cream, and set suddenly down again. Every bone in my body ached.

The woodland around us was still. The mare stood immobile. The owl made no sound. They were waiting for me to do something. I forced my body to move, and half-slid, half-fell from the mare's back to the ground. My legs were like jelly. I stayed on my feet only because my hand still gripped her mane. She stood steady, unperturbed; a rare gift of a horse, this one.

Down a gentle slope before us there were more trees, and water glinting silver in the soft light of the moon. And there was another small light as well, a warm, flickering sort of light. I detected a faint smell of something savory in the chill air: surely it could not be oaten porridge? Then the mare gave a little whickering sound, and from down the hill there was a reply, a soft whinny. I saw a figure rise to his feet beside the glowing camp fire, and turn slowly toward me. Leaning heavily against the horse's shoulder, I stumbled forward.

Then a lot of things happened quite rapidly without a single word spoken. Soft running footsteps and a sharp intake of breath. An arm around me, supporting my faltering progress to the fireside. A cloak over my shoulders, blissfully warm. I could not sit down, my body was too sore; a folded blanket smelling strongly of horse was produced, and I was eased to a half-lying position, as close to the fire as was safe. There was a tiny clank of metal, as of a pannikin being used to fill some other vessel. Then a hand curled my frozen fingers around a cup of something hot and fragrant. Tremors coursed through my body, my teeth chattered, I could not have uttered a word even if I had known what to say. Darragh busied himself building up the fire, throwing on a log or two, blowing on the coals. The flames licked up; my face began to thaw. I took a sip of the beverage he had provided. It was a tea, very hot and very sweet. I had never tasted anything so good. At last Darragh settled himself across the fire from me, and looked at me direct.

"That's a fine wee mare you have there," he observed. "Learned to ride, I see, since you left me."

For a moment I was speechless. Was that all he could think of to say? On second thoughts, it was typical.

"The way I remember it, *you* left *me*," I snapped, but my voice came out sounding shivery and pathetic. "But yes, I can ride. A bit. Just as well. I have to be back before dawn."

Darragh looked at me. "Is that so?" he said.

"You don't need to sound like that," I retorted.

"Like what, Fainne?"

"Like you know best. Like you think I'm stupid for coming here. I don't know why I bothered." A new bout of shivering seized me, and I clutched the cloak tighter around me.

Darragh watched me in silence for a while. The little gold ring in his ear glinted in the firelight.

"Why did you come?" he asked eventually.

"I—to tell you. To tell you something important."

Now he was stirring his pannikin over the fire. The savory smell arose again. Peg and Molly and the others always cooked an oaten porridge in the mornings. Kept out the chill, that was what Peg said. He took the pot off the heat, and brought it around to me.

"No golden platters here," he said. "No silver spoons. Not used to catering for fine ladies, you see. But the food's good. Come on, Fainne. You must eat."

"I'm too tired to eat."

"Here," he said gently, and settled himself by me. "Eat, and don't talk." He dipped the horn spoon into the pot, and I found myself opening my mouth and being fed like a bird in the nest. It would have been humiliating, but the cautious expression on his face, the great care with which he went about the task, somehow made it all right between us. Besides, the porridge was delicious, and I discovered I was very hungry indeed.

"Good," said Darragh from time to time. "Well done. Good girl." And soon enough it was all gone.

"I'm sorry," I said, my voice somewhat stronger. "Was that going to be your breakfast?"

Darragh did not reply. He was sitting close by me, looking into the fire, arms folded. The silence drew out. At length he spoke with some diffidence.

"Better tell me. Better tell me what it is."

"You tell me first. Why you came to Glencarnagh. What you're doing so far from home, and in the middle of winter. Aren't you supposed to be working for O'Flaherty?"

"I am. On our way back there now, me and Aoife. He wasn't overkeen to let me take the time to come to Sevenwaters. Had to get Orla to sweet-talk him. In the end he said I could go, but I've given my word to be back there by dark of the moon. Not a lot of time."

I did my best to take this in. "Who's Orla?" I asked.

Darragh glanced at me sideways. "O'Flaherty's daughter. The younger one."

"I see."

"No you don't, Fainne."

"Yes I do. I suppose she's good with horses, is she?"

"Very good," he said, his teeth gleaming white in the darkness as he grinned. "A capable rider, for a girl. Understands all the tricks."

"Yes, well, she would, I suppose. And no doubt she's a beauty as well?"

"Oh, yes," said Darragh, stretching out his hands to warm them at the fire. "Long golden hair, cheeks like roses, eyes blue as a summer sky. Same as her sister. They've suitors lining up from here to the Cross, the two of them."

He was teasing me.

"Forget I asked," I said crossly. "Now answer the question. Why are you here?"

"I got anxious. Worried about you. Seemed to me you might be in trouble, and need help."

"What?"

"No need to sound so shocked. Rode to Sevenwaters, was told you were gone. Came on to Glencarnagh, discovered you'd no need of me whatever. Now I'm on my way home. Simple tale. I made a mistake. Not the first."

I could not think what to say, so I remained silent. I was starting to feel almost warm at last, what with the fire and the cloak and the porridge. My body felt better, for all the aching and the shivering. It was my mind that didn't seem to be working very well. All I could think of was how short one night was, and how many things there were to say, and how every time I opened my mouth it was the wrong words that came out.

"Fainne?" His voice was gentle in the darkness.

"Mmm?"

"Tell me. Tell me what's wrong. Why would you ride all that way in the dark to find me? What is it? What can be so important that you let yourself near freeze to death?"

His kindness came close to overwhelming me. It all flooded back, my father, Grandmother and the amulet, Maeve and the fire, Eamonn. I longed to tell him everything, every part of it; to unburden myself of my guilt and my fear. But I could not. He must stay outside it. I must keep him outside it.

"I came to tell you to go home, and never come back," I said flatly. "You mustn't come back, Darragh. You mustn't try to see me again. It's important."

There was a pause.

"You rode out here in the dark to tell me this?"

"Yes. It's what must be. Believe me."

"I see," he said tightly.

"No, you don't." I could not disguise the misery in my tone. "You don't see at all. But we are friends, despite everything. I must ask you to trust me, and do my bidding."

He narrowed his eyes at me. "Tell me. What's this fellow to you, the lord of Glencarnagh? Unpleasant piece of work, that one. What's he to you?"

"None of your business. What did he say to you?"

"Sent me on my way, quick smart. Suggested an armed escort to the border. And me a traveling man. I declined his kind offer. He told me no, I couldn't see you, today or tomorrow or any day in the year. Said you were there as his very special guest, and you were not to be disturbed. Riffraff such as myself should know better than to pester a lady. Words to that effect. Made me wish for a moment or two that I was a fighter, not a musician. What does that mean, Fainne? Very special guest?"

"I'm sorry he treated you thus." My voice was shaking. "I was ill. Indisposed. I did not know you were there."

"And are you happy to let this fellow make your decisions for you? Content to have him choose your friends?"

I did not answer.

"Fainne. Look at me."

I turned my face toward his. He seemed very pale, and very serious.

"Would you wed this man? Is that what it is? Tell me the truth."

"None of your business," I whispered.

"Oh, yes, it is. Now tell me."

Reluctantly I nodded. "It's not impossible."

"A bit old for you, isn't he?" said Darragh bluntly.

"Such a match is not unheard of. It's the woman's age that is more important, surely, if a man wants to get an heir."

Darragh never got angry. That was one of the good things about him. I thought he came close to it then. His jaw tightened. But he kept his voice calm.

"So, you would wed for a name and a fortune. You would bear an old man's sons, for that."

"You wouldn't understand."

"Try me."

"You couldn't understand."

Darragh was silent for a moment. Then he observed, "Told me that plain enough before, didn't you? Something about a stray dog, I think it was."

"I spoke without thinking, that time. I'm sorry if I hurt you. But this is something I can't explain to you. I'm simply asking you to stay away, that's all." Oh, but I ached to tell him the truth.

He waited a little. As the night wore on, the air about us was growing colder and colder. Now the small fire, the warm cloak were not enough to take away the frozen feeling which seemed to come from deep inside me. I thought, if I were able to weep, my tears would turn to drops of ice before ever they could fall from my eyes. "Do you love this fellow?" asked Darragh flatly, not looking at me anymore.

"Love!" I exclaimed, sitting up in my shock and suppressing a groan of pain. "Of course not! Love has nothing to do with this. Who'd wed for love, anyway? That's just foolishness. There's nothing in such a match but sorrow and waste." I thought of my mother and my father, and how both their lives had been destroyed by the bond between them.

"Then you'd advise my sister Roisin not to wed Aidan, would you? They've plans for a wedding in the autumn, when she's seventeen. Aidan has his own little bit of land now. You think they'd best not go ahead with it?"

I scowled at him. "That's different," I said.

"How different? You mean, because they're simple folk, unlike yourself and your great lord back there?"

"Of course not! I thought you knew me better than that!"

"So did I," said Darragh mildly. "But you keep surprising me."

"It's different because—because—I can't tell you. But it is."

"Uh-huh," said Darragh. We sat in silence for a while. The cold seemed to come in from all sides. The only parts of me that were even half warm were my hands, which I was holding out close to the fire. The rest of me ached with the chill, not to speak of the damage the ride had caused. I thought, vaguely, of how I must climb back on the horse before dawn and do it all again.

Darragh sat with his hands around his knees, looking into the flames. He was solemn; not his smiling self at all.

"You haven't convinced me," he said.

"Convinced you of what?"

"That you're all right. That you don't need keeping an eye on. I don't believe it for an instant. Your words are giving me one story and your eyes another. Come on, now. You can talk to me. There's no secrets between us, you and me. What is it that's troubling you so badly?"

"Nothing." My voice quavered, despite my best efforts. "Nothing. I'm just telling you, go away and never come back here."

"And what will you do, when I'm gone?"

Put on the amulet and finish my grandmother's work, so I can keep you safe.

"Ride back to Glencarnagh, and be in my chamber before they know I was gone," I told him. "Get on with my life. That's no concern of yours."

"I have another suggestion," Darragh offered.

I said nothing.

"We wait until dawn, and then I put you up on Aoife, and the two of us go home to Kerry. That's what we'll do."

The simple confidence of this took my breath away, and for a moment I was unable to reply. Longing swept over me. If only I could say yes. If only I could go home, back to the Honeycomb and to my father, back to the time when it all made sense, and the worst thing in my life was having to wait through the winter until Dan Walker's folk returned to the cove. But I could not go. If I were not wearing my grandmother's amulet at dawn she would appear at my side, angry and seeking answers. And once I wore the amulet she could see me, whenever she chose. To go back to Kerry was death for my father, and for Darragh. Not to work my grandmother's will was the end for all of us.

"I can't," I said. "Besides, what about O'Flaherty and his horses? Haven't you a job to go back to? What about Orla?"

Darragh threw a stick into the fire.

"Forget O'Flaherty," he said. "Don't concern yourself with that. I'm offering to take you home. You're tired, you're scared, you don't rightly know which way to turn. I shouldn't think your father would be happy to see you thus."

I forced myself to speak. "I can't go back." My voice was as cold as the chill that numbed my heart and froze my unshed tears. "You must go. You and Aoife. I must stay here. I know what I'm doing, Darragh."

Then he said nothing for a long time, and as the silence drew out I began to yawn, and my eyelids began to close, despite the cold, and I thought dimly that it was rather a long time since I had slept. But I must not allow myself to sleep. I still had to ride back to Glencarnagh, I still had to . . .

"Here," said Darragh. He'd found another blanket, not much more than a strip of sacking, perhaps used to keep Aoife warm, for like the other, it smelled strongly of horse. "Best rest awhile. You're weary to death. Come on, lie down and I'll cover you up."

"I can't," I protested through my convulsive yawns. "Told you . . . back by dawn . . . long way . . ."

"Aoife's quick," said Darragh. "We'll have you back in plenty of time. I'll wake you."

"No—you don't understand . . ."

"Yes, I do, Fainne."

"But . . ." The blanket felt good, so good. I put my head down and closed my eyes even as I mumbled my protest.

"Hush now," said Darragh. "I'll keep watch for you. Rest now."

Sleep rolled over me like a great wave, sudden and unstoppable. Once or twice I half-woke, aware of the winter cold that pierced through blanket and cloak and gown alike to touch the very spirit with its frosty fingers; aware that I was trembling and shivering again, despite the still-glowing coals and my efforts to curl up on myself as tight as possible. And then suddenly I was warm, wonderfully warm, and I was safe and well and somewhere in the back of my mind the sun was shining down on the sparkling water of the cove, and it was summer. Later still I stirred again, knowing the night was passing, but unwilling to wake fully lest this fair vision be lost forever. There was an arm across me, holding the cloak around me; and the same old blanket covered the two of us. Darragh lay behind me, his body curled neatly against my own, his living warmth a part of me, his slow, peaceful breathing steady against my hair. I kept quite still. I did not allow myself to return to full consciousness. I thought, if it all ended right now, I wouldn't mind a bit. Let it end now, so I need never wake. And I slipped back into sleep.

"Curly."

I hugged the blanket around me, and screwed my eyes shut.

"Fainne. Wake up, sweetheart."

I put the blanket over my face.

"Fainne. Come on, now."

I blinked, and stretched, and gave a groan. I sat up with some difficulty. It was still dark. Across the fire, Darragh was moving about, and I could see that Aoife wore her saddlebags and the folded blanket on her back. The gray mare stood by her quietly. The brightness faded from my mind as if it had never been.

I tried to get to my feet. It wasn't easy. The ride had done me more harm than I realized.

"Darragh."

"Mmm?"

"I meant what I said. Go back to O'Flaherty's. I'll ride to Glencarnagh by myself."

"Uh-huh."

"Stop saying that!" My voice was as weak and wobbly as a weeping child's. What was wrong with me? "You can't come. I'll go by myself."

"Let's see you walk over here, then."

"That's not fair!" I took a step, and pain lanced up my back. "I can go. I will go."

"Sit down, Fainne. If you insist on going back, Aoife and I will take you. I told you."

"Why won't you listen to me?" I protested, sinking awkwardly to the ground again, for my legs would not carry me. "You cannot come. You cannot be seen with me. Not at Glencarnagh. Not anywhere."

"Embarrass you, does it, to be seen in company with a traveling man?" He had his back to me, tending to the mare.

"Of course not!"

"You might be stupid enough to try to ride. I might let you, because I was tired of fighting with you. But you can't ride this mare all the way to Glencarnagh. She's old, and she's gone a long way for you tonight. She's not fit to carry you back, not in the dark. I'll take you. Don't worry, I won't shame you by showing my face before the great man himself. Wouldn't want to spoil your prospects, now would I?"

I said nothing. What was the point? I would do what I must do, and every moment of it I would thank the goddess that he was far away in the west, and could not see me. Every day I would give thanks that I had been granted this one chance to send him away safe from my grandmother's eyes. But I needed his help to get back to Glencarnagh. I would have to accept it, this once.

"Well, now," he said pleasantly after a while. "We'd best be off."

"I'm sorry," I said in a small voice.

"For what?"

"Sorry that I made the mare go so far in the dark, in the cold. Sorry I tired her out. I didn't think. All I thought about was . . ."

"Don't trouble yourself with that," said Darragh. "She's a little weary, but nothing a rest and a warm stable won't mend. Not used to such excitement, poor old thing. But she's a sound creature. Don't fret over her. She'll make her way back easy enough, following Aoife's tracks. Seems to me you've enough troubling you already, without adding to it."

Then he lifted me onto Aoife's back, and got up behind me, and we set off into the night.

It was a strange ride; silent for the most part, and quicker than my journey here, for Aoife moved both swiftly and smoothly, with little apparent need for directions. In her wake the gray mare followed, some distance behind. At one stage Darragh said, "There's an owl there. Following, or leading. Do you see it? Puts me in mind of that raven that's always near your father, wherever he goes. Like a guardian."

I nodded in the darkness. "Another of the same kind," I said.

"I see. Fainne?"

"Mmm?" I was refusing to let my mind go forward beyond the moment; beyond the pony's steady pace, and the white gleam of her coat under the moon, and Darragh sitting behind me with his arm around my waist and his own warmth flowing into me, thawing the chill in my heart. I felt safe. I thought, foolishly, I will hold onto this as long as I can; for this will be the very last time.

"I know you won't come with me. I know you won't go back to Kerry. You've told me I'm not welcome here. But . . ."

"But what?"

"I wish you would heed an old friend's advice. I wish you would at least not stay at Glencarnagh. You'd be safer back at Sevenwaters. There's good folk there. Your uncle's a fine man. My father has great respect for him, and for all that family. And—and you should take your time, before you make any choices. You're young yet. You have all the time in the world."

Oh, no. I haven't. I have until summer. No more than that. My fate is measured out over two seasons. But I can buy a longer span for you.

"Finished?" I asked him.

He did not reply.

"Not so long ago you were advising me to find a husband and rear a brood of children, I seem to recall," I told him. "Now you're telling me to wait. Which is it to be?"

"Don't mock me, Fainne. If you must wed, at least choose a kind man."

I was silenced. Somehow, he had a knack of saying the simplest things, and turning me to joy or misery on the instant. We rode on, and I thought I could see the very slightest lightening of the sky, as if dawn were not so very far off. The frost began to creep into my spirit once more, as if the best and truest friend in the world no longer had the power to stay its icy fingers.

"Darragh," I said quietly, and even to me my voice sounded strange, as if I were fighting tears. But my eyes were dry. I was a sorcerer's daughter, and strong. I would not weep.

"Yes?"

"If you knew the things I have done, you would not want to be my friend. If you knew, you would understand why I ask you to stay away from me. Terrible things. Evil things that don't bear speaking of."

"Why don't you tell me, and let me judge?"

My heart gave a thud of alarm. "I can't. I can't tell you."

"I could guess."

"No, you couldn't. Nobody could guess. It is—it is beyond the imagination of ordinary folk. Just believe that you are better off well away from me. Please believe that."

Aoife moved steadily forward, and now there was a distinct grayness to the sky, a change in the pattern of shadows around us.

"I could guess," said Darragh again. His hand was relaxed on the reins, his arm around me steady and sure. "There was a fire. Auntie told me. A man died, and another was hurt. A child was injured. Freak accident. You were always good at making fires."

I said nothing.

"You're right, that was a terrible thing to happen. You might persuade me, without too much trouble, that you had something to do with it. You'll never convince me that you'd do such a thing on purpose. Hurt the innocent, take the life of a holy man. That I'll never believe."

"There's more," I whispered.

Darragh waited.

"That girl, in the cove. The fishergirl, the one who disappeared. Remember that?"

He was silent.

Every word was a trial. I forced them out one by one, my heart hammering. "I—I used the craft, Darragh. Used it wrongly. I changed her, and she died. Something went wrong, and she died. I never told anyone, until now. After that, surely you cannot be my friend."

And now he would go, gladly. He would despise me, and leave me, and I would not have to worry anymore, because he would be safe. Too bad if this hurt, too bad if it felt like a knife in the heart, twisting and turning. I could never suffer enough to make up for the things I had done, and the things I must go on doing.

"She was a good little lass," said Darragh quietly. We came down a gentle slope, and between tall elms, and there in the dawning light was the long, low house of Glencarnagh, and there, not so far away at all, were two guards in green tunics with weapons at their belts. Aoife halted.

"You must go now," I hissed. "Leave me here, I'll make my own way to the house. You've come too far already."

Behind me, Darragh did not move.

"Darragh!" I whispered urgently. The sky was growing ever lighter. I must be back indoors, with the amulet around my neck, before day. That was what I had promised Grandmother. And Darragh must be gone before we were seen. I feared Eamonn's anger.

At last Darragh stirred, slipping from the pony's back, reaching up to help me down. My legs were unsteady, and he held me by the arms, frowning as he scrutinized my face in the pale predawn light.

"Maybe I'll ride to Kerry myself, and fetch your father," he muttered. "Maybe that's what I'll do."

"No!" I gasped. "No! Don't do that! Just go, just go and leave me! How plain do I have to put it, to make you understand?"

"You need looking after. That's what I always said, and it hasn't changed. You're mixed up in something that's too big for you. It's not right, Fainne."

I took a deep breath. "Don't be stupid," I said, and I made my voice as cold as I could. "This is quite simple. I want to forget you. I want to wipe every trace of you from my mind. I wish you would go away, and I would never see you again. Believe this. It's the truth."

Darragh went very white, and he took his hands slowly away from where they held me. I found I could stand without support, just. His gaze remained steady on my face. His brown eyes, looking into mine, were deeply searching.

"Give me your hand," he said.

I opened my mouth to argue, but found instead that I was putting my hand out, and he was taking it in his own. We both looked down.

"I don't believe you," said Darragh, as his fingers touched the little circle of woven grass I wore on my smallest finger; the tiny token my hands had encountered, as if quite by chance, in the most secret corner of my wooden chest, when I had thought to challenge my grandmother and had been defeated. This she had not seen, and never would, for it would be safe again in the chest before the amulet went back around my neck. This was a symbol of innocence; and I was no longer fit to wear it. Still, tonight I had borne it on my finger to prove that I had not forgotten.

"I don't believe you," he said again, and released my hand. "Now, it's almost dawn, and you'd better go in. Won't those guards see you?"

I shook my head. "There are ways of doing these things."

He frowned. "I don't like this, Fainne. I don't like to leave you here."

I said nothing. We stared at each other for a moment, and then I made to move away.

"Well, then," said Darragh gently, and his hand reached out to brush a wayward lock of hair back from my face. His fingers lingered by my temple, and withdrew. "Farewell, Curly. Keep out of trouble, now, until—"

"No!" I exclaimed. "Don't say it! You cannot come back! Never, you understand, never!"

And I turned away from him, fleeing as fast as my bruised body could carry me beneath the shadows of the elms, casting the spell as I went so the guards would see nothing but a trick of the dawn light, the merest trace of movement against the pattern of bushes and long grass, and I never looked back, not once. I ran past the hedge and across the garden, I slipped in by the kitchen door and away along the passage and into my chamber where the fire was out and the candle reduced to a misshapen lump of wax. The air was bitter cold, but not as cold as the deathly chill that gripped my heart.

I slipped the little ring off my finger, and thrust it away deep in the chest under the silken shawl. I would never wear either again. Then I took out my grandmother's amulet, the triangle of strangely worked bronze, and I sought for a cord or ribbon, any means by which I might put it around my neck, for I would not risk her return, not while Darragh still traveled within the boundaries of Glencarnagh. Once I wore the amulet, she was secure in her control of me. I need only perform her will, and my dear ones would be safe.

I remembered something. A cord, a strange one, that had adorned my doll, Riona. I had removed it for safekeeping, and the little white stone that went with it. Where had I put that? In the pocket of a gown, I seemed to recall. The russet-colored gown. I had it here, folded in the chest. Yes, there it was, a strong cord woven of many fibers, so strong it seemed unbreakable, its ends bound with leather. Before, I had found it difficult to untie. Now, curiously, the knot unfastened with ease. It seemed this thing which had been my mother's was not unwilling to bear such a perilous charm. I placed the small white stone away in the chest and strung the bronze triangle in its place. As I fastened the cord about my neck I found I was whispering, *Sorry. I'm so sorry*. The amulet felt lighter now, as if the cord which bore it were of far stronger stuff than the one which had frayed and broken under such an ill burden. Perhaps, even at the darkest times, my mother's spirit watched over me. I shuddered. Better that she did not watch; better that she did not know I was my grand-mother's tool once more. For it seemed to me that from this moment on, my steps would follow the sorceress's path and my tale would be her tale.

Chapter Nine

I knew what to do. It was a matter of discipline. Control the will and concentrate the mind. Focus the energy on the task and let nothing get in the way. It should have been thus from the moment I climbed onto Dan Walker's cart and left the shores of Kerry. It was what I should have done in the forest of Sevenwaters, instead of letting the little girls slip under my guard and establish a place in my heart, against all sense. It was how I should have protected myself, instead of listening to a druid, and heeding the tales of those that called themselves Old Ones.

There was a strategy to be followed, and its first step was Eamonn. Eamonn was not so difficult, I told myself as I washed and dressed with unusual attention to detail, frowning at my ghost-white face and shadowed eyes in the mirror. At least I did not care about him, I thought, as I gave my hair one hundred hard brushes, and plaited it up on top of my head so I would look older, seventeen at least. It was just a matter of remembering what to do, and why I was doing it. Think of my grandmother's voice, saying, *He'd as likely be murdered by the road for his little pack of cheap goods.* Think of that, and do her bidding with the sure hand of a sorceress.

I ventured out, knowing it was late and questions would be asked if I did not appear for a second day in a row. I was tired and cold and covered with bruises. I did not look as a girl should look who had been resting for a whole day and night. A little pallor was one thing; the appearance of complete exhaustion quite another. At least I was tidy. And I would not use the Glamour. If I must do this, I would do it as myself.

I was lucky. The girls were nowhere to be seen, and I found Eamonn alone, frowning over documents in very small script as he sat in an antechamber where tall narrow windows caught the cold sunlight of this winter morning. I stood in the doorway watching, thinking his face seemed worn and lined in the unforgiving light, noting his brown hair was touched with gray at the temples, reminding myself that I must learn that people were pieces in a game, no more, no less. I made no sound, but suddenly he was aware of me and sprang to his feet, almost as if on guard against an enemy.

"Good morning," I said politely. "I'm sorry if I startled you."

"Not at all." He recovered quickly, coming forward to guide me to a bench by the small fire. It was deathly cold; the tapestries stirred in the draft. I could not suppress a shiver.

"Come, sit here," said Eamonn. "You're still not well. Have you eaten?"

I shook my head, and immediately a serving woman was summoned and dispatched, and bread and cold fowl and an ale jug were brought on a tray and set by my side. The woman was dismissed. The door was closed.

"Please," I said, "I have disturbed you at your work. Please go on. Ignore me. I will be quiet. Or, if you wish, I can take this elsewhere. I did not intend—"

Eamonn gave a grim little smile. "Not at all. I'm making slow progress with this; the task is not to my liking, and I cannot concentrate today. The interruption is welcome. Besides, I was just about to send a woman along to see how you were. Here, let me pour this for you."

I waited silently while he did so, thinking of Darragh's fingers warm around my own, remembering him feeding me like a child.

"There," said Eamonn. "I've been concerned, Fainne. We did not have the pleasure of your company yesterday."

"As you see, I'm quite well now." I sipped the ale and crumbled the bread between my fingers.

"I—" Eamonn was unusually hesitant. "I did wonder if your indisposition was a result of—I thought perhaps I had offended you, distressed you. My behavior was not altogether appropriate, I realize that."

I looked up at him.

"It was not so much your behavior as—it was what you said. I was—I was somewhat upset, it's true. But as you see, I am recovered now."

"Then I did offend you. I regret that." He sounded sincere enough. He had seated himself on the bench opposite and was scrutinizing me closely. I sipped the ale. In fact I was quite hungry, for the oaten porridge had not gone far, but a hearty appetite was at odds with the picture I wished to create. I left the bread.

"We must discuss this," said Eamonn, his tone less than enthusiastic. "Still, I scarcely know where to begin."

I glanced up at him. He looked like a man who had gone without sleep, and I sensed the scrolls strewn on the table were the least of his worries. "You mentioned compromise," I reminded him. "I believe that's possible between us. But we won't speak of it this morning. I am still weary, and you appear somewhat distracted. If I might make a suggestion?"

"By all means."

"Perhaps I might remain here quietly for a while. No need to speak of what occurred between us. I have some needlework with me; I will eat and drink, and occupy myself with that, for the light is good in this chamber, and I wish for no company but yours this morning. You can get on with your work, as if I were not here. Later, after supper perhaps, we might speak of other matters."

For a few moments he stared at me in silence. Then he said, "There was a fellow here asking for you yesterday. Rough sort of man. Rode straight in demanding to see you, and reluctant to take no for an answer." He was frowning. I exerted the utmost control over my features, and kept my voice calm.

"Really?"

"Fine pony he had with him, too good a piece of horseflesh for such riffraff. Pure white. Fellow said he knew you, from Kerry."

"It would be one of the traveling folk, I suppose. They brought me north to Sevenwaters."

"Unusual arrangement," Eamonn said, scowling.

"Maybe. But safer, in its way, for a girl traveling alone than a more obvious escort. Folk let the travelers by unhindered. This man is related to a woman in my uncle Sean's household. That is all."

"And what is this fellow to you, Fainne? He was very persistent. Foolishly so. He seemed slow to understand, when I ordered him off my land. What's he to you?"

And all of a sudden there was a note in his voice, and a look in his eye, that made me very uncomfortable indeed. I remembered that this was the man who had nurtured his jealous resentment for eighteen years or more. This was the man who had said, *A man who takes what is mine, pays in kind.* I did not like that look, but my grandmother's voice was saying, *Yes, oh yes. Play on that.*

I attempted a sweetly dismissive laugh. "Him? Nothing at all. They're good folk, but simple. They've a habit of dropping in, asking after the welfare of a friend, riding away again. It means little."

"Friend? Surely a lady would not be classed as friend by such as this, a tinker's boy, no more?"

"There's no harm in it," I said, offhand. "Besides, I am not so much of a lady. You recognize that yourself, do not deny it. A man in your position could not consider such a girl as a wife, after all. A girl whose parentage is, at the very least, irregular. A girl brought up in isolation, knowing more of books and learning than the ways of a fine household."

"Fainne—"

"Ah. I broke my own rules. I'll tell you what we'll do. You'll sit down and continue deciphering that very small script. I'll eat what you have kindly provided for me, and get on with my sewing. And we won't talk. Not until later. Agreed?"

Eamonn gave a wry smile, and retreated to his seat by the table.

"Somehow," he observed, "I feel I am not being consulted here so much as instructed."

"This is not pleasing to you?" I inquired, my brows raised in imitation of my grandmother's style.

"I didn't say that."

I finished my breakfast and applied myself to needle and thread. It was just as well my grandmother had taught me how to sew. Perhaps the quality of my stitchery might not have satisfied her, but at least I was able to make a suitable picture of domestic competence. And the light was good. This man had spoken of white skin and red hair as if both pleased him well. I sat exactly where the winter sun would touch my pale cheeks with its brightness; I knew its rays would catch the burning flame of my hair and turn it to a dazzling halo. I concentrated on my work, my fingers moving industriously. I knew without looking that Eamonn's eyes were fixed more often on me than on the documents before him.

Time passed in total silence. All too soon the sun moved across the sky, and the best of the light was gone. It was not so long until midwinter. For a moment I allowed myself to think of Darragh, and Aoife carrying him back westward across the miles to Ceann na Mara. He would return to O'Flaherty's, and settle, and perhaps he would wed Orla and raise a brood of small dark-haired sons and beautiful blue-eyed daughters. All of them would swim like fish and ride as if born in the saddle. He would have his sister close by, when she married Aidan. Their existence would be simple and happy and full of purpose. He'd live to see his children grow.

"Fainne?"

I flinched as if struck, and wrenched myself back from my dangerous thoughts. I must not do that again. I must concentrate.

"Mmm?" I queried, finishing my thread with a neat little knot, and biting the end off.

"I—nothing. Forget I spoke."

"You broke the rules," I said lightly, folding my work. "No talking. Still, I've finished this task. Perhaps I should go."

"Don't. It is pleasing to me to have you sit thus quietly while I work. It seems strange, yet in its way fitting. I used to—I used to dream that it would be so, with—I used to imagine how it would be, if I were a married man. How different it might be. There was a picture in my mind, of riding home to Sídhe Dubh, and—no, this is not appropriate. I should not speak thus to you."

"Tell me," I said quietly.

He stood up and came over to stand by me, staring out the tall, narrow window at the winter landscape: bare elms, a well-dug garden awaiting new planting.

"You will think me foolish," he said. "Soft."

"No, I won't, Eamonn. I would not judge you."

He glanced down at me, his expression bleak. "Then, you understand, I thought I would wed and sire sons, as any man does. It was at that time I first encountered the Painted Man; that spawn of evil who was to become my lifelong nemesis. I did not know, then, that he would snatch from me all that I held dear; that he would seize my very hope of the future and take it for his own. Then, I still believed my life would be like other men's. And, as I felt the darkness of that man's influence begin to enter my spirit, I saw a small picture, like the one pure image that would remain true: my wife standing in the doorway at Sídhe Dubh, with my child in her arms. That was my reassurance that things were as they should be."

I said nothing.

"Foolish thoughts, for an old man," observed Eamonn bitterly. "That's what you think."

"It was Liadan you saw, of course."

"Of course. But he took her. It was his sons she bore. Her sons should have been mine."

This seemed an extraordinary thing to say, so much so I could scarcely frame a response.

"We said we would not speak of these things until later," I managed. "Why would you choose to tell me this?"

Eamonn was avoiding my eye. Still he stared out the window, watching a man go down the path with a pitchfork over his shoulder and a pair of dogs at his heels.

"I don't know," he said after a little. "I suppose, watching you there across the room in the quiet, I felt a sense of—of rightness, of the way my life might be if things were different."

I said nothing.

"I did not wish to speak of this; I have told you, despite myself. It is folly and weakness. One cannot recapture something that never was."

I rose to my feet. "I'm going now," I said quietly. "I must see the little girls, and then I should rest again. The ride to the waterfall caused me more aches and pains than I would have imagined."

"That was very thoughtless of me." Eamonn frowned, staring at me. "Very thoughtless."

"Nothing to worry about," I said lightly. "After supper, perhaps we might play at brandubh again, and talk further of these things."

"I don't think—"

"Perhaps we might." My tone was firm. "And before then, I want you to consider one question."

He waited.

"The question is," I said carefully, "what is it you need to do before you can move on? What is it you are waiting for before you seize hold of your life, and ensure your return home will be greeted with open arms and a warm hearth and the laughter of children? What ghost is it you need to lay before you do this?"

"You cannot—"

"Ah," I said. "I already have. I have asked the question, and I want the answer."

"I will not speak further of these things. They are best left untouched."

"I don't think so," I said. "You have lived but half a life. If you throw away the rest, then your enemy has indeed conquered you. Now I'm going. Will you do something for me?"

He inclined his head courteously, but his jaw was tight.

"Put your hands behind your back," I said. "And shut your eyes, until I say."

Startled into compliance, he did as I asked. I placed my palms on either side of his face, and felt tension grip his body.

"Eyes shut," I said sternly. Then I forced myself to kiss him, a kiss which began as the sweet touching of lips one might expect from an innocent young girl such as myself. But Grandmother had taught me many things. I knew how to make this kiss change, with a slight parting of the lips, and a little flicking of the tongue, into something more, something which would make a man's blood race and his breathing quicken as Eamonn's did now. I waited for the moment when he could no longer manage to hold his hands behind his back, and at that moment I withdrew my lips and stepped away.

"Fainne!" he breathed, staring at me. "What are you trying to do to me?"

"Nothing," I replied in round-eyed surprise. "I wished only to show you that I, too, believe compromise is possible. By the way, if in future you have difficulty with your reading, I would be able to help you. I'm well practiced at it, and my eyes are younger."

I turned my back and left the room, and Eamonn said not a word.

It wasn't easy. I despised myself for what I was doing. I shuddered to imagine what Darragh would think if he could see me. My father had always let me find my own path and make my own mistakes, but this would have shocked him deeply. Still, I found the strength within me to go on. There was a little image of my father, coughing blood. There was another, Darragh and Aoife moving on into the west, and away from danger. And what about the little girls, each one of them different, each one in her own way precious? They had given me their trust without question; I could not expose them to my grandmother's destructive anger. I need only think of that, and it was not, after all, so very difficult to go on.

I spent a little time with the girls. They were unusually subdued; Eilis showed me her sewing, the twins sprawled on the rug before my fire, and Sibeal sat by the window as still and silent as if she were a girl carven of pale stone.

"Very good, Eilis," I said. "Your mother would be proud of you. I'm sorry I could not help with this yesterday. I've been ill."

"I helped her," said Deirdre with a touch of smugness. "You were shut in here all day. You didn't even answer the door. What's wrong with you?"

"A very bad headache. I'm better now."

"You don't look better," observed Clodagh. "Your face is white, and you've got bags under your eyes. We thought maybe you'd had a fight with Uncle Eamonn."

"Uncle Eamonn's in a really bad mood," said Deirdre.

I did not reply. Better that I spend less time with them from now on. Better that I step away as quickly as I could, even if it hurt them. To stay close was to put them in danger. Besides, they were getting altogether too clever at puzzling things out.

"You missed him," said Clodagh into the silence. "Darragh. He was here, and you missed him."

"So I heard," I said tightly.

"We never thought they were real." Deirdre lay on the floor, head propped on one hand, looking up at me where I sat by Eilis on the bed. "Him and the white pony. Not really real: just a boy and a pony in a tale, having adventures. But they were. He let us pat Aoife."

"He said he'd been to Sevenwaters, and then he had to leave again. He saw Maeve, did you know that? He said she was getting better." Clodagh was holding a twig into the fire, letting it catch. "Can we go home, Fainne?"

Suddenly it was very quiet in the room. All four of them were looking at me intently.

"Soon," I said. "Very soon. I have to talk to your uncle Eamonn again first. I'll ask him what he thinks, if you like."

Clodagh glanced at Deirdre, and an unspoken message passed between them.

"He'll say no," said Clodagh. "He'll want you to stay at Glencarnagh. And you could hardly stay without us. You should have seen him yesterday, when Darragh was here. He was furious."

"Darragh was nice," observed Eilis. "He let me give the pony a carrot."

"Don't you mind?" Clodagh asked me. "That you missed him?"

I drew a deep breath. "It was a shame," I said as firmly as I could. "But I wasn't well enough to see anyone, not even an old friend. Your uncle Eamonn did the right thing."

I could feel Sibeal watching me, even though she was behind me. But she kept quiet.

"If you say so," said Clodagh in a tone of complete disbelief.

When they had gone I tried to rest, but could not. It came to me, that day, that the fair visions I had seen while I lay by a little fire, with Darragh's arm around me and the warmth of his body against my own, were the last good dreams that would ever visit me. Now, as soon as I dropped into a half-doze, images crowded my mind: my mother stepping from a ledge and falling, falling with her bright hair whipped by the wind, and the rocks below reaching up in anticipation of one final, ungiving embrace; my father, chalk-pale, retching blood; Darragh lying by the road with a knife in his back and Aoife nudging him gently, her faithful eyes bewildered when he failed to wake. And later, more pictures which seemed to me to tell of things that were to come, or that might come. A girl sobbing and sobbing, eyes screwed shut, tears flooding down her cheeks, nose running, mouth stretched in a rictus of anguish, her dark red curls and milk-pale skin revealing her as myself, as if I had not known already. I had seen this before. Words came with the picture: *You will not know how much you have to lose, until it is already gone*. And then, a sudden darkening, as if the whole world had gone awry, and day turned to night by the force of this grief. Men muttering and crying out in fear. And a great wave, a wall of water from nowhere, a surge so high one looked up and recognized death, even as one snatched a last shuddering breath. *I will sweep you bare . . . bare . . . I will take all . . . all . . .*

I noticed, at supper, that Eamonn had changed his clothes and that his hair, like my own, bore signs of careful brushing. I observed the serious dark brown eyes, the square, uncompromising features, the way one lock of hair kept falling across his brow. I thought that once, a long time ago, he must have been a fine-looking young man, one whom a girl might well have thought highly suitable for a husband. When one considered his wealth and the position of power he held, it was hard to imagine my aunt Liadan rejecting him for another man, especially one as unappealing as her strange husband sounded. It did not seem to make sense. I considered what kind of woman she was, to treat a faithful suitor so cruelly that his whole existence had been blighted by it. Then I told myself, again, that I must remember men and women were just pieces in the game, to be manipulated to advantage. It was not appropriate for me to feel sympathy for the solemn, pale, middle-aged man seated silent across the table from me, eating little, drinking steadily. It was not appropriate for me to feel anything at all. *Good girl*, said my grandmother's voice.

We finished our meal. The platters were cleared away and wine brought. Eamonn instructed the serving man that we were on no account whatever to be disturbed. There were two carven chairs by the fire, with a small table between. The box with the brandubh pieces, the elaborately patterned board stood there ready.

"You wish to play?" queried Eamonn as he settled himself opposite me.

Not this game, I thought. "Maybe not tonight. I don't think I'd be able to concentrate very well. Won't your folk jump to certain conclusion, if the door is closed and they are told to keep away? Whatever good reputation I may have had will be gone forever."

Eamonn regarded me levelly. "As you see, I did not bolt the door, nor will I. You are under no threat from me, Fainne. I am not a seducer, whatever opinion you may have formed."

"My memory of your behavior the other day does not quite support what you say."

"I have apologized for that, and do again. I don't know what came over me."

I raised my brows. "I could hazard a guess."

"You have not made it particularly easy for me. This morning, you—I am at a loss to understand what it is you want from me." He poured wine into my goblet, refilled his own. The wine was very strong, with a mellow flavor that spoke of sun-drenched hillsides and meadow flowers. I sipped cautiously, conscious I must keep all my wits about me.

"First things first," I said. "Have you an answer to my question? For it seems to me, if the two of us are to move on in any way whatever, the past must be dealt with. And I can help you with that. Believe it."

"I cannot see how, Fainne." Eamonn stared into his wine cup as if it might hold the answer to some puzzle. "With all the good will in the world, you are, after all, very young and quite inexperienced. You could scarcely comprehend what lies between me and—"

"And Liadan?"

"Her, and others. You said it yourself. That you had been brought up in isolation, away from the halls of men. You could not conceive of the evil things that have taken place. You are an innocent. How could you help me?"

"I see." I rose to my feet. "Then there's no point at all in this, is there? I may as well return to Sevenwaters. The girls have been asking when we can go home. I'll tell them we can leave in the morning."

"No." Eamonn was up in an instant, and I felt hand close around my arm. "No. That was not what I meant. Please, sit down, Fainne."

"Difficult, isn't it?" I asked quietly when I was seated again, and he had unclamped his fingers from where they gripped me, and returned to his place. "You don't understand what I want, and I have no idea what you want. I'm not sure you know that yourself. Why don't you start by answering the question I gave you?"

Eamonn did not reply. His jaw was tight, as if he clenched his teeth hard to keep words back.

"You dismiss my question?" I queried. "You think it—what is that word you favor—inappropriate?"

His lips stretched in a smile completely without mirth. "It was appropriate enough. I suspect you could give me the answer."

"Maybe. But I want you to give it."

Another silence.

"I have never spoken of these things," he said after a while, his tone muted, almost apologetic. "Not in all these years. Why should I do so now? Besides, I am bound by a promise. I cannot tell you the full truth, and will not."

I said nothing, but waited.

"What you said, one thing you said, has been in my mind all day. That if I did not act now to change the path of my life, he would indeed have conquered me. If you want me to name the ghost I must lay, it is that one. The Painted Man. He killed my men, he stole my woman, he robbed me of my sons. He took my future for himself. I cannot contemplate another life until I place my two hands on that man's neck and squeeze the last breath from him. I want to see him suffer and die. Is this what you wanted to hear? Is it?"

"Tell me." My voice was not quite steady, but I kept control. "Doesn't it trouble you that the woman you once loved would then lose her husband, and face a future of grief and loneliness? For you still care about her, do not deny it."

"Love? You use that word again. The word is meaningless, Fainne. You'll grow to realize that. Liadan condemned me to a life of emptiness. Does she deserve any better? Besides, Inis Eala is bristling with men. Feral creatures like him, every one. She could take her pick. Her bed will not stay cold long when he is gone."

"That's a little harsh."

"You think so? After what she did?"

"Tell me. Is there not the tiniest hope, somewhere beneath your lust for vengeance, that once this man is gone, Liadan will have a change of heart and come back to you?" I was watching him closely, timing my words to his mood. "Is this why you have remained so long unwed? Did you not say, once, these halls are kept bright for her?"

"Huh!" It was an explosion of scorn. "I'm not a complete fool. Nor am I entirely without pride. She debased and sullied herself by letting that man take her. She is no longer a fit partner for a man of quality. That was her choice. I would not offer her another chance, not if she begged me."

"Besides, she is no longer of an age to bear your sons with any safety."

Eamonn looked at me, and I willed myself to gaze steadily back.

"So," I said. "You must kill this fellow, the Painted Man. Then you can forget, and have your life back. If this is all, why did you not take the initiative years ago? Why waste so much time? You have the resources, surely? I understand the man is some kind of outcast, rejected by all respectable folk, for all he holds an estate across the water. And he's a Briton. An enemy. It should be simple. Why wait so long?"

"You think I have not tried?" Eamonn's voice grew harsh, and he got up and began to pace across the room, to and fro, to and fro. "The fellow's slippery as an eel, and not to be cornered; devious and quite devoid of scruples. With his marriage he put on a thin coat of respectability. In time he acquired Harrowfield as well as his bizarre establishment in the north. So now he has powerful allies as well as enemies. You say I have resources. They are nothing to his. He is ingenious, a trickster who will turn anything and anyone to his own advantage. He knows how to slip through the finest net, how to out-pace the swiftest hound. My pursuit of him has been relentless, Fainne, through the years. I have never even come close. That's the man he is."

"A clever one."

"Clever? Rat-cunning, that's all. Sewer scum."

"This man is Sean's ally, and the father of his heir. That must be a little difficult. Wouldn't it jeopardize my uncle's venture against the Britons if the Painted Man were killed? Muirrin told me each of the partners in the alliance has a vital role to play if Sean's great endeavor is to succeed."

"That's as may be," he said, scowling. "My quest to destroy this man is not Sean's concern."

"Still, the warriors of Inis Eala will fight alongside your own forces in the battle for the Islands. Will not the Painted Man be your own ally then?"

"That man is evil," he said coldly. "He cannot be viewed as an ally, not under any circumstances. He was marked for death at my hands long ago."

"What are you telling me?" I asked him. "Is your thirst for vengeance stronger than your desire to see the Islands preserved for Ulster? How can that be?"

Eamonn muttered something, still pacing.

"What?"

"I can't discuss this further. I told you, I am bound by a promise."

"A promise to whom?"

"To her. Don't ask me, Fainne. This is something that cannot be told."

"Very well. I understand what must be done. It seems to me you need inside information. A spy, maybe."

"Nobody spies at Harrowfield. Nobody gets in and out without that man's nod. And he always knows. I've tried. As for Inis Eala, it's impregnable. Not one of my men got as far as the settlement on the landward side, let alone over the water. The Painted Man has a network of intelligence to rival that of Northwoods himself. He travels often between Ulster and Britain, and far beyond, but he does so in secret. Nobody tracks him. Folk used to say he and his men were some sort of Otherworld creatures, outside the laws of humankind. Sometimes I find myself half believing it, fool that I am."

"Right," I said. "No spies. Not human ones, anyway."

"What other kind can there be?"

"Ah. I'll come to that later. But believe that I can help you. More wine?"

I refilled his goblet; added a drop or two to my own. Eamonn was gazing at me in disbelief.

"You, help? Forgive me, Fainne, but I cannot see how."

"No, you wouldn't. I'll explain in time. First, I have another question."

"I hope it's not as difficult as the last. It seems to me this is somewhat more taxing than brandubh."

"I want you to tell me honestly why you think me unsuitable as a wife. Make your words plain."

He opened his mouth and shut it again.

"You think this question inappropriate," I said coolly. "That much is obvious."

"Your education has certainly been somewhat lacking," he said, tight-lipped. "This is not a question a young woman asks a man."

"I have asked it, and I want your honest answer. And if you want to consider what is inappropriate, perhaps it is not so appropriate for a man in your position to take his kinsman's niece out riding alone, and put his tongue in her mouth and his fingers—"

"Stop it, Fainne! You sound almost—coarse."

"I knew nothing of such matters until you taught me," I said demurely, hating the look of distaste in his eye.

"I made an error. I have already said I'm sorry. You are a lovely young woman, and you have a manner about you that catches the eye, and the imagination, and makes a man itch to take you in his arms and do those things of which you so bluntly remind me. It is natural for a man to feel thus, Fainne. Even an innocent convent girl must understand that."

I nodded, eyes downcast. "And for a woman to feel the same. That is what brings two people together, a stirring of the blood, a longing to be close. I understand. But I have told you, I will not give myself to a man outside marriage. And you have made it plain enough it is not your intention to wed. Yet you brought me here; and you do not seem eager to see me go."

Now he was looking into the fire, reluctant to meet my eyes. "Indeed no. As I told you, I find you pleasing as a companion, quick-witted, clever, competent. Good with children; patient and sweet-tempered. And full of surprises. I'm coming to realize I do not dislike surprises as much as I thought. I cannot deny that I hoped you might—that you might let me teach you the arts of the bedchamber, Fainne. This has been in my mind, disturbingly so, since first I saw you with your cousins at Sevenwaters, so out of place in that house, like an exotic bloom set among wildflowers. But marriage? I could not consider it."

My heart was cold with fury. I breathed slowly and carefully. Feelings were irrelevant. Feelings only got in the way, and stopped you from doing what had to be done.

"So you thought I might stay as some sort of—unofficial wife, was that it? To warm your bed, and sit demurely by you as you worked, and be whisked out of sight whenever folk of consequence came to visit?"

"No, Fainne." He sounded quite wretched, but this time I could not summon a shred of sympathy. "I had no such thoughts. I behaved foolishly, from self-interest, and without thinking things out. A lapse of judgment which I will not make again. It was as if you were a bright flame, which I wanted at my hearth to warm me."

"Poetic. But you would not take me as a wife. Why not?"

"I had not thought to wed at all. It seemed too late. Besides, when a man in my position takes a wife, she must be a woman of proven pedigree. Don't imagine it did not occur to me, when first I met you. I made inquiries. I asked my sister, and I asked Sean. I asked the druid. All of them were remarkably evasive about the identity of your father. That was sufficient to alert me to an irregularity. A man does not put his prize stallion to some wild mare, Fainne. The progeny would be tainted, not worth raising."

I swallowed my humiliation with great difficulty. I wanted badly to hit him. Instead, I allowed myself to blush faintly, and took a sip of my wine.

"I see. You understand, a good marriage could make a great difference to me. I am not without skills and talents; indeed, I have some you could scarcely guess at, Eamonn. But in my uncle Sean's house I am no more than a poor relation. Without a good match, and a worthy man to guide me, I face a future of obscurity. Servitude, almost."

Eamonn scowled. "I would offer you a place here. You would be well cared for. Everything you wished: fine clothes, adornments, the run of my house and my estate, my company when I am here. I could provide a life of quality for you, Fainne. You need not return to be a drudge in my sister's household. And—and I would initiate you gently into those pleasures you spoke of. I think you might not be averse to that."

"But you would not place your ring on my finger, or give me your name, or have me bear your sons. Rather than endure that shame, you would have no sons at all. In all things, I would be a poor substitute for her, would I not?" My voice shook, despite my best efforts.

"Oh, Fainne. I've done this badly, and I've distressed you. Marriage is out of the question, my dear. It would be frowned upon by everyone. Such a match would be viewed as foolish and wasteful, an indication that my grasp was slipping. I'd become a laughingstock."

"If you do not wed, you have no legitimate sons. When you die, carrion descend on your estates and tear them apart. Is that what you want? Have you lost the will to fight for what is your own, to preserve a birthright for your children? You disappoint me. You have let your enemy win, after all."

There was silence again.

"Tell me then," said Eamonn, putting his goblet down heavily on the table and taking both my hands in his. "Tell me who you really are, and why you came here. For one thing is certain, I will not wed a woman who has no father."

My strategy was fraught with risk, and this was the trickiest part. A man with such a strong sense of propriety would recoil from the truth. I must tell him, and I must keep his interest long enough so he would hear what came after.

"Very well," I said with a hesitancy that was quite natural, "I will tell you the truth. You won't like it. I'll have to extract a promise from you, I think. That you will let me finish. Give me your word."

"Of course," said Eamonn, and his thumb moved slightly against my wrist, as if in the back of his mind the pleasures of the flesh still held him in their grasp, despite his better judgment. If it were so, that gave me an advantage, and I must use it though it sickened me.

"Very well," I said again. "This is difficult for me, you under-stand? It is like admitting I am—somehow flawed. I am not what you have believed me, Eamonn. I never told you I was raised in a priory, by Christian sisters. I let you believe what you chose, that was all. I grew up with my father in Kerry, just the two of us alone. My father taught me all I know. He was once a druid, but is no more, since he met my mother and took her away. His name was—is—Ciarán, and he is half-brother to Conor of Sevenwaters."

There was a very long silence. Eamonn kept hold of my hands, but now his own were still as if frozen in time.

"What?" he said so quietly I could barely hear. There was deep shock in his eyes.

"My father is the child of Colum of Sevenwaters by his second wife. She took him away when he was very small; but his father brought him home to the forest, and they raised him as a druid. He is a good man, a wise and honorable man. He has been my only family, my guide and mentor, all these years."

"But—but that means—do you understand what it means, Fainne?" Now he released my hands.

"Oh, yes. It means the union between my mother and my father was forbidden. They were too close in blood, for her mother was his half-sister. But they did not know that when they fell in love. Nobody told my father whose son he was, until it was too late."

"But—but your mother, Niamh, she was wed. She was wed to one of the Uí Néill, and she was abducted from my own fortress at Sídhe Dubh. She was taken away by—by—the Dagda guide me! You cannot tell me that Liadan knew of this incestuous passion, and helped her sister flee to the arms of her lover? That Liadan aided this, with the assistance of—this is abhorrent beyond belief! That such a thing might occur in my own home, with my own sister present! Did Sean know of this?"

"He knew of their love for one another. That was why my mother was given to another man, and sent away to Tirconnell. She was very unhappy. Her husband was cruel to her."

"He punished Niamh, perhaps, on finding she had committed an act of base depravity. It seems her judgment was as flawed as her sister's."

I bit back my rage.

"Now you know who I am, Eamonn. This is the truth. You can understand, perhaps, why my kinsfolk were evasive in their answers."

He seemed to have no more to say, but stood glaring into the fire, arms folded. I though maybe he was considering what a lucky escape he had had; thanking the gods that he had not, after all, taken me to bed.

"Enough of that," I said with a lightness quite at odds with my heavy heart. "We have other matters to discuss: your enemy; your vengeance. For it seems to me that is foremost in your mind; so powerful it outweighs your loyalty to your allies and kinsmen."

"It doesn't matter," Eamonn said dismissively. "This is over between us. Return to Sevenwaters if you wish, and take the children. Let all be as before. I have no future, Fainne. If I choose to spend my life pursuing a phantom, what concern is it of yours?"

"None, perhaps," I said quietly. "But I hate to see a good man go to waste. Besides, I said I could help you. I spoke the truth, and I will show you how. It was necessary, first, for me to explain about my father. He was raised as a druid. After he left the wise ones, he delved further into the realm of sorcery. When my mother died, he became my sole companion; and he taught me a great many things, as a master teaches an apprentice. This was what I meant when I spoke of skills."

"This is no longer of interest to me."

"You promised to hear me out."

Eamonn stood there stony-faced. I poured a goblet of wine and put it in his hand, and he drained it. I doubt he was even aware of what he did.

"Imagine a set of scales," I said evenly. "On one side hangs your chance to finish the Painted Man, once and for all. The certainty of vengeance, a knowledge that you hold his life between your fingers. On the other is a young woman; one who, on your own admission, makes your heart beat and your body stir. One who saves herself for you; saves herself fresh and untouched for your wedding night. Maybe she is not the one you love; but she will give you what Liadan never gave. She will give you her youth and bear you fine sons and lovely daughters, she will never so much as glance at another man, she will keep your house bright and your hearth warm, and welcome you with open arms when you return. You will never be bored by her; she will always surprise you anew. There's only one problem. Her pedigree is somewhat flawed. You tell yourself you will not have her. You cast her aside. And so you lose both. The scales unbalance; you lose your future, and at the same time you throw away the chance to destroy your old foe and wipe out the injustices of the past. For to have one, you must take both."

"You speak like a druid. I don't understand you." His curiosity was awakened, despite himself. I had chosen my words with care.

"To defeat this enemy, you need inside information. You need intelligence of where his weakness lies; information on his movements, identifying perhaps a time when he will be alone and unguarded, and at his most vulnerable. The two of you fight side by side next summer. There will be opportunities for you."

"But—"

"Yes, there's a problem. On one hand, an estate in distant Northumbria, in enemy territory, and well guarded. One could scarcely attempt that. On the other, an island fortress, remote and secret, with a network of protection so complete it seems almost Otherworldly in its construction. This man can be found there from time to time. But how can one penetrate such defenses? Not by sending in some warrior trained in the art of spying. This man will always have another, better than your own. No, you need something more. You need a spy who can go quite undetected, who will blend with the surroundings as if she is not there at all. A spy who can travel unseen to the most secret council, the most covert meeting. One who might even uncover the confidences of the bedchamber, if you wished to know them. This I can provide for you."

Now he was staring at me, both shocked and bemused. His cheeks were flushed; maybe it was the wine, but I thought I detected a new excitement there.

"My father taught me some skills that are a little—unusual," I said softly. "I will demonstrate for you. Call in your serving man; ask him to bring food, perhaps, or logs for the fire."

Without further question, Eamonn did as I instructed. The man came in and stood before us, a square-framed, youngish fellow with a hard sort of face and little eyes. My heart was thumping even as I summoned the craft, for I could see the image of that woman using her knife to slit open a fish that was her own daughter. I must make no errors this time. As Eamonn gave his servant quiet instructions, I spoke a spell under my breath, suppressing the temptation to change Eamonn himself into another form while I was at it, maybe a stoat. And as I spoke, the man's form began to alter, his nose to lengthen, his skin to grow darkly hairy, his form to shrink before Eamonn's fascinated, horrified gaze, and there in front of us was a fine black hound, panting a little, tongue hanging out, ears pricked up, tail wagging hopefully.

"Good boy," I said. "Sit."

Eamonn set his wine cup very carefully down on the table.

"Can I believe what I see?" he breathed. "Is not this some trick of the light, that will vanish the instant we move? How did you do this?"

"Here," I said. "He's real. Touch him. Then I'd better change him back, and send him on his way."

Gingerly Eamonn stretched out his hand, and the hound licked his fingers.

"The Dagda save me!" whispered Eamonn. "What are you, a practitioner of the black arts? I've been a fool to listen to you. It was your grandmother who seduced and bewitched Lord Colum, and in doing so destroyed him. This is perilous, Fainne. You frighten me. And yet—" He broke off.

I touched the dog's head and murmured a word, and in a trice the serving man was back before us, blinking in confusion. A wave of relief ran through me; it had worked, I had done it safely this time.

"Fetch more wine," I told the man kindly enough. "And some wheaten bread, if there is any. Lord Eamonn is hungry." When the man was gone, I said, "I'm no evil witch. My father is a sorcerer. He taught me. But we are not necromancers. We use our craft with wisdom and caution. Can you see how this might be employed to achieve the goal which has thus far eluded you?"

"You'd better tell me, I think. Come, we should sit, and perhaps wait until he comes and goes again. Will he remember nothing?"

"It depends. It depends on how the spell is cast. This man will think he had a slight dizziness, a momentary confusion, no more. Had I left him in his altered form for longer, it might have been different."

"You would—you would send a man, in the form of a creature, to gather information? He could do so, and bring it back to you?" He was eager now, his mind sifting possibilities.

"No, Eamonn. I'll explain it to you. And you will see why the image of the scales is apt. Ah, here is your man with our wine. Thank you." I smiled as the fellow set down a tray with a fresh wine jug and a small loaf of soft bread.

"That's all for tonight." Eamonn could not help staring, as if he expected the man to develop pointed ears or a wagging tail at any moment. "You can go to bed. The others too. Shut the door when you go out, and remind the household not to disturb us."

"Yes, my lord."

The man retreated, and Eamonn stooped to put another log on the fire. The room was dark enough, save for the flickering glow from the hearth, and the candles set here and there. Outside, the wind keened through the winter trees. Here before the fire there was a feeling of conspiracy, of secrets shared under cover of darkness. I took a mouthful of the wine, then set my cup down. Not too much. So far, this had gone my way. I could not afford to grow reckless.

"I'll explain it to you, Eamonn. I cannot turn a man to a dog, or a fly, or a bird, and send him to spy for you. In his creature form, he will not remember your instructions, and he cannot comprehend human speech. I could change you; I could make you a toad or a weasel. But you are the same kind as your servant; you, too, would lose your human consciousness until I brought you back. So, you see, that would be pointless."

"How, then, can this be done?"

"An ordinary man or woman cannot change thus, and retain the knowledge of both forms, man and beast. To do so is the preserve of a seer. Or of a sorcerer."

"You mean—?"

"I mean that if you want this done, you must trust me to do it for you. For I can change, to owl or salmon or deer, and I can go into my uncle's house, or to the secret halls of Inis Eala, and listen. I can return and bring you the key to this man's destruction. I have the skills, and will do it."

"You really mean this," said Eamonn slowly. "It is true, and not some young girl's wild fantasy."

"My grandmother turned six young men to swans, and came close to destroying the house of Sevenwaters," I said grimly. "Do not believe that I am incapable of such a deed. It is your own resolve that might be questioned. For if this goes ahead, my uncle Sean's campaign is doomed. Aunt Aisling is your sister, after all. Would you see Sevenwaters fail, and the Britons keep the Islands?"

Eamonn gave a bitter smile. "We have the child of the prophecy, don't we? Perhaps it may not fail."

"The son of the very man you seek to destroy? Is not he just such a wretch as his father, the man you think less than human?"

"Oddly enough, the boy is a sound leader, much admired among the alliance. He is strong, skillful, wise beyond his years. I find it unthinkable that that man's son will one day be master of Sevenwaters, that much is true. But a son does not choose his father."

"I see." He had surprised me. Such was his hatred, I had assumed it would spill over onto everyone connected with the Painted Man. I wondered, again, just what sort of man this Johnny was, that they all had such faith in him. "You think, then, that if his father dies, he will lead the allies into battle?"

Eamonn scowled. "In any event, he will lead. The prophecy makes that clear. As to his father's role, that has been kept from me. Allies we may be, but Sean gives out only as much as suits him, and that riles me. I cannot judge whether the loss of the Painted Man will affect the campaign or not. Nor do I care, for I must confess to you the one far outweighs the other in my mind. I want you to show me, Fainne. Show me you can do as you say." Now his voice was shaking with eagerness. "Show me you can change."

"Ah, no. I will not do that."

"Why not?"

"Because it's fraught with danger, Eamonn. It depletes the craft; afterward, one is drained and exhausted. Such high powers are not to be used lightly, as a mere demonstration. Believe me, I can do it, and when the time comes I will."

"I can scarce comprehend this," he muttered, and I could see his mind was turning over the tantalizing possibilities I had held out before him. "With this, I can have him before the summer is over. I can know his very thoughts, be privy to his darkest secrets. With this, surely my quest cannot fail, and the man must perish at my own hand. Are you sure, Fainne? Are you certain you can do this for me?"

"Oh, yes," I said calmly. "There's no doubt that I can. But there's a price, Eamonn. You are not the only one with a vision and a goal."

"What price?" I could hear the excitement in his voice; at that moment I could have asked for almost anything.

"I told you before," I said. "The scales, the balance. You accept one side, you accept the other. If we are to be partners in this, then we are partners in all things. I perform your will, I gather the intelligence you seek. I share your hearth and your bed. You will find that there, too, I can work magic. I bear your children and you give me your name. I need that security. I need respectability, a home, a place where I can belong. Without that, I will not do it. For if you kill this ally, and my uncle's campaign is lost, my only future lies with you."

There was a deathly silence, interrupted only by the small crackings and poppings of the fire and, outside, the hooting of an owl. I waited for him to tell me that he would not wed a woman with tainted blood, despite all. If he said that, I might not be able to retain control; to remain calm. Magical powers do not arm one against that kind of hurt.

"Fainne?" he said quietly. He was looking into the flames, and I could not see his expression.

"Yes?" Curse it, my voice had gone wobbly, as if I were about to weep. I had been foolish to have so much wine. Control was everything.

"Come here. Come closer."

I got up and moved to kneel before him, so that the firelight would shine on my hair and warm my pale skin to a rosy glow. I looked into his eyes, schooling my expression to an innocent hope, fresh, guileless.

"You swear that you are telling the truth? That you can do this and succeed?"

"I swear it, Eamonn." I toyed with the idea of casting just one more spell; like an opposite of the charm I had used on him in an awkward moment, up by the waterfall. But I saw the expression in his eyes and knew I needed no such aids. There was desire in his look, but it was more than that. It was the look of a man so eaten up by hatred that he would stop at nothing to get what he wanted; a look that told me, while his bodily lusts might need attending to from time to time, the only thing that really excited him was the thought of his enemy's neck under his hands, and the sound of the last breath being slowly squeezed from his body.

"Touch me, Fainne," he whispered, and I heard the same excitement in his voice, edgy, dangerous. "Let me taste your lips; let me taste my vengeance there."

There was a very strong wish in me to spit in his face, for it seemed to me the man did not see me as a real woman at all, but merely some tool to be used toward his own dark purpose. Anger and self-disgust rose in me; I suppressed both. *Control*, said Grandmother's voice. *Don't lose it now, at the end. Do as he bids you. You said you would be a good wife, didn't you? Show him how good. Make him want you.*

"You did say—" I murmured.

"Just a kiss, just one," Eamonn said softly, and he took me into his arms and pressed his lips against my neck, and my cheek, and because there was no choice, I let him kiss me on the lips. That was the hardest moment of all; pretending to him that I was willing, winding my arms around his neck, opening my mouth so that he could probe deeper with his tongue, feeling his hands on my body and knowing all the time that there was no honesty at all about it. I was filled with a cold distaste even as I gasped with simulated pleasure and moved my body against his own. As for Eamonn, he wanted me, I could feel that, but I did not fool myself that my charms had anything at all to do with it. He had proved, tonight, that it was the thought of vengeance that brought him alive. Interesting, I thought as his hand began to move against my leg, to think what might come later. I could not imagine myself as this man's wife. If it ever came to that, I had the tools to punish him for his arrogance. But it would never happen. Whatever occurred, there was no future for me after the summer. I had asked for marriage only to make my offer of magical help more convincing, for it was hardly plausible that I would make such a gesture out of the goodness of my heart. Perhaps, also, I had done it to salvage some sense of pride. His hands were wandering somewhat further than they might. Maybe he had misunderstood my meaning.

"Eamonn . . ." I gasped. "You promised . . ."

"Just once," he muttered. "Just once, Fainne. You'll enjoy it, I'll make sure of that. Just tonight. Then I'll wait . . . don't say no to me . . ."

He was quite strong; strong enough to deny me any chance of escape without using the craft, and I could hardly try that trick again. I did not wish to annoy him, for after all he had not yet said yes, not in so many words. Besides, I could not speak the words of a spell while he had his tongue in my mouth, and he seemed in no particular hurry to remove it.

I heard the small sound before he did. It was no more than a creak, a rustle, as the door was opened and someone came to a sudden halt on the threshold. Eamonn withdrew his lips from mine and his hands from my body. He drew breath, ready to reprimand whatever serving man had dared to intrude where he had no business. He looked toward the doorway. There was a stunned silence.

"I've come to take my daughters home." The voice was my uncle Sean's, and chilly as a dawn frost at Samhain. "And not a moment too soon, it appears."

I turned around slowly, feeling a hot blush rise to my cheeks, despite my efforts at control. My uncle was dressed in riding clothes, and the look in his eyes was as wintry as his voice.

Behind me Eamonn took another careful breath, and I felt his hands as they settled on my shoulders in a gesture which, it seemed to me, indicated ownership.

"Sean. You surprised us," he said with commendable smoothness. "Fainne has done me the honor of agreeing to become my wife."

If I had read shock and distaste on Sean's face before, it was nothing to the way he looked now. He took two very deliberate steps into the room, without speaking, and the set of his mouth was very grim indeed. And then I winced with pain as Eamonn's grip tightened convulsively on my shoulders, and his body froze.

My uncle had not come alone. Behind him in the doorway stood a woman, previously masked from view, for she was a small, slight thing who came barely to Sean's shoulder. For a moment I thought it was Muirrin; and then I looked again. This woman had the same dark curling hair as my cousin, fastened up neatly in a coil of plaits, with wayward tendrils escaping around her delicate features. She had the same fey green eyes and tiny, slender form. But Muirrin had not such a sweetly curving mouth, a mouth a man might think made for kissing. And Muirrin had no such air of authority, for this woman was considerably older, and as she stepped into the room, untying the fastenings of her hooded cloak, she seemed as formidable as my uncle himself, a woman who would command instant obedience from all, without even needing to ask. As an enemy she would be daunting. I had no doubt at all that this was my mother's only sister, my aunt Liadan.

"I—I—" Eamonn, who had handled my uncle's unexpected appearance with surprising aplomb, seemed now completely lost for words.

"A cold night for riding," I observed, and I put one hand over Eamonn's for a moment, then moved away from him as he relaxed his grip. "You'd welcome a goblet of wine, I expect?"

"Thank you." Liadan appeared to be capable of speech, if the two men were not. She moved forward, discarding her cloak on a bench to reveal a gown and overtunic of extremely plain cut, the one a dark gray, the other a lighter shade, with a hint of violet in it. For all the severity of her appearance, her voice was warm, and her wide green eyes surveyed me tranquilly enough. I poured the wine and passed her a goblet, keeping my hands steady.

"We didn't expect you," I said.

Liadan glanced at Eamonn, and back at me. Her mouth tightened. "Indeed. I will not apologize, for it seems to me our arrival was impeccably timed. We plan to take you and the girls home tomorrow morning. Maeve is somewhat improved, and fretting for her sisters."

"I—I'm glad she's better," I said. I forced myself to go on. "What of the man who was burned, the young druid?"

"I was able to ease his pain a little. But not even a young, strong man recovers from such injuries. I explained this to him. Conor took him back to the forest."

"I'm sorry." My voice cracked, and her gaze sharpened. The two men had neither moved nor spoken. The air in the dimly lit room was alive with tension. Then there were rapidly approaching footsteps, and Eamonn's serving man was at the door, fastening his shirt, smoothing his rumpled hair, full of apologies. Eamonn gave quick instructions. Food to be prepared, sleeping quarters got ready immediately, horses stabled and cared for.

"It appears we have matters to discuss." Sean moved at last, but only to fold his arms and frown. "Matters that cannot wait for tomorrow. I want the girls out of here as early as they can pack and be ready."

"There's no need for such haste, surely." I had come to know Eamonn well enough to hear the deep unease in his voice, and to see how carefully he was not looking at my aunt as she settled herself on a bench, straight-backed, managing somehow to look like a princess in her plain gown.

"I've no intention of staying here beyond one night," said Liadan coolly. "It's time the girls went home. As for what you spoke of, it is quite out of the question. In the light of day, upon a little reflection, even you will see that, Eamonn."

"I think not. The match appears to me quite suitable, and I'm confident that Aisling will agree. My sister has been urging me to wed for so many years I grow weary of it. And you are unlikely to see your niece so advantageously matched elsewhere, I think."

"It's not possible," said Sean heavily. "For reasons best not discussed here."

"If you refer to Fainne's parentage, I know of it, she has told me herself, quite bravely. I think, if we are to debate this tonight, we should excuse her first. Fainne has been unwell, and is very tired. These matters are best settled between men."

I saw my aunt Liadan's mouth quirk up at the corner, but her eyes were deadly serious. She looked at her brother, and he looked back at her, and I was reminded that Sean was Liadan's twin. I was reminded of what Clodagh had told me; that messages flew between them in silence, no matter what the distance. From the dark, shadowy forest of Sevenwaters to the impenetrable secrecy of Inis Eala or over the sea to Harrowfield, messages of the mind, straight as an arrow and swifter than the fleetest deer.

"For once I find myself in agreement with you, Eamonn." Liadan rose to her feet, yawning. "We can spare Fainne the details, surely; and as for myself, I am quite weary, and have need of nothing but a warm place to sleep. I will see that our escort is settled, and then retire. Believe me, I have no wish to remain here one moment longer than I must. Come, Fainne. Shall we go?"

As the two of us made our way out of the chamber, leaving the men in a charged silence, I looked back at Eamonn over my shoulder. His expression was a wondrous blend, where the agony of hopeless love warred with a vindictive hatred nurtured through long years of frustration. I had been right before. It was on her his eyes were fixed, and the darkness in them showed how he struggled with himself. To him, nothing else mattered but this.

Chapter Ten

S he was tiny, graceful, and well-mannered. She was completely
in control. Eamonn's folk snapped to attention and ran to do
her bidding. I followed her, feeling like a clumsy giant,
tongue-tied and awkward, until all was settled to her satisfaction and
she announced with no consultation whatever that she would share
my bedchamber for the night, since that would be easier for all. As we
made our way there by candlelight, I asked her bluntly, "Don't you
trust me, Aunt?"

She glanced at me sidelong, her green eyes coolly appraising.

"I don't trust Eamonn," she said grimly. "I know him to be capable of many things. It seems taking advantage of young girls must be
added to the list."

I did not reply until we were in the chamber, and the door closed
behind us. Liadan had a little bag with her containing a nightrobe
and a comb. It was plain she had not intended to stay long. I watched
as she began to unpin her coil of plaits.

"Are you angry with me?" I asked.

She paused, giving me a very direct sort of look. "No, my dear,"
she said. "Not angry. Just a little sad. I've been so looking forward to
meeting you. Indeed, I'd have fetched you straight back, but Maeve
needed me at Sevenwaters and Aisling overruled me. If I'd been
there, none of you have come near this place. Now the occasion has been marred for both of us, but the fault is Eamonn's, not

yours. I know you have acted in innocence; it could hardly be other-wise for a girl of your years."

Now she had really confused me. "Looking forward?" I asked, sitting on the bed to take off my shoes. "Why?"

"Why?" Liadan sounded astonished. "How can you ask such a thing, Fainne? Can't you imagine how it was for us, to be cut off from Niamh for all those years? Ciarán never let us near. Once he took your mother to Kerry, that was the end of it. I understood his reasons, but I could never agree that he was right. Niamh was my sis-ter, and Sean's. We loved her. It was a terrible blow to hear that she had died; and another to be prevented from seeing you. It is a gift that you are here, Fainne. A gift it seems we have come close to los-ing, in our carelessness. We'll leave early in the morning. I don't want you to see Eamonn alone again."

"Love," I said bleakly. "Why does everyone use that word? My uncle Sean, and Conor, and the others, they did not show much love when they sent my mother away from Sevenwaters. There was not much love in raising a young man to think he could be a druid, and throwing those long years of discipline and devotion back in his face. I don't believe love exists; or if it does, it causes only sorrow and loss. My mother killed herself. Doesn't that mean anything to you?" I had not intended to speak thus. I had wished to show control. But she made me angry, sitting there neat and pretty as could be, with her glib words of welcome. Couldn't she see, couldn't any of them see that my father and I would never belong here? Couldn't they under-stand what they themselves had begun?

"You're very like her," said Liadan softly, looking at me with those huge, fey eyes. "Far more so than you realize, I expect. Do you remember your mother at all?"

I shook my head, furious with myself for saying too much. My discipline was slipping again, when I could least afford to let down my guard.

"That's a shame," she said. "Niamh could be quite—difficult at times. Blunt, even hurtful. She never meant it. She was just so full of feelings, bursting with them, that they spilled out sometimes. You cannot dismiss love, Fainne. If you do, it is only because you have not yet learned to recognize it. Niamh loved your father; loved him more than anything in the world. She'd have changed her whole life for him; and did, when it came to it. And he did no less for her. That's why it's so hard to believe."

"What?" I slipped my nightrobe over my head as quickly as I could, for I did not care to undress in company.

Liadan looked thoughtful. "That she would put an end to it. That her choice would be death. I heard her threaten to kill herself once, when she was still wed to the Uí Néill. I had no doubt she meant it then. But to do it after Ciarán came for her, and after she had you . . . that always seemed to me impossible. I could not understand it. All she wanted was to be with him, and to bear his child. She longed for that. And she loved you dearly, Fainne. I know it."

"You can't know," I said flatly. "You told me yourself, you never saw her again after she went away. You can't know." I lay down on my bed and stared up at the ceiling.

"Oh, dear," said Liadan, and it sounded as if she were torn between laughter and tears. "We have started on the wrong footing, I see that. Forgive me, I must keep pinching myself to remember it is you lying there and not my sister, for she'd just such a way of conducting a conversation when she was cross with me."

"I thought you said you loved her."

Liadan sighed. "Everyone loved her, Fainne. She was like a beautiful creature of summer, lovely, merry and full of life. What happened changed her terribly. There was a great wrong done, to her and to Ciarán. I acknowledge that; indeed, your father and I spoke of it, long ago. But Ciarán and I were never enemies. And as for Niamh, she told me once how much she wanted to have his child. I understood what she meant, for at the same time I was carrying my own son within me, though his father was far away, and it seemed unlikely we could ever be together. I understood how much she longed for it. She kept hold of that hope, even in her darkest moment."

"Maybe," I said grudgingly. "But she did not love me. How could she? If she'd loved me, if there were any such thing as love, how could she choose to die, when I was too little even to remember her?"

"I do know how she felt about you." Liadan's voice was soft but sure in the darkness, as she blew out the candle. "I saw it. These visions are granted me sometimes. It was long ago, before you were born, that I saw this. An image of the Sight. Niamh was sitting in a strange place, a place of blue light and soft shadows, like a little cave half-buried beneath the sea, where a gentle tide washed in. Niamh and her child. The two of you were making patterns in the sand, careful, quiet. I'll never forget the look on her face as she watched you. After that, I found it hard to understand that she would . . ." Her voice trailed off.

For a while I could say nothing. Her words had brought it back: the little cave beneath the Honeycomb, the place of the margins, the refuge where I had sat silent many a time, alone or with Darragh by me, watching the play of soft light on mellow stone, and let the pure sand trickle through my fingers, and heard the gentle wavelets washing in and out, in and out. That place called me back to Kerry. I tried to picture my mother sitting there on the little beach, watching as a tiny Fainne played on the sand. But that was all it was: a picture. I longed to remember, but I could recall nothing of her. Just as well, perhaps. I was in danger of feeling too much, and feelings only made things more difficult.

"Aunt Liadan?"

"Mmm?"

"Is it such an impossibility that I might wed Eamonn?"

There was a long pause.

"Yes," she said finally.

"But why?" I asked her. "You know my background. Where else would I find a husband of such standing? Has he not honored me greatly by his choice? I don't understand."

"I won't talk of this here, in his house, Fainne." It was a tone which allowed for no discussion whatever. "This can wait. You can wait. Unlike Eamonn, you are only in your sixteenth year, and have all the time in the world. Now, best sleep, for we've an early start tomorrow."

I said nothing, since I had no answers for her. I thought her asleep, but after a while she said, "It is possible, you know, to wed for love. Indeed, our family has been noted for choosing to do so, against all odds. It would be sad to marry with no more than security or strategic interests to aid your choice of a mate. Practical, maybe, but sad. Have you a sweetheart, Fainne?"

"No," I snapped, much too quickly.

"Well, then," said Aunt Liadan into the darkness.

Sometimes attack was the best defense. "Surely you did not wed for love?" I challenged.

"Why do you say that?" Liadan did not sound offended, merely surprised.

"Forgive me, but to all accounts your husband does not sound the kind of man for whom a girl would give up the prospect of an excellent marriage and leave her home forever. How did you meet him?"

There was a brief silence.

"As I recall," said Liadan, and I could tell she was smiling, "his men hit me over the head and abducted me. I thought him quite fearsome in those days, and he considered me no more than a nuisance."

"So," I said, wondering if she was telling tales to make fun of me, "you did not wed for love?"

"Love found us, and surprised us," she said softly. "I wed for nothing else, Fainne. When you see this man, you might think him strange; wild; most certainly not a dignified chieftain such as Eamonn of Glencarnagh. Bran is no respecter of laws and conventions, save those he makes himself. And his appearance sets him apart as much as his reputation. But he is fifty times the man Eamonn ever was. What is between us is beyond love, Fainne. He is my husband, my lover and my soul-friend, the one to whom I can confide the deepest secrets of the spirit. I hope, one day, you have the joy of finding such a mate, for nothing surpasses it."

My aunt had a way with her, I was forced to admit it. I fell asleep with my fingers in my ears, lest I start to believe what she said was true.

We were ready for departure not long after dawn next morning. The girls were excited to be going home, and chattered like a flock of small birds until Sean silenced them with a firm but kindly warning. Eamonn seemed withdrawn. Whatever had been said between him and my uncle, it had not put him in a good humor. There was only one moment to be snatched, when Sean's back was turned and Liadan was answering some lengthy query of Clodagh's. The little horse which had carried me so bravely in Aoife's footsteps was saddled ready for me; Eamonn had said I might ride her home, since she seemed to suit me so well. I could hardly point out she might be too tired after her nocturnal adventure. Now I stood by the horse's side, and Eamonn made pretense of adjusting the bridle. He glanced at me, his eyes narrowed, his jaw tight.

"Promise me," he whispered. "Promise me you'll do what you said."

My heart thumped. There was death in that look, a vista of shadow on shadow. "It's a bargain, remember?" I said, shivering. "There are two sides to it. How can you keep yours, now?"

"You doubt me?" Eamonn's hand clamped itself around mine, the fingers tight enough to bruise. I willed pain and fear into the background, and stared back unflinching.

"I will keep my part of it, if I can rely on you to do the same," I said steadily. "If my uncle refuses this marriage, why should I take any such risk for you?"

"He will not refuse." There was no room for question in Eamonn's tone. "He will comply with my wishes. They're fools if they don't realize what power I hold over them. Sean's endeavor cannot go ahead without me. I will have the Painted Man; and I will have you. Make no doubt of it."

"I—"

"Promise me, Fainne!"

I nodded, feeling the chill all down my spine.

"Say it!"

"I promise. You will have what you want by summer."

His grip relaxed and he lifted my fingers to brush them with his lips. "Then so shall you," he murmured. "And that, too, I shall look forward to with keen anticipation, my dear. The waiting will try me hard, I fear."

It should not be too hard, I thought, as long as Mhairi was available. I restrained the comment that sprang to my lips.

"Goodbye, Eamonn," I said, and then my aunt Liadan rode up alongside and the moment was over.

"This is your entire escort?" Eamonn ran his eyes over the three men in Sean's colors, who now sat ready on their horses, with the four little girls between. "This is inadequate, surely. I'm astonished that you would come out thus unprotected. I'd better arrange some of my own guard to ride with you." He frowned in Liadan's direction.

"Please don't," she said coolly. "I've my own men."

"Really? Are they creatures of the Otherworld, that they render themselves thus invisible? I see no men."

"No, you wouldn't. They're good at that. I go nowhere unprotected, Eamonn. Bran makes sure of it."

He stared at her, wordless. Then he spat, very deliberately, on the ground at her horse's feet. It was shocking; a gesture quite at odds with all I knew of the man, for outwardly at least he was ever bound by what was correct. Liadan said nothing, but turned her horse and rode away with never so much as a glance behind.

It was strange. We made our way eastward through Eamonn's gardens and woods, past his fields and his settlements, and Sean and his three men rode ahead and behind, keeping a lookout, though surely while we remained within the borders of Glencarnagh there could be no danger. It was not until we had traveled beyond the wooded country and out into a terrain wilder, more open, and studded with rocky outcrops, that I became gradually aware of others riding alongside not so far away, a constant unseen presence. My skin prickled. I though of Otherworld creatures, messengers of the Túatha Dé Danann maybe, come to follow me and find out my secrets. After a time they became visible, as if it had only now become safe to show themselves. There were six or seven of them, and they did indeed have the appearance of some creatures from an old tale, for they were clad all in gray-brown, blending with the winter landscape, and over their heads they wore close-fitting hoods which concealed their features save for the eyes, nose and mouth; there was no telling these warriors one from another. And warriors they were; all were armed with dagger and sword, and some bore bow or staff, axe or throwing-knife. I was alarmed, but the others continued riding as if the presence of these fearsome creatures was nothing out of the ordinary, and I realized belatedly they must be my aunt Liadan's men. Now they had formed a silent guard all around us, and my uncle, whose role as part of the escort seemed suddenly superfluous, reined back his horse to ride by his sister, who was just ahead of me.

Eilis chose this moment to speak up.

"Next time we go to Uncle Eamonn's, I'm going to ride that big black horse," she announced brightly.

"Fainne," said Deirdre, "are you going to marry Uncle Eamonn? Clodagh said you were."

"I did not!" Clodagh exclaimed. "What I said was, who'd marry Uncle Eamonn if they could have someone like Darragh? You weren't listening."

"I was too!"

"That's enough." Sean did not need to raise his voice to silence them. Deirdre scowled. She did not like to be in the wrong.

"Who's Darragh?" inquired Aunt Liadan casually. No one answered. It appeared the question was intended for me.

"Nobody," I muttered.

Liadan raised her brows as if she found my reply less than adequate. We rode through a narrow way between rock walls; the silent escort was before and behind, their work a seamless demonstration of control, achieved with never a word. I was spared from response, as we must go single file. When we emerged, Clodagh answered the question for me.

"Darragh's a boy in Fainne's stories about the traveling folk. He rides a white pony."

"Her name's Aoife," put in Deirdre. "They came, when we were at Glencarnagh. We never thought they were real, but they came to see Fainne. Uncle Eamonn sent them away."

"He came all the way from—from—" Clodagh faltered.

"Ceann na Mara," I said grimly.

"I gave the pony a carrot." Eilis must have her say.

I could not let this go on any longer. "He's nobody," I said repressively, feeling Sibeal's eyes on me as well as Liadan's. "He's just a boy I know from home, that's all. From Kerry. That old woman, the one who sits in your kitchen, Janis I think her name is, she's some sort of relation. He came to see her."

Sean and Liadan glanced at each other.

"This is the lad who came to Sevenwaters looking for you?" asked Sean. "One of Dan Walker's folk?"

"His son," I said.

"Dan played the pipes at my mother's funeral," Liadan said softly. "That was the loveliest music I heard in my life, and the saddest. He must surely be the best piper in all of Erin, that man."

"Darragh plays better," I said before I could stop myself. My fingers moved up to touch the amulet. I must not speak of him. He was gone. Forgotten. I had to remember that, so there was not the slightest reason for my grandmother to be put in mind of him at all.

"Really?" said Liadan, smiling. "Then he must be a fine musician indeed."

But I made no comment, and we rode on in silence with our strange escort keeping pace like watchful shadows.

It was on the second day that it happened. We had stopped overnight at one of my uncle Sean's outer settlements, and I had shared my sleeping quarters with the girls. This arrangement pleased me. Their incessant chatter could be wearisome, but anything was better than having to endure another of those strange conversations with my aunt, in which she seemed to comprehend so much more than I put into words. Aware that I must go on as I had begun, aware of the implications of what I had promised Eamonn, I had no wish to let Liadan befriend me, or to reveal to her any secrets. Indeed, it was time for me to put aside all friendships, and concentrate on what must be done. I had to remember that. I must be strong; I would be strong, for had not my father himself trained me in self-discipline, and him a very model of control?

We rode along a narrow track overlooking a tree-clothed valley. It had been snowing in the night, and the pines still wore a white dusting on their thickly needled branches. Sean's dogs raced ahead, leaving twin sets of neat tracks. It was a still day, the sky a mass of heavy low cloud. Between that and the encroaching trees, I could not escape the old sense of being trapped, shut in. I rode glumly along, trying to find, somewhere in my thoughts, a clear image of the cove, with the wild gulls soaring in the open sky, and the air full of the smell of salt spray, and the thunder of the ocean on the rocks of the Honeycomb. But all I could see was my father's face, wasted and white, and all I could hear was his struggle for breath as he coughed and retched in his shattered workroom.

Our horses picked their way carefully along the track. It was quite narrow, and for a short stretch the hillside went steeply upward on our right, and plunged sharply downward on our left, where tumbled boulders marked the site of some old landslide. Three of the masked men were in front, and then my uncle, followed by Clodagh and Sibeal. I was next, with the others behind me. Lucky, I thought, that my little horse was such a remarkable creature, for I still had no skills whatever in horsemanship. But this gentle mare knew her way, and could be trusted to carry me safely. I owed her a great deal; I had mis-used her, exhausted her, and still she bore me willingly. When we got home I must ensure she had rest, and care, and whatever it was horses liked, carrots maybe.

It was sudden. There was no saying what it was: a bird, or a bat, or something more sinister. It came from nowhere, moving swift as an arrow, swooping down and up again in complete silence, gone almost before I had time to see it. My heart thumped in shock. The mare trembled, and halted. But in front of us, where the shadow had passed, Sibeal's pony shied, lifting its forelegs high, and she was thrown. There was no time to think. I saw her small, cloaked figure flying through the air, down toward the rocky slope on our left. I heard Deirdre's scream from behind me. The craft flowed through me, though I was barely conscious I had summoned it. The long years of practice served me well. *Stop*. The child hung suddenly in midair, suspended not three handspans above a jagged boulder where her small head would have struck with some violence. *Now gently down*. I made the necessary adjustments. A little to the right, so she would come to rest on a narrow ledge beside the ungiving rocks. Not too sudden; she would be frightened and might still fall. Now it was over. I was shivering from head to toe and incapable of speech, as if even this limited use of the craft had drained me.

Aunt Liadan's men were good. Almost before Sibeal had time to realize what had happened, two of them had descended the precipitous slope to the place where she lay, and were supporting her small form to ensure she did not tumble down further. With reassuring words they carried her carefully back up to the track. Liadan, white-faced, checked the child quickly for broken bones; Sibeal herself was remarkably composed, a sniff or two, a slight tremble of the lip her only signs of distress. Eilis, on the other hand, was sobbing with fright. As soon as Sibeal was pronounced unhurt, she was put up in front of her father, and our guard led us with quiet efficiency down the hill to a safe place under the pines, where we might pause for a little and recover ourselves. A small fire was made; tea brewed. I busied myself comforting the now-bawling Eilis, for the last thing I wanted was questions asked. I had acted instinctively; I had taken the only course possible. If it happened again, I knew I would do no differently. Yet I still wore my grandmother's amulet; I still trod her path. I sensed a change, in myself or in the talisman I bore. Since the night she had come to me, the night when she had threatened to destroy all

I held dear, it seemed I could no longer do her will blindly, without question. Was the amulet's power muted somehow by the cord which now bore it? My heart was chill. Perhaps today's incident had been mere chance. But maybe it was Grandmother's doing, a kind of test. If that were so, there was no doubt I had failed it miserably. I had done the exact opposite of what she would have wanted. Perhaps I would never know. Perhaps, from now on, I would have to watch every fall, every little accident, not knowing.

"You're such a good rider, Eilis," I said quietly, smoothing the child's curls. "When we get home I'll tell your mother how you kept your horse under control, even when that happened, and were as brave as could be." Slowly she grew calmer, and after a while Deirdre brought the two of us tea, and I watched from a distance as Liadan checked Sibeal again, more thoroughly this time, peering into her eyes and asking her questions. The child's pony seemed none the worse for wear; it now stood by the others, cropping the meager winter grass.

"Funny," remarked Deirdre. "When people fall off a horse, they usually just—fall. But Sibeal—she sort of floated, the last bit. I've never seen that before."

"Magic," hiccuped Eilis. "Like in a story."

"She could have died." Deirdre was thinking hard. But before she could reach any conclusions, Liadan was there beside us, and the girls were off to cluster around Sibeal and ply her with more tea and questions.

My aunt sat down by me on a fallen branch. Her expression was unsmiling, almost severe.

"My brother did not see what happened here; but I did, Fainne," she said quietly. "At first I thought I was imagining things. But Sibeal said, Fainne saved me."

I did not reply.

"You do not know, perhaps, that your father saved my life once, through the use of the druidic arts. You did a fine thing today, Fainne. Ciarán would be proud of you. So quick; so subtle."

Misery settled on me; I might have wept, if I could.

"You seem sad," said Liadan. "Do you miss him terribly?"

Despite myself, I nodded.

"Mmm," she said. "It's a long way from Kerry. I've wondered why Ciarán did not come with you, for you are overyoung to make such a journey on your own. Conor would have welcomed him. I'm sure he welcomed you. Such talent would doubtless have my uncle busy trying to recruit you to the brotherhood. He has never found another with your father's aptitude."

"Don't be foolish!" I snapped, furious with myself for letting feelings get the better of me again. "Our kind cannot aspire to the higher paths of druidry. We are cursed, and can never walk the ways of light."

Liadan lifted her brows. Her eyes were the green of winter leaves in cool sunlight; her face was snow-pale. "It seems to me," she said softly, "that you've just disproved your own theory."

She was wrong, of course. She did not know the other things I had done, terrible things. She did not understand what I must still do.

"You're shaking, Fainne. You have had a bad shock, my dear. Come, give me your hand, let me help you."

"No!" My voice sounded harsh. I would not let her look in my eyes, and read what was in my mind. Perhaps she thought I did not know she was a seer. "I'm quite well, Aunt Liadan," I added more politely. "What I did was—was simply what one does, a small trick, no more. I'm glad I was able to help. It was nothing."

She did not comment, but I sensed her gaze on me, shrewdly appraising. She rode home beside her brother, and they did not speak aloud, but both seemed very serious. I wondered if they spoke of me, mind to mind, in the strange manner of the Fomhóire folk from whom, if my grandmother were to be believed, they had inherited this skill.

Something had altered at Sevenwaters since we had been gone. I could not quite put my finger on it; it was just as if the feeling had lightened, the shadow had passed, and an order and purpose had come back into the place. It was as if, somehow, the family had regained its heart. Aisling hugged her daughters, smiling; Muirrin hovered behind, and there beside her was Maeve, with a big bandage around her head. Her sisters rushed to greet her, all talking at once.

"Careful now," Muirrin cautioned. "It's only for a moment, then she's to go straight back to bed."

There were smiles and tears all around. I stood back, for I had no part in this. I waited for them to be finished, so I could go to my room and shut the door and be alone. So I could go somewhere and not see. Saving one child did not cancel out harming another. It was not so simple.

The girls were beaming. And Deirdre was blushing. The widest smiles, the most effusive greetings were not in fact for Aisling, or for Maeve, but for someone else entirely. Close by the family stood two more of Liadan's men in their plain dark-colored clothes, though these two were not masked. I had thought them guards. Both were young; one took the eye immediately, for his skin was as dark as fine oak, and his hair was in small braids like a druid's, but decorated with bright beads and scraps of feather at the ends. He stood by Maeve, supporting the child with his arm. I saw Muirrin whisper something in his ear, and he smiled, a quick flash of white teeth.

But it was the other young man who had my cousins' attention, though I could not for the life of me see why. He was an ordinary enough sort of fellow, pleasant-featured, shortish but strongly built, his curling brown hair severely cropped. He turned slightly, and I saw to my surprise the markings on his face, a delicately incised pattern of some subtlety which encircled one eye and swirled boldly onto brow and cheek. It was very fine work; there was a slight suggestion of beak, and feathers, no more. Around us, the men who had made up our guard had dismounted and in turn removed their mask-like hoods, and I saw that every single one of them wore some similar marking on his face, mostly quite small, a few more elaborate, no two quite alike. Each had the hint of a creature about it—badger, seal, wolf, stag. I was the only one staring. To the others, this band of painted warriors must be a familiar sight.

"Fainne." It was Clodagh, who had appeared at my side, and was tugging my sleeve. "This is Johnny."

The ordinary-looking young man was standing behind her, with a friendly grin on his patterned features. I gaped. This was Johnny, the fabled child of the prophecy? This unprepossessing young fellow who seemed no different from one of his own guard? Surely this could not be right. I had expected—well, I had at least expected a warrior of formidable stature, or maybe a scholar steeped in craft and learning. Not—not someone who might just as well be a stablehand or a kitchen man.

"So many cousins," Johnny said, "and all of them girls. I am glad to meet you, Fainne. Maeve has spoken a great deal about you, and told us all your stories." He reached out and clasped my hand. His grip was warm and strong. I looked into his eyes, and realized on an instant that I had been quite wrong. His eyes were gray and deep. They assessed me quickly, recorded what they saw, and put it away for future reference. The man was clever. He was a strategist. And his smile was hard to resist. I found myself smiling back.

"That's better," he said. "Now, here's my friend Evan. Evan's Mother's apprentice. She'll tell you he has the makings of a first-rate healer. He and Muirrin have done wonders with young Maeve. The two of them make a fine team."

He grinned at the dark-skinned man, and then at Muirrin. Muirrin blushed; Evan looked down at the ground. Then Liadan said Maeve should be back in bed, and in the flurry of getting indoors and sorting out baggage, I was able to flee upstairs and into my own chamber, where I bolted the door behind me, though against what, I hardly knew.

I won't like him, I seemed to be saying to myself. *I can't like him. That makes it too hard.* I sat on the floor before the hearth, but I did not light the fire, for all the freezing chill of the winter day. I feared what visions I might see in its heart, the evil things that lay before me, those I might do myself, and those I might be powerless to stop. *It should be easy*, I told myself. *It's a game of strategy. Like brandubh. You know what must be done. Just do it.*

Easy enough to say. Things had indeed changed here at Sevenwaters, and it was not solely that Liadan had come, and that Maeve was now improving faster than anyone had dared to hope. It was him, Johnny. You could see it in the way the men came to him for answers, and the way he spoke to them, friendly, respectful, but confident, as if he were a far older man, seasoned and wise. You could see it in his smile and in his bearing; in the way he wore his plain clothes with pride, as if being part of a team gave him greater satisfaction than any mark of leadership. Yet he was a leader. Older men fell silent to hear him speak. Women hastened to provide his meal or refill his goblet, and blushed when he offered a kind word. He was everywhere, drilling Sean's men in the yard, inspecting the building of a new barn, chatting to Janis in the kitchens. Often enough he could be found by

Maeve's bedside, telling a story, or listening as she whispered confidences. It was his sweet smile that had warmed these halls; his ready offers of help that had brought the color back to Aisling's wan face; his counsel that Sean sought in the evenings, as the men talked long over maps and diagrams. Because of him the household had regained the sense of strength and purpose which had vanished at Samhain, the night of the fire. I had brought the darkness. Johnny had restored the light.

It was close to Meán Geimhridh. Often, at the cove, the weather was so wild in this season that the day could not be read from the stones; all was in shadow as clouds blocked the midwinter sun. Still, I would know; I would go up the hill in rain or gale, and sit beneath the dolmen looking out to the west, thinking if I could see far enough I might catch a glimpse of Tír na nÓg, isle of dreams. But I never did. Then I'd just sit, cloak up over my head against the wind, feeling the strength of the rock at my back like a great supporting hand, and I'd dream my own dreams of summer. Summer would always come. It was just a matter of waiting and being strong. That was all finished now, of course. I had said goodbye to the cove, and to my father. I had sent Darragh away, far away where he could be safe, and for me there could be no more summers.

It was necessary to practice. To do what I must, an exercise of the craft was required which went far beyond what my father had allowed me to do. Indeed, he had expressly forbidden it, and with good reason. So, I must sharpen my skills again, discipline my mind and make myself strong. Then, only then might I attempt a transformation from human girl to wild creature and, still more difficult, a return to myself. The prospect terrified me. What if I had overestimated my own ability? What if I condemned myself to life as a duck or a toad, or worse still, found myself trapped between one form and another? Then I would indeed be powerless to protect those I sought to shield from her. This was a potent charm, one of the most challenging forms of the craft; it drained the strength and taxed the mind. My father had not thought me ready to try it. What if that were still so? Time was passing quickly; already, in the chill of the solstice, it seemed men gathered for some imminent departure, and Aunt Liadan spoke of returning home. Even in winter's darkness, these folk set their gaze on summer's victory. It was not so long. I must prepare.

But how might I rehearse this skill here at Sevenwaters? There was no solitude, no privacy save within the confines of my own chamber, and even there I was constantly interrupted. The house was full, the family busy, and my help in great demand for a variety of tasks, not all of which I was accustomed to. I learned things, but they were the wrong things: how to sew tucks into a bodice, how to preserve apples in honey and to make jellied pigs' tongues, how to pluck a goose, the best way to doctor a sprained wrist.

In the evenings it was difficult to escape unnoticed. With the coming of Johnny and his band of painted warriors, supper had become a more festive occasion, followed as often as not by the telling of tales and the singing of songs. One of the young men had a fine voice, and another was not at all bad on the whistle. There was a small, finely carved harp in the household, and both Deirdre and Clodagh could coax a voice of some sweetness from its delicate strings. In Dan Walker's camp there had been something of the same sense of well being; the same joyful fellowship. Strange, though. These were my own kin, yet I felt less a part of this than I had of that simple, colorful family of traveling folk. I thought more kindly of Peg, who had given me a kerchief and her smile, than of Aunt Liadan with her searching eyes and her silences. I heard their music of celebration and longed for the solitary lament of the pipes.

I considered the forest. Out there, surely many places were open, untenanted: clearings amid winter trees, deserted stretches of lake shore, great lichen-encrusted stones. Those were places well suited to the secret practice of the craft. But I had no druid to walk by me, and the guards were many. Besides, who knew what strange beings looked on in that dark wilderness, all too ready to spy out my secrets and anticipate my moves? I could not go there.

I was beset by doubts and terrified by my own lack of progress. If I left it too long, if I let myself think too hard about what I intended to do and what it meant, then I knew I risked losing the will to act at all. Now, when I touched the cord around my neck it did not seem to focus my mind on the task ahead, but whispered a different message: *You are a child of Sevenwaters*, it told me. *You are one of us*. But I had not forgotten my grandmother's warning. She wanted to see progress. If there was no progress, then she would come back, and she would make others pay the penalty for my disobedience. Yet, when I put my mind to it, it seemed to me that no matter what I chose to do, the folk of Sevenwaters were doomed. I might protect the innocent from my grandmother's wrath by obeying her commands. If I did that, there would be no more fires or unexpected falls, or those other things she had listed such as poisonings or disappearances. Those I sought to protect would be safe, here at Sevenwaters and in Kerry and far west in Ceann na Mara. I might achieve that. But, in the long term, if I carried out her quest the battle would be lost, and the Islands as well, and this family would be plunged into chaos and despair. Was not that a catastrophe far greater than the personal losses I sought to prevent? Indeed, if I heeded the voices of those who called themselves Old Ones, the failure to win the Islands, this time, would signify no less than the passing of the great races of Erin: the Fair Folk, the older folk, the many and strange Otherworld dwellers beneath the surface of things. As for the human kind, they would lose forever the mysteries of the spirit. What sort of man or woman could you call yourself, without those? They would cease to be guardians of earth and ocean, and become no more than parasites living off them, with no heed for what it meant, with no regard for the sacred trust laid on them. Could it be true that this was my grandmother's intention? The choice I faced was no choice at all; both ways ended in darkness. It was no more than I could expect, with the cursed blood that ran in my veins, and in my father's; tainted blood which meant we could never walk the paths of light. I was no child of Sevenwaters. Whichever way I went, I could do no other than destroy my kinsfolk and what they sought so hard to keep safe.

I practiced as well as I could within the confines of my chamber late at night. In the mornings I would emerge white-faced, yawning and ill-tempered. Aunt Liadan watched me, her small, sweet features giving away nothing at all. Aunt Aisling watched me too, frowning, and ordered me to rest in the afternoons, and her daughters to give me a little peace and quiet. I snatched the time gratefully and used it for more practice. I did not dare attempt the full transformation, not yet, but I grew ever closer. I warmed up with other things: the manipulation of objects, which had become easy for me, the dropping and catching, the subtle moving, the cunning adjustments of shape and size. I gave myself a fright once with a giant cockroach; fortunately I was able to reverse the charm with a click of the fingers. I lost one spider, making it so small I could not see it to turn it back. I had not yet mastered the knack of performing this trick blind. I rehearsed transformations before the mirror, easy ones at first, since time was always limited: the prettier, more graceful girl of the fair; a very plain version with a squint and sparse, frizzy hair; a matronly one with a child in her belly and wrinkles on her brow; an ancient crone who bore an uncanny resemblance to my grandmother. I did not keep that guise long, for it chilled me to think there might be a future in which I was just like her. Then, somewhat more difficult, a Fainne who was about eight years old, the same size as my cousin Sibeal. This child stared at me from the polished copper surface of the mirror, her features innocent, unformed; her hair flowing across her small shoulders like a cloak of fire. On her finger she wore a little ring made of wild grasses. And behind her, instead of the dark stone walls of my chamber, I saw the cliffs of the Honeycomb, and the waves of the southern ocean, and the cloud-tossed sky of Kerry. I thought I heard my father's voice saying, *Well done, daughter. You've an aptitude for this*. I made the change back to myself abruptly, too abruptly, for I came close to fainting with the sudden loss of energy that accompanies such transitions, and when I looked back in the mirror, I saw myself wan and drained, like some shadow-girl. Day by day, night by night I polished these skills. Soon, very soon, I must take that last step, girl into wild creature, wild creature into girl.

A letter came from Eamonn. Not to me; that would have been inappropriate, and Eamonn believed in abiding by the rules when he could. The letter was to my uncle Sean, and it was a formal request for my hand in marriage. Such a letter could not be ignored, nor might it be dismissed with a straight refusal, not if the writer were a kinsman and ally. It did not seem to make any difference that Eamonn had already been told such a match was out of the question. Indeed, the man did not appear to understand the word no. He made his request with courtesy, indicating that there was no expectation of a dowry, my circumstances being what they were; he added that, in view of the impending risks of the summer, it was his preference that the marriage take place in spring, at Imbolc maybe. There was another message to be read behind these words. I would be established at Glencarnagh before summer, and accepted as his wife. There was every likelihood he would get me with child before his departure on the great campaign. If he were slain, he would at least have left an heir behind him. This unwritten message would be clear enough to Sean. As for me, I could see Eamonn's true intention. He wished to stamp the brand of ownership on me. Now that he knew what I could do, he wanted to be certain it was his will I worked, and not another's. Information; secrets; intelligence. With me by his side, no opportunity would be closed to him. Best establish that before the campaign began. It had occurred to him, perhaps, that there were possibilities in our union that went far beyond the elimination of one particular enemy.

Sean showed me the letter in private. That I appreciated, not wishing to have Aunt Liadan watching over such an encounter. I read the missive quickly and gave it back to him.

"Very formal," I commented.

My uncle raised his brows. "You're skilled at reading, I see," he said.

"My father taught me. Conor taught him. I suppose I might be called a scholar. Maybe, if you do not allow me to wed, I could seek employment as a household scribe."

Sean glanced at me quizzically. "I think not. Conor saw you as a druid. Would you consider such a calling?"

"My kind cannot do so." My tone was cold. "You should know that, Uncle. I am my father's daughter, after all."

"And your mother's, Fainne. She was my own sister. I owe it to her to make the right choices for you."

"You chose poorly for her," I said bitterly.

"Maybe; and maybe not. It is true that ill fortune befell her. Still, at the time the family did what seemed right. Nobody could have known how it would unfold. Don't think me heartless, Fainne, but in a way, Niamh brought what happened on herself. She chose a man she could not have."

I glared at him. "But for that, I would not exist, Uncle. I am the child of a forbidden liaison. Don't you think this marriage is my best chance to make something of myself?"

Sean sighed, and went to sit by the small table. "You should talk to Liadan about this," he said. "Some aspects of the matter are best discussed between women."

"No," I said quickly. "That should not be necessary. Just give me one good reason why Eamonn and I should not wed; one reason beyond the difference in our ages, for that should be of no import provided I am willing."

I thought I had backed him into a corner, where he must reveal to me the truth about whatever it was between Eamonn and Liadan, some secret they both guarded tightly, from which great bitterness had come. But he was too good a strategist for that.

"Very well," he said. "We need your father's permission. Liadan tells me she is certain he will not give it. But if you are set on this match, let us put it to the test. Tell me where Ciarán can be found, and I will send a messenger with this news, and ask for his blessing on the marriage."

"No!" I could not control my fear. "No, you can't do that!" Once the words were out, they could not be taken back.

Sean looked at me very shrewdly. "I see," he said. "However, we must respond to this letter one way or another, or Eamonn will be on the doorstep demanding answers. You've put me in a very awkward situation, niece."

"I'm sorry," I muttered.

"Never mind. Conor arrives in the morning to perform the solstice ritual; we'll discuss it with him, and with Liadan, before we decide how to word our response. Brighid save us, I think sometimes I've slipped back to a time when such an offer came for your mother, and she refused so much as to listen. Already, then, the sorceress who was our family's old enemy had her hand on us once more, moving us like pieces in some game of her own devising. Perhaps, when it came to it, poor Niamh didn't have a chance."

I turned cold. I thought of my mother, stepping off a ledge into nothingness, and of Liadan's words. *That always seemed to me impossible.* A terrible idea lodged itself in my mind and refused to go away. Perhaps Niamh had not given up. Perhaps her second chance had been snatched away from her.

"You need not be afraid of Liadan," Sean said with a little smile. "She loved her sister, and means you no harm."

"Afraid? Of course I'm not afraid." Even to me this sounded unconvincing. I looked at my uncle again. He sat relaxed, his fingers stroking the head of the great dog that sat by his side. The hound's eyes were half closed in sheer pleasure. At Sean's feet the other dog lay sleeping. "It's just—"

"Tell me, Fainne." His voice was kind. "I wish you to feel at home here, you know that. I want you to consider yourself no different from my own daughters, while you remain with us."

"It's just—the—the power, the ability to speak without words, to look into people's thoughts—she has that, I know. I am—I'm afraid of that, Uncle. Afraid that Aunt Liadan will look into my mind and see things that are—private." Why had I said such a thing? It could do nothing but arouse his suspicions. "A girl of my age does have secrets," I added hastily. "Things she might tell her best friend, maybe, but no one else."

"You should speak to her," Sean said again. "It is true, there are those of the family with this ability. Its strength varies in us; Liadan has a powerful gift, shared by only one other that I know of. But she never uses it to spy, or intrude where she is unwanted, Fainne. Such a gift brings with it great responsibility. It cannot be used lightly. It would, perhaps, be only at a time when she believed those she loved to be in mortal danger that she would be tempted to use it thus."

His words did nothing to reassure me. "I see. Perhaps I will talk to her. Must this be discussed in some—family forum, aired in front of all, Conor, and the others?"

My uncle nodded gravely. "I believe so, Fainne. We must choose our words with care when we frame a reply to Eamonn. He's an influential man; we cannot afford to anger him."

I had not seen Conor since the time of the fire. He had not seen me since he bore the ancient druid home to rest in the deep quiet under the great oaks. I did not know what I would say to Conor. It seemed to me my guilt must show plain on my features to one who knew how to read such things. It seemed to me the evil spirit I had inherited from my grandmother must show stark in my eyes to one as skilled as an archdruid.

I was sitting by Maeve, telling a story. Despite my best efforts to say no, I found I could not deny her repeated requests for me to visit her, and that once seated by her side, I was unable to refuse her a tale. This time I had begun a story of two small friends and how they nearly got trapped by the tide. Maeve and I were not alone; Muirrin was busy with a mortar and pestle, and the dark-skinned young man, Evan, was in the next room tending to a fellow with a nasty gash on the buttock. Wild pigs roamed the forest, and in his efforts to spear a fine specimen for the midwinter feast, this man had got more than he'd bargained for. The tusk had gone in and out cleanly enough; Evan was talking reassuringly as he stitched the wound. Before the small fire stood Johnny. He'd come in after I started, and I had thought to cease the tale, being unwilling to reveal myself thus before him. But Maeve said, "Go on, please, Fainne," in her polite little voice, and Johnny gave his wide, disarming grin, and I continued.

"Well, what were they to do? The waves were getting higher, and the day was growing darker, and all that was left of the beach was a tiny little strip of sand scarce wide enough for Fainne's two feet to stand on. She was scared, but she wouldn't let on to Darragh, so she didn't say a thing, just clutched Riona tight and looked at the water coming closer, and felt the rock wall steep behind her; too steep to climb up."

Maeve watched me solemnly. Her head was still bandaged; the eye, at least, had healed, the swelling gone down, the vision still intact. Her hands were swathed. I knew Muirrin took off the linen strips twice a day, and made Maeve move and bend her fingers. I had heard the child weeping with pain as she stretched the damaged skin. Muirrin herself tended to emerge from these sessions red-eyed.

"Then Darragh said, 'We'll have to swim. It's not so far—just to those rocks there, and then we can scramble to the jetty. Give Riona to me, I'll carry her.' And Fainne said in a little wee voice, 'I can't swim.' Darragh stared at her, with the water coming up around his ankles, and then he said, 'Don't suppose I can leave you to drown, can I? Think you can float on your back, and not panic? I'll swim for the two of us. Have to go out a way; the waves come up quick.' As he spoke, he was fastening Riona into his belt and wading into the sea. The waves were splashing onto the base of the cliff now; Fainne felt the water up to her knees, dragging at her skirt. The very thought of going in deeper made her tremble all over. But she would not show Darragh she was frightened. So she did as he bid: moved out into the frothing sea, and let it come all around her so she was chilled through; felt Darragh's arms under her own and across her chest, holding her safe, and then they were moving through the water, letting it carry them. Fainne had never been so scared. Sometimes the water splashed over her, into her mouth and up her nose, and once Darragh's grip slackened and she nearly went right under. It was cold as ice, and she felt the power of the ocean as it bore them up and down, up and down. Once, she dared to open her eyes and look back; but she closed them again quickly, for they were far, far out from shore, so far it seemed impossible that Darragh could ever swim back in again, not with her weighing him down. She screwed her eyes tight shut.

" 'Look, Fainne,' said Darragh. 'We've got company. Now that's a rare sight, that is.' He sounded quite like himself; not at all like a boy who was in danger of drowning. He was hardly even out of breath. Cautiously, she opened one eye just a bit. And there beside them, to right and to left, swam great sleek creatures of the deep, keeping pace like graceful guardians. Selkies they were, children of Manannán mac Lir, come to see them safe to shore. All the way across the bay they played, diving and circling, dancing in the water, and Fainne stared spellbound, quite forgetting to be afraid. And at length, there were the smooth rocks at the end of the bay, and Darragh and Fainne scrambled out of the water, shivering with cold and grinning from ear to ear. The two selkies swam away with never a look back, but for a while they could be seen playing a game of chase out beyond the waves.

" 'They do say,' said Darragh, watching, 'that the selkies are part human. Did you know that? Sometimes they come ashore and take off their skins, and become men and women again, for a while. But they have to go back. The sea calls them. It's an enchantment laid on them. That's what they say.'

"Fainne nodded, and the two of them walked home, cold, wet and tired, but not unhappy. As for Riona, she'd had a bath she didn't want, but she dried out soon enough before the hearth fire, and what she thought of the whole thing, nobody knew, for she wasn't saying."

Maeve gave a little sigh of satisfaction, and I looked up, and there in the doorway from the next room was Conor.

"A true story, no doubt," he observed gravely, coming forward to greet Muirrin and Johnny, and to touch the child's head with a gentle hand.

"Oh, yes," said Maeve with certainty. "All of Fainne's stories are true. Well, maybe not the one about the clurichaun. But Darragh's real."

"Indeed?" Johnny was grinning, eyebrows raised as he looked at me. "Such a fine swimmer, too. I'd like to meet the lad myself, I think. Sounds a useful sort of fellow to have around."

"Well, you're unlikely to," I said repressively. "He lives far away, in the west. And the stories are not quite true, and not quite untrue."

"That's the way of it with all the best tales," said Conor. "You learned this art from your father, I think," he added quietly. "He'd the same ability to hold us all spellbound with his words."

"Excuse me." I jumped to my feet and fled, muttering something about things to do. When I was safe in my room, I willed myself to calm, and stood before the mirror, and summoned the craft. But my mind was jumbled and sad, and I could not escape my own haunted features staring grimly back at me. In the end I gave up. I opened my wooden chest and, rummaging deep, took out the silken shawl which once, long ago in another life, I had worn to ride to the fair. I sat on the floor with its drift of summertime colors around my shoulders, and I shut my eyes tight and rocked back and forth, and I whispered, *I'm sorry, I'm sorry*. But whether I spoke to my father, or to Darragh, or simply to myself, there was no telling.

To give in to such weakness was dangerous. It showed a lamentable lack of self-control. My father had never let his feelings get the better of him thus. How disappointed he would be if he could see me. And yet—and yet there were those long times when he shut himself away in the workroom and would not let me near. Did he wrestle with the complex practice of the craft, or was it something else he fought? I had seen him emerge at the end of the day with just such an expression of confusion and self-loathing as I read on my own features now. Then, I had put it down to the great challenges he set himself as a master sorcerer. Now, suddenly I was not so sure. As a child, I would have done anything to take away his sadness, to bring that rare smile to his lips, and yet, when this mood was on him, he would shrug off touch, would cut short my anxious queries. Later he would do his best to make up for it, sharing a tale by the fire, listening patiently as I recounted the small events of my day. I had longed to make his world right, and had known I could not. My love for him had colored my life then, and it did so still. It was my grandmother's strongest weapon, and it bound me to a future of shadows and betrayal.

I could not escape Conor. He found me before supper, as I undertook an errand for Aunt Aisling. I was in the kitchens, where there was another set of eyes that I'd sooner have avoided. The old woman, Janis, had not said much to me since I returned from Glencarnagh, but what she had said had made me more than uncomfortable.

"I always knew," she remarked, fixing her dark, probing gaze on me, "that your mother would invite trouble. And she did. Seems as if you're no different."

"What do you mean?" I snapped, outraged at such a ridiculous accusation.

"Did he find you?" was her next effort.

"Who?" I glared at her.

"Who do you think?"

There was a pause. I realized I had clenched my hands tight. I forced myself to relax them.

"I didn't see him," I told her coolly.

"Didn't, or wouldn't?"

"What's it to you?" How dared she interrogate me thus?

"Lass, I'm old enough to speak the truth without fear. Maybe you won't listen. Niamh didn't care to listen, if what I had to say didn't suit her. You'll do a thing you regret forever, if you break that boy's heart."

"That's nonsense," I said, shivering, but my tone had lost its certainty. "Hearts, and the breaking of them, don't come into this. Darragh is—was—my friend, that's all. He's gone away now. He has a sweetheart in Ceann na Mara, a lovely girl who knows all about horses and has a rich father. It's—it's very suitable. There's no hearts in it, not for him and me."

Janis sighed, and gave a little smile which had no joy in it at all. "I saw the look in his eyes, lass. Seems to me you don't know the worth of what you cast aside. Seems to me you can't see your way at all."

"I can," I whispered, wondering why it was I stayed by her listening, letting her hurt me so much with her words. "It is—it is just because of this, because I do know these things, that I must do as I do. It is better this way. Better for Darragh. Better for everyone."

Janis was scrutinizing me closely. "That's not the way it works, lass," she said quietly. "You can't order other folks' lives, and their feelings, to suit what you think's best. Grew up with Darragh, didn't you?"

I nodded, tight-lipped.

"Mm. He told me. And did he ever once let you make his choices for him?"

I shook my head.

"Well, then."

"I know what's best," I said fiercely.

Janis reached out her knobbly old fingers and took my hand. Her touch was surprisingly gentle.

"There's a lot of weeping in it, lass," she said.

All I could do was nod, for her words brought back the little image I had seen in my dreams, night after night, ever since the day I turned a girl into a fish and let her own mother make an end of her with a kitchen knife. I saw myself racked by such anguish it threatened to tear me apart.

"I can't help that," I said in strangled tones, and then I fled.

After that I did my best to stay away from Janis. Still, there were errands, and it was unthinkable not to do them, for in this household Aunt Aisling's word was law. So I was there in the kitchen, asking the cook to send some men down to some barn or other to collect chickens, and Janis sat silent by the fire, watching me. And on the other side of the hearth was Conor, doing just the same.

"Ah," he said with a smile, "the very girl I need to see. Come, Fainne, let us take a short walk together. I've a proposition for you."

There was no refusing. I found a cloak hanging near the fire; Conor put his hood up. It had been snowing again, and we left the mark of our boots in the pristine white as we walked down the track toward the forest. There was that strange sort of warmth in the air which presages more snow before nightfall. I waited for the druid to speak. I tried to anticipate what his questions might be, and to form convincing answers in my head. He might ask me about the fire and my part in it. He might speak of deaths and injuries. He might ask me, again, why I had come here. Perhaps it was of my marriage he would wish to speak; to tell me how impossible it was.

"We celebrate Meán Geimhridh tomorrow," said Conor. "You proved an able assistant last time, Fainne. Will you perform this duty for me again?"

I struggled to find a reply. "I—I cannot imagine why you would want me to do so. It would not be at all appropriate."

"No?" asked Conor, smiling a little. "And why would that be?"

I could not tell the truth: that my acting thus would be a travesty. On the night of Samhain I had let myself pretend that I was one of the family. On the night of Samhain my grandmother had come, and I had made the fire.

"I can't," I said bluntly. "You know I can never belong to the order of the wise ones. You knew my father could not, but you lied to him and let him think it was possible, all those years. That was like— it was like promising someone a wonderful prize, if they worked hard enough for it, and then, when they'd earned it, snatching it away. No wonder my father still speaks of you with bitterness. I cannot be a druid, Uncle. I cannot do these things. I am not fit for it."

It was a long time before Conor replied. If I had upset him, I told myself I did not care; it was time he faced the truth of what he had done. He sat down on the stone wall, near the place where the track made its way under the leafless trees into the shadows of the forest. I stood by him looking out over the lake.

"I remember your grandfather rebuilding this wall, stone by stone," he remarked eventually. "A wise and patient teacher, was Hugh of Harrowfield. He taught the men here the right way to do it, but he played his own part; always, he showed by example. There's a trick to it, a knowledge. You have to run the stones with the length of them across the wall line, and their thinnest section must be laid horizontal; that way the stones support one another, and do not break under pressure. Like a great family, these stones; the strong support the weak, but each plays its part in the enduring whole."

I made no comment. It seemed this was a learning tale.

"What you said is not correct, Fainne," Conor said gravely. "I understand why you might think it so, for it was what your father believed: that because he was the son of a sorceress, he was forbidden the powers of light, the higher practice of the craft. Once that idea was fixed in his mind, no argument could shake it. I tried to tell him, that night when he came to the house and we let him know the truth about his parentage. But he would not listen."

"How can it be wrong? Our blood is evil. No matter how hard we try, all of our choices lead to darkness. There's no controlling that. I know."

Conor sighed. "You're very young, Fainne. How can you say this with such certainty?"

"Because—because that's what happens to me," I whispered. "There's no point in pretending any differently."

"I cannot believe that, child."

"It's true, Uncle. It's not just what my father chose to believe. It's an old, old thing. The tale of what we are. We are descended from one of the Túatha Dé, the Fair Folk; from one who was cast out for practicing a dark form of the craft. She summoned up something evil and let it loose in the world. So the Fair Folk banished her, and forbade her the higher magic. It is so for all her descendants."

Now Conor was looking at me very intently indeed. "An interesting tale," he said. "But just a tale, after all. Where did you hear this, Fainne?"

"My . . . my father said it is so."

"And where did he hear it, I wonder? One can choose to believe such stories or not. But I will give you a counter-argument which you cannot but believe, for it is based on proven fact."

I waited.

"Now tell me. Have you ever seen your father employ the craft for an ill purpose?"

"No," I replied reluctantly. "But that's different. My father made a choice. He told me. He said, our kind are drawn to evil. But one can always choose not to use the craft."

Conor nodded gravely. "So, he does not exercise his skills at all?"

I frowned. "He practices; for what, there is no telling. Perhaps merely to challenge himself; to fill the empty days. He used to demonstrate, in order to teach me. But—he did use it once." I glanced at the druid. "He saved the folk of the cove, when the Norsemen came. They still tell of it."

"So," said Conor, "the only time he used it, it was to do great good."

"Folk died," I said. "There was a flaxen-haired warrior, washed up on the shore among the splinters of the longships."

"It's a complicated business. Sometimes it's hard to extricate right from wrong, Fainne. And you are young yet, and barely started on your training."

"What does that mean?" I snapped, somewhat affronted that he considered me a mere beginner.

"We've spoken of your father. But what of you? You say you can only walk a path into darkness, because of what you are. I tell you that is wrong. You do have the choice. Yes, you are the granddaughter of a sorceress. But your other grandmother was my sister Sorcha, whom they sometimes call the daughter of the forest. She was the strongest of women; great of heart, pure of spirit, well-beloved in this household and this community. Your grandfather, Hugh of Harrowfield, was a stalwart and admirable man, for all he was a Briton. You carry that heritage too, Fainne. You are one of us, whether you wish it so or not. And you're wrong about the craft. Liadan told me what happened with Sibeal, on the way from Glencarnagh. You used your skills for good, then. I'm sure there have been other times."

I felt as if I were going to cry. "I've done some very bad things, Uncle." It felt as if the words were being squeezed out of me despite myself. "Terrible things that I cannot tell you. If the family knew these things, I would be cast out as my father was."

"Ciarán was never cast out." Conor's voice was calm, but the shadow of an old pain still lingered there. "He chose to leave. He chose a perilous path. I believe he sought her out. The lady Oonagh."

"The lady Oonagh?"

He raised his brows. "His mother, the sorceress."

"Is that her name? I always just called her Grandmother."

Sometimes, you say something, and once the words are out, you know they should never have been spoken. But it is too late to unsay them. I watched Conor's expression change; saw the serene confidence vanish to be replaced by a pallid tightness that almost suggested fear. I wrenched my gaze away, looking again down to the empty waters of the lake, today gray and sullen under the heavy winter sky.

"You—" he ventured, and cleared his throat. "Tell me, Fainne," he said with more control, "was—was your grandmother present, during your growing years in Kerry?" I thought he chose his words with the utmost care. As for me, I had let the conversation stray into very dangerous waters. I had lost control of it, and of myself. That was druids for you. With my upbringing I should have known better.

"No, Uncle. She was there for a little. I grew up with just my father, as I told you."

"If he believed the craft would lead you into evil, why did he teach you thus?"

I had no answer for this.

"Come," he said. "It grows chill. Let us walk back."

"Yes, Uncle."

We made our way up to the keep in silence. I was torn by conflicting feelings, chiefly fear of my grandmother's fury if she had observed this interchange. But beyond this fear there was a terror far stronger, that perhaps Conor might be right. Was it possible that, after all, I might not be evil through and through, but might aspire to something different? That thought was cruel. Surely it was no more than the vain hope that had once been dangled before my father, then rudely snatched away. And yet—and yet, I had saved Sibeal. I had done good without even thinking about it. As we made our way up to the main door, where boys were busy sweeping snow from the pathways, and girls well wrapped in scarves and shawls were hanging garlands of greenery about the entry, I remembered that time at the fair. There had been no reason to stop that fellow from playing his nasty tricks; no need to release his furred and feathered captives, beyond a sense of what was right. But I had done it. I had been wearing the amulet and still I had done it.

The idea Conor had put into my mind was so terrifying I wished with all my heart it had never been spoken. But once there it lodged firm and could not be shaken. Indeed, I realized the truth had been creeping up on me for a long time now. From the moment I had restrung Grandmother's little charm on that strange cord of many fibers, this new possibility had been growing in my mind. Something in that necklace seemed to work against the evil of the talisman, something bright and fine. Maybe it was love, or family; perhaps both. I was glad my grandmother had never mastered the art of look-

ing into a person's thoughts; the art my aunt Liadan was said to possess in abundance. For this was an idea my grandmother must not be
allowed to see.

That night I put out the hearth fire in my chamber and sat shivering in the light of a single small candle, as shadows danced across the
walls, keeping time with my thudding heart. It was snowing outside;
the quiet was profound. I had believed I had no choice but to do as
my grandmother wished: attempt a fearful task of grandiose propor-
tions. Impossible as that seemed, I had planned to do it, for I was
bound by fear, and by my belief that sooner or later, I could do nothing but work her will and follow the evil path to which my cursed
blood bound me. Daunting, but in its way easy, because it was
inevitable, and outside my own control.

But I had been wrong. The power of the amulet had twisted my
mind and dulled my ability to reason. It had made me blind to all but
what she wanted me to see. Through it she had worked her ill deeds,
and made me believe they were my own. A powerful sorceress
indeed. But maybe not so powerful. She had never explained why she
could not simply kill the child of the prophecy herself and end this
once and for all. All she had said was that events must unfold according to the ancient foretelling. And that night when I had taken off the
amulet, she had come rushing to find out what I was doing. She really
had been afraid of me; afraid of what I might do if I escaped her control. *A momentous unfolding of events*, my father had said, and something about finding the right purpose for my gifts. Very well, it
seemed I had found that purpose now, though I trembled to contemplate it. I could give my father back his life. I could show him that our
kind might indeed aspire toward the light. I could ensure these folk
were not robbed of the chance to win their battle and save their
Islands. They were my family: wise Conor, so disconcertingly like my
father, and Sean, who seemed to want only the best for me. Aunt Aisling treated me as if I were her own daughter. Then there was Liadan,
whose love for her sister still showed in her eyes, and Johnny, the perfect son. And what about the girls, now so much a part of my life I
was hard put to imagine the time when their tears and chatter had not
sounded like a sweet, discordant music through the quiet of my days?
When this was over, whatever happened, there could be no place for
me here among them, I knew that. And Kerry would be lonely now,

even in summertime. I could never make up for the terrible wrongs I had done. The past could not be remade. But I could tread a different path if I dared, from this point on. It would be a path of fear and sacrifice; in time, perhaps a path of redemption. The lady Oonagh was strong. I must be even stronger.

Chapter Eleven

y mind began to work very quickly indeed. She would come if she thought I was too slow, of that I had no doubt at all. I must act first. I must preempt her visit. I must summon her myself, though the prospect of her coming anywhere near Sevenwaters chilled me. I would take control; I would demonstrate my compliance. I wished her to be in no doubt whatever that I was still her puppet, and dedicated to work her will. It was a perilous way I contemplated; none must know the truth. Thank the goddess Darragh was safe back in Ceann na Mara, which was surely far enough away for my grandmother to forget him. As for my father, he trusted me to make my own decisions, and though this was the biggest decision of my life, the same rule applied. He had brought me up to do things without help, and I would be true to his teaching.

I would need some reason to summon Grandmother; a progress report, that should please her. The plan I had outlined for her involved spying for Eamonn, finding out the information he needed to destroy his old enemy, the one they called the Chief. What was the fellow's name? Bran? I must do it, and glean some news to show her I had not been idle. And I could not spy unless I could transform. It was time for an exercise of the craft.

"Good," said a strange little voice right behind me. I froze in shock, there where I sat before the cold hearth in the semi-darkness.

For a moment I had thought—I had really thought—but no, this soft hooting tone was nothing like my grandmother's.

"You think so?" I asked cautiously as my heart went back to its normal pace, and I turned to observe the owl-like creature as it stood round-eyed by my window in its feather cloak and little red boots. I must indeed have been absorbed in my thoughts if I had sat unaware while it flew in, and changed.

"I know so, fire child. I see it in your face. A different look. So what's it to be? A ginger cat, maybe, all hiss and danger? A flea? That would give you an intimate insight. You'll learn something tonight, for they all sit up by lantern light, behind closed doors. Best be quick."

I frowned. "Reading my thoughts now, are you?" I queried, wondering whether I might risk trusting this small personage which seemed to understand so much without being told.

A gurgle of laughter. "Not us. Just waited for you to work it out, that's all. And we're everywhere, though folk don't see us. We read it in your eyes. Took you long enough to find your way through this puzzle, and you a druid's only daughter."

There seemed no possible answer to this, save maybe a question. "Do you think—do you think my father intended—?"

"You'd have to ask him that question. Now come on, time's passing. What's it to be?"

I shivered. "I must make my way unseen to the chamber where they meet, enter by a locked door in the dark, remain there unobserved, and return safely here. No cats, that's certain. A creature of night, quite small; one which can enter through the crack between door and frame."

"A cockroach?" the creature suggested helpfully.

"I thought, a moth," I said, my voice shaking with the very idea of it.

"Good idea. Go on, then."

I recalled, belatedly, that an owl was also a creature of the night, and I remembered the camp of the traveling folk, and a certain miniature predator swooping down on its prey with needle-sharp claws and snapping beak.

"I hope you're not here just for an easy supper," I said, frowning.

"I've eaten already, thank you," replied the creature politely. "Come on, hurry up. Can you do it or not?"

"I've never tried this before."

"We know. That's why I'm here. A watcher. You need one, the first time. This sort of thing's second nature to our kind. Be warned. You'll feel it afterward. Takes quite a toll. Be sure you're back in here before you undo the charm."

The first step. It was necessary to create a picture in the mind, a sort of map of what must be done, plain enough for even the smallest and simplest of creatures to retain. I closed my eyes and made myself visualize the path I must follow, out of my chamber, beneath the door where a gap admitted a chill of winter draft, along the dark passageway to the chamber where they would be meeting, a smallish, private room at the top of the stairs. I captured in my mind the faint outline of that doorway, light showing dimly from within. I must make my way through the crack at the top of the door, then simply cling to wall or ceiling, and listen until I heard something, anything I might use to convince my grandmother I was moving forward with my plan. Then I made myself feel and see the return journey, back through the tiny slot, along the hallway on rapid wings, coming to rest at my own doorway, creeping under, safe again. This pattern must be very clear in my mind before I began, and so must the charm of reversal. These two things I must hold, and my knowledge of myself, or be lost forever in that other form. My heart pounded in anticipation. I must do this. I would do this.

"Now," said the owl-creature.

The second step. I thought *moth*. I felt the shape, the lightness, the alteration of balance, so that instead of up and down, floor and ceiling, there were simply different sorts of planes, and different kinds of touching. I felt the power of the wings, and the strange pull of the light. I felt my consciousness dwindle and alter and focus into something far simpler and more direct. In my head I spoke the words, and changed.

For a moment there was only blind panic. I could not sort out legs from wings, my eyes did not seem to be working properly, I blundered and toppled and fluttered in helpless circles on the floor.

"Door," said a voice, and it scared me, but somewhere there was a pattern and I understood I must follow it. I flew erratically to the faint crack of light and crept through beneath the door. Brightness. Warmth. I wanted that. I wanted the light, and it was there, not far above. I flew, more boldly now, drawn to its glow, knowing I must go to it, I must get closer . . .

"No, fire child. Not that. Remember who you are. Remember the pattern."

The voice. I should heed the voice. But there was the light. The light called me so strongly . . .

"You will burn if you fly into the lantern. Follow the pattern. Do not lose yourself."

Somewhere, the sense of self, deep within, my father's training. I was Fainne, daughter of Ciarán. This moth-form was only a shell, and I must disregard the way it pulled me toward that sweet glow of warmth. My fragile wings carried me high along the hallway, safe above the tantalizing flame of the lantern. I could not see my strange companion; perhaps the creature had stayed behind the closed door of my bedchamber. But its voice still guided me.

"Good, fire child. Remain yourself. Do not give in to that other mind, or you are indeed no more than an owl's next meal, and not much of one at that. Now go in."

I had reached the entry to the small council chamber. There was only just space enough to crawl between oaken door and frame. Inside there were lights again: two lanterns, and candles. They summoned me the way a stream of clear water calls to a thirsty man after a long day's journey. With an effort of will, I held myself on the wall by the door. My vision was strange: there were no colors, only light and dark, and I could see right around me, not just in front. I could scarcely begin to interpret what my new eyes showed me; to do so, I would need to learn to see all over again. I concentrated on hearing and, with an effort, made out the separate voices of Conor, Sean and Liadan, and, to my surprise, Johnny. It came to me that I owed it to Johnny that any part of the conversation was spoken aloud. But for his presence, they might have used the voice of the mind, and conducted it in total silence. None but a seer might have spied on such a council.

It was hard to listen and harder still to understand. Part of me heard only sounds, sounds of danger, and part of me saw and felt only darkness and light: the darkness of unseen predators lurking in the shadows, the coaxing, wonderful, flickering light there on the table that called me, called me so strongly. Focus. The words, the pattern. I must not lose myself in that other. The pattern was listen, door, fly, door, safe. Then the charm of reversal. First, listen.

"What it means, I cannot guess," Conor was saying gravely, as if he had just reached the conclusion of some narrative. "What influences there have been, I shudder to contemplate. The question is, what action do we take now?"

There was a brief silence.

"Are you telling us," Sean's tone was careful, "that you believe young Fainne has come here as an emissary of the lady Oonagh? That seems quite fanciful, and I cannot bring myself to believe it. I've never concurred with your doubts about the girl. She's a good child. Aisling speaks quite highly of her. She's had a strange upbringing, and is a little shy and awkward, but no more than that, surely."

"You forget the use of sorcerer's magic." Liadan's voice was chill. "We have seen that. She's strong; strong and able, like her father. And it would be just the lady Oonagh's way, would it not, Uncle, to seek to harm us by using as her weapon a child we long to take to ourselves, to love and to welcome? Niamh's own daughter. It's cruel indeed, and has the unmistakeable stamp of the sorceress on it. Did you not say Fainne knows how to conjure fire with her fingers? Doesn't that tell you anything?"

"You can't be suggesting—but that's preposterous, Liadan!" Sean spoke in a shocked whisper. I crept closer to hear, moving from wall to ceiling so that I clung upside down in the shadows. Below me, one of Sean's great dogs twitched its ears and began a low, ominous growling. I sensed the scurrying movement of other small creatures close by me; I felt a sudden terror without understanding its cause.

"That can't be right, Mother." Johnny spoke with absolute confidence. "I've seen Fainne with the children. She loves them. You should hear her telling stories, or see her by Maeve's bedside. There's no evil there; indeed, there's a simplicity about her that makes the very idea unthinkable."

Liadan sighed. "You can't know. But Conor could tell you, I think. Wasn't it just so with the lady Oonagh?"

"Not exactly," said Conor heavily. "We never trusted the sorceress, not from moment my father first brought her home as his intended bride. But she had a kind of charm; like a faery Glamour she would put on to convince people she was sweet and well-meaning; to trap them. My father was ensnared thus, and my brother Diarmid as well. A sorceress has the ability to do this. It will not succeed with one such as myself or Liadan. But with you, son, or with Sean here, it might."

"Impossible," said Johnny flatly. "I may not be a seer, but I know how to read a man's character, or a woman's. Fainne is confused, scared; that's the truth. Underneath that, she's a child, and innocent. What is it you're afraid of?"

"I'll tell you," said his mother in an oddly constrained voice. "Once, long ago, I was presented with a choice. The Fair Folk came and ordered me to remain here in the forest so that my child could be kept safe from the influence of the sorceress. Conor will vouch for that; he gave me the same advice. They came close to saying that the prophecy would not be fulfilled unless I did as they bid me."

"But you disobeyed," said Johnny. "Why?"

"I suppose there seemed no choice really. I could keep you safe, or I could risk your future, and the future of Sevenwaters, the forest and the Islands themselves. Most folk would find what I did hard to understand. But there was Bran. He could not stay with me, here in the forest. To protect my son, I would have had to cast away the man who is the other part of me; to deny him his own child. That I would not do. I defied their orders and set my back to Sevenwaters. I went against Conor's good advice. And it was through my own intervention that Niamh escaped her husband and fled to Ciarán. But for that, Fainne would never have existed. They warned me. The Fair Folk warned me that—that—no, I cannot put this into words. I hoped I would never have to tell you this, Johnny. I have never told your father."

"You're saying Fainne's presence is somehow a threat to me? To my safety?" Johnny was bemused. "How can that be, Mother?"

"The lady Oonagh sought control of Sevenwaters once," Sean said slowly. "She was defeated then by my mother's strength; by human strength. It may be the sorceress tried again, through Ciarán; and now tries once more through his daughter. That was what my mother believed. When Niamh and Ciarán first set eyes on one another, and cast a darkness on this house, she saw that as the lady Oonagh's hand reaching out over us once more. She believed that old evil would continue to make itself known, generation by generation, until the prophecy was fulfilled and all made right again. It could be true. If the lady Oonagh indeed still lives, she must move swiftly to thwart us now, for our venture seems likely to succeed by summer. But if we do not have the child of the prophecy, we are doomed."

"The girl is troubled," said Conor. "She has much of her father in her, with his intelligence and his sensibilities. Were it not for this foolishness with Eamonn and the pressure that places on us, I would prefer to take the time to gain her trust, and convince her she may be a power for good, whatever she may have been taught. Fainne does not seem to me bent on a course of evil."

"Forgive me, Uncle, but I think your own feelings blind you to the truth," Liadan said tightly. "You felt the loss of Ciarán keenly; you never found another with such talents, and the brotherhood dwindles. Be careful you do not trust too much, seeing in Fainne only what you want to see."

Conor's response was immediate. "She saved Sibeal. She is your sister's daughter, and only in her sixteenth year. What would you have me do?"

"Common sense tells me, send her straight back home," Liadan said flatly. "Let Ciarán take responsibility for her, since he chose to raise the child in the knowledge of a sorcerer's arts, and exposed her to his mother's influence."

"I don't think we can do that." Sean spoke with authority. "My niece is frightened; I saw it when I told her we must seek Ciarán's permission if she were to wed Eamonn."

"You *what*?" His sister's voice was shocked.

"The idea's unpalatable, certainly; but I have learned a little from experience. I could hardly dismiss her request without explanation. She refused to countenance the idea of sending a message to her father. The girl's terrified for some reason; terrified of making contact with him."

"But not frightened of him," put in Conor quietly. "She speaks of him with the greatest loyalty and respect."

"I won't send her back to Kerry," Sean said, in a tone which indicated a decision had been made. "Not against her will. We cannot know what forces are in play here. It's hard for me to believe Fainne might mean any harm to us, but I trust your judgment, sister. I would not wish to jeopardize our venture, nor to risk my family."

Liadan was silent.

"There's only one solution, then." Johnny spoke with cheerful confidence. "We'll take her north with us. Put Eamonn off politely; say his intended bride wishes to wait for her father's approval, and that Ciarán cannot be reached just now. Meanwhile Fainne is whisked out of harm's way, and all's well. There'll be no shortage of enthusiastic suitors for her on Inis Eala, and every one of them younger and likelier than Eamonn of Glencarnagh, if somewhat less well-endowed with worldly goods. She'll forget him soon enough."

"You haven't been listening to a single thing I've told you," Liadan said wearily.

"I always listen, Mother," said Johnny with a smile in his voice. "I'll make a wager if you like. I'll wager I'm big enough and strong enough to stay out of harm's way, sorceress or no sorceress. How's that? Besides, if you think Fainne's confused or frightened, what better place to seek guidance than Inis Eala? If she wants answers, that's where she'll find them, surely."

"The lady Oonagh tried to kill you once."

"I'm still here, aren't I?" said Johnny blithely.

Listening with all the concentration I could summon, I had forgotten for a while that I was moth as well as girl. I moved my feet to go closer, but one foot was caught in something, and I sought to free it, and my legs were suddenly tangled. I flapped my wings, struggling to break away, and the sticky thread tightened around fluttering wing and fragile limb, and could not be broken. In the darkness behind me I sensed a presence, hungry, waiting. The part of me that was still Fainne told me *Web, spider. Free yourself now, quickly.* The part of me that was moth was seized by a blind terror that held me fast as I beat my wings in frantic, futile effort. The presence came closer, moving like a clever dancer on its delicate cobweb bridge.

"Quick!" said the voice of my feathered guide as I felt my death at my back. "One short, sharp jerk. Quick now."

I pulled to the side, using all the weight of my body, slight as it was, moving my wings as hard as I could while the spider made a sudden dart out toward me, and at last breaking free, spiraling downward out of control with fragments of the sticky fiber still clinging to my legs. My blundering flight took me into the side of the lantern; hot. I fell to the table, landed on my back; felt death close again. The dogs were barking. I was lifted in a large hand; another hand came over, trapping me between. I struggled, flapping, until I regained my feet. I waited for one final, crushing blow.

"Poor thing," Johnny said. "Doesn't rightly know which way it's going." There was movement, and the hands opened, and I crawled off the warmth of human skin onto the stones by the doorway in the shadows. Having thus released me, my cousin went back to the table, and with my strange insect-sight I thought I saw him lay a reassuring hand on his mother's shoulder. "That's settled, then," he said as I crept out through the crack above the door and flew away down the hallway, high above the lure of the lantern, all the way along until I reached my own door. Quickly down and under. Safe. Rest.

"Now the charm." My Otherworld companion stood by the window; I sensed the small red boots not far from me, felt the threat of their hard heels. I did not want to move for now. It was dark here; I could be still.

"The charm. It is not finished. Speak the words, fire child."

Dimly it came to me: the charm, the pattern. Door, fly, door. Listen. Door, fly, door, safe. The charm. Somewhere the words of the counter-spell still dwelt within me, and I sounded them out in the silence of my moth-mind, words that seemed to have no meaning, only power. Around me the room tilted and changed; dim colors appeared, the candlelight gold, the russet of a gown laid across the bed, the green and crimson of a holly wreath Clodagh had tied up over my window to welcome spirits abroad at Meán Geimhridh. The chamber faded and brightened, faded and brightened; the figure of the owl-creature swam before my eyes. I looked down and saw that I was myself again. I looked up, and around me candle and window and owl-being shifted and merged and jumbled all together. Then I was falling, and everything went black.

"I'd never argue with your father on a point of strategy, and I won't with you. The men rely on you to make the right decisions, and so will I."

The voice made its way into my consciousness as I came slowly awake. I kept my eyes shut. I was in bed, tucked up warmly, and there was the little crackle of a hearth fire. A lovely smell; some drink with ginger and cloves. I was tired; I was so weary, and the bed felt soft and good. My body ached all over. I thought maybe I would just go right back to sleep . . .

"Besides," it was Johnny's voice this time, "in your heart, you want her to come. I see through that stern demeanor. You must agree Fainne's a lovely girl, sorcerer's daughter or no. Can't you just see her, shining like a little bright lamp in our grim house of men?"

"Her mother certainly drew them like moths to a flame," Liadan said wryly. "And indeed sometimes I think this is Niamh all over again, so stubborn, so prickly, and yet a fine girl and easy to love. You read me well, son. I cherish my four boys; but I have longed for a daughter. Maybe it's true. Maybe what Fainne needs is protection. But there's a terrible risk as well, I know that better than anyone, save Ciarán himself."

"Trust me, Mother. This is right."

"I suppose there's no point in speaking to you of danger, just as there never was with Bran. The concept of self-protection is unknown to the two of you. I hoped he'd become a little more cautious, as a man of near forty with grown sons. But still he must be in the forefront of it all, risking himself as if he'd as many lives as a cat."

"Hasn't he?" Johnny chuckled.

"He need not do this himself. There are others, younger men, who would jump at the chance. It sounds—it sounds perilous, Johnny. I fear to lose you both."

"You know the Chief. He calculates his risks. This has been planned to the last detail, and for all his advanced years, he's one of our strongest swimmers, and knows the terrain and the layout of their mooring better than anyone. We'll hand-pick the other men. It's true, there's danger, but there's always danger in winds and tides. And look what's riding on it. You don't sink your enemy's fleet by stealth without exposing yourself to peril."

"There will be so few of you, and such a long way from help. If word of this got out, you'd be vulnerable as chicks in the nest."

"You imagine we haven't made allowance for that? As for intelligence, who'd believe even the Painted Man crazy enough to attempt such a sortie? Nobody sails around the Needle on the eastern side. As for such a swim, it's never been attempted before, the currents being what they are. Such rumors would be instantly discounted as fantasy."

"Your words do little to reassure me," Liadan said. "I am reminded that it was my choice to have you brought up in your father's mold; a warrior and strategist, with no concept of fear. Things might have unfolded very differently had you been raised as a scholar and mystic in the nemetons."

"Do you regret your choice, Mother?"

"Until that moment, when Conor told us the lady Oonagh still lives and threatens us, I did not. I have had years of such happiness; I do not know how Bran and I could have lived our lives without one another. I rejoice in my boys, and in the fine community of Harrowfield and the fellowship of Inis Eala. I am proud that we were able to give heirs not just to my father's estate but to Sevenwaters as well. There are regrets; Niamh's sorrow and suffering remain in my heart, as does Ciarán's estrangement from his family and his calling. For that reason, I longed to welcome their daughter as my own. But now . . . once, long ago, I was told, *You want more than you can rightly have*. I was told there was blood and sorrow in my choice. Perhaps it is time for me to pay the price for those years of joy. Ask me again, after the summer, if I have regrets."

"You miss him," Johnny said softly.

"More than I can put into words. My home is here; but my heart is there, wherever he is."

"We'll leave as soon as Fainne can travel," said Johnny.

Then I heard a knock, and the creak of the door, and Clodagh's voice. There was a conversation about whether I had had fainting fits before, and how I had been sick at Uncle Eamonn's house for a whole day, and missed seeing the white pony. Eventually it seemed safe enough to open my eyes and let them see I was awake again.

I'd been unconscious for a whole day and night, they told me, from the time Sibeal had found me lying on my bedroom floor early in the morning, until the next day. Longer maybe, for I was freezing cold when my cousin discovered me and raised the alarm, though I had had a blanket over me and a pillow beneath my head, which was strange. I had slept right through the midwinter ritual, which Conor had performed on his own. I had missed the burning of the great log, Eilis informed me, and the cider and cakes. Indeed, I was still so weak I could scarcely stir from my bed. I had plenty of small visitors and was told many stories. Johnny came, and broke the news to me that I was to ride north with him and his mother, and meet the other part of my family. Sibeal slipped in alone, bringing Riona. My protest was overruled.

"I've explained it to Maeve," the child told me, solemn as an old woman, "and she agrees. We'll make Maeve her own doll, all of us. Mother's going to show us how. But you need Riona back now. You need to take her with you when you go."

The weariness went on. I was astonished at the way the effort of transformation had drained me, even though I had been forewarned. The body trembled and retreated from any challenge; the mind still held the terror of the helpless insect, tucked away somewhere within the human consciousness. Next time, I thought, I would choose something bigger and stronger and better able to look after itself. Three whole days passed before I had recovered sufficiently to move on with my plan.

I sat before my fire, that third night. I had put away anything that might be dangerous. Riona was deep in the wooden chest, along with Darragh's shawl and the tiny ring of woven grasses. If I had had the strength, I might perhaps have thrown these precious things away; destroyed them, lest they catch my grandmother's eye and give her ideas. But, sorcerer's daughter or no, I was not as strong as that.

When all was safely stowed and the door bolted, I put my hand around the bronze amulet and focused on the flames. A mind-twister has a dual purpose. It links the wearer with the bestower; it binds one to the other's will. It is also a type of conduit, an eye which opens between the two when it chooses. It was thus, I believed, that my grandmother had been able to see me from time to time, to know what I was doing, although she was far away. She had said she could not see me all the time, only now and then in snatches. Such charms possess their own quirks, their own tricks. The link had always seemed stronger when I touched the amulet or held it. If I did that now and spoke an invocation of summoning, I thought she would come. I breathed deep, and opened the eye of the spirit. I spoke the ancient words, and I called to her.

She was there in an instant; not present in the flesh, as at our last memorable encounter, but there in the heart of the fire, a pair of beady dark eyes and a powerful, demanding voice.

"Ah! This I did not expect, that you would bring me to you thus. I'm thirsty for your news, child. Tell me!"

"I've done very well, Grandmother." I could not quite keep the tremble from my voice.

"I'm all ears. Go on."

"My plan is in place, as I told you it would be. The man Eamonn has offered for me, formally, in return for information I can give him. He wishes to destroy another who is part of the alliance. I performed a transformation to obtain what he wanted. If he acts on this it will surely spell the failure of the campaign. They cannot win without this man they call the Chief."

"You performed a full transformation? Successfully?"

"Yes, Grandmother."

"Without any help?"

"Yes, Grandmother." I looked straight into the fire, and kept my expression guileless.

"I see. And what was this information?"

Somehow I had known she would put me to the test. It would not have been enough simply to fabricate a story. Yet I was reluctant to tell her; in her hands such information could be dangerous indeed. "It—it would mean little to you, Grandmother; it is simply something which may give Eamonn the opportunity to do what he wishes. Once I have told him, he can work out how."

Grandmother's eyes narrowed alarmingly. "Fainne," she said very softly, "you're worrying me, child. I thought you understood what the result would be if you attempted to disobey me. It seems you did not. Must I show you again?" The fire seemed to glow brighter around her features, a fierce flame of gold and red, save for the dark coals of her eyes. Surely she had not guessed the truth already? Surely she could not know I planned to defy her?

"I—I did not mean—" I stammered.

"Tell me, Fainne! What is this highly significant piece of strategy you have discovered? Not trying to play games with me, are you? Games make me think of children. Children love games, don't they? Climbing, balancing, swinging high. Risky business, especially for the smaller ones. Still, your uncle has many daughters; too many, really."

I was shaking. It enraged me that she still had the power to manipulate me thus; her casual dismissal of the girls terrified me. There seemed no choice but to tell her. The amulet felt hot against my breast, as if it held something of her own anger.

"It's to do with swimming," I said, trying for as little detail as I could. "A small group of them. And it's hazardous."

"More," Grandmother commanded.

"They'll swim across from one island to another to sink the enemy's ships. During this venture the man Eamonn despises will be at great risk. I plan to tell Eamonn of this; let him seize what opportunity he can from it."

"Mmm. It's not much. What if this doesn't work?"

"It will work, Grandmother. And there's more. I am to travel north with my aunt Liadan to Inis Eala. There, I will be close to the heart of the campaign; near to its secrets. I will be ideally placed to carry out your work."

"I see."

"Aren't you pleased with what I have done, Grandmother?"

"There are bad influences in that place. It's old, and full of presences. Your father would feel quite at home there, no doubt. Just make sure it's not the same for you. Remember, the only sound advice is mine. And don't be tempted to remove the amulet. You need it, for this is your most dangerous time. Take it off and that may well be the end for you."

"I understand, Grandmother," I said in suitably meek tones. Indeed, I understood all too well, for it had happened before, the day Darragh came to Glencarnagh. Take it off, and she would know immediately, and harry me to do her will with every weapon she possessed. She needed me. She could not do this without me, that was clearer all the time. Although I might long to remove this dark talisman, I must wear it to the end; until the moment of final conflict. I must carry her charm until the instant she learned I was not her tool, but her adversary. What would happen then I could not say, but I knew deep inside me that this must play itself out to the end, as the Old Ones had said; as she herself had said. *A momentous unfolding of events . . .*

"What about this fellow Eamonn?" Grandmother asked suddenly. "How do you feed him the information he wants if he's in one place and you're in another?"

It had not taken her long to discover this weakness in my strategy. I tried not to let my misgivings show. "I'll find a way," I told her with what I hoped was an air of confidence. "He must be part of the final campaign; there must come a time when all are assembled together. Inis Eala is the key to this, Grandmother. That's where I must be."

"You seem different, child. Something has changed. Don't forget. Don't forget what I showed you."

I shuddered at the menacing sweetness of her voice. "I have not forgotten, Grandmother. And I have changed. Now that I know—now that I have felt the satisfaction it gives to make a man beg for my touch, now that I have experienced the power of transforming, I am beginning to understand. I am starting to know why you act as you do; I am realizing that to be a sorceress has its own rewards."

"That's as may be," she sniffed, but I could hear in her tone that she was pleased. So far, then, she had believed me. It was just as well she was not fully present, or she might smell my cold fear. It was a perilous game I played with her.

"What if it doesn't work?" she demanded. "Do you know what you must do then?"

"It will work. If not, I will find another way."

"You needn't find one, Fainne. I'll tell you. It should be obvious. Now answer me one thing. Is he there, the son, the one they call the child of the prophecy? Have you seen him?"

"Yes, Grandmother," I said cautiously, not liking the tone of her voice.

"Remember," she said, "at the end, the only thing that matters is him. He's the only piece of real value in this game. The rest of them, the druid, the warrior, the chieftain, the lady, they'll stand by him and give their all for him, and die for him if need be, to achieve the long goal. He's in the prophecy, and they all rely on that. Their confidence comes from that, from him. At the end, all you need to do is remove the child of the prophecy, and the whole thing collapses. Wait until the last moment, and see he fails. If you haven't the stomach to kill again, there are other ways. You know those already. It's easy enough to find someone else to do the dirty work for you. What's the fellow like? Not letting yourself grow fond of him, I hope?"

"No, Grandmother. I am not so foolish."

"Hmm. I'm not sure if that's the truth. You were softhearted with those children. I expect this is a charming young man; and you are your mother's daughter, after all."

I saw my mother stepping from the rock again; felt the air passing, the touch of the salt spray. Stepping off to oblivion. *That always seemed to me impossible*. I shivered.

"Believe me," I said with hard-won steadiness, "I would not dare to lie to you."

"Very wise, Fainne. Still, I think I'd like a little demonstration of loyalty. Here's what we'll do. We'll put this young warrior to the test, and you as well. We'll see just how strong he is; just how much pain he can endure. It'll be helpful to know that for later. This trip north is an ideal opportunity. No need for you to work a spell, granddaughter; save your power for the end, you must be at your best then. I will do what is necessary. I won't kill the fellow, that's your job and comes much later. I'll just play with him a little."

I felt a prickling down my spine; it was difficult to look into her fire-circled eyes and keep my features calm. "I don't understand," I said. "What purpose can there be in this?"

"I told you, Fainne. It's a test. An easy one for you, since there's no need for you to do anything at all. Indeed, that is your part in it: precisely nothing. You'll simply watch him and take no action. It isn't much to ask."

I stood silent as the meaning of her words became clear to me. "I understand," I whispered. "What kind of charm do you plan to use on him?"

Grandmother cackled with amusement. "You need to ask me that? You with your disfigurement of children? Come now, where's your imagination? What would you use?"

This was indeed a test. I held my expression impassive while my stomach churned with disgust. "You'd need to be subtle," I told her. "My aunt Liadan sees a great deal. If you plan to reverse the charm later it should be something invisible."

"Night terrors, maybe," said Grandmother encouragingly. "I could drive the fellow mad with visitations of death and disaster."

I recalled the steadiness in Johnny's gray eyes. "I don't think that would work very well," I told her.

"Well, then?" She grew rapidly impatient. "What's it to be?"

I knew the answer, though I did not want to tell her. At least what was in my mind would be easily reversible. And to keep her trust, I must continue to play this game. "A pain in the belly," I said, "that could be natural, something that starts as a minor disturbance and grows worse. What do you want from Johnny? Grovelling sub-servience? An acknowledgment of his own frailty? What are you hop-ing to prove?"

Her lips curved, showing the lines of neatly pointed teeth. "How long he can endure," she said. "More important, how long you can watch without helping him. If you are both strong, the final conclu-sion of our venture will be so much more satisfying, Fainne. So much. Indeed, I can hardly wait to watch that. Very well, a bellyache it shall be; you'll know all about that, since I've demonstrated it to you myself in the past. Rows of little teeth gnawing their way through living flesh, a pain that makes the nerves jangle and the sinews tremble, an agony that makes a man dream of death as a bliss-ful release. And just remember, there's no expectation of you at all, my dear; only that you watch and not act. Only that."

I nodded, trying not to shiver.

"You won't see me," Grandmother said. "But I will see you, Fainne. Make sure you act as I have instructed."

"Yes, Grandmother," I said.

"Don't worry," she went on, "I'll let the fellow recover in time. I want him well enough to take his place in the final battle, after all. I want these folk to savor the taste of success until the very last moment. Then we'll snatch their victory away, only then. Human folk and Fair Folk will go down together, before our very eyes. What a sight that will be! I'll probably add a few little touches of my own, I think. I won't be able to resist."

"I will do as you bid me," I said. "And my plan will work with Eamonn, I promise you. But I'll be a long way away. You may not hear from me now until the last."

"I'll know where you are, and what you're doing," said the lady Oonagh. "I always do."

Not quite always, I thought. "Farewell then," I said.

"Farewell, child. I have great hopes for you. Don't disappoint me. Don't forget your father, and that other one who's never far from your thoughts."

"No, Grandmother." I made my words firm and sure as the flames died down, and the glowing eyes faded quite away, and the evil voice fell silent.

I waited a long time, and when I judged it safe, I went to the chest and took out Riona, and I lay on the bed hugging her like a child. I could not stop shivering, even with a blanket over me, and after a time I got up and went to stand by the window, watching the gentle fall of snow through the shadowy air of the winter night. I thought of my father, all alone in the dark halls of the Honeycomb, and I spoke softly, using the tool he had given me to maintain my courage; to focus on what was and is and must be.

Whence came you?
From the Cauldron of Unknowing.
What do you seek?
Wisdom. Understanding. I seek the way to the Light.

It was a strange time of year to travel, the weather inclement, the days at their shortest. I asked no questions about that. A message had been sent to Eamonn, along the lines Johnny had suggested. It was anticipated the recipient might be less than pleased with this missive, and waste no time in paying a call, and asking questions. Our departure, therefore, took place on the day this letter was dispatched. By the time Eamonn could ride to Sevenwaters I would be well gone. This was not stated in so many words, but I understood it. Maybe I should have made a show of protest. But my mind was taken up with other things, and I let it pass.

To my astonishment the girls were distraught that I was leaving. Eilis wept. I had never thought the child had much regard for me; after all, I was a hopeless rider. Perhaps her tears were no more than habit. But Clodagh hugged me, and so did Deirdre, and their expressions were identically woeful.

"Come home safe," said Clodagh.

"We'll miss you terribly," sniffed Deirdre. "It'll be so boring here when you're gone."

"Goodbye, Fainne," Sibeal said gravely. "You'll need to watch out for cats." I stared at her, understanding she had seen ahead, perhaps to a time of transformation. I could not ask her what she meant, not while the others stood close by, but I nodded acknowledgment. Muirrin kissed me on both cheeks, and gave me a gown of soft gray wool, which she said would be nice and warm, for the winds bit hard up there. Muirrin was not weeping. My aunt's apprentice healer, Evan, was to remain at Sevenwaters in the period before the campaign, since he'd the strength for bone-setting and a skill with surgery my cousin lacked. I had seen the way the two of them touched hands and exchanged shy glances when they thought nobody was looking, and understood the glow that brightened Muirrin's pale features. As for Maeve, I had made that farewell in private, and the little last tale I told her was just for the two of us. The image of this child's injuries, and her courage, was lodged deep within me; now I would use it to give me strength.

Before we left I made myself go to the kitchen and seek out Dan Walker's old auntie, Janis. She sat in her chair by the hearth as always, like an ancient guardian of this domain, a kind of house-spirit watching with benign discipline over all. That was fanciful; this was no Otherworld creature, but a mortal woman of advanced years. The wrinkled skin and sunken cheeks told me that; the knobbly hand clutching a stick confirmed it. But her dark eyes were still bright and shrewd.

"Well, child. Going away, I hear? So what do I tell our lad when he comes after you?"

"He won't," I said decisively. Perhaps great age made one bold. She certainly had a way of coming out with whatever she had to say, however unpalatable. "He knows that. He's not to come, not anymore. Anyway, he's settled in the west. I told you."

"A traveling man never settles. What do I say to him? No message? Or shall I make it up? Tell him what I see in your eyes, maybe?"

"He won't come. But if—but if he did, I would tell him . . ." The words I needed fled. The only message that was in my heart was one that was all wrong; one that could not be spoken. Darragh must not know it; he must be given no reason to come after me, not while my grandmother might work her evil magic against him. "If he did," I made myself say, "I would tell him, indeed I would command him to return home and never come back. I would say, he and I are no good for each other, and never will be. If he follows me it can only lead to pain and sorrow. Tell him, I will look after myself. It's better that way."

"Anything else?" Janis had pursed her wrinkled lips, and raised her black brows. Clearly she was unimpressed.

"And—and tell him," I whispered, "tell him I haven't forgotten. Tell him I'm trying to do what's right."

There was silence between us, amid the creaking turn of the spit where a whole side of mutton roasted, the clatter of dishes, the laughter and joking of warriors as they snatched a moment of warmth and company before returning to the endless drills and sorties of campaign preparation.

"It's a lonely way you've chosen," observed Janis quietly. "And you not sixteen years old; a child still. A long, lonely way."

"I'm used to that," I said fiercely. Perhaps it was the look in her eyes, perhaps it was the kindness in her voice, I cannot say. But it brought back images of time past, sharply, and if I could have wept then, I would. "I have memories," I told her. "There's always those."

"Not a lot, to build your life on," said Janis.

We rode north. From the moment we departed the keep of Sevenwaters, Johnny became one of the guard, the uniform dark hood rendering him indistinguishable from his fellows. All seemed well. My grandmother's small voice had been silent since the night I had summoned her and heard her plans for Johnny. All rode on swiftly; none showed signs of illness or pain. There was no telling when she would strike him down, though the amulet felt warm all the time now, and I took this as a sign that she watched me. Our guards maintained their silent, vigilant presence around me and my aunt Liadan as we traversed wooded slope and wide forest way, by frozen pond and icy streamlet. They led us across narrow tracks in a marshy wilderness; through high passes where great hunting birds soared overhead and the ground was iron-hard with frost. They camped with us in a place of standing stones, where we slept in the shelter of an ancient barrow marked with secret symbols. All the way they kept their masks on, except to eat. There was no knowing one from another.

"A form of protection," Liadan explained. "Necessary, in view of the markings they wear."

"If those are so dangerous, why adorn themselves thus?" I asked.

Liadan smiled. "A symbol of pride; of belonging. Our warriors consider it a great honor to be allowed the mark. Not all are accepted into this band."

"What are the—prerequisites? Noble blood? Brave deeds?"

"Each man is unique. Each brings his own qualities. If he has something to contribute, something of which we have need, he will be accepted as long as he passes the test."

"Test? What sort of test?"

"A test of skill and of loyalty. It varies. You'll find folk of many kinds at Inis Eala. Men of all sorts; all colors and creeds."

"And women?"

"Ah, yes, a few of those as well. It takes a very particular breed to live in such a place, Fainne. A special kind of strength."

"Aunt Liadan?" I said as we settled to sleep in the strange arched space of the old barrow. "This place here. Have you read the signs? The inscriptions?"

There was a pause.

"No, Fainne," she said in an odd sort of voice. "This is a language more ancient than any I have learned to decipher. I cannot read them." There was a question behind her words.

"You understand," I said, "that this is so old no living man or woman knows the tongue. But I grew up in a place of standing stones; the markers of the sun's path were the daily companions of my childhood. Some of these signs I recognize."

"I know it is a place of the Old Ones," my aunt said softly. "A place of great power and wonder." She hesitated, then went on. "They spoke to me here. The Fomhóire."

I stared at her. "You mean—you mean those creatures that seem part rock, part water, part furred or feathered thing? Those small beings that call themselves our ancestors?" Perhaps I spoke incautiously. Here in the belly of the earth, it seemed safe.

"I never saw them," Liadan said in wonder. "I heard voices, only. Deep, dark voices from earth and pool, guiding me. Somehow I never thought them small. They seemed huge, old, and immensely powerful. And they bade me follow my heart; follow my instincts. It was here in this place that . . . that decisions were made of great import, decisions that changed the path of things. Have you seen these folk, Fainne, that you speak of them thus as familiar beings?"

I nodded. "The signs tell of an ancient trust. They speak of blood and darkness. And they speak of hope. That much I understand."

My aunt stared at me in silence. Our lantern glowed softly in the darkness of this subterranean space. Farther down the huge empty chamber, some of Johnny's men had settled to sleep, and we kept our voices low. After a while Liadan said cautiously, "Do these same folk guide you, my dear? Do you believe them—benign?"

This was dangerous territory. I could not know, at any time, if my grandmother were listening or no. It seemed a safe place; but nowhere was safe while I wore the amulet, and to remove it was to summon her instantly. "They have their own theories about how things should be. But they have a habit of not explaining, of leaving me to work out what things mean. What happened with you? Did you follow their directions, or make your own choices?"

Liadan sighed. "Both, I think. It was others' orders I disobeyed. What of you, Fainne? Whose path do you follow?"

A perilous question. "A lonely one," I said. "So I've been told."

"Like Ciarán's?" she asked me softly.

"I don't wish to speak of my father." I lay down with the blanket over my face. The weight of the amulet was heavy on me; its small, malign shape seemed to burn most of the time now, as if I could not avoid my grandmother's scrutiny however well I played this new game. I wondered if she had heightened its power somehow, now that we were coming close to the end. Perhaps what I had suspected was true. Perhaps she feared me. I disregarded the burning. Pain was nothing. My father had taught me that lesson early.

I learned soon enough that Johnny was not simply a kind young man who rescued blundering insects and held the hands of sick children. It was the habit of our silent guard to ride two ahead, two behind, with several men on each flank, not always in sight of us, but close enough to be quickly by our side if need be. Liadan and I were clad in plain dark cloaks, serviceable tunics and skirts and sturdy winter boots. She rode a brown mare, I the small gray which Eamonn had lent me. Liadan had no qualms about that.

"She's mine," my aunt said simply. "A gift, and not from

Eamonn. And it was certainly not my fault that she was once left behind. That creature's seen a lot, Fainne. Sad things; terrible things. I think it's time we took her home."

We rode through a clearing. It was a bitterly cold morning, the ground crisp with frost, and scarcely a bird astir in the bare branches of the blackthorns before and behind us. This was a terrain where strange piles of stones dotted the hillsides, where one could not tell if their seemingly random heaps were in fact a work of man or of something older, the winter shadows turning rock into goblin or bogle, giant or crouching earth-dragon. The very undergrowth seemed malign, squat dark bushes reaching out long strands in thorny embrace to tear at skirt or stocking. Our pace was brisk; it seemed even the hooded warriors had no desire to linger in these parts longer than they must.

The way narrowed until only one of our escort could be seen, the man in front of us. Someone shouted, and he stopped dead. The two of us drew our horses to a halt behind, and Liadan reached out a reassuring hand toward me.

Ahead of us on the track stood a group of ferocious-looking men armed with knives, clubs and small axes. Their apparent leader, a huge fellow with a patch over one eye and yellowed, rotting teeth stepped forward and pointed his weapon at our guard.

"Down you get," he ordered. "And no funny business. There's six of us and one of you, not counting your lady friends there. Nice and slow. Give me that sword. And the knife. Turn around. Now . . ."

To my astonishment our man did exactly as he was told, without a word of protest. The attackers relieved him of his weapons, and took the reins of his horse as if to lead it away. I stared in growing alarm as the man with the eye-patch sauntered over to us, grinning. My aunt sat quietly, her gaze quite calm. Now they were stripping off our man's hood. Of the rest of our escort there was no sign.

"Well, well, well," sniggered the leader of the group, coming up alongside my little horse. "What have we here?"

I raised my hand, summoning the words of a spell.

"No, Fainne," Liadan said softly. "No need for that."

Behind the leader, his henchmen had peeled back the warrior's mask to reveal the distinctive markings on his face. Someone swore, and I heard the words "painted man" spoken in a terrified mutter. The fellow by my side froze, then backed away, his face suddenly chalk-white around the black of the eye-patch. Then there were several small sounds; a whirr, a twang, the thud of an arrow finding its mark; the man they had disarmed whirled about, felling one of his attackers with a strategically placed kick. Without any sort of struggle what-ever, suddenly there were six men lying on the hard ground, groaning or gasping or, more ominously, quite silent. Behind and before, to left and to right, Johnny's men emerged from the cover of rock or tree, stowing small items away in belt or pocket. An arrow was retrieved, messily. A short knife was used, effectively. I shut my eyes.

"Fainne? I'm sorry. Were you frightened?" This masked warrior spoke in Johnny's voice. The man the attackers had disarmed was reclaiming his weapons, replacing his hood as if such encounters were no more unusual than, say, rounding up sheep or slicing a loaf of bread.

"I can look after myself," I snapped, forcing my heart to slow. "It seems an odd way of countering an ambush, that's all. You might have warned us."

"We've our own ways. And that could hardly be called an ambush, far too inept."

"You didn't need to kill them."

"They were fools to attempt what they did, and deserve no better. Besides, not all are dead. Some will carry a tale home; a tale of the Painted Man. This pass will be safe for a while, until they forget and try again. They chose their victim poorly this time. Nobody touches my mother. Travel with her and you're assured of the best protection there is." His voice was steady, his manner assured as always. Had Grandmother not yet worked her spell, then? Could I hope that, for her own reasons, she might choose not to enact this particular piece of cruelty?

We rode on, and I pondered the oddity of it, that the very man my grandmother had bound me to destroy was the one who now ensured this expert force kept me safe from all harm. He carried his own death with him, and guarded it as carefully as the most precious treasure. It was good that he was strong, for if she did go ahead with her little plan, the trial would tax him hard. My grandmother's mas-tery of such spells was matched only by her complete lack of scruples. She had presided over the thrashing, fluttering death of many a small creature as she demonstrated one charm or another; she had viewed dispassionately my own agony as she punished me with knives of glass in the head, with bizarre swellings of tongue or throat, with cruel alterations of sight or hearing. Did not she watch calmly over her own son's slow, wasting demise? Grandmother would use the craft coolly and effectively against my cousin. I just hoped she would not keep it up for too long.

I had learned to recognize Johnny among our identically masked attendants in their plain garments. He was the shortest of them, in height not so much taller than myself, and his back was as straight as a small child's, his head proud, his shoulders set very square. They changed horses from time to time, but I knew him. As we rode ever northward to the farthest shore of Ulster I watched him, thinking soon, very soon, he would have to halt and dismount, or fall from his horse convulsed with pain. I knew the spell; she had used it on me once. Even the strongest man could not endure it long.

The hills and valleys, the hidden streams and misty woodlands passed us steadily by. Ahead of me my cousin rode on, his carriage as upright as ever, his hand relaxed on the reins. I watched in vain for any sign of illness, but there was nothing. Indeed, by dusk I began to wonder if the child of the prophecy was somehow protected against this charm, perhaps by those powers of the forest that my grand-mother so loathed. I felt the heat of the amulet against me and knew that she was close; the small triangle seemed ever more finely tuned to her presence, its burning a clear message that she was watching me, watching Johnny, that she would indeed test us both.

We camped for the night in the shell of an old building, where crumbling stone walls and the remnants of beam and thatch offered a precarious shelter against the winter chill. The men took off their hoods and ate a frugal meal. Johnny seemed a little pale, and I did not see him partake of the food, but his voice was steady; he smiled at the men's jokes, and bid us a courteous good night before retreating to take his turn on watch. There seemed not much amiss with him.

We should reach the coast in another day and a half, Liadan told me as we rode out the next morning. There, a boat would take us across to the island. There was a note in her voice which spoke of anticipated delight; she could not disguise her longing to reach our destination. She did not ask her son if all was well, and nor did I.

I watched my cousin as the track became steep and dangerous. I kept my eyes on him as he led or followed or guided, and still his back was straight and proud, and his horse moved steadily onward. Johnny held his head high as if he were a hero from some old tale. The amulet was burning me. She was watching me, watching him. It came to me suddenly that I had been quite wrong. Not only had she already worked her charm, perhaps days ago, but she tightened it all the time, piercing, stabbing, grinding. It was not the lack of magic that made this malevolent thing invisible, but the sheer fortitude of the man who endured it. I rode along with jaw clenched and brow beaded with sweat; my hands shook as I held the reins. *Give in to it*, I willed him. *Don't be so strong. The sooner you give in, the sooner it stops*. Around us the others rode on, quite unaware of the battle being played out in their midst. There were only three who knew anything was amiss: my cousin and I, and the sorceress whom nobody could see.

We made camp again for the night. Johnny retired early. He did not eat. I glimpsed the gray pallor of his face, and noted the way he took care to avoid his mother's scrutiny. In the night I awoke and heard the sound of retching out beyond the rocks, in the shadows, and I heard Liadan stir, but she did not wake. Soon after dawn we rode on, and the men rode by us, silent. The smell in the air was like home, sharp and salt. Gulls passed overhead screaming. I could hear the distant roar of the sea. But there was no enjoyment in these dear familiar things, not in this far place, with the whole length of Erin between me and my father. Not when I would never walk these cliffs with a friend by my side, and sit in the shelter of the stones in a silent companionship of total trust. Such things I would never have again. I did not deserve them; never had. The amulet was hurting me; I would bear its brand on the flesh of my breast. That was nothing beside what my cousin must be enduring. She watched; she was close. I could not help him, even though I knew the charm of reversal, even though I had it at my fingertips. I must not use it.

The land opened up. The sky seemed to lighten and broaden as we moved steadily northward. There were few trees here; those that clung on in this windswept corner of the land nestled into gullies, or clustered in pockets of shelter beneath small hills. Two men rode off at a gallop, no doubt gone ahead to announce our arrival. The others were spread out along the track, still quiet. Our journey would be ended soon. Now, as we came up a rise and the first, distant view of a northern ocean came in sight beyond a pale line of cliffs, I heard her whisper inside my head. *Tempting, isn't it?* she goaded me. *You know how it eats at him; you recognize it. The boy's strong; he's one of those Fomhóire throwbacks, and a warrior besides, trained to endure. That's his father's doing. I underestimated him; we won't make that mistake next time. And you're nearly there; running out of opportunities. I'll just take this one step further, I think. Close to the point where the body gives up in defeat, close to the moment when the heart flags and fails . . . so, so close . . . you know how it is, Fainne . . .*

I did know. Imagine some wild creature feasting on your living body as you lie there aware and helpless before its rapacious appetite. Imagine the pain as it flows into every corner of your body, every fiber of your being. I knew that was how it was for him. I waited, trembling as I watched him. My fingers shook with my effort to hold back the counter-spell; I made myself swallow the words that would free him. And at last there was a reaction. His mount trembled, and halted, and Johnny slid from the saddle to the hard ground of the track. I could hear his breathing; sharp, quick. Still he kept on his feet, where any other man would have been writhing on the ground, screaming and clutching his belly. Behind him my own horse had stopped still, shivering.

I was incapable of speech. Was this enough for Grandmother? Why couldn't Johnny fall, or scream, or give some acknowledgment of defeat, so she would stop it? I knew she could take this no further without risk of killing the man where he stood. What was he, Cú Chulainn reborn, that he could withstand such agony? Another of the men rode back, and a quiet exchange took place. Liadan was well behind us, out of sight.

Now the other man dismounted and stood by the track, holding the reins of both horses. Behind his mask, Johnny was looking at me. He indicated with the smallest jerk of his head that I was to follow, and set off on a side track to the east, where a group of three ancient stones had been placed atop a slight rise. On them grew a crust of gray lichen, and I was reminded of that strange, rock-like creature which had spoken to me once of age-old trusts and future paths. I got down from my horse and left her with the others. Johnny walked, and I followed, and if my steps were unsteady, what with my limping foot and the uneven ground, his were more so. Still he walked, and spoke not a word, but I could hear in his breathing how he forced himself silent when everything in him was screaming pain. I wondered, then, that my grandmother did not simply screw this charm up to its fullest force, and kill the child of the prophecy once and for all. That would be easier, surely, then this cruel game of tests and trials. She had no need of me to quench Sevenwaters' hope of victory. Already Johnny teetered on the brink of death, and without Johnny the battle could not be won. We halted in the shadow of the ancient stones, on the eastward side out of sight of the path where the others waited. My cousin peeled back his mask. I looked at him, and he looked at me, his face ashen, his eyes bright with pain and fierce with determination. *There is something here she cannot defeat*, I thought. *Perhaps it's raw courage, perhaps something more; a magic older and deeper than her own, a power that guards his steps, that guides him toward the destiny foretold for him.* Johnny drew a shuddering breath, and at that moment the throbbing heat from the amulet dwindled and died, until it was simply a small triangle of metal on a cord around my neck. She was gone, and the spell still held him.

"I don't think," said Johnny in a voice that was a very thread of pain, "that you understand quite what it is you're dealing with here." His hand, laid against the weathered stone to support him, was white-knuckled.

I drew a deep breath. "What do you mean?" I asked him.

"Tell me," he managed, gasping for control, "how much longer? Not for myself; we are trained to endure. But I don't want my mother worried."

I stared into his pallid, sweat-drenched face with its bold raven-pattern; a face whose look of raw courage did not seem to have faltered for an instant. He thought that I had done it. He thought I was the one responsible for this cruel torture. No wonder he had said nothing. And now Grandmother was gone, and she had not released him. With a muttered word and a slight movement of my hand, I reversed the charm. It was only then that his control was momentarily lost. He let out his breath all of a sudden, and slumped to the ground with his back against the stone and his eyes closed. As for me, I was instantly drained of energy and I sat down abruptly beside him.

The sky was clear, the breeze fresh and clean; birds wheeled and cried high overhead. That seemed somehow all wrong, as if we were quite out of place. These things belonged in a time of long ago, a time of innocence, not here where all was danger and difficulty, hurt and fear.

"Understand," Johnny said after a while, not opening his eyes, "that I have a path to tread and a mission to accomplish, and nothing's going to stop me. Nothing." His voice was a ferocious whisper, daunting in its certainty. If I had ever doubted that this was the hero the prophecy spoke of, I doubted no longer.

"I was not responsible for this," I said shakily. "But I don't expect you to believe me." I could tell him no more than that. I had already failed my grandmother's test; she had left me no choice but to intervene. I would not risk revealing the truth to him.

"I see," my cousin said in a tone which could have meant anything.

"Why did you bring me with you?" I asked him bluntly.

He opened his eyes and managed a very small grin. "I overruled my mother," he said shakily. "She did not want you at Inis Eala. As to why, I cannot say, save that you seem to be in trouble, and in need of protection, and that that is something we do quite well."

"And do you regret your decision now?"

"No, cousin, I do not. My judgment seldom fails me."

"Some folk might think that extremely foolish," I said cautiously.

"Do you think it foolish, Fainne?"

I would not risk answering aloud. But I shook my head, and offered him my hand as he got slowly to his feet.

"You have great strength of will," I said as we began to make our way back. He walked gingerly, as if testing each part of his body to be quite sure the pain was really gone.

"I'm my father's son," said Johnny.

And I my father's daughter, my heart told me. So we returned to the track, and mounted our horses as if we had merely taken a stroll to stretch our legs, and we rode on to the northern shore of Ulster and to Inis Eala: Isle of the Swan.

Chapter Twelve

had my mind not been otherwise occupied, I would have remembered that to get to an island one must go by boat, and that a boat must be on the sea, and that, even though I had grown up on the shores of Kerry, I was afraid of the sea. Only when we came to a small, heavily fortified settlement atop a tall, deeply indented cliff, and looked out to a low-lying island in the north, and I observed the considerable expanse of rough-looking water between us and this inhospitable place, did I feel the clutch of terror at my vitals. But there was no way I would let my cousin or my aunt or a single one of these stern young warriors know of my weakness. There was an anchorage in a bay. This too was very well guarded, by men mostly somewhat older than Johnny's band, and all of them extremely odd-looking. These wore neither hoods nor masks nor any uniform raiment, but garments of great individuality, made with fox fur or rabbit pelt, with what seemed a serpent's skin, with leather and silver and bronze all playing a part in their construction. The men themselves were as distinctive, with the same patterned skin as the younger warriors, but each with some extraordinary touch of his own: hair to the waist, maybe, bound back neat and tight; a semi-shaven head; a ring pierced through brow or nose; a collar of dark feathers. For all their flamboyant appearance, they behaved like professionals, doing their work quickly, quietly and with no fuss whatever. They treated Liadan like a queen. As for me, they afforded me great respect, with never a wink or a whistle or a comment out of place, for all Johnny's talk of likely suitors. There was, however, a very close scrutiny, especially from a fellow whose name appeared to be Snake, a daunting-looking man of middle years, whose eyes narrowed in his hard-featured face as he helped me into a smallish and alarmingly rocking boat, and made sure I was seated squarely in the middle, out of harm's way. The men rowed. The boat went up and down. I forced myself to keep my eyes open and my features calm as my stomach churned and beads of sweat broke out on my face. I clenched my hands tightly together and watched the island coming closer. I did not look back. I thought I made a convincing pretense of composure, until the fellow named Snake observed, glancing my way, "You'd want to watch out for the sea serpents. Just the sort of day for them, today."

I stared at him in horror, my heart thumping, and beyond him at the high crests of the waters and the dark, mysterious troughs between, where anything might be lurking. Then Liadan looked at me, and at him, and said briskly, "Shame on you, Snake, to tease the poor girl thus! You're old enough to know better."

Snake grinned at her. "Nearly there," he said in a different tone.

Liadan gave a nod. Her eyes were fixed on the island now, and there was a bright anticipation there which gave her the look of a far younger woman.

I'm not sure quite what I expected. At least, that her husband would be down to meet her at the jetty where we disembarked, though he had not come across the water. But while there were many men there to help us off the boat, and to carry our bundles up a steep set of steps cut in a low cliff above the anchorage, I could see no figure which seemed to match my expectations. There was a young man there much like Johnny, with the same charming smile and steady look. He greeted Liadan with a kiss on either cheek; her son, then, the one the girls had said fancied himself a warrior. He looked every bit of one to me, with his strong-jawed face and capable manner, not to speak of the large knife and throwing-axe at his belt. And there was a boy, though this one had a look of my uncle Sean about him, with pale skin and dark curling hair which fell in his eyes. That would be the youngest, Coll. There should be four altogether, but one was at Harrowfield. Where was their father? Liadan seemed unperturbed. Men crowded to greet her; there were smiles all around, but also a sort of deference that kept them always at a slight distance, as if they thought themselves unworthy to come too close. We climbed the steps; there were thrice nine of them. My legs ached. At the top there was a plateau, treeless in the main part, and a group of low buildings surrounded by a sturdy stone wall. In the distance the contours of the land rose and fell, and rocky outcrops, slick with spray, seemed to guard hidden hollows, secret beaches, caves maybe.

"It's a wild place," said a quiet voice on my right. "But a good place, when you get to know it."

I looked around. The man who spoke had skin as dark as coal, and very white teeth, of which a couple were missing. He wore a feather in his braided hair.

"Welcome to the island," he said. "You'll have met my son, maybe."

I stared for a moment, regained my composure and made a guess. "Evan? I—yes, I have."

He put out a hand in greeting and I took it, and felt immediately the disfigurement; his grip was very firm, but this hand bore surely no more than three fingers.

"Come, then," he said, "we'll get you indoors, find you a bite to eat and a place to sleep. A rarity here on the island, young lady to visit. My name's Gull; you'll get to know us all in time."

Liadan had vanished; Johnny and his brothers had merged into the group of men who now headed off toward the longest of the stone buildings. Farther away I could see a few sheep grazing ; smoke from a chimney; cloths flapping in the breeze. A cozy domestic scene, however remote the setting.

"What sort of a place is this?" I ventured as I followed the man, Gull, indoors. "What do they do here?"

He paused, staring at me with dark brows raised. "You came this far without asking? It's a kind of school, lass. A school such as you'll find nowhere else from Wessex to Orkney, from Munster to the far shores of Gaul. A school of battlecraft, you might call it. And more. And a great deal more. Now, you'll want something to drink, and somewhere to rest. Biddy!"

The building was mostly one long open space, furnished with great tables and benches. At one end there was a cooking area, and here a large, capable-looking woman with a sweet face was ladling soup into bowls for the men, each in his turn.

"The young lady's here," Gull said to her. "Liadan's niece Fainne."

So, they had known I was coming; my name, even. Johnny's messengers were efficient.

"My wife, Biddy," Gull added. "She'll look after you. Here, sit down, rest yourself."

But I was staring out beyond the kitchen entry, to a little patch of garden with a wall around it, a sheltered place where herbs or vegetables might be coaxed to grow in defiance of the salt spray. Through the doorway I could see my aunt Liadan, and a man who must be the Chief, for they were standing completely still with their arms wrapped around each other and their eyes closed, like young folk who had just discovered love for the first time. His hands were buried in the dark silken fall of her hair, which had escaped its neat bindings and flowed loose down her back. Her brow rested in the hollow of his neck. I was quite certain neither of them had the least awareness of a single thing but the closeness of that touch, the beating of heart on heart. I could not drag my eyes away, and it was not just the intricate, finely graven pattern that seemed to cover the body of this man all down one side which held my attention, startling as it was. I had never thought that men and women of five and thirty, or even older, might still possess such feelings for one another that it drove all else from their minds. I had thought love a fantasy, a delusion of youth, like the passion which had destroyed my father and mother, or the blushes and downcast eyes of Muirrin and her young man, which surely could not last long after the advent of marriage and the loss of youthful comeliness in the cares of calling and family. So I stared, and knew in my heart that what I saw was as lovely and enduring as it was completely unexpected. It filled me with a strange, piercing sadness.

"He'll not greet her before other folk," said Biddy softly. "Not him." And she reached across and closed the door, so nobody else might disturb the two of them with prying eyes. I flushed with embarrassment. "It's all right, lass," she added kindly. "Now, a drop of ale? Some soup? And we'll find you a bed somewhere. What can you turn your hand to? Mending? Cooking? There's work for all here."

"I—well, they tell me I'm quite good at looking after children," I said, clutching at straws. These folk seemed immensely capable, in the mold of Liadan and her sons. I dredged my memory for anything of any use at all. I could hardly tell her I might employ the craft to light her kitchen fire, or form stones into a fine new storehouse maybe. "I can read and write, a bit. And I can catch fish with a hand line."

"Really?" Biddy grinned. "Won't be long before you find yourself a husband, with talents like those. I've two big sons myself, apart from Evan. Smiths, the both of them, fine strong fellows. I'll wager there'll be competition, with a pretty thing like you wandering among the sheep and the chickens. Now you're blushing. Drink your ale, lass. You're safe here. We've rules, and folk stick to them. The lads worship the ground Johnny walks on. Not one of them'd risk his place here on the island; not for the bonniest girl in the world."

It was another kind of life. Folk thought, perhaps, that I would be ill at ease, and find it hard to settle in this harsh place with its biting winds, its perilous cliffs and its isolation, not to speak of the mysterious activities of its menfolk. But then, they knew little of my upbringing. Opposite corner of the land it might be, but in many ways Inis Eala was like home. Here no blanket of forest shut out the light. I awoke to the sound of the sea, in the little hut I shared with three other unwed girls. I had my own corner. They found out soon enough that I preferred to keep to myself. Anyway, there was always work to be done. One girl helped Biddy with the cooking; another seemed to turn her hand to anything, whether it be killing and cleaning chickens, or prising shellfish off the rocks with a big knife. The third girl, Brenna, was a fletcher. I must have raised my brows in surprise; she volunteered with quiet pride that it was her father's trade, and when he died, she took it over, so to speak. Now she was one of the best in Ulster. If she hadn't been, she wouldn't be here. Only weapons of the very highest standard were used on the island.

Some of the business of Inis Eala was carried out quite openly. There was the bakery and the forge; there was the place down in the bay where they seemed to be building big curraghs, and cunning little ones as well; there was a shed where fish were dried and smoked. There was an infirmary, which was run by the man called Gull, the one with a feather in his hair and but five fingers on the two hands together. There was a Christian priest and also a druid. These two spent most of their time together in amicable debate. Both performed rituals: folk attended one or the other, or neither, as it suited them. There was a small tannery, and a place where they did spinning and weaving, and a sailmaker's.

And then there was the other business, which was the reason they were here. One saw a hint of it at the forge, where two brawny individuals named Sam and Clem beat out not just pitchforks and shovels and implements for tilling the stony ground, but also a wide variety of weaponry: swords, spearheads, daggers, throwing-axes and numerous other items the uses of which one might only guess at. Sam and Clem were Biddy's sons, but not Gull's. Fair as milkmaids, the two of them, with rosy cheeks and hair sweet buttercup-yellow, and limbs like tree trunks. In the evenings after supper, Sam would play the bodhrán and Clem the whistle, and I marveled that such giants might possess such deftness of touch. There was a woman who played the knee-harp, but there was no piper. While the winter wind whistled outside, and the sea roared its hunger to the freezing air, folk clapped and sang, and even on occasion danced, in the shelter of that snug building and the warmth of its hearth fire. I did not dance. I watched. I observed, and thought how different things could be from what one had imagined. Take that man, the Chief. Bran, his name was, but the only one who used that was Liadan. Once, I had thought him a piece easily sacrificed in this game; I had thought I might let Eamonn destroy him, and break the alliance, and so lose the battle. I had told my grandmother I would do that very thing. For what had I heard of the man, until that point? I'd been told he was an outlaw, scum of the earth; that he had cruelly stolen Eamonn's sweetheart, and ruined his life. He was considered, at the least, somewhat odd. He had made so many enemies over the years that he could never come to Sevenwaters. And even more strangely, he managed at the same time to be lord of a substantial holding in Britain. It was a position surely impossible for such a miscreant to sustain. I expected an enigma. But nobody had told me the man's wife loved him more than life itself. I had not known his sons respected and admired him; that his men and women viewed him as something quite above ordinary folk. It became ever clearer to me the longer I dwelt on Inis Eala that although Johnny ran the place, the taciturn, grim-looking Chief was the cornerstone of the whole community, the unifying force of the entire enterprise. And enterprise it was; for all the inclement weather, men came and went by ship, and behind the high walls of the practice yard skills were endlessly perfected, and inside locked rooms another set of skills was taught: map reading, covert intelligence, poisons and antidotes, subterfuge and disguise. One could not remain there without knowing a little of it. Still, there were rules, and one of the main ones was secrecy. It was just as well I no longer needed to gather information for Eamonn, for I could not have done so without a total transformation. That I could not attempt without arousing Liadan's suspicions. She watched me closely; another mysterious period of illness would certainly have given me away. I was immensely grateful to Johnny for bringing me to Inis Eala, where I need no longer think of Eamonn at all.

The Chief was nothing much to look at. There was that flamboyant body-marking, to be sure; the pattern was a work of art, and covered him all down the right side, from the top of his shaven head to the tips of his fingers and his toes. But apart from that, he was much like Johnny, a shortish, strongly built man with shrewd gray eyes. His mouth was hard; he had not his son's charming smile. The only time I ever saw a softening of his features was when he looked at Liadan, and even then, I thought he did not wish others to see such a weakening of his stern image. But he revealed himself in little touches, in little glances. It was clear they could not bear to be long out of each other's sight. Always, he sought her opinion gravely; always, he treated her as an equal, to be duly consulted and respected. I did not much care for him, but I liked that.

There was an inner circle here, a group of older men who seemed to play the major part in councils and decision making, and to have control of various aspects of the enterprise. The Chief's visits were rare; his estate at Harrowfield needed his presence, and he and Liadan spent most of their time at home in Northumbria. It was these others, led by Johnny, who managed the work of Inis Eala. One thing this group shared was their odd names, which were not men's names at all but those of wild creatures. As well as Gull, the healer, and Snake, who looked after matters of battlecraft, there were warriors called Spider or Rat or Wolf. The younger men had not such an affectation, though their names did speak of a variety of origins: Corentin, Sigurd and Waerfrith; Mikka, Gareth and Godric. After a time, Biddy explained to me kindly that in the old days, when the Chief first set up his fighting force, the men who joined him had shed their old names and taken a new identity. Their animal names told nothing of their origins or history; they spoke only of each man's own qualities, a dog's loyalty maybe, or a gull's ability to travel far and see clear. With their names, they got their mark: that pattern graven on the skin which was at once a sign of belonging and of fierce individuality. Now that they were settled, so to speak, there was no need for the names; but even the young ones still had the mark. You'd know who'd been with the Chief since the beginning, by the names. You'd know who'd proved his worth, by the skin. All answered to Johnny; his youth was no impediment to his authority.

There was work for me. Scribing, for instance. I demonstrated my skills on request, and was allocated tasks. Nothing concerning strategies and dealings of war, of course; nothing touching on the summer campaign or other secret matters. The priest and the druid took care of those. Nor was I given maps to work on, though maps and sea charts were used aplenty by the inner circle. Still, there were books to be copied, and letters written of domestic import, and records to be kept of stock. There were household reckonings to perform, tedious work, but, for me, so easy I could do it without even thinking, and still receive praise for my accuracy. I was asked questions about who had taught me so well, and I told them a druid, and tried not to think about my father.

And because I had so foolishly mentioned children, I was put in charge of my cousin Coll. That had been Johnny's idea, not his mother's. Maybe, I thought grimly, it was a sort of test. I discovered soon enough that small boys are somewhat different from small girls. One could not expect them to listen enraptured to such tales as I had in my repertory, or bite their lips in concentration over sewing, or occupy themselves with dolls. Indeed, I had done none of these things myself as a child. Riona had always seemed less a plaything than a companion in adventures. It was winter, and Coll was restless. He was too young to learn the arts of war; he did not concentrate long on practicing his letters with waxen tablet and stylus; he thought ringstones boring; he did not care to play the whistle. Instead, he would wander to the shuttered window and peer through the cracks at the sleeting storm outside, and sigh heavily. I saw in his eyes the longing for summer, and felt its echo in my own heart as so many times before.

I was trying to copy a book of herb lore. It was in Latin, and I was translating as I wrote, which required a deal of concentration. Coll kept interrupting. I could imagine him teamed up with Eilis very well. In the end I put my quill down and went to join him at the window.

"When the weather clears," I said optimistically, looking out into the lowering gray of the storm, "maybe you'll show me the rest of the island. I'll wager there are caves there, and beaches the selkies visit. Do you go down to the far point?" In the gloom outside the whole of the landscape was veiled in slanting rain.

"Sometimes," he said guardedly.

"Only sometimes? Is it too dangerous?" The cliffs were higher there, that was certain. The waves made an explosion of white as they lashed the rocks at the base. Still, it was no steeper than the Honeycomb.

"Of course not," said Coll immediately, scowling. He was indeed very like Uncle Sean; long thin face, dark brows, black curling hair. I regarded him gravely. Another like Sibeal? Surely not. This one was—was—well, to put it frankly, he was too much of a *boy*. I remembered something my grandmother had said once, about what children might have been born if my father had chosen Liadan instead of her sister. If Liadan had had a daughter, I thought cautiously that I might have quite liked her.

"Where do you go, then?"

"There are little bays on the west side. There's a cliff, with puffins. Caves. Tunnels. Selkies do come in sometimes. It's good there." He frowned. "Shouldn't think you could manage, though. You have to climb down a long way."

"You'd be surprised," I said dourly. "Where I grew up, you had to climb cliffs like those every time you wanted fresh water. Nimble as a goat, that's me."

Coll looked unconvinced. "The only thing is, you're a girl."

"Mmm. Well, my best friend back home was a boy, and anything he could do, I could do." This was so patently untrue I felt obliged to correct myself. "Except for swimming. And music. And horses."

"And could he do everything you could do?"

I attempted a smile. "Not quite," I told him.

After that, Coll and I became friends, and together we counted the days until the storms of winter should abate, and the sky open again to the pearly hues of Imbolc. We reached a sort of agreement. He would work on his letters for a time, while I labored with quill and ink. I would correct his work. Then we would take turns telling a tale we had invented, about a boy who sailed to strange lands in a little boat, and had all sorts of adventures. Coll was supremely confident, with the innocent assurance of a seven-year-old, that this was exactly what he would do himself in a few years' time; not just the voyage itself, but the discovery of spice islands, and the vanquishing of sea monsters, and probably even marrying a princess, but not that part until he was really old, one and twenty at least, because he'd be having too much fun.

Time passed. The amulet remained cool to the touch, and I lost the constant fear that Grandmother might show herself unexpectedly, perhaps to berate me for delivering Johnny from her spell. Cautiously, I began to wonder if this place was safe. Perhaps that was why she had not wanted me to come here. She had said something about *influences*. But there had been no sign of Otherworld folk; neither the grand ones nor the smaller ones had manifested themselves since I rode away from Sevenwaters. There was merely a strong contingent of highly capable human folk, and rather a lot of dangerous-looking weapons, and the wind, and the sea. There were no horses on the island; these they kept at the settlement on the landward side. And there were no dogs, not even to help herd the sheep and goats. There was a cat, which lurked in the kitchen and got under Biddy's feet. It was the oddest creature I had ever seen, with a little hollow on its rump where the tail should have been, and a hopping gait not unlike a rabbit's. Coll told me it came from Manannán's Isle, where all cats were tailless. When I raised my brows in disbelief, he said everyone knew the story. It was the doing of the Finn-ghaill, with their propensity for highly decorated headgear. They had developed a fashion for hanging a cat's tail from their helms as a kind of plume, brindle or tabby or white. And the shores of Man were heavy with Viking settlements now. So, the mother cats would bite the wee tails off their own young, as soon as they were born, to prevent a cruelty befalling them later. It was an interesting story, and no less plausible than some of my own.

Apart from Coll, the family kept its distance. The Chief was not a man easily befriended, and I was glad he restricted his discourse with me to a greeting here and there, or a stiff nod as we passed. Still, I had learned enough of him to be aware that while he was on Inis Eala nothing at all could occur there without his knowing of it. Johnny was the friendliest. He always had a smile and a kind word for me, and would tease his little brother for monopolizing the prettiest girl on the island, which just went to show how few girls there were, really. Johnny had never once mentioned what happened between us on the journey north, and nor had I. There was no way of knowing whether he still believed that charm had been my own doing. The other brother, Cormack, was so heavily involved in the work of the practice yard and armory he had no time at all for talk. They said he was as good as his father in hand-to-hand combat, and him but fourteen years old.

And then there was Liadan. I had heard what she said about wanting a daughter, and I sensed she would have liked to talk to me, perhaps of my mother and the times of their girlhood. But Liadan was anxious. I thought she counted the days until summer in the same way I did, but her pale features were sober and her green eyes very solemn. Her menfolk looked ahead and saw only challenge, and conflict, and victory. Liadan, I thought, sensed a summer which would also bring blood and loss, as she had once been told. She feared for them all, but especially for Johnny. She watched him with shadowed eyes. My aunt did not ask me any awkward questions, perhaps knowing she would get no answers. Still, she let me befriend her small son. It was his presence, lively, questioning, uncomplicated, that allowed me to get through the winter in a reasonable state of mind. That, and Grandmother's silence.

The season passed, with rain and gale and shivering nights, and the closer the spring came, the clearer the task appeared in my mind; the clearer and simpler. To satisfy my grandmother I must be there at the last, at the point when the allies were about to defeat their enemy.

Once there, I was supposed to take whatever action was necessary to ensure the victory did not take place. One could turn an army into toads, I thought, though the use of that charm on such a massive scale was probably beyond my abilities. Or one could do it the simple way, as she had suggested. One could kill the child of the prophecy. There was no doubt whatever that without him the venture could not succeed, even if he were lost at the very point of victory. A prophecy was a prophecy, after all, and every one of them depended on it. Why else was it Johnny who would lead this venture, instead of Sean of Sevenwaters, or a chieftain of the Uí Néill, or indeed Bran of Harrowfield, who seemed the kind of man who had never lost a fight in his life? Why not that wealthy and influential leader, Eamonn of Glencarnagh? But this would be no ordinary campaign, no mere territorial dispute, swiftly settled. It was an old struggle, steeped in mystery, heavy with symbolism. They had failed against the Britons in the past because they had not had Johnny. They could conquer only when the child was there to lead. Everyone knew that. Lose the child, and they would lose their heart and their hope.

Very well, then. I must appear to go along with my grandmother's plan until the last moment. I would wear the amulet until the very end; that way she would believe me still her creature. Then, when it came to it, instead of doing her will I must defy her; I must stand between her and Johnny, so he could win his victory and save the Islands. I supposed she would punish me. If she killed me, perhaps it was no more than I deserved, for the bad things I had done.

I went over it in my head, my quill poised motionless above the parchment as I focused my mind on how it must be. The battle would be on the Islands; the Islands were near to that very land of Norsemen and tailless cats. A long journey. A long way from Kerry and from O'Flaherty's farm in Ceann na Mara. So much the better. Ships must travel there. There must surely be some stopping place on the way, some safe harbor where the Chief's forces might join with those of Sean and Eamonn and the Uí Néill, and ready themselves for the final onslaught. Then there was a swim; a perilous swim from some place they called the Needle, to sink the Britons' fleet. A masterstroke, if they managed it. All hinged on that. Then, I supposed, they would simply go across in their curraghs, and land, and slaughter the opposition. It was most certainly not the kind of venture on which men took a young female cousin. In order to be there, I would need another transformation. No moths. Not this time. No help, either; my Fomhóire friends appeared to have deserted me. Still, I could do it. I would choose another form for myself, and I would accompany the Chief's mission, and then . . . and then I would have to change back again, and for a time I would be too weak to use the craft. That was the big flaw in my plan. I had no idea whatever how long such a battle might last; how well armed the Britons, how diffi-cult the terrain, what effect the loss of their fleet might have on the enemy's resolve. I did not know how long my grandmother would be prepared to watch, and wait for me to act. I would need to change back and then hide myself until I regained my strength. Johnny could win his battle by himself, I could see that in his eyes. But at the end my grandmother would come, and he would need me; and without the craft I was nothing.

They were beginning to test their skills on the sea, storms or no storms. There were no half-made ships in shelters now, but craft of many kinds hauled up on the narrow strip of beach or at anchor in the bay. We saw less and less of the menfolk; I learned that from now until the summer, none would visit Inis Eala to learn the crafts of war. All resources were for the campaign. All men worked for that purpose and each had his part to play in it. There were crossings to the mainland any day the sea allowed it, and much movement of men and supplies.

Sometimes, when it wasn't raining, Coll and I would sit on the clifftop above the bay and watch them. For him it made a welcome change from the discipline of writing, with which he struggled despite his quick intelligence. For me, it was good to be out-of-doors and feel the wind in my hair. Gull had left the responsibilities of the infirmary to Liadan, and now worked all day on the boats. His dark figure could be seen moving nimbly about the decks, and his voice came up to us on the wind, issuing curt orders. They appeared to be rehearsing a particular maneuver, out beyond the northern tip of the promontory where the tide flowed swift between rocky islets. The small curragh, rowed by six men, was held just beyond the clutching swirl of the current, oars used with great skill to keep it motionless there until an order was given, and they let the tide carry them through the gap and out into open water. Again and again they practiced that, incoming and outgoing, and once I saw men in the freezing water, swimming, and others hauling them up into the boat. Even at such a distance I identified Johnny.

"Your brother's a strong swimmer," I observed, hugging my shawl around me against the wind.

"So am I," responded Coll immediately. "When I'm bigger I'll be better than him. I'll swim all the way to the mainland. Nobody's ever done that."

I was reminded sharply of Eilis. Perhaps this sort of confidence ran in families.

"Can you swim?" Coll asked.

I shook my head. "I don't like the water much."

"I'll teach you, if you like. In the summer. If you want to." I could tell from his tone that this was a gesture of extreme generosity.

"Thank you," I said gravely. "Maybe. I'm not sure it's something I could learn."

"Everyone can learn," Coll said. "It's easy."

Like horse riding, I thought.

"You'll need to be able to swim if you're going to live here," he observed.

"I shouldn't think I am. Not after the summer."

"That's not what Johnny said. He said you'd wed one of the lads, probably Corentin because he's clever and speaks three languages, but maybe Gareth because he's a nice, patient fellow, and that you'd stay here on the island. That's what he said. But you don't need to marry them if you don't want to," he added hastily, no doubt reading my bemused expression.

I was saved from response by the unexpected arrival of the Chief, approaching us from the direction of the practice yard.

"Coll! I've an errand for you, son. Go down to the jetty and wait for Gull to come in. Let him know his supplies have arrived at the settlement. He'll want to send someone across with a bigger boat."

"Yes, Chief." There was a look of pride on Coll's face as he scampered away down the track, fleet-footed as a little goat. I made to get up and go, but the Chief stopped me, and then surprised me by sitting down on the rocks by my side, gazing out over the bay. There was silence for a while, a silence in which I realized he had sent Coll away for just this purpose.

"Your men will be well prepared for the campaign," I observed eventually. "Gull drills them hard in seamanship."

"Johnny's men, not mine," the Chief said mildly. "Harrowfield plays no part in this; it has always stood outside the feud. You're right about Gull. His skills with small craft are unsurpassed." His gray eyes were intent on that curragh poised on the flow between the smaller islands. "Each one of these men is the best at what he does."

"And yet, it seems astonishing that a man with such crippled hands can do so much. That must take remarkable strength of will."

"Indeed."

He sounded friendly enough. I thought I might venture another question.

"How did he—how did Gull come by such an injury, to lose fingers from both hands?"

The Chief's tight mouth stretched in an unpleasant sort of smile. "A man named Eamonn sliced them off with a sharp knife," he said quietly.

I froze. "What?" I whispered.

"It was done in an attempt to get information from me, rather than Gull. Eamonn wished to see us both beg for mercy before he finished us off. Liadan would not tell you this, and nor would Gull himself. My wife promised Eamonn her silence, and Gull has put these things behind him. But some promises, I think, are meant to be broken. It's best that you know this. The man you thought to marry is a butcher, Fainne. His hands reek of blood and betrayal. The full tale will never be told, I think; few know it. You're well away from him, and should stay away."

"But—" I was about to say, But he seems a good man, an honorable man. I was about to say, He is a respected chieftain, and your son's ally. But I recalled what Eamonn had said about the Painted Man, and I remembered the light in his eyes as he realized I could give him his vengeance, and I held my tongue.

"If your father wants a good marriage for you," the Chief went on, still gazing down at the point, where men now slipped quietly over the side of the curragh into the icy water as others strained to hold it steady, "he need look no further than Inis Eala. I'd be surprised if Ciarán cared much for such trappings as wealth, respectability or great landholdings. He'd want a good man for you, a steady sort of man, and there are plenty to choose from here. You'll have offers. Not yet, of course; they've all been told, no dalliance of that kind until after the summer, and they obey the rules. But later, there'll be the opportunity. And there's work for you here. The community is lacking in scholars."

"You speak of my father as if you knew him," I said in surprise.

"I met him once. And your mother. A long time ago, well before you were born."

"W—would you tell me about it?"

"Not all can be told. I was impressed by Ciarán. A young man of considerable strength; of depths I could only guess at. A man driven by strong passions, I think; love, anger, determination. We met under difficult circumstances."

"And my mother?"

He thought for a little before he replied. His hand rested still on the rock beside him; the swirling, complex pattern flowed across his skin like an ancient, cryptic language. "Again, the circumstances were—unusual. She was not at all like her sister."

"You mean," I said bitterly, "she was weak, stupid and selfish? That beauty was her only good quality?"

The Chief turned his head toward me. His eyes were very grave; they seemed to read me without judgment. "Everyone has something unique to offer," he said. "In some, that quality may be harder to find. I would never dismiss a man or woman thus, Fainne. Your mother was in severe distress when we undertook the task of bringing her to safety. She was indeed beautiful, a loveliness that is the stuff of tales. She was also confused, hurt and frightened, and the appearance of Gull and myself did little to reassure her. Niamh was not in our care long. Ciarán made sure of that. But I can tell you three things with complete truth. Your mother was a very courageous woman. One who goes doggedly on when frightened near out of her wits shows greater bravery than the warrior who charges into battle without thinking of the odds. She loved Ciarán deeply. There was a bond between them that endured, despite all. A bond as strong as—" He broke off.

"As strong as that between Liadan and yourself?" I ventured softly.

He gave a nod.

"What was the third thing?" I asked.

"This may distress you. We heard she killed herself. I am a sound judge of men, Fainne, and of women. I saw the look in your mother's eyes when she began to realize that she was at last safe, and that Ciarán would come for her. It was not the look of a woman who would throw away the unexpected gift of a second chance. Whoever told you she took her own life, lied to you."

"My father believed it," I said, my voice shaking. "How could he be wrong?"

"This upsets you. I regret that. But you should consider the possibilities. Had such a death occurred in my own home, I should have investigated thoroughly. A fall from a cliff, unwitnessed, could be many things. Suicide, certainly. An accident. Or murder."

"Murder! How could that be? There was nobody there but the three of us, and I was only an infant. You're not suggesting—"

"Indeed, no. Your mother was Ciarán's most priceless treasure. Still, you should be aware of my doubts. I do not believe she would ever willingly have left him; or that she would have abandoned you."

I sat quiet, staring out to sea as my head seemed to fill with the tears of an ancient grief.

"There was a time," the Chief said quietly, "when I swore I would never take this path, the way of family and community, for it has perils all its own. The ties of love are very strong. They bring a pain beyond any suffering of the body; dilemmas unsolvable save by anguish and loss."

"But you took it, all the same. The path."

He nodded. "And I do not regret it. But it is necessary, now, to avoid being paralyzed by fears. My sons speak highly of you, Fainne. They respect you."

I did not reply.

"I rely on Johnny's opinion. He believes you should be here with us."

"But?"

"I cannot disregard Liadan's misgivings. Her visions make her uneasy; she will not tell of them. I understand that, for the Sight does not always show true, and to act on its every message would set one adrift in a sea of terror. But what she sees gives her sleepless nights. I find it hard to believe she might be afraid of you; yet that is how it seems. So, despite my own opinions, I must make one thing plain. Who tries to hurt my wife, or my sons, is answerable to me."

"Her fears are unfounded." As I spoke, I felt the weight of the amulet heavy around my neck.

"Then why not tell her so?"

"I don't think she'd believe me," I said in a small voice.

It was close to Imbolc, the festival which heralds the first approach of spring, and I had been at Inis Eala long enough to learn folk's names and to gain a little of their trust. I had also discovered Johnny did not make idle threats. One of the young men, still fresh to the island's way of life, had made the mistake of trying to visit a girl by night, uninvited. I did not witness what took place between him and his leader, but I saw him leave the island under guard next day, his face ashen, his eyes betraying his anguish that such a foolish error had cost him his chance to be a part of this. It was the only way, Johnny told me. And there was no risk that such a man might tell of what he had seen. It was part of the training, to learn what fate might be expected if one were stupid enough to reveal secrets. The Painted Man had a long reach.

After that the young men were very quiet for a day or two. Dark, handsome Corentin, who on occasion had brought me ale or spoken to me of life in his native Armorica, now gave me a wide berth. As for laughing Gareth, who was one of Johnny's closest friends, he always abided by the rules. The most he ever did was glance at me shyly from time to time. Now even Gareth was somber. All of them knew such things must wait. Sam and Clem had plans for the autumn; one would wed Brenna, the fletcher, and the other Annie, the young cook. For folk such as these life might be hard at times, but at least it was straightforward.

Aware of the unease in the camp, Johnny proposed a trip to the mainland to collect supplies. While we existed comfortably on fish and mutton and the cabbages, carrots and leeks from the walled garden, we could not grow grains on the island, nor did we run cattle, so it was necessary sometimes to bring in oats or barley, cheeses or butter. And there was a need for more specialized supplies. This time Brenna was going across to check and collect some equipment she had ordered, and so I was allowed to go too, it being more seemly for the two of us to travel together. It was interesting Johnny saw no need for a chaperone, such as Biddy or another of the older women. Deliberate, I thought; thus he shows these young men that, despite what has happened, he trusts them.

The day was clear, the sea choppy. Brenna chattered away happily as the boat went up and down, and I clenched my teeth and kept my eyes on the far shore, and at length the voyage was over, until it should be time to come back again. Johnny's choice of Gareth and Corentin to guard us was perhaps a little unkind. Both were heavily armed. Brenna unfastened the bundle which was waiting for her in the storage hut, and began a close inspection of the contents, muttering to herself. I watched Johnny and Godric and the others as they hefted various parcels and packages onto their shoulders and headed down to the boat. The settlement was busy today, carts of goods having come in but recently; armed men patrolled everywhere. Snake took no risks, and maintained a substantial force on this side of the water. There was no casual sailing across, and no unannounced entry to this fortified place. Brenna was taking her time. I went to sit on a bench outside, enjoying the clear day and wondering if maybe the air was just a little warmer. My thoughts drifted back to the island. Soon I must venture out and find myself a secret place to perfect the exercise of transformation, and sharpen my skills for the task ahead of me. Maybe tomorrow, or the next day.

"Fainne?" I jumped at the sound of Johnny's voice.

"Is it time to go?" I asked, getting up.

"Not quite. The lads'll want a drop of ale first. There's a fellow over yonder says he knows you."

"Fellow? What fellow? It must be a mistake. I know nobody."

Johnny grinned. "I have a feeling you'll know this one. Quite persistent, he was."

A trickle of cold fear went all the way down my spine. I followed my cousin without a word to a place where a couple of old nags were tied up loosely, and empty carts stood in a row. And there, patting the nose of an ugly-looking bay mare, was a lanky sort of fellow with black hair to his shoulders, and a bit of a beard, and a gold ring in one ear.

"Hello, Curly," said Darragh.

My heart gave a thud that was mostly horror and only the smallest part joy. If I could have summoned my wits, I might have told

Johnny the man was a complete stranger, and to send him on his way. But I could not even find my voice; I stood there gaping. And suddenly Johnny was gone, and the hovering Corentin with him. I cursed my cousin's tact.

"You're looking well," said Darragh.

I managed, at last, to speak. "What are you doing here? You shouldn't be here! Where's Aoife?"

There was a pause.

"Sold her, didn't I?" he said.

I couldn't have heard right. Sold her, beautiful Aoife who was so much a part of him she seemed half-human herself? Aoife who was his luck?

"Sold her?" I echoed. "You can't have."

Darragh looked down at the ground. "A man doesn't break an agreement to work, and travel halfway across Erin without some sort of wherewithal, Fainne. That was the bargain. I got my freedom; O'Flaherty got the mare. She'll be well taken care of."

"But why?"

Then there was silence. He looked at me and away again. I thought there was a new sorrow in his eyes, as if even he doubted the wisdom of his choice.

"There's nothing for you here," I said in a fierce whisper, furious with him for coming, and with myself for the feelings which welled within me, feelings a sorcerer's daughter had no time for, not when there were momentous deeds to be done. "You should not have come here. It's dangerous. You must go home, Darragh. Now, straight away."

"Ah," he said casually, but I could see his hand shaking as he stroked the horse's long muzzle with gentle fingers. "I don't think I'll be doing that."

"You must!" I hissed. "You can't be here! It'll ruin everything! You've got to leave at once! I can't do it if you're here—"

"Do what, Curly?"

"Do what I have to do. Please, Darragh, please, if you care anything for me, you'll go now, quickly, before . . . before . . ." *Before my grandmother sees you.* I could not say it.

"Well, now. It's not so simple."

"Why not?" I glared at him. Darragh looked up and over my

shoulder, and suddenly there they were, four of them, Johnny and Gareth, Godric and Corentin, bristling with weapons and ferocious of aspect. Every one of them wore the mark on his face; every one of them looked ready to kill. In this setting, Darragh was like—he was like a meadow lark among birds of prey, I thought. In quite the wrong place. Surely even he must see that.

"Friend of yours?" inquired Johnny, with a smile which did not reach his eyes.

"I do know the young man a little," I said stiffly. "From long ago."

"Your name?" Johnny's gaze was sharply assessing. I thought his behavior a little odd. Had he not spoken with Darragh already?

"Darragh, son of Dan Walker, from Kerry."

"And what cause would you have to travel to these parts? I'm surprised you got so far."

Darragh glanced at me. "Looking for an old friend, you might call it. Helped a man with a horse, on the road; got a lift."

Johnny made no comment. He simply waited. Behind him Gareth shifted uneasily, and there was a little scrape of metal.

"I heard," said Darragh, "I heard you might be wanting men, in these parts. A campaign. I came to offer my services, if you'll have me."

"What!" I exclaimed in shock before I could stop myself. Johnny's companions made no attempt to conceal their amusement.

"I see," said Johnny politely. "And what skills do you have, which you think we might find useful?"

"Nothing!" I snapped before Darragh could open his mouth to reply. My voice was less than steady. "Nothing at all! This man cannot fight, he does not know how to use a weapon, he's never killed anyone in his life. He would be quite useless to you. I know him; take my word for it."

Johnny looked at me calmly, and back at Darragh. "You heard the lady," he said. "We need warriors here. I think we cannot employ you, unless you have some other skills."

"I can play the pipes," Darragh ventured. "And I've a good hand with the horses. Warriors need horses."

"Not this time," said Johnny. "This venture is by sea. You might find work in the stables, on the landward side, if you proved yourself."

"No." Darragh's voice was raw with feeling. I stared at him in amazement. Couldn't he see how impossible this was; how foolish he was being? Had he lost all his common sense? "That's not good enough. I want to be over there on the island. I can learn to fight. I'd work hard. You seem a fair sort of fellow. Give me a chance, at least."

Johnny looked him up and down. "I don't think so," he said.

"Too much of a fine lord, are you, to have a tinker's lad like me in your band? I'm not ashamed to be the son of a traveling man. I'll prove my worth."

"At Inis Eala," said Johnny, who was now regarding Darragh very closely indeed, "we care nothing for a man's father. It is what he himself has to offer that counts. How far have you come?"

"From the west. From Ceann na Mara."

"I see. You are persistent. Still, as my cousin here says, you are not a fighter; and a source of music, while desirable, is not one of my major priorities. Are you sure there is nothing more you can do?"

Don't say it, Darragh, I willed him.

"I can swim," Darragh said. "A bit."

"So I've heard," said Johnny smoothly. "Well, I'll have a think about it. I may be back here before the spring is over. If you're still in these parts, we might talk again." And he turned on his heel and headed off down to the curragh, where Brenna was supervising the stowing of her precious bundle. I followed my cousin blindly, making myself breathe slowly, forcing myself not to look back. It had been cruel, maybe; but it was the right decision. Darragh could not come with us. He must not.

The men had to pull harder on the way back, against an incoming tide, and we made more gradual progress. My mind was troubled, my heart heavy. Foolishly, what seemed to distress me most was that I had not bid my friend goodbye. I could at least have managed a kind word, I thought; the clasp of a hand or a little kiss on the cheek. It would have been better never to have seen him again, than to meet thus and part so soon with no farewell.

The men were rowing hard, their backs to the island. They were still managing a conversation of sorts.

"Pigheaded sort of fellow," observed Corentin.

"You'd need to be crazy to try it," Godric grinned. "Against the tide and all."

Johnny wasn't saying much. He was simply gazing back across the sea, the way we had come, with the same carefully calculating look on his face as I had seen, often, on his father's. I recalled his saying once that he was a sound judge of a man's character, or a woman's. I watched him, and felt myself grow cold with horror as the meaning of the men's words hit me. I twisted around and looked back.

Somewhere between our small boat and the retreating shore, a dark head bobbed in and out of view in the choppy waters. Sleek as a selkie's, it came up for air, then disappeared in the dark trough, to surface once more after a heart-stopping, immeasurable wait.

"You did say he was a good swimmer, I recall," observed Johnny. "Just how good, I think we're about to find out."

I clutched Brenna's arm in terror. What about the sea serpents? What about the biting cold? And hadn't Coll said nobody had ever done this?

"Johnny," I said in a small voice. "It's a very long way. You wouldn't—?"

"All men must pass a test. Still, we could hardly let your sweetheart drown, could we? Besides, we need him. Halfway, maybe, or a little more. He's already come farther than any of us could manage, and his progress is steady. We might ship oars by the rocks out yonder and let him catch up, I think."

"Fellow can't wield a sword; hasn't the stomach to kill a man," growled Gareth. "Maybe he can swim, but what about after?"

"Just a liability," grumbled Corentin, hauling on his oar.

"He can learn." Johnny's tone was level. "He said so, didn't he? And we have the best teachers, on Inis Eala."

It felt like forever. The tiny, doggedly swimming figure grew smaller, and the waves grew higher, and the air colder as we moved farther away from the shore. Every crest seemed topped by long clutching fingers; every trough shadowed by menacing monsters of the deep, long-toothed, slippery, strangling. I do not know what my face showed. Johnny glanced at me, and his mouth quirked a little, but there was concern in his eyes and something like surprise. Brenna held my hand and said, "It's all right, Fainne. We're nearly level with the rocks. They'll wait for him there." Gareth glowered. Corentin was tight-lipped. Godric and Mikka had a bet on whether they'd be fishing an upstart tinker from the water, or a corpse. I could feel the ache all through my head, so hard were my teeth clenched. I clutched Brenna's hand tight, and kept my eyes on that distant dot of black as it appeared, and was lost, and appeared again. Perhaps she did this, I thought. Perhaps Grandmother brought him here, and now she means for me to watch him drown, so she can show me the price of disobedience. She means to show me how foolish I was, to think myself strong enough.

"Your young man is very brave, Fainne," said Brenna as we came level with the rocks, and Johnny ordered the lads to hold the boat still against the tide.

"Very stupid, more like," I muttered, but she was right, of course. He came on steadily, as if he did not know the meaning of fear, as if he did not understand the limitations of a mortal man. Despite my terror and my fury, I was so proud of him I thought my heart would break with it. "And he's not my young man."

"No?" queried Johnny. "Well, one thing's certain. It's not the prospect of lessons in swordsmanship that drives him thus."

We waited; the men used the same technique they had been perfecting at the point, a balancing of the oars on either side which held the curragh tolerably still against the pull of the incoming tide. They kept their distance from the rocks. The wait seemed endless, but was maybe not so long; the dark head became less like that of a sea creature and more identifiably that of a man, and the strong rhythmic movement of thin brown arms could be seen through the swell, and the pallor of the face, and the dark eyes filled with grim determination. Then, at last, he reached the boat, and was hauled in and dropped unceremoniously at my feet, white, shivering and quite unable to utter a word. The men shifted their grip on the oars, and pulled for home.

There were tears there, somewhere, but I could not shed them. Tears of joy, tears of terrible sorrow, tears of fear and of frustration. I unfastened my thick shawl and wrapped it around his trembling shoulders.

"How dare you frighten me like that?" I hissed in an undertone. "You ought to be ashamed of yourself!"

Then he leaned forward, just a little, and put his head against my knee, and I heard him whisper through chattering teeth, "D—d—don't make me say g—g—goodbye again."

The most powerful sorceress in the world could not have stopped my fingers moving, at that moment, to touch his cold cheek and rest

there for a heartbeat of time. I saw a crooked smile curve his lips; and
then I took my hand away and closed my eyes tight. I would not look
at him; and yet I longed to, I yearned to look and look and store it all
up, like a treasure hoarded for bleak times ahead. I wanted to warm
his chill hands with my own, to hold him close in the circle of my
arms until the shivering stopped. I wanted to watch the color return
to his frozen features, and to see the sweet smile and the merry eyes. I
wanted what I could not have. It was my great weakness, and if I did
not quell it now it would be my own downfall, and Darragh's, and
the ruin of the great campaign of Sevenwaters. It would be the triumph of Lady Oonagh over all that was right and good. In my wanting, Grandmother had the perfect tool with which to manipulate me.
I could not let this happen. Somehow, I must make Darragh understand. So I kept my eyes shut, and knew with every single part of my
body just where he sat, and how he looked, and felt the need to have
him stay, and the need to have him go, tearing me in pieces.

From the moment Darragh set foot on the jetty at Inis Eala, shivering and bedraggled, he was a man with a reputation. One does not
easily escape the effect of such a display of strength and courage.
These folk liked that. It was something they understood. And they
liked him; who could fail to do so? Whether it was the lack of preten-
sion, or the crooked grin, or the willingness to learn, within a few
days he was everyone's friend. Even Gareth and Corentin admitted,
grudgingly, that the fellow was a hard worker. He'd need to be; there
was a lot to be mastered, and not much time. Johnny expected miracles, maybe.

It was as well for me that Snake took personal charge of educat-
ing a traveling man in the arts of combat, for it meant Darragh was
out of my sight for the best part of the day, concealed behind high
walls, and all I learned of his progress was from suppertime talk. I
made sure I sat away from him at table. I kept my eyes on my platter,
or maintained conversation with Brenna or Annie, to the exclusion of
all others. Though I longed to look at him, I did not. Though I
longed to speak with him, I made sure there were no opportunities.

The weather began to clear and the season to change. Imbolc was
past; it was almost spring, and I needed to act quickly. I found
Johnny alone one morning, looking at maps in the hut we used for
scholarly pursuits. It was early; Coll was not yet abroad.

"Johnny?"

"Mmm?"

"I need to tell you something. Ask you something. It's important."

He looked up, eyes narrowed. "What is it, cousin?"

"D—Darragh. He should not be here." I spoke furtively, glancing around me; foolish, that was. If my grandmother chose to look, she could see, I had no doubt of that. "I want you to send him away."

Johnny raised his brows. "I've a job for him. Certainly, your friend is somewhat lacking when it comes to the finer points of combat; all the points, to tell true. But he's learning. He's willing and clever. He's quick, and light on his feet. I need him, Fainne."

"Please," I said, furious to hear how my voice cracked. "Please send him home. Darragh is not a warrior. He doesn't have it in him to kill. Please, Johnny. You can find another swimmer. This is—it is really important." I lowered my voice. "It has an importance beyond what is—apparent."

He looked at me for a moment.

"It is a momentous mission, and its unfolding may be beyond what any of us can comprehend," he said gravely. "My own part in it may be both more and less than what folk hope for." There was a sadness in his eyes which I did not understand.

"What do you mean?" I asked him, startled out of my own dilemma by his words.

"A man might think it easy, to have a destiny laid out for him since birth; a grand and glorious path, the fulfillment of an ancient prophecy, no less; the deliverance of his people's sacred ground. Folk see it clear: the battle won, the Islands restored, and the heir returned to Sevenwaters to guide and protect his people, when it is his time. That, I have known since I was no more than an infant."

"But it's not so plain, is it?" I ventured, recalling what I had been told by the Old Ones, in snippets, and never really understood. "Winning a battle is not all of it."

Johnny gave a nod. "So I believe. There is a part of this untold, a part which does not match the expectations of these good folk; not at all. The path is not all glory. My mother sees death for me, though she will not say so. I see something that is like a death, but is not so; something far from the straight path of the warrior. Who can say how this will unfold? It frightens me."

"You, frightened?" I found this hard to believe. "But they all have such faith in you. Not a single doubt."

"I never had the freedom to choose my own future," Johnny said. "That is a loss to be regretted. But I will do what I must. I will win the battle, and face what comes after with my eyes open. Your Darragh, now, he is a man who goes his own way. And the way he wants is this one, Fainne. Would you deny him that?"

I bit my lip. "He doesn't know. He doesn't understand what it means. He wants to help me, or to protect me, and he keeps on following me, and he doesn't realize that's the worst thing he can possibly do. He must go home, Johnny. Please send him away."

Johnny stared. "You have changed since he came here," he said softly. "I would almost think you might weep, as you plead for this man. But it is his choice, cousin, and not yours. I respect a man's choice. Besides, we need him. There must be five swimmers; we have only four with the strength and endurance to undertake what is required. Myself, my father, Sigurd and Gareth. It was indeed a miracle that delivered this tinker's lad to our door. I cannot do as you ask."

I felt misery descend on me anew. Who would help me, if he would not?

"Fainne." Johnny's tone was gentle. "I seldom lose men; my forces are unsurpassed at what they do. And I would hardly place a fellow with barely one season's training in my front line."

"It's not that, though that is part of it. It's—it's—" I could not tell him. I could not say, if you let him do this, she will put him in peril and then . . . and then . . . I do not know if I will have the strength to go on. I do not know if I can bear it. It may be proven, after all, that I can be no more than my grandmother's creature.

"You see visions?" he asked me. "Shadows of things to come, as my mother does?"

I shook my head. "No. But I have heard warnings, and—no, I cannot tell you. I should not have spoken thus. I see you will not help me."

"My instincts and my training tell me my decision is a sound one," Johnny said. "I would not risk a good man if it were not necessary. Now here is Coll, and I'd best be away before I find myself set tasks with stylus and wax, never my favorite occupation. Farewell, cousin."

I spoke to the Chief, but it was not much good, for the only argument I could use with him was Darragh's inexperience as a warrior, and how little help he might be to them on land, for all his strength in the water. And, that I would rather he did not get himself killed quite yet. The Chief listened gravely, and then told me Snake was very pleased with the lad's progress; for a skinny fellow, he'd good strength in the arms and a knack with the staff, and he was not at all bad in unarmed combat, either. Maybe that was something you learned on the road. As for sword and dagger, those needed work, but there was still time. When I tried to protest, the Chief said this was Johnny's decision, and he trusted his son's judgment. Besides, wasn't it what the lad himself wanted?

There was one last possibility. Liadan was in the infirmary, grinding something pungent with mortar and pestle. There was nobody else about. Empty pallets awaited victims of warfare or domestic accident or seasonal ague. Strings of garlic hung from the beams above her; jars of herbs were stored on neat shelves.

"Fainne!" she exclaimed in surprise as I came in. "I did not expect you." She wore her customary dark gown and plain overtunic, demure as a nun's garb; her hair was caught up in a linen band, but curls escaped over her pale brow. She frowned.

"You are come, no doubt, to ask me to send this young man home?" she asked as she resumed grinding the reddish powder in her bowl.

I stared at her. "Is no business private here?" I asked.

My aunt smiled. "We do talk to one another, Fainne. That's usual in families. Besides, Darragh came to see me."

"He what?"

"He's very worried about you. And I know you are anxious for his safety. Darragh offered a solution which I might be prepared to support, if you agreed."

I wasn't sure I wanted to know, but I asked anyway. "What solution?"

"That the two of you leave here together and travel quietly back to Kerry. You will preserve him that way; and he will have what he came for. You will both be well gone before this campaign commences. Safe."

"Safe?" I echoed with some bitterness. She was watching me

closely, green eyes very intent. I hoped she was not reading what was in my mind. "That would not be safe at all, Aunt. It won't do. I must be here; I cannot return to Kerry. But Darragh must go. He does not belong at Inis Eala. He was never meant to be part of this. He just— he just put himself in it, uninvited. That's what he does."

"It seemed a sensible suggestion to me," she said mildly. "Darragh argued his case well. He loves you, Fainne. Can you not see that?"

"It's not love," I snapped. "It's just—it's just stubbornness. The boy doesn't trust me to look after myself. He doesn't understand what's good for him and what's not. He never has."

"And what about you?" Liadan asked. Her hands had ceased their work and now rested on the table before her. "Is it love that makes you so eager to see him gone, when he has risked his very life to be by your side?"

"Our kind do not feel love," I muttered, knowing as I said it that this was a lie. "It makes life too complicated. It—it stops you from doing what must be done. Like my father. Love ruined his life."

"He has a daughter," she said softly. "I imagine he feels great pride in you, my dear. You are clever, accomplished and—subtle, like him. And you're as bonny as Niamh was, in your own way. And as headstrong. Ask Ciarán if he regrets that he ever met my sister, before you dismiss love so lightly. Set it aside, and you will not live a life, but only the shadow of a life."

"Anyway," I said, not wishing to take this any further, "Johnny won't let Darragh go. He says he needs him."

Liadan sighed. "If you were prepared to go as well, I would speak to Johnny."

I shook my head. "I must stay here. I can't go home."

"Yes," she said wearily, and sat down on the bench. "I suppose I knew that; still, I wished to try. Darragh's a good lad, Fainne. He does not deserve this."

"It's his own fault," I said in a whisper.

She nodded. "Perhaps you are right. These men, they have a habit of putting themselves into the tale, where they've no right to be, and making themselves a part of it. It is pointless, maybe, for me to try to change the course of things, but I have never been able to—just to sit back and let it unfold, as my uncle Conor usually advises. It seems to me one must seize hold, and move ahead, and make the tale bright and true, if one can. Darragh does so; he has great strength of will."

"He has no understanding of this," I said flatly.

"And you do?" Her voice was very quiet. It sounded almost as if she were sorry for me.

"At least," I whispered, "at least I know what must be done."

"And you will be there at the end," Liadan said in a tone that frightened me; a tone that spoke some sort of incontrovertible truth. "How, I cannot imagine, but Johnny will be there, and you will be there. I've seen it."

I turned cold all over. "What did you see? What of Darragh?"

"I do not tell of these things. It is too easy to misunderstand."

"Can't you tell me anything? Anything at all?"

"My son faced death. You wept. You wept as one weeps who has cast away her only treasure. Never have I seen such grief."

I swallowed. "I've seen that part too. If it's to come, it will come, I suppose."

Liadan nodded. "You should ask Coll to take you down to the north point some time," she said in quite a different tone. Our conversation was over, and I had lost my last chance to send Darragh away safe. "The season's turning; there will be clear days. You need time away from your tasks, fresh air and exercise. It'll do you good." She sounded quite ordinary, like someone's mother. Somewhere beneath the jumble of fears that crowded my mind, I thought that it might be quite good to have a mother who fussed about whether you were getting fresh air and exercise. Perhaps, if my mother had not died, she would have been like that. Perhaps, if the Chief was right, she had never meant to leave us; maybe she had loved us and had hopes of a future. One day, if I were granted time, I would find out the truth about her death. I owed that to her. Meanwhile I would remember her, and I would remember Liadan's words. *I imagine he feels great pride in you, my dear.* I would keep these things in my heart, and I would make the tale as bright and true as I could; and never mind the tears. There was simply nothing else to be done.

Chapter Thirteen

Over and over they practiced the thing with the boat in the current and the swimmers. And now Darragh was among them as they slipped over the side of the curragh and into the freezing grip of the tide. They did it by day. They did it by night, with lanterns on the prow. They took to doing it with the masks over their faces, and dark clothing close-fitting from neck to wrist to ankle, so that they did indeed resemble creatures of the ocean, some strange children of Manannán himself. They did it by moonlight and left the lanterns behind; I heard them as they came up the steps from the cove afterward, laughing. It seemed to me they were quite fearless, a band of comrades bound together by their unshakable belief in themselves and in each other. It worried me that Darragh had so soon become one of them. And it was not only my fear for his safety that gave me sleepless nights. It was something I was ashamed to admit even to myself. He was mine, and I did not want to share him. I did not want him to change, and become hard-jawed and ruthless like the rest of these warriors. Sometimes, it had only been the little image of Darragh, riding quietly along some sunlit pathway between rowans on his lovely white pony, and smiling his crooked smile, that had kept me going at all. Once that was gone, what had I left?

Then Coll fell sick. One day he had a slight headache, nothing much, just enough to make him grumble a little more than usual over his work. The next day he had a fever and could not get out of his bed. I did not go to see him. I stayed at my table, busy with quill and ink, recording the medicinal uses of a herb named scrophularia, commonly known as figwort. I spoke to nobody.

Liadan was not present at supper, and neither was Gull. The Chief was very quiet, but that was nothing unusual. Johnny wasn't saying much either, and I thought he was watching me.

"Boy's been taken real bad," Biddy muttered to me. "Hot as a blacksmith's fire, and babbling nonsense."

I retired early to my sleeping hut, thinking, But for me this child would be well. This is my fault. How could I forget? How could I let myself make another friend? How could I be foolish enough to believe Grandmother would let me be, even for a moment? I had only just lit the lamp when they sent for me. In the infirmary they were waiting, Liadan sitting by her son's bedside as he lay sweating and mumbling and turning his small head restlessly from side to side, and both the Chief and Johnny standing grim-faced and silent behind her.

I am a sorcerer's daughter, I reminded myself as I stepped forward to face them. It didn't seem to help much.

"I'm sorry Coll is sick," I said as calmly as I could. "I hope it is only a spring chill, and that he'll be better soon." I clasped my hands behind my back to keep them still.

"Sit down, Fainne." Liadan's voice had lost the warmth of our last encounter. When I had seated myself on the other side of the boy's bed as indicated, I saw that her eyes were red and swollen, and her mouth tight. The Chief's expression was alarmingly fierce, Johnny's cautious, as if he were weighing a dilemma.

"I suppose you know why we have called you here," said Liadan as she wrung out a small cloth and used it to sponge Coll's burning brow.

"Perhaps you had best tell me." I managed to keep my voice under control, despite my thumping heart.

It was the Chief who spoke then, in a very soft voice, a voice designed to put fear into men. "My wife tells me such a fever, burning so hot in so short a time, is unlikely to have come about without some — intervention." There was a question in his tone, but I did not reply. "If my son dies, those responsible will not escape punishment."

"Coll was well yesterday," Liadan said, and now her voice shook. "He was running around and getting in everyone's way and he was quite well. There is no reason for him to be stricken thus. This fever does not respond as it should to the herbal drafts; he burns as if gripped in a fire-dragon's jaws. If this does not break soon, I do not know if he can withstand it. Fainne, have you done this?"

I flinched. Although I had been expecting blame, I had not thought she would confront me so directly.

"No, Aunt Liadan." Was it my imagination, or did my voice sound less than certain? Indeed, I had not done it; I had laid no spell on the child, nor would I ever have considered such a thing, even if Grandmother had bid me; even if she had threatened direst punishment. Coll was only little. I would never have hurt Coll. But I was guilty all the same. If not for me, my grandmother would never have noticed the lad. She would never have taken it into her head to hurt him. This was as much my doing as if I had indeed used the craft.

"I have not used any magic since I came to Inis Eala," I said as steadily as I could. "It's the truth. I would not hurt Coll. He's my friend."

"Wouldn't that be a greater test of will?" asked Johnny carefully. "A demonstration of strength? To hurt a friend, rather than a foe?"

I stared at him. "There's nothing wrong with my will," I whispered, shocked that he came so close to the truth. "I've no need to demonstrate it by hurting children." And then I felt a cold horror come over me, because of course there was Maeve, and the fire. Hurting children was something a sorceress could do with no hesitation at all; and I was a sorceress. I put my head in my hands, so they could not see my face.

"Look at us, Fainne."

The Chief must be obeyed. I looked up. It was like facing a brithem who has already decided you are guilty, without hearing the evidence. And it hurt. I did not want to be judged thus by these good people; my own people.

"I did not do this," I said in a small voice, rising to my feet. "That is the truth. Maybe—maybe it is just a spring fever. Maybe Coll will be better soon. I would help nurse him, if you wish. I would—"

"I don't want you anywhere near my son." Liadan's voice was harsh with feeling. "I saw what happened at Sevenwaters; I did not want to believe you responsible, but I know you can make fire when you choose. I know Ciarán allowed his mother to—to influence you. No wonder Eamonn was unformed clay in your hands. No wonder your young man is so desperate to get you away. He recognizes the evil that you can do."

Her words turned me cold with anguish. Not so long ago, I had heard her speak with affection, as a mother would. So soon, my grandmother had turned that to bitter enmity.

"I didn't do it," I said again, feeling my head swim and my eyes tingle with tears that could not be shed. "That's the truth! I swear it!"

"You'd best go to your quarters, until we see what's to be done." The Chief spoke calmly, but I had seen the look in his eyes as he glanced at his small son. "Perhaps, after all, we must allow Darragh to take you home. You cannot remain among us, after this."

"But you've no proof! It's not fair! You can't send me away, you can't! Johnny? Surely you don't believe I would do such a thing?"

Johnny looked at me with a strange little smile, but he said nothing at all. The goddess aid me, it was all collapsing around me, every bit of it. A total failure; could my grandmother's wrath be far behind? "Oh, please," I breathed. "Oh, please. I swear I had no part in this. I didn't do it this time."

There was a moment of terrible silence. Then Liadan said, "What do you mean, this time?"

I made some sort of sound, halfway between a sob and a scream, and then I was bolting for the doorway, and I was out in the night, in the dark, and I was running, running as fast as my limping foot would carry me, away from the feverish child and the judging eyes of my family, away from the settlement of good folk with one bright purpose and one straight path before them, away from my friend who was caught up in something he could never be part of, away across the sheep fields and over the wall and beyond. I ran until my head throbbed and my heart pounded and my breath came in great agonizing gasps. The moon lit my path; my boots crunched on small stones and slid on great, wet rocks and sank in patches of soft sand. I ran up little hills and crashed down small valleys, I blundered into bushes and came mind-numbingly close to launching myself off a cliff into white water far below. An accident; still, as I teetered there I thought that would be one way out. But I fought for my balance and regained it. That was a weakling's solution, and, frightened and hurt and confused as I was, I would not take it. There was one good thing

I could do, and whatever stood in my way I was going to do it. I would make my father proud of me, despite all.

I ran on. Under the spring moon the landscape took on a silver shine, glittering rocks, pearly sand, gleaming bushes as if I fled through some realm beyond the mortal one. And there were strange sounds: above the roaring of the ocean came low, sad cries, like those of some great creature of the deep, mournfully singing of something lost, some treasure never to be regained. There was an anguish in it, a sorrow that was beyond comforting.

I ran as far as I could go, all the way to the rocky headland at the north of the island. I never looked behind me for folk following with lanterns or torches. What would they care if I fell off a cliff and broke my neck? Why would they bother if I blundered into the sea and let the inky waters swallow me? They would think themselves well rid of me. Darragh was wrong about family, and Liadan was wrong about love. Both brought nothing but unnecessary complications. I was better off with neither.

Now I was at the rock face, and there was an entrance, a little tunnel with a sandy floor, perhaps leading to a place of shelter, and it was quite like home. Still panting hard, with my hair tumbled over my eyes and both hands stretched out in front of me to find the way, I stepped inside. I thought I would go in far enough to be out of the wind, and then I would curl myself up into a ball, and shut my eyes tight, and pretend, until morning, that there was nobody else in the world. No Coll, no Liadan, no Johnny, no Darragh. Especially, no Grandmother. I would lie down on the sand and will them all away until the sun rose. Then I would get up and go back, and be strong again.

I edged forward in the dark, fingers touching the rock walls on either side, feet moving cautiously. I made no sound. Some way in, the tunnel seemed to open out; I could see little, but there was a movement of air and a sense of space, and a little ripple of water which was not the sea. I glimpsed something white ahead of me amid the shadows, like a fold of cloth, or a swathe of feathers. I reached out my hand in front of me and instead of hard rock or empty space, my fingers touched something that was soft and warm and unmistakably alive. I gave a yelp of fright, stepped back, trod on my gown and sat down painfully on the ground. There was an answering exclamation of alarm in the darkness, and a sound of soft footsteps retreating. I sat there, working on my breathing. In, out. Calm. Discipline. Some way off light flared, and then there was the steady glow of a lantern coming closer. I got slowly to my feet, staring at the man who bore it, and blinking in disbelief. He stared back at me. No doubt the expression of shock on his pale features mirrored my own. But it was not the sudden fright of the encounter that made my heart thump now. It was not the similarity this man bore to my uncle Sean, and to Liadan, with his long pale face and shock of wild dark hair, his slender, upright form and neat, clever features. Nor was it his ragged robe, his tattered cloak, his unshod feet that shocked me. It was the wing he bore in place of his left arm; a great shining thing, a gleaming swath of gold and pink and cream in the lantern light. My grandmother had said, *You'll need to watch out for that fellow with the swan's wing*.

"You ran away," the man observed as he stood there looking at me.

"Who are you?" I managed, still somewhat short of breath. His voice was very odd; unaccented, but still with the hesitancy of one who speaks a tongue not his own.

"It seems my tale has not yet spread as far as Kerry," he observed dryly. "Come. You've run a long way. You'll want to rest, and maybe drink something. I don't have a fire here, but I can provide fresh water and a place to sit in comfort. I hope you didn't hurt yourself."

"It's not those sort of hurts that are the problem," I said grimly, following him as he walked ahead into the cave. There seemed no alternative, really. I could hardly sit down and refuse to budge.

We reached a place where there were rock shelves against the cavern walls, and a still pool gleaming before us. Above it the chamber was open to the sky; in the dark waters stars gleamed remote and mysterious. The man set his lantern down and fetched a little cup of dark metal. He bent and filled it from the pool, and I heard him mutter words, familiar words. He passed me the cup with his right hand. I was trying not to stare at the feathers, only part-concealed by the ancient, raggedy cloak.

"Thank you," I said, and drank, feeling the cold and purity of his offering flow into my being. My breathing slowed; I became calm. "You honor the earth as you take from her," I observed.

"I am no druid, child. My mother taught us early to respect that which gives us life. It is a lesson one does not forget."

"Us?" I delved into my memory. I knew the story, of course; but even though it was so close to home, perhaps I had not quite believed it. I should have done. This creature, part man, part swan, was of my grandmother's making. "You, and Conor, and your other brothers, you mean?"

He inclined his head. "And my sister. Why have you come here?"

"By accident. I did not know there was anyone here. They never told me. I wanted—I just wanted a hiding place. Just for a bit."

"You have found one, then. Won't they come looking for you?"

"They don't care," I said miserably, so enmeshed in my woes I hardly thought how odd it was to be speaking thus to a stranger. "They said I did something bad, and I didn't, but they wouldn't believe me. Nobody cares where I am."

"Still," said the ragged man, "we'd best perhaps let them know. Then you can stay here undisturbed until you have regained yourself."

"Let them know?" I stared at him blankly. "How?" And then I saw his eyes; deep, colorless eyes like light on still water, eyes that were the image of my cousin Sibeal's. There was no need for him to answer.

For a time I sat there on the rocks, and sipped the water, and watched the shadows dance and sway around the cavern in the lantern light. The pool was very still now; the faint rippling I had heard before was quite gone. It was a place of great calm; of immense silence. It was like the little cave below the Honeycomb; a place of the margins. I breathed slower still; the throbbing in my head subsided.

"This is a place where secrets are safe," said the man in a soft voice. "It is protected by forces older and stronger than time. I am surprised they did not send you to me earlier, for I see you are deeply troubled."

"What are you offering? Good advice? A brisk talking to? I've a friend who's all too ready to offer both, and won't understand I don't need them. I go my own way. Why should I tell you anything?"

He waited before replying.

"I do not offer advice. Sometimes I see things, and sometimes I speak of them. Sometimes I have visitors, and they talk to me. Liadan's sons come here. She herself does not need to come."

"Because you talk mind to mind?"

"You do not share that gift? That surprises me."

I frowned. "Why would it surprise you? You seem to know who I am. Doesn't the Sight come from your Fomhóire ancestry? My mother had no such gifts, and even my father has not that particular ability. Our skill is limited; it was decreed thus by the Túatha Dé, long ago."

He raised his brows. "Who told you that story?"

I did not answer.

"Secrets are safe here. All secrets. You were not told of me. So we scared one another. My name is Finbar."

"Mine is Fainne," I said stiffly. "How can it be safe? Nowhere is safe. Not while—"

"Not while you wear what you wear around your neck?"

I realized that, in my headlong flight, the amulet on its strange cord had broken from its concealment and now lay fully visible against the bodice of my gown. I put my hand up in a futile effort to hide it. The metal was quite cold.

"A powerful charm," Finbar observed. "If you have withstood its influence thus far, you are indeed your father's daughter. I recognize this cord on which it hangs."

"You do?" The man was full of surprises.

"Oh, yes. It was your mother's, made for her by Liadan when Niamh was sent away. She who gave you this amulet most certainly did not give you the cord."

"No. I restrung it. And it seemed to me . . ."

"Ah, yes." Finbar nodded. "The one counteracts the other, as far as it can. You must thank the strong women of our family for this token of kinship, for it weaves a powerful protective spell, Fainne. Not a spell of sorcery, but something simpler and purer. Liadan worked into it the very fiber of all who dwelt at Sevenwaters. She tried to keep Niamh as safe as she could. Your mother was much loved, though you may doubt that."

I stared at him, unable to find words.

"That is an amulet of malign and potent influence," he said gravely. "But here in this place it cannot perform the task it was designed for. Why don't you take it off?"

I turned chill with fear. "No!" I whispered. "No! I cannot do that! We must not even speak of such things, lest—"

"Lest she hear us? Look around you, Fainne. Liadan tells me your father raised you in a knowledge of the druid lore; an understanding of the pattern of all existences. Look around you with the eye of the spirit. This place is safe. Here, all secrets are guarded."

I could scarce bring myself to consider it might be true. He had terrified me by suggesting I might remove the amulet, here, with Darragh so close; didn't he know Grandmother would come after me as soon as I slipped the cord over my neck? I stared into the dark pool, silent.

"You fear to speak. Indeed, there is a great burden on you, one too heavy to bear; and yet you bear it stoically, Fainne. This strength you owe to your father's teaching, I think. You need not speak; if you wish, simply remain here silent and rest until the morning. You have no reason to trust me. I understand that. Perhaps it will help if I tell you I know what it is to be alone; to be shut off from everyone else in the world, so there is not a soul who understands your dilemma; not a single friend to help you. When you are thus isolated it takes great strength to carry on. There were times when I would have given up. I had such hopes; such great and stirring dreams, before the lady Oonagh came and I was changed forever. I wanted to make the world right. I wanted to make tyrants just and miscreants honest. I wanted to put an end to cruelty and oppression. Those were the dreams of a boy your age, Fainne. Before I was twenty, the fire of those dreams was turned to cold ashes, and I became what you see before you: a thing neither man nor beast, a creature of the margins, with no place in the world of affairs. But I am still here. I did not take the way of the small, sharp knife, or the high cliff and the flight to oblivion."

"Why? Why not do so? Have you remained here because you seek vengeance for what she did to you?" His words both shocked and fascinated me, and I forgot to be cautious.

"Vengeance?" He spoke the word as if he had forgotten what it meant. "I had not thought of that. If we had not the strength to act against her then, myself and Conor and all the others together, then we would hardly possess it now. It has been a long time. No doubt the sorceress has regained and reinforced those powers that were undone by my sister. I would not dare confront her. I could not face that a second time, and lose myself again."

His pale face was calm, but there was a deep fear behind the words which I recognized, for I had felt it myself, looking into my grandmother's mulberry eyes.

I nodded. "Then why have you carried on?" I asked him. "Why not end it, as you said?"

"I would not take that path while my sister lived. To throw away the life she won for us would have been to spurn her sacrifice and her love. And after that, there was Johnny."

"Johnny?" I was taken aback. "What has he to do with this?"

Finbar smiled. It seemed to me this was something he did so seldom he had almost forgotten the way of it; like speaking aloud. "He is the child of the prophecy, isn't he? Such a one cannot grow up unguided. It is not simply the strengths of the body that he needs to develop. I have helped him all I can; though I fear not enough. Conor might have done more. Liadan made a safe place for me here. I cannot live as men do. I—I am not quite as I once was. You may know, as Ciarán's daughter, how the mind of a wild creature differs from that of a man. I do not know how far your father's teaching took you—?"

"I have experienced what you mention," I said tightly. "I know what you mean. There are—instincts, which call strongly. It can be difficult to disregard those, and keep a sense of oneself."

"You do know. Then you may begin to understand how it is for me. Since that time, since the sorceress changed us, I have kept within me a little of both, man and swan. I am never quite free of those fears: the frost, the hunter, the snapping jaws of the hound. That is why I live here and do not visit the settlement. Liadan has been wise, and treated me with kindness. You seem doubtful, child. Your aunt will learn in time what stuff you are made of."

"How can you know?" I asked him. "Have you seen that?"

"No. But I believe it. I see you will not remove the witch's charm you wear around your neck. Tell me what you believe its purpose to be."

I glanced around, lowered my voice. I put my hand over the amulet and felt again the cool hardness of the metal. "Are you sure it's safe?" I whispered.

"Quite sure, child."

"It is—it is so that she can see me," I said in a little thread of a voice. "So that she can track me, and make sure I do what she tells me to do. She does not watch all the time; but if she chooses to see me and hear me, she can, as long as I wear this. It seems to get hotter when she is close, and when she is watching. And—" I hesitated.

"And—I think there is another kind of control, as well. The only time I took it off, I became myself, as I once was. Able to see clear; able to remember that I could be good, and wise, and make sound judgments. While I wear it, it is all too easy to see the darkness in myself. Without this cord, without the charm of family, I don't know how I could have kept going."

"Why do you not remove the thing straight away, since it does only harm?"

"Because," I said in a shaking voice, "the only time I did that, she was very angry, and she came after me, and punished me."

In the flickering light, it seemed to me Finbar's pale face turned even whiter. There was no doubt he shared my own fear, and understood it. "Punished you how?"

"First, by hurting me. Then, when she saw that didn't work, by—by threatening those I loved. She—she made me do some very bad things. Things that can never be made right again. There's only one person who knows that, apart from her and me. I have such terrible evil in me; I would never have believed that I could hurt the innocent, but I did. Three good folk have died because of me. And now, today, my little cousin Coll is sick, and I didn't do it, but Liadan won't believe me, and they're going to send me away."

"I could tell her—"

"No! No, you must not do that. They must not know the truth. You said it was safe—"

"Do not distress yourself. I will not reveal what you want kept secret. Why would the sorceress wish harm to your cousin? The boy is only a child."

"To punish me," I said haltingly.

"To punish you for what?"

"For—for disobedience. For slowness. I have not acted directly against her will, not yet. But if she has cause to doubt my loyalty, she shows her power by—by threatening those I befriend. Thus she commands my actions. I have been very foolish. I allowed myself to get close to Coll, and to others. That only provides her with fresh ammunition. I was stupid. I should have learned by now."

"A most difficult lesson," he said gravely. "Now, I wish to put a theory to you. I have no evidence for it, but I think it strong nonetheless. I believe this amulet has still another purpose. I will not ask you what task it is the sorceress wishes you to perform for her; I have some idea of what its nature might be, and I understand Liadan's misgivings. If I were you, I would be applying my mind to the question of why the lady Oonagh needs so badly to be sure she has you under her control. And I would hazard a guess that this charm provides not just a window to your whereabouts, but a curb on your abilities. It is only thus that she can limit your strength: a strength which builds on Ciarán's, and on her own, and on a whole line of folk, human, and Fair Folk, and Fomhóire alike. She uses this charm to weaken you, because she knows you have the ability to defeat her."

"*What?*"

"It is only a theory. Still, think about it. You remove the amulet, and straight away you see your path clear; you are again yourself, Ciarán's daughter, a child of Sevenwaters, strong and true. And she comes rushing back before you escape her control forever. She acts thus because she's terrified of what you might do. Once she called me her old enemy, and I wondered what she meant. I think, now, she saw in my eyes, even as she changed me, the spark of my youthful ideals: justice, courage, integrity. Perhaps she sees her old enemy reborn in you. Most certainly she sees your strength, and plans to use it for her own gain. But she treads a perilous path, for you possess several things I never had: the wisdom of the druid, the craft of the sorcerer, and the blood of four races. Her behavior reveals that she knows this, and fears it above all."

I fingered the amulet in wonder, and felt my lips curve in a hesitant smile.

"You really believe that? You're not just saying it to make me feel better?"

His laughter rang out in the silent vault of the cavern, startling me. He was instantly solemn again, "No, child. These are great and weighty things; desperate matters. It seems to me cruel that such a burden should rest on shoulders so fragile; but you have an inner strength. Johnny too is strong, in his way." He sighed. "Liadan fears for the lad, and rightly. But it is not you she should fear; it is his own lack of readiness for the task he must undertake."

"He seems a fine man," I offered hesitantly, not understanding. "A leader, wise beyond his years, brave and balanced. He has at least some understanding that he must do more than simply lead his army to victory. But—but he is sad about it, at the same time."

Finbar nodded.

"Do you know what it is that he must do? Do you understand what the Fair Folk want?" I asked him. "I heard—I was told—there was a mention of a kind of sentry, a guardian. The Watcher in the Needle. It sounded odd at the time. But there is an island called the Needle. And—and they said the old ways would die. That the wisdom of the earth and the ocean and the ways of sun and moon would be lost forever, unless the watch was kept. Is this, in some way, what Johnny has to do?"

Finbar was staring at me in amazement. "I see," he said slowly, "that others besides the lady Oonagh have guided your steps. Who revealed these things to you? The Fair Folk themselves?"

"No," I said softly. "Smaller, older ones; creatures of earth and water; Fomhóire folk. They have watched over me since I had cause to help one of their kind, by use of the craft. But they have not come here."

"They are everywhere, I think," Finbar said. "But they do not show themselves lightly. This is wondrous indeed."

"You have the Sight. Tell me. Liadan says she saw Johnny, and she saw me, at the end. What have you seen? What will happen to us?"

But the man with the swan's wing only shook his head. "I cannot tell you," he said. "I think it is for you to determine the path of it; to make the vision."

"Bright and true," I said softly.

"You should rest," Finbar said. "It is late, and cold. I have a blanket somewhere. In the morning your friend will come for you."

I hesitated. "It's possible I may not come here again. They want to send me away. The Chief and Liadan. Even Johnny believed I had cast a spell over his brother, to make him sick. I—if I cannot speak with you again, I would rather not waste the time in sleeping. I wondered if—?"

"Ask, child. If I can help you, I will."

"I need to regain my strength. To do what must be done, I have to—to employ a branch of the craft which is somewhat perilous to the user. I have done this only once before, and then I had help. Do you understand what I mean?"

Finbar nodded. "It had occurred to me as unlikely Johnny would be persuaded to include you in his special forces. To be there, you will need to change. And change back, I think. Liadan's vision was of a girl, not of a fish or a grasshopper."

"My cousin Sibeal told me to beware of cats. There will be a need to traverse both sea and land, to be close to men, but able to retreat quickly. I think this time it must be a bird."

"Perilous indeed. And draining. I have assisted with something of the kind at Sevenwaters. The young druids must experience metamorphoses as part of the discipline. But those are more of the mind than the body, and never unsupervised. This is of quite a different order. Ciarán had a gift for this."

"I know. He taught me. And he told me not to use it. But I have no other choice. There's a difficulty, though. How do I regain my strength and my craft quickly enough to act, after I return to myself? Last time I was weak as a babe for all of three days, and had not a scrap of magic in me. If that happens again I cannot do what must be done."

"I imagine what Ciarán has taught you goes considerably beyond my own skills. Still, there are techniques which will aid you. Those you can learn. But not in one night, Fainne."

"Then may I return here to visit you?"

"You will be more than welcome, child. But time is short."

I thought of the Chief's grim-set mouth, and Liadan's red eyes. "Maybe only tonight," I said, "if they send me away."

"That is not what I meant. Still, we can make a start. What, do you think, is the core of your training? The essence of it?"

"The lore."

"Then, as we have but one night, we will use it to focus on that. I am no druid; I have not these things by memory. But I can listen, and help you to rid your mind of what jumbles and confuses it. In the morning you will be stronger. After that, we shall see."

We sat cross-legged by the subterranean pool, and he quenched the lantern. As our eyes became accustomed to the deep darkness of the spring night, the tiny stars in the pool seemed to brighten and become clearer, jeweled echoes of their heavenly counterparts. The eye of the body fixed on those fine points of light. The eye of the mind moved upward and outward, to soar in the vaulted realm high above. My voice a whisper in the profound stillness of the cave, I began the litany of question and answer.

Who were the first folk in the land of Erin?

The Old Ones. The Fomhóire. People of the deep ocean, the wells and the lake beds. Folk of the sea and of the dark recesses of the earth.

And who came after?

The Fir Bolg. The bag men.

And after them?

Then came the Túatha Dé Danann, out of the west . . .

One cannot tell all the lore in one night. Nineteen years in the forest, it takes, for a man or woman to become a druid; and many seasons for the memorizing of the ancient wisdom. I barely touched on it, though I went on steadily until the time just before dawn, when the sky begins to brighten and the first hesitant chirrup floats out in the still air as birds commence their call to the sun. Finbar sat quiet and listened, and I felt a deep calm which seemed to spread itself from his mind to my own as if for a time the two of us were one. Though my lips told the ritual words, my thoughts were visited by images of the past, good things I had almost forgotten. There was my father, white-faced, black-cloaked, his hair the color of a midwinter fire, showing a tiny girl how to point her finger and make pebbles roll uphill. There were traveling folk on the road, bright-scarved, laughing, and a child hiding in the bushes watching and waiting. Maeve, smiling wanly as I tucked Riona in beside her and settled to tell a story. The sound of the pipes. Somewhere in it there was a lovely white pony, and a shawl with rainbow colors. And . . . and faintly, a tiny image of a woman, a frail young woman with huge blue eyes and honey-colored hair to her waist. She was sitting on the sand, and I was making the letters with my finger, and I looked up, and she said, *Good, Fainne*, and smiled at me. These images came and went as I continued my telling. I felt the warmth of them in my heart, and for a little while, I was not afraid.

Outside it was dawn. I fell silent. Finbar rose, and filled the cup, and put it in my hand. I noted again how chill the water was; it gave the head a strange clarity.

"Will you not drink?" I asked him.

He shook his head. "I don't seem to need those things anymore.

Food, drink, a soft bed for the night. Strange, I suppose. I have become used to it."

I gaped. "What are you saying? That you have transcended the need for bodily support, and live by the spirit alone?"

"Nothing so impressive, I'm afraid. I cannot say what this is; save that I cannot seem to live quite as one or the other, as man or bird. And yet I live. Her punishment was, in my case, very effective, and lifelong."

"Tell me something."

He waited politely.

"You were as frightened as I was when we first bumped into each other. I heard you. But you made up your mind to trust me, right away. I don't understand that."

"Part of me is beset by fears, Fainne. I fear the howl of wild beasts; I fear the ice on the lake; I fear human touch. Your hand, in the darkness, would have been quite enough. But your face . . ."

"My face? Am I so monstrous?"

"I looked into your eyes and saw the eyes of the sorceress," he said in a shadow of a voice. "Without any need for light, I saw them right before me. That brought back a moment of terror which has never really left me; the moment of irrevocable change. The loss of human consciousness; the theft of young lives, and the destruction of my sister's innocence."

"I—I'm sorry," I said inadequately. "Maybe I do look like her. I'm sorry I frightened you. But—"

"I have learned to look deeper. Liadan was right to be wary of you. You have the power to make us or break us, I think; and it will not be until the last that you will choose which way to go."

His words shocked me, and I spoke without caution. "I have chosen. I will be strong enough. I must be. Anyway, you can hardly pass judgment on me. Your life seems that of a creature that hides itself away; wise, maybe, but a sad end for a youth who once burned bright with the will to make the world better. What became of that fire, that you lock it away here beneath the earth?"

I had startled him, no doubt of that. Probably nobody had ever spoken to him thus before. Indeed, I regretted it instantly. He had been kind to me.

Finbar pushed back the worn cloak to show the swath of white at his side. He looked down at the wing as if it were both a burden and in some way a familiar friend.

"I cannot go forth into the world of men," he said quietly. "Such a deformity brings not just unwelcome attention, but ridicule and scorn; a place, maybe, on the sidelines of a fair somewhere, for folk to gawk at me and let their children hurl soft fruit. I would be a millstone around my family's neck; no more than an embarrassment. Here, I can share what things I know, and I am out of folk's way. It's better thus."

"Nonsense!" I told him sharply. "What you call a deformity is a mark of honor. It is a sign of your strength and endurance, and singles you out for a great purpose. If you let that boy's dreams die, if you forget what you once were, then my grandmother has indeed triumphed over her old enemy. Here, you hide from life. And yet you bid me go forth and make the vision. What about your vision? We are family. Surely we all have a part in this."

There was a long silence. Finbar looked at me, and I observed how thin he was, wraith-like, the bones of his face jutting under the white skin. His strange, pale eyes were ringed with shadows, and his dark hair was matted and tangled, as if he had never thought to care for it.

"I'm an old man," he said eventually.

"In years, maybe. You don't seem so. Indeed, you look no older than my uncle Sean. You think to dwindle and die here in your prime. A terrible waste."

He did not answer me. No doubt I had offended him. My words had been scant recompense for his patience and understanding. I was framing an apology when a familiar voice was heard calling outside.

"Fainne! Fainne, where are you?"

I scowled. "What did they have to send *him* for?" I snapped. I had been so careful to avoid him, so careful, and now I would have to walk all the way back with him. "I could have gone on my own," I grumbled.

"Come," said Finbar quietly. "I'll take you back to the entry. Who is *he*?"

"A friend," I sniffed as I followed him out along the shadowy tunnel, barely lit by the faint creeping light of the dawn. "He followed me to Inis Eala, and now he won't go back. And he must go back; you know why."

Finbar made no comment, but after a while he said, "I expect he's here for a purpose. In any event, it may already be too late."

"Too late?"

"Too late to send him back."

We emerged from the tunnel's entry to a pale, clear morning. Long ragged strips of rose-tinged cloud spread across the sky, and the birds had woken and chorused energetically to the new day. And there was Darragh waiting for me, clad in serviceable gray of the very plain kind favored by Johnny's men. At least, I thought grimly, he does not bear the mark on his face. His honest eyes, his sweet smile, those are still his own.

"Fainne! You're safe, then." The relief in his tone was undisguised.

"Of course I'm safe. There was no need at all for you to come here."

"Thank you for coming, young man." Finbar spoke a little awkwardly, as if unused to strangers. "I am Liadan's uncle, and I can assure you your friend has been in good keeping. Now best go home, the two of you, and tell the little lad I'm thinking of him, and that I expect a visit as soon as he's better."

Then Darragh stepped forward and put out a hand in greeting, and Finbar, clearly startled, took it in his own.

"Thank you, my lord," said Darragh, smiling. He never once looked at the swan's wing; it was as if it were no different from any other part of a man's body. "Thank you for keeping her safe. She never did learn how to look after herself properly."

There was the tiniest hint of a smile on Finbar's austere features. "You intend to do it for her, I see," he observed dryly.

Darragh withdrew his hand. "It seems ridiculous, maybe, for a traveling man to mix with warriors, and lords, and seers. But I do what I must do. If the road brings me here, then this is where I must be."

Finbar nodded. He was not smiling now. "As long as you understand your own choice. A path of great difficulty; of strange perils and few rewards."

"That's not going to stop me," said Darragh.

Finbar turned to me. "Farewell now, Fainne."

"Farewell and—thank you."

"Perhaps I should thank you. A clarion call. That was not at all expected." With that, Finbar stepped back down the tunnel and was lost from sight.

"Best be going," said Darragh, suddenly restless. "Got your cloak? It's cold on the track, in the wind."

"Stop fussing, will you?" I said, as the calm and certainty of the lore began to fade from me, and the familiar fears and misgivings came crowding back. A long walk, out in the open, and still I wore the amulet. My fingers moved to check it; it seemed no warmer. Still, we must go as quickly as we could.

"I'll race you as far as those bushes," said Darragh unexpectedly. "Good way to get warm. Ready? One, two, three, go!"

Old habits die hard. I ran, limping, on the narrow stony track, knowing I could never outpace him. I pushed myself as hard as I could, not easy after a night of no sleep. And I hadn't had breakfast. His soft footsteps could be heard right behind me.

We reached the rocks together; together our fingers stretched out to touch the surface. Thus had all our childhood contests ended. I was quite out of breath; he, completely unaffected. He waited while I recovered myself. The wind whipped his dark hair back from his face; the gold light of early morning spread a glowing warmth over the smooth skin of his cheek and brow.

"I was worried," he said. "You ran away."

"What was I supposed to do? Stay there while they accused me of something I didn't do? They said I hurt Coll. It wasn't true. And now the Chief's sending me away."

"Got your breath back? Good. We'd best walk on."

"Darragh?" I whispered.

"What?"

"Coll. Is he—?"

His expression was grave. "They weren't saying much. He still lives, I know that. We'll find out more when we get back."

I was silent, my thoughts full of shadows.

"I told them," Darragh said. "I told them you didn't do it."

"You what?"

"They were concerned when you ran away. Johnny came to ask

me where you might have gone. I wanted an explanation; he gave one. Then I went to see the Chief and your auntie, and I told them you'd never do such a thing."

I risked a sideways glance at him. "Why would you say that? You know better than anyone what I'm capable of. You're the only one I've ever told. Folk have died. Why would you stand up for me? You couldn't know."

"I did know," said Darragh very quietly, giving me his hand to help me over a low rock wall. "You didn't do it, did you?"

"Of course not!"

"Well, then."

"Anyway, why tell them so, even if it is true? Isn't that what you want, to get me sent back home?"

There was a little silence.

"Stop it, Curly," he said unevenly. "Stop fighting me. Maybe you think it doesn't hurt, but it does, and I don't think I can bear it much longer. I know you don't want me here. I know you're angry with me for coming. But we're still friends, aren't we? You shouldn't need to ask me these things. No matter what I want, I'm not going to stand by and let folk punish you for something you had no part of. Anyone can see you're fond of the young boy. I just told the truth, that's all, and I'm not sorry for that. It's best to tell the truth, even if it means you don't get what you want."

I said nothing. His goodness put me to shame. We walked on up the small hills, and down into the little gullies, and past sheep grazing on the scant tufts of foliage and goats making their way along precipitous tracks high above the sea. It was important to hurry, yet in a way I wanted to go slowly, for memories stirred in me, long-ago memories of times in Kerry when the world was a simpler place, and two friends could spend all day out-of-doors together with never a fear or an awkwardness between them. The first buildings of the settlement came in sight in the distance. We had been silent a long while. Now, both of us slowed our pace.

"Fainne?" Darragh sounded very serious.

"What?"

"You know I have to go away soon. That's what I'm supposed to be here for, after all. A warrior. There's a mission, and a battle. I want you to give me your word you'll take care while I'm gone. Look after yourself, and think before you do things, and—and be safe. I want you to wait here on the island for me."

I stared at him, not understanding at all. "Wait for you? I don't think I can promise any such thing. Wait for what?"

His cheeks turned red. "I was hoping that—that when it's over, the battle and all, you might let me take you home. Back to Kerry. I'd like that. See you safe with your father again. I know I can't have everything I want; that's what he said, isn't it, the seer? But I'd dearly love to know you were away from harm, and back where you belong. Would you go with me, after the summer?"

He had offered once before, and I had said no, and thought my heart would break with the longing to be home again. Now I felt only a cold, hopeless finality.

"I can't promise. I don't know what is to happen; but I don't think I will ever return to the cove, Darragh. You made a mistake in coming here. You'll be disappointed, I think."

"Ah, no. I'm here, and you're here. Better than nothing, that is. And you're speaking to me today. That's an improvement. If I work hard enough at it, maybe by Lugnasad I might get a smile. That'd be a fine thing."

"I—I'm sorry. There hasn't been much to smile about."

"There's always something to smile about, Curly. Silly things; good things. The sound of a whistle in the evening; the candlelight on a girl's hair. A joke between friends. You've just forgotten, that's all. Ah now, what's the matter? I've upset you. I never meant to do that."

Stupid, how his words seemed to get into some little part of me that nothing else could touch, and stir feelings I wanted left alone, so I could just get on with what had to be done. The pain was so bad I had to put my hands over my face, for fear I might actually shed tears. They were there, not far from the surface. But a sorcerer's daughter does not weep.

"What is it, Curly? What's wrong?" Gently, his thin fingers came around my hands and lifted them away. "Tell me, sweetheart. Tell me what it is."

"I—I can't," I muttered, unable to avoid looking into his eyes, which were full of concern and something else I did not want to interpret. "I can't tell you."

"Yes, you can. Now come on. We're friends, aren't we?" One hand came up to brush the hair back from my temple, and stayed there, stroking softly.

"I—I don't want you to get hurt." The little whisper escaped despite all my efforts at control. "If something happens to you it will be my fault, and I don't think I can bear that." I pressed my lips tight together to stop more foolish words from slipping out. His touch was very sweet, so sweet I might melt with it, I thought, and do something even more stupid such as put my two arms around him and hold on tight, to keep him by me. What had got into me, that I was suddenly so weak? I blinked, and stepped away.

"We should be going," I said with a lamentable effort at control. My voice shook like a birch in autumn. "I shouldn't have said that. Please, forget I said it." I walked on, cloak hugged tight around me. And Darragh walked by me, quiet, keeping pace with me step for step.

"Maybe you won't promise," he said after a while, "but I will. I promise I'll never leave you on your own. Not if you want me near. Just this one time, just this one campaign, because I gave Johnny my word. After that, things'll be different. I swear it, Fainne. You mustn't fear for me. I'll always be there when you need me. Always."

Was it accident, that a cloud came over the morning sun as he spoke that word? Was it chance that a great dark bird passed high above, cawing harshly as we made our way up to the settlement, now completely silent, the two of us?

It was very early; still, folk were abroad. Smoke rose from the cooking fire and there was a smell of fish frying, and fresh-baked bannocks. Men were carrying things down to the cove, purposeful and silent. By the outer wall Johnny sat on the stones, sharpening a knife, and there beside him perched a large raven. The creature turned its head to the side, and fixed its small, intense eye on me.

"Fiacha!" I exclaimed. My heart thumped. "Is my father here?" I asked, torn between fear and impossible hope.

"Just the bird," said Johnny, slipping the knife away in its sheath. "Mother said he'd likely be familiar to you, as he once was to me. Too long ago to remember; I was only an infant. Creature's here for some purpose; he follows me everywhere. Perhaps he's brought you a message."

"Unlikely. I've never found a method of communicating with a raven, and I don't think I want to. Fiacha has a sharp beak. I've cause to know it." My fingers moved instinctively to touch the place on my shoulder, under my gown, where the bird had pecked me long ago. It had hurt, and I had disliked him ever since. "What about Coll?" I made myself ask.

"Better," Johnny said casually. "Eating porridge, and grumbling when Mother says he must stay in bed."

There were plenty of things I could have said, as an immense tide of relief washed through me, but I held them back. What was the point?

Darragh was less circumspect. "Then you owe Fainne an apology, I think." He looked straight at Johnny with grim mouth and narrowed eyes; I had never seen such an expression on his face before.

"It's all right, Darragh," I said, laying a hand on his arm. "A reasonable mistake, under the circumstances."

"It's not all right." His voice was very firm. "You were distressed and frightened. It's far from all right. Your aunt should apologize, if Johnny will not."

"Unfortunately," Johnny said softly, "this proves nothing. Fainne is as adept at undoing these charms as she is at casting them. I've personal experience of that, friend. Now, as we're on this tack, tell me why you went to fetch her on your own instead of taking Godric with you? Don't you understand orders?"

Darragh reddened. I did not like to see him angry. He never used to be angry.

"Johnny," I said, stepping between them. "I've had no sleep, and nothing to eat since breakfast yesterday. I don't care what you think; I know what's the truth, and so does Darragh, and that must be good enough for us. I want to see Coll, and then I want to rest. And no doubt Darragh has work to do. Can we stop this, please?"

Johnny grinned, and glanced at Darragh. "Was she always like this?" he asked.

But Darragh was frowning, and did not reply. Instead, he turned and spoke to me, very quietly. "Will you be all right?"

I nodded, not trusting myself to reply. Then he was off without a word, and after a moment, Johnny followed him. The bird spread its great, glossy wings and flew after, circling, now ahead, now behind. I hoped its bond with my father made it more friend than foe.

Coll was indeed better. He was sitting up in bed, still a little flushed, while Liadan adjusted the pillows.

"Fainne!" he exclaimed as I went in. Gull was there, packing a bag with items from the shelves, tincture and salve, ointment and unguent. He grinned at me, white teeth flashing against night-dark skin. His crippled hands moved deftly as he lifted tiny bottle or delicate bowl. "Where have you been?" Coll went on. His eyes were overbright; still, the change in him was remarkable.

"To the north point," I said, advancing to the bedside. Coll lay back; his mother smoothed the blanket across his chest. I looked at her, and she looked back calmly. There was no telling what she thought, but I did not see an apology in her eyes. "May I sit here a little?" I asked her.

Liadan inclined her head. "Very well, Fainne. Not too long." She got up and went to help Gull with his packing. They began a conversation about knife wounds, and whether vervain or all-heal provided the best protection against ill-humors.

"Did you really go all the way to the north point?" Coll asked. "By yourself? In the dark?"

"I did."

"Weren't you scared?"

"Why would I be scared?"

"You might have fallen over a cliff or broken your leg. And what about Uncle Finbar?"

"Don't talk so much," I told him sternly. "You've been very sick. You must rest and get better, so we can start our lessons again before you forget everything I've taught you."

Coll heaved a sigh. "Lessons! Maybe I will stay in bed after all. Fainne?"

"Mm?"

"They said you might be going away. Are you going away?"

I glanced over at Liadan. "I don't know, Coll," I said.

"Perhaps not quite yet." My aunt's tone was grave. "If you continue to make progress with your letters, we may keep her a little longer. Besides, I'm going to need help here."

"Good," said Coll sleepily. "I'm glad you're not leaving. It'll be

quiet as a tomb here when everyone's gone. Even Cormack's going."
He closed his eyes.

Belatedly I came to a terrible realization. Men bearing bundles
down to the cove. Gull packing medicines. Finbar saying there was
no time.

"Aunt Liadan?" I asked in a shaking voice.

"What is it, Fainne?"

"The—the campaign. Isn't it supposed to be in summer?"

There was a delicate sort of silence. Then Gull spoke.

"The Chief sets great store by false intelligence," he said, tighten-
ing the lid on a small earthenware jar before he wrapped it in cloth
and stowed it deep in the bag. "Summer's official. But we're ready to
go any time, and it looks like the time's now."

"N—now? You mean—straight away? Today?" My heart quailed.
That meant I must do it with no preparation, with no help whatever.
It meant that before dusk I would have to watch Darragh get on one
of those boats and sail away to battle.

"Tomorrow," Liadan said. "Tonight is for feasting and farewells.
Bran would not go while Coll was in danger. But—"

"It's so early," I said, shivering. "So soon. I had not thought it
would be so soon."

Liadan surprised me by coming over to sit beside me, and putting
her arm around my shoulders.

"It gets no easier, saying goodbye to them," she said. "Each time
is like a little death; each time one begs the gods, just one more
chance, just one more. Men do not understand what it is like to wait.
Women endure it because they must. It's the price of love. For you, I
suppose this is the first such farewell."

"It's not like that with him and me," I said fiercely, for her kindness was somehow harder to bear than her disapproval. "He
shouldn't go, that's all. He doesn't know what he's doing. At least
these men, Johnny and Snake and the Chief, at least they are warriors.
It's what they do. Darragh is—he's an innocent."

"Ah, yes." Liadan's hand came up to touch my hair, and to tidy it
a little off my face. I expect I looked quite a sight, with bags under my
eyes and curls all tangled by the wind. "You recognize that. Sometimes the innocent walk through a battlefield unscathed, Fainne. It is
that very quality which protects them. We must hope all will be safe,

and return victorious. Now, I think Coll should rest. You must be exhausted and hungry. Biddy and Annie were up early, and there's a fine breakfast waiting. Why not go through, and enjoy some food and good company, and then sleep awhile? You cannot change what will happen by fretting about it."

Gull had finished packing, and was strapping the bag up neatly.

"Have you ever gone with them?" I asked my aunt. "They must have desperate need of healers at such times."

"A field of war is no place for a woman. I would go, believe me; it's like a knife in the heart to have them out of my sight so long, and in danger. But Bran would not allow it. This is too perilous. Gull travels with them; he will tend to their injuries. Meanwhile, I will keep an eye on things here."

"Liadan?"

She looked at me, but I could not find the words for what I wanted to ask. She gave a little smile, a kind of recognition.

"Finbar tells me we've no choice but to trust you," she said. "If he can do that, I suppose I can. He has more reason to be afraid than I do. Now go on. And no long faces. We need to see these men on their way with smiles and confidence, not with tears. Those are for later, when we are alone."

I ate, but not much. There was a sick feeling in the pit of my stomach. I slept, and was visited by dreams so evil I will not tell them here. I woke, and washed my face, and changed my clothes. I braided my hair neatly down my back. Then I went out and sat on the clifftop above the bay, and thought about birds. The weather was calm. The curraghs stood at anchor, ready to go. There were three large ones and many smaller, some well-laden with bags and bundles, some empty of cargo. There would be weapons, I supposed. Supplies. There must be some sort of camp on the way. I had no idea where, and they had not let me see the maps. I would have to fly, and I would have to go straight after them, or instead of finding them I might travel on and on across that vast stretch of water until my wings gave out and I plunged down into the jaws of some long-toothed sea creature. That was if I did not first perish from cold. I thought of men swimming by night, and shuddered. Surely summer would be better. Why hadn't they waited until Beltaine, at least? The air was bitter chill; the sea would be unforgiving.

Birds. Seabirds: gull, tern, albatross. Good for the long distance across the ocean, blessed with endurance and strength. Not so good on land, maybe. Too loud; too wild. It might be necessary to get close; it might be essential to be unobtrusive. A wren; a sparrow. No. Too vulnerable, too weak. No more than a tasty mouthful for some predator on the wing. One might be a hunting creature oneself, a goshawk or eagle. That did not seem right either. What was smallish, and plainish, and not too frightened of man, yet able to fly long distances? There were little gray birds in Kerry; they came down sometimes when I was sitting under the standing stones, and strutted around watching me hopefully, in case I had brought a handful of grain or a scrap of rye bread. Plump things with small heads and neat little beaks. Rock doves, they called them. Didn't folk sometimes send doves with messages? But then there was pigeon pie. Still, nobody was likely to be doing much fancy cooking where we were going. A dove was small, but not too small. It had a soft, sweet voice and plain, unobtrusive plumage. It could fly a fair way, as far as I knew. That was it, then. As soon as they left I must do it, and without any help. And at the other end, I would just have to hope I would be strong enough.

These folk had made farewells many times before, but even for them, this was unusual. At other times, a group of the men might be called away on some mission, and return again after a while with one or two missing, and one or two injured, an eye put out, an arm or shoulder damaged maybe. They were used to that, Biddy told me as I sat in a corner of her cooking area making myself swallow a bowl of soup. I could not afford to be weak in the morning, not with such a long way to go. In those days, Biddy went on, before the Chief came to Inis Eala, they'd been on the run all the time, never safe, always in hiding, or risking their lives in some impossible enterprise. They'd earned a reputation for achieving what others could not. She'd lost one good man already; she'd just have to hope she wouldn't lose another. Thanks to the Chief her boys had a trade, and weren't fighters, and so they would stay on the island. But Gull must go; she couldn't stop him. His first loyalty was with Johnny, she said wryly, sprinkling sprigs of rosemary on the side of mutton Annie was turning on the spit. Johnny was the Chief's son, and the Chief had given Gull a life. She understood that. It didn't make Gull any less of a stupid fool, though, and she would tell him so. A man who'd passed forty was too old to get up to such nonsense, and didn't deserve a good woman keeping his bed warm for his return.

Still, this time was something more. Never before, since they had come to the island and built their school and their community, had so many gone forth together on such a mission. Their job now was teaching the arts of war, not making war themselves. The word was, the Chief hadn't wanted them to take part in this undertaking. He was a landowner now, with responsibilities of a different kind, and settled at Harrowfield. He maintained his interest in Inis Eala because he couldn't help himself; it was in his blood. Still, he had wished to stay outside this particular venture. But Sean of Sevenwaters was family, and they owed him something. It had been Sean who had helped them get established; who had put the word about that if you wanted your men well trained, Inis Eala was the place to go. And Sean was Liadan's brother. Besides, there was Johnny, who was the heir to Sevenwaters. There was no denying a prophecy. So they went, all of them save the very old and the very young, and those whose trade meant they did not bear arms. All of the fine young men who had guarded us so silently and cleverly; all the strange and skillful band with their odd names and motley garb. Even young Cormack was going; he was indeed a warrior.

There was a feast, with the mutton, and chickens stuffed with garlic, and a pudding with spices and fruit in it. There was ale, but not in abundance; clear heads were required for a dawn departure. Afterward there was music. Sam and Clem played their hearts out; the woman with the harp excelled herself, first with jig and reel, and then a slow air floating from the strings as sweetly as a faery tune. When she finished that, someone called for dancing and the band struck up again.

Tonight, touching seemed to be allowed, and glances, and whispered words. Their men being fully occupied with whistle and bodhrán, Brenna and Annie danced together, giggling. The young men were on their feet, and in a flash there was scarcely a woman in the hall who was not out there on the floor twirling and clapping her hands to the sound of an energetic tune and a thundering beat. Nor was the activity confined to the youthful. Big Biddy danced with tall, lanky Spider; the girl who reared chickens circled with the ferocious, battle-scarred Snake, resplendent in his tunic of serpent-skin. Gull took Liadan out on the floor, the two of them laughing like old friends. The Chief did not dance. He sat very still, his gray eyes never once leaving his wife's slender, plainly dressed figure as she passed under Gull's arm, or circled gracefully around him, or wove a pattern with him between the rows of dancers. I understood the Chief's look, intense, hungry. He was storing up memories, to last until he might return and take her in his arms once more.

Johnny came over, grinning, and asked me to dance, and I said no, politely. Then Gareth tried, falling over his words and blushing, and I said I was too tired. Corentin looked at me, his dark brows crooked in a frown, and he looked at Darragh, but he did not come over. Darragh was not dancing. He sat near me, but not too near, and I could see from the way his foot tapped and his fingers snapped that he was itching to be part of it. He'd music in every part of him, that boy. But he didn't get up, and nor did I. The reel finished and Liadan came back, flushed and smiling, to sit by the Chief again. They did not look in each other's eyes; simply, his hand came out to clasp hers as she sat down by his side, and their fingers twined tight together. Tonight they were less careful of what folk might see, for time was very short.

"Play another!" demanded tow-haired Godric, who had claimed Brenna as his partner. This showed some courage, as her beloved Sam would be watching every move as his blacksmith's arm drew a throbbing pulse from the bodhrán. But the harper was weary, and wanted a rest and some ale, and Clem said it was time he had a dance with Annie.

"Hey, Darragh!" called Godric, not to be thwarted. "Didn't you say you could play the small-pipes? How about a tune, then!"

Darragh gave a slow smile. "Packed away, they are," he said.

"Well, go on then, fetch them! Nothing like the pipes for a bit of a dance."

That was true enough. I could see from the looks on their faces that they half-expected rough, untutored playing, the fumblings of a lad who has picked up his skills in dribs and drabs, by copying something heard on occasion, or by guesswork maybe. I could have told them different, but there was no need. Soon enough Darragh had the bag inflated and tucked neat under his arm, and his long, thin fingers began to fly over the holes in the chanter, and a stream of melody poured forth into the air, hushing every voice in the long hall. All stood still and quiet, until Sam took up the beat for the jig, and the older folk started to clap in time, and the dancing began again.

Storing up memories. The Chief wasn't the only one who could do that. He'd need his until the end of the campaign. I thought mine would have to be forever. But I didn't need to look at Darragh to see what I knew I could not have. I could shut my eyes, and let the sound of the pipes make the image for me: the dark-haired lad on the lovely white pony, and above them the pale, wide sky of Kerry, and the soft air, and the sound of the sea.

"All right, lass?"

I blinked, and looked up. Biddy stood by me, panting from her exertions, her broad, sweet face flushed, wisps of fair hair giving her a shining halo.

"You're looking pale as milk; not coming down with the fever, I hope."

"I'm fine." At least, I was until Darragh brought the frenetic jig to a close and, with a sidelong glance in my direction, began a slow lament. The dancing ceased; the laughter and talk died down. Folk stood hand in hand, or sat quiet, and their eyes softened, and here or there a tear fell as the melody soared and dipped as gracefully as a swallow, the intricate pattern of decorations clothing it in a fine fili-gree of light and shade. A good tune, like a good tale, speaks to every listener at once, and to no two does it tell the same story. It brings forth what is deep inside the spirit; it awakens what we scarcely know was there, so buried it was by the clutter of our daily living, our cloaks of self-protection. Darragh played from the heart, as always, and in the end I found I simply could not bear it. Any more and I would weep, or scream, or tear off the amulet and shout that I couldn't do it, and nobody was going to make me. But I had been well trained. I got quietly to my feet and went outside, not far. I sat on the wall by the kitchen garden, under the pale moon. Inside the lament rang on; a song of love and loss; a song of farewell. It spoke of what might have been. I clenched my teeth, and wrapped my arms around myself, and reminded myself that I was a sorcerer's daughter, and had a job to do. I must forget that I was a woman, and Darragh was a man, and remember that tomorrow I must be a creature of the air, flying high above treacherous seas. I must remember my grandmother and the evil she had wrought: a family near-destroyed, a household shattered. Finbar, a fine young man turned into some walking wraith. The death of my mother's hopes, my father's dreams; all had begun with her. I must remember what she had made me do, and what she would have me become. If that did not give me the strength I needed, then we were indeed lost.

The music ceased. The lights were dimmed; folk streamed out of the long house and away to their beds. I would wait, I thought, until Brenna and the others were abed, and then slip in quietly. I had no wish for talk. I needed to be strong tonight, full of hope and confidence. Instead, I felt alone and helpless and afraid. How could I transform if I had no faith in myself? Now that the music was over, I must breathe deep as Father had taught me: in slowly, fully, from the belly; out in three stages, like the cascades of a great waterfall. And again. Control was everything. Without control I was at the mercy of feelings, and feelings were nothing but a hindrance.

"Fainne?"

I jumped. He was right in front of me, and I had neither heard nor seen him.

"There's no need to creep up on me like that! Anyway, you shouldn't be here alone with me, not at night. It's against the rules."

"What rules?" said Darragh, hoisting himself up on the wall beside me. "Now, we'd best have a talk. No time in the morning. Upset you, haven't I?"

"Of course not."

"You went out. I thought you liked to hear me play."

"It made me sad. Darragh, you must go, or I must. There are still lights on, and folk abroad. Someone might see us."

"Just two friends having a bit of a chat, that's all. Where's the harm in that?"

"You know that's not all. Now go away, please. Don't make this any harder than it is already." My voice shook. It was taking all my strength to sit still and not look at him. Darragh said nothing for a while. Then he slid down from the wall and turned to face me where I sat, his eyes on a level with mine, so I could not avoid them.

"What do you mean, that's not all?" His voice was very soft in the darkness. Behind him, through the half-open door, I could see the glow of lamp light, and hear the voices of Biddy and Gull as they moved about tidying up.

"Nothing. Forget I said it. Please."

"What did you mean, Curly?" He put out one long hand and curved it around my cheek, and the look in his eyes made me feel very odd indeed. It made me want to do things I knew I must not do.

"I can't tell you." I looked at him, and kept my hands quite still in my lap, and made my breathing into a pattern: in, two, three; out, two, three. Control. I managed not to reach up and touch. I managed not to put my arms around his neck, and lay my cheek against his, and give in to the great wave of warm longing that flooded through me. It was cruel. In an instant, I could have achieved what I had wanted so much. I could have smiled as I had smiled at Eamonn, and bid him shut his eyes, and kissed him in the way Grandmother had taught me, a way that made a man burn for a woman, so that he would do any-thing to have her. I could have made a little noise, and brought Gull or Biddy out to catch us. Then they would have sent Darragh away, and I would have saved his life. But I could not do it; not even for that. This was my friend. He was the only person in the world I could trust, besides my father. I could not bring myself to cheapen what was between us. And yet, what I longed for then, with every single part of me, was to hold him close and to bid him goodbye as a girl farewells her sweetheart, with tender words and the warmth of her body. I kept very still. I said nothing. But I could not school my eyes.

"Curly?" said Darragh very carefully, as if he had just seen some-thing he could not quite believe.

Touch me again, something inside me said, despite all my efforts at control. *Put your arms around me and hold me close. Just once. Just this once.*

But Darragh turned his back, and shoved his hands under his arms, and his voice, when it came, shook with some sort of feeling I had no hope of understanding.

"You'd best go," he said. "Go on, Fainne. It's late. Best leave now."

I slid down off the wall, suddenly cold. What had I done wrong? He seemed angry; yet I had thought . . .

"Go on, Fainne." Still he had his back to me, his arms tightly folded, as if the very thought of looking, or touching, was suddenly repugnant to him. I could not believe how much it hurt; it was as if the last, sweet remnant of my childhood were turned suddenly to ashes. I reached out my hand, and for just an instant it rested against his sleeve.

"Best not," he said in a choked sort of voice, and edged away like a nervous horse.

"Good night then." I forced the words out, fought to recover my breathing. I must be strong for the morning, strong for the journey. I could not afford this. It was wrenching me in pieces.

"Farewell, Curly. Keep out of trouble, now, until I come back for you." Still he would not face me. But his voice was the same as I remembered it from long ago, strong and true. I fled, before I said something I would regret forever. I ran through the long house, where Gull and Biddy now sat before the embers of the fire, talking softly together. All must make a farewell, but I thought none was more terrible, or more final, than my own. I reached my little sleeping hut and went in quietly, and I lay down on my pallet open-eyed. Two of the girls were gently snoring already. Brenna's voice came in a whisper.

"Are you all right, Fainne?"

"Mm," I said, and pulled the blanket up over my face. I was not all right, and it seemed as if I never would be. I had got so many things wrong. I had hurt so many good folk on the way, just as the owl-creature had said. *It seems to us you don't give a toss what casualties you leave behind.* But I did care, that was the problem. That was what held me back. Feelings. Friendship. Loyalty. Love. So much easier for a sorceress to be like my grandmother and not give a fig for what was lost on the way. *All that matters is power*, she would say. I could almost hear her saying it now, deep inside me: a small, dark voice long silent, and now awake once more. *As long as you understand that, Fainne.* I fell asleep with my jaw clenched tight and my eyes screwed shut, and my body curled into a little ball under the blankets. I dreamed of fire.

Darragh had been right. There was no time in the morning. I rose before dawn, and as I crept across to the scholars' hut I could see lights down at the bay, and hear an orderly, purposeful movement of men on the steps. Sails crackled; there was already a northerly breeze. By candlelight I found a scrap of parchment, took the stopper from the ink, picked up a quill. What could one write? How could such things be said? In the end it was brief indeed. *I have to go away for a while. I'm sorry.* I signed my name, and sprinkled sand to dry the ink. I folded and sealed the message, and wrote Liadan's name on the front, and I propped it up where the priest or the druid would soon find it. Then I went out to the place I had chosen, a narrow ledge not far below the clifftop, looking out over the bay. A growth of scrubby bushes would conceal me from view in the half-light, yet give me partial sight of the fleet as it prepared for departure. Perhaps I should have chosen my clothes with a view to my destination. Perhaps I should have stolen something of Cormack's; to go clad as a warrior would be to have a chance of remaining unobtrusive for a little, when I returned to myself. But I had dressed, instead, for courage. I wore a simple gown in stripes of blue and green, the sort of gown a traveling girl wears for a special occasion, such as the horse fair. Over it I had tied the loveliest shawl in all Erin, its silken folds resplendent with bonny creatures in all the colors of the rainbow. My hair was loose; the first rays of the morning sun turned it bonfire-red. I dressed to show I was my own self, and nobody's creature. But still I wore the amulet, for I was leaving this place of protection and heading out into the unknown. Take it off, and she would come, I knew it. She must not come, not yet. She must watch and believe me loyal right up to the last, not knowing the power my mother's cord possessed, not understanding that at last I had begun to recognize the strength I had in me, the strength that flowed both from my father and from my mother. Was I not both sorceress and daughter of Sevenwaters, a potent mixture by any measure? As my grandmother had said, this must unfold according to the prophecy, to the last, to the very last. Then she would understand how ill she had chosen her instrument of vengeance.

Riona was fastened in my belt; I could not leave her behind. I waited as the men came down and boarded the curraghs; I waited as the women waved, calling their brave farewells. I waited as oars flashed in the dark water, until the wind filled the sails and the craft began to move eastward out of the sheltered bay into open sea. Then I closed my eyes and summoned the charm. With every part of me, mind, body, spirit, I thought, *dove.* The words of the spell vibrated through me. I felt the power in my fingertips, in the soles of my feet, in the hair on my head, up and down my back like a great current, carrying me forward. I opened my eyes, and spread my wings, and flew.

Chapter Fourteen

It seems simple. A bird moves its wings up and down, and turns to the south or the north or wherever it wants to go. It follows the flock until it reaches a destination, and comes down easily to land in a tree, something like an elm with plenty of convenient perches to choose from. But this was not simple at all.

Part of it happened instinctively; beating the wings, riding the current, feeling light and shadow, far and near, warm and cold and adjusting to them as I went. But something was wrong. This way was danger. It was away from food and shelter and homelands. These things pulled me; they called a strong warning. Back! Come back! Not that way! And there was no small Otherworld being to offer guidance this time. I was alone, a tiny speck of feather and bone adrift on the very breath of the air, high above the freezing grayness of this northern sea where the small boats, brave-sailed, now breasted the swells of open water. The boats. The mission. Somewhere down there was my cousin, the child of the prophecy, embarked on the great campaign of his life. Somewhere down there was a traveling man who barely knew one end of a sword from the other. Now, because of me, he was going to war. I must not forget who I was; what I was. Dove was a guise only. Dove would get me there. I must not lose myself in the creature, or all would be lost indeed. Keep moving, keep working, for the curraghs moved swift over the ocean, carried on the same north wind which chased me hard across the pale sky. The sea was such a long way down; farther than the fall from a high tower; greater than the dive from a clifftop; a plunge that would kill before the icy grip of the water could do its work, or the teeth of the sea creatures tear and rend a small victim. In its way, a fall would be merciful.

My eyes saw a different world: wider, brighter, clearer. It was confusing, for I did not see objects so much as patterns of light and dark; shadows above me which might be danger; patches below me which might be places of rest. I felt my body suspended in air; borne by the current. Part human, part creature, I saw with bird-sight and must constantly remind myself of what things were, and how I must act. Boats. Sails. Follow them, said the human part of me. Home, said the bird. Turn for home. Too far. But I flew on, for the one thing that never left me was the fear that I might be too slow, or too weak. I was afraid I would lose them, and myself be lost.

It was a long way. I had not thought how long it would be; had not calculated with chart or map. That showed a lamentable lack of self-discipline. My father would never have undertaken such a journey so ill-prepared. I must go on; I could not let my grandmother win this battle. The prophecy foretold a great victory; my cousin would lead the forces of Sevenwaters and win back the Islands. Now Johnny sailed forth and I must follow, for he would need me at the last. I felt a warmth against the feathers of my breast; the amulet was still with me even in my birdlike form, and so was she. Her eyes were open once more, her presence shadowed me. So be it; I would lead her after me until the moment when I must turn and confront her. For at the end she would be there; of that there was no doubt whatever. She would be there to watch and gloat over her great triumph. I must go on. But I was tired, and the wind was getting stronger, and the air seemed colder. Weren't the curraghs further away now, not below me and just ahead anymore, but over on my right, and I much further offshore and being carried steadily eastward? I was moving my wings, and trying to find a level where the currents would help me, and every time I looked the boats seemed smaller, and the land beyond them more distant. Would this cruel wind carry me all the way to the shores of Alba?

A shadow moved above me. Large, swift, an echo of that dark presence which had terrified Sibeal's horse, and nearly caused the child's death. Fear, danger. Wings outstretched, I tilted and dropped, then fluttered back to a level path, out of reach. The shadow moved;

it hung in air, above and behind, waiting. Terror, death. I flew lower, less controlled now, panic threatening to undo my precarious control of this wind-harried flight. The gray swell of the sea moved closer; I imagined dagger toothed monsters beneath its choppy surface. The menacing presence above me was driving me back to the west, staying just out of my sight, but close, so close I could sense the outstretched talons, the tearing beak of a hungry predator. I fluttered, terrified, as the wind gusted and the slate-dark sea stretched up toward me, still closer now. Turn for home; fly back before it is too late, said my instincts. Wait, cautioned the part of me that could still think. Control, that is the key.

But it is not easy to maintain control when death is as close as the snap of a beak away. Terror lent strength to my wings; my mindless fluttering gave way to a steady beating, up and down, up and down. I set my course south west, flying low above the sea's surge, and the unseen presence behind me kept pace as if it were my own shadow. At every instant I expected a fatal blow, a final dive to seize and kill. I flew on, and now the curraghs were nearer, and nearer again, so I could see clearly the scraps of black and brown and cream that were their small sails, and the dip and flash of many oars, and at last, the figures of men I recognized: the Chief with his intricate body-markings; Gull's dark features; Johnny standing in the stern of one small craft, shading his eyes against the sun as he gazed southward.

Behind and above me, something gathered its strength, perhaps preparing to strike. Quick. I must land, I must find a place there on the boats among the men, before those claws fastened themselves on me and I was reduced to a limp bundle of lifeless flesh and feathers. Quick. But where? Where was safe? Might I not make a landing, and straight away be caught and strangled, and put away for tonight's supper?

There was no choice. The creature swooped, a dark destroyer swift and purposeful. I veered sideways, a hair's breadth from its grasp, and landed awkwardly, not on the rim of the small curragh, not on a taut rope or convenient wooden thwart, but on a man's shoulder, my small bird-feet clutching instinctively for purchase on the soft cloth of his well-worn cloak. The thing behind me flew past and made a precise landing at the stern of the boat, right beside my cousin where he stood motionless and silent, his gray eyes fixed on the ocean ahead. And it was Fiacha: dark-plumed, bright-eyed, knife-beaked Fiacha, who had pursued me thus until I reached a place of safety. I liked his way of doing things even less now that I, too, was a bird.

"Ah," said the man on whose shoulder I had landed, and reached up his right hand toward me. Dove sensed danger. I edged away, claws catching in the fabric of the man's cloak. And now I could see his face; even with bird-sight I knew those gaunt, pale features, those shadowed, colorless eyes. Even without the flash of white feathers beneath the ragged garments, I knew who it was.

"A long journey," said Finbar softly. He might have been referring to me, or to himself, or to the two of us.

So he had come. Against all my expectations, he had heeded my clarion call.

Gareth was hauling on an oar, brows creased in effort. "Must have been swept across by the storm winds," he observed. "Such a creature belongs in a sheltered wood, surely, not far out to sea."

"My mother used to make a tasty pigeon pie, with leeks and garlic in it," put in Godric.

"Not this time." Finbar moved his arm cautiously; I walked back up and settled on his shoulder, ruffling my feathers. Fiacha, it seemed, had driven me forward to precisely the safest place I could be among these grim warriors. "It's a gentle little creature; we can afford it shelter, surely."

"Unusual," Gareth remarked.

"What?" frowned Godric, bending to the movement of the great oar.

"He means the plumage." Finbar's voice was placid. "A rock dove has very plain coloring, shades of gray, subtleties within that, no more. I've never yet seen one with a crest of such brilliant red as this small bird bears. A sign of luck perhaps. The goddess smiles on our endeavor."

"Hm," said Godric, eyeing me with a certain disappointment. Doubtless the effort of driving the curragh forward through this wind-tossed sea made for hearty appetites.

Supper came a very long time later, and there was no pigeon pie. It was already dusk, and even the strongest of these warriors was gray-faced with exhaustion. For a time we traveled within sight of land, a long, green island to the east. I wondered if this were the shore of Britain, close to Harrowfield, home of Bran and Liadan who had so curiously chosen to settle there as neighbors of the family's arch enemy.

"It is not Northumbria," Finbar observed quietly, "but Manannán Isle. Here we make camp, and rest a little, and meet our allies. It will not be for long."

If the men eyed him rather strangely, finding it odd that he needed to state what was already known, he seemed unperturbed by it. Indeed, he had sat calm and still throughout the voyage as if, now that he had decided to confront his fears, they had ceased to trouble him. As for me, I stayed on his shoulder, where Fiacha could not reach me. I watched as the curraghs were anchored, or drawn up on the shore, and the men stretched, and cursed their aching bodies, and then unloaded the boats and made camp swiftly and silently in the dark.

Clouds had been gathering all through the day, and the rain began to fall almost as soon as the men had begun their frugal meal, cooked over a small fire. There was a general retreat to what shelter could be found. Johnny had set a well-armed guard about the camp's perimeter, but the rain became a deluge, and I thought none but frogs would wish to be abroad tonight. Finbar pulled his hooded cloak up over his head, and I nestled closer to his neck, quite dry in this small shelter. We moved to a place where the rocks opened to a shallow, cave-like space. Here one might sit on the earth and be tolerably dry, though the heavens opened outside.

Others had found this place of refuge before us. There were three of the young warriors seated on the ground, barely visible in the dark, their cloaks wrapped close around them against the chill: Waerfrith, and Godric, and Darragh. They moved over to make room for Finbar, and as he sat, he slipped back the hood and reached up to touch me gently, as if to ensure I was safe. If I had been myself, I would have used the craft. If I had had the craft, I would have made a little fire to dry us out and keep us warm. It was chill, with spring no more than a thought in the earth's heart, and the storm seemed to be right above us. The part of me that was dove was scared; scared of the dark, feeling the wrongness of being out in it awake, and so close to humankind. That fear made me tremble; it made me move my feet restlessly on Finbar's shoulder, longing for a safe place to sleep, hidden amid the thick branching twigs of a great tree, or in the crannies and crevices of a rocky hillside. Back in Kerry in the sunshine, under the standing stones, pecking for crumbs left by children as they sat and shared their small repast, that was where a dove should be, not here.

For a little the rain abated, and a faint glow of moonlight entered our narrow shelter.

"There," said Finbar in a whisper. "There. No need to be frightened. You are safe now, and among friends."

"Creature seems to have attached itself to you, my lord," said Godric, grinning. "Funny, I thought a familiar would be a wolf or an eagle, something strong and impressive; not a shivering scrap of a bird like that."

"Druids don't have familiars, stupid," said Waerfrith, digging his friend in the ribs. "That's sorcerers. My lord here is hardly one of those."

Darragh wasn't talking; just watching very closely, with a little frown on his brow.

"I'm no druid," Finbar said calmly. "My brother accompanies Sean of Sevenwaters on this venture; he is the wisest of the ancient kind, and will perform the auguries and prepare the rituals such a great undertaking requires. I am here—I am here because—"

"Because you were called to it," Darragh said quietly. He was still staring at me, and now he stretched out his arm, very slowly so as not to frighten, until his long brown fingers were just by my breast, almost touching but not quite. "Come on, little one," he coaxed. "Come here now, come on. I won't hurt you. You know I'd never do that."

There was something in his voice that soothed me and called to me at the same time. Perhaps it was the same something that had lured the white pony away from her herd; the same thing that had made him the only friend of a lonely little girl at the cove. Back then, I had feared to be seen; and yet, I could not wait to see him, on that magical day of the year when the traveling folk came back to Kerry. I had been awkward and tongue-tied with Dan and Peg and Molly and the fisherfolk; but Darragh had shared my deepest secrets. I had feared touch; but not his touch.

"Come on, Curly," he said softly. "Come on, now."

I took a little step with my neat bird-feet, and another, and perched cautiously on the fingers he held out to me. Then I felt the warmth of his hand beneath me, holding me safe as he stroked my head with one finger, and I heard his voice, no more than a whisper. "That's it. That's it, small one."

"Curly?" queried Waerfrith. "What sort of a name is that?"

"It suits her," said Darragh, his voice held very quiet. "See, she's got a little tuft of red feathers on her head, all curling round."

"Her?" Godric raised his brows.

"Undoubtedly, her," Finbar said. "Now, we'd best try to rest, for I understand we have but one day to assemble, and then we shall all be extremely busy for a while. This may not be comfortable, but at least it's dry."

Once before I had slept in Darragh's arms, and wished that I might never wake. Now, as I nestled warm between his cupped hands, so close to his cheek that I could feel his steady breathing ruffling my feathers, I wished something different. This strange night was an unexpected gift, for I had thought our last parting over when he turned away from me, in the darkness on Inis Eala. A gift, then, to be so near, to feel his careful touch and share his innocent sleep. But I wished, oh, how I wished I was a girl again, and the others gone. There was a longing in me that near shattered my small heart, that I could reach out and take him in my arms; that I could give back the same gentleness he bestowed so generously, never thinking of himself. I wished I had a woman's voice, and not a bird's, so that I could whisper in his ear. I would tell him . . . I would tell him . . .

We slept; and then it was dawn. A bird sings at dawn, and moves forward into the day, seeking light and warmth, food and water. But I was not a bird, for all the outward appearance. When a sorcerer transforms, he does not become that other; he merely remakes himself in the semblance of it, to deceive folks' eyes. The more successful the transformation, the more one is likely to feel of the essence of the chosen form: the instincts, the changes of balance, sight and hearing. And yet, the best of sorcerers retains at the same time his own full consciousness. A delicate balance. While in the altered form, one cannot use the craft. When I had made myself into a farmer's wife, and confronted the trickster at the horse fair, I had used only the lesser form of the Glamour, and that sparingly, and so I had been able to perform charms and cast spells, to make bird into snake, to release latches, to half-strangle a man. But I could not do that today. All I could do was watch and listen. All I could do was keep out of Fiacha's way, and observe these men, and try to ready myself for what would come tomorrow.

I left the shelter of Darragh's hands, the sweet warmth of his body. Finbar was awake, standing motionless outside the shelter of the rocks, gazing into the paling sky. The storm was over; there was the merest whisper of a westerly breeze. Finbar's expression was strange; the eyes intense and bright. As I alighted on his shoulder I felt the way he paced his breathing, slow and deliberate: a pattern. Thus he calmed his racing heart, his head full of visions, I thought. I could not speak to him, but if I had had a voice, I would have offered words of recognition. *I know how hard this was for you, to come here; to face the terror we share. And I salute you for your courage.*

"Well, Fainne," said Finbar quietly. "Another morning. The last before our great endeavor begins, if my brother reads the signs and finds them fair. You keep this form skillfully; I trust it serves you well. Today is a day for observation, I think; for looking and learning. In this form you are vulnerable, to the elements, to wild predators, to the carelessness of man himself. Of us all here, there will be but two who recognize what you are. Your young man is sick at heart to see you in this guise, for he knows he cannot keep you safe. There is no place for such a small creature at the heart of a great battle, nor in secret endeavor by sea. As for me, I will watch over you as best I can. We share the same enemy and the same fear, you and I. But I do not know your exact purpose here. You will fly forth, no doubt, and return when you please. Know that I am close by, and will provide what protection I can for you."

I could not reply, and so, as the sky lightened and a flock of gulls passed overhead, plumage glinting in the dawn light, I spread my wings and flew, scarcely knowing where I was going or for what purpose.

Early as it was, men were stirring, emerging from their various places of shelter, gathering in small groups, making a fire, preparing some sort of meal with practiced efficiency. I found a perch among the bare branches of an old apple tree. I was ill concealed, maybe, but safe for now, and well placed to look and listen. I did not feel the need of food and drink; perhaps I would take neither until I was myself again.

Before us was a bay, not broad and open like the cove of my childhood, but a place of safety and secrecy, with deep water and high, sheltering arms of land on either side. Here the curraghs lay at anchor, here the smaller vessels were drawn up on a pebbly shore. As well as Johnny's fleet there were many other boats, some of skins stretched over a frame, some all of wood, blunt small craft, sturdy and strong. Among them, like stately swans amid a flock of common brown ducks, were three much larger ships, the sleek long lines of them a wondrous sight, plank laid against curving plank in perfect balance, the prows high and graceful, with carven figure of mermaid or princess or horned god of war giving each the semblance of some mystic craft from an ancient tale: the very ship in which some great voyager went forth to find the end of the world; the very vessel in which a legendary warrior sailed out to win his lady and his kingdom. I had never seen such ships before. Each was large enough, I thought, to bear a fighting force of considerable numbers. With a full complement of oarsmen and a favorable wind, each could be employed in lightning attack on slower vessel or on unprepared coastline, to sail in fast and disgorge its cargo of armed men while the helpless inhabitants were still rubbing the sleep from their eyes. I had no doubt these were ships of the Finn-ghaill; vessels of the Norsemen, such as my father had devastated once, long ago, in Kerry.

And yet, there was no panic. Below my tree, the young warriors of Johnny's band ate their breakfast and readied their weapons as if this were a day like any other. There, too, were the older men, Snake and Gull and the Chief himself, talking quietly together with never a glance at the fearsome sight out on the quiet waters of the anchorage. It was as if nobody had seen the threat, save me.

Now there were other men here, and Johnny was greeting them, and I saw that some of them wore the symbol of two torcs interlinked: the emblem of Sevenwaters. Others had a different sign, their tunics blazoned with an image in red, a serpent coiled around to devour its own tail. And there were men in green: Eamonn's men. The morning was growing brighter; after the storm, the air seemed clean-washed, the land breathing deep, as if spring were not so far

away. Below the branch where I perched quiet, a traveling man finished his meager breakfast, a meal taken abstractedly as he glanced
here and there around the campsite, as if seeking to find something
lost. I shifted slightly on my branch; he looked up and frowned. An
instant later, Finbar was there by his side, speaking quietly.

"There is a council, I understand; a meeting of these leaders, and
a final decision to be made. You must let Fainne do what she will;
you cannot alter the course of events here. You cannot protect her
from this point on. We must trust, simply, that she has the strength
to do what must be done."

"It's not right." Darragh's voice was tight with feeling. I did not
like to hear him thus distressed.

"Nonetheless," Finbar said gently, "there is nothing you can do
about it. You must leave her be; she will go her own way."

"That's what I'm afraid of," said Darragh.

The council took place under cover and under guard. In the end I
did seek Finbar's aid, for I could hardly fly into the long, low building
where they met and settle as if by chance on the rafters to hear their
secret interchange. I entered the council room on the seer's shoulder,
half hidden in the folds of his cloak, half shrouded by his tangle of
dark hair. And I saw, straight away, why there had been no shouts of
alarm, no hasty setting of arrow to string at the sight of those elegant
ships at anchor in the bay. For here at the council table, alongside
Sean of Sevenwaters and his uncle Conor, alongside the chieftains of
the Uí Néill and the child of the prophecy himself, were several very
large men with broad, fair faces and long flaxen hair neat-braided.
They wore gold about their necks and in the clasps of their cloaks;
gold fine-wrought in the shape of war-hammer or dog's head or rising sun. They were leaders of the Finn-ghaill, the very Viking war-
lords who had raided and plundered the coastlines of Erin and of
Britain alike these long years. Was not this an ungodly alliance?
Would a man such as my uncle Sean break bread with such savages,
even to ensure victory over his oldest enemy? But then, hadn't my
uncle said something about a dispute being settled by marriage
between a lord of Tirconnell and a Viking woman? Perhaps, after all,
this was not so impossible. I sat quiet, listening and wondering
greatly.

This was a select council. Of our own band, only Johnny and his father were there, and Snake. Sean and Conor represented Sevenwaters. My uncle was grim-faced and purposeful; Conor glanced once in Finbar's direction, and gave a nod of recognition. The Uí Néill seemed wary; the Norsemen spoke among themselves, and one of Bran's men, a large, dark-bearded fellow named Wolf, appeared from nowhere to address them in their own tongue.

"Wolf will translate for us," the Chief said calmly. "Now, can we begin this? The morning is passing; there is surely little more to be resolved at this stage. Each of us knows his own part in this."

One of the Vikings made a rumbling comment.

"Hakon asks, what of these empty places at table?" Wolf translated. "Are we not yet all assembled here? Decisions made in this council must be agreed by all, or may we not expect a knife in the back?"

Sean frowned. "Eamonn is already here on the island, encamped not far away. He will come. We should wait a little longer; Hakon speaks wisely. As with the rest of us, Eamonn has brought his men over gradually, and by various routes, not to draw undue attention to the magnitude of our endeavor."

Then one of the Norse chieftains clapped his hands, and a lad brought a great drinking horn which was passed around. It occurred to me belatedly that not only were these Vikings some sort of ally in the endeavor, but that this place was theirs, a whole settlement perhaps, on the fringes of Manannán Isle. Someone had struck a very useful bargain here. It was clear I had a great deal to learn about warfare.

There was a stir at the entry and three men came in; men in green. I watched as Eamonn stalked across the room to take his place at the council table. His men settled themselves on his left and his right, as if to separate him from the others. He looked up and across the table, and straight into the steady gray eyes of Bran of Harrowfield.

"Well, well, well," said Eamonn affably, smiling. "It has been a long time: How is your charming wife? A girl of unique talents, I always thought."

The Chief did not reply. Instead, his gaze swept over Eamonn as if he did not exist. He turned toward Sean and Conor. "Time passes swiftly," he said. "Let us make our decision and move on."

"We are all assembled," said Sean gravely. "At this meeting we confirm our plan of action and renew our pledge to support one another in this alliance. My uncle, the archdruid, will perform the augury, and if the goddess smiles on us, tomorrow's dawn will witness the enactment of our strategy. A great victory must surely follow." He glanced at Johnny. "My nephew leads this campaign. Johnny is heir to Sevenwaters; he is at the same time born to Harrowfield, the British estate of my father. The prophecy which has guided us toward this final encounter names just such a one as the leader ordained to carry us forward to victory. In Johnny is born the child of the prophecy; in him we witness the fulfilment of the old truth. He is the shining light which guides us forward to triumph over Northwoods. The Islands will be ours once more; our enemy banished forever to his home shore, never again to set his heedless foot on our sacred ground."

"I don't question the lad's ability to lead," said one of the men who bore the snake-symbol on his tunic. "But what about his father? Is there not room for doubt when one of our number is a Briton himself, and close neighbor to the very chieftain we oppose? Bran of Harrowfield shares a border with Edwin of Northwoods. Indeed, there is some tie of kinship, I understand. What assurance is afforded that this alliance will hold firm, when we set Briton against Briton?"

"I don't think that will be a problem," put in Eamonn smoothly, before either Sean or the Chief could speak. "It's never been difficult in the past for this man to change his allegiance, or turn against his own kind. Just make sure you've enough silver for an incentive. That's the only language he understands."

There was a difficult little silence. Snake's eyes narrowed to dangerous slits, and his hand moved to his sword hilt. There was a scrape of metal. Wolf made no attempt to translate. Bran, tight-jawed, maintained his control and did not speak. It was Johnny who rose to his feet.

"My lords," he said, "there is no doubt of the strength of this alliance, no question of the loyalty of its partners. My father's role in this is not as battle-leader. He has won for us the support of these fine chieftains, Hakon and Ulf, and the generous loan of their strong vessels. But it is I who lead here, and not Bran of Harrowfield. These men are under my command. Tomorrow my father returns home to Britain; he will not war with Northwoods, save in times of threat to his own borders." I noted he did not mention anything about swimming, and putting holes in boats. It seemed that part was secret even from their own allies. "Now," Johnny continued calmly, "let me set out for you the course of this venture, for each must understand well his part in it. Each part is vital; each part is separate until the end, and must be carried out independently and precisely. Each of you is responsible for his own forces. Without trust, this great venture is doomed to failure."

There were murmurs and rumbles of assent around the table. Eamonn wore a crooked smile; the Chief was impassive.

"If the goddess wills," said Johnny, "the venture commences this very night. At dawn we must be in position to strike . . ."

I watched him as he paced to and fro and gestured in illustration, as his gray eyes shone with hope, lighting the solemn chamber with the flame of his enthusiasm. And I watched the men there, seasoned battle-leaders every one, men far older in years and experience than him who addressed them, men used to their own command, accustomed to making their own decisions. They listened transfixed. Not a muscle stirred; not a whisper was uttered. With the confident flow of his voice and the ardent hope on his face, Johnny held every one of them silent as he set out the bold plan by which they would at last triumph over the old enemy. Indeed, so impressed was I by my cousin's authority and bearing, I lost track of his words for a time, and did not catch every detail. He said nothing at all of the perilous venture planned for tonight. He did not tell them the small boat would sail across after dark, and lower into the icy grip of the sea a very special group of five men including both himself and Bran of Harrowfield. Perhaps his father would not set foot on the islands, perhaps he would not actually be seen with a sword in his hand facing up to Edwin of Northwoods, but he most certainly intended to help sink the five vessels of Northwoods's fleet this very night. I knew that, but it became plain none of these men were to be told. Johnny simply said one boat would go in first, and if all seemed well, a signal would be given: a red flag to advance. Before dawn the three great ships of the Finn-ghaill would be in place, crewed not by Viking warriors but by our own men, the men of Sevenwaters and of Inis Eala, the warriors of the Uí Néill and the forces of Sídhe Dubh and Glencarnagh; the men in green. The sun would come up, and the Britons would rise from their beds unsuspecting. Then, from the direction least expected, from the perilous channel between knife-edged rocks, skirting the great whirlpool which they called the Worm's Mouth, would appear the deadly longships with their cargo of armed warriors. Hakon and Ulf would each take charge of a ship; Gull would control the third. Their skill would guide these craft through waterways hitherto thought impossible. They would go in swiftly, attacking the Britons fiercely before they could mount a defense. I knew, though Johnny did not say it, that for the forces of Northwoods there would be no escape. Their ships would be gone; they must surrender or be annihilated. The men of the Uí Néill would land on Little Island, Johnny said, to subdue the lesser forces there. The rest would go to Greater Island and surround the enemy's encampment. By dusk tomorrow it would be all over.

Johnny's exposition drew to a close, and as one the men rose, and moved from the table, and with gripping of hands and clasping of shoulders, and with fierce grins and fighting words, the strange allies of this venture confirmed their commitment to one another; Viking and Ulsterman, Briton and chieftain of the royal blood of Erin. Conor was leading the way outside; there were still omens to be read, and guidance to be sought beyond the merely human, before the final decision might be made, to go tonight, or wait. It was very early in the season, so early the elements were predictable only in their unpredictability. On the other hand, the sooner the allies moved, the more effective the factor of surprise.

From my vantage point on Finbar's shoulder, I watched as Eamonn strode up to the Chief, hand outstretched in a display of apparent amity.

"Let us seal this agreement, then," he said with a strange little smile, "since it appears you have become respectable, and now deal at council tables and not by stealth, in the darkness."

But Bran only gazed at him a moment, gray eyes cool, patterned features devoid of expression, and then he turned away, as if what he had seen were beneath notice, something of no import whatever. I watched Eamonn's face, and the look there made me tremble. Anger, offense, bitterness I might have expected. But I had not thought I would see gloating triumph in those dark eyes.

Outside this meeting-house there was a flat expanse of sandy ground, neat-raked. Around its perimeter were assembled many men, warriors all, each in the colors of his leader. Some held banners: the coiled snake which seemed to be the sign of the Uí Néill, the torcs of Sevenwaters, the dark tower on a green field which was the emblem of Eamonn of Sídhe Dubh and Glencarnagh. The house of Harrowfield was not represented; the Chief, it was clear, was not officially an ally in this venture, and wished to conceal tonight's mission and his own vital part in it.

Now Conor came forth, birch staff in hand, and began the slow pacing, the solemn words of a ritual of augury. A small plume of pungent smoke rose into the air: herbs of divination were being burned. I left Finbar's shoulder and flew to the roof tree of the low building, a better vantage point. The druid cast the circle; he sought the blessing of the four quarters and expressed the respect of all for the power of the elements, and those deities to whom each pertained. Some of those present were not adherents to the old faith; I had seen crosses worn around necks, and observed a man who seemed to be a tonsured Father among the forces of the Uí Néill. Still, all were quite silent; all watched intently as Conor stepped to the center of the circle he had made, and brought out a little bag of soft kidskin, fastened with a golden cord. He took out the coelbrens, the slender sticks of pale birch wood with their carven Ogham signs, and, with an invocation to the goddess, strewed them before him on the raked earth. All eyes were on him; all but one man's. Eamonn stood to the side, flanked by his green-clad guards. An odd little smile still played on his features; the smugly anticipatory look of a cat which holds the mouse alive but helpless in its claws. The crowd watched Conor as he bent, now, to study the fall of the rods of augury. But Eamonn was looking at me. I shifted uneasily on my perch, wondering how he could possibly know; how he could possibly guess. I reached down with my beak to preen my feathers nervously, stretching out a small wing, folding it back again as I had seen that ragged owl do. I tried to look as any other bird might, going about its business on a fair morning. Eamonn's smile widened in apparent amusement; he gave a little nod of acknowledgment, never taking his eyes off me. I remembered the way he had been at Sevenwaters, always watching, silently observant, as if he were putting together the pieces of a puzzle in order to discover whatever might be to his advantage. I had thought he could not uncover this secret, but it seemed I had underestimated the man yet again.

The silence stretched out as Conor crouched by the scattered rods, unmoving. The augury should have been a simple one, for but a single answer was needed: to go now, or to wait. But the archdruid had turned very pale, and a frown creased his ageless brow. The men began to mutter among themselves. Why didn't the fellow tell what he saw? Did the divination show ill tidings, that he did not stand, and speak?

Conor raised his head and looked at his brother. Finbar's fear was almost palpable to me as he walked slowly across to stand by the druid, a straight, slight figure in his worn robe and tattered cloak, the sweep of snowy feathers by his side plain for all to see in the bright light of this spring morning. There were a few gasps of surprise, a few exclamations, quickly suppressed. I saw one man make the sign of the cross, furtively. Somewhere, a dog barked, and the man with the swan's wing froze momentarily. I felt the trembling terror that ran through him as if it were my own; I, too, was part wild thing until the time should come to change. But Finbar could not change. *Be strong*, I thought. *Be strong, as you once were.*

Finbar moved again, squatting down by his brother's side. The two men studied the pattern of the coelbrens closely. Neither spoke. Perhaps there was no need. The silence drew out again, and the assembled warriors began to shuffle in restless unease.

"Tell us." It was Sean of Sevenwaters who broke the silence, speaking calmly from where he waited among his men. "What are the signs? Does the goddess smile on our venture?"

"Come on, man, out with it." The war-leader of the Uí Néill, Christian as he might be, knew well enough that the timing was dependent on this, for those who led the campaign would not proceed unless the signs were favorable.

Conor stood upright, his features grave but calm. It seemed to me his mask of serenity was held in place by a strong effort of will; beneath it, there was some great misgiving. His white robe settled about him, its folds full of shadows even in the morning sunlight.

"I will tell true," he said in a voice which seemed quiet, and yet somehow carried to every corner of that great assembly of men. "The signs are not all good. There is an obscurity here, some darkness that clouds the path of our endeavor, that conceals the full pattern of it. It is as if even the great powers of the Otherworld cannot be certain how this will unfold. And yet, the message of the augury is clear in one respect. We must move now, and not delay. By dawn tomorrow our fleet will touch the shores of the Islands, and before the sun sets the land will run red with the blood of those who dared to set foot on our sacred ground. We will drive them thence, or see them perish under arrow and blade; perish to the last man. This we swear by all that is true."

There was a great roar of approval from the crowd; Conor's words had been carefully chosen, I thought, for just such an effect. The reservation in his augury would be soon forgotten; the men scented victory, and now strained at the leash like hunting dogs. Maybe there was blood and death in it, but what brave young warrior of one and twenty thinks it will be his own? There was a light in their eyes, a spring in their steps as they made their way back to their various encampments, to ready weapons, to make the final adjustment to ship and sail and instruments of war. They did not see the pallor of Conor's features, nor the shadow in his brother Finbar's strange, clear eyes as the two of them stood talking quietly with Sean of Sevenwaters, and Johnny, and the Chief. They did not notice the grim set of Sean's jaw, nor the fierce, frowning determination on the fair young features of the child of the prophecy. But I did; and I heard my grandmother's voice as I sat there on the roof of the meeting house, a voice long silent, awake again within me as the amulet glowed warm against my breast. *Good, Fainne. Good, child. All is in place. Do not fail me now, so near the end.*

My heart lurched at the sound of it. I had been right; she watched me, she tracked me even in my bird-form. Conor had seen a darkness; I knew what that darkness was, and whence it came. My grandmother was part of it, and I was part of it, whether I wished it or not. A terrible fear ran through me, remembering how I had slept last night, sheltered in the warmth of Darragh's hands. I must not go near him again; not from now until it was all over. Nor would I bring her close to Finbar, already so damaged by her cruelty. This day, and the night, I must spend quite alone.

There was not much in the way of trees. Low scrubby bushes, a few leafless apples. There were buildings half-hidden by folds of the land, or constructed deep, with a great turf-cloaked mound of earth covering them, secure from wind and frost. These offered no hiding place for a small bird to avoid wandering fox or tailless cat or the prying eyes of a chieftain with too much of an interest in solving puzzles. And there was Fiacha. I understood that he was somehow on my side, but still I feared his sharp beak, his clutching claws and his swiftness. Near Fiacha, perhaps I might have been safe from other predators. But my bird-self froze in terror at the glimpse of his dark form as he followed Johnny about the encampment, now before, now behind, keeping pace, keeping watch. I could not bring myself to go near.

I found a spot in the bushes close by the track leading down to the anchorage. It was not a place of concealment; I kept as still as I could, hoping to stay unnoticed. Curse the red crest. The charm I had used to change myself had said nothing of that; some malign power had done it, and made it all too easy for those who knew me to identify me. Even Darragh had known; Darragh who knew nothing of magic.

The day passed; the men went about their business, faces grim with concentration or bright with purpose. There was no fear of death in their eyes. They passed by me on the track and did not look at me. But once, as the warriors in green made their way down to the ships, which lay so gracefully there on the calm water, the chieftain of Sídhe Dubh and Glencarnagh halted on the pathway, and motioned his men to go ahead of him. He stood there with hand shading brow, as if inspecting the fleet, or the clouds, or the wide expanse of sea beyond the bay.

"Well, Fainne," he said under his breath. "A strange meeting indeed. My men would think me crazed, that I hold a conversation with a wild creature. But I cannot let the opportunity pass us by. I imagine you have waited here for just this purpose. I owe you the greatest of debts, my dear. The information you sent me has served me better than you could possibly have imagined. Tonight I have him at last; tomorrow the world is a better place for his demise. Oh, Fainne, what you have done for me is beyond price."

His strange words made me shiver. The look on his face struck a deep fear into me. What information? I had not spied; I had sent him nothing. What could he mean?

"It will be easily explained," he went on. "No finger can be pointed at me. The man was simply too old for such a venture. That is what folk will say in the morning. It will be dark and cold; the distance is long, the task taxing even for a young man at his peak. Better that he had sent another; still, he was ever a fellow who liked to be in the forefront of things. But by then it will be too late." He smiled, and I saw the spark of madness in his dark eyes. I fancied I heard my grandmother's voice. *Oh, yes. Play on that.*

"It is passing strange to see you in this form," Eamonn said, glancing at me sideways, then back across the water. "And yet, not so strange maybe. Our partnership, I think, will be one of great advantage to us both. This form you have chosen is a vulnerable one, my dear. You must be cautious; I would not wish you to come to any harm. The anticipation of the marriage bed stirs my body even now. There is a whole new world of discovery there. Indeed, there is a new life ahead for the two of us."

I shuffled nervously on the perch, longing for him to go away, not quite prepared to fly off myself, since I had nowhere else to go. His earlier words had unsettled me deeply; I struggled to make sense of them.

Other men appeared behind Eamonn on the path. It might not have bothered Finbar, or Darragh, to be seen talking solemnly to a small gray bird as if she could understand them. But Eamonn was too dignified to be caught in such foolishness.

"Farewell now," he muttered. "Take care, my dear. I want you safe." Then he was away down the track, and the others after him.

He knew, then. He knew of the swim, and the terrible risk that would be taken, tonight, by five men, to ensure the Britons would be crippled before ever the fleet of the allies touched the shore of the Islands. He knew, and planned to strike when the Chief was at his most vulnerable. But how had he learned this secret? Why had he thanked me for this knowledge? I had told him nothing. I had told nobody what I knew; nobody except . . . except my grandmother. I remembered, suddenly, how I had spoken to her of the swim, because it had been necessary to convince her I still followed her orders and worked to her purpose. Somehow she had ensured Eamonn found out; had done it in a way that made him believe the information came from me. It would be easy enough; some sort of unsigned message; a whisper in the darkness, almost like a dream. A safeguard, she'd said. I'll need a safeguard. And when none was forth-coming she had made her own, just in case I did not perform, at the last. She did not trust me; she probably never had.

My heart was beating fast, my body chill. I must warn them. There was little time, the day was passing quickly, and I did not know how soon the small curragh must set sail for the swimmers to reach the British anchorage and return to safety before dawn. I must tell them there was a traitor in their midst who put his own crazy quest for vengeance before the balance of a great campaign. But how? How could I tell them? I was a dove; I had no human speech, and I could not make myself a girl again, not yet. It was tomorrow's battle that would decide the final unfolding of things; and to be there I must remain in this form, so I could fly to follow them, and be strong. Change back, and my uncle Sean would bundle me off home to Erin and safety, no matter what I told him. If that happened I could not do as I must, and prevent the lady Oonagh from performing her dreadful work of destruction. That was my task and mine alone. And in the long term, that mattered more than anything.

How could I warn them? I did not know what Eamonn intended. He could hardly mean to join the group himself. I could imagine what the Chief would have to say about that. What did he plan? Perhaps I could follow, and listen. Still, I would be powerless, for I had neither words to use nor the voice of the mind. And there were only two who knew my identity, save Eamonn himself. Finbar, and Darragh. I could not approach either; I would not draw to either my grandmother's interest, for to do so was to put them at grave risk, and to provide her with powerful weapons against me.

I flew back to the main encampment, itching with frustration that I could not be myself again. I perched in a tree; on a rope suspending a shelter; on a post in the open. Men worked quietly, or rested in preparation for long effort without sleep. Prayers were spoken, of one persuasion or another. Sean sat with Eamonn and the war-leaders of the Uí Néill, and looked at charts. Eamonn's pale features were calm and serious; his eye revealed no light of madness now. He was like any other chieftain who plans a foray with his long-term allies: he looked, in a word, trustworthy.

Johnny was engaged in more active pursuits. I saw him leave the sheltered area with three other men, those who were to swim with him tonight: Sigurd, and Gareth, and Darragh. They slipped away quietly, perhaps for some final rehearsal of the night's risky maneuver. Some time later, I discovered the Chief down at the cove with Snake and Gull by his side, checking the small curragh with the dark sails; in this vessel they had moved to and fro between the islets back at Inis Eala, balancing the craft like some great skillful seabird on the swift ebb and flow of the tide. I flew down through the salt touch of splashing wavelets to alight as neatly as I could on the stern of the curragh; but once I was there, I could think of no way to convey to them any message at all. A dove could not make pictures in the sand, or cast the coelbrens to mark out disaster. A dove could do no more than flutter its wings anxiously, and make small, worried chirrups.

"Bird seems bothered," Snake observed with a half-smile as he adjusted a rope tighter. "Hopping around like some chicken that knows it's next for the pot."

"Came over from Ulster on the boats, that's what I heard," said Gull. "Maybe it's an omen."

"Good luck, I hope," Snake said. "Creature's quite agitated; almost as if it were trying to tell us something. Aren't they normally timid little things?"

"We need no luck, nor any omens." The Chief's patterned features were solemn, his gray eyes clear and purposeful, his son's eyes. The sunlight shone bright on the fair, unmarked side of his face, and for a moment it could almost have been Johnny standing there. "Skill, and planning, and good preparation will ensure success here, as they have done in all our past ventures. Disregard the bird; perhaps it is lost, blown off course by the west wind. Our own strength will suffice, with no need for auguries and portents."

"Still," said Gull, glancing at me again. But he took it no further, and I could see there was no way for me to tell them what I knew. Then, suddenly, Gareth was coming down the track to the anchorage, his amiable features tense with strain, his face white. The Chief straightened slowly from where he bent to adjust the ropes.

"Well?" he demanded. "What is it?"

"Sigurd's taken sick. The flux; a bad dose of it. Came on all of a sudden. He's not going to be able to swim."

The Chief's hard mouth tightened further. "Gull? Can he be doctored with something? Have you a potion for this?"

"How severe is it?" Gull was leaving his task, ready to hasten up to the encampment, dark features creased in a frown.

"Bad. Purging and retching as if he'd taken poison. You'd have to work a miracle to have him ready in time."

I felt my insides knot with fear. Poison. There were only five swimmers, and one of them was Darragh.

"What about the backup?" the Chief asked quietly. Like the seasoned campaigner he was, he did not panic, but assessed the possibilities swiftly and calmly.

"Mikka? Not up to it, Chief. Slit his hand this morning in a practice bout; hasn't the full use of it yet. He'll do well enough tomorrow in the battle, but he can't do this. Johnny says he won't risk him."

Snake muttered an oath under his breath.

"Have we no men here but invalids?" the Chief asked softly. "Are we undone so easily? I cannot believe this."

"Cormack says he can do it if you'll give him the chance," ventured Gareth with some hesitation. "He hasn't swum the distance before, but he's strong, and he says he can manage it."

"I think not." There was a finality in the Chief's tone that closed off any thought of argument. "I may risk one son in this venture, but not two. Cormack is too young, and untried. He will take his place with pride tomorrow among the men; but he will not be part of this. We must find another, for there must be five, one for each vessel. As it is the venture is risky; with less than five, it becomes simply foolhardy. No man would wish to be discovered there close by the Briton's ships, with a mask over his face and a neat iron spike in his hand. With five, we strike together and retreat together."

Gareth nodded, his blunt features serious. "Johnny's asking, discreetly," he said. "There may be one among the Uí Néill, or among Lord Eamonn's men, who could attempt this."

Bran spat, efficiently, at the side of the path. "One of the Uí Néill, maybe; or the Norsemen," he said. "I'll trust none of the men in green."

That was how it came to pass that five men sailed south into the dusk on their covert mission, and that one of them was an assassin. That was how it came to be that I saw them go, and could not do a thing to stop it. There was indeed a man of the Uí Néill who was a strong swimmer; his fellow warriors backed up his claims, and spoke highly of his strength and endurance. He had fair hair plaited down his back, and an irregularity of build, so that one shoulder was higher than the other. It did not impede him in the water, they said. Johnny tested him in the chill embrace of the sea, out beyond the bay, and pronounced himself satisfied. The Chief was less than happy; still, there was no choice but to accept the fellow. They could not wait for Sigurd to recover. He was reduced to a shivering, sweating wreck, unable to keep so much as a drop of water in his stomach. He would not be ready tomorrow, or the next day, or the day after. And the druid had said the time was now.

As for me, I had seen this swimmer before. Maybe he was one of the Uí Néill's men. Certainly, he wore the symbol of the coiled snake. But it was at Glencarnagh I had observed him, through a slit of doorway, in secret council. I knew he was Eamonn's creature, a spy and a killer.

So, when they sailed away, I had no choice but to follow. It was dusk; it was cold. A rock dove's instinct was to fly for shelter and hide from predators of the night. But I flew out in the fading light, my heart thumping with terror; fear of the waves, of the dark, of the cold; of owls and other hunting creatures; of getting lost, and flying on over open sea until I dropped from exhaustion. I had to go, though I could do nothing to aid them. If this went wrong, it would be my fault. For who had told of this secret venture, save myself?

The five were not alone. Their foray depended on support; the small boat had six rowers, and the swimmers silent on the thwarts, clad all in black, with the tight dark hoods over their faces. Beneath the woollen clothing their bodies had been thickly coated with goose fat, to help keep out the cold. In the silver light of the moon you could scarce tell one from another. Each wore strapped to his back a strange implement fashioned of hard wood, with a sharp iron spike at the end, and a small hook a handspan back from it. Each bore in his belt a sheathed knife; for a warrior, unexpected attack is always a possibility, even on the most meticulously planned of missions. Besides, there were the sea monsters.

The breeze was moderate; they raised the small sail and the curragh slipped over the water as swift and secret as some silent dweller of the deep. I followed, cursing the bird-sight which belonged to a daytime creature; the bird-instinct which made every corner of my small body vibrate with the wrongness of being out here alone at night, and scarce able to see ten paces before me. The moon shone; I followed the curl of foam at the curragh's prow, where it cleaved the swell, and the pale faces of the rowers, who bent to their oars as one. Only the swimmers wore hoods; their mission took them into the very heart of the Britons' territory. If they were seen they would be taken, for so near that shore they would be far outnumbered. It did not require a great stretch of the imagination to work out what would come next, as Northwoods sought to discover their true purpose. Curse Darragh. Why had he come here? Was the boy stupid, that he could not understand how wrong it was for him to pretend to be one of these fierce, ruthless fighters, and not the simple traveling man he was? Didn't he realize they could all be dead by morning?

I was growing weary. The night was very chill; the cold grasp of the ocean seemed not so very far below me, as I flew doggedly on. I could not land on the boat. Darragh would see me. He'd more than enough to worry about, without that. And might not my grandmother be watching, even now? My body ached; I could scarce move my wings up and down. If I fell behind all would be lost. I must keep going. I was not a dove, after all, but a sorcerer's daughter. I must be strong, as my father had taught me.

At a quiet command from Johnny, the men began to take down the sail. The movement of the oars changed. Ahead there was a roaring sound, like a voice of challenge from the ocean itself, a deep, threatening swirl of noise. *Who goes there? Approach me if you dare.*

Not far ahead of us in the moonlight I could at last see land, a rocky island so narrow and high its pinnacle seemed to pierce the dark sky. The water frothed and boiled around its base, white and treacherous. And there were other rocks nearby, their jagged forms near-invisible save where their slick surfaces gleamed in the cold light, or the sea threw itself against them in a wild curtain of spray. The oarsmen held the small boat steady. This maneuver was second nature to them; rehearsed so many times they could surely perform it almost without thought.

"Ready? It's time." Johnny's voice was calm. "Pull hard toward the Needle; remember what you've been told about this current.

Don't let the sight of those reefs tempt you to go out too wide, for then it will grip you and suck you down. This is no practice run, lads; we have one chance. The Worm's Mouth is unforgiving. Use its force to pull you through. We can do this. Summon the strength and the will. And may the hand of the goddess guide us."

Nobody answered, but the oarsmen gripped harder, and seemed to brace themselves, and then, with a suddenness that made my heart lurch, they dug with their blades, hard toward the knife-sharp rocks which encircled the tall, steep island, and the curragh shot forward, faster than human effort could possibly drive it. Some tremendous current had seized it, and now it disappeared into a dark emptiness where the only landmark was the churning, frothing surface of the water; the only signal its endless, hungry roaring. For long moments I fluttered, panicking helplessly, above the raging water. Surely the sea had swallowed them and would spit them out again in a spray of shattered wood and splintered bone. No man could survive such a cauldron of seething power. They were gone. I was alone in the night. Once I had feared to bathe myself in the still waters of a small lake, in case I slipped and went under. Below me the sea boiled and grumbled. Behind me the long empty miles stretched back to the camp; with nothing to follow, how could I find the way? Before me was the impossible channel; the secret way to the Britons' anchorage. No wonder none had thought to use it before. It was impassable; the attempt an act of complete stupidity. But Johnny was not stupid. The Chief was no fool. And somewhere through there was Darragh, who would not be here at all if not for me. Somewhere down there was a man with a sharp knife in his belt, and death on his mind. With a silent plea to Manannán, I gathered my strength and flew after them, straight across the furious maelstrom and on to the open water beyond.

The boat was there, well past the narrow channel, and already dark-hooded men were slipping over the side into the cold embrace of the sea. There were larger islands not far away, looming up like broad-backed ocean creatures. Somewhere, close by in a sheltered bay, the fleet of the Britons lay at anchor. Somewhere on these grassy slopes the fortified encampment of Northwoods housed a strong contingent of battle-hardened warriors. There would be archers in the towers; guards at the perimeters. These swimmers now ventured deep into the heart of forbidden territory. I could not follow them there; I must do nothing to draw attention to them. Besides, I was weary, and could go no further. Reluctantly I fluttered down at last, and settled on the stern of the curragh.

The rowers sat quiet. They held the small craft still on the water.

"You again," whispered Waerfrith, who had the oar closest to me.

"What?" Godric hissed.

"Druid's familiar," Waerfrith said. "Tinker's little friend. Still with us. Good omen. Here's hoping."

"They'll need all the good omens they can get," someone else observed. "Timing's close. In, do the job, out, and in place to hoist the signal at dawn, bring the fleet in. Not much margin for error."

"Johnny doesn't make errors." Godric's tone was confident, though still he kept his voice to a whisper. "They'll be back in time. A triple blow for Northwoods, this'll be; first the fleet, second the attack from this side, against all odds. Third our pact with the Norsemen. They won't expect that."

"Got the Chief to thank for Hakon's support," said Waerfrith. "Just goes to show, calling in old favors can be very handy at times."

"Ssh," said someone else, and they fell silent once more.

Time passed. It was very cold under the spring moon; I ruffled up my feathers, but still the wind bit hard. The young warriors waited uncomplaining. Such privations were part of their long training, the discipline integral to their way of life. I understood that all too well, remembering winter in the Honeycomb. It grew still colder. I thought of those men, in the water. Between the freezing grip of the ocean, and Northwoods' watchful guard, and the traitor in their midst, it seemed to me they had little chance. If the assassin struck, the Chief would die, and my aunt Liadan would lose the man she called her lover, her husband and her soul-friend. It would be she who bore the brunt of Eamonn's terrible vengeance. Perhaps that had been his intention all along; to punish her for not preferring him. And I had helped him.

I waited, trembling, as the night wore on. There would be no rest for these men. When the dawn broke, the fleet of the Irish would sail in, and they would descend with the others on the Islands, there to strike with arrow, and cleave with axe, and slash with sword, until the

Britons fell to their knees in surrender or were slain every one. It was a very long night, and it would be a longer day.

At last the moonlight faded and the sky began to brighten to the dull gray that presages dawn. These men would not express doubt. Johnny was their leader, and the child of the prophecy. And everyone knew the Chief's reputation. He had never failed in a mission, no matter how difficult. They would return. They must return. So, nobody said, *Where are they* or, *It's getting late*. Indeed, nobody said a word, but as the sea's surface changed from an ink-dark blanket to a rippling expanse of deepest greens, and gulls began to circle over the curragh, I saw a grimness in the men's eyes and a set about their jaws that alarmed me. Who knew better than I what might have delayed the swimmers? Still perched in the stern of the boat, and trembling with fear and cold, I watched the shapes of the larger islands become slowly clearer as the sky lightened, and doubted I would have the strength to fly when I must.

Perhaps my bird-sight was an asset after all. I saw them first, no more than dots in the water, making their way toward us in the rise and fall of the swell. I stretched my cramped wings, and moved along the rim of the curragh, and I tried to draw the men's attention, but a dove's voice is not made for loud alarms, for calls to action. Soon enough they sighted the group of swimmers, and seized oars to edge the curragh closer, for the return was almost too late; they must sail back to the point where they would be visible to the waiting fleet, and raise the signal to advance: the red banner of action. If they delayed too long, and Northwoods realized what was happening, it would give him the chance to mount a solid defense, boats or no boats. That was not part of the plan.

"There's but three of them," Godric muttered as the craft drew closer. "Three—no, four—but—"

"Something's amiss," Waerfrith said, and gave the signal to hold oars balanced, so the craft lay still in the water. The swimming men were alongside now; I could hear the labored rasp of their breathing, and see their shadowy eyes through the holes of their close-fitting hoods. I could see, too, that of the four men who floated there in the chill tide, there was one who lay limp and helpless, held up only by the strong grip of another around his chest; and I could see the red ribbon of blood which streamed forth, bright as spring poppies on the dark surface of the water.

"Quick," said a voice. "He's hurt. Get him aboard." That was Gareth, who swam alongside, who now reached to push the injured man upward as Godric and Waerfrith hauled him into the curragh. The black-clad form sprawled across the benches where they laid him; Waerfrith peeled back the mask with cautious fingers, to reveal the ash-white features and flaxen hair of Eamonn's man. The clear light of dawn played on his staring blue eyes, and his bloodless lips, and the gleaming hilt of the dagger which had been driven deep into his chest.

"This man's not hurt, he's dead," said Godric, rolling the fellow off the bench and into the bottom of the curragh, out of the way. "Get the rest of them up quick; it's close to sunrise."

First came Gareth, now ominously silent. Then a taller, thinner man. I breathed a prayer of thanks to the goddess, though doubtless it was not out of any consideration for me that she had preserved Darragh's life thus far. Then the last man, shortish, well-built. They stripped off their hoods. Godric passed around a metal flask, and all three drank, and gasped, and shuddered. The silence was palpable.

"Where's Johnny?" somebody said eventually, asking the question nobody had been quite prepared to put into words.

"Lost," said Gareth heavily. He took another mouthful of the drink, and wiped his hand across his lips.

"Lost? What do you mean, lost? He can't be." Godric was incredulous.

Gareth glanced at the Chief, who sat beside him on the bench, quite silent. "Drowned," he said. "We don't know what happened. The task is done; each of us crippled one ship as we planned. But when we assembled again to make the swim back, there were only the three of us. We searched, though time was short and the risk of discovery high. We found Felim here floating on the tide, with a knife in his chest; but there was no sign of Johnny."

My heart turned cold; the struggle was over. She had won. My grandmother had won, almost by accident, before ever I had the chance to stand against her. She had not achieved the victory by cleverness or stealth or cunning use of magical craft. She had triumphed simply because Eamonn's assassin had made an error; had mistaken one man for another, out there in the dark. Who knew how long the two of them had wrestled together in the water before one let go, the dagger in his breast, the lifeblood flowing swift, and the other drifted away on the tide, perhaps strangled, perhaps drowned, perhaps himself the victim of a none-too-subtle knife thrust?

"We must make sail." The Chief spoke now, his voice constrained, as if he exercised the tightest of controls. "The longships will be waiting. We must not delay the attack, or the element of surprise will be lost."

"But, Chief!" Godric's tone was of complete outrage. "We can't just leave him there!"

Bran regarded him levelly. "He is lost," he said, and despite his best efforts, his voice shook. "Believe me, we searched; we hunted until we had barely time to reach you before dawn. He is drowned, and swept away. There is some work of treachery here; but it seems the only witness is silent." He glanced down at the dead man sprawled at his feet.

"How can we go without Johnny?" one of the men asked blankly. "How can the battle be won without the child of the prophecy?"

There was a silence.

"That's Johnny's knife," said Waerfrith, eyeing the dead man. "I'd know it anywhere. I could hazard a guess at what happened. See, the man's own dagger sheath is empty."

"The truth will be discovered; the guilty punished." The Chief's tone was again controlled; that of a seasoned battle-leader. "For now, we must make a swift decision. Hoist the sail; whatever choice we make, we must be away from here without delay. We cannot wait, hoping for miracles."

I thought for a moment the men would not obey. They stared back across the empty water, faces pale with shock. This was not just the loss of their leader, it was the snatching away of their very purpose. Still, they were professionals. The sail was raised, the oars taken, and the curragh began to move rapidly away from the land.

"Never have got this fellow back aboard, save for Darragh here," said Gareth. "Towed him all the way. Thought he might have had a chance."

"Scarce worth the bother," muttered Waerfrith. "Man's stone dead. The Uí Néill will be answering a question or two before the day's over."

Darragh himself sat silent. Perhaps he was exhausted from the night's swim, perhaps shocked by his first sight of treachery and loss. I stayed behind him, out of his view. Our small craft slid through the waves, swift as a gull's flight, and soon enough there was an order to heave to and wait.

"This is the point," Waerfrith said. "From here we can be seen by the leading longship; the signal must be given. Red to advance; white if we want them to hold, and delay until another day."

There was silence.

"The fleet is sunk. The mission is accomplished. We must raise the red banner," Gareth said. I thought I saw tears glinting on his broad cheeks.

"How can we?" snapped Godric, voice shaking with rage. "Our leader is lost. The child of the prophecy is dead. No wonder the druid didn't want to tell us what the divination showed. We cannot win this battle without Johnny."

"He's right," said Waerfrith heavily. "The prophecy makes that clear. Go in without him, and we'll like as not all be slaughtered. The whole thing depends on Johnny. Without his leadership there can be no victory."

"Seems to me," all turned in surprise as Darragh spoke up quietly, his tone calm, "that we might as well go on with it. We've fine ships, good men, strong allies behind us. We've sunk the Briton's fleet, so he starts at a disadvantage. And there's something even more important. What would Johnny want us to do? Would he want his men to retreat for fear of failure, or show their courage and put up a good fight for the things he cared about?" He paused. "I know I'm no warrior, but that seems to me plain common sense."

Oh, no, I thought. Not common sense but foolish courage. You will die; you will all die. Go home. Save yourselves at least, since it seems there is nothing else to be saved here.

But Gareth looked at Darragh in surprise, and gave a nod; Waerfrith scratched his chin. Godric was still hostile; it was his grief, perhaps, that fueled his anger now.

"We have no leader," he said grimly. "How can we raise this banner and call forward the forces of the allies when they have lost their rallying point, their very reason for going on? The whole campaign would be a lie."

"I will lead." The Chief spoke very quietly, but there was a core of iron in his voice.

"You, my lord?" Godric raised his brows. "Fine champion you may be, but you are still a Briton. Did you not swear you would remain apart from this confrontation, for the sake of preserving your truce with Northwoods? How can you lead us?"

Bran turned his cool gray eyes on the young warrior. "My son is lost," he said. "I will lead."

Godric fell silent. Gareth drew a deep breath, and squared his shoulders. "Right, men," he said firmly, with the marks of his tears still stark on his amiable features. "We do this for Johnny. If he cannot wield a sword today, we use our own blades to honor him. If he cannot fulfill the prophecy, we can at least ensure the men of Erin do not go down without a good fight. We may yet triumph." He glanced at the Chief.

"Well spoken, lad." Bran gazed ahead toward the third island, the tall, stark pinnacle of rock whose treacherous base concealed the secret channel, the place of the Worm's Mouth.

"Hoist the red banner," he commanded. "This is the dawn of our great endeavor. Tonight we sleep the sweet sleep of victory; or the long, dark sleep of death."

Chapter Fifteen

It was a sight to stir the blood; the stuff of the old tales. They raised the scrap of scarlet cloth to the masthead and, as the first rays of the sun spread out across the water, lighting the high, rocky tower of the Needle to a bright glowing gold, Sevenwaters' fleet emerged from the impossible channel: three great longships balanced with immense skill against the fierce tug of the maelstrom, their prows high and proud in the dawn light; and after them the smaller craft, curragh of wattle and tarred skin, squat fishing boat blunt and practical, each with its complement of fighting men. Once they were clear of the whirlpool's perilous currents, the ships parted. One of the Viking vessels made for the smaller island with two lesser craft in its wake, while the main part of the fleet made direct for the larger mass of land, where the ships of the Britons now lay beneath the sea; where my cousin's body now drifted, somewhere, in the arms of Manannán mac Lir. Our own curragh turned and followed. From a place of concealment in the bows, Godric and Waerfrith now took out weapons, sword and dagger, axe and knife, and leather helms; every man must go prepared to play his part, even those who had spent the night in the water. For them, there was dry clothing; a man could not fight if he was numb with cold. I watched Darragh fitting a helm over his dark hair and buckling on a sword belt, and then I spread my wings and flew, for the heart of a battle is no place for a woman, and no place at all for a bird no bigger than a man's clenched fist.

I summoned the strength of my true self, and flew to Greater

Island, heedless now of sea-eagle, goshawk or human predator, for it seemed to me this was beyond fear, beyond grief, that the great battle should go ahead, the brave banner of Sevenwaters be raised, when the venture was doomed before ever it began. If the child of the prophecy was slain, the long goal of the Fair Folk could never be achieved. The Islands would be lost; the old ways would be forgotten. A prophecy was a prophecy. The men would go in and die, and all the time the lady Oonagh would be laughing, laughing with scorn that the blood of these strong young warriors was spilled to no purpose at all. I could not believe, still, that she had won so easily. And yet I must believe it. With my own incautious telling of a secret, I had ensured that she would win. It was wrong. It must be wrong. Surely it had not all been for nothing?

The old tales tell of great battles: the exploits of heroes such as Cú Chulainn; the warlike deeds of Fionn mac Cumhaill and his outlaw band. They tell of strength and courage, of triumph and reward. They speak of the routing of enemies. But they do not tell of the sights I saw that day, as I moved across the low grassy hills of Greater Island. I saw the bright light of commitment in a young warrior's eyes change to stark terror the instant before his opponent's axe struck the head from his shoulders. I saw Snake, a hardened fighter if ever there was one, weeping as he stood over the form of young Mikka lying on a red-stained ground with the blood pulsing from his severed arm; I heard the maimed youth calling for his mother in the voice of a small child suddenly gripped by a nightmare. Snake's face was pinched and old as he muttered, "Rest now, son; you fought bravely," and used his knife to grant Mikka the gift of a dreamless sleep. The suddenness of it stopped my heart. No story can describe the look in such a man's eyes as he rises and turns straight back into the fray, bloodied blade in hand. As for Johnny's men, they wielded their weapons even as Bran of Harrowfield did: as if they did not care if they lived or died. Such a force is fearsome indeed, and the Britons fell back before the unearthly light in these warriors' eyes.

I lost sight of Darragh. He was somewhere out there in the midst of it, but the tunics of the opposing armies were stained with earth and blood, and all was confusion. The forces of Sevenwaters had secured the anchorage and the western cove; here Gull could be seen moving about giving sharp orders; here the limp forms of the dead and the tormented ones of the injured were laid out in what little shelter could be found. Not all could be brought back here. There were many slain; by afternoon it seemed each fold of the land was studded with the broken bodies of Briton and Irishman alike, and the waters around the island ran red with the mingled blood of these old foes. Among the injured moved the archdruid and his brother, the man with the swan's wing. Perhaps they could do little but murmur a quiet word or two; perhaps they could only hold a man's hand as he screamed and writhed there on the ground, beyond help of surgeon or healer, waiting only for the goddess to be merciful and grant him his final release. I had been shocked to see what Snake did, earlier. Now I understood it had been an act of great compassion.

The day wore on, and it was close to dusk. There had been talk of victory before nightfall. But it was clear there was no victory, not yet. The Britons were well armed, and for all the element of surprise it seemed they had soon rallied and put up an orderly and disciplined defense. And they had the advantage of possession. On the highest point of Greater Island there was a fort, and it was to this place of safety they withdrew their forces as the day drew to a close. Behind it, sheer cliffs fell to the sea; on the landward side it was protected by a deep ditch, within which a high earthen rampart shielded their dwellings, their armory and storage huts. In the center was a sturdy stone tower, built round and tall. From such a place a strong defense could be maintained. Still, they could not last there forever. The Uí Néill would by now have vanquished the establishment on Little Island, for they far outnumbered the British forces there. Perhaps all Sean of Sevenwaters had to do was wait.

As dusk fell each army retreated to its rallying point. A strange sort of quiet spread over the land as the light faded; a kind of understanding, as if each side recognized the losses of the other. Indeed, in pockets of the land, where the dead lay limp and broken like discarded playthings, small groups of men with lanterns could be seen stooping to gather up their slain, and if a grizzled warrior from Northwoods happened to glance across, and see a pale-faced Ulsterman not so far off, about the same grim task, he simply averted his gaze and got on with what had to be done. For all the deceptive peace of the evening, it was acknowledged that at dawn both sides would pick up their weapons, and venture forth, and start the killing again.

That night I flew over two camps, and learned that a Briton and an Irishman shed the same blood, and feel the same grief. The day had shown me that such challenges, such impossible choices bring out what is finest and bravest in a man. They let his courage shine forth. At times of conflict a plain man can become a hero. But in every battle there is a loser, and the loser, too, may be a man of bravery and endurance, of steadfast valor and greatness of heart. The tales do not tell of the blood and sacrifice; of the heartache and waste.

Down by the shore were little fires, and around each, silent men gathered, seeking in this reflection of the hearth's warmth some reminder of home and loved ones, now far away. They had had the best of it today, but their losses were terrible, and none worse than the loss of him who had symbolized their certain triumph: the child of the prophecy. Nobody said it, but I thought all knew it in their hearts; without Johnny, there could be no true victory. Still they would go on: for Sean, for Sevenwaters, for their own battle-leader, whether it be Bran of Harrowfield, strangely present in their midst and bearing arms against his own people, or the high-born chieftains of the Uí Néill. They sat quiet around their fires, and gazed into the flames. Not far off, in the shelter of quickly improvised tents, men lay wounded and dying. Some were already shrouded for burial; if the battle was over soon, they might be conveyed home and laid to rest with a mother's tears, a sweetheart's lament. Amongst the fallen were three of Johnny's brave young warriors. Mikka lay there, helped to a quick end by Snake's merciful knife. Beside him lay the two friends, Waerfrith and Godric. The men told a tale that made my heart sore: how Waerfrith was wounded, an arrow taking him in the belly, and how Godric bore his comrade on his back, all the way down from the northern ridge, through the thick of the battle. When they were nearly at the cove, and safety, a British warrior stepped out in challenge. Holding his friend's unconscious weight, Godric was too slow to dodge, too burdened to flee; and he would not drop the injured man to save himself. The Briton's sword took him in the chest; and as he lay bleeding, he lived long enough to see the enemy draw the blade with casual efficiency across the neck of the man he had carried. So the two of them died together; forever they would be young and laughing, bright-eyed and fearless. Today these two had fallen, and many another besides. Tomorrow it might be Gareth or Corentin. It might be Darragh. Generations of men had been slain for these islands; the brothers of Finbar and Conor, the brothers of their father, who, strangely, had been my own grandfather. These were my people; but so were the others, for my lineage was that of Harrowfield as well as Sevenwaters, and Harrowfield was kin to Northwoods. I flew through the night, heedless of danger, and alighted on the wall of the British fortress. And there, not far away, perched a great dark bird, its eyes fixed on me, fierce and bright.

I discovered I was no longer afraid of Fiacha. Fear seemed suddenly a waste of effort. My grandmother had won; I was powerless now. Surely there was no more to do but watch, and grieve, and wonder only that the lady Oonagh had not come to gloat, now that the final victory was hers. So I sat quietly by the raven on the wall, looking down into Northwoods's encampment. I heard them talking; I saw them grieving. There were many dead, and even more wounded. And they had another problem. In this outpost, long thought safe, several men had wives and children with them, a whole small settlement. Now their leaders, gray-faced, stood around their fire debating a terrible choice. If the savages of Erin should triumph, and breach their fortress walls, what of the women? There would come a point, maybe tomorrow, when they must decide whether to put their own wives to the sword, or leave them to the mercy of the invader. Best, perhaps, to let the women go armed themselves, and trust each had the will to plunge a dagger in her own breast, or her child's, before they could fall victim to the horror of rape, or the brutality of torture and slavery. They spoke of my uncle's men as of monsters. I thought of those bright young warriors, of Johnny and his companions. I thought of kindly, capable Sean of Sevenwaters, of courteous, smiling Gull, and of the Chief, a hard man maybe, but in every choice a fair one. This was all wrong; this long feud had bred a terror based on ignorance and misunderstanding. Did not these grim-faced Britons comprehend that all Sevenwaters wanted was for the Islands to be left alone? Did none of them understand what it had been all about?

I would have flown away, thinking to find some place of shelter and keep sleepless vigil until a blood-red dawn, but Fiacha's gaze was intense. Something in his manner held me where I was, looking down on Edwin of Northwoods, and a broad-shouldered young man who seemed to be his son, and the four or five others with them. One was a Christian priest, tonsured and robed, a cross about his neck. One was old, gray-bearded, stooped; too ancient for such a place of danger. It seemed they had made their decision. The women would remain in the tower with Brother Jerome. They would be given knives. When the time came they would make their own choice.

"Now, to what rest we can find," Edwin of Northwoods said gravely. "Tomorrow we fight on. We fight until the last man falls. I will not see my name set down as the coward who let the islands go. Pray, friends, that the Lord will be with us. Pray for a miracle."

At that moment there was a sudden flare of light at the far side of the enclosure, close by the around tower which was their last bastion of defense, and a small group of men came into view. One bore a flaming torch; two held between them a young warrior clad all in black, a man whose skin showed chalk-white in the torchlight, whose face was bruised and swollen, whose eyes glowed with defiance as they brought him forward to stand before Edwin of Northwoods. The British leader stared at the captive; stared into the fierce gray eyes, whose youthful intensity was heightened by the delicate pattern marked on the skin of brow and cheek, on the left side; the sign of the raven.

"Look what the tide washed up, my lord," someone said.

"Perhaps," Edwin said softly, "our miracle is here. With such a prisoner, who knows what bargain may be struck?" He turned to his captains. "You know who he is?"

There was a murmur of acknowledgment. They might not have seen the man before, but it seemed he was well enough known by description.

Johnny spoke. His voice was very soft; I could barely make out the words. His clothing was dripping wet, his flesh starkly pale. I wondered how long he had been in the water, before the sea cast him up into the hands of his enemies.

"They will not deal," he said. "My uncle will not compromise the mission for my life, or my safety. This is not our way."

"You think not," said Edwin quietly. "Perhaps Sean of Sevenwaters will not do so; but what about your father?"

Johnny was silent; he could not quite conceal the shock in his eyes.

"Oh, yes," said Edwin. "He fights there among the others; he wields the sword against his own countrymen. Will he see his son perish before his eyes for the sake of a principle, do you think?"

"He will not make bargains with you; not for me, not for anyone."

Edwin folded his arms. "We'll put that to the test in due course. I think you may be surprised." He turned to the men who held Johnny. "Lock him up for the night. Set a strong guard. Give the fellow a blanket, he's wet through."

"He's hurt, my lord," said someone hesitantly. "Bleeding from a flesh wound; broken a rib or two as well. And he's half-drowned. A wonder he survived so long; cast up on the rocks, from the looks of it, and somehow crawled to safety. Found him by accident."

"Will he die before morning?"

"No, my lord."

"Very well then. As I said, give him a blanket, and lock him up. Tomorrow is a new day."

I watched them drag the captive away; and I watched as Edwin and his men departed to rest, their faces alight with a fresh hope. I looked at Fiacha, and he looked at me. Then he spread his wings and flew away from the island, swift and straight, making a path southwestward in the darkness. I had never liked his way of doing things.

I came very close to mindless panic that night. Johnny was alive; against all odds, the child of the prophecy had survived. That made my heart thump with joy; it awoke new hope in me. And with that hope came the terror. After all, it was not yet finished. I had a chance to win, to make it all right again. But before it was ended, I knew she would come, and I must face her and hope I would be strong enough. The final battle, the only one that counted, was still before me. Fiacha was gone; my Otherworld friends seemed to have deserted me. I would not seek out Finbar. I would not reveal myself to Conor, or to my uncle Sean. There would be no more victims scattered by the wayside. I would bring my grandmother's wrath down on nobody but myself. I must wait until it was light, and change my form, and hope to regain my strength again quickly. For there was no doubt in me that I would not defeat the lady Oonagh without using every scrap of craft, every morsel of will, every single element of control my father had taught me.

Fire child I might be, but my upbringing had ensured I was a creature of cliffs and rocks, of caves and secret places, and it was to such a wild corner of the land that I retreated to seek a place for changing. I had not forgotten last time, and the crippling weakness which had followed the transformation. I must be out of sight, out of the path of battle, and pray that I regained my strength before my grandmother realized the end was almost upon us, and hastened to witness her final victory. Then I would—I would—I was not sure exactly what I would do, but I knew I must do my utmost to turn the tide of things before she noticed and came rushing to force me to her will. When she came, I must stand against her and hope some aid would be forthcoming, whether from human world or Otherworld. Increasingly, as neither Fair Folk nor Fomhóire showed themselves, it seemed I might have to do this all by myself. I must trust that when the time came, my path would be clear to me. Focus. That was what my father would have said. Make your mind empty, your spirit receptive. Then you will find the answers.

There was a place on the south coast of Greater Island, not far from the British fortress, where the land rose in sheer cliffs from the sea, stark and treacherous. Earlier in the day I had seen a refuge here as I flew overhead. A little way down from the top, just for a short length of the cliff, there was a narrow ledge, and this held indented hollows like shallow caves, where clinging creepers softened the rock walls and the pebbly ground allowed a space just wide enough for a man or woman to sit in relative safety, looking out over the wide expanse of water below and beyond. There were few places of concealment on this featureless island, but this was one, and I chose it as my place of transformation because of that. Here I could wait out the time of weakness if I must; here I could make some decision about what to do, and when, and how. One thing was certain: nobody must see me in my true form until the moment when I stepped forth and played my part in the end of things. Act too early, and all that would happen was my uncle Sean sending me back to the boats with orders to keep out of harm's way. Once I was a girl again I could not move about freely. There was indeed but a single chance to make things right.

It all hinged on Johnny. He was a captive; he was crucial to the outcome. Northwoods would use him to try for a bargain, and probably as soon as possible, before more men were lost. Soon after dawn, I thought. What would the deal be? Johnny's life in return for an Irish retreat? If that were so, my uncle's forces had quite a dilemma before them. They knew they could not win the battle without the child of the prophecy. To sacrifice him was to admit defeat, and fight on with only death ahead. The prophecy was quite clear about it. But I did not think they would be prepared to give up the struggle in order to save him. As Johnny had said, that was not their way. I had seen the light in their eyes as they charged into battle; the look on their grim faces as they followed the banner of Sevenwaters into the fray, screaming their leader's name. Somehow, retreat did not seem an option.

I must act early, then, before my grandmother saw, and knew, how easy it might be for her to win. The child of the prophecy was a prisoner; how simple for me to end his life and their hopes in one swift, spectacular act of magic. How simple to take the easier way, and let Northwoods do the job for me. For she had been quite right; all centered on Johnny. I had better work the charm now, in the dark, here in this small depression in the rocks with the sea frothing in and out far below. I had better move in closer to the cliff face, just in case. There would be time, surely; time to recover myself and make my way out to the center of things by dawn. I moved cautiously along the narrow ledge on my little bird-feet, seeking the place where the crevices were deepest and afforded best shelter. I took one step, two steps, and a hand came out of the darkness to close around me. My heart hammered with fright, and I let out a strangled chirrup.

"Ah, now, no need for that." The voice was soft; this was the tone that had so often soothed frightened creatures. "Hush, now. See, I'll let you go, if that's what you want. I didn't mean to scare you. Found the same hiding place, didn't we? Fine spot this, good for time on your own, or with a friend. Quite like Kerry, with the sea and the sky, this is." Darragh withdrew his hand slowly and settled back, cross-legged on the rock shelf. It was not so surprising, perhaps, that each of us had sought out this corner of the land which was so vivid a reminder of the carefree summers we had spent as children. In just such a refuge we had once whispered our deepest secrets.

I knew I should go and seek some other place for my purpose. The last thing I wanted was for the lady Oonagh's attention to be drawn to Darragh. Why else had I tried so hard to send him away, time after time? But I could not make myself move. Here in the dark, perched high up above the treacherous sea, with him by me, at last I felt safe.

"Curly?" Darragh said quietly. I could not answer, but I settled on the rocks near where he sat. "I want to tell you something," he went on, and I could see, in the darkness, that he was twisting his hands together, and frowning. "I saw some terrible things out there. I suppose you saw them too. Things I couldn't have imagined in my worst nightmare. And I did some things I'm not proud of. Proved I could be a fighter maybe; but it doesn't feel right to shed a fellow's blood, just because he's a different kind." He looked down at his hands. "I always thought we'd go home, you know, go back to Kerry, when this was all over. I thought I just had to wait, and stay by you, and hold on. But—but this is different, it's not what I expected at all. In the morning there'll be more killing, and I'll go out and join in because that's what I'm here for. And I have a feeling that this time there might be no tomorrow, Curly. I don't like to ask you this, but I'm going to ask it anyway, because it seems to me there's nothing more to lose. If I have to die, if that's the way of it, I'd—I'd dearly love to see you one last time. I mean, see you as yourself, as a girl. Say goodbye properly. There's things I'd like to tell you; things I can only say if—but I shouldn't ask. It wouldn't be safe for you, I can see that. I don't want you risking yourself."

This had always been my weakness, and my folly. I had tried to fight it, but now I could no more resist the gentle, hesitant coaxing of his voice than could the wild white pony he had brought down from the hills. There was a longing in me to feel his touch, to comfort him with mine, to be by him once more in silent companionship, as so many years ago. I ruffled my feathers, and in my mind I spoke the charm of transformation, and changed.

I heard Darragh's exclamation of shock, and felt his hands come out toward me as he rose quickly to his feet. I gasped, "Don't tell any-one—don't tell them where I am—promise—" and then his face swam before me, and the stars above us began to spin in crazy circles. I buckled at the knees and fell into a dead faint.

It was an unconsciousness deeper than an abyss; a darkness devoid of dreams. I did not come to myself until dawn was already touching the sky with its first trace of gold. I opened my eyes to that; I felt the bone-deep weariness that filled my whole body, as if I myself had fought a long battle, and I knew without looking that I lay there with my head pillowed on Darragh's lap, and his hand stroking my hair. For a long moment I did not move, and then I forced myself to sit up, and then to stand, reaching out to clutch at the strands of creeper as my vision blurred and my head reeled with dizziness. Darragh was on his feet in an instant, his two hands firm on my arms, steadying me. The goddess aid me, I could hardly keep upright, I could barely summon a sensible thought, let alone be ready to perform some great feat of magic. At this rate I would be no use to anyone. And it was already day.

"Whoa—steady—take it slowly," Darragh said, supporting me with a strong grip. He was scowling; his dark eyes were deadly serious as he scrutinized my face. "I'm a fool," he said flatly. "I shouldn't have promised. You're sick, Fainne, you need help. Let me fetch someone—let me tell them—"

"No!" I summoned enough strength to snap back, terror giving a sharp edge to my voice. "No, you mustn't! I must be left alone to do this—" my words trailed off as a wave of nausea swept through me, followed by a strong desire to weep. This would not do, it would not do at all. Control. Strength. I was a sorcerer's daughter, with a mission.

"Fainne—" Darragh began.

"No," I said, summoning a coldness into my tone with great effort. "Don't say it. Don't say anything. Just go, and leave me. I'll be fine. I can look after myself. Go on now, Darragh. I hear men abroad. There's a battle to be fought."

Darragh stared at me. "That's what you want, is it? For me to be out there running fellows through with a sword, and leaving you on your own, up on a cliff, hardly able to stand up by yourself, miles from home with nobody to look after you? Is that it? That's not what you said before."

But he had taken his hands away. I held myself upright by clutching at the creepers with my two fists, and leaning back against the rocks. Where were the Fomhóire when I needed them?

"Please go," I said in a tight little voice. "There isn't much time. Please do this for me." *Oh, let him go, let him go quickly, before this became just too hard.*

There was another small silence.

"Right," he said. "Right. I'll say goodbye then." But he did not step away. Instead he put his arms around me, with never a by-your-leave, and held me close, and I felt his fingers in my hair and his warmth against me, and in an instant everything changed; for there was a longing in me, a yearning for him that was in every part of my body. I could not help it, I clung to him, and he kissed me, and for a long moment I forgot Grandmother, I forgot everything in the sweetness of it.

"Ah, Curly," muttered Darragh, his hand stroking the back of my neck, beneath the heavy fall of my hair. "I'm sorry. I'm sorry."

"Sorry?" I breathed. "What have you to be sorry for?"

"I wanted so much to keep you safe. I did my best. I'm sorry things didn't come out different for the two of us. I wish I could have been good enough for you."

For a moment his arms tightened around me, and I felt his heart hammering against my breast. I opened my mouth to tell him he had got it all wrong; that it was I who was not good enough, and never could be. But before I could say a word he stepped away from me, and I saw what he held in his hand.

At first I could not believe it. The realization was like a cold knife in the heart. I stared and blinked. I put my fingers up to the back of my neck, and as my skin began to crawl with fear, I fumbled inside my gown and knew I had been betrayed by my dearest of friends.

"Give it back!" I hissed, and saw his face go white, and his jaw clench. "Darragh! Give it to me!"

Darragh said nothing, but he took a little step away, still clutching in his long brown fingers the bronze amulet and the strong, unbreakable cord that had held it.

"Give it to me! How could you! How could you touch me like that, and say those things, when all the time it was just so that you could—Darragh, you must give it back! You don't know what you're doing!"

I moved closer and tried to snatch it from him, but he was too quick; and besides, he was far stronger than I. He always had been.

"It's for the best," he said.

"How can you say that? You know nothing! How could you understand? Oh, quickly, quickly, give it back! You will bring a curse on all of us!"

But Darragh stood there stubbornly with his hands behind his back, looking at me with eyes that seemed full of sorrow.

"You're wrong, Curly. They all say so. Lord Sean. Lady Liadan. Johnny, and the Chief. This thing's evil. It's making you crazy; it's making you lose your way. That's why—"

"That's why what?" I spat, distraught that some misguided conspiracy had snatched away my chance to save them all. "You're a pack of fools, and time's running out. Don't you understand, as soon as I take it off she knows, and she comes to find me, and I don't have my strength back yet—oh, please—"

Above us, cloud was starting to roll in, strange, coiling swathes of it, slate-gray, thick as a woollen cloak, and with it a chill wind. Above us, gulls screamed a warning. I thought I could hear a voice, familiar though still distant, a voice that turned my heart to ice. *Fainne. Fainne, where are you?*

She was coming. She was coming already, and driving wind and cloud before her. She was coming, and she would kill and maim until she forced me to do her will. I summoned up the words of a charm to force Darragh to let go; to make his hand yield up its treasure. I muttered the words and fought to find the will. But there was nothing. My mind was empty, drained; my spirit hopelessly depleted by the transformation. There was not the smallest scrap of craft left in me.

Darragh was backing away along the ledge; he was obeying my orders, and leaving. Not far off, I could hear men's voices, and the clash of metal.

"Please, Darragh," I whispered, using the one weapon left to me, and I stepped toward him and put my hand up to touch his cheek.

"Don't," he said tightly. "Save those tricks for your fine chieftains. Don't try them on me. If you can't touch me honestly, and say what's in your heart, then best do nothing at all." His tone was fierce, almost angry; now I felt his tears falling onto my fingers where they lay against his face. I was frozen; I could not move, though I heard the voice of the sorceress, somewhere out over the ocean. *Do you dare disobey me, girl? Do you dare flout me now, at the last?*

I opened my mouth to say something, anything, and then I looked into his eyes and my words halted. In that moment, I saw how he had changed; how the carefree lad with the crooked grin and the whole world of opportunities in front of him had become pale and weary, with eyes shadowed and somber as if he bore a weight of anxious cares on his thin shoulders. I saw what I had done to him.

"Curly?" he said very softly.

I stared at him, hoping beyond hope that he would see sense, and give back the amulet, now, quickly; give it back and save himself.

"Maybe I did this because they bid me," he said. "But that was only part of it. I did it for you. It's what I'm bound to do."

"Bound?" I whispered, as the wind rose and streamed across the sea, and the air came alive with salt spray and the shaken cries of birds. "How, bound?"

He looked into my eyes, and shook his head slowly, as if in disbelief. "Bound to keep you safe. Safe from those who would harm you, and safe from yourself. Bound by love, Curly."

And before I could move, before I could stop him, he raised his arm and threw the amulet, threw it high into the wild air, and I saw the glint of it in the low sunlight as it spun up and out above the cliff face, as it fell away down, far, far down to the hungry ocean rolling in below. My heart stood still with terror. A voice was saying, "No, oh no, oh no," over and over. I buried my face in my hands and registered, dimly, that the voice was my own.

"Curly?" Darragh's voice was gentler now, the anger gone. I could not find it in me to respond. If this was love, then I had been right all along; love was only confusion and pain.

"I have to go now," he said. "You're right, there's a battle to be fought. I can't stand by and not help them; not while I wear Johnny's colors."

"Don't—" I began, my hands stretching out before me like a blind woman's.

"Ssh," Darragh said, and he reached out to touch my hair, to tuck back a stray curl. "No more." Then he bent to give me a kiss, a little kiss on the cheek such as a boy might give a girl when the two of them are too young and too shy to put what they feel into words. I closed my eyes, but I could not shut out the sound of my grandmother's voice.

"Goodbye, Curly," said Darragh. "Keep out of trouble, now."

I waited for the next part, but the silence drew out, and when I opened my eyes again, he was gone.

As if I were a child playing a game, I made myself count up to one hundred, slowly. I waited until he would be well out of sight before I made my stumbling, uneven way along the ledge and up over the rocks to open ground. Out in the field of battle, he could take his chance with the others. There, he might be one of the lucky ones and escape with his life. With me by his side he was surely doomed.

The sky was alive with angry cloud, and the air with salt spray whipped high. The few low shrubs which clung to the windswept landscape now bent in surrender; a storm was coming, a storm whose ferocity was born of a sorceress's fury. There was no time, no time for anything. What could I do? She was coming, and I had no weapons for the battle, none save my own weary body and wretched, confused mind; none save my flawed spirit and my treacherous heart which felt, now, as if it were being ripped apart. I stood teetering on the cliff's edge as the wind whipped my hair forward like a banner. Think, Fainne. Focus. The red banner of victory. I carried my own. I did not wear the emblem of Sevenwaters, but I bore my own colors, in a shawl as dazzling and lovely, as full of life and wonderment as the bounty of the earth itself. Perhaps my own spirit was damaged, my heart cracked in pieces, so that I could never be fine and good; so that I could never say what I felt, however much I wanted to. But Darragh's spirit shone bright; his heart was the truest and best in all of Erin. While I wore his gift, a gift of love, I could move forward. And I had Riona, still tucked in my belt, her pink skirts crumpled, her dark eyes reflective. Riona was family; she reminded me of whose daughter I really was. Right, then. Forget the aching limbs, the fuzzy head, the eyes full of unshed tears. Forget the limp and the weariness, and just get on with it. I began to walk, following the sound of voices from over the small rise ahead of me. There was no point in trying to find cover. The landscape was almost bare of features. As soon as I reached the top of that hill, they would see me.

"Not that way, stupid."

There was a flutter of wings, and a slight disturbance in the fabric of things. There was a cracking of the earth, and a brief rumbling sound. In front of me, now, there was a medium-sized boulder which had not been there before, and by it an owl-like creature with snub nose and bright red boots.

"Don't just walk out there," the owl-creature admonished. "Raw courage is all very well, but you need to be canny with it."

"What else can I do?" I asked weakly, irritation warring with profound relief that help had come at last. "The sorceress is on her way; I can feel it. I must act now. And there are no hiding places here. What can I do but walk out, and tell them—tell them—"

The rock-being gave a gravelly sort of cough, and was silent. The owl-creature raised its bushy brows.

"Tell them what? That you think they should pack up and go home? Come on now, use your head. Use your training. We can help you. We can provide cover; we've a talent for that, for merging, so to speak. But the solution's in your hands, fire child, not ours. The last little piece of the puzzle, that's what you have to work out for yourself, and then it's yours. Didn't your father teach you to find answers? This one's right in your grasp; but you must discover it before the lady Oonagh does, or we're all gone."

I scowled in exasperation. "It's not some kind of stupid game! Doesn't everything depend on this? The future of the Islands, the future of Fair Folk and Fomhóire and human folk alike? How can it all hinge on some—some riddle? Why don't you just tell me the answer, curse you?"

There was a little silence.

"A prophecy's a prophecy," observed the rock-being eventually. "That's just the thing. Unfortunately, it does all depend on you. We'll help you all we can. But we can't tell you. This one's for human folk to settle. That's why the Fair Folk are standing back, even now. Itching to step in and do something, all of them. But they can't. As I said, a prophecy's a prophecy."

It seemed to me there was a crying, a screaming in the air around us, and it was not the voices of gulls, but a terrible sound of rage, a searching, eldritch sound that set my teeth on edge. *Where are you? Do not think to thwart me. Act against my will, and I will destroy you.* Last time it had taken from morning to evening, before she came. Today it would be quicker; she could not see me without the amulet, but she knew the end was close. It would not be long.

I began to walk on, and as I neared the top of the rise I observed a little row of feathery bushes which had not been there a moment ago; a round boulder which seemed to have grown in an instant from the plain grassy sweep of the hillside.

"Keep down," the owl-creature whispered. "Keep out of sight until you know it's time. There'll be one chance, and one only." It settled by my side under cover of the bushes; the lichen-crusted rock at my left, with its mouth-like crack, edged in closer, so that I was well concealed.

"What about Fiacha?" I hissed as I craned my neck to see out toward the British fortress. "Has he a part to play in this? He just flew off and left me."

"Oh, yes. That creature has played a part already, and will again, no doubt. He has powerful connections. You speak of him with distaste."

I shivered. "I don't like him. He saved my life, I think, on the flight from Ulster. But I've never cared for him."

"Why not?" The rock-creature's voice was low and soft now.

"Because—"

And suddenly, I was completely lost for words. Suddenly, the last piece of the puzzle slipped into place, and my heart gave a great thud like the tolling of some ancient bell, and my head cleared to the recognition of an unbelievable truth; a solution so simple that it was astonishing I had not thought of it before. My fingers went up to rub at a little place on my shoulder, under my gown; and I thought; perhaps if I had been brave enough to take off the amulet before, perhaps I might have thought of this, and folk would not have suffered and died. Perhaps.

"She doesn't know," I said hesitantly. "My grandmother. I'm sure she doesn't know, or she'd never have sent me here."

"She suspects," said the owl-creature. "Not this, precisely; but she senses your power, and seeks to ensure you use it only for her own ends."

"No wonder she's afraid of me," I said in a whisper. "But—but I have no magic now. No craft at all. It takes a long time to come back after a transformation. Days, even. How can I do anything without that?"

"You'll have to fake it," the rock-being said casually. "These are human folk, easily fooled. We'll help if we can. Pretend. Confound them with surprises. Just until your powers return."

"Use what you can," the owl-creature advised. "Use what exists, as a druid does. The natural magic of sun and moon, wind and water, rock and fire. Tap into that power, and channel it to your own purpose."

"But—" I shrugged with exasperation, while my heart still thumped with the revelation that had come to me; the truth that changed everything. It filled me with dismay and terror; and it filled me with pride and hope. Never mind the terrible things I had done. Never mind the evil path the sorceress had set for me. Never mind my weakness. Today, I would be my father's daughter.

The allies had used their time well. In the brief span since dawn, they had advanced across the island and up to the perimeter of Northwoods' fortress, so that their forces were now deployed all along the outer rim of the ditch below the earthen rampart. So far they had not moved in, for Edwin had a strong contingent of archers posted atop the defenses, under cover, and everyone knew the British skill with the longbow. Instead, they seemed to be waiting for something. Below a central point in the wall, where stone fortifications marked some kind of guard post, the leaders of the Irish waited beyond the ditch. They were all assembled there. In the center stood Sean of Sevenwaters, solemn and pale, his tunic bearing the interlinked torcs, world and Otherworld, symbol of the folk of the forest and their mysterious counterparts, whose future today depended on the human kind. There was Eamonn of Glencarnagh, resplendent in green, brushing a stray lock of hair from his brow as he narrowed his eyes to scan the fortifications for signs of movement. His face was shadowed; perhaps his sleep had been visited by ill dreams, dreams in which the smallest of errors denies a man his long-sought prize. Something as little as a father and son who look too much alike, clad all in black and under water. There were the chieftains of the Uí Néill, richly dressed and handsomely armed; and there was a chalk-faced Bran of Harrowfield, with Snake and Gull by him, and those of Johnny's band who had survived the first day. Big, fresh-faced Gareth; intense, handsome Corentin; and Darragh. And, to my surprise, along with these warriors waited the archdruid Conor, upright and grave in his white robe, with the golden torc about his neck; and beside him his brother Finbar, the man with the swan's wing. Nobody was standing too close to *him*; they viewed him with respect, but such a difference tends to engender fear as well, even in the most hardened of men. And yet Darragh had not feared him, not for an instant. Darragh understood wild creatures; knew them so well it was no wonder folk said he was half one himself. He knew how to turn fear into love, with patience.

Such an assembly was surely the precursor of some major development. They must have issued some sort of challenge: surrender or we storm the fortress; give up or we lay siege and starve you out. Now they awaited a response. Or maybe it was Northwoods who was issuing a challenge, for now atop the earthen wall a small group of Britons appeared, one bearing a white flag, to denote the wish to exchange words without fear of harm. There was a stirring among the men of Erin; a chink of metal, a shuffle of boots.

"My lord of Northwoods wishes to discuss terms," one of the British warriors called out across the ditch, straining his voice against the increasing roar of the wind. He spoke in the tongue of Erin, strongly accented. The white banner tore at its bindings, threatening to launch itself into the air at any moment. The lad who carried it held tight to the pole. "He has a proposal for you. If Sean of Sevenwaters and his chieftains will step forward to the point below the guard tower, he will come forth and lay it before them. This is on understanding of no further attack from either side, until all parties agree that these negotiations are over. My lord offers this in good faith."

I saw Sean glance at Conor, brows raised, and Conor give a little nod. Perhaps they had expected this. Northwoods was driven back inside his last line of defense, and he had no way off the island. What could he do but surrender? But there was doubt on the hard features of the Chief, and in Snake's narrowed eyes, and also on my uncle's solemn face as he bade a man call back in agreement. This was too easy. It was too simple a victory, for all their losses; and what about the prophecy?

Now, among the party of Britons gathered in the guard tower, there appeared a man I already knew as Edwin of Northwoods. Last night, by firelight, he had seemed weary to death, oppressed by terrible choices. Now he was clad in field armor, and over it a russet tunic, and his gray beard was neatly combed, his hair bound back from his face. His expression was calm, his voice steady.

"Lord Sean. You know me, I think. Do your chieftains under-stand this tongue?"

"My druid will translate for the men." My uncle spoke in the language of the Britons. It was, after all, his father's native tongue. "What do you want, Northwoods? We stand at your very gates here; you are in our grasp. Have you at last seen sense, and come out to bargain for the safety of your men?" There was a touch of impatience in Sean's voice. Conor glanced at him, then rendered his words into Irish, his tone level.

"Indeed." The wind was howling now; Northwoods raised his voice to span the gap of the ditch. "I come to strike an agreement with you, Sevenwaters, but not the one you imagine. I want safety for my men, and for all our household within here. I want a ship, and I think you will give me that, and more besides."

Sean's brows rose. "I cannot imagine on what terms such a bargain might be reached, unless you agree to quit the Islands forthwith, and return with your men to Britain. I'd need an undertaking, signed and sealed, that Northwoods would lay no claim to these shores ever again. I can be magnanimous if I choose. A ship comes even now from Harrowfield, captained by my young nephew Fintan. On this vessel your men can be conveyed home with some dignity at least. But none of you will return to Britain until I have your sworn word that you will never again set foot upon this shore. Those are my terms."

"Harrowfield!" Edwin turned to one side and spat upon the ground. "Harrowfield, whose lord stands even now among your men, a traitor to his own kind? I would not set foot on such a ship if my life depended on it."

"It is your choice," said Sean levelly. "Accept, and retreat in safety. Refuse, and be overrun. You will die, every one, and the islands will be ours once more. It matters little to me which course you choose."

There was a pause.

"I think you may find," Northwoods said carefully, "that it is I who will make the terms here, and you who will choose." He turned to his guards. "Bring him up," he ordered, and looked again at Sean. "I have something of yours here, something you may have thought lost. What will you pay, I wonder, to get it back?"

Then his man mounted the steps to the elevated guard post,

pushing before him a captive whose hands were bound behind his back; whose exhausted eyes were nonetheless alive with hope and defiance; whose fair skin bore, unmistakeably, the mark of the raven.

"Sweet Christ!" exclaimed Snake. "He's alive!"

I could feel the great wave of excitement as it swept through the Irish forces, *He's alive, the child of the prophecy is alive*, with never a touch of reservation. He was back; Johnny was back. They had not lost him after all. That meant they would win; they must win. The prophecy said so.

The Chief's gray eyes were very bright. He was even paler than Johnny, and he now moved to stand by Sean's shoulder, staring up at the bound figure of his son. He, at least, had seen beyond the wild elation to the peril of the moment. Johnny stared back, meeting Bran's gaze, and he gave the smallest of nods. I thought it meant, *I'm the leader. Leave this to me*.

"You wish to offer us this prisoner in return for a boat and safe passage?" Sean asked. I saw his hand tighten on his sword-hilt, but his voice was steady. "We will grant neither without an assurance that you forfeit this territory, captive or no captive. This is not the way we do business, Northwoods. I thought you knew us better than that."

Edwin folded his arms. "That's a bluff, Lord Sean. I know who this lad is. I know of the prophecy that drives your folk, the foretelling that Sevenwaters can never win this territory back without the child spoken of in ancient lore; the warrior who bears the sign of the raven, offspring of both Erin and Britain. This is your chosen one. Ask your men what it will mean, if I draw my knife across his throat. Ask them about their will to win once his lifeblood is spilled here. Without this boy you will never triumph. His death would be the death of your hopes, the end of your dreams."

"His death will be yours, Northwoods!" shouted Bran of Harrowfield, no longer able to keep his silence. He spoke in the British tongue, which was his own. "Do not judge us so hastily. Harm my son, and your fate is sealed. Our long years of truce will be over until I wipe you from the face of the earth, and your own sons with you!"

There was restless shuffling among the men; Conor was ominously silent.

"What's he saying?" someone ventured. "What's the Briton saying?"

Conor cleared his throat.

"Tell us what you want, Northwoods." Sean's voice was heavy. "What is the price you demand for Johnny's freedom?"

"The same price you thought to ask of me, Sevenwaters." The British leader's voice was quieter now; perhaps he sensed a weakening; perhaps he scented victory. "A complete withdrawal of your troops from the Islands, and a signed undertaking that you will never attempt such an invasion again. Relinquishment of all claim to this territory. You will leave one ship behind; you may retain the others to convey your troops and those of your dubious allies away from our shores. I too can be generous. As for my neighbor of Harrowfield, I will make known his act of treachery across Northumbria and beyond. He may find his own territory somewhat less secure than he thought it, from now on."

"We cannot accede to such a request." Sean's face was grim as death, his mouth a hard line. "The Islands are ours. We are pledged to recover them. To agree with this proposal would be to make a mockery of our fathers, and their fathers before them, who fell in this cause. I will not do so."

"No?" Northwoods' tone was suddenly savage. "Very well, then." He drew a knife from his belt, and laid it against Johnny's throat. There was a roar of outrage from the warriors assembled around the perimeter of the ditch, and all along the line swords were drawn, and daggers flashed. Here and there, small groups of men surged forward. From behind the rampart came the sound of many small clicks, as arrow was set to bow, and string tightened in readiness.

I half-rose, knowing I must act, still uncertain.

"Now?" I ventured, glancing to the side where the owl-creature had been watching the scene in silence. But instead of its round, quizzical eyes, I met a gaze dark as mulberries in a face as milk-pale as my own, but creviced and old, and crowned with a shock of wild white hair.

"No, Fainne," Grandmother said in a soft small voice that turned my spine to jelly. "Not now. This is much too interesting to be interrupted. Don't you just love it when men quarrel? I'll tell you when to step in. Not until the very last, girl."

I could not stop shivering; she held me transfixed with her gaze as a hunting creature holds its prey, terror preventing flight. After all the panoply, the wind and clouds and baleful voices, in the end she had crept up on me as subtly as a shadow.

"Where's the amulet?" she hissed suddenly. "What have you done with it? You promised me. You promised you would never take it off. You lied to me, Fainne. How can I know you will not betray me now, at the end?" And it seemed to me she grew bigger, and darker, so that she was no longer a crazy old woman, but a great queen, mysterious and powerful. No wonder the Fomhóire had gone to ground, so to speak.

"I will not betray you, Grandmother." I might have no scrap of the craft left in me, but I was still my father's daughter, well disciplined to control. I kept my voice steady, my gaze calm. "I'm afraid the amulet is lost. I was hiding on the cliffs, and it fell into the sea. But I don't need it anymore. You are right here beside me, after all. Will you help me when the time comes?" I even managed a smile, though beneath it I was sick with dread.

"Why would you need help? Ssh, now. They're moving."

Down by the ditch there were developments. Sean and his leaders had formed a tight group, and were conferring. As for the warriors, they were making a lot of noise; the meaning of the British leader's words had spread among them, and they were angry. Along the edge of the ditch, Snake was hastily deploying the fighting men of Inis Eala to prevent any premature forays across, any suicidal acts of heroism. Only a mass onslaught could hope to penetrate such a defense, its upper rim thick with archers. Gareth was out there holding them back, and so was Corentin, and the older men, Wolf and Rat and many more. Up at the southern end, where earthen rampart gave way to sheer cliffs, the ultimate defensive barrier, I thought I saw Darragh, knife in hand, taking his place among them. I turned quickly back to Grandmother.

"Quandary," she said with a little smile. "Sevenwaters can't win, whatever choice he makes. Let the boy be killed, and they must lose; it's in the prophecy. Bargain for his life, and they're bound to retreat. Honor demands it."

"It seems to me," I told her as I watched them debating, as I saw Finbar looking up toward Johnny where he stood swaying slightly in the tower, pale as death, "that whatever is decided, they'll have trouble holding their own men back. Johnny inspires great loyalty. These men will do anything for him."

And, almost as if he had the very same idea, Finbar now stepped up to my uncle Sean and began to speak quietly. A strange hush spread over the crowd; by the time Finbar had finished, they were all silent. Even the wind had died down.

Sean of Sevenwaters squared his shoulders and looked up again at his old enemy.

"We have a counter-proposal," he called.

"You've heard my terms," growled Edwin of Northwoods. "I said nothing of any compromise."

"Hear me, at least," Sean said. "You have told us all hinges on the prophecy. That much is true, for this place is the very heart of our faith; it is no mere anchorage for us, but a symbol of our bond with the earth itself. I cannot expect you to understand that; but I sense you know its significance to these men. Strategically your position is weak indeed, so weak that without this convenient hostage you would have been overrun by nightfall. I think you know that, Lord Edwin. But you are not a fool. You know that if this man is lost, my forces cannot triumph here. Today, they may storm your fortress and slaughter every Briton within it, but it would be no victory. Without the child of the prophecy, without his intervention, this feud cannot be ended."

"So?" Edwin's gaze was sharp; perhaps he guessed what was coming.

"So, ask him. Ask Johnny, who is heir to Sevenwaters and at the same time your own kin, what the decision must be here. Let him determine this. He is our true leader. The men will accept his choice."

And when Conor translated, this time, a cheer of acclamation came from the Irishmen which made the very ground rumble with its power.

"Pack of fools," muttered my grandmother. "To risk all, on that. The boy's half-dead, from the looks of him. Can't even stand up straight. What sort of choice is it, anyway? He'd hardly choose to have himself killed. Just as well you're here, Fainne, to do this for me, or it might all slip through my grasp once again. And we can't have that, can we?"

"No, Grandmother."

Now Edwin was speaking to his captive, and Johnny was saying something in return. The Briton had little choice in the matter, and I imagined he knew it. He'd just the one bargaining tool, and the best he could hope for was safe passage away, and maybe a chance to return later. Edwin was a seasoned campaigner. Perhaps, in his heart, he knew that once he drew the knife across Johnny's throat they were all dead men.

Now Johnny took a halting step forward, and looked down at the assembled men. A profound silence fell.

"This cannot be decided in such a way." His voice was steady but faint; it must have taken quite an effort of will to keep it under control. His face was wan with exhaustion. "Men of Sevenwaters, of Glencarnagh and Sídhe Dubh; men of Inis Eala and of Tirconnell. I put it to you that we settle this by single combat. The winner takes the Islands; the loser has safe conduct to his home shore, with an undertaking never to return here. It is time for the killing to end; for the losses to cease. Both sides undertake to accept the outcome and abide by it. If I am slain in this fight, there will be no breaches of the walls here, no indiscriminate slaughter. A clean fight; a clean ending. If I die, you will return to Erin and claim these Islands no more." He turned to Edwin of Northwoods. "I will fight what champion you choose from among your warriors. If he is vanquished, you will take advantage of my uncle's offer, and ferry your men home in the vessel my brother brings from Harrowfield. My father will go with you; he is your neighbor and kinsman, and I believe fought here only because he thought me lost. You will mend your differences with him. Have I your agreement to this proposal?"

Edwin stared at him. "You? Fight against one of my warriors? You've been a whole day in the sea, you're injured, and—" He stopped short.

Johnny gave a little smile. "Then you have an added advantage," he said calmly.

And so it came about that the very fate of the Islands, the very working out of the prophecy itself came down to the simplest of things: the outcome of a fight between two men. The troops of Sevenwaters were excited, elated. They knew Johnny's prowess with the sword; even better, they knew his near-mythical place in the scheme of things, and in their minds, he could not possibly fail. They had not understood Edwin's last words; they had not seen, as I had, the child of the prophecy half-drowned, exhausted, with broken ribs and battered body, sent off to spend a night alone in some stark cell. They thought him more than human; but, blazing with courage and goodness as he was, he was no more than a mortal man, and both weary and injured. I heard Bran arguing fiercely with the others, *He cannot fight! Let me fight! Let me do this!* and in turn, Conor, and Sean, and Finbar telling him the prophecy must be allowed to run its course; that Johnny's strange decision must in some way be right. It seemed they too believed he would win, against the odds, because it was foretold. All the same, Snake maintained the guard right along the ditch's edge; his own men might be trusted not to break ranks, perhaps, but he'd a sharp eye on the others, and in particular the men in green.

As for my grandmother, she was chuckling to herself and grinning from ear to ear. "Oh, this'll be easy, Fainne, easy. Almost a shame, really, such a fine young fellow, though there'll never be another Colum of Sevenwaters. Still, this one's a sound enough specimen: good shoulders, strong legs. Fainne? Are you listening? What are you looking for, up in the crowd there? Pay attention, girl! You must be ready when I give the word. Know what to do, do you?"

"Yes, Grandmother," I whispered, fists clutched so tight my nails dug into my palms.

"Got the courage for it?"

"Yes, Grandmother." Oh yes, I had the courage all right. It was the craft that was the problem. I could not sense its power in me at all, not yet; I was still so weak I could scarcely keep upright. And I could not test it; the two of us were barely concealed behind low bush and ancient boulder, and I must not let her know how helpless I was. Soon enough I must walk out there and hope, when I spoke the words of a charm, that something would happen.

"Sure?" Grandmother was frowning now, her dark beady eyes piercing as she scrutinized my face.

"Completely sure," I told her, voice rock-steady as I returned her gaze with eyes I knew were the image of her own.

I had thought it folly beyond belief that Johnny would stake all on this, when he was so weakened. But the men trusted Johnny's judgment, and for a while it seemed they were right. I should not have been surprised, maybe, for he was a son of Inis Eala, born and bred to the song of sword and spear. He was good; so good, in fact, that it soon became obvious that without the handicaps of weariness, and bruising, and a broken rib or two, he would have vanquished his opponent quite quickly. The British champion himself was not without strength or skills. It seemed Northwoods, too, could take risks, for the broad-shouldered young fellow who now circled there below me, wary, shifting his sword in his hands, was none other than Edwin's own son, who had stood by his side last night, speaking of knives. The balance of it, the symbolism, gave this combat the resonance of an ancient tale.

The men were gathered in a great circle now. On one side, farthest from the ditch and wall, were the men of Erin, and on the other assembled Northwoods's warriors, for they must be present to protect their champion and see fair play done. The men of Inis Eala still patrolled, wary and watchful, to ensure things did not get out of control. Whatever agreement the leaders had struck, the situation still balanced on a knife-edge, and the smallest lapse of discipline was liable to precipitate a bloodbath. Only yesterday these men had been hewing each other's bodies, and clubbing one another's heads, and screaming the harsh language of war. It was a miracle they stood so close together now, and kept their weapons sheathed. So Johnny's men walked the edges of the crowd, hands on dagger-hilts, eyes narrowed. And in the center of the open space around which the crowd gathered thickly, the two young warriors fought on. They used their heavy swords two-handed, whirling and ducking, the weapons whistling through the air, their own grunts and gasps a counterpoint to this deadly music. No shields; this was a direct and brutal encounter, and could surely not last long. Johnny was tiring. I could see the way he shifted his feet, struggling for balance. I could see a change in his steady gray eyes, as if he sensed death close. If he lost this, he would indeed lose all.

Edwin's son was bleeding from a deep wound to the shoulder and a cut to the thigh. His face was flushed with effort and sheened with sweat. Johnny was deathly pale; I sensed a shadow over him, and steeled myself. There would be a moment soon when he was pinned down, with the other man's weapon at his throat, and I would have to run out in the open and—and—

Edwin's son lunged with his sword, and this time Johnny's balance was not quite perfect. His foot slipped; he teetered for an instant, and his opponent's weapon sliced down his side, tearing through cloth and flesh. Johnny's eyes widened a little; his mouth opened and closed. Edwin's son took a step back; gripped his sword anew; readied himself for a final blow. Johnny stepped neatly forward, and turned on his heel, and his foot came up to strike the other man's weapon from his hand. The heavy sword flew through the air as the crowd gasped with one voice. A moment later, the Briton was sprawled on the ground with Johnny standing over him, the point of his sword a finger's breadth from the other man's throat. Johnny wore black; but I could see how freely the blood flowed from the great gash Edwin's son had laid open, and how my cousin's face grew ever paler as the sun came up above the clouds to light the scene below with eerie brightness.

For a moment, Johnny was poised there quite motionless, and the crowd stood, hushed now, waiting. The leaders were together in a group, Sean, Conor and Eamonn, with Bran of Harrowfield not far away; my eyes sought out Finbar and found him strangely alone on the far side of the circle. Hidden as I was from view, nonetheless he seemed to be looking straight at me, and stranger still, I thought I could hear what was in his mind.

Now would be a good time. We will help you.

"Now would be a good time," I muttered. "Don't you think?"

"Ssh," hissed Grandmother, suddenly not in the best of tempers. "What's he saying?"

Johnny's eyes were dark pools; his mouth was set grim. He looked over at his father, and at Sean. He looked across at the ashen-faced Edwin of Northwoods.

"Is this supposed to be a fight to the death?" he asked politely in the voice of a man close to losing consciousness.

There was a roar from the crowd, and then silence. It seemed to me that, whatever the response, we were poised on the brink of a disaster. And if there was anyone whose judgment I respected, it was Finbar's. I stood up, and walked out slowly from the concealment of bush and rock, my arms by my sides, my hair quickly caught by the

newly freshening breeze to stream out around my head. The red banner, signal to advance. My heart thumped with terror.

Behind me, my grandmother gave a chuckle of delight. "Good,
Fainne, good! Make me proud of you, girl!"

I had not a scrap of magic in me. My Otherworld helpers were
gone. My grandmother was right here watching. And now I limped
forward, quite unarmed, a girl in a striped dress and a silken shawl,
with a childhood toy tucked into her belt, and a great army of fearsome warriors parted, muttering, to let me through. Why, I cannot
tell you. Maybe it was no more than simple surprise that so unlikely
a figure should appear here, on this lonely island, in the middle of
such grave and perilous endeavors. Some, perhaps, thought me a
creature of the Otherworld myself. A hush fell as I approached the
open area where the two warriors still held their frozen posture.
Blood now pooled on the earth by them, the mingled blood of two
races.

Go on now, my grandmother's voice seemed to whisper. I
glanced over my shoulder; she was right behind me, now dark-
cloaked, dark-hooded, and she halted at the edge of the crowd,
watching my every move. *Finish it. Finish him. He's half-dead already.
A simple matter. Quick now, before he plunges that sword in the Briton's
neck with his last strength. Quick now. They're watching. They're all
watching. I want to see the looks on their faces when the child of the
prophecy chokes on his own lifeblood. Do it, Fainne. Do it for me, and for
all our kind.*

It was not so far across to where Johnny stood waiting. Ten
paces, maybe. A lot can happen in ten paces. I glanced up and around
the circle: saw the shocked face of my uncle Sean, the horrified
expression of Eamonn, the dawning comprehension on Conor's
grave features. I saw Finbar's nod of recognition and approval. I saw
the confusion and doubt on the faces of Briton and Irishman alike.
And beyond the circle, I saw others standing, waiting silently, their
strange eyes intense and piercing: a woman taller than any mortal,
pale as spring snow, with long dark hair like silk; a man crowned with
flames, whose garments flowed about his stately form like a curtain of
living fire. And there were others, many others, beings with rippling
locks like weeds in river-water, and skin translucent as glass; lovely
creatures clad in feathers and berries, in grasses and leaves, in lichen

and bark and soft mosses. Every one of them was tall beyond imagining, and every one of them was looking at me. *It's time*, they seemed to say, though perhaps only I could see, only I could hear them. *At last it's time*. The Fair Folk were come, now, at the end. But they would not help me. I must do this by myself.

Go on, Fainne, my grandmother's voice urged. *Quick, now. There's only one way for this to end. Kill the child. Hurry, girl!*

I took another step, and another. I was halfway across the space. Then there was a shout, in the tongue of the Britons, "It's a trick! Stop the girl!" I heard a sort of whistling in the air behind me, and a general gasp; I heard someone running toward me, and I was roughly knocked sideways, so I sprawled on the ground, with something heavy on top of me. There was a roar of voices, and the sound of weapons being drawn, and the voice of my uncle Sean shouting, "No! Keep calm! Keep back!"

I struggled to my feet, dislodging the dead weight that pinned me. There was blood on my gown, a lot of blood; Riona's rose-pink skirts were stained scarlet. A man lay at my feet, and it was his blood that soaked me, for a slender spear had pierced his chest from back to front, its barbed point now protruding from his body and catching at my skirt as I stood by him. The man was choking; a red stream gushed from his mouth, and from his nose, and spilled over his green tunic. As I bent to touch his brow, to brush back the lock of brown hair that fell into his agonized eyes, he wheezed a word that might have been my name, and fell back lifeless on the earth. Against all odds, Eamonn had been the one to act on impulse, and to save my life; against the whole pattern of things, he had died a hero. A chill came over me. There must be no more of this. No more blood. No more death. It had to stop. I had to stop it.

"Keep back!" Snake yelled. "You can do nothing here!"

"We must follow due process!" It was Edwin's voice that called now. "Keep your discipline, men! We have an agreement, and will honor it!"

"Hear Lord Edwin! Keep ranks! Keep back!" This was Sean of Sevenwaters, whose own men now were clamoring loudest for blood; for it was a British spear that had killed Eamonn of Glencarnagh, though it was meant for me. It seemed only a matter of moments before these warriors, thirsty for vengeance, would break through the guard set by Snake and his men and be at one another's throats once more, fighting and killing until the whole island was awash with blood.

A circle. A circle of protection. That was what I needed. It should be fire, because fire was easy, and it scared folk enough to keep them out. I raised my arms, and spoke the words of a spell, and turned in place where I was. I knew even as I went through the motions that I had not yet the strength even for this simple trick; the most I could summon was a tiny tingling of the fingertips, too weak to make a single spark. Nonetheless, as I turned and pointed, flames burst forth in the path of my outstretched hand, so that Johnny and the young Briton and myself were encircled by a ring of fire three handspans high, and hot enough to send the men jostling back out of the way. For the time being we were safe. Across the circle, Finbar now stood with his arm outstretched, and his great white wing unfurled. And opposite him Conor the archdruid did the same, arms spread wide, hands stretched out in a gesture of power. The flaming circle ran from him to his brother, and back again. It is useful, sometimes, to have druids in the family.

At the edge of the circle my grandmother still waited, a slight, dark-robed figure, now silent as I walked up to Johnny. Even then, even as I reached him, I was not sure what I would say, or how I might make a difference here without the craft. But they were all waiting now; the warriors, the seer and the druid, the leaders of Britain and Erin. On the rise behind the men, many small creatures were now gathered, an owl-being, a mossy rock with holes for eyes, a little bush with finger-like foliage; a hare, a wren, a thing like water in the shape of a child. And all around, behind the others, the Fair Folk themselves, guardians of the earth's secrets, holders of the mysteries of our faith; even they held their breath now, awaiting my words.

But I had no magic. I was only a girl, and a pretty poor example of one at that. I had no goodness or nobility. I could not inspire men as Johnny did. I could not charm wild creatures as Darragh could. I did not know how to heal a man bleeding from a deep wound, I could not swim or dance. Without the craft, I was nothing.

Use what is already there, the Fomhóire had told me: the natural magic of earth and water, air and fire. Druid magic. Use that. And at the moment I stepped up beside Johnny, the sky began to darken. It was full morning; the clouds had dispersed as quickly as they gathered, and the sky was clear. But now the sun's brightness began to dim, and an eldritch twilight to fall across the landscape, as if day were turning to a strange half-night. The men began to mutter uneasily; some made signs in the air before them.

Quick, Fainne! Where's your backbone, girl? Get on with it! My grandmother grew impatient.

I'd have been scared myself, of this strange darkness, if other things had not already driven me near-witless with terror: Eamonn's blood, my grandmother's voice, my own terrible weakness. Focus. Control. I thought about my father and all I owed to him, and I knelt by the Briton where he lay prone, so that Johnny could not finish him off without risking my own life.

"Fainne! What are you doing?" my cousin hissed. Now that I was close, I could see how his hands were shaking; soon he would be unable to hold the weight of this sword. As for the Briton, he was whey-faced, and lay in a pool of blood. The sky grew darker, and the ring of fire glowed bright in the uncanny dimness of the morning. Words came to me at last.

"I am Fainne of Kerry, daughter of the sorcerer Ciarán!" I called out in a voice as solemn and grand as I could summon. This must be quick, or both these men would bleed to death where they were, and it would all be quite pointless. "I am of a great line of mages. I am come to bid you put down your arms and leave this place forever. See how the sky darkens; it is a sign of warning to you all. There has been enough blood shed here; enough waste of young life over the generations. The child of the prophecy lives, and has returned, and the great quest of the Fair Folk nears its end. Your sons stand here wounded close to death. Their blood soaks the very land that divides you. Would you lose them both in your lust for power? Retreat, save yourselves, and fight no more!" I glanced upward. It did indeed seem that some Otherworld shadow blotted out the sun's light; it was enough to make the heart clench tight with fear. From the edge of the fiery circle I could hear a voice, I thought it was Corentin's, rendering my words into the British tongue so each man there could understand. And now the assembled warriors were beginning to glance behind them nervously, their eyes sliding to those tall, mysterious figures who looked on silently; whose gaze seemed ancient and wise under the strange dark sky. "The sun hides his face," I went on. Beside me, Johnny had withdrawn his sword from the Briton's throat; the two of them watched me in astonishment. "You must leave this place, for I tell you words of truth when I say no man can live here after tomorrow; to stay on these shores is to measure your life in the span of a single journey of the sun from eastern rim to western ocean." The words seemed to flow from me now without being summoned at all; indeed, I hardly understood them myself. "The Islands are the Last Place. They are not for the grasping hand of man; neither Briton nor man of Ulster, neither Norseman nor Pict shall hold them from this day forth, for they will vanish in the mists of the margins, and reveal themselves to none but the voyager of the spirit. Come, men of Erin, men of Northumbria, hear me now. This long feud is over."

The sky had grown still darker, almost as if it were night. The sun was obscured, a mere rim of gold, its center quenched by some malign shadow. The strange light gave my words a power beyond the ordinary, and now all around the circle men muttered and whispered, and some cried out in fear, or called upon one god or another to save them. A few were already edging away from the crowd, and heading down to the boats.

"The girl speaks no more than the truth." My heart thudded as I heard the voice of the lady Oonagh. She threw back her dark cloak, and took one step forward so that she stood on the edge of the fiery circle, the flames licking at the hem of her gown, yet never catching it alight. It was as if she were impervious to its heat. She did not wear her old-woman image now, but the guise of a tall, lovely lady, white-skinned, auburn-haired, her voice sweet and strong as fresh-brewed mead. "Retreat is your only choice, poor foolish human warriors. It has all been for nothing, all these deaths, all these losses; quite pointless. The prophecy will never be fulfilled; it was no more than the ramblings of some ancient druid, age-addled and witless. There are no winners here save my own kind: I, the lady Oonagh, and my granddaughter Fainne, who shows herself now in her true colors, a sorceress even as powerful as myself!"

She turned toward me, and as she spoke, I saw my uncle Sean staring at me, horrified; and Bran of Harrowfield, grim-faced, stepping into the circle of flames, heedless of the risk, only to be pulled back by Gull and Snake, one on each side. Nobody would cross this barrier, save one stronger in the craft than those who made it.

"Now, Fainne!" My grandmother gave a gloating cackle of laughter. "Now do as we planned! Kill the boy; finish these upstarts and their Otherworld masters. End this farce about a prophecy here and now. Even now the fellow staggers with weakness; his fingers can no longer grip his weapon. Do as you promised me, and make an end of him!"

There were shouts of outrage from the crowd; I heard Bran yell, "No!" and I sensed the rage and frustration of the men around us, Ulsterman and Briton alike. Yet none might step across the barrier, while it held; the balance was in my hands. I glanced up, and felt a deep pain, to see those men who had treated me with respect and friendship now staring at me as if I were a creature too foul to be contemplated. Gareth, Corentin, Gull and Snake, even my uncle Sean looked at me with shock and loathing. Perhaps it was no better than I deserved.

Johnny had fallen to his knees; he held his hand pressed close to his side, the fingers stained with seeping blood. Edwin's son lay prone on his back, eyes staring, breath harsh.

"Quickly, girl!" the sorceress hissed. "Use the craft! Or use the sword, if you must. Do it! I must see him die by your hand."

"I'm sorry, Grandmother," I said politely, my voice shaking like an autumn leaf. "I don't think I can do that."

I watched her face change; I shuddered at the expression in her eyes. With such a look a sorceress might turn a hapless mortal to stone through sheer terror. Beyond my grandmother I could see Conor, still holding his arms outstretched, still maintaining the protective circle. Impervious to fire she might be, but the lady Oonagh could not move inside this charmed space, not yet; even now she struggled to break through, her brows knotted in fury. Perhaps a force stronger than any of us held her back.

"*What?*" she screamed. The sky remained dark; now the wind rose again, a moaning, eerie wind that whipped her skirts about her. Strange shadows spread around her on the ground, and she seemed huge and menacing. Her eyes were slits in a chalk-white face, her lips blood-red, and her teeth like little sharp knives. To her left and to her right, the circle of flame began to waver and die down.

"Hold fast, brother!" called Conor. His hands were shaking;

behind me, I heard Finbar's gasp of pain and fear. She was doing her utmost to break it, and she was strong. The druid and the seer, after all, were no more than mortal men. If only I were not so weak, if only I had but a fraction of my true power.

"You think to thwart me, girl? You, a mere slip of a child, with a half-baked education and a featherbrain for a mother, you with your foolish notions of love and loyalty? Either you have a very short memory, or you think me exceptionally stupid."

And now she turned, facing outward, looking up the line of ditch and earthen wall to the place where the fortifications gave way to the sheer southern cliff face. Here small birds nested, and tiny plants clung. Here, there were no sheltered ledges wide enough for man or woman to rest on; no places of safety on the precipitous surface. Instead, the ground simply rose gently, and stopped, and there, far, far below, was the sea. Snake had posted his men all the way up the slope to prevent premature incursions into the ditch and over the earthen wall; he had deployed them right up to that sudden end. And who better to take the farthest place, the place deemed easiest to guard, where sloping ground gave way to nothingness, than a traveling man who had no business pretending to be a warrior anyway?

"Now," breathed the lady Oonagh. "Now, oh now you will do as I bid you. For this you surely cannot endure!"

Darragh's attention had wandered from the job; he was looking up, watching a flock of terns as they flew overhead in neat formation, perhaps in search of springtime. As I stood there staring, my whole body frozen in terror, the sorceress sent the wind ahead of her up the rise, and men blundered aside, thrown to their knees by its force. The blast caught Darragh unawares, whipping his dark hair back, tearing his short cloak away, sending it spiraling up, up into the air. He staggered sideways, clutching for purchase, a rock, a bush, anything at all; but there was nothing he could hold onto, and the violent gale drove him steadily backward, backward up the slope, his feet staggering nearer and nearer to the point where the ground vanished, and the great space opened out above the sea. Now men were running toward him, the wind at their backs, but slow, too slow. Broad-shouldered Gareth, dark-haired Corentin, shouting, *Hold on! We're coming!* It was clear they could not reach him in time.

"Now!" screamed the lady Oonagh, her berry-dark eyes fixed on me, her snarling mouth as feral as a weasel's. "Do it! Do it! Kill the child, or watch your little tinker perish! Do my bidding, curse you! Do it or watch him die!"

Johnny was kneeling by me, his steady gray eyes looking up at me. I saw the recognition of death in them, but no fear. If ever there was one born to be child of the prophecy, it was this man, a model of courage and dignity. Without him the folk of Sevenwaters would be set adrift once more, their flame of purpose snatched away, their path once more in darkness. Without him, there would be no point to any of it; no point at all.

"I can't," I whispered, and learned how it feels when your heart breaks.

I knew a charm. I knew a little charm well-mastered before ever I ceased to be a child, and learned what love is. *Stop. Drop. Now gently down*. Once I knew this trick, I never broke the glass ball once. Today, I had no magic.

There was no need to look. With eyes squeezed shut, with my two hands over my face, I saw it all. I saw the mad fury in the sorceress's eyes, an unholy light of pure evil. I saw the wind pick Darragh up as if he were no heavier than an autumn leaf, I saw the cruel way the lady Oonagh held him poised a moment, right there on the edge, teasing me, taunting me, as if even now a cry, a word, a single gasp might bring him back again, if only I would utter it. And I saw how, at the very end, the traveling man turned his long, last descent to oblivion into a thing of wonder and beauty, a thing as lovely as the dying notes of a piper's lament. For he did not fall, but twisted his body in air, and laid his arms by his sides, and dived head first, swift and straight as a swallow, down and down into the merciless clutch of the cold sea, down to the knife-edged rocks and the white surge of the waves.

Chapter Sixteen

Someone was screaming. Someone was wailing, a terrible sound of anguish that set the teeth on edge, a sound fit to shred the very spirit. It was a cry to make the strongest man tremble. My fists were tight in the sockets of my eyes; my jaw was clenched hard; my head vibrated with pain. At last I had learned to do something I had always believed a sorcerer's daughter could not do. I had learned how to weep. I wept as surely no girl had ever wept before, a river of tears, a gushing torrent of grief. I stood there and screamed my loss to the wind, and the lady Oonagh watched me with a little smile on her face. Beside me, Johnny stretched out a hand to the enemy who lay sprawled at his feet.

"Come," he said. "This is over. Both of us need a surgeon, and then we need to talk. Let me help you." The Briton staggered to his feet; the two of them stood by me, supporting one another.

"Not so fast." She was not done yet; not so easily thwarted. "You think you have won, maybe; you think this task is beyond me, without your aid. Foolish girl. You've cast away the only one who ever cared a scrap about you, and for nothing. I will break this circle; I will break these human folk as I did once before, long ago. One by one I will take them, these sons of Sevenwaters, and then I will kill you both: I will kill the child of the prophecy, and you, my disobedient grandchild."

I heard my uncle Sean shout, "No!" and start forward, to be beaten back by the very flames that protected us; I saw my grandmother raise her hands, and send a ripple of green light along the line of the fiery circle, a ripple which touched Finbar first, and sent him crumpling to his knees, wheezing with pain. Conor was ready for it, and held fast, but his face was gray, and his eyes less than calm.

"Quick, Fainne!" he said. "We cannot maintain this much longer. Help us!"

But I could not. The craft was returning slowly, my fingers tingled, my blood ran swift, I could feel it flowing into me now like a deep anger that built and built, inexorable, unstoppable. But still I stood there frozen by my grief, paralyzed by my loss, and beside me were the sons of Sevenwaters and of Northwoods, both like to bleed to death where they stood if I could not help them soon.

"Which shall be first?" hissed the lady Oonagh, baring her teeth like a hunting cat, and she sent another wave through the circle, deep red, the color of heart's blood. Finbar cried out, and she laughed. I could see what looked like smoke rising from the soft feathers of his wing; his face was drained of color, ashen and terrified. The next time, surely he would be unable to hold against her. She raised her arms high, a fierce smile on her face, and as she did so the sky began to brighten once more, the sun to emerge from its strange obscurity, and a great bird flew across the circle, diving so close to the eyes of the sorceress that she flinched away; passing by to alight on the shoulder of a dark-cloaked figure who had appeared among the onlookers, as abruptly as if by magic. The sorceress lifted her hands again, and she seemed to draw sparks downward from the air into her fingers. Her body was clothed with glittering brightness. She seemed far taller than any mortal woman might be.

"You," she shrieked, "you who defied me once, you who endured what no man should endure, this time I will finish you!"

She swept her arms downward and pointed them straight at Finbar, who knelt there gasping with pain, his eyes still clear and true as he fought to maintain the protective fire.

"This time!" she hissed, and the strange flame seemed to flow from her fingertips and out across the circle. The dark-cloaked figure pushed back his hood and raised his hands, holding them out at his sides, palms up, in an echo of Conor's posture. The line of sparks from the sorceress's fingers fizzed and died.

"I think not, Mother," said Ciarán, standing quiet with the raven on his shoulder. His gaze was level, his face pale but calm. If he had been sick before, sick to death, he seemed well enough now. She had lied to me. She had manipulated me, and I had believed her. How many more of her threats were merely that, merely poisonous false-hoods she used to frighten me into compliance?

"You!" she spat furiously. "How dare you meddle in this, you misguided weakling with your headful of druid notions! No wonder your daughter failed the test in the end! You ruined her, you and that useless little wife of yours, your precious Niamh with her soft ways and her empty head. Just as well I got rid of *her*, or I'd never have made anything of the girl. But Fainne didn't live up to my expecta-tions. Lost her grip, just when it mattered."

My father took a step forward, very slowly. He, it seemed, could cross this circle with no difficulty at all.

"What did you say?" he asked softly.

"Girl's no good. Like her mother." There was a change in the lady Oonagh's voice, an edge, as if she were surprised, or frightened. Above us the sun was emerging fast now; the day grew ever brighter.

"Not that. You said, you got rid of Niamh. What does that mean, Mother?"

"A little accident, no more. A little slip on a ledge. A slight push in the back, and down to oblivion. She was no good for you, Ciarán. You could have been a great man; a man of power and influence. She was spoiling you and weakening the girl. She had to go."

My father's face blazed with fury. There was such danger in that look, even a sorceress might quail before it. As for me, her words made me tremble with horror. I knew her well, yet I could hardly believe the depths of her ill-doing. It was she who had snatched away their happiness in the end, not Sean, not Conor, not a cruel husband or uncaring family, but the sorceress herself; Ciarán's own mother. My father's eyes were like dark ice. His voice was deathly calm.

"So it comes to this," he said, regarding his mother across the cir-cle. "A test of wills; a test of strength. But first . . ."

He glanced at Johnny where he stood by me with Edwin's son leaning on his shoulder. I could hear both young men's labored breathing; it was hard to say which of them was more ghastly pale. "Go forth from the circle," Ciarán told them quietly. "Go forth under my protection." I felt rather than saw the effect of the charm he was using, a guardian cloak, invisible, unshakable, which wrapped itself around both young warriors. He would not hold this enchantment on them for long, but while he maintained it, this was a screen no weapon could penetrate, neither arrow nor spear nor sorceress's curse. Clothed in this spell, they could cross the fiery barrier unscathed. Johnny hesitated, feeling the magic, no doubt, but slow to comprehend its meaning through the clouds of exhaustion and injury.

I looked up at my cousin. "Best go," I managed, my voice coming out cracked and hoarse, for I still could not keep the tears from flowing. "Go, seek help, make a truce. All must leave this place by nightfall. There is a wave coming, and a mist; none can be safe here." Words, again, which seemed to come from outside me; words which made a curious sense.

Johnny stared at me. "But—" he said faintly.

"Ssh," I said. "All will be well. Go, ask Gull to staunch that wound. Mend matters with these men. That is your part; to lead. There is no further need for you here."

"Fainne—"

"Go on, Johnny. Trust me. I am family." I saw the sorceress's head snap around toward me as I spoke these words. Her eyes narrowed sharply. At the moment her attention was diverted the circle of flames died down a little, and the two warriors stumbled through, cloaked by my father's protective spell, and collapsed into the arms of waiting healers. Bran of Harrowfield and Edwin of Northwoods each went to his son; they conveyed the wounded men away to a place of safety. Still the forces of Inis Eala kept a tight control of the crowd; the warriors were growing ever more restless and fearful. They had come here expecting an honest battle, not some eldritch display of magic tricks that turned the very day to night before their eyes. My father lifted his arms again and the fire sprang up anew. The sorceress gave a little smile; her pointed teeth glowed red in the flames. She took one step, two steps inside the circle. It had not taken her so very long to find a way through.

Ciarán stood calm and steady with the flames at his back. On his shoulder Fiacha crouched still as a carven effigy. Behind my father the fire still burned fiercely. Conor stood still and silent, outstretched arms holding the circle unbroken, and on the opposite side Finbar played his part, crouched on the earth with visage ghost-white and eyes darkened with pain. Mother and son faced each other not six paces from where I knelt, my head still reeling from the knowledge that my mother had been murdered, and a terrible lie told all these years, a lie which had filled my father's days with guilt and shame. All this time he had believed his love was not enough for Niamh; all this long time he had believed she chose to leave him. Beneath this new grief my heart still ached with emptiness, with the loss which could never be made right, not if I lived thrice the span of mortal woman. Maybe my mouth no longer howled my pain, but inside me the song of grief wailed like the banshee's cry, keening, screaming, sharp and savage as a shard of ice twisting deep in the vitals. And all the while I felt the magic flowing back into me, stronger and still stronger, powerful and true, yet I could not move; I slumped on the ground, held fast by shock and misery.

Beyond the flames the great throng of warriors had fallen silent, but for occasional mutterings and whisperings; prayers, maybe. This was far beyond the experience of ordinary man, be he hardened warrior or Christian priest or merely fisherman or shepherd called to arms in service of his chieftain. Terror blanched their faces; fascination held them watching as this strange game played itself out before their eyes.

"So," the lady Oonagh said, and it seemed to me as she faced her son she drew up dark power from deep within her; she grew taller, and grander, and her mulberry eyes glowed with malevolence in the smooth pallor of her terrible, fair face. "So, you think to do battle with me; you, my weakling son, corrupted by druids, tainted by family, crippled by love. Have you forgotten who gave you birth, you apology for a sorcerer, that you manifest yourself now at the last in some futile attempt to save these fools and their pathetic scrap of rock? Or do you seek merely to protect your daughter, who has proven no apter a tool for my purposes than you yourself were? Look at her crouching there, a shivering, pathetic wreck! Some sorceress she is! Cared more for her common little tinker than for the great task I set her, got it all mixed up in the end, let it all go. Now she's got nothing left, no power, no influence, no lover, no family, for they will cast her out now they know what she's done. Maiming children, killing druids, spying, watching, insinuating herself among them with the will to destroy in her heart. There'll be no going back for your precious student, Ciarán. You should have seen your sweet little girl in Eamonn's arms. That would have opened your eyes well and truly. Oh, yes, she did inherit one or two skills from her mother. Niamh was good under the blankets, wasn't she? Why else would you have wanted such a featherhead?"

All the time my grandmother spoke she was watching Father; her eyes never left his face. His lips were tight, his jaw set; his eyes burned with rage. But he did not lose control. I sensed each waited for a moment when the other's guard might slip; the instant of opportunity. The air seemed to crackle with magic; spell and counter-spell, in the mind but not yet on the lips, warred in the air above the fiery circle. Fiacha's dark form was outlined in little sparks. My own body tingled with the craft; I felt its force in my hands, in my feet, burning in my head.

"It's over, Mother," Ciarán said quietly. "There are forces ranged against you here that you can scarcely dream of. You have failed. The young warrior lives to lead his men forward; I see peace in his eyes, truce in the strength of his hand. Your venture is pointless. And if Fainne could not do the deed you set for her, tell me, tell us all, *why did you not do it yourself?*"

Oonagh stared back at him. Her face was not that of a beautiful, regal lady now but had changed again; I saw the skull beneath the tight-stretched skin, I saw the look in her eyes and knew it for fear.

"That means nothing!" she snapped. "The boy was useless! Child of the prophecy, huh! He's not fit for it, he can never fulfill the task foretold for him. What matter if he lives or dies? You've lost, all of you! This can only turn to dust and ashes, whatever you do. Dust and ashes, desolation and despair!"

"Answer me," Father said in the quietest of voices, and I saw Fiacha beginning to edge down from his shoulder and along his outstretched arm, as if preparing for flight. "Answer my question. No? Then let me answer it for you, Mother. You sent my daughter to kill the child of the prophecy because you could not do it yourself. You could not do it because your strength is waning, day by day, season by season. Even as my daughter grew, even as she worked and studied and became strong in the craft, so your own powers diminished. You never recovered from the defeat you suffered at the hands of human folk. You will never be what you were. You cannot destroy the secrets of the Islands. Admit the truth. In what was to be your great moment of triumph, you have already lost."

The lady Oonagh blinked. For the merest instant her eyes were unfocused, and in that moment Fiacha rose, dark wings spread wide, to fly swift as a spear straight at her face. She was quick; her eyes grew sharp again and with a little snapping sound she set a guard in place. One hand went up, and now a ball of green light was pursuing the raven as he circled her head, dipping and swerving to escape its eldritch fire. The bird could not fly away; she held him to her. The charm would burn him to a crisp the instant it touched him. My fingers moved subtly, and now Fiacha was a tiny raven no bigger than a bee, a little speck of darkness that spun out of the fixing charm as easily as a fishling escapes the herring net, and darted away to the shelter of a small feathery bush which might or not have been there an instant before. My father did not so much as glance in my direction. Oonagh glared at her son.

"What is this?" she snarled. "A game of tricks? Dog eats cat, cat eats rat, rat eats beetle and so on? We are above such conjurer's gimmicks, surely. And you are wrong. I have a power beyond yours, beyond theirs." Her glance of scorn swept around the great circle of dumbfounded, staring warriors, taking in the ashen-faced Conor, the grim-jawed Sean, the crouching, gasping Finbar, and passing over the tall, stately figures of the Otherworld beings who stood behind, silent, grave observers. "You've never understood how to defeat your enemy, Ciarán; you've never grasped it, and you never will."

Then she changed. At the Glamour she was a master, even more skillful than my father; I had seen that demonstrated many a time as she stood before the mirror back in the Honeycomb and showed me simpering girl and wondrous queen, slithering serpent and sleek hunting cat. But she had never shown me this. Quick as a heartbeat the change was on her, and there stood a girl of eighteen, her pale cheeks flushed with delicate rose, her wide, guileless eyes blue as the summer sky, her hair flowing down across her bare shoulders red-gold as fine clover honey. She wore a gown the color of wood violets and on her feet soft kidskin shoes, dancing shoes. I heard my uncle Sean's exclamation of shock, I heard the lovely girl who was not my mother say, "Ciarán?" in a soft, sweet voice that trembled with hesitant joy. I saw the look on my father's face; his guard had dropped away, and for that moment he was quite without defense. The girl held something loosely in her hand, half hidden in the silken folds of her gown; something shining, something deadly. I opened my mouth to warn him, to speak a spell, anything, but I, too, hesitated; the girl looked at me, her eyes full of love; it was my mother . . .

Finbar moved. Quick as sunlight he moved, up from his knees, into the circle, running, flying, wing unfurled to stop the lethal bolt as the girl raised her arm and hurled it toward my father's breast. Crumpling, falling, writhing enmeshed in the deadly, burning charm meant for his brother, Finbar sprawled at Oonagh's feet, a great black scorch across the white wing feathers, a bloody, gaping wound in his chest where cloak and tunic and living flesh had been torn away by the force of the death-bolt. The thing lay harmless by his side now, smoking, its force all spent. Ciarán stood mute, his eyes not on the man who lay dying at his feet, but on the figure standing opposite, now an old woman, her mouth a gash of crimson in her wrinkled face, her hair a wild crown of disheveled white.

"You killed my brother," Ciarán said in a voice like a small child's. "You killed him."

Conor had let out one great cry of anguish as he saw Finbar fall. Now he was chanting, his soft words falling like tears into the bitter silence. I saw Sean's face twisted with grief; I felt a wrenching pain in my own heart, I who had believed I could hold no more sadness. As the sound of my grandmother's cackling laughter rose in the air, my father knelt by Finbar's side and took his hand, heedless of danger.

"The earth receive and shelter you," Ciarán said softly. "The waters bear you forth gently to your new life. The west wind carry you swift and sure. The fire you hold already in your head, brother, strong and subtle, for you were ever a child of the spirit. You have given your life for me this day; I will not squander that gift. You have my word; a brother's word."

Then Finbar smiled, and died, and for a moment the air darkened as if a shadow passed over us all. And when I blinked again, it seemed to me the man who lay there lifeless on the hard ground was a man untouched by evil, a man who bore no disfigurement at all, for his two arms were outstretched at his sides and his clear eyes gazed up into the sky as if searching for an answer that lay, far, far beyond the realm in which his family stood by him, their hearts stricken with loss.

Then my father rose to his feet again and turned to the sorceress, and her face changed as she saw the look in his eyes. I must not let him do this; it was wrong that son should be the instrument of mother's punishment. This was my own task; this was my time.

"No, Father," I said quietly, rising and stepping forward. "This must be done well. Your part is ended."

The lady Oonagh's head whipped around toward me again; her lips parted. She seemed to scent victory. "Fainne," she cooed, "my dear, how valiant. Best stay out of this, I think. This is well beyond your limited powers. And I see how weakened you are. The transformation took a lot out of you. Don't make a fool of yourself, dear. Leave this to your father." Then her eyes widened, and she swallowed, and her hands clawed themselves into tight fists as she felt the grip of my spell, a charm which held her where she stood, able to see, able to speak, quite unable to break free. In her wild gaze I saw the recognition that she had completely underestimated me.

"Clever," she said tightly. "I've taught you well. So be it, do your worst. It's all useless anyway. I've won this battle, regardless of your cunning little devices. Perhaps Sevenwaters has not lost the battle; but the Islands are surely lost, and the long goal of the Fair Folk thwarted. Oh, yes, they stand there watching; look over your shoulder and you will see them, the Lady of the Forest and her Fire-Lord, the fine ones of stream and ocean, of lofty heights and echoing caves. *Sevenwaters cannot win*. The child lives, but he cannot fulfill the prophecy. He just doesn't have it in him."

My father gave an odd little smile. He looked at me, and I looked at him.

"What do you mean?" asked Conor. His face was wet with tears; he looked gray and old. "Johnny has led his men valiantly, almost at cost of his life. He has triumphed here on the field, and so the Islands are won for Sevenwaters. What more can there be?"

The lady Oonagh laughed, a youthful, carefree laugh like the pealing of tiny bells. "The battle was only the first part, my dear little druid. It's what comes after that counts. The child of the prophecy is to keep watch; a very lonely watch, no less than the long guardianship of the very secrets of the lore; the heart of the mysteries the Fair Folk hug to themselves so jealously. He must climb up there, to the top of that pinnacle out yonder in the sea, and live alone, live his whole life in solitude, keeping those things safe. Without the Watcher in the Needle, the old things will dwindle and die, and the Fair Folk with them. Maybe it's not all in the prophecy, but it's the truth. Ask Ciarán. He worked it out. Ask these grand lords and ladies of the Túatha Dé, they'll tell you."

"The Watcher in the Needle?" Sean's voice was harsh with shock; bitter with disappointment. "He must live there, in the cell under the rowans, alone? Johnny is the heir to Sevenwaters; he is a war-leader, future guardian of the túath, he is vital to our people's security and well-being. Are you telling us that after all this, the slaughter, the loss, still the true battle is not won? That unless Johnny makes this sacrifice, the prophecy cannot be fulfilled and the balance restored?"

There was a silence. Then Conor put his hands over his face, and bowed his head.

"All is lost," he said. "For the boy cannot do this; all of us know it. Johnny is a warrior; his heart beats to the rhythm of the sword, and not to the slow unfolding of the lore. His mother cut off this path for him, long years ago, when she chose to take him away from the forest. He is no scholar, no mystic; in such a place he would last no longer than the turning of the year, from Samhain to Samhain, before he grew crazed with it. Johnny cannot do this; and if this is the truth of it, then all has been for nothing."

"Wise words, brother," said Ciarán gravely. "The boy must return to Sevenwaters and in time take up his rightful place in the scheme of things. He will be guardian of forest and folk, and will in his turn perform the task nobly, as his uncle does now."

"Ah!" the lady Oonagh said sharply, still struggling to free herself from the spell in which I had trapped her. "So you agree with me. You see, I was right all along. The Fair Folk are finished."

"I cannot believe it, and yet I must," said Conor in a voice heavy with defeat.

"Not so," said my father. "A prophecy is never simple. It has as many twists and turns as the lore itself. Like a puzzle, it may have more than one solution."

There was a small disturbance in the air beside me; a ruffling of feathers. And on my other side, a creaking sound, a slight rolling of pebbles. Suddenly, I was flanked by the Fomhóire. A general rustling, a snuffling and twittering told me there were more behind me.

"Ahem," said the owl-creature. Around the circle, the men stood completely silent, staring; such entertainment had not been seen for many a long year, and so strange was it that they had almost forgotten their fear. "You overlooked us, I think. Again. But no matter. Come on, Fainne. Time to tell the truth. Time to tell them what a good idea it is to keep a little in reserve, so to speak, just in case things don't work out the way you plan them. The Fair Folk don't understand that, but we've been here a long time, oh, so very long. We know the value of a backup."

"Uncle," I said, choking back the tears which still seemed to be rolling down my cheeks, blinking so I could focus on Conor's weary face as I moved to stand before him. "All is not lost. Johnny cannot go to the Needle and fulfill the prophecy; but I can."

"You?" It was Sean who spoke, frowning at me ferociously. Clearly, he was still far from sure which side I was on.

"It is true," said my father, coming up beside me. His voice was deep and resonant. "There was a pattern, set by the Fair Folk. Liadan changed that. She ensured her child could not play the part intended for him. But the prophecy does not speak of a man, or of warriors and battles. Fainne, you had better explain this to your uncle."

I stared at him. "You knew," I breathed, torn between astonishment and anger. "You knew, all the time, and you didn't tell me?"

Ciarán shook his head; a tiny smile curved his severe mouth. "Suspected, that was all; one does not know these things. If I had been certain, maybe I would have told you, daughter. But maybe not. If you had known, your journey would have been different; its ending perhaps failure. This way, your errors have strengthened you, your difficulties have prepared you for the long vigil ahead."

"What!" the lady Oonagh spluttered, still held firm in the grip of the spell. "What are you saying, wretch? It cannot be so! The girl bears no mark—she cannot be the one!"

I turned again, so the sorceress could see me quite clearly. "You called my education half-baked," I told her. "One thing my father did teach me was how to solve puzzles; to look for signs. I would have known this sooner, had I thought to study the words of the prophecy more closely. It speaks of a child of Erin and of Britain, who is at the same time neither. My mother, whom you so despised, was a daughter of Sevenwaters, a child of the forest. But her father was Hugh of Harrowfield, a Briton, who by his own choice wed a woman of Erin, and lived his life exiled from his native land. My father is a sorcerer, and he too is a child of Sevenwaters; son, indeed, of Lord Colum, once a strong leader of the folk of the forest until you entrapped him; until your lust for vengeance made him lose his way. The human folk of Sevenwaters fought against you then, and triumphed; and they do again today. I am indeed a child of Erin and of Britain; and yet I am neither, for I am more than that. I carry in my blood the seeds of four races, the heritage of the Fomhóire ancestors, and the strain of the Fair Folk themselves, through you, my grandmother. Are you not yourself descended from the very people you so despise, through a line of outcasts?"

My grandmother's whole body was shaking with fury and disbelief.

"This means nothing!" she spat. "Clever words, tricky arguments, druid's rubbish! You can never fulfill the prophecy! The Fair Folk cannot win! What about the sign of the raven? You pathetic, crippled apology for a girl, how can you claim that? You are no hero; you're as weak and useless as your mother was!"

My fingers touched Riona's butter-yellow hair, her bloodstained skirts. At my feet Finbar was stretched out on the earth, dark hair tangled around his head, features pale and calm. Farther across the circle, Eamonn's body still lay where he had fallen. If not for him, I would have died, and the lady Oonagh would have won this battle. Words no longer seemed to hurt me. All I could feel was an emptiness. My heart was numb. But I knew I would go on, I must go on, or these losses would indeed have been for nothing.

"You're wrong, Grandmother," I said quietly. "Prophecies are a little like the Sight, I think. They show things distorted, or changed subtly, so you need to be good at solving puzzles to understand." I drew aside the neckline of my gown, and my fingers touched the tiny scar that still marked the white skin of my shoulder. "Fiacha pecked me once, when I was a child. A raven has a sharp beak; I still bear the scar of it. Even so arbitrary can the working out of a great mystery prove to be. I do indeed bear the mark of the raven. I am a child of Erin and of Britain. In every respect I am the child of the prophecy, as much as Johnny is. Besides—"

"Besides," said Conor with dawning realization, "you were raised as a druid, whether your father intended it or no. Raised in discipline, in the endurance of hardship and the knowledge of the lore. Raised in a love of solitude and trained in the craft of magic."

"What are you saying?" Sean stared at me, now apparently torn between horrified understanding and a budding hope.

But I was suddenly weary, oh, so weary, and could hardly think how to respond; and before my eyes, my grandmother began to strain anew against the charm, wrenching at its unseen bonds with bony hands, her pointed teeth bared in a terrible rage.

"No!" she hissed. "This cannot be!"

"I think it can," said my father quietly, moving behind me to lay a hand on my shoulder; to lend me his own strength. "I think you will find, Mother, that you made quite an error of judgment in sharing your knowledge with me and then dismissing me as not worthy of your attention. As a druid I too learned to solve puzzles and to respect what is. As a sorcerer I learned to play games, and I always play to win. You settled on my daughter to work your will; and in doing so you have crafted the weapon of your own destruction. In the forge of your cruelty, with your tests of will and endurance, you have yourself created the child of the prophecy, and the instrument of your downfall. I prepared her as well as I could; you sharpened her to perfection."

"Come."

There was a sudden hush, for this was a different voice, and the men fell back in amazement. From each quarter of the circle a wondrous being stepped forth, all taller than any man or woman of mortal lineage, and so dazzling bright it was as if the sun had burst forth anew here on this desolate hillside. They were the folk of the Túatha Dé; they had watched and waited until this combat, this debate were over. Now they came forward, faces grave and pale, voices like the shimmer of clear water over pebbles, or the distant thunder of an autumn storm.

"I am Deirdre of the Forest." A woman stepped toward me, long white hand outstretched. Her hair rippled down her back in a curtain of dark silk; her eyes were the deep blue of the sky at dusk, a color echoed in the flowing folds of her cloak. "Time passes. We are ready."

"Come, fire child." It was a man who spoke, if such a wondrous creature could be called a man; his hair was brightest red, a halo of flames that danced and sparked around his head. His eyes, too, sparked; mischievous, dangerous. "Your long work awaits you. Come, now."

"We will convey you there." This being had a voice like the ocean, soft and powerful, a sound like the waves washing into the echoing chambers of the Honeycomb. "The sea will carry you." I could not say how she looked, save that she was a thing of water, transparent yet real, a moving, changing being with fronded hair and wild eyes, and hands and feet fluid as the ebb and flow of the tide in rock pools.

"Not yet!" The fourth being spoke, and all turned to gaze on him. He was little more than a disturbance of the air; the hint of a shimmering robe, the glow, now here, now gone, of a pair of deep, shining eyes, the glitter of hair like strands of tiny jewels, moving on the breeze. "This must be ended now. Move forward!"

It was a command not to be refused; a voice of power. But it was not to me these words were spoken. The spell I had cast broke abruptly, shattered by some higher magic. I felt my father's hands on my shoulders, gripping firmly as the lady Oonagh stepped toward me, a little unsteady on her feet, stretching out her long, predatory fingers.

"I will destroy you!" she shrieked, shaking from head to toe, and the menace in her dark eyes was enough to freeze the strongest will. "I will shred you limb from limb, you little weakling!"

Around her the great lords and ladies of the Túatha Dé Danann stood silent and still. My father's hands were strong and warm; in their touch I felt his love. Conor chanted ancient words under his breath. Still the barrier of flame burned, holding back those who might have attempted a foolish intervention with sword or spear.

I felt no fear at all as I watched her coming closer, though the venom in her eyes was real and chilling. I felt nothing but the emptiness inside me and the knowledge of my own power.

"This is for you to do, Fainne," said the Lady of the Forest quietly. "It is meant thus. End the long darkness. Use what you have learned."

And so I looked straight into my grandmother's eyes, which were the very reflection of my own, and I spoke the words of a little spell long ago perfected under her tutelage. I had always been good at this, and now the magic flowed through me as strong and sure as in the days of Kerry, the days before ever I rode away from home, and learned that love is the cruelest thing of all. In the moment before she changed, I saw the recognition in her eyes, the knowledge of her own defeat; and the terror.

"Of all the evil that you have done," I whispered, "there is one thing, just one, that I can never forgive. But I will not kill you. You can take your chance, like the rest of us." Then I clicked my fingers, and the fearsome sorceress became a farmyard chicken, clucking and pecking this way and that at my feet, frightened by the crowd. I clicked my fingers again, and a little snake slid and coiled there, shining, dark as ripe mulberries, darting swift now for escape, until I turned it into a scuttling cockroach, glossy black. Somewhere behind me there was a ruffling of feathers, a slight change in the manner of things. I moved my hand and whispered; the cockroach became a plump barn mouse, well fed on last season's hoarded grain. It scampered away, for now there was a great mossy stone there, good cover for a small wild creature. But as the mouse reached it the stone rolled subtly away; and in an instant, a bird swooped down, swift and deadly, to rise again with the squeaking, struggling creature gripped firmly in its beak. The ragged owl landed neatly atop the mossy boulder; it swallowed once, and all that could be seen of the mouse was a frantically thrashing tail protruding from the beak's end. The owl gave another gulp, and the mouse was gone. Not one of us uttered a word.

"Come, Fainne." The Lady of the Forest reached out her pale, smooth hand again, making to lead me away. "It is time." She turned to the men assembled there, to Sean and Conor, to the leaders of Britain and Erin alike. "The girl spoke truth," she said. "Heed her warning, and mine. After tonight, none may remain here in safety. After tonight, no human foot will touch these shores, save this young woman's. Use what ships you may, convey your men hence without delay, and sail to safe harbor. For if you remain on the Islands you perish every one. The prophecy is fulfilled. The quest is over. Go home, and begin your lives anew."

"Even now your sons make terms of peace." It was the flame-haired Lord who spoke, his voice as solemn and deep as thunder. "Even so easily is this settled, by one as wise and courageous as the child of the prophecy. For make no doubt of it, the young man too has played his part here; without him the battle would not have been won, for it is he who gives your men the very heart that sustains them. Without him peace will not be made between Northwoods and Sevenwaters; between Harrowfield and its neighbor. Johnny is the child of our own making; his lineage of our devising." I heard a little cough behind me; the Old Ones appeared to have a somewhat different opinion on this issue, but they were not arguing the point. "The boy is a rare and shining example to you all. Follow him, and you may enjoy peace on both sides of the water. Follow him, and you may preserve both lands and forest, for a time. For a time." There was a deep sadness behind his stirring words.

"Come, Fainne."

I could no longer refuse to follow; it was indeed time. The warriors were dispersing fast; some, under Snake's orders, headed for the anchorage to load ships and make ready for departure. There were many men to carry away from the shore, and a miracle of organization would be required. But the men of Inis Eala were good at these things. By nightfall, all would be away safe. Green-clad warriors were lifting Eamonn's broken body; dealing with the spear. Men of Sevenwaters were covering the ragged, peaceful form of Finbar with a white cloth which bore the symbol of two torcs interlinked. Sean was looking over toward the guard post, for Edwin of Northwoods stood there waiting.

"Just a moment," I said to my Otherworld guides; for I thought, since this parting was forever, they could grant me a little time at least. I turned to my uncle, the lord of Sevenwaters.

"Tell the girls I won't forget them," I said as steadily as I could. "They taught me about family, and a lot of other things. I would like to be sure Eamonn is given a good farewell, with lights and music and honor, for though he made many errors, in the end he died bravely. And tell Maeve—tell her I'm sorry. I'm so sorry."

There was pain in Sean's eyes, but also a certain respect. He nodded, and kissed me on one cheek and then the other, but he said not a word.

"Goodbye, Uncle," I said to Conor.

"Goodbye, my dear." His expression was very grave. "This is a long farewell. I wish I could help you. You are so young, for such a trust. So young, with your whole life ahead of you."

"It doesn't seem to matter," I whispered, the tears beginning to flow again. "I may as well do this, since it is all I am fit for."

"All?" Conor echoed. "A great and wondrous *all*, I think."

He didn't understand. None of them understood the hollow emptiness inside. I turned to my father.

"Father?"

Ciarán looked down at me, his face very pale, his dark eyes still guarded, even now. "I have great faith in you, daughter," he said. "I always did. Great faith, and great pride. And I love you. Never forget that."

"Father, will you go back now? Home to Sevenwaters? They need you. Conor is old and tired. It is time for the ties of family to be remade, and for the wisdom of your own kind to be renewed in the forest. And there is a little girl there who might be a great mystic, if only you would teach her. I have done a lot of harm, Father, thinking only to protect those I loved. I wanted to keep you safe, and—and—"

My words trailed into silence.

"You have been very strong; strong enough for all of us, in the end. I will consider what you ask." He glanced at the white-shrouded form that lay on the ground near our feet. "Perhaps it is time at last for these wounds to be healed. Now goodbye, daughter." He bent to kiss me on the brow. "May the hand of the goddess rest gently on you; may the sun warm your days, and the moon light your dreams."

"Goodbye, Father. I'll hold you in my heart, always."

But it seemed to me, as the Fair Folk led me down to the shore where a long, dark boat lay on the pebbles waiting, that my heart was empty now, washed clean of all it had ever held, and that it could never be filled again. It did not seem to matter what was in store for me, how lonely and perilous the task. It did not seem to matter what I was leaving behind. They did not understand that. None of them understood. The Old Ones had been right. I had cast away my only treasure. I had not known how much I had to lose, until it was already gone. Now, by my own choice, I had lost everything.

The boat slid away from shore with never a sail or an oar in sight, with never a crewman to guide her on the perilous way to the Needle. Behind me on the shore the Fair Folk stood watching, grave and silent. I clutched Riona tightly in my arms as if I were a little child again, as the boat moved ever swifter away from the land.

"It wasn't fair," I whispered fiercely. "Darragh was so good, he never did anything wrong, and she killed him, and it was all because of me. And Finbar died because of me, because I made him come here. Nobody understands. Nobody knows. They expect me to feel like some sort of hero; as if I were full of a grand purpose. But there's nothing left in me but emptiness."

And it seemed to me I heard the small, silent voice of the doll as I looked into her dark, inscrutable eyes. *I know,* she said. *I, whom Niamh made with her own two hands, stitch by stitch, thread by thread; I know what love is.*

I looked back toward the shore, where Conor and my father now stood side by side, each raising a hand in salute and farewell. Their figures grew smaller and smaller, and at last could be seen no longer as the little boat surged forward, gripped by the current, dragged ever faster toward the treacherous rocks of the Needle. I closed my eyes and gave myself up to what would be.

The Fair Folk travel swifter than the west wind; more subtly than a shadow. They were waiting there, when the boat came through swirling waters to the Needle, and swept into a cavern under the rocks, and stopped abruptly beside a rough-hewn shelf. This formed a jetty of sorts, though what vessel other than a faery craft might make its way to such a strange anchorage, I could not imagine. The Lady of the Forest extended her hand again, helping me to scramble out, leading me up a set of impossible steps cut in the precipitous rock face. Who could live in such a place? The slightest wind might blow you down to the reefs below; and how could you survive? I saw myself wasting away to a lonely death on a diet of seaweed and the occasional shellfish prised from the rocks with bleeding fingers. A hermit's life. It was possible, of course. There was that place in Kerry, the Skelligs, and the Christian monks who had held on there through Viking invasions, through pillage and murder, through the storms of Meán Fómhair and the hard clutch of winter. Year after year they had clung to their pinnacle, its isolation strengthening their faith and sharpening their minds, the better to contemplate the mysteries. I did not understand the Christian way. My studies suggested to me it was somewhat lacking in respect for the things that *are*: for the power of earth and sun, the force of water and the purity of air. Those are the cornerstones of the old faith, for without them, without the knowledge of moon and stars, without the understanding of all existences, how could one make any sense of things at all? We are a part of those wonders, tied to them as a newborn child is tied to its mother; if we do not know them, we do not know ourselves. There are so many manifestations of beauty: swift deer and sleek salmon, delicate wren and mysterious starfish, strong oak and slender birch. And there are the things beyond the margin, which show themselves but rarely: the inscrutable, changeable beings of the Otherworld, who walk beside us through our short lives, unseen save when they choose, or when we ourselves learn to cross that divide. At Samhain we may see them, or in dreams and visions; but it is not as it once was, when the Old Ones walked the land, and the boundaries were scarce visible between the great things that *are* and those who are their guardians. As for the human folk, we are a small part in the long way of it, so small; yet each of us is precious, a jewel of great worth, and each of us is different. The Fair Folk might not see it that way, I supposed. They could not understand how the loss of a single human life could weigh so heavy, for their thoughts were on the grand scheme of things; my importance lay only in the part I would play for them.

We came to the top of the steps. I was breathless and dizzy, for I had eaten nothing since I left Inis Eala. Here the precipitous surface gave way to a small plateau, sheltered by a natural rock wall. There were rowan bushes growing, thick with both leaves and berries, though it was as yet barely spring. The wind did not batter this small place of shelter; indeed, there was a strange sense of calm about it, as if it were in some way isolated from the rest of the world, from storm and frost, from the passing of the seasons, perhaps even from time itself. In the center of the open space a spring welled up between flat stones, to pool in a basin of rock before it ran through a narrow channel to the edge, and tumbled away down to the sea far below. A little cup stood by the basin. Either someone lived here, or had done; or the place had been prepared for me.

"It is a long time," said the Lady of the Forest, "since man or woman dwelt in this place. There was a druid, once. It is a difficult calling; the Needle has been untenanted now since long before the memory of man or woman living, or their fathers, or their fathers' fathers. We came very close to losing all. Sevenwaters let the Islands go; the invaders hacked at the sacred trees and defiled the holy spring;

they walked in the caves of truth. But they saw nothing. They understood nothing. The mysteries reveal themselves only to the few, only to those who understand the pattern."

"If that is so," I asked her, "why not just leave things as they are? Why should you need a weak human tool like myself, to stay here for you and watch over this place as a sort of—caretaker? Doesn't it look after itself? You could keep folk out by magic, couldn't you? Mists, storms, sea monsters? Why would you need the child of the prophecy?"

The fiery Lord appeared by her side. I had noticed a certain flamboyance in his style; he seemed given to sudden showers of sparks and colorful flashes of light.

"Ah," he said with a grim smile. "The explanation lies in the words themselves. A prophecy must be respected. One can help it along a little, but in the end it governs the falling out of things. We have known for a long time that our days were numbered; we have known this prophecy must be fulfilled if we were to have any chance of preserving what is precious to us all. Our age is drawing to its close at last. The Old Ones fared better for, weak, crippled breed though they are, they nonetheless possess the wisdom of the earth itself, the ability to blend and go unseen right in the midst of things, and to endure. The Túatha Dé have different arts. Once we were great indeed, rulers of the realm of Erin, supreme and powerful. We did indeed shine bright; in us was the very embodiment of mystery and wonder, magic and enchantment. But the world changes. In this age of human kind, our places of refuge are few. The forest of Sevenwaters is one of the last; and while Lord Sean rules there, and after him the child, Johnny, we may walk beneath those oaks in safety. The archdruid is one of the true folk of Sevenwaters; he will keep the observances of the old faith, and inspire others. And Ciarán, too, will have his time and his influence, for all he is *her* son. The man is strong-hearted and has much to give. They will win a season, a year, a lifetime for the forest and its dwellers. But there will come a time, soon enough, when even that ancient wood will fall to the axe, to grant man his grazing land, his settlements, his towers and walls. He thinks, in his ignorance, to tame the very earth, to force the very ocean to his will. And so he will lay waste the body of the mother who gave him birth; and will not know what he does. The old ways will be forgotten, Fainne, no matter what we do. A new age begins; an age of darkness in which those who walk the earth are cut off from the very things which give them life."

"Without you, all will be lost." The being spoke who seemed made only of air and light; all I could see of him were his luminous eyes and the golden threads of his hair. "For while the mysteries remain alive in the heart of a single human creature, while the knowledge of our kind dwells there in safety, then we do not pass away forever, but simply wait, dreaming, until the time comes for renewal, for rebirth of the sacred trust, the understanding of the great circle of existence."

"You must keep these things alive, Fainne," said the watery being, whose long hair waved around her shoulders like delicate strands of pond weed. I thought I saw tiny, glittering fishes swimming there, darting in and out of the fronds. "This is the trust laid on you."

"But—" I began, one quite obvious question springing to my lips.

"Come, let us show you."

The Lady of the Forest took my hand again and led me to the rock wall, and now I saw there was an opening there, a mere slit cunningly concealed, so one would think it no more than a slight irregularity of the surface, perhaps only a shadow.

"There's a great deal more here than meets the eye," she said gravely. "These portals are not easy to find; thus do we guard what little is left to us. Once within, you will discover this is a larger realm than you imagined."

"As the spirit burns bright, and seems sometimes too great to be contained within the small shell of the body, so it is with this place," the water-being said softly. "The inner world is wider and more complex than the outer, deeper and more intricate. Here you will see many things; you will see what was, and is, and what may be. You will watch, and you will remember."

It was indeed as they said. The slit in the rocks gave way to a passage, and the passage to a cavern, greater far in height and width than the narrow plateau outside had indicated was possible. And there were other caves leading off the central chamber, on every side; through one opening I glimpsed a warm gold lamplight, and a place for sleeping, with pillows and soft linen, and a coverlet which looked like the shaggy pelt of some great wild creature. My eyes widened.

"Look here, Fainne."

The purpose of this central chamber was immediately evident to me, brought up as I had been in the knowledge of the mysteries and the practice of ritual. In the middle was a wide, shallow bowl of bronze, empty now; by it was an ornate jug of similar make, placed on a granite slab. Above these ceremonial vessels the roof of the cavern arched high; and in the center it was open to the sky. It seemed to me the round hole in the rocks was precisely placed, just as the standing stones in Kerry had each its position and its purpose. This opening showed a tiny patch of blue sky, quite cloudless. It was perhaps midday, perhaps a little later. Tonight I might look above me and see one lovely star; or a velvet darkness profound and quiet. At a certain time of year the rays of the sun would pierce the stone, touching the ritual water beneath with living fire. This was a cavern such as the place Finbar had inhabited alone, far away on Inis Eala. An ancient place. A safe place. The hand of the goddess stretched over it, her cradling body supported it. If the old ways were to be preserved, held intact in the memory of a single human mind, the beating of a single human heart, it would be here. But for how long? I opened my mouth to ask the question, and the ocean-being waved her strange, weed-like hand over the bronze bowl, and it was filled on an instant with clear water. I closed my mouth without speaking. The Lord who was more airy light than substance leaned forward and breathed on the water, and its surface came alive with a patchwork of tiny images, bright as summer flowers, moving and changing in a complex, dazzling pattern.

"Come, fire child," said the Lord with hair of flame. "We will show you."

The Lady of the Forest took my left hand, and he took my right, and together we looked down into the water. There was so much there, too much; it was jumbled and fragmented, and yet within the intricate movement I could see familiar things, now here, now gone; a fish flapping on the earth; cages opening, creatures fleeing swift; a fire burning, and a man's face contorted in pain. I screwed my eyes shut.

"I don't know how to scry," I said tightly. "I'm no good at it. If this is the task you want done, you've got the wrong girl."

"Focus," said the Lady.

"Control," said the fiery Lord. "You find this difficult not because you have too little ability, but because you have so much. You must narrow your range; fix on a time, a place, a sequence. Find a pattern, and shut out the rest until you need it. Here is the working of all existences, Fainne. Here you can find what was: the endless movement of the stars, the voices of the ancient rocks, the mysteries of the depths of the ocean. You can read the stories of our kind, and your kind, and the other kind as well. You can see what is: even now your father and the others leave the shores of Greater Island, even now the Britons ship for home, leaving behind them a promise of peace. The master of the vessel which conveys them is a cousin you have never met: Fintan, heir to Harrowfield. There is a bright time ahead for these folk; a brief, bright time."

"You will see these things," said the Lady, "and you will be shown what will be, or what may be. There is a peril in that which I am sure you understand. You have been chosen for this, Fainne, because of what you are. There is no barrier for you; there is nothing to prevent your attainment of the highest realms of the craft, if that is what you aspire to. She who told you otherwise lied to you, and to your father. Even then, even when you were but a child, she sensed the power in you; a power, in the end, far greater than her own. Her error was to believe she could channel it to her will. She underestimated both Ciarán's strength and yours. It is a paradox, for without her blood, the blood of the outcast, you would not be strong enough for this task. The lady Oonagh was one of us. Her kind are our shadows, our counterparts who walk by us, keeping the balance. The one cannot exist without the other; and yet we war together eternally. So, she has made you strong. You have a deep understanding for one so young. Those skills of which you have not yet the mastery, we will teach you. Oh, yes," she raised her brows, smiling at my start of surprise, "we will come, from time to time, at least until you are settled in this place. Now look again; choose a single image, and concentrate your mind on that. Make it work for you. Block out the rest."

I gazed into the pool, remembering small Sibeal and her total, silent concentration. She was only eight years old. I had a lot of ground to make up. Among the chaotic swirl of images, there was one that drew me. Three children lying on rocks, by a lake. The lake of Sevenwaters, not far from the keep. It was summer; two trailed their fingers in the water, watching the fish. The third, a boy with a tangle of dark hair, lay on his back with arms outstretched, staring up into the sky. The boy had a look of Coll; he had a look of my uncle Sean. But there was only one man I knew with those clear, deep eyes, eyes with no color save that of wisdom. Without a doubt what I saw was an image of long ago, and this child was Finbar, looking beyond the realm where his small brother and sister played and into his own strange destiny. The tiny image changed, yet was the same. The rocks, the lake, brown ducks dabbling there. The three children, sons and daughters of Sevenwaters. It was still summer, but a different summer, and the children were different too. A pair of twins, boy and girl, fey and dark-haired, reaching down to tease the fish that swam there among the reeds; and another girl, lovely as a spirit of autumn with her wide blue eyes and fall of red-gold hair. The tiny black-haired child who was my aunt Liadan said something, and Sean poked her in the ribs, and my mother laughed, her sweet, pure features alight with mirth. I bent closer to the water, longing for more, longing to see this child as she had been once, before her joy was snatched from her. But the image blurred and changed again, and I saw my cousin Sibeal, cross-legged on the selfsame stone by the lake, hands folded in her lap. Her eyes seemed to see nothing, and everything. She looked right at me and smiled; and the image was gone.

"You will learn quickly," the Lady of the Forest said as I blinked and rubbed my eyes. "You will learn to hold these things in your mind and in your spirit; to preserve what is precious. You will recite the lore; you will observe the rituals. The sun and moon will guard you; the sea will be your fortress wall, the living stone your safe refuge. Guard well the mysterious bond between the earth and the life that dwells there, and our great mother will sustain you."

I felt a little faint, and more than a little bemused. Perhaps my questions did not matter, really. The trust they placed in me was a grave one; I should feel honored. But I did not feel much at all, save the emptiness of the heart, and the cold paths of my tears.

"You wish to ask us something, before we leave you?" The Lady of the Forest spoke more gently now; still, one did not forget what she was. These folk knew nothing of human kindness; to them, surely our small lives were of no consequence in the pattern of things.

"I wondered . . ." I ventured.

"What is it, child?"

"I have two questions. A human girl needs food, warmth, clothing to wear; the means to stay warm in the winter. I am prepared to be alone; that is nothing new. But how will I find time to perform the duties you require, if I must also scrape a living from these barren rocks? I do know how to catch fish with a hand line, but—"

The four of them laughed, high, deep, the sound of it a kind of music ringing through the chamber.

"You will be provided for," said the fiery Lord. "Through an act of unexpected kindness, you have won strange and loyal friends. The Old Ones will ensure all is here for you, as you need it. Indeed, they insisted this duty be theirs alone, odd creatures that they are. There will be no requirement for—fishing." He broke into chuckling again.

"Very well," I said, glancing around me and wondering how many eyes watched us. The Old Ones merged well; one never knew what wisp of shadow, what jumble of broken stones might without warning transform itself into a living, breathing creature. At least there would be company of a sort. "There's one more thing you don't seem to have thought of," I said. "My grandmother told me our kind live long. Because we have your own blood, our span is greater than the ordinary human kind. But I will not live forever. I may hold these secrets safe until I am a wrinkled old crone like the lady Oonagh. But eventually I will die, and the mysteries will be lost with me."

The ocean-being's liquid eyes widened, her fronded brows rose. "Oh, no," she said in surprise. "The secrets do not die with you; that is not the way of it at all. Our vision is far greater than the life of a single guardian. You will teach your daughter these things so she in turn can hold the trust; in time she will pass on the wisdom to her own child. It will be long, oh, so long before this knowledge can be made known again to the world. It is for this reason that we conceal the Islands, tonight, from the realm of man. A great wave will wash over; a mist will arise and blanket them from view. Voyagers may search, but none will find this place again."

"My daughter," I said blankly. "I see. Correct me if I am wrong, but I thought it took a man, as well as a woman, to make a child. Is this infant's father to be a crab, or a seagull maybe? Or were you planning to shipwreck some likely sailor on my doorstep, so I can make convenient use of him?"

There was a sudden silence. Perhaps I had missed something. The four great beings of the Túatha Dé regarded me gravely. Then the fire Lord reached out a sudden hand, and there before me in the air a fragile glass ball hung suspended, as lovely and glittering as a star.

"You know the charm," he said. "Show us."

I stared aghast, struck dumb by such cruelty. I bit back the words that sprang to my lips. *Drop. Stop. Now gently down*. How dared they? How dared they play such tricks?

The ball did not smash to the ground. It fell, and halted, and hung suspended now a handspan above the rocky surface. But I had worked no spell. The shining orb twinkled in the glow from the fire Lord's flaming hair. He stooped and took it up in his hand.

"You see?" he said softly. "You are not the only one who can per-form this feat of magic."

"Crabs, seagulls, wandering sailors; I think not," said the Lady of the Forest. "I think we can do a little better than that."

My heart lurched. Terrified that I had misunderstood, I whis-pered, "What do you mean?"

"What kind of father might such a child need, growing up in this place of isolation?" she mused. "Such a child would need to be resourceful, and merry, and wise. She'd need to be able to climb and balance; and to respect wild creatures, for they are all around us in this sea-circled realm. It would be useful if her father could teach her to swim, since her mother cannot. What else, do you think?"

"What are you saying?" My voice cracked with anguish, I was shaking like a winter birch. I feared they were tormenting me, for it could not be so, surely; how could it be so? The cliffs were high, the rocks were sharp, the ocean gripped like an icy hand. And yet—and yet the hope in me rose like the saps of spring, welling sweet and strong.

"A bit of music to while away the time," said the Lord of air and light. "A little laughter, a little kindness. Patience, and a reason for keeping on. That'd be love, maybe."

"It seemed to us there was only one choice," said the ocean-being.

"You mean—you mean he is alive?" I hardly dared form the words, fearing the answer. I thought my heart might leap from my breast, for it was pounding like a great drum. "You saved him? But how can that be? How could he survive in that treacherous sea, after such a dive? And where is he now? Do not lie to me, oh, please—"

"Hush, child. We must soon be gone. This is no simple matter, for it was not easy to snatch him thus from the very jaws of death, and to preserve him." The Lady of the Forest was grave indeed; there was some shadow over her expression. "It was necessary to make a slight adjustment to the manner of things, so this could be possible. And he is not here, not yet. He will not come to you so easily, for there is another test, of sorts; one you have set for yourself."

"What test?" I was cold again, quite baffled by her words. "What must I do?"

She sighed. "He has followed you to the ends of the earth. All that he treasured, he has given up for you. You tremble with joy, now, that he is alive; and yet you sent him away, time after time. Perhaps once too often; perhaps, this time, he will not return, knowing himself unable to endure another banishment."

The four of them were starting to fade, starting to leave already. Their forms grew transparent and attenuated, until I could see little of them save the eyes, sorrowful, proud, not entirely without pity.

"Tell me! Oh, please, oh, please tell me what I must do!"

The Lady of the Forest was last to go. Her voice now seemed as fragile and ephemeral as the sigh of a breeze over the leaves of a great forest, a soft rustle of farewell.

"You must go down to the sea and wait for him," she said. "There will be but one chance. Waste that, and he is lost to you forever. You must open your heart, and speak truth from your lips. Ah, not yet," she added as I sprang toward the entry. "Not until dusk. You must wait until the time of changing. It is only then that you can bring him home." Her shadowy figure blurred, and faded into nothingness.

At the time when the clear blue of late afternoon began to dim and darken, as if a brush had been drawn across the vast expanse of sky to paint it the shade of dried lavender, the hue of a dove's wing, the color of lichen on ancient stone, I went out barefoot, down the rough-hewn steps, all the way down to a place where great flat rocks raised their backs above the sea on the south side of the Needle. There would be times when the water washed the creviced surface of these monumental stones; even now, their secret corners held tiny pools, each with its delicate share of life: fragile sea creatures, clinging, fronded anemones and iridescent fishlings no longer than a single eyelash. But now the high surface of the rock was dry; here I seated myself cross-legged, straight backed, and fixed my gaze on the darkening waters before me. I felt the warmth trapped there in the ancient stone, and the earth's embrace as she gave the sun's life back to my body.

Words came in silence, as once before. *This rock is your mother; she holds you in the palm of her hand. This warmth is your father; he gives you his life, his spirit and his strength.* For all the serenity of time and place, my heart was beating fast as the light faded; the sea was growing dark, and I saw no swimmers there in its cold embrace, no sons and daughters of Manannán mac Lir playing in the swell as the sun sank lower in the west, somewhere beyond the green hills of Kerry. The water whispered in at my feet, bathing the old stones, laving, lapping, as if it would wash away things past and make all new and clean. A great flood; a great welling of tears. But there could never be enough tears to make up for what I had done. If there were treasure to be cast up on this wild shore, who less deserving to receive it than this sorcerer's daughter, who had wounded so many good folk on her blundering way? How could that ever be made right?

Words came again, secret words borne on the whisper of the west wind, sighing in the deep surge of the sea. *This breath is a promise, a gift of love and loyalty. The tide turns; all things change, and are reborn. The earth suffers and endures; the ocean trembles, waiting for renewal. Fair things perish, and innocence dies. But hope survives while the Watcher keeps faith, high in the Needle. This is the way of truth.*

I trembled to hear the words, but still I sat quiet there on the rocks, for it seemed to me there was nothing else to be done but wait and hope. If hope were gone, then there was indeed nothing left, nothing at all.

Out in the darkening water there was a sudden movement that was surely not just the swell, or the tangling of shining seaweed borne on its breast. Surely—surely those were creatures, sleek-bodied, round-headed sea creatures, playing, diving, dancing in the tide, their forms the very essence of the shifting, fluid element they inhabited so joyfully. I narrowed my eyes, peering closer. Yes, they were selkies;

five or six of them moving and circling some way off shore. From time to time they would raise their heads from the water, the dark skin slickly gleaming in the last light, and fix their liquid, plaintive eyes on me where I sat perched on the rocks of the Needle. Surely they would come closer. Surely, here where the stone sloped quite gently to the water, a selkie could slip ashore and . . . and . . . but they did not come in, and now the sun was sinking below the horizon, away in the west, and it was almost dusk. This would be my punishment, perhaps, for daring to hope that, after all, I might be granted such a wondrous gift, to hold in my arms once more what I loved best, and had thought lost forever. This was my doom for daring to believe, even for a moment, that the goddess might think me deserving of such kindness. I breathed his name as the selkies seemed to drift away from the island, and still farther away until I could barely see them in the half light. *Darragh*, I whispered like a foolish lovesick girl. *Oh, please. Oh, please.*

"You'll need to do better than that," said a dry little voice on my left. I started, and looked down. This time it had not even taken the time to transform; it was the small, ragged owl I saw, though there had been no sign of a flight, or a landing. "You'll have to do some real work, and quick. Dusk doesn't last long; soon it'll be dark, and too late."

"Think, girl, think," said a cracked, deep voice on my right, a voice which seemed to come from the very rocks themselves; was that crevice a kind of mouth, that neat, round hole studded with a bright shell, a kind of eye? The Fomhóire were everywhere. Thus had they survived for countless eons, while others were slain or exiled. "Think," said the voice again. "Use your head. Think back."

"I can't," I whispered. "I can't see him. Surely it is too late." And yet, out in the water, was not there a single selkie left, alone in the dusk, bright eyes gazing back toward the land, seemingly reluctant to swim after the others as they made their way eastward to the sheltered bays of the bigger islands? He waited; but he would not wait forever. What was I supposed to do? I could not call; this was a wild creature, my voice would only frighten him away. *Think, Fainne. Remember. Remember.*

"Singing," I muttered as it came back to me. Darragh playing the pipes, so sweetly, and coaxing me, trying to get me to join in. What had he said? Something about seals, that was it. *I bet you could sing fit to call the seals up out of the ocean, if you tried*, he'd said. The goddess help me. How could I sing this wonderful creature to the shore, I with my cracked and weeping voice that was like the cry of some small, lost marsh creature croaking alone in the reeds? I looked into the dark, liquid eyes of the selkie, and he gazed back at me, and I knew this was exactly what I must do; that mine was the only voice that could sing him home. For, choked and broken as it was, was it not the voice of love?

"Hurry up then," urged the owl-creature. "Too late, when it's dark."

And indeed, out in the sea, the selkie turned his head to look after the others; and turned back to look at me. So I took a deep breath and began to sing. My voice was weak and tuneless; a little thread of sound snatched away by the west wind, surely a song too small to carry as far as the creature that bobbed there in the swell. He was watching me.

"Good," said the owl-creature with patent untruth.

"More," encouraged the rock-being. "More. Louder. He hears you. Quick, now."

It seemed he did hear me, for he swam closer, and I imagined I saw something like recognition in those strange eyes, dark, sorrowful eyes with the wildness of the ocean in them. I began again. The warmth of the great stones flowed into me, the west wind gave me breath, the voice of the sea lent a deep counterpoint to the halting flow of my melody. I sang on as the light faded and the water grew ink-dark, as the shadows stretched out their long hands over me, and the sky turned to the deep violet of dusk. My voice was a pathetic shred of ill-formed sound in the vast expanse of this remote place, my tune unformed, my words halting. But I made my song from the depths of my heart, and I poured into it all the love and longing I had held hidden there. All the things I had never told him, because I could not, I sang to him now. I sang on into the dusk, waiting for the time of changing.

> Come to me now, my bonny one
> Sleek-coated, wild-eyed selkie
> Son of the ocean, strong swimmer, come.

The night grows dark, the air grows cold
Swim in to safe shore, seek your shelter
Wild is the west wind, chill the spring tide.

Lad of my heart, my bonny one
Come home, come home to me now
Long have I waited to hold you close
Long have I ached to hold you by me
Safe in the circle of my arms.

The last light faded. At my feet, close by the margin of sea and land, the selkie waited, smooth dark head barely visible above the water, around eyes fixed on mine. My song drew to a halting close. I reached down my hand as dusk turned to dark, and my fingers gripped the strong hand of a man. I pulled with all my strength, as tears began to flood my cheeks anew, and at last, there on the rocks beside me, sprawled shivering in the first dim light of a rising moon, was my dear one, soaking wet, shivering from head to toe and without a stitch of clothing on him. I put my two arms around him as I crouched there by his side, and wondered why I had ever doubted he would come back to me. Had he not always been the truest of friends?

"I'm sorry," I whispered. "I'm sorry, Darragh, oh, I'm so sorry I have done this to you."

He blinked, and turned his head this way and that, as if he were not quite sure which one he was, seal or man. Perhaps, if the tales were to be believed, from now on he would never be quite one or the other. He was shivering so hard I felt the spasms through my own body where I held him. I reached to unfasten my shawl, thinking to put it around him.

"I'm sorry," I said again through tears of joy and pain.

Darragh rose cautiously to his feet. His body was very pale in the moonlight; pale and naked and quite, quite beautiful. I swallowed.

"It is possible to live here," I went on, wanting him to speak, yet fearing it too, for I had laid my heart open and now I began to wonder if that had been very foolish. After all, he had turned his back on me once before, when I had longed to feel his touch. "There is food and water and shelter. But it is not much. We cannot leave this place. I'm sorry. Because of me, you have lost all that you might have had."

Darragh looked at me in the half-dark. "You always said you c—couldn't sing," he observed through chattering teeth. "I'd dearly like to hear that song again. Loveliest tune I ever heard, that was. Would you sing it to me one more t—t—time, if I asked nicely?"

I felt a blush rise to my face. "I might," I said. "Right now, we have to find some way of warming you up, before you freeze to death."

"I could think of one or two," said Darragh, himself blushing fiercely as he spoke. He reached out his arms to me, and I wrapped him in mine, never mind the lack of tunic or trousers or a scrap of anything at all, and I felt the steady beat of his heart against my body, such healing for the wounded spirit I thought I might die with the sweetness of it.

"Darragh," I said. "There's nothing for you here. Nothing at all but me and the seabirds and the weather. It's no sort of life for you." All the same, I held on tight to what I had; I understood, now, that some things are too precious to let go.

"All I ever wanted was you by my side, and the road ahead of us," said Darragh. "I'm well content with that."

"Not much of a road," I said, feeling the flood of longing begin to flow through my body, feeling the need to be closer still rising fast in me, near overwhelming.

"A great adventure." Darragh's voice was soft against my hair. "That's what it is." Another deep shudder went through his body, and I made myself step away.

"Tell me something," I said. "That night on Inis Eala, when you played the pipes, and upset me. Why did you turn away from me? Why wouldn't you say goodbye with a kiss, or a hug, or some little thing? I thought—I thought—"

"Silly girl," Darragh said gently. "You never saw it, did you? You never saw how much I loved you, and longed for you, so that I couldn't trust myself to touch, knowing if I started I couldn't stop, and I might do something that would frighten you away forever? It gets to a lad like that, Curly, the wanting; even now—" he glanced down at his naked body, and up again, "even so cold, you see—?" He gave a helpless sort of grin.

"Come then," I said shakily, reaching out my hand to him, "let us waste no more time."

And together, the two of us began the long climb upward to warmth and shelter; to a life reborn. For it seemed his destiny was to be mine, and mine his, here in this place of the margins, this place where earth and fire, air and water so sweetly and mysteriously met and parted and met again in their eternal dance.

Epilogue

In the years after the great battle for the Islands, many tales grew up about the events that took place and their aftermath. For a time something resembling the truth was told; a tale that might be called history. This tale told how Sean of Sevenwaters defeated the Britons, with the help of his allies, and the leadership of the young man Johnny, a warrior of near-supernatural powers. Such was this victory, that Northwoods renounced his claim to the disputed territory forever. Yet in a way Edwin did not lose. New alliances were formed between old enemies. In time, the daughter of Northwoods wed the heir to Harrowfield, and so, ironically, by making peace at last these two great estates of Northumbria achieved exactly what that villain Richard of Northwoods had once desired: a strong, united holding in the north west of Britain. There was an even stranger alliance, that between Northwoods and Sevenwaters, no less than a pledge of peace and goodwill between Briton and Irishman. That was Johnny's doing, and it led to long years of content and prosperity on both sides of the water. Nobody spoke much about the battle itself; all knew there were oddities about it, such as the use of ships suspiciously like those of the Finn-ghaill, and the intervention of some powerful strangers, and how it all hinged, in the end, on a sword fight between two men. Some folk said there had been a woman there, and some said an ogre or a faery; but most dismissed that as wild imagination.

As time passed the tales developed a life of their own. Fishermen, in particular, liked to exchange them on cold nights around the fire, their telling embroidered by the effects of a tankard or three of good ale. The funny thing was, everybody spoke of the Islands, and how they were won back at last by great courage and skill. But when you asked someone where they were, nobody seemed quite able to say with any accuracy. Some said south of Man, but that couldn't be right, for they had all sailed there in their curraghs, and everyone knew there were no such islands there, only a bit of rock the sea washed over every high tide. Some said maybe north, but others argued the point. Wherever the Islands had been, they were not there now; not so as you could find them, anyway.

But sometimes, they'd hear a tale from one fellow or another who thought he'd seen something, and when you put these tales together, there was a sort of story to it, a story so strange it was past believing; and yet they did believe it, almost. You'd be rowing along, and a mist would come down as sudden as if by magic, and when it parted for a moment, you could see a tall pillar of stone, like a tower built by giants, only this stood in the sea with the waves crashing in all around it. And sometimes you'd see folk there at night, sitting on the rocks by moonlight, or climbing up and down as if they were crabs, so nimbly did they move on the precipitous slopes. Little folk like children, with hair as red as the leaves of an autumn beech; and sometimes a man or a woman, but all you'd catch was a tiny glimpse of them before the mist closed in and hid them once more. One fellow had seen lights, right on the very top, and another swore he spotted a creature with a feather cloak and scarlet shoes; but the others told him he was letting his imagination get away from him. Another had told how there were many selkies there, all around the rocks on the south side; and a woman sitting by the water, singing. A mermaid, he thought it was. Nonsense, said the others. But still they told the tales.

The stories make me laugh. I watch the ways of men in my mirror of clear water, and as the years pass I see our tale twisted into a strange distorted reflection of itself, evolving into something more acceptable to folk, without the blood and loss, without the cruelty, the terrible errors and the waste, and I smile and let it pass me by. I hear my daughter recite the lore, and praise her efforts, *Well done, Niamh,* but not too much, or she will have nothing to strive for. I give her time for play, with her father and small brother. They laugh and sing and tell tales as they sit in the sun under the rowans. They make whistles of whalebone, and invent new names for fish and bird and scuttling rock creature. They see no strangeness in Fomhóire folk.

Danny may choose to leave us when he is grown; but we think he will stay. He has two homes here, the sea and the land, and he revels in the freedom of one and welcomes the warmth of the other. Our daughter's path is more difficult. For her, perhaps the Fair Folk will indeed shipwreck a likely voyager, a man of courage and vision to be drawn through the mists to this hidden place, and captured by love.

It will be a long time. It will be after my time, and my daughter's, and her daughter's as well. We will see terrible things in the caves of truth; we will see the rape of the earth, the fouling of the oceans, the burning of the great forests. We will see man's cruelty and his greed, and the loss of the old faith save in the hearts of a dwindling few. But the time will come. It must; have not the Fair Folk said so themselves? Wisdom will prevail at last, when the world is all but lost; and man will find his bond with the earth, his mother, once more. This is a great and solemn trust, and we will fulfill it faithfully.

I learned many things on my journey to the Needle. I learned about loyalty and courage and forgiveness. I learned that love is the cruellest thing, and the kindest. I learned that friends are found in the strangest of places, if you know how to look. My life here is rich beyond measure; the goddess was indeed kind. She granted me the wondrous gift of a second chance; and I will not fail her.